SHADES
OF
PERCEPTION

BOOK 2

BOOK 2

FiniteVoid

Podium

Podium

SHADES
OF
PERCEPTION

BOOK 2

CHAPTER 1

ANOTHER SIMPLE MORNING

Wiping away the steam fogging the mirror, Vern leaned over the basin and stared at his own reflection. Damp and dark tousled hair framed his pale face and sharp features, primarily his intense eyes. The black pupils expanded to allow in all the light needed to focus on the dim surroundings lit only by the sunlight seeping in from the small ventilation.

Nothing seemed out of place until—

Balance.

And like a phosphorous match struck inside an abyss, his irises flared. They didn't burn bright orange or some fiery hue but instead imbued a white hotness.

It was, however, a little more complicated than that. A ring of white had etched itself within each of his irises, bringing light to his otherwise inky eyes. Yet, this wasn't the extent of this pattern. The white ring had some width to it, and within even that was a circle of darkness.

He didn't know if it signified anything but was happy it wasn't just white—one "extreme" of the spectrum that depicted his viewpoint.

Steam from the bath he'd just taken began reclaiming the lost surface of the mirror as he continued to scrutinize his eyes. They made him look . . . distant and . . . detached. And would obviously make him stand out, which was enough reason for him to want to keep them hidden. It was either looking cool or being unable to use his powers discreetly.

It was a cruel choice, but what could he do? There was a reason he had spent the past couple days cooped up in the hotel room while the Vigil cleaned up the mess at the steamscript relay station and handled Asea's believers in the city.

Vern's actions in the station weren't anything too outstanding for those not in the loop. Luckily, he hadn't painted too big a target on his back as a blasphemer, unlike some loudmouthed dancer he knew. However, Captain Akira had his plans, for he made Vern wait until the situation had calmed down entirely, and he wasn't on anyone's radar.

Apparently, Asea's believers weren't very happy when the blame for the destruction of a big chunk of Starfall Heights fell upon their laps. Yet, nothing came of it because a good number of the jury were believers of Asea themselves.

A lot of them had surely benefitted from the "healing," after all.

At least that's what Butler De Flanc's last letter had said. Vern had been told to lie low until the dust settled and those mother-lovers calmed their boilers. The only time he'd been out farther than a couple blocks was when De Flanc had taken him to meet Lady Amelia, or . . . um, Master Amelia? Mistress Amelia?

He still didn't know how to feel about having a literal and actual reaper as his mentor. Not that he had received any classes just yet. When they'd met, she had glanced at him once and nodded before zipping off to somewhere else—probably to reap more souls with her scythe.

De Flanc said she wanted to meet him before actually accepting him into her fold, and apparently, that one glance was all she needed.

But it let him gauge exactly who he would be learning from. It would be an understatement to say he was honored as well as terrified. Training regimes of armies were never easy, much less that of Kingsmen. He could only hope he wasn't about to be forced into years of grueling training. He didn't have time for that.

Not when there were religions to be upended.

Drying himself with a towel, he walked out of the bathroom and threw his sweat-soaked shirt in a basket.

He had rearranged his hotel suite quite a bit. There was now a lot of space in the center of the room, allowing him to use all the makeshift contraptions he had created to train his body.

Five days were obviously not enough to bring about any tangible changes in reaction speed or the like, but he had at least moved past the stage of his muscles being sore the next morning.

He had quickly realized the utility of stability inducement in helping him relieve the aches, but after careful deliberation, he chose not to abuse it.

The vision forcefully stabilized his body's structure, which helped alleviate the pain, but he wasn't an expert on human anatomy. He was surely creating more problems than he was solving by randomly applying visions with unclear effects on himself.

So he only used it once a day, but even that was a great help for someone like him, whose extent of exercising until last week was moving stacks of books from one place to the other.

But he definitely felt the progress. Hopefully, he could learn more ways to go about enhancing his physical abilities from the Vigil or Mistress Amelia today.

He had finally received another letter from De Flanc last night, prompting him to visit the headquarters. It would be a lie to say he wasn't excited. He was finally going to get his hands on the Vigil's library, and after that, he would have his first task assignment, too.

He was practically oozing with energy. He had waited long enough. A lot of answers were close at hand.

Grabbing a loose-necked stretchy shirt from the closet, he draped it over his lean muscles and buttoned it closed. He furthered his attire by following it up with his most flexible pants.

Then came his pocket dweller for the day, for one can never have enough pockets in their coat. He didn't need it for the cold as much since shading the perception came with more than a mental upgrade. It was a navy blue peacoat that only had two pockets outside, but the interior had over six!

He combed his hair with his fingers as it naturally settled into his trademark messy side part. Then came his genius invention. Opening the drawer on the table, he pulled out a pouch, relaxed its string, and out came a pair of glasses.

The somewhat rectangular glasses framed the bridge of his nose. He looked at his reflection and invoked his perception again.

Balance.

This time, however, the glow that made him look ethereal didn't shine through the glasses. His reflection looked back with a gentle, scholarly aura as he checked it from multiple angles.

This was his method of staying discreet. Not a perfect one, but this was all he could manage with his limited resources.

They used a photochromic lens that absorbed any light beyond a certain threshold. It was perfect for him, since his eyes weren't too conspicuous except for the glow. It would still look weird if one paid attention, but it was about balance. He felt these precautions were enough for the situations he might encounter.

Strapping the vapor blaster he received as a gift in the mail—probably from Cera—to the holster, he picked up his notepad. He had replaced some pages within the notepad with ones from a convergence note.

He could always differentiate them from regular pages because those golden glyphs were a little too eye-catching not to notice—only for him though. He had done it more for the sake of convenience than hiding some secret, though he didn't mind that it worked both ways.

Finally, he hung the badge of Vigil around his neck and tucked it inside. Slipping his feet into a pair of socks and then into his boots, he locked the room. No top hat this time, sadly. He didn't want to lose more of them.

His stay at the hotel had been quite serene, and those two memory wipers hadn't really bothered him. Not that he would be any wiser if they had cleaned his memories. But he liked to think that he now had some kind of resistance against others' observation now that he was a proper observer himself.

With these random thoughts in his mind, he walked through the corridor toward the grand staircase that cut through all floors of the hotel.

Bright sunlight shone through the glass roof, and chatter and gossip filled his ears as he descended past the many groups that hovered around their respective landings. However, today was far more boisterous than usual because it was the—

"Happy New Year, young man! Care to join these old people for a chat?" came the gravelly voice.

A polite smile appeared on Vern's face as he looked at the group of two men and a woman. He had chatted with them a couple more times since that morning, and talking to them had become something of Vern's pastime.

When his thought space became too dim to envision anything and he was too tired to train anymore, he would come down and talk to them about the city's happenings.

Following the etiquette of juniors, he spread his hands a tad and bowed as he replied to the group, "A very happy New Year to all of you as well."

The calendar had indeed begun its new cycle. The month of Winterveil was the last month of the year and had thirty-two days, whereas Luminar, the first month of the year, had twenty-nine, just like every other month.

This stray thought, however, led Vern to a saddening realization. If things hadn't gone the way they did and the world hadn't spiraled down such a disturbing path, this would've been his last day in Elmhurst, and he'd probably be spending it with Ari before taking the train back to Nvoria.

Not letting any of his somber thoughts appear on his face, he stood back up and looked at the flattered couple, Benedict and Martha, and the government servant, Wilfred, who still had too much energy for it being so early in the morning.

"You, too, young man. You, too," Benedict chortled.

And Martha interjected as usual, "A new look? Glasses, huh?" A teasing smile formed on her face as she narrowed her eyes. "It's a girl, right? Who is she? You can tell me. I can give you lots of tips on how to properly court ladies. I am sure you'll do a far better job than Benedict right here."

Wilfred, Martha, and Vern chuckled as Benedict ignored them and pulled a cigar from an antique case.

Already knowing them enough not to be awkward, Vern relaxed and teased back, "Well, I was hoping to find someone that can match your class and poise, Lady Martha. But it seems I am either down on my luck, or there aren't many like you."

Martha scoffed, grabbing Benedict's arm. "Hahaha. Sorry, but I like tobacco money more than young ones like you."

Vern simply shook his head and asked, "Anyway, what are you all planning for the day?"

Putting the cigar in his mouth, Benedict replied, "Well, I fancy sitting here by the balcony to watch the police being just as lazy as me. However, my friend Wilfred here thinks I am wrong."

"Hey, let's not act like you didn't lose this argument already. Right, Martha? Well, you tell me, Vern, what else can we expect the police to do in this situation? Go into every house and interrogate the civilians and check if they're sheltering any insurgents?"

"He's not wrong, Benedict," interjected Martha, a knowing smile on her lips, "I would rather not have them come check our rooms."

Vern acted like he didn't hear that and simply watched as the men bickered. Benedict harrumphed and lit his cigar as he continued, "You're ignoring the truth, Wilfred. The Calidian Empire is not what it used to be a decade ago. The rot that has infested the parliament hasn't cleared up even after such a divine intervention. What else would it take for them to finally come to their senses?"

Blowing out a puff of smoke, he pointed at the streets past the window and said, "You see those policemen down there? They have not seen war. Heck, they haven't even seen real criminals. The worst they handled in those inner districts from their sandcastles is probably some dishonest merchant or a sexual deviant."

Wilfred couldn't hold himself back and butted in, "Well, that's what we have Kingsmen for! Police have their own jurisdiction and boundaries in which they act."

Benedict sniggered. "I don't see any Kingsmen in the party that Duke Neagan brought to 'claim' back the borough. Nor do I see the 'state-of-the-art' weapons you were so excited about. Surely, there's no reason for them not to be here. I wonder why they wouldn't participate in such an important mission?"

"They're busy, obviously! Haven't you heard?" Wilfred suddenly tamped down his loud shouts and continued in a more controlled manner, "I don't remember which one, but a whole outer district had to be cut off from the rest of the city. Not figuratively, but literally. Since no one could put a dent in the bridges, they had to set a burning barricade at every entrance and monitor all the periphery waters. Who do you think is handling all that? It's obviously the Kingsmen."

Vern asked, curious, "Why is that? And how's it any different from the general inner-outer district situation? Aren't most of the outer districts barricaded in one sense already? No one can enter the inner districts from there, after all."

A complacent smile etched itself on Wilfred's face as he replied with faux arrogance, "You didn't know either, huh? Well, since you're more affable than this odious tobacco consumer, I shall tell you the news I heard through the grapevine."

Wilfred motioned for all to come closer. Benedict rolled his eyes while Martha leaned in with great interest. A smug smile from Wilfred, two puffs of cigar smoke followed by a nagging look from Martha, and a deep sigh later, Benedict leaned in as well.

Ensuring no one was paying them much attention, Wilfred spoke in a low voice, "I heard from my sources that the whole district has caught a plague."

"A plague?" Martha's face turned pale with fright at the mere mention, and she clenched Benedict's hands harder. He himself had turned aghast.

Vern wasn't unfazed either. Plagues used to be the primary cause of the end of cities and empires before alchemical fundamentalists, or simply alchemists, delved deep into related fundamentals and found cures to some of the deadliest threats.

Wilfred nodded and continued to whisper, "Indeed. No one knows for sure what it is, but rumor has it that it's the same plague that ended the reign of Empress Sinatra."

Hmm, isn't she the empress that built Eleonora's archive and catalyzed the acceptance of fundamentalists in the society? How is she related to any of this?

"But did those alchemy fundamentalists, or whatever, not manage to find a cure in all this time?"

To this, Vern shook his head and added, "Some plagues simply don't have a cure. The best one can do in these situations is quarantine it." Such was the way of life for the alchemists.

Benedict asked, not in a mood to joke anymore, "How does it spread? Can we do something to avoid it?"

Wilfred shook his head. "We don't even know what it is exactly. How can you avoid it? If I get any more news, I will share for sure."

After another round of paranoid queries and circular discussion, Vern bade them farewell and made his exit. He would get far better information about things like this at the Vigil than listening to gossip from some bored upperclass men.

Descending all the way to the lobby, he motioned for Butler Beaumont to open the door, and the old man in black-and-white overalls hurried over.

"Happy New Year, Master Vern. Hope this year treats us better than the last."

"A great New Year to you, too, Beaumont. We can only hope."

Beaumont opened the door without wasting any more time, and Vern let himself out, bidding farewell to the good man.

Not needing to block the sunrays because of his masterful glasses, he walked through the foggy street toward the bridge to Mosaic Miles, the same one he had crossed in a deadly situation last time.

It wouldn't be like that this time though. For, even though Benedict derided the police, they had managed to reclaim the market area of this borough from multiple unsavory factions in just a couple days. This meant Fulham borough was once again connected to Mosaic Miles, and he wouldn't have to risk his life just to cross the bridge.

His destination today was Ferrovane Heights, all the way toward the center of the city. There were no carriages in Fulham borough just yet, but he could surely find one once he was in Mosaic Miles.

Not having much else to do other than survey the streets tainted by the blood from the bloody struggle last week, he slipped into his perception. A ring appeared within his iris, and the world took on new shades.

He had figured out many new details about his perception, like how his balance sight had multiple facets, and if he figured out their essence, he could see far more than harmony or disharmony or fulcrums in a structure.

He could—

Tweeeee.

The piercing trill of the whistle came from behind him. "Hey, you! Stop right there." Vern froze in his tracks and lamented his bad luck. Footsteps of authority drew near, thumping on the cobblestone street with mighty vigor.

Go arrest some insurgents. Why waste your time on me? Maybe Benedict wasn't wrong after all.

CHAPTER 2

MISCOMMUNICATION

Vern waited as the policeman came marching in his slow steps and stopped right in front of him, a scowl on his face. He wore a high-collared coat crafted from a dark, sturdy fabric with a row of brass buttons that caught the dim light filtering through the fog. A vest just as dark and flashy alongside the pants of the same material added a hint of formality to this practical uniform.

On his head sat a distinct helmet, notable for its integrated goggles that used more brass for intricate detailing, surrounding the lenses that served Lady knows what purpose. Many little pieces of equipment hung onto his service-issued belt, including a baton, light lamp, and an ammo box.

An ammo box for the rifle that was gripped tightly in his hands. He looked on with his stern and vigilant expression and barked, "State your identity, purpose, and religion!"

Disgruntled thoughts ran through Vern's head as he tried to keep up his friendly expression, and he replied in a diffusing tone, "A happy New Year, officer. My name is Vern Lockwood, a fundamentalist, and I'm headed to Ferrovane Heights for the first day of my work." Then, putting one hand on his chest, he finished, "And I only believe in the Lady from beyond."

The man squinted, the suspicion in his eyes only growing heavier, "I haven't seen you round here, and I've been here for three whole days. Not just that, what fundamentalist goes to work without a briefcase? And what work is there for a fundamentalist in Ferrovane Heights anyway? I apologize, but I'll need to verify your claims."

Vern sighed internally. He couldn't even tell them that he worked for Vigil. According to his understanding of the matter, Vigil was formed on the eve of duskfall itself, and not many knew it even existed. The government wasn't very happy about having another group of power within its city, so he might just be inviting more trouble by telling this policeman about it.

He assessed all his options and used his tried and tested method. "If you wouldn't mind me reaching into my pockets, I can show you my badge from the Coven of Truth."

The man kept the rifle aimed in Vern's general direction with those hands wrapped in leather gloves and nodded.

With slow, deliberate movements, Vern reached into one of his inner pockets and pulled out that badge with an hourglass etched on it, extending it toward the policeman.

The man seemed to calm down a little, but his eyebrows remained knitted together. Taking one hand off the rifle, he snatched the badge and checked it from all angles.

"It is the real deal. But we've had at least a dozen cases where people looted such badges from the remains of the people lost in the duskfall and tried to pass themselves off as the owner."

However, after switching back and forth between Vern's innocent and scholarly expression and the authentic badge a couple times, he sighed and lowered his rifle. Returning the trinket, he said, "But my judgment says it belongs to you."

Then, with a shake of his head, he softly whispered, "I am a little too sensitive, maybe."

Tucking the badge back in his pocket, Vern dipped his head and said, "Thank you, officer. Can I go now?"

The man seemed conflicted for a second before replying, "Yes. But after a quick body search."

Vern's expression, which had just turned for the better, took a nosedive as he realized a fatal mistake. Civilians weren't allowed to carry guns.

Fuck.

He had never even considered this could be an issue given the current state of the society. But in this situation and under this light of suspicion, this was sure to become a problem.

He didn't have a license for carrying the gun, and he doubted the man would listen to his arguments as to why he would need to carry one in a "lawful" district.

What the hell do I do?

The policeman walked toward him, slinging the rifle on his back as he pulled those gloves tighter.

Should I make a run for it?

He looked around, and it was quite foggy. If he could manage to make a little distance from the man, he should be able to slip into an alley and escape easily.

Yet, not even a moment passed before he discarded such a stupid plan. A little search on their end would lead them right back to the hotel, where they could figure out all about him. He would have to give up all his possessions there for nothing, only to later skulk around like some criminal.

No. That would be stupid. I can't have myself shot or put in jail for such a stupid reason. Not on such an important day, at least. Something major was going to happen at the Vigil today. He was called straight to the headquarters, not at a random hideout in some district.

He couldn't miss that. Not for this.

Vern stood there frozen as the man began frisking him from top to bottom.

His heart raced faster and faster as the man patted down his pockets and moved farther down at a brisk pace.

Vern's frustration mounted rapidly. This was such a petty problem. He should have asked Butler De Flanc about this beforehand.

Surely, Captain Shinsei, Ambrose, and others didn't get frisked by a common policeman every day. They must have some official method to ignore such insignificant hassles.

"You okay, mister?"

The policeman met Vern's shaky gaze and paused his search. "Something wrong?"

Vern's brain churned, and he quickly responded, "Oh, there's something I forgot to mention."

The policeman instantly turned vigilant and alert, focusing on Vern's hand, expecting some trickery to follow as he gripped his rifle again. But instead, a ring appeared in Vern's eyes, and he pulled one flap of his coat to the side.

"Please wait, officer. I just forgot to mention that I have the prototype of a weapon I am currently working on latched on to my waist. It can be dangerous if handled without care."

But before Vern could explain any further, a kick landed on his stomach, and the force sent him crashing toward the wall with intense ferocity.

"Haghhh! I knew it! I fucking knew it! I knew you were one of them. The moment I laid my eyes on you, I fucking knew it. You're going nowhere! You're not taking down anyone with you today. I'm not like the others."

His eyes bulged wide, darting frantically as his voice cracked and pitched high. He pulled back the rifle's stock to his shoulder and aimed at Vern, screeching, "You aren't fooling anyone with your bullshit! Not me!" And without any hesitation, he pulled the trigger.

Click.

His brows furrowed as he turned his eyes toward the rifle, puzzled over what went wrong. But his eyes continued to flicker intensely as his face turned hot from exertion.

Discarding the current bullet and bolting the next shot, he pulled the trigger another time.

Click.

The man began to hyperventilate, his breaths coming out in uneven bursts. His hands trembled, and his lips quivered as he discarded the whole chamber and shells clanked on the ground.

"Not me! Not them! You won't destroy anyone's family! I won't let you!" he continued shouting as he grabbed a fresh bullet from his ammo box and loaded it into the chamber, aiming at Vern.

Vern stood there against the wall, calm and unfazed, a distant and indifferent look in his eyes.

With a soothing voice, Vern consoled the man, "Calm down."

But the policeman was having none of it and pulled the trigger in rapid succession.

Click.

Click.

Click.

Click.

"This can't be! My comrades! We need to finish him! Nip it in the bud before he enters in there. WHY!? Why the fuck is this junk not working!"

He stared at his rifle without blinking, resetting every latch and lever frantically before shooting again, only for it to do nothing except for clicking uselessly.

Frustrated, he threw the rifle aside, discarding it for an infallible weapon. With a useful click, he pulled out his baton and charged toward Vern.

"Haghh! You won't! You thought you could fool me and go kill more innocent children!?" he bellowed, a twisted grin stretched across his face. With an intense fervor, he made a beeline toward Vern, ready to beat him to a pulp.

Vern simply stared back silently, a placid look on his face. The baton headed for Vern's head, which would almost certainly be a fatal hit if it connected, but he didn't seem like he had any intention to move.

"Die!"

Thump.

"Stand down, officer!"

Just as the thing was mere inches away from Vern's head, a hand intervened and instantly halted all that momentum in its tracks. Vern had seen this man running to interject here quite a while ago.

A man taller than Vern himself snatched the baton from the policeman's hand and ferociously struck the man on his shoulder.

"Aghhh!" Vern heard a bone crack before the baton went tumbling on the ground.

"What the hell are you doing, officer?!"

"Commander, ahh! But this. This man!" The policeman supported his broken arm with the other and pointed toward Vern with a distorted expression. "He is one of them! It will be just like back then. He will kill them all! No one will survive."

"You're telling me this guy who stood there stupidly in front of a gun is the mastermind here?"

The taller man held his forehead and sighed. Then, with a voice that boomed throughout the street, he said, "Who's squad does this one belong to?!"

"I will go get him, sir," replied another policeman without a moment's delay as he dashed past many men.

A crowd had gathered around them as they watched the display with looks of fear and trepidation. Quiet murmurs spread around them, and Vern registered a few.

"These men are supposed to . . . protect us? Like this? He didn't even listen to the kid."

"That guy didn't do nothing, brother. Nothing. But that bastard? He kept trying to gun him down. Woulda peppered him with holes if that thing worked."

"Well, that's police for you." Another man shrugged. "This is where all that tax we pay is used. All so one day they can stop you randomly and take your life for breathing."

But before it could get any more heated, the tall commander bellowed, "This is not a show. Get out of here!"

And as if his voice held an unknown pressure, the crowd cleared up almost instantly, and the fog reclaimed its rightful space.

Another policeman came running, pushing down on his helmet to keep it from falling off. He gasped for breath, yet stood tall and saluted toward the tall one. "What can I do for you, commander?"

Muscles bulged underneath the commander's arms as he gripped the shoulders of Vern's assailant and barked, "What you can do for me is keep your men from causing a fucking commotion! If they can't control their trigger fingers, chop 'em off for all I care."

Pointing at the shadows in a couple alleyways, he continued, "This district is not fully secure. We can't have them losing grip in public like this! Duke will strip us of everything if something goes wrong with the operation because of stupid bullshit like this."

However, Vern's aggressor interjected, "But, commander, captain! This one has a gun! He's carrying a gun! He is a threat. He wants to go to Ferrovane Heights. He'll kill more people, captain. He should be kil—"

"Shut up and get a grip!" The commander roared, smashing his head into the man's.

The squad leader jumped in the middle and tried to de-escalate. "Commander, let me handle this, please. He has gone through a lot. His wife and daughter were caught up in that incident with patients of a mental asylum in the Athenaeum district last week. Please let me take care of this."

"Yes! Yes! Commander, listen to me. This man is just like them. A madman, I am telling you! A madman! I am not making it up. He acts calm and lies without a hint of emotion on his face. We shouldn't let him—"

The squad leader slapped him in the face. "Kenny, shut up! If you keep acting like this, you're the one who will need to go to the asylum!"

The slap finally seemed to jerk the man out of a trance as he looked at Vern with a complicated expression.

But before Vern could try and lodge his grievances, the tall commander walked up to him and looked down. "And what's your deal? That one might not be right in the head, but there's no fire without smoke. Why did it come to this?"

CHAPTER 3

WHAT HAPPENED TO THEM?

Vern barely suppressed the rage that bubbled from within him. He would've been killed in cold blood without even getting a chance to appeal simply because he possessed a gun. What the fuck kind of logic was that?

If the policeman had something wrong with his head, why was he allowed to be in this position and have control over others' lives?

But all this could wait. He wasn't completely in the clear just yet. Not bothering to mask his anger, he recounted the situation.

After showing the man his coven badge, he pulled the edge of his coat to one side, and the metallic revolver peeked through the holster. This time, however, the man opposite him had a realistic reaction.

"So you're saying it's a prototype gifted to you by Von Industries to provide feedback?"

Vern nodded, not feeling even a hint of guilt for lying about it. Not that it was entirely untrue, anyway. But the man didn't seem persuaded with just his nod, so Vern continued, "If you're still suspicious, I can do a little demonstration of my skills."

The commander looked at him with a side-eye. "What demonstration?"

Vern pointed at the rifle on the ground. "I can fix it. Right now."

"Without any tools?"

Vern smiled. "Won't need them for something so simple."

The tall man seemed to consider his words for a while before he walked over to the rifle and held its muzzle up in the air. With a strong grip, he pulled the trigger. *Click.*

As expected, nothing happened. Vern had destabilized more than a couple mechanisms, after all. At the start, when he made up his mind to come clean about his vapor blaster, he had only destabilized a small section of the rifle as a precaution. But it soon became clear that his paranoia wasn't unfounded.

When he noticed that the policeman was hell-bent on peppering him with holes, Vern went ahead and destabilized the whole thing so it wouldn't work no matter what.

The commander walked back with the muzzle of the rifle pointing downward. Shoving the tip in a corner, he held it from the stock and looked at Vern. "Fix it."

Vern didn't mind this. This was at least a reasonable situation. Though he would have to ask De Flanc what the hell to do about situations like this in the future. He would rather not be captured by the police of the city when he was about to be in the same line of work as them.

Except, I won't be raring to murder innocent people at the drop of a hat.

Shaking his head, he knelt and began fiddling around with the weapon. He had enough know-how to act like he was actually doing something.

With his head facing away from the commander, he traced the structure of the gun with his hand, and the very next instant, the world took on shades of gray.

The broken and misaligned lines of the structure within the gun that he had induced just a second ago became clear for him to see. Removing one component after another, he fiddled around with them.

He could honestly have fixed this without using his vision, but what would be the point of that? He had experience fixing thousands of mechanisms but very little doing that with his visions.

So he imagined how those structural lines would have to bend and connect to go back to their prior state.

Stability inducement.

Sure enough, a ring appeared in his eyes as lightning crackled in his thought space. A set of notions that perfected his crude imagination ran through his mind, and the broken mechanism seemed to have gone back in time—as neat and pristine as it had been a couple minutes ago.

"All good to go." Vern refitted the components in their position and patted the muzzle one last time before getting up.

The commander still seemed to hold his doubts. Nonetheless, he aimed the rifle in the air, and Vern clamped his ears—

Dang.

A flash appeared from the firearm's muzzle, and the fog was sliced through in a neat line upward.

"That's indeed something only a fundamentalist can do." The commander looked back toward the other two police officers. Vern's assailant sat on a barrel as the squad leader poured water down his face, pointing toward Vern. The mad policeman stared at the ground, trembling violently.

The tall commander sighed again. "I guess it's time I apologize for my subordinate's mistake." Putting away the rifle, he stated, "We already don't have enough fundamentalists around, and my stupid man would have taken another one from mankind."

Then he took off his hat and bowed. "Please accept my sincere apologies, mister fundamentalist. My men are currently under a little too much pressure and are going on for days without any rest."

"I understand that it doesn't excuse the behavior and attempt at your life, but I hope you can find it in your heart to let this go. All of us have lost a lot, and many have left or disappeared from our ranks, so we have had to make do with whoever answered our call."

Vern held the man's gaze, not really sure how to go about dealing with this. The apology was a little too sincere, and it was clearly coming from someone of a grand station.

He was never really in any danger except for the possibility of being put in jail, so he didn't know if there was any point in trying to escalate this. There was no way general courts had the time to deal with something like this. Neither did he, for that matter. He had better things to do.

Vern looked at his aggressor. The man had fallen off the barrel and held his head while huddled in a corner. Even Vern was quite surprised at the turn of events. That man had looked very normal and upright just a while ago.

There really is no telling what's going on inside someone's mind.

Obviously, that man was dealing with some issues. So, not taking the edge off his voice, he made his first demand. "I sympathize with your cause, officer, but I can't accept that you let men like him roam the streets with guns in their hands."

Then, with his best frightened look, he lamented, "Lady had blessed me with luck today, for this rifle was busted. Or I would've survived the culling only to die at the hands of a traumatized man who needs help."

Not waiting for Vern to continue, the commander shouted, "Harry, fine the man three hundred crowns and demote him to ground staff. Transfer him to the port offices outside the city and make sure he gets a doctor, not a rifle!"

The squad leader turned around with a start and saluted back. "But, sir, we're barely fulfilling the duke's minimum quota as is."

"I'll deal with that."

"As you command, sir!"

The commander turned toward Vern and asked, "Anything else, mister fundamentalist?"

Vern pondered for a while before sighing as he pointed at his vapor blaster. "Can I get a permit to carry this around so next time I can show that first?"

"That should be easy. You were headed toward Ferrovane Heights, right? I can get you one at the hub in Mosaic Miles in a jiffy. Please walk with me," said the commander as he led the way.

Clearly, the commander wanted to wrap this up as soon as possible. Even though he managed to scare away the people on the streets, there were still many eyes watching them from beyond the curtains in the houses.

Vern looked at his aggressor, who seemed to have calmed down a bit, one final time and left it at that. What else was he supposed to do? Kill him for having a screw loose in a fucked world?

This should be fine. It was an acceptable balance of punishment.

Following the tall man in his dark uniform gilded with badges on its epaulets, Vern cleared his mind.

In no time, they crossed Timekeeper Lane in silence when the commander spoke up, "Nowadays, it's rare to come across a fundamentalist. Would you mind if I asked where you live? The city can always use some help from your expertise in these trying times."

But these words confused Vern beyond measure. It didn't make sense. So he asked, "Rare, you say? How could it be hard to find fundamentalists in the month of the annual conference? Even if many of us were culled just like everyone else, how could there be a shortage?"

"Tch." A flicker of realization dawned on the man's face as the corner of his lips twitched imperceptibly. It seemed he had unintentionally let on some information he wasn't supposed to.

"Well?"

After a while, he sighed and replied, "It's . . . complicated."

This didn't bode well.

"Could you please elaborate? If it's related to my very life and death, I really would rather not be in another situation where I'm at the mercy of some lunatic or the like."

That last remark caused the man to wince as he seemed to consider Vern's words. After they crossed another intersection in this foggy ambiance, the man spoke, "It is my observation that more fundamentalists disappeared in the duskfall of sorrows than anyone else."

Huh?

Why would that be the case?

If Vern remembered correctly, he had conjectured that those with the willpower to hold on in that horrifying landscape were the ones who managed to survive the culling.

By that logic, fundamentalists should be leagues better than ordinary people. They handled hundreds of bizarre sights when they delved into fundamentals. There was no way they would be done in where weak-minded people like those in his hotel had managed.

This didn't make sense.

"Are there any more such patterns? Is there anything connecting these special cases?"

The man nodded. "It is no secret, but we've lost more than two-thirds of the kids in the city compared to the general trend of one-third of the population disappearing."

He followed this with a dry chuckle as his shoulders slumped. "I guess I lucked out by not having kids of my own. Don't know how everyone is holding it together after losing their children."

Vern looked up at the sky beyond the fog.

He remembered. Master's son was quite a naughty one but a little too smart for his own good. He would have survived, right? What about Gestalt? His senior in apprenticeship had recently become a father, too.

I guess I lucked out as well.

"For fundamentalists, however, I guess there is more than just that. They disappeared in places that were found to be anomalous anyway."

Vern reeled in his distant thoughts and asked, "Anomalous, how?"

"I can't provide many details, but in certain places within the city, no one survived. Not a single person. While in all other situations, one-third of the people perished, in these specific locations, there were no survivors—only the remains of those who vanished."

Taking all this information in, Vern couldn't help but ask, "What are these places?"

"Can't tell you. They're being handled by even my superiors. So, if you really want to know for your safety, you will have to file a petition at the head office. And I can assure you it'll be a long while before you'll get an answer."

Well, he could just ask a different set of people. But this was some damning information. The fact that more children died than adults was in line with his conjecture that it depended on one's willpower to survive that terrorscape.

But that didn't explain the disappearance of everyone in so many unrelated establishments.

Wait.

That's when a familiar possibility reared its ugly head, and a shiver went down his spine.

C H A P T E R **4**

THE GLOWING LISTS OF CONVERGENCE

Someone actively murdered them before the time rewound itself! That is why they weren't brought back.

That had to be it. He remembered the scene in the library. Everyone but Ari had turned into some kind of bloody liquid, escaping through the roof into the skies beyond.

Ari also had cuts and scrapes on her body, but they were healed like nothing had happened when time turned back. But anyone who was already dead due to the fire only had their clothes floating to represent their selves.

They were gone. Didn't matter if they were fundamentalists or if they could have survived the terrorscape. They were squeezed dry of their very blood, flesh, and bones. There was no bringing them back.

Could the same have happened to all the people in these establishments?

But all this still didn't clarify how exactly they died. Eleonora's archive was a special case because it had caught on fire; what was their reason? And on top of that, why only fundamentalists? If everyone in those buildings died, were fundamentalists really the target or just unlucky collateral damage?

So he asked to clarify, "Are these the only two patterns? Fundamentalists and children?"

The tall commander nodded. "As far as I know."

"By your estimate, how bad is it? Like you said, about two-thirds of the children disappeared, but what about my colleagues?"

The man rubbed his stubble with those leather gloves for a while before replying, "You're the third fundamentalist I've met in the last ten days, and I used to see about a hundred every day of the conference. No one bothered to do the numbers, but if I had to wager, it'd be around five out of a hundred?"

Vern gasped involuntarily at the distressing number. "That's . . . that's it? Why is no one investigating this?"

The man shrugged. "There is nothing to investigate. We've already matched the remains of thousands of fundamentalists to their identities from all over the city. They're gone. Just like everyone else, there's no explanation unless you want to believe in one of those scammy religions."

Then he gave Vern a dubious look and added, "No offense, but apparently, the lady was more furious with your kind than the others."

Vern's mind slipped into a whirlwind of questions and confusion as he kept his head down and continued following the man. Those shoes passed over cobblestone, the bridge's metal, and the inner district's concrete in what felt like a second.

Finally, when the footsteps halted, Vern followed suit.

"We're here. Before I go get the permit, can you tell me your name as well as your place of residence, if you don't mind? For both purposes—the permit and for my own knowledge."

He absent-mindedly replied, "Vern Lockwood, and I am currently staying at Hotel Inkwell."

"I will be right back."

Vern waited in front of what seemed like a barrack that, along with similar buildings, had been repurposed to act as administrative checkpoints in all the "free" districts. There was one on each side of the bridge. And no more Kingsmen this time.

Vern monitored the street full of graves, but surprisingly, the atmosphere wasn't as stifling as last time. A couple shops had opened, and people were going about their day with something akin to smiles on their faces.

It seemed that time was performing its magic—healing the inner wounds.

Or it could just be temporary bliss brought on by the new year. They probably believed things were going to get better.

Vern didn't know.

"There you go," came the commander's voice, snapping him out of his reverie. The man presented him with a paper that had the Crown's stamp on it alongside a signature by an Oberon Derleth.

"This is a level three ownership certificate, perfect for a fundamentalist. It allows you to carry any kind of weapon on your person. No matter the type, length, or weight."

"Thank you, Commander Oberon." Vern nodded, eyeing his name badge as he folded the paper and slipped it into his inner pockets. He didn't miss the overcompensation he was receiving.

It wasn't because he had been wronged, but due to his profession. It was ironic that the death of his colleagues made him more valuable to the city.

The certificate might come in handy later. Or not. It would depend on how Vigil handled these issues. But it was good to have, nonetheless, just like connections with people in power. One can never know enough of such people.

So he walked away, leaving one final sentence in the air. "I will remember this favor. Please feel free to send me a letter if there's something I can do for you."

"My pleasure. I will do just that." Oberon tipped his helmet.

Vern stood on the edge of the sidewalk next to the tombstones and raised his arm, making eye contact with the drivers passing by. However, two drivers quickly approached him before he could even close the buttons of his coat with his free hand.

After an intense exchange of looks and implied threats, the one on the left backed away and continued past Vern. The other driver stopped in front, and the door opened automatically.

Fancy.

Vern didn't think much of it and got in. "Ferrovane Heights, please."

"Don't worry, good sir. We'll be there before you know it."

Vern settled down on the comfortable seat and opened his notepad. As the carriage started with puttering sounds, he began scribbling the new information he had found today.

He would ask De Flanc if the Vigil knew something about this. This made him wonder if there was something of an intelligence squad in the Vigil. *Surely, there was one, right?*

However, when he flipped the page to continue writing, he reached that one page. In what seemed like words penned by a crazed murderer, it read *Shut the fuck up!*

This one was very weird. It had allowed him to gain some major insights on how those golden glyphs worked, but damn, did it give him the scare of his life.

When he had first felt that weird notion in his mind, he had assumed Esther had finally found the time to write to him, but there was no way this was Esther.

They had parted on good terms. Esther had no reason to say something like that to him. So, who the hell sent him that message? There was no way anyone else was in possession of his viewpoint's trace. That left De Flanc's guess.

Fate.

Except, he didn't believe in things like that, and the man had scared him right after. Sending messages into the void was one thing, but receiving was another. Apparently, some people in the past had communicated with malevolent spirits in this manner, only to turn mad soon after.

This was one of the reasons he had completely stopped his experimentation with the thing. And it was saddening to say the least.

Unlike observation, where experimentation could only be done by taking on mortal risks, he had believed this was heaven. All he had to do was spend some of his representation, the same thing he used to execute visions, and the glyphs would follow a pattern.

Before receiving this . . . threat, he had done over fifty tests. The tests comprised sending a very specific string of messages and then observing how the glyphs changed to represent that message.

But there were so many variations, even with a message as simple as the letter *a*, that he had all but given up on figuring out how they were encoded in the short term. Primarily because looking at these glyphs hurt his head.

If he just stared at them passively, it didn't matter, but whenever he tried to understand their course, his eyes strained, and he found himself getting tired in a dozen seconds.

Sending these small messages cost him next to nothing, but the observation and studying after dimmed his thought space almost entirely every time.

He had pages full of notes that tried to decode the movements of the glyph and the set of lists that appeared after it for a short instant.

It was an enigmatic process. Once he was finished penning the message, there was a consistent delay of about two and a half seconds in which the glyphs didn't change at all. After that, golden rectangles appeared, and the newly combined glyph would channel itself into one of them.

But the window for which these golden rectangles appeared was too short for him to figure out anything. He had made over fifty attempts but barely managed to trace out a drawing of them.

He was making slow progress toward understanding what all that meant until he felt it that day. When he sat back down in the carriage after meeting Mistress Amelia, a glyph appeared in his mind.

It was such a complex shape he couldn't understand any of it, so he had done exactly as one was supposed to do with messages received through convergence notes—pen them.

But doing so had sent the glyphs into a new routine. Usually, the rectangles appeared momentarily after the glyphs converged. But this time, those golden rectangles appeared first and stayed etched on the paper. That was when he had concluded they were lists.

This gave him the opportunity he needed to study them, but the wording of that message and the reaction of De Flanc had disturbed him enough that he had failed to glean too much.

From what he remembered, it was a set of lists, each with ten or so items in them. But obviously, he had no clue whatever the hell they meant since they were written in that glyph language, too.

If only he could study them for longer . . .

He let out a sigh and slouched back on the cushioned seats.

Why hasn't she sent me anything?

Esther seemed so pumped about wanting to exchange letters with him, but it had been so many days. Why hadn't she sent anything at all? If she did, he would have a chance to look at those golden lists again.

He was hoping she'd begin the conversation.

Did women generally not do that?

But it'd be weird if I sent the first message, right?

"Fuck me!" he muttered, rustling his hair. He would have to take the loss here. Curiosity was killing him. And it would be nice to know if she got back home safe.

No. It's only gentlemanly of me to begin the conversation! Also, when she responds, I can study those lists. It's a win-win.

He looked outside for a solid minute before he managed to convince himself that this was really a good idea. Nodding to himself, he picked up the pen and . . .

Wait . . .

It was like lightning struck in his mind, and his serious expression slowly morphed into one of joy. He couldn't believe he hadn't thought of this before!

What if I . . . send a message to myself?

This way, he wouldn't have to be the one to initiate the conversation . . . Uh, that is, umm . . . more like he wouldn't have to depend on others for research. Yeah. That was it.

There was nothing to lose by trying this.

Feeling a little squeamish, he placed the nib of his pen beneath that disturbing text and wrote *aaaaaaaaaaaaaaa*. While doing so, he considered his own viewpoint and face.

Glyphs birthed around his every stroke and soon moved in one direction. After two and a half seconds, they converged, and . . .

What?! His eyes widened in surprise, and he gripped the pen harder than ever. The exact same glyph that was on the paper had appeared in his mind, urging him to release it on the note.

That's . . .

He had gone through this, almost as a joke, and to rid himself of stupid reasons to not message Esther first. But it actually fucking worked?

However, his disbelief was quickly picked apart by the growing urge in his head to put the notion on the paper.

So, he didn't waste any more time and let the notion guide him. The moment he put his pen on the paper, his arm moved on its own like it knew what to do. But his focus wasn't on that.

A golden glow seemed to shine in his eyes as his vision was populated by an array of rectangles, lines, and glyphs.

He intentionally slowed down his writing speed, trying to make the most out of this situation. It was fascinating, but he knew he didn't have much time because of his weak eyes, so he focused on analyzing the details beyond the mundane.

First, he leaned in, almost shoving his face into the notepad. The lists were very small in size, after all. The golden things took up most of the space around where he had begun writing. Sadly, many of them were cut off, reaching beyond the canvas of the paper.

Out of the four or five that he could make out, the one in the center was glowing. No, not the whole list, but just one of the items inside it—the very first one out of ten or so. Small golden threads emerged out of that glowing glyph, combining to make a path for his next strokes.

So that's how it works? he mused, his eyebrows raised a little too high.

But that wasn't the most interesting part. If he remembered correctly, the last time he was in the carriage with De Flanc, the second glyph on the list was the one that was glowing. Not the first.

And in every second that passed, he became more and more confident that these ten glyphs on this specific list were exactly the same as last time.

Did this mean something?

He had previously hypothesized that these "items" or glorified glyphs were actually just traces of viewpoints that one used to send messages to others. But then, why was he first on the list? And why had they been second for that strange message he had received?

Was it really the so-called fate?

Then should he interpret this as he was most fated with himself, and hence first on the list? And other people on the list shared his fate, the extent of which decreased the farther down he went?

That sounded oddly reasonable.

Is there any other criteria that I am glossing over just because De Flanc planted this idea in my head? And what even is fate exactly?

But even his slow writing began approaching the end as he sat there without a better answer. So, he focused on other nuances. Could he send a message to other entities on this list, too? And what were those other lists?

The items on the list to the right of the "fate list" changed every second. What could be the essence of that column?

However, as he continued to write more letter *a*'s due to the notion that guided him, the carriage came to a sudden halt, and a voice filled his ears. "We're here, good sir. As fast as wind, ain't it? That would be eleven crowns, please."

Vern sulked, for he wasn't done yet. But right when he was about to shout to make the man wait a while, something changed in those golden rectangles, and an excited gleam appeared in his eyes.

The list with rapidly changing glyphs next to the fate list had settled down. Just like the carriage.

Did that mean . . . ?

With bated breath, he shouted, "Sorry, but can you drop me off at the next block?"

"You sure, sir? Entering the district would cost me toll, and by that, I mean cost you."

"Yeah, whatever. Just go!"

He was almost at the end of the message he had sent himself. The list would disappear at any moment.

So when the carriage started again and the list began changing rapidly, Vern's heart burst with excitement.

These are the traces of people around me!

As the carriage moved about, the people within some range around the convergence note changed, and so did the traces in that list.

"We're here. That would be sixteen crowns."

The list settled down again, confirming his suspicion, and so did the message as his hand halted. Vern closed the notepad and exited gingerly. He gave the man two ten-crown notes and said, "Please keep the change."

The moment he turned away from the carriage, his breath caught in his lungs as he looked at the scenery in front of him.

He believed things couldn't get any better. But it seemed today was one of those days.

Ferrovane Heights was truly a sight to behold.

Carved into the mountain, the towering spires of the castles pierced the fog. Below, a sea of mist swirled through cobbled streets, veiling the lower quarters. Gas lamps glowed intermittently, casting dancing shadows and lending an air of mystery to the shrouded alleys and byways.

Craning his neck, he took in the breathtaking view. Stone and steel bridges spanned the mountain's chasms, connecting various structures. High above, he could just discern people moving within the tall, gilded towers.

The city extended to the riverbanks, where the fog obscured all but the lights in the buildings, revealing the undimmed heart of the Calidian Empire. As his gaze swept across the expanse, mechanical marvels revealed themselves.

Here, trams clattered along serpentine viaducts, their steam engines chuffing rhythmically while far in the distance, an intricate network of gears and pulleys operated a massive elevator, easing access to the upper castles.

Sentinel-like smokestacks rose against the bright sky, their plumes mingling with the fog. In the distance, airships dotted the horizon. Their propellers added a soft hum to the industry's symphony, silhouetted against the sun's orange sheen.

Indeed, this was the capital of one of the largest empires on the continent of Quartzford.

Chapter 5

FERROVANE HEIGHTS

Vern looked out at the bustle as the tram zoomed past one neighborhood after another and up a winding path. The tram's interior was nothing to write home about, but it was the mechanical art of the work that mattered.

Just from the sound and smoke of the engine, he could tell it was state of the art. The previous generation engines—the same ones used in trains—didn't use a purifier and ran on coal. This one was definitely running on a steam core.

But he didn't have the mind to appreciate the beauty of his ride like usual. All he wanted was for his representation to regenerate as soon as possible. He hadn't realized it, but he had spent around 80 percent of it in the short time he had stared at those lists.

He would have loved to find out more about them right away because the possibilities excited him to no end, but he had a long day ahead of him. He wouldn't want to go into this special occasion already drained of juice. First impressions mattered a lot, after all.

Not like the convergence note was going anywhere. And since he didn't need anyone else to help him research it, he could always figure out its nuances at a more opportune time.

So he continued to scrutinize the structure of everything that passed by the windows. He had realized the fastest way to regenerate his representation was to do just that.

It seemed counterintuitive that one had to think harder to generate usable thoughts, but it also had sound logic. How representation worked used to be an enigma before he had a thought space.

But now? He could clearly gauge the amount he had left and plan his expenditure around it. All he had to do was look at the intensity of those lights within his thought space. Though it would probably make more sense to call them insights.

So, all he had to make those insights bloom brighter was to analyze structures. He had been doing this within his own room for a while now but had begun to see diminishing returns in the rate at which it recharged his representation.

Right now, however, the dark sphere within his mind's eye was rapidly reclaiming its glow. It was very curious. So much so that he had devised a couple mathematical equations to try to quantify the amount.

But it seems they need to be further modified now, he thought as another new insight blossomed within his thought space. This was the tenth time it had happened in the past half hour he had spent on the tram.

It started with that fleeting feeling of having figured out something new that he couldn't put his finger on. But unlike the dreadful past where such insights were lost in the next moment, his thought space immortalized it.

His smile grew wider every time the islands within his mental insight sphere extended further. He barely managed to keep himself from forgoing today's primary task and just traveling around in the tram all day.

The feeling of his capabilities growing further simply by virtue of gaining deeper insight into a topic thrilled him to no end.

He looked with sharp focus at that grand cathedral in the distance, its arches and its bows, and then at that forge by the next tram station. Those underpass sections of the tramway or the flyovers made the residences look small. All of them hid something new for him to glean.

The crowded market that had more shops than he'd ever seen in one place or that thousand-step staircase that led all the way up to the mountaintop. It was all . . . mesmerizing.

Except that it was probably not the most efficient method to go about progressing his viewpoint.

At the current rate, he'd have to spend months or even years looking at these buildings before he could fill in an octant within his thought space. And who was to say there wouldn't be diminishing returns?

So, after a couple more stations passed by, he calmed himself down and reoriented himself.

One station after another, the tram crossed multiple kinds of sections of the district. Heck, he felt awkward calling it a district. This "district" was larger than many cities he'd been to.

At one odd station, a rush of people entered the same car as him and occupied every seat of the previously empty tram.

A little distracted eavesdropping told him some priest was giving a sermon, and this whole party was going there to worship. The thought left a bad taste in his mouth.

Still, he understood the need for religion. Especially in times like this. People wanted to believe that they mattered. That there was something above, watching their actions and caring about them.

Hah.

The only things watching them were beings that probably considered them less than ants. The only god that existed was that of make-believe. A symbol. It'd be fine if all they did was believe in a collective symbol.

But these people expected this symbol to care for them.

"Tch."

He shook his head and focused back on the scenery outside. He needed the progress this scenery allowed him. Only then. Only then could he create the balance. Something higher than a symbol.

In another few minutes, the conductor shouted, "Hillside Park."

Vern squeezed past the believers and exited the tram. He paid when he got on, so he wasn't committing his second illegal act of the day.

Purified white smoke from the tram cleared up, and he walked up to the little map painted on a signboard. He had to get to the former imperial palace. He had never been to the place, the very reason he left almost an hour before he needed to.

He didn't know if and how big of an organization Vigil was, but he was in safe hands if their location was anything to go by. Not just any random nobody could establish themselves in the previous empress's palace.

So that was reassuring. Obviously, someone as powerful as Shinsei wasn't joking around, but Vern didn't know. He had only met three people from the organization in person.

Shinsei had taken him to one of their "hideouts" in the Athenaeum district to test his "blessing," but he only saw a couple hooded faces there, so there was not much to judge them on.

He now understood that blessing, which Shinsei talked about, was a very loose term that included a viewpoint's moral and physical ramifications. If someone had a pollution quotient higher than a certain threshold, they would have to explain and have their viewpoint thoroughly tested before being allowed to join.

That was because there were only two reasons for a viewpoint to have a high pollution quotient. One was that the observer had chosen a very illogical viewpoint and somehow managed to achieve enlightenment with it. So, each vision they performed was "inefficient" and caused unintended side effects.

The other reason was the viewpoints that had an evil tendency right from the start. They were the kind that didn't care or bother about the internal consistency of their logic and just imposed their will on reality.

In hindsight, it sounded like the visions they could create around such a viewpoint would be very potent, but a closer look revealed an obvious limitation. The more inefficient one's viewpoint was, the more representation it cost them to envision even simple things.

Vern could safely say this was the most interesting tidbit about observation he had learned so far that didn't come from his own testing. Shinsei had told all this very easily, and Vern remembered feeling like a fool.

And there's more of that up there!

Butler De Flanc had praised their library so much that Vern was more than pumped. It held so many answers that he couldn't wait to get in on.

So he quickly figured out the route to one of those elevators he'd seen from the bridge. It was not even five minutes away.

He checked his pocket watch, and it read half past eleven. He had to be there by one. That was more than enough time.

He sauntered in the beautiful weather, feeling rather refreshed. His balance of the wins for the day quite outweighed the setbacks.

Life wasn't perfect after duskfall, but there was clearly a lot to be happy about.

Click.

Crrrrank.

He leaned on the railing and looked beyond the glass window of the metallic capsule as it began to slow its rapid ascent. Surely, they didn't want their customers going up so fast they'd have their guts turned upside down.

But damn, was this commute getting expensive. He had already spent more than fifty crowns just getting here, more than half of it on this elevator ride alone.

Can I lodge this as a business expense? He chuckled at the thought.

It was worth it though. Just looking at the mechanism of this elevator working had added a couple insights into his thought space, much less the view of the city itself. And it was . . . fun. He hadn't been on a ride like this since . . .

Since Mom, Dad, and Ari were around.

"Please mind the gap when exiting. Especially if you're wearing heels," shouted the handler on the platform as he escorted people out safely.

Vern made his own exit and asked the old man, "Excuse me, but which direction is the former imperial palace?"

The man looked Vern up and down before nodding. "You're the tenth person who has asked that question today. Mind if I ask what's going on?"

"You don't know?"

That wasn't Vern. Someone else had answered that question with a question.

Vern glanced back and noticed a handsome man with a middling fashion sense walking up to both of them, his long blonde hair moving to and fro. He probably had been in the elevator with Vern.

The old man took it in stride and shook his head. "Not a clue. They won't talk."

The blonde-haired guy asked back in kind, "And what makes you think we will?"

The handler took off his beret and began dusting it as he replied, "Because neither of you have your nose pointing up to the sun like those stinking nobles."

Vern looked around and sighed. Luckily, the rest of the group from the elevator had cleared out, or this was sure to become a problem real quick. Nobles wouldn't take that lying down. However, Vern wasn't the best judge of the customs of this city. Maybe commoners weren't as oppressed as other places?

At this remark, the blonde guy seemed impressed and checked Vern out. "You really sure this guy isn't a noble? He's dressed like one."

The old man scoffed. "Hah, a greenhorn wants to teach me how to judge people?"

After scrutinizing Vern a little more, the blonde-haired guy laughed. "Well, I guess you're right, given that he's looking at me like I am stupid for even asking that."

Huh? Did he really make such an expression? Well, maybe it was because of the man's poor clothing choices. It wasn't about his clothes being dirty or anything. No, Vern couldn't fault one for that. It wasn't even the quality, branding, or any stupid materialistic idea like that.

It was about synergy. This man had picked the horrible combination of shiny red pants paired with a yellow jacket and a blue vest. It wouldn't have been a disaster if the jacket matched his hair, but it was too light for even that.

To make it even worse, he had a black hair clip, too. It surely had to be his inner repulsion to this abomination of an outfit that was visible on his face. And you know what? He didn't blame himself. The man deserved this for choosing to wear that atrocity.

A simple all-black outfit would have been ten times better.

"Hey! Are you mesmerized by my killer dress? I'll have you know I got it tailor-made for this occasion."

Flap. Flap.

The old man waved his beret in front of Vern, ignoring the blonde guy. "What occasion? Come on, tell me."

Vern was only thankful for the interruption. He didn't want to answer that previous question. What he did want, however, was to get out of here as soon as possible. What if he caught this man's fashion sense by sticking around him?

The thought gave him goose bumps. And the realization that they were going to the same place only made his heart sink even deeper.

Accepting his fate, he replied with a pinch of truth and lies, "There's an interview for some new organization there."

The blonde lightly smacked Vern's back and added, "Right! What he said. Now, can you tell us how to get to this palace?" But the touch of that horrific non-synergized yellow only made Vern feel like he was being wronged.

Suppressing his nonsensical disgust, he eyed the old man, who obviously didn't buy his bullshit. Still, he told them exactly where to go. Apparently, it was the building of two castles to the left.

As they walked on, the blonde man patted him one more time and retracted his putrid arm before saying, "Nice to meet you, man. I am Lucian. What about you?"

He somehow managed to say, "Vern. Nice . . . nice to meet you, too."

Then, in an attempt to counter his illogical loathing for the blonde guy just because of his outfit, Vern restarted the conversation as they walked past one gaudy cathedral-like building. "So, what exactly are we here for?"

The guy smiled sunnily and said, "Well, isn't it an interview?"

Wow. He was trying to be funny now. It wasn't endearing at all—not paired with that outfit.

Taking a deep breath, Vern tried again, "So you don't know either?"

But then, as if a switch flipped inside him, Lucian suddenly turned serious and replied, "Well, it really is an interview for me. I am going to meet my new mentor for the first time today. So if they don't like me, I am fucked. What about you?"

That was interesting. They climbed the stairs and began on a sloping path toward their destination, and Vern replied, "I guess by that logic, it's my first day on the job."

"Lucky bastard. Anyway, what district are you from?"

"None, really. I'm not a local."

"Oh? Then why join the Vigil here and not some organization back in your hometown?"

That was a deeper question than Vern bargained for.

What is home?

Was Master's research station really home? He surely liked the man. A lot.

But was that the place he'd want to go back to and settle down in had the world not gone to hell?

Unlikely.

Too many bad memories there. Not enough good ones to outweigh the bad, at least.

Then, was it here in Elmhurst?

He had thought so. At least until Ari was here.

Now? He had no clue . . .

"Damn. Me and my mouth. My bad, man. Didn't mean to make you think about family and home."

Well. Either this guy was too good at reading him, or Vern's skin was too thin.

He began looping a strand of his blonde hair and mumbled, " I guess . . . all of us could benefit from not having to think about family."

Vern couldn't deny that one.

So they walked on in serene silence until they reached "just the second palace on the left."

"Damn! We sure this isn't the current emperor's palace?"

Vern agreed with the man for the first time as he let out an involuntary gasp himself. He stood before a castle, its grandeur not just a presence but an encounter. Its structure loomed over him with an air of regal opulence, each spire reaching toward heaven as if to weave the very clouds in its design.

The stone from which the facade had been hewn gleamed like polished onyx in the daylight, reflecting the sun's rays with a luster that bordered on divine. Elegant flying buttresses arched gracefully from the main structure, supporting the lofty towers that were adorned with intricate filigree.

The craftsmanship was exquisite, with every detail contributing to the overarching sense of splendor. Ribbed vaults and pointed arches bespoke of a lineage from a previous era, yet the overall effect was uplifting. The architecture seemed to defy gravity in its ascent.

The gateway itself was a triumphal arch, its keystone bearing the symbol of an eye—the same one as the badge Shinsei had given him. Dozens of carriages stood in front of the palace, cluttering the walkway.

Stained-glass windows arrayed across the facade, their edges adorned by the marvel of ornamental stonework, each carved figure and filigree imbued with significance. When the light struck them so, the ground was bathed in a kaleidoscope of warmth that played upon the flagstones and ivy-clad walls.

Just looking at this structure caused a couple new insights to blossom within Vern's thought space. It seemed he really had missed out by not having seen this majestic castle before.

"You know what, man? We should head in. We're looking like country bumpkins, staring like this," said Lucian, his eyes glued to the tallest spire.

"Indeed."

Chapter 6

PRELUDE

After having their invitations verified at the giant door, they were finally allowed in without any other hassle.

The interior was as luxurious and opulent as the exterior. It was definitely the finest of the work, but at least his jaw wasn't hanging open this time around. He had some experience in this department, after all.

He had worked as a tutor for some noble's kid once, and the decor there was at least on par with what was presented here.

But something else had him scratching his head. There were too many people in here. He wasn't feeling sure anymore. What the hell was going on? What exactly was Vigil organizing?

"Hey, man. Are you sure we're at the right place?" whispered his poorly dressed fellow bumpkin.

"I am pretty sure I got the time, date, and place right," answered Vern hesitantly, eyeing all the people in their exquisite gowns, resplendent attires, and opulent robes.

Each hallway and corridor had groups of people standing together, laughing, chatting, and making small talk.

What the hell was this?

From the looks of it, it seemed like a banquet would begin any moment. The atmosphere wasn't really what one would expect from a somber organization like this.

Was it going to be some kind of party to celebrate the foundation of the Vigil? For the new year? If it was anything like that, he would much rather go find the library than stick around to mingle with these people for the sake of it.

But that's when his eyes glanced at the people in the side halls, and he reflexively let out an "Oh."

It seemed like he had underestimated this situation a little. The nobles here weren't just nobles. They were observers, too.

In one group, motes of lights surrounded a guy while he played with his glowing fingers. One second, he was standing next to a pillar, but next, he swapped places with a mote of light.

On the other end of the hall, he saw a girl in black with double-edged knives floating around her as she launched them one after another into a dartboard hanging on a wall.

Then there was also a group of girls who had cups of tea floating in front of them, and they each took sips from them in between sharp giggles.

One guy stood in the corner all alone, the light turning fragmenting into random colors as it neared its vicinity. But this was only the beginning. He could easily make out thirty or so people doing random things like this. How could—

"Whoa whoa whoa, what the hell is going on here, man? Are you seeing this? They're using their powers in front of everyone like it's nothing," Lucian stage-whispered.

Vern was also wondering about the same thing. He replied, "Everyone in here knows about observation." And now that he said it aloud, it only made sense. They only allowed people in with invitations, so everyone here had to have come in contact with observation one way or the other.

Lucian grinned a big one. "Hey, so does that mean we can show off, too?"

But before Vern could reply, a voice resonated throughout the halls. "Ahem, Ahem."

He turned around and noticed a familiar face, and his expression instantly perked up. It seemed that Lucian knew him, too, for he reacted with, "Butler De Flanc!"

Luckily, the guy had just murmured to himself, or it'd have been beyond embarrassing. Because De Flanc hadn't come for either of them especially.

The old man stood in the center of all the halls with his gray hair parted in the middle, sticking neatly to the sides, and addressed the whole crowd with a loud clap of his white-gloved hands.

"Ladies and gentlemen The time is nigh. Vigil's leader will be arriving soon, and since the address will take place atop ichor tower, we should begin gathering right about now. There's only so many elevators, after all."

"Finally! Let's go, girls." And as if on cue, a large group began moving toward the inner hall. It was those girls who had been drinking from floating cups.

However, De Flanc barred their way, bowed formally, and said, "I apologize for inconveniencing you, but the invitation rules clearly mentioned that only the candidates are allowed up the tower. The family members will have to wait down here for the address to be finished."

Candidates, huh? So these were the people who could be joining the Vigil? Was this going to be some kind of inauguration speech, then?

A couple of disgruntled murmurs passed around the hall, and the large group of ten or so girls quickly turned aggressive. One of the older women walked up to De Flanc, shouting at him, "Who the hell do you think you are to tell the women of the Garmen family what to do?"

"Yeah, get the hell away, or don't blame me for using force."

But right as the eyes of one of the women began to glow, someone stepped down from the central hall's stairs, and the whole castle instantly turned silent.

The only disturbance came from the footsteps of that figure. Vern examined her, and the first impression he got was that of immaculate grace.

It was a woman garbed in sleek armor designed to match every curve of her body. It almost acted like a skin suit, but the metallic sheen made it clear it wasn't.

The dark armor had circular golden etchings all over it that radiated an aura of celestial elegance. However, what was contrasting to this menacing form was the layers of silky blue veil that hovered around her.

The thin cloth swayed with her every move, allowing her bewitching countenance framed by her short dark hair to peek through every few seconds. Vern saw a pointed nose, thin ruby lips, and sharp blue eyes that ruthlessly bore down on everyone with their sheer indifference.

As she glided past the gathered onlookers and vanished into the chamber beyond, a wave of collective sighs rippled through the crowd, and at last, the room seemed to draw a long, liberated breath.

"Holy fuck, man. Was she a goddess?" chirped Lucian, blinking rapidly as if wanting to make sure this wasn't a dream.

"Lady Antonia. Oh my god, I saw Lady Antonia!"

"It was worth coming here just for this. I can't believe this—"

"Did you see how she acted so high and mighty? What a bitch."

Similar conversations filled the room, but De Flanc didn't let them go on, instead hammering it home another time by saying, "Elevators this way, please," while pointing toward a set of double doors.

It was clear that the butler had anticipated this situation and coordinated the timing of that woman coming down to match his declaration.

A subtle balance of power play, huh?

Five women backed out from that group in the front without another word, but their scrunched-up faces told Vern how enthusiastic they were about it.

Like birds dissociating from their flocks, many left their group to head toward the elevators while the rest found themselves seats to waste time. The ones who waited were obviously the family members of the candidates.

His fellow bumpkin glanced back at Vern and asked, "Let's go?"

Vern shrugged. "Sure."

So they followed the group that marched in the direction De Flanc had pointed.

"Wait, Master Vern. Master Lucian."

Both halted in their tracks, and a few from the mass ahead of them glanced back, eyeing their interaction with giggles.

Vern ignored their nasty looks and turned toward De Flanc. He wanted to chat with him anyway, but he had assumed it would be rude to disturb the man by asking silly questions when he was clearly busy managing all this.

So the moment he was close enough, Vern greeted, "Happy New Year, De Flanc."

Lucian gasped and joined him by saying, "Me, too. Yeah, happy New Year, sir." However, there was a hint of betrayal in his eyes.

Yeah, strangers with abominable outfits don't get a New Year's wish from me. Sorry, not sorry.

"A prosperous New Year to you gentleman as well. Did you have any trouble finding your way up here?"

Lucian swept his hair back and rubbed his hands together before replying, "Well, you see, I didn't have a problem, but my wallet? Yeah, it's not very happy. Can we, uh, do something about that?"

Vern wanted to ask something along these lines at some point in time, but not right now! He stepped back a little, trying to reduce his association with this walking embarrassment.

"Hahaha, don't worry about that, Master Lucian. We will set you up with a pass from the Crown itself so you can use most public services without having to worry about your wallet ever again."

Lucian clapped his hands. "Great!"

Before the man could ask any more mortifying questions, Vern interjected, "De Flanc, can you give us a little idea of what's going to happen? Why are there so many nobles here? It's not some kind of party, right? Because I'd rather go check out the library you praised so much if that's the case."

Lucian looked at him like he was inspecting some insect, but Vern ignored him and focused on De Flanc's response.

The old man waited for a while until their surroundings cleared up, then spoke in a low voice, "Please don't worry, Master Vern. Master Akira doesn't have patience for anything like this, either. But trust him. All this is just to increase the effect of the revelations that will follow."

"I knew it, man!" interjected Lucian.

Right.

Nodding to De Flanc, Lucian walked ahead. "Let's get up there. I'd rather not be the last one."

"Indeed, it isn't something that should be missed. Especially for you two," said the butler with a smile before bowing and heading to the room that the graceful woman from before had entered.

Soon, they found themselves in another hall where four large chambers that looked like huge lamps moved up and down.

"Please just wait a couple more seconds," said the handler in a soothing tone as an elegant chamber encased in wrought iron descended from the top of the dizzyingly high hall without any sound. The intricate ironwork resembled delicate filigree, creating a harmonious blend of strength and elegance.

Once it eased onto the ground, the handler opened its brass door and gestured to the group of five at the front to enter. But that was only the start. More than a hundred candidates were waiting in this hall.

It was gonna be a while.

Since Lucian was too busy admiring himself in the mirrorlike wall, Vern decided to pick up some clues from the exchanges nearby. Surely, they would give him some idea about what was going on.

"Come on, you've never even squashed a bug. Do you really think you can deal with the monsters and horrors of the city? There's still time to back down. We go back once this is over and leave this mess for others to deal with."

"Enough, brother! We've been over this a hundred times. I don't care what you have to say about this anymore. If you don't want to do it, you can leave. I am going to help as many people as I can. I believe there's a reason I awakened this power. I am not going to squander it like everyone else in the family."

With that, the girl stepped away, and the guy gnashed his teeth in frustration. It seemed like some conflicting notions of responsibility were at play here.

Wanting to hear more varied opinions on the matter, Vern shuffled around the crowd a little and soon came in earshot of another conversation.

A girl exclaimed, "We're going to learn from the best! Oh my god, I can't believe this! I am sooo pumped! Do you know that even the young Master Finnesse also works for Vigil?!"

"You mean Ambrose? That hypocrite bastard? What the hell, man? Great, as if getting an audience with Lady Antonia weren't tough enough. With him around, it's practically a lost cause."

A third chimed in with a depressing tone, "I suppose that is unfortunate—"

"Hey! Watch your mouth about young Master!" the first girl protested. "Don't you know his reputation? His sister's only stronger because she's older. Did you miss the news about him taking down a templar from some top-tier order?"

Vern's mind clicked. *So that woman was Ambrose's sister, huh?*

Now that they had mentioned it, Vern saw the similarity. They did look a little alike. She even had the aura of a real "dancer." Not a phony scammer like Ambrose, who liked to cuss eleven times while hiding behind the facade of a gentleman.

Even he can have admirers, huh? Vern mused silently, amused by the thought. The whims of the nobility were ever elusive, their passions and loyalties a constant source of entertainment.

With a soft chuckle, he drifted away from the debate, his curiosity leading him to the next cluster of gossiping attendees.

"Hey, you see those two? Do you know them? What family do they belong to?"

Hmm, they were talking about him and Lucian, weren't they?

Chapter 7

ASSEMBLE

S ome commoners, I bet. Look at that buffoon's dress. No family would let a son of theirs walk out of the house like that."

Vern didn't agree with their tone and the way they put it, but damn, did he agree with the sentiment.

The whole group giggled. Then one added, "But did you see the audacity of that butler? He treated our families like shit, calling that dancer bitch right at that moment."

"Yeah, not just that. He even called these two low-borns from whatever backwater district to the side for a chat. As if those rats mattered more than our Garmen familia members."

I see. It was the group that tried to argue with De Flanc. That explained it. A bunch of stuck-ups, for sure.

"Hey, commoners got to stick together and all that, you know?"

"And they call us classist. Who's the real classist here, huh?"

"Hahaha"

"Hah, I can't."

Yeah, this wasn't very informational. He had long become immune to jabs from stupid ones who liked to think simply being born into a noble family put them above everyone else.

He had been at the same tables as many nobles because of his profession, so he knew exactly what went through their minds. The depths of their depravity were nothing new to him. But obviously there were all kinds of nobles in the world—just like commoners. He wasn't one to generalize for the sake of it.

"Next group, please," hollered the handler, and luckily, it was directed to the set of bitches that wouldn't stop with their disdainful commentary.

Taking a deep breath, he let it go. It wasn't worth arguing with people like them. Moving his attention over to another group, he closed in. That guy who was playing with motes of light was also here.

One of the men grumbled, "This is ridiculous. I've only been an observer for ten days. Just ten days! Why did my family even accept this absurd invitation? I'm nowhere near prepared for whatever this is."

A second man bobbed his head in agreement. "Exactly. I've got no interest in being a guinea pig for some untested venture. Bet they're just winging it. We'll sit through their spiel, then make a quick exit, right?"

The first man's resolve firmed as he spoke, "Indeed. We should wait and see if this organization is worth joining or not. If this organization proves itself, joining later won't be an issue. They'll need us nobles eventually—commoners lack the observation records, after all."

But that's when the light manipulator interjected with serene composure, "It's about the first mover's advantage."

Shoving his hands in his pockets, he leaned on the wall and continued, "If we don't join it during its early days, we will be giving up the golden opportunity to shape the future. Once the groundwork is laid and internal alliances are formed, changing anything gets exponentially harder."

Then he narrowed his eyes and declared, "So if you all want to chicken out, go right ahead. I am nabbing my place with the founders."

"But Arthur, aren't you concerned about the risks?" another questioned, skepticism lacing his tone. "You think it's going to be that simple?"

A different voice piped up, somewhat reluctantly, "He does have a point though."

Then the handler interjected again, and three more groups were sent to the top of the tower, including the one he was eavesdropping on.

Vern looked at his pocket watch. They still had about twenty minutes, and only a couple more groups were left ahead of them.

Now he didn't even need to strain to hear what was being discussed. It was a group of two guys and one girl.

The girl whined, "Why are we here? I could've gotten my nails done in this time."

The taller one mumbled, his voice getting louder by the second, "Who cares about your stupid nails? I had to ditch a date for this charade. Daddy made me cancel it. What was he thinking, for Lady's sake?"

The third one tried to pacify them, his eyes fixated on that outer room. "Hey, come on, guys. Don't be like that. We got a chance to see Lady Antonia. I say it was worth it."

The girl pulled out a file and began shaping her nails as she snarled, "Don't care. Didn't ask. She is much more of a bitch than she lets on."

The tall one banged on the wall and moaned, "Ah, who the fuck cares about her? She's out of our league. But my date? MAN! I've been courting her for three months. Three fucking months, and she never bothered with me. But now that her lover died in duskfall, she finally gave me a chance. It was my only opportunity! Shit. Shit. Shit. I can't believe it!"

The girl threw him a disgusted look while checking the shape of her nails. "You're annoying. Just leave and go to your stupid date."

He pulled his hair, letting out the words through gritted teeth, "And have my old man bury me alive? He's definitely lurking around here somewhere. If I don't do this correctly, I am going to get my allowance cut for who knows how long."

Ugh. That was it. Vern didn't need to hear any more of their stupid gossip. He had heard enough opinions to get a picture of what was going on anyway.

There were all kinds of opinions on the matter. Some were going into this naively, while others understood the risk but still wanted to join the Vigil.

A few just tagged along because of the hype while some came because of family pressure. There were then obviously the ones who wanted to use this as an opportunity to further themselves.

But what surprised Vern was the nonchalance of these people. A lot of them acted like duskfall hadn't just wiped a third of the world out of existence without any explanation.

They didn't feel any sense of responsibility toward society, even with their great powers.

Vern shook his head. Such was life. Everyone was the main character in their story, and he had no reason to try to tell them what was wrong and what wasn't.

As three more elevators came back down, the handler opened their brass doors and gestured everyone in. Vern and Lucian finally managed to board one for themselves alongside three other people. The handler fastened the latch back on, and soon, the contraption began its ascent.

Crank.

Vern took this opportunity to admire the structure of this different kind of elevator. It was such a rush when simply analyzing those curves and thinking about their design, which caused a new insight to blossom within his thought space.

When they stepped out of the elevator up top and then into the enclosing room, a chilly wind picked up and quickly cooled him down. It was nearly the height of winter, after all.

Luckily, Nvoria used to get far colder than this. So this somewhat chilly weather felt nostalgic instead.

"Hey, I am gonna go talk to some of these beauties. It should be a walk in the park to start the conversation with such a gorgeous view right in front of us. Care to be my wingman?" said Lucian with a conspiratorial look.

Vern held back a sigh and advised, "It's not a good idea."

"Your loss." Lucian shrugged and left his words hanging in the air, walking past him.

Vern shook his head and ignored the guy who was about to become the butt of many jokes, focusing on his surroundings instead. Many slimmer sub-towers were connected to this landing, reaching higher into the skies supported by flying buttresses and large pillars.

But he quickly forgot all about them. The real beauty of this tower wasn't up here. It was in the wide expanse on display.

Vern walked to the parapet, and the entire city unfolded before his eyes. Not just the immediate vast district but the entirety of the urban sprawl. He could even spot the clock tower next to his hotel in the Fulham borough.

To the north, his gaze landed on a half-ruined peak—the remnants of what used to be the steamscript relay station. This perspective cast that crater Ari had inadvertently made in a new light.

Seconds turned into minutes as he took in this breathtaking sight, moving from one edge of the tower to the other. It wasn't long before he began to draw a map of his own.

Right when he was outlining some port district on the outer edge of the city, he heard the doors of the adjacent elevator room—one that no one else had been allowed to use—open with a bang.

Soon, a rhythmic thump of majestic footsteps resonated in the environment, and an array of handsome men and gorgeous women walked out. The air seemed to crackle as uncanny phenomena transpired with each of their steps.

It was getting started, it seemed. So Vern pocketed his notepad and focused up.

The candidates parted like a sea before this unstoppable ship, their eyes wide with awe. Each stride of the procession appeared to synchronize with some unseen machinery, creating an aura of power and intrigue.

Vern even thought his senses were playing tricks on him, for the air seemed to become tangible around one of them, while he didn't hear any sounds from the vicinity of another one. The space seemed to distort while the temperature on the roof dropped even lower.

Not even a moment passed, and he spotted a couple familiar faces in this set. Captain Shinsei walked in in his usual unkempt attire, facial stubble, sword on his side, and wearing a red scarf. But even he seemed to have a unique oppressive charisma about himself today.

All seven of them wore hooded capes each with the symbol of an eye etched on it with an insane amount of detailing. However, no one had their hood on except the man in the center, who walked in the lead.

Heck, the hood was just the beginning. A pure black blindfold covered the man's eyes, and the shadow of his cloak hid his features.

That beautiful lady with a floating silk veil and black-gold armor with hundreds of plates walked next to the blindfolded man while a redheaded man flanked his other side.

But the parted candidates seemed to grow surprised after glancing at that blindfolded figure, some even pointing at the man with trembling hands.

These should be the other captains that Ambrose mentioned, Vern mused.

Clank.

However, right at this moment, something latched on to the stone railing right behind him, and Vern jumped out of the way with a start.

He quickly put his guard up and backed out of there, but soon a figure pulled itself up the railing and vaulted over effortlessly.

It was . . . a Kingsman.

That tricorn hat, face cover, and thick leather trench coat crisscrossed with leather strings—corroded by wind and weather. A dark gray capelet billowed with the man's every move as he cut through the candidates without any effort.

And then another dark figure leaped over the railing from the other end of the tower. And her mere sight caused Vern to perk up instantly. A scythe gleamed behind the lithe figure of the woman as she moved to join the group too.

Mistress Amelia! He cheered in his heart but stood his ground. It would seem off if he tried to start a conversation with Mistress in such a solemn atmosphere.

The tension began to mount as everyone around him became jittery. Their stances grew unstable, their faces masks of confusion and alarm. A few straight-up retreated to the elevators, almost tripping on their own feet.

Muffled chattering began again, and a surge of incomprehensible sentences backed by fear, confusion, and excitement bombarded his ears.

"Who . . . who-who do you think is that man in the middle? I think I've seen him before somewhere."

"It can't be. But that can't be! Wasn't he exiled as a kid?"

"Hey, fuck that! What the hell are Kingsmen doing here? They're not even observers. Who gave them the right to encroach here?"

"Shut up! You wanna get us all killed, don't you?"

"Wasn't this supposed to be a simple recruitment speech? What the hell is going on?"

"Is that Lady Amelia!? The Eclipsed Reaper? I heard she cleansed our city of at least a thousand of those stupid insurgents in just one week! Oh my god, I can't believe she's here! Will we get a chance to work with her?"

"Look at you—"

Thump.

Suddenly, the footsteps came to a halt as they reached the end of the tower. All the captains turned around to face the crowd, and the blindfolded man walked out of the formation. Taking off his robe in a smooth motion, he took a deep breath and let out a fierce yell.

"Observers!"

The shout resonated like a thunderclap in everyone's mind, plunging the terrace into utter silence. Vern, too, felt an invisible force pressing down upon him.

As the oppressive silence grew, the man broke it with a dramatic flair of his arms. "I, Akira Ferrovane, stand before you today," he declared, "to shatter the veil of ignorance you have willingly draped over your eyes."

CHAPTER 8

FORMER PRINCE

Before the man could even finish the sentence, the floor rumbled.
Thump.

Thump.

Thump.

Vern watched on in astonishment as, one after another, everyone around him fell on their knees, and it only hit him a little too late. *He is a Ferrovane!* Not wasting another breath, Vern bowed his head and fell down on one knee.

Even the men and women who followed behind the prince were down on their knees. The only exceptions to this demonstration were the two Kingsmen who looked on apathetically from the sides.

Then as if everyone had rehearsed this a million times, the whole crowd bellowed in unison, "We greet the former prince!"

Vern simply mouthed the words, barely keeping up with all that was happening.

However, this didn't seem to faze the captain at all. Amid the looming towers and the oppressive weight of silence, he stood—a figure both enigmatic and imposing. His hair, long and pale as moonlight, fell about his shoulders wild and untamed.

A blindfold, as dark as an abyss, concealed his eyes, yet it didn't evoke an ounce of pity but instead suggested a vision far more penetrating. Clad in an onyx coat adorned with intricate yet delicate tracery and the subtle sheen of velvet, he bore the weight of authority and finesse of the regal aristocracy.

Epaulets heavy with ornate embellishments spoke of rank and burden of command while the cravat embedded with a ruby brooch wrapped around his neck in delicate folds of lace, expressing his eye for detail. Finally, his cuffs, edged with patterns of delicate frost, added a touch of gentility amid the strength.

As the winds toyed with his alabaster locks, his high cheekbones—sharp as guillotine blades—cast deep shadows, imbuing him with a sculptural quality. Even without the shape of his eyes obscured by the blindfold, his face was a landscape of power, every contour meticulously crafted by nature to demand respect and evoke a sense of enigmatic allure.

With a dismissing wave, he commanded, "Rise, observers. Today, I am not here in my capacity as a former prince but rather as a fellow observer. Someone who reveres the laws of the world as much as a criminal venerates the laws of the land."

None dared to laugh at his witty remark, but everyone still stood back up. Vern, not really sure what to make of this, looked at the others to gauge the weight of this revelation. Fervor, panic, and a hundred other emotions were bare on everyone's faces to see, clearly suggesting no one expected this.

Vern chided himself for not knowing scrapshit about this city's political situation. However, it did make some sense that the "former" prince would establish his organization at the "former" imperial palace.

It was still surprising in its own right though. Not one of the three members of Vigil he had talked with let it slip that Captain Akira was a former prince. And what was the meaning of "former" here? Was he a candidate in the last succession?

But that didn't make much sense. From what Vern knew, the current emperor was well into his fifties and had been at the helm for over twenty years. He considered it a miracle that he remembered even this much.

Vern shook his head. He couldn't just analyze his way through questions like these. Context mattered a lot, and he didn't have it.

"Now, let us begin . . ." The blindfolded prince held up his hands and clapped softly. And the moment he did, the whole scenery changed.

The city beyond the tower's parapet suddenly turned dark, and a moon hung high while the skies took on a dark hue. What was interesting, however, was the fact that there was no gash in this sky. Maybe because it was just an illusion?

A quick look at the flabbergasted candidates told him that he wasn't the only one seeing this.

The girl next to him, the one that was messing with those double-edged knives in the hall downstairs, muttered, "How did he force us into a vision? This . . . this shouldn't be possible, even if his perception is shades beyond ours—not when there are hundreds of us."

Vern was wondering about the same thing himself. But most of the others seemed to ignore that fact for the spectacle it created out in the city. Before things could devolve into a hubbub again, Captain Akira spread his arms and stated, "This is the day that will live on in infamy forever."

Everyone moved closer to the edges of the tower, looking beyond the parapet at the sprawling cityscape, illuminated by countless lights and outlined by masterfully crafted structures. Even the destroyed peak in Starfall Heights was back to its original pristine state.

Vern realized what was going on. *It's what the city looked like on the night of duskfall.*

After letting the crowd take in the sight for a while, the captain continued, "This is the day when the world lost its charm. Wives lost their husbands, and fathers lost their sons. Families lost their heirs, and cities lost their leaders. The day when the skies wept fire."

Boom.

An intense explosion went off far in the distance, a mushroom of fire growing rapidly, but the prince didn't stop. "This is the day when billions vanished into thin air and civilization halted."

Shriek.

The haunting sound of emergency sirens echoed, fading into ghostly wails, but the prince's words cut through, "This is the day when laughter died in the streets and children lost their protectors. Homes turned to ashes, and communities crumbled."

Crash.

Hundreds of buildings, a distant silhouette against the night, collapsed under their own weight, sending clouds of dust throughout the city. Yet, the man's voice remained unyielding. "This is the day when the fabric of reality was tainted and the representation of the planet itself was polluted."

Then he stopped and faced the sky and suddenly everything halted in its steps. The expansive city turned quiet all at once, and the world lost its radiance. With an inordinate amount of emotion in his words, he yelled, "This is the day when objectivity was shattered!"

Crack.

Everything exploded in a frenzy of particles. The buildings making up the city underneath turned hollow and transparent while the sky twisted and turned. The fiery explosions became white, and the moon distorted.

When nothing was left but darkness, the prince calmed down and shook his head before continuing, "It was the day that could have been the end of the world. Just like in the tale of the first observer. But we survived."

The man waved his hand, and the darkness beyond the tower receded, making way for the day sky of the real city underneath. The mountain to the north was back to being in shambles, its peak missing entirely.

Yet the prince went on, "But know that true objectivity is shattered. You may think it a blessing to view the world subjectively, but it's just as much a curse. Every law you change, every vision I impose, every possibility we observe—we bend the very fabric of reality."

He then held up his hands, and everyone turned their eyes over unanimously. With a snap of his fingers, a minor black distortion appeared in his palms, and he spoke, "However, unlike in the genesis era, the world now knows to heal. To return to its objective state."

As if to prove his sentiment, the black distortion was ripped to pieces and eroded away as his words came to an end. Even Lucian nodded alongside many others, already privy to such a simple fact of life.

Captain Akira's gaze swept over the crowd, capturing every eye with the gravity of his words. "But it's getting weaker. Every day. Every minute. Every second. Even in this very instant, objectivity is getting polluted. The hold of reality on itself is slipping, spiraling down an inevitable doom."

He paced slowly, his every step measured. "Now, there's one simple solution to fix it—have all observers forfeit their viewpoints and let the world heal." Conflicted expressions appeared on everyone's faces, but none dared deny the point.

But Captain shook his head. "Yet, it is nothing but a flight of fancy. Ten or so unrecognized observation records are already circulating throughout the city, and one can only imagine what's happening in the rest of the world. Pandora's box has opened, and it is impossible to shut it."

Captain turned slowly, his posture an embodiment of solemnity, facing the spire that pierced the twilight sky. His voice, when it emerged, was a soft murmur laden with an ineffable dread. "But there is yet a deeper, more profound disturbance that plagues us. In the wake of our tampering with reality and barely surviving, we have invited the inexplicable into our midst."

He stood still as if sensing the very air around him. "These entities, these anomalies, defy all attempts at explanation. They are not creatures of logic or reason, but manifestations of the world's growing madness, born from the depths of the unfathomable."

The crowd grew restless at this mention, but he carried on, "Their influence seeps through the cracks of our world, an invisible miasma that warps the mind and matters alike. Their very presence rends the fabric of sanity, turning the familiar into the bizarre, the rational into the absurd."

"So tell me, observers." He snapped his head toward the crowd, his blindfolded gaze piercing deeper than the captains standing behind him. "Tell me. What have we done to stop this? What are we going to do to stop this? Every one of us jumped at the opportunity to enlighten ourselves, to observe the world through our chosen viewpoints, to bend the reality to our will."

His voice softened, betraying a hint of sorrow. "But what have we done? What have our families done? When the dusk fell, the very nobility that was supposed to protect the city from such dangers turtled up in their shells, refusing to lend helping hands."

"Thousands upon thousands have been converted into destructive ideologies in a mere span of days. Forced enlightenments, mass observations, large-scale sacrificial ceremonies, systematic mental manipulation, or anything you can imagine that could push our reality further onto an edge—it's being committed right now."

"Why? Because our government decided to 'tighten the net' and secure the inner districts. Because most of the latent observers in our city were too busy cowering in their homes. Those early days after duskfall were when the public was most susceptible to these antics, and if our latent observers had done something about it . . ."

His head bowed slightly as if shouldering the weight of their collective negligence. "I tried. All my friends and colleagues behind me tried. Many who you don't see right now because they're risking their lives at this very moment tried as well. But we were not enough. We are not enough."

Taking a short breath, he shouted, "Yes! We live in a cruel world where selfishness is one of the most essential qualities. Yes! Your life is more important than everyone else's. Yes! It's not your fault that the world went to hell."

"But let me hammer this home. If we don't do something about this right now, the city of Elmhurst as we know it, will be no more."

"The world as we know it will be no more. It will be nothing but an echo of the past. Our streets, homes, families, societies, our very personalities—everything you can conceive of—will undergo a subtle yet relentless transformation. Their inherent characteristics will be tainted, corrupted beyond recognition. Gradually, imperceptibly, we'll reach a point where we will fail to notice the changes, and all that we cherished will have lost its essence irrevocably. And that will be the end."

He stilled. "Now I know. Many of you are still beyond skeptical of every word I've spoken. And I don't blame you. So . . . let me offer you proof."

Extending his arm to one side, he slowly drew it back, pressing his hand close to his heart. His voice resonated with a deep, unwavering conviction. "I, Akira Ferrovane, will show you the pure subjective reality. What the world looks like without the reinforcement of its objective counterpart."

CHAPTER 9

BEHIND THE VEIL

A heavy silence hung atop the tower for a while before it devolved into chaos as if Ferrovane's words had lit a match and set the crowd on fire. Vern looked at Lucian, and the guy had a serious expression on his face.

Then a girl from that group of annoying bitches suddenly shouted, "Hey, I don't consent to this! What if something goes wrong? What if—"

The blindfolded prince interjected with a cold tone, "Then you can leave. Vigil has no need for you."

"Huh? What the hell is wrong with you? You're the one who invited us here! You think I wanted to come here so you could tell me your sob story and guilt me into working for you? What a joke! I showed you respect because of the Crown. You're nothing but an exiled prince. Know your place!"

The captains standing all the way to the back broke out in chuckles, and the "exiled" prince tilted his head before responding, "I suppose your families don't trust you enough to tell you the truth, huh? Well, then, let me fill you in on what's going on.

"When I proposed the creation of Vigil to our emperor, my suggested plan was to select talented individuals from the masses and help them become observers who will fight for the cause."

A disdainful smirk replaced his affable smile, and he continued, "It was the chancellor and archons of your families who pleaded to our emperor to not let 'commoners' be in charge of saving the city.

"So please, I beg of you, don't listen to this exiled prince, and sit this one out. It would mean I can bargain for spots for more talented individuals in the next meeting," he said, chuckling with mirth.

But the girl's face only grew nastier at those remarks, and her companions were just as furious. One of them forced through her teeth, "Okay, keep lying to yourself. Don't come crying on the Garmen family's doorsteps when you can't find a luck-attuned viewpoint in those lowborn."

Captain Akira raised a hand and glanced back. "Arthur, please escort these ladies out of here. Make sure any requests for aid from the Garmen family are denied in the future."

"Yes, sir," replied a tall man with bandages on his arms standing to one side of the long array of captains. And when he moved, he made no sound. None at all.

As he walked toward the group of girls, he pointed and said, "You dare look down on the Garmen family—" Suddenly, their annoying screeches became silenced. They looked about themselves, confused by their loss of speech, and the tall man soon "escorted" them back to the elevator room without giving them a chance to cause any further ruckus.

Vern was only happy he wouldn't have to work with people like this. But before things became too heated in light of this political drama, the blindfolded captain clapped.

"Anyone else who is too scared can leave right now. If you can't confront the simple reality of our situation, you won't be much use to the Vigil anyway." The words were as cold as ice, and it was clear they brooked no argument.

Vern looked around and quickly noticed many unsure faces, but no one really moved. It seemed the gravity of the situation was slowly becoming clear to everyone. Even the brother who tried to persuade his sister to leave gritted his teeth and stood firm.

When no one else complained, the blindfolded captain nodded. "Good."

"Captains. Take positions and defend the observers!"

At his command, the set of men and women standing behind him walked out and encircled the candidates, settling equally far away from each other. Ambrose's sister stood a little behind Vern while Captain Shinsei manned the other end.

Captain Akira sighed. "Now, before we do this, let me give all of you a couple of warnings. Do *not* look behind you. Do *not* look at the sky. Do *not* speak in any language. And most important of all, do *not* focus on anything for too long."

Vern furrowed his brows, unsure of what to make of this. And before he could ponder it further, the crowd destabilized again. Lucian gripped his fist tighter while the girl next to him sheathed her double-edged knives and took a deep breath. Some hyperventilated, while others finally couldn't take it and ran out of the encirclement to the elevator room.

No one stopped them, and the captains didn't seem to care. Many others looked conflicted, but in a few more seconds, solemn expressions replaced their unsure ones. Vern, on the other hand, felt a weird mix of excitement and fear.

If he understood it right, they were about to see a world that wasn't reinforced by objectivity. That was to say, it would be an amalgamation of all the twisted imaginations of city dwellers as well as a certain amount of global fears. Just what would it look like?

However, he was far more curious about those esoteric warnings. Why should he not look back? What was wrong with speaking? And why not look up at the sky? Was it because of the gash, or was it something else?

All very interesting questions, but he had no plans of tempting fate. He was going to follow those warnings to the letter. So he took off his glasses and slid them into their velvet case.

The prince pointed at all the captains and added, "My colleagues will ensure your bodies don't lose their objectivity, and they will defend you from other inherent dangers of that realm. As long as you keep a level head and heed my warnings, it will be over before you know it."

The crowd hesitantly nodded, and a smile bloomed on the prince's face. He took both his hands and pressed them on his heart, and his lips moved. One word resonated in the air: "Gazebinding." The very next instant, a black glow spilled from behind that blindfold. Then before Vern knew what hit him, the scenery changed.

A sense of profound disquiet swept over him as he surveyed the altered surroundings. The floor beneath him took on a bony texture, and its shape resembled that of a rib of some titanic being. Rotten white flesh pervaded the gaps between the skeleton's bones, its foul smell threatening to make his guts churn.

But Vern quickly shifted his focus, making sure not to fixate on one aspect of this reality longer than necessary. His heart raced as faint, anguished cries and unchecked screams emitting from everywhere filled the air.

The faces of the people around him were in constant flux, features melting and reshaping into expressions of joy, sorrow, and terror. Their bodies contorted, elongating and twisting in impossible ways as if each person were trapped in their own personal nightmare.

Luckily, the captains maintained their forms even in this distorted reality, allowing him to reorient a little.

He shifted his gaze beyond the rotting parapet of the skeletal tower, and the sight sent his heart thumping uncontrollably. Thousands upon thousands, if not millions of carcasses floated above the streets—impaled by pikes and stakes originating from blister-like tombstones.

The unclear features and churning flesh of the cadavers being gnawed at by the spikes made his skin crawl. But the sight soon felt . . . mesmerizing, and he quickly realized it was the side effect of having fixated on it a bit too long. So, he bit his tongue and forced himself to focus past all of them without a delay.

The previously tall spires twisted and turned, extending upward infinitely, and Vern dared not follow them to their ends up in the sky. Heavy red fog permeated every street, nook, and cranny, vague outlines emerging from them.

The otherwise elegant and ornate structure of the buildings lost their shapes, becoming lurid amalgamations of grotesque materials that curled, twisted, and churned into sinister abominations. Their mere sight sent a shiver down his spine.

A putrid blend of all that was uncanny—yellow, red, and white flowed through the mazelike city in place of water. It was a mixture he had no wish of further identifying. Trees bled shadows, and their branches reached out all over the world like fingers extending into one's very soul.

That's when he heard a voice. "This . . . is what our reality would become without objectivity." And the words reminded him to breathe. Still, they did nothing to calm his overstimulated mind.

He wanted to look back at Captain Akira, to just stare at the man until he could get his nerves back in control, but what if focusing on him for too long was against the warnings, too?

So he gritted his teeth and kept shifting his sight from one ghastly vista to another, ensuring not to linger on any for too long. Then in his peripheral, he noticed Captain Akira pointing in one direction before saying, "Slowly turn your eyes toward—"

"Agh!"

A piercing scream originated right next to Vern, drowning the captain's words, but the captain simply amplified his voice and carried on, "Toward Crescent Bay."

When Vern reflexively looked to his side, his gaze fell on a fellow candidate, whose unclear shape was letting out a piercing shriek, her face stretched disproportionately as her sinuous arms coiled around her own neck.

He couldn't even be sure if this was real or not. But the bone-piercing scream frayed his nerves, overlaying upon the already saturated cries and screeches from the surroundings.

Still, he recalled Captain Akira's last words and tore his gaze and mind away from the banshee-like wails to focus on Crescent Bay, which was about four bridges away on the outer edge of the city's baleful silhouette.

The moment he perceived what the captain had directed them to, his breath hitched in his throat, and he barely trapped the scream that threatened to burst out of him.

"Agh."

"Save me!"

"Let me go!"

"Stop this!"

However, his fellow candidates couldn't manage to do the same and screamed out one after another. A cacophony of wails assaulted his ears, but he was too stunned to do anything about it.

His mouth went dry, and he swallowed as he stared at that gigantic hand far in the distance. Five bony fingers jutted out of the putrid rivers, constricting the district of Crescent Bay within it. Bloody liquid oozed out of each of its joints and elevated toward the sky.

However, an oval shape peeked through the gap of the fingers, and some hairlike substance outlined humanoid features on it that moved. It was so far away he couldn't be sure, but the rows of teeth were moving.

It said . . .

It said . . .

"Shred me scratch me eat me crush me."

How could he even make these words out? A cold, numbing terror gripped him, freezing him in place, and his knees felt weak.

"Stifle me drown me shatter me maim me."

A sense of impending doom settled over with each word, and he found it impossible to tear his eyes away. Fuck. He tried and tried, but every time his irises were about to change their target, the thing pulled them toward itself!

But how!?

"Rend me drown me thrash me burn me cut me bleed me fester me scar—"

Agh!

All sorts of pain began claiming him, and every word he heard became his reality. He was losing it. He was fucking losing it!

Not caring about any future repercussions, he considered his own body for the shortest of a second, and . . . *Stability inducement.*

His devolving senses became sharp for an instant, and he snatched the chance to rend his eyes away from that thing.

But the moment he did so, the shape hidden beyond the fingers snapped open its bloodshot eyes, teeth made of hairs peeking from within its pupils. But Vern entirely ignored the terrifying thing and focused only on Captain Akira's voice.

"This is what the minds of our populace conjure when they're not affirmed by objectivity. Imagine living in this nightmare. Envision your friends and families slowly losing their grip on reality, turning into inhabitants of this realm."

The words helped, but his skin prickled with fear, every hair standing on end. He could feel it. That thing was staring right at him. And not just that, another feeling of being watched originated from behind him—gnawing at his slim sense of rationality.

Tip.

A sense of panic fluttered in his chest as he felt the one behind it getting closer. And closer.

Tap.

He wanted to look back. He had to look back! How would he prepare for it if he didn't understand it?

No. No. No. No. He shook his head from side to side. He wasn't going to violate another warning, no matter what. He refocused on the sounds he had been intentionally ignoring until now—the terrified screams of his fellow candidates. It helped drown out the steps behind him.

His breath came in short, ragged gasps, but he kept pushing through. He felt exposed and vulnerable, like prey in the sights of a predator, but Captain Akira was saying something. He should listen to that instead. He should. Yes.

Then, the captain turned back toward the crowd and asked another time, "So tell me, dear observers. Do you understand the gravity of our situation?"

"Aghhhhhhhh."

"Zxkoraxx."

"Ygshtohtu."

"Yes!" shouted Vern with all his might, hoping that would get the man to put an end to this.

"Kraxhenzansen."

Tip.

A cold sweat broke out on his forehead, and a deep, unsettling chill coursed through him. His gaze darted frantically, trying not to remain on one thing for too long, but his mind couldn't really drown out that sound anymore.

Tap.

A sense of helplessness washed over him, and he wished to use stability inducement, only to find that trying to do so caused his eyes to slow down and be pulled back toward the face behind the fingers. A lump formed in his throat, making it harder to breathe.

"Rend me drown me thrash me burn me tell me," came a whisper right in his ears with a bloodcurdling timbre. Right after that, something touched his back, and his nerves exploded.

Holding back all his screaming impulses, he instead limped forward on a bony rib of the floor, barely avoiding the shapes of his fellow candidates.

Tip tap tip tap tip tap.

The steps chased him without a moment's delay, and before he could even think about it, it was upon him. His eyes widened, the whites showing in stark terror as something pushed his neck to one side—forcing him to look back.

He wanted to scream. But that seemed to do nothing for his colleagues, so he used his arm to push back, only to feel a cold touch that scraped across his skin and numbed it instantly.

Fuck fuck fuck fuck.

His heart thumped with explosive rhythms as he kept pushing forward, only to barely move an inch, the reverse force threatening to rend his neck in half.

And then it happened. The force twisted his neck around, and a—

Light.

A woman in a tricorn hat and face cover stared back at him. Her pure white locks that spilled out of the hat tried their best to hide her sharp eyes, but they failed miserably.

He soon felt the grip on his head loosen, and she backed away, her hands falling to either side.

But that question left his mind instantly as he stood amid dozens of men and women who were lying down on the ground—convulsing, trembling, and shaking violently.

He was the only candidate standing.

CHAPTER 10

JOINING

"Good work," came the words from his front, and for a second, he couldn't reconcile the voice with the face. For some reason, he had expected Mistress Amelia to sound . . . masculine.

Before he could even acknowledge her words, she turned around and walked back toward the other Kingsman, their voices barely an undecipherable whisper.

Not that he had the mind to understand their words anyway. His heart was still pumping a ridiculous amount of blood through his veins, and his brain felt like mush. He staggered over to the parapet and leaned on it before his knees gave way as he slowly slipped down.

Sitting, he closed his eyes and rested his head against the wall. He tried to ignore the low cries of pain of people around him, but it wasn't working so well. That scene from before, that touch, those voices, those landscapes kept coming back to him.

The very thought of what could have happened if he stayed there for another second sent shivers down his spine. A maid offered him water, and he drank all of it like he had been parched for a week.

His hands trembled still, and he gripped one with the other, hoping to get his nerves back in control. The idea of repeatedly using stability inducement on himself sounded so alluring, but he held on.

It would pass.

Minutes went by as he sat there, not really thinking about anything. His heart slowed, and his pulse was normal again. His body stopped shaking, and he wasn't unknowingly clenching his teeth anymore.

Another few minutes passed, and the amount of moans and cries reduced by a lot. He then finally opened his eyes. Most of the candidates were still on the ground but weren't shaking and convulsing anymore.

That's when he heard some words he hadn't expected. "Akira, only ten or so seemed to have passed the test. How could this lot of observers be so rough?"

When Vern followed the sound to the source, he noticed the redheaded man talking to Captain Akira.

What do they mean by test? Was this a test?

Vern's mind was still a little overheated, so he didn't bother analyzing further and just waited to hear the captain's response.

The blindfolded prince looked up at the sky and replied, "No, Roland, you're expecting too much of observers who enlightened themselves a mere week ago. To be honest, the results are better than I expected. It should be fine to accept them in our fold as long as they wake up within the next five minutes."

The man named Roland seemed unsure but eventually sighed. "Whatever you say, boss." But then he suddenly began whispering, and Vern strained to hear, "Anyway, are you sure we did the right thing? This move is going to make a lot of nobles mad at us. We didn't disclose in the invitation that we'd be thrusting their beloved sons and daughters into the worst nightmare known to mankind."

Captain rubbed his hands together before replying, his words taking on a cold tone, "My only regret is that I couldn't have done it sooner. Do you know just how wanton and reckless the nobility has become? Every day, I get dozens of reports of séances, spirit circles, spectral communions, and whatnot from our informants. All committed by these very nobles."

Blowing some warm air on his hands, he continued, "What's worse is we can't even prosecute them because they're protected from us by the imperial law. So, I had to send a message."

Roland rubbed his chin. "But there's a reason all the latent observers in the nobility kept the existence of pure subjectivity hidden from others. Are you sure it's not going to cause a panic? I am pretty sure at least half of the failures here will be running their mouths like hell—justifying their incompetence by exaggerating the horror of pure subjectivity."

Captain continued warming his hands and nodded. "Yes, that's my hope, too. It should at least spread throughout the nobles of this district, and we would be lucky if it gets to others. As for the risks? Everyone should be panicking to an extent. This world's their responsibility, too, after all. Sure, this new rumor won't stop them from being entirely stupid, but many would err on the side of caution when it comes to their lives."

Roland stood there, amazed, before murmuring, "Just how many birds is that with one stone?"

Captain Akira didn't respond.

Soon, the redhead turned around to leave, only to suddenly stop and point at Vern, who instantly dipped his head in his knees, pretending like he hadn't heard anything. Soon came Roland's voice, "What's up with that one? The guy didn't even scream throughout the whole thing. I was paying attention to him, you know? He seemed so . . . unfazed."

After a while, the captain answered in an intrigued tone, "Almost as if he's seen something like this before, huh?"

Whoa! What kind of logic is that? Just . . . How? He could have been unfazed because of his strength like other captains, no? Luckily, Vern's face was still hidden in his knees, or his wide, trembling eyes would've given himself away.

The problem was that he'd indeed been into situations like this. First, during the duskfall itself, then in the land of dark sun within the third rune. Both of them had surely expanded his resistance to uncanny to a higher degree.

Roland then asked, his voice serious, "What do you mean, Captain?"

Vern felt those eyes boring at him, and his heart went cold. Would he look guilty if he didn't look up? They obviously knew he'd been listening, and they hadn't cared about it. But it would seem suspicious if he acted like he hadn't heard them talking about him.

Taking a deep breath, Vern wiped the shocked expression off his face and looked up, staring at that blindfold with a puzzled expression, sure that the eyes behind the cloth were staring right back.

Fortunately, he wasn't up against those eyes, or he would've cowered almost instantly. The intensity of Captain's face was a sight to behold.

After another few seconds, Captain looked back at Roland and responded, "Oh, nothing. He's a fundamentalist, after all. They've seen things we'll probably never witness in our lives."

A look of realization appeared on Roland's face, and he tapped his fist on his other palm. "Right. That makes sense. Good for him, I guess."

Roland then broached a few more random questions before he left Captain alone and found someone else to chat with at the far end of the tower. Vern felt like Captain Akira was still watching him, but he dipped his head back, not wanting to confront him unless necessary.

His heartbeat had picked up the pace again in this veiled interrogation. Captain had clearly deflected Roland's question with a secondary explanation, and he knew more about Vern than he had let on.

Vern wondered if that was a bad thing. He didn't like the idea of anyone knowing his secrets, but he wasn't about to go full paranoid either.

There was a silver lining in this situation—Captain hadn't really done anything to hamper Vern, nor did he try to put him down. He had instead assigned Vern under a legendary Kingsman and was treating him the same as every other candidate.

So what if he knew more than he let on? He probably knew a lot about everyone. Vern recalled both captains' conversation before it took a turn toward himself. Roland had asked a great question: *Just how many birds is that with one stone?*

This simple demonstration of pure subjectivity had first acted as a test to weed out the weak-minded. A little extrapolation of matters also suggested that having fewer nobles passing the captain's test meant he would have more leverage in the next meeting with the emperor.

Beyond that, he sent a very personal message to the nobles of the city. These candidates were clearly heirs and heiresses of noble families, and by showing them the truth behind the veil, he had forced the secret out in the open.

It was a very delicate balance. He hadn't revealed it to the public—avoiding outright hysteria, but instead demonstrated it to the chosen few who had a lot of weight to their words. He knew when this information spread, it wouldn't be dismissed easily.

This should garner more support for Vigil's noble cause, all the while reducing the reckless tainting of reality by the nobility who they couldn't prosecute directly. This should cause the people participating in rituals and séances to be afraid.

The more he pondered it, the more layers he found in each of the man's actions, and he couldn't help but be awed. It was a very simple move, but the subtle control of information and intention was just . . . genius.

If he had to put it in his own terms, the Ferrovane had struck a perfect balance between stability and instability. The timing, scope, and audience of information revealed would destabilize the societal structure of the city just enough to achieve his goals of hammering home the dire state of the city, stop people from dabbling in risky practices, and give him a better negotiation position in the future.

It was . . . fascinating.

But suddenly, a novel feeling of . . . correctness spread through Vern, and a weird notion surfaced in his mind. It felt like he had comprehended something important about his viewpoint, but he couldn't put a finger on it.

It was different than having a new insight blossom within his thought space. It was like he understood balance . . . better? As if he grasped his viewpoint more clearly.

But he couldn't revel in the ecstasy for long. It was gone as abruptly as it came. Unsure what to make of this, he peered into his thought space and was pleasantly surprised.

Many new insights had blossomed within his thought space. And not just in one octant; they had cropped up everywhere—in all eight areas of his mental insight sphere.

No, this isn't right, he mused. He was pretty sure these new insights hadn't blossomed just now. What had just happened was some form of deeper internalization of these insights. Also, his reflection a second ago was related to stability and instability of societal "structure," his primary octant, not all eight of them.

So that could only mean one thing.

These new insights developed when he was observing pure subjectivity.

Yes, that has to be it. he concluded. He was too focused on surviving to realize any changes in his thought space.

This was to say, he had two distinct advancements in a very short period of time! That had to be a good thing, right? If only he understood the bigger picture of progression as an observer.

He sighed. *Just a while longer.* Yes, the library here was going to give him all the answers he needed.

Feeling a little more at ease, Vern shook his head and pulled out his notepad. He should write it down before he forgot the details.

Minutes passed, and other candidates began waking up one by one. Some had pale faces, while others had bloodshot eyes. But the general trend was that once they woke up, they weren't shaken for too long.

Did they not have the same experience as me? That could be the case because that thing at his back only took notice of him once he used stability inducement on himself. If others didn't use their visions, it was possible that they didn't run into the same problems as him.

But things could have gone way worse if I had held back. He didn't regret his choice but still wondered how others managed to survive without it. Or maybe the unconscious ones were in that state because they used their visions recklessly?

Clap clap.

The five minutes were over. Butlers and maids helped carry out the ones who were still fainted, and the tower soon cleared up. Vern got up and joined the twenty or so remaining candidates.

Captain Akira dusted his coat, looked at the bunch that was worse for wear, and started, "My dear observers. All of you have proved yourselves worthy by surviving the nightmare that's pure subjectivity. You're the ones who hold the keys to change the fate."

He waited for the observers to take in his words and continued, "However, I believe there's some lack of communication between you and your archons regarding this situation. So, let me fill you in on what Vigil has in store for you if you decide to join."

The tired and scared faces perked up, and the man continued, "It's an opportunity. Vigil isn't just a frontier that will fight against the horrors of our new reality. It's a gathering place for observers to come together and hone their viewpoints as the sharpest blades of mankind."

He paused, surveying the room with a solemn gaze, and his voice suddenly turned grave. "As we all know, most observation records we have nowadays are erroneous or incomplete, which means the majority of us have no hope of advancing beyond a certain shade."

Vern's eyebrows furrowed at this assertion. That was unexpected. For some reason, he had assumed these observation records were the be-all and end-all path to becoming a powerful observer. It appeared things were more complicated than that.

Others around him also seemed quite down at the mention of this fact, which seemed to suggest this was a common problem.

Captain's expression softened slightly, a glimmer of hope entering his eyes. "But as much as not having objectivity is lamentable, it opens up many doors that were closed before. Multiple ruins of the previous era of subjectivity, which used to be impossible to track down, have finally been located. That is to say, lost knowledge will resurface, and there's hope for us to mend those broken paths."

This proclamation instantly caused many to stand straighter, their eyes shining with a newfound light.

He began to pace slowly, his hands clasped behind his back. "And at Vigil, the contribution of its members doesn't go unrewarded. Weapons, perceptual artifacts, memory packets, even observation records that we find are up for grabs if your exploits warrant the reward."

He stopped and faced the crowd directly, his covered eyes scanning the faces before him. "We have talented observers in our midst with multiple shades that can aid you in the comprehension of your viewpoints. We are here to provide you any kind of aid you might need to better fight off the terrors that haunt the city. Anything you will need to progress far in your shade sequence as an observer, Vigil has it."

The captain's voice suddenly hardened, his eyebrows turning fierce. "But all of this comes at a cost. You have to be willing to do everything in your power to save this city from the horrors that threaten to end our very civilization as we know it."

He let those words hang in the air for a bit before roaring, "So tell me, observers. Do you understand the gravity of our situation?"

"Yes, sir!" thundered the crowd, and even Vern knew what to say this time. He had long made up his mind. He wasn't exactly in it to save the city, but his personal goals aligned well with the general direction of this organization. So he would give it his very best effort.

"Are you willing to fight for the Vigil?"

"Yes, sir!"

"Are you willing to fight for this city?"

"Yes, sir!"

"Are you willing to fight for humanity?"

"Yes, sir!"

If it meant gaining a deeper understanding of the essence of balance, he'd gladly fight for the cause.

The atmosphere was charged with fervor and passion, and a beautiful smile bloomed on the captain's face. Letting out a deep breath, he rested one hand on his heart and bowed to the crowd. "Then I welcome you all to the Vigil of duskfall."

Vern, alongside everyone else, bowed back in solemn respect, each chirping with their own form of greeting, turning the atmosphere into an incoherent mess.

When the former prince stood, he commanded the ones behind him, "Captains, choose the candidates you think will best supplement your teams. You already know their viewpoints and potential. I trust you to nurture them and employ their uniqueness to the best of your abilities."

Everyone but Shinsei rushed into the crowd, and Vern let out a sigh of relief, feeling a mix of excitement and ... anxiety? After all, he hadn't taken on such a grandiose responsibility before.

But he had to quickly push these thoughts to the back burner because Lady Amelia was walking toward him. And well, it made sense. She was the captain assigned to him, after all.

So he took the initiative to meet Mistress Amelia halfway. He had been hoping to express his gratitude for a while now. So the moment she was within his range, he bowed formally. "Thank you, Mistress Amelia, for agreeing to teach me the ways of Kingsmen. I—"

She interrupted him with her serene, flaccid tone, "Don't worry about it. Meet me in the training ground by four."

His eyes lit up, and he nodded seriously. "I will." That was about two hours from now.

Before he could say any more, she extended her other arm, and all he perceived was a zipping sound and a blur before she was gone from the tower. That was not all. The other Kingsman who was talking to Lucian a little distance away also disappeared with a brandish of his arm.

Lucian walked toward Vern right after and grinned ear to ear. "Do you think they left us here because they couldn't bother waiting for the elevators?"

Vern shook his head, not keen on going down such a line of thought. So he ignored that question and asked with a chuckle, "So, did you pass the 'interview'?"

Lucian smacked him lightly on the shoulder and replied, "Very funny coming from you. Why the hell didn't you tell me you were also assigned under a Kingsman? And Lady Amelia at that!"

Vern shrugged. "Well, you didn't tell me either. How was I supposed to know things would end up like this?"

Lucian tilted his head, his blonde hair pivoting with it, "Eh. Whatever." Then he squinted his eyes and rubbed his hands. "Anyway, do you think our unique status is going to give us some points with the hotties in our group?"

Vern rolled his eyes and ignored him again. "Did your master call you for training, too?"

"Yes! I'm pumped! Though, I don't know where this training ground is."

Just then, a new voice cut through their conversation. "Well, then, let me show you around," announced Captain Shinsei, stepping forward with a warm smile.

CHAPTER 11

TOUR

Vern, Lucian, and Shinsei sat in what could only be called a dining hall. Its decor was nothing to scoff at, but Vern focused on finishing his meal as soon as possible.

He didn't want to exert himself physically after stuffing himself full of delicious food. Filling up another spoonful of pudding, he eyed the captain, who had brought them straight down here.

After a little deliberation, he said, "Captain, I have a few questions."

"Fire away, my friend."

"Do you know why only two of us were assigned under Kingsmen? Does it have something to do with us not being nobles?"

Captain nodded, using chopsticks to shovel rice into his mouth. After a few seconds, he added, "Akira picked you two because of that. I remember him saying Kingsmen didn't want to nurture nobles."

"Oh? Why is that?" chirped Lucian, showing off his lackluster table manners.

Captain Shinsei gave a helpless smile and put his bowl down before replying, "Kingsmen were established during the previous empress's reign, and I think it has been a tradition ever since? I . . . I don't know exactly why."

So, Vern asked something else that had been on his mind for a while, "Captain, do you know what the Kingsmen are expecting from both of us? Or why they agreed to teach us at all?"

The swordsman pondered for a while before replying, "I think this is a joint attempt from both organizations to foster observers who aren't just . . . you know, good for their visions, or Kingsmen who can't observe anything subjectively."

Oh. Pieces of the puzzle fell into place, and Vern nodded slowly. That made sense. Except that the captain phrased his words in a way that put both organizations on a similar level. Yes, Kingsmen were feared and all, but were they really a match for observers who could change their very reality?

So he asked, "But, Captain, does it mean Kingsmen are as powerful as observers? Aren't they just . . . humans?"

Captain didn't even wait for him to finish before he started shaking his head side to side. "Don't make that mistake. Never underestimate the Kingsmen. You haven't fought one, so you don't know, but they are far more than just . . . humans. How could they be normal when they don't even appear in our perceptions? It's almost as if they're some kind of observers themselves."

Vern furrowed his brows. That was unexpected. He had believed that Kingsmen were just highly trained individuals. Though he'd been doubtful ever since he saw Mistress Amelia fight back on that bridge.

Lucian gave the captain a what-the-hell-are-you-talking-about look, and the swordsman sighed before adding, "See, I wouldn't go so far as to say they're as versatile as us observers, because all they have is their physical strength, but with all the outlandish gears that fundamentalist friends like you have made for them, they are more than a fair match for most observers."

Lucian dropped his fork and asked, "How? How does that work? Where does that power come from?" Vern leaned in, very interested in the answer himself.

But Captain gave them a saddened look and shook his head. "I don't know, my friend."

That was disappointing.

Lucian closed in farther. "They've been around for so long. Surely the secret would've gotten out?"

Captain Shinsei looked around, trying to recruit some help, but Vigil members at other tables ignored his pleading look, focusing on their own new squad mates.

Lucian kept pressing, "Are they going to share that secret with us? Will we become as strong as them?"

Captain drank some water and sighed another time, melancholy drowning his tone. "I am really sorry, my friends. But I don't know. I am a foreigner and was never really interested in the affairs of the city. Neither did I bother asking Akira about it. Please forgive my ignorance and incompetence."

Lucian was taken aback at the sincere disappointment in the captain's words, and he fumbled, "Uh, umm, don't worry, sir. I was just asking, you know?"

"No, my friend. I pride myself on helping new friends like you to the best of my abilities, but it seems I am failing already." He clutched his forehead and looked at the ground, utterly disappointed in himself.

Vern couldn't sit back anymore and tried to clear the air. "It's okay, Captain. We can always go and read about these things in the library. I remember De Flanc told me there's all kinds of confidential information in there." Then he squinted and turned to the blonde, the knife in his hand gleaming sharply, "Right, Lucian?"

The very mention of books caused a terrified expression to surface on Lucian's face, but he gritted his teeth, looking back and forth between the despondent captain and Vern's menacing gaze. However, he soon gave up and admitted, "Yes. Yes. Vern's right, we can just go . . . read about it." It almost seemed like someone was holding him at gunpoint.

Anyhow, these words seemed to have done the job. Captain looked up and nodded very seriously. "You guys are done eating, right? Let's go to Vena's archive. I can introduce both of you to Irene so she won't give you any trouble later on, and you can read all about Kingsmen."

Vern instantly stood, wiping his hands and lips with the napkin provided, and exclaimed, "Let's go!"

Lucian looked at them, then at his mushroom and truffle pastries. Sensing his hesitation, Captain added, "I have to give both of you a tour of the rest of the Vigil before I hand you over to our Kingsmen friends anyway. We should get going."

Lucian continued to drag his feet, so Vern picked a tissue and placed a couple of the pastries on it. Handing it over to Lucian, he pretty much forced the guy up and set him in the direction toward the mess hall exit.

Captain didn't care about Lucian's antics and led the way. "The archive's entrance is on the ground floor, though it spans at least three floors."

"Just how it should be," Vern replied, his smile a little too wide.

Lucian appeared to be more interested in his pastries and the castle's interior as he followed them from a distance. Vern took the opportunity to ask very sensitively, "Captain, don't worry if you're not sure about the answer to my next question. I'm just curious, but why is the library called Vena's archive?"

Captain tapped the finger resting on his sword's handle and replied with a repeated nod, "I know this one, my friend. The previous empress of this kingdom, Lady Sinatra, had two daughters, Eleonora and Vena."

"Lady Vena was apparently displeased that her older sister alone had been immortalized with a library named in her honor. So, to appease her younger daughter, the empress renamed their in-house library after her."

Oh, right. Vern nodded. He remembered hearing somewhere that Eleonora's archive was named after the previous empress's daughter.

Still, Vern stared at the captain dumbfoundedly, unsure why his knowledge distribution was so skewed. How did he know so much history about the previous empress but not the Kingsmen of the present?

And it seemed his confusion was too obvious, for Captain smirked, adding, "Don't look at me like that, my friend. I know all this because this is Akira's family we're talking about. Lady Vena was Akira's mother."

Before Vern could reply, Lucian butted in, extricating himself from his sinful gluttony. "Oh, were they as beautiful as Captain Akira, too?"

Vern rubbed his chin, connecting the dots in his mind. This answered some of his burning questions, but more cropped up right after. Lady Sinatra was the previous empress, and Captain Akira was her grandson. But the fact that neither Lady Eleonora nor Lady Vena became the next empress suggested that something had gone wrong with the succession.

Mix in the fact that people called Captain Akira an exiled prince who was shunned at an early age, and one had the plot of an insidious political drama. Though the current emperor had the same last name, so he was probably some uncle of Akira's.

The whole thing intrigued Vern, but Lucian was too excited about the question he had asked. So when they stopped, the captain pointed at some painting far down the hall. "That's Lady Vena. You can go and judge for yourself."

Lucian ditched them instantly and walked up to the painting while Vern focused on the large door with transparent panels right next to them.

Captain disregarded Lucian and pointed in the room before saying, "That's our communication hub. Currently, we have only managed to connect to a couple of our hideouts in the inner districts. There's even one in the Athenaeum district now. If we had that beforehand, we could have called reinforcements at Starfall Heights right from the start."

Vern, who was curiously feeding his brain on all the delicate machinery on display, responded with a shake of his head. "It's great that wasn't the case. Who knows how the 'vessel' would've reacted to a bigger group." Hopefully, he didn't sound sympathetic to the "vessel" at all.

Shinsei nodded and made to walk away, calling Lucian back. Vern asked, "Can we not go in right now?"

"Uh, not much to see, honestly. And we shouldn't disturb our ordinary staff for no reason."

Vern nodded reluctantly and sighed before joining them. Shinsei resumed their tour, and after crossing another corridor, he pointed at a hall that had a reception area. A lady sat behind the desk, looking utterly bored.

"That's the resource allocation hall. You can receive a gem for your vigil badge over there. The type of gem depends on your contribution to the vigil. Think of it as something akin to clearance levels. The more shades in your gem, the higher your clearance."

Vern questioned back, "Shades? In the gem?"

Captain chuckled, "Haha, don't worry, my friend. It's not what you're thinking. Someone came up with the idea of using gems that can show different colors when observed, and no one disagreed. So the more colors in your gem, the higher your clearance."

Vern let out a sigh. "Fair enough." He was expecting it to be some mysterious affair.

But then Lucian rubbed his chin and said, "Hmm, Captain. You said we can receive gems for our badge? Do you mean me, too? Should I go get one right now?"

Captain responded, clearly amused, "I said 'you' to Vern. Not you, my friend. He's contributed quite a lot to our coffers and arsenal because he helped save some very rich ladies. You have yet to do anything of the sort. Don't worry though. I'm sure it won't be long before you have a high-shade gem on your badge as well."

Lucian looked back and forth between Vern and Captain, mouthing soundlessly. After a while, he gave up with a grumble.

But the captain didn't take them to the resource allocation hall and instead turned them into another section of this labyrinthine castle.

I guess I'll have to go get that badge later. Wonder what my "clearance" is, Vern thought as they passed one chamber after another.

Finally, after a while, they stood in front of a huge door with a signboard proclaiming VENA'S ARCHIVE in gorgeous fonts. Captain wordlessly pointed at the sign and then pushed open the door.

A blue hue filled his vision, and when his eyes adjusted, inordinately tall shelves greeted him, each one filled to the brim. A smile began forming on his face, but he soon noticed something was off.

His eyesight had improved quite a bit since he had shaded his perception, and he could read most of the titles on the books' spines. They were . . . mundane. He obviously hadn't seen all of them before, but he didn't need to read them to know they weren't anything special.

A little worried, he whispered, not forgetting library etiquette, "Captain Shinsei, umm, is this really the archive where information regarding observers is stored? No offense, but all I see are ordinary books."

Captain smiled back and gestured with a dismissive wave of his hand. "You need clearance."

Oh, right. That had completely slipped his mind.

In what could only be called a muffled shout, the captain called, "Irene. Hello, Irene? Irene? Are you here?"

He tilted his head and looked around past a couple of shelves with nothing to show for them. After trying another couple times, he became despondent and staggered back to Lucian and Vern.

Looking all downcast, he said, "My friends, it seems Irene isn't here right now, and I have no idea where you could find more about Kingsmen in this mess of a library. I—I really couldn't do anything about such a simple request. I failed you. I—"

Lucian's smile returned, and he started backing out of the library, but Vern cut in before things went any further, "Umm, it's okay, Captain, don't worry about it. We don't have the time to read anything right now, anyway. If it's about putting in a good word, you can always do so whenever you meet Lady Irene."

"I suppose . . ."

"Please don't worry so much—"

But Vern suddenly stopped mid-sentence. And he felt it. Again. It was that feeling of being watched. He didn't know if this had become some kind of talent of his now, but he was pretty sure someone was watching him.

And this time, no one warned him not to look back. So he snapped his head backward in an instantaneous motion, focusing above and behind himself. It was a rack above the archway of the door, books stacked atop it neatly, but he saw it. For the briefest of moments, two green eyes stared him down from the gap between two books.

He instantly turned alert and pointed at the position of those eyes, shouting, "Someone's there!"

Rustle.

It was a little dark above the archway because a hanging scroll blocked the light, and he couldn't be sure what had actually happened there.

Lucian seemed to catch his drift and quickly took on a fighting stance—something Vern didn't have. So he instead backed up behind a shelf and readied his perception.

He was just waiting for Captain Shinsei.

But what was he doing?

Instead of taking cover, he looked at both of them with a strange expression.

Thump.

But Vern felt it again, and he jerked his head toward the source. It was coming from right above him! He saw those green orbs for a fraction of a second again before they disappeared.

He took a deep breath and made up his mind. It wasn't the greatest idea to recklessly use a vision on his first day in the organization, and in front of a captain at that, but he could always observe, right?

Not waiting for the swordsman anymore, he opened his perception for general structures, and a black . . . blur shot from above him toward the captain. Stunned, he yelled, "Captain! It's coming for you!"

But then he heard a sound, and his perception shattered on its own.

Meow.

Chapter 12

WHISPERING REPOSITORY

They walked atop the bridge connecting one section of the castle to another, and the cold wind buffeted their faces. The small bridges were in open air, after all. Captain Shinsei stopped and pointed at some tower on the other end of the castle.

His other hand, however, cradled the prettiest cat in existence. Vern only paid minimum attention to Captain's words when he explained about the infirmary and how they didn't have the magic recovery fluid like Asea's believers.

The cat was too pretty, after all. Those green eyes followed Captain's fingers, and Vern took the chance to creep closer.

One step.

Two steps.

Right hand up.

Extend elbow.

Open palm.

And pet—

Mrowr.

The kitten growled, puffing up its tiny body covered in white and gray fur as it slapped his hand away. Those large green eyes looked at his palm like it was the dirtiest thing in existence, and the fingers of Vern's still outstretched hand slowly curled into themselves.

Captain retracted his palm and petted that cute head. He even had the audacity to look at Vern with pity as he rubbed those shiny whiskers and said, "Come on, Luna, don't be afraid. He's a good friend."

She hissed, swatting a paw in the air.

Vern's shoulders drooped, and his budding smile faded into a thin line. Was she like this because of the first impression he'd made? No. No. No one's going to talk about that.

But he felt some vigor return when he looked back at Lucian, who was two paces away from them, a scratch mark on his arm. *That's what you get for trying to be forceful.* Vern snickered to himself.

Soon Captain continued on their previous track. Luna accepted all his pets with a lazy yawn as he started, "Now we're heading toward the most dangerous place in the Vigil." And almost as if reacting to his words, Luna hissed at the other end of the bridge and climbed on Captain's shoulder.

With a mesmerizing jump, she landed on a balustrade. Seeing an opportunity, Vern made his final attempt, but she swerved from under his palm and jumped on the roof of the bridge, growling at him with a *rraow.*

Vern's soul died a little at his nth failed attempt, but this instead only reaffirmed his determination. He was going to pet Luna one day, no matter what. And she would like it!

Lucian growled back in a beastly tone at the retreating ball of fluffiness and walked up close to them. "What a little devil, man!"

Vern glared back at his disgusting outfit and barely stopped himself from going any further. Captain ignored their shenanigans and started again, a little graver this time, "So, like I said, this is the most dangerous place in the Vigil. Even worse than some of the high-clearance texts in the archive. I'd like both of you to clear your heads and prepare your minds."

These words instantly erased any playfulness from Vern's thoughts, and he nodded solemnly. Lucian did the same, and Captain continued, "We have come to call it the whispering repository, primarily because the combined effect of all the anomalous perceptual artifacts stored in there is just like the whispers we perceive during our insight sifting sessions."

Vern caught the keywords *anomalous perceptual artifacts* and *insight sifting sessions*. The former seemed to suggest that something was wrong with the perceptual artifacts in question—items like Captain's scarf or Esther's mother's gauntlets.

The latter, on the other hand, was quite a peculiar term. It hinted at some form of meditative process where one just sat and sorted through their insights.

Was that how one progressed their viewpoints? By analyzing and introspecting the existing insights? That sounded very intriguing and . . . right. Though he would first read up on it in Vena's archive when he had a chance.

But Captain also mentioned that it was possible to encounter the whispers in this process. That didn't sound safe.

He wanted to ask about it, but he didn't want to flaunt his lack of understanding when all of it could be solved by simply reading up on it later. So he instead asked something that wasn't personal.

"Captain, what exactly are these anomalous perceptual artifacts?"

He nodded. "Good question, my friend. Anomalous, just like in our language, is a vague word we use to describe effects that are out of the norm."

"Can you give us some examples?" asked Vern without delay.

Captain slowed down and pondered his words for quite a while before replying, "I will give you examples, my friend. But, I have a suggestion for you." Then he glanced back at Vern and said, "Understand that knowing too much is never a good idea. Especially about things we don't comprehend."

Vern was taken aback, not expecting to hear the same words that Cera had told him before they entered the steamscript relay station.

Captain continued in his grave tone, "Their very knowledge can pollute your thought space and invite the attention of beings your perception can't handle. You must have felt it when Akira threw you into pure subjectivity, right? Things beyond our understanding are always watching us—waiting, hoping, and expecting us to recognize them."

"The simple act of accepting their existence makes them a bigger part of our reality, affirming their place in objectivity. Usually, it won't matter because they can't steal your representation because your viewpoint is simply more potent than theirs, but what if it's not?"

Every word sent a chill down Vern's spine, and he realized he had indeed gotten a little hasty in his approach. The lack of new knowledge in the past five days had made him a little restless, maybe causing him to undermine the risks of delving into mysteries surrounding this whole world of observation.

Taking Captain's words to heart, he replied, "Yes, sir. Do you have any guidelines on when to pry further and when to stop?"

Vern's question sent the captain deep in thought, and he only replied when they were almost at the door of their destination at the other end of the bridge.

Captain said, "That's a good attitude, my friend. However, I might not be the best person to answer this question, so take my following advice with a grain of salt. I judge my questions based on whether they serve a purpose beyond mere curiosity."

Vern knitted his brows, trying to understand the point, when Captain elaborated, pushing open the door of the corridor and said, "Ask yourself: 'Does the answer aid in my duties or the safety of others? Does it contribute to a deeper understanding that's crucial for my growth as an observer?' If the answer is 'yes,' proceed with caution; if it's 'no,' then perhaps it's a path best left untraveled."

He paused before adding, "In our line of work, curiosity isn't just about seeking knowledge; it's about balancing the risk and reward. The allure of the unknown is powerful, but so are the dangers that lurk within."

They passed by an array of ordinary guards into the only visible corridor as they reached what looked like a platform for the elevator. Captain Shinsei gave Vern and Lucian a meaningful look and said, "Above all, trust your instincts and viewpoint. They are your best guides in navigating the murky waters of the unknown. And when in doubt, seek counsel from those more experienced. We're a team here, and none of us is alone in facing the mysteries of this world."

Vern nodded solemnly. "Thank you, Captain. I'll keep that in mind," he said before focusing on internalizing the advice. It wasn't exactly in line with his general style of doing things, but this was the beauty of being in the company of accomplished individuals who had diverse mindsets and ideologies.

They didn't try to mold their words to please you and instead provided a fresh perspective. He valued such words greatly. He wasn't planning on integrating all contrasting ideas, but it gave him a broader perspective on what was closer to the right approach.

They allowed him to tweak his own internal balance subtly toward the correct side of the spectrum. In this case, he concluded that risks should only be taken when they clearly benefited him in some way. In other circumstances, he'd have to tone down his curiosity a little.

However, before he could ponder this for too long, the sound of clattering chains resonated in his ears, and he looked up. Another lamp-like elevator stopped in front of them, and all of them boarded it without much fanfare. When the gate clicked shut, it automatically began its screeching descent.

Captain reminded them again, "Clear head."

Vern dismissed his wandering thoughts and focused.

Then, Captain started again as the elevator continued its descent, "You asked for examples, right? Let me tell you about a couple that should be harmless for your cognition. There's this goblet we found in an abandoned church, which refills itself with the blood of nearby people."

Lucian asked, his brows furrowed, "How? Does it puncture a hole into its holder or something?"

Captain shook his head. "No. Anyone in the vicinity will suddenly turn pale and feel weak—almost as if they had lost some blood."

Vern asked, "So if one doesn't empty it, it's pretty much harmless?"

Captain smiled wryly. "If only it were that simple. It compels those in its surroundings to drink it."

A shiver crept up his spine at the thought. What if one was left alone with this goblet? Would they drink their own blood? Until when? The idea alone was disturbing.

"Then will we also feel that urge when we get close to it in a minute?"

"You would if it weren't for the tireless efforts of other observers who built this repository. They have turned it into something akin to a vault where the effects of these artifacts are suppressed. The only problem, however, is that there's no automatic way to quell the objectivity pollution that they emit."

"So someone has to be down there all the time, resisting the assault of those whispers to manually suppress the pollution?" asked Lucian, surprising Vern with his fluent use of the vocabulary.

Captain nodded.

"Anyway, another one I can tell you about is the lute of Gremwick, a famous artifact from a village with the same name to the east. It used to be known for helping children sleep, but ever since duskfall, it has . . . changed. Its melody now also causes anyone who's asleep to . . . gouge out their own eyes. And the lute plays on its own."

Both Vern and Lucian stared at Captain Shinsei with a hint of fear in their eyes, and the swordsman continued, "And that's just the start. There are a lot more of those in there that have terrible consequences that can't even compare to this. So it's important we keep them hidden away down there."

Clank.

With a loud rumble, the elevator came to a halt, and they deboarded gingerly. Walking in the dim corridor, they quickly reached a giant metallic door made with mechanical arts Vern hadn't seen before. It was a few notches above in terms of security and complexity than even what his master back in Nvoria had had in his residence.

Captain knocked thrice at the door and extended his necklace toward the peephole.

After a dozen seconds, the metallic latches opened, all the gears moving in great harmony. Vern pondered if it made sense to use these doors given the unique abilities of observers, but who was he to tell them what was right and what wasn't?

For all he knew, these doors might have been reinforced using some kind of vision, making them resistant to observation. So, he did a quick test by trying to perceive the door from his perspective, which was, indeed, elusive to his perception.

More assured in Vigil's methods, he let it be and cleared his mind. Before the doors even opened, something he hadn't heard for a while greeted him in full force.

"Nexarionth zulmestra gyrinthol exaraphon teryxial."

Vern's heartbeat slowed down, and he recalled his previous encounters with the whispers. None of them were pretty.

"Vorinthex quillarion phloxenthras umbraxio zentharim."

But things had changed. He had advanced as an observer, and these whispers were . . . different. They were . . . lesser than the actual thing, if that made sense. They weren't the all-consuming and self-destructive kind he had heard in his head before.

"Cryomorphix lyranthor voximyth quintalos vermoran."

Taking a deep breath, he walked in alongside Captain. The room inside was dimly lit by gas lamps, their glow illuminating the dancing motes of dust and the large circular table in the heart of the room.

But in this dim ambiance, at the far end of the room, stood another door. Heavy chains jutting out from either end encased it while various patterns subtly glowed on its surface. Vern's heart thumped louder simply looking in that direction.

It had a magnetic pull to itself, and Vern had to grit his teeth to wrench his eyes away from that door. The whispers seemed to grow louder, and a prickling sensation arose all over his body.

"You're early today," came a new voice, and Vern snapped back toward the source, feeling more than a little jittery. A man stood next to the door they had entered from, a unique hat perched atop his head. It was elongated lengthwise but was quite slim otherwise, its tip almost hiding the book that the man held in his fingers.

Captain nodded. "Yes, Cedric. I wanted to get these new friends introduced to the whispering repository as soon as possible."

Cedric put away his book and asked with interest, "Oh, these the kids we hired today? Does that mean I will finally not have to stay here alone in this hellhole for four days a week?"

Captain chuckled. "Hopefully. We need more people here, anyway. The more artifacts we put in there, the worse it gets."

Cedric nodded, his face hiding behind the shadow of his elongated hat. Then, he asked, "So, they're gonna guard here with you today?"

"Oh, no. They've got to be in the training ground in about twenty minutes. I brought them here because I'd rather not make the walk alone, and it's better to be accustomed to this place sooner than later."

Cedric nodded. "Fair enough. So, can I go?"

"In a minute. Take them back up with you and direct them to the training grounds. Allow them a few minutes to get acclimated to the whispers."

"Sure." Cedric shrugged before flipping the page of his book and ignoring all of them.

CHAPTER 13

KINGSMEN

Vern strode past one chamber after another while Lucian continued to nag, "What's the hurry, man? We still got like five minutes."

"Yep. And I'd rather be there five minutes early," Vern replied.

"No, no, no. You got it wrong. Being on time means getting there *just* in time and not early. What if they're busy, and we disturb them by getting there before they expected?"

Vern countered with a smirk. "That just means you need to keep your mouth shut so you don't disturb anyone. Simple."

Lucian rolled his eyes and actually piped down. They were close to their destination, after all. Cedric had left them as soon as they got off the elevator, giving them some vague directions. Apparently, he had to finish reading his book in the next thirty minutes, or there would be terrible consequences—whatever that meant.

Framed by a dozen elegant arches and tall columns, they finally found the training grounds. When they walked in, it quickly became apparent that it used to be the royal court. There was a stepped pedestal and a high throne at the end of the hall dotted by a clear path in the middle with seats on either side.

Now, however, it was retrofitted entirely. Dueling grounds with clear demarcations were drawn on the floor, and another group of people was already using it. Surprisingly, he had seen them not too long ago.

It was Captain Arthur and his group. Vern also saw the girl who had used double-edged knives. She was facing someone in what looked like a friendly spar since wooden blocks floated around her instead of actual knives.

Lucian quickly swerved his trajectory to go watch the show, but Vern grabbed him and turned him toward the other end of the hall where two Kingsmen stood in front of a giant painting.

An excited gleam appeared in his shabby colleague's eyes, and he quickly forgot all about the battles, making his way toward the reapers, and Vern followed.

The moment they were in range, Vern greeted them in his usual style, "A good evening, Mistress Amelia and Lord Kingsman."

Lucian fumbled, "Good . . . good evening, Lord and Lady."

Mistress Amelia simply nodded, her wayward locks following the motion, while the other Kingsman looked both of them over for a while before replying, "Name's Osric. Glad to make your acquaintance. The kings' parity court and Vigil expect a lot from both of you. I hope we can do you justice."

Vern nodded alongside Lucian, but his mind lagged. He knew the reason for Kingsmen to be willing to take on commoners like him and Lucian, but what were their expectations? To run around the city and catch criminals? It seemed a bit . . . rude to ask that directly now.

Captain Shinsei didn't know, but maybe De Flanc might? Well, no time to do that now. Lord Osric turned back to the painting before asking, his gear gleaming against the sunlight streaming in from the floor-to-ceiling windows, "Do you recognize the portrait?"

"Yes," replied Lucian.

Vern admitted, "Only a guess, sir," not having a solid idea of who the woman might be.

"Hmm, curious. You're not a local, right?"

"Indeed, sir."

"Why Elmhurst, then? Trains have yet to get going, but a couple airship routes are running again. You could go back to your roots if you want to."

After Lucian had asked him something along these lines, Vern came up with a more suitable answer. So this time he wasn't as lost and replied, "I used to apprentice under a great fundamentalist in Nvoria, sir, but my only family—my little sister— lives here in Elmhurst. However, she's been missing since duskfall. So, not much for me to really go back to."

That was the story he had decided to settle on.

Lord Osric swiveled back, his cape jerking the other way around. With a dark light in his eyes, he followed up, "Missing, you say? Not to burst your bubble, son. But too many missing ones are just . . . gone. If finding her is your reason for fighting, you might as well stop while you're ahead."

Vern could hear it wasn't coming from a place of malice, so he admitted with a heavy voice, "I know, sir. I don't expect a miracle, but I still have to do my best. With or without her."

Lucian's and Amelia's gazes seemed to turn a touch softer at these words, and Osric replied, "As long as your expectations are tempered. Anyway, if you guessed this portrait to be Empress Sinatra's, then you'd be right."

Vern nodded. That was his best guess, too. However, it could have been Lady Vena or Lady Eleonora for all he knew—they all had reasons to have their paintings here. Though the painting really reminded him of Cera for some reason. Maybe it was the dress? Also, the hair color, and style. But the painting had a clear advantage in terms of bearing.

Lord Osric continued, "Milady Sinatra took this empire that was down on its luck, plagued by a thousand problems, and turned it into a powerhouse rivaling the world's greatest kingdoms."

"What do you think was the biggest factor in the explosive rise of the empire?"

Vern gave it a little thought and answered, "Military might?" That was the most standard answer for an empire's growth in history. Lucian agreed with Vern.

Lord Osric nodded. "Yes. You aren't wrong, but where do you think this might suddenly came from? Training a capable army from scratch can take anywhere from a few decades to half a century, especially when it's constantly being ground down by internal and external factors."

He remembered reading a few tidbits about the Calidian Empire's rapid expansion that happened around forty years ago, but he never dug deep on the topic. Seconds passed, and neither Vern nor Lucian, who was scratching his head, had a real answer.

Osric's eyes beneath the tricorn hat flattened to match the smirk that appeared underneath his facecloth, and he carried on, "Now, that was a rhetorical question because there's no way you could've known. And I wouldn't be telling you if the game board hadn't been flipped so violently. But here we are, trying to train the new era equivalent of magicians and fighter hybrids."

But then his voice suddenly turned grave. "Anyway. The answer is—blood." Something around them changed the moment he said it. Vern felt a primal urge to bow down and let himself be consumed. It was like he was surrounded by feral things, and they wanted a piece of him. He could almost make out a red glow within Lord Osric's eyes.

Lucian was looking around, too, his brows furrowed. But as if that discomfort wasn't enough, the intensity of the feeling abruptly turned a notch higher. Vern's heart began thumping wildly out of nowhere, and he barely stopped himself from staggering.

It was the most fundamental of the urges, something within the deepest recesses of his mind, calling out to surrender. In front of him, Lord Osric seemed to grow taller, his form appearing evermore threatening, sending shivers down Vern's spine.

It took him a second to come to terms with it, but apparently, Captain Shinsei was right. Kingsmen weren't your standard humans, either. Something was very wrong with this aura, and he was sure it wasn't just some psychological gimmick.

Once he factored that into the equation, he quickly realized it had to be a show of power, and just like Akira had done, Lord Osric was testing them before giving them a real chance.

That meant he had only one way to go about this.

Hah . . . Vern wasn't joking when he decided to do everything in his abilities to gain the power needed to find balance in his life. This was his chance to learn from some of the best fighters on the planet and maybe even employ their . . . secrets.

So when the intensity of the primal compulsion grew yet another time, a white ring appeared in Vern's eyes, and he stood taller. He had yet to see any repercussions from stabilizing himself, and since the situation called for it, he wasn't going to shy away from using it.

A sharp look appeared in Lord Osric's eyes, and Vern saw the outline of the lips on the man's face cover growing wider before—

"Agh!" yelled Lucian, barely holding on. But Vern gritted his teeth and feigned calmness. Yet, this only seemed to ignite a fire within the Kingsman's eyes.

A tangible red aura pulsed from behind the man, and the surroundings distorted. Vern braced for another surge of that wild thumping from within and envisioned another wave of stability for himself.

But then came a soft voice. "That's enough, Osric." Mistress Amelia had a hand on the radiating Kingsman's shoulder. "There are other people in here, too. Don't be rude."

Her words alone shattered the pressure, and as if he'd come to the surface after being underwater for too long, Vern took a deep breath and closed his eyes. Lucian was handling it worse than him, clutching at his heart, but in contrast to that was the wild smile that played on his face as he took rapid, short breaths.

Vern couldn't help but be impressed that the guy was still standing. He wasn't sure he could've done the same without stability inducement, at least not at the end.

Then there was a sigh and some words. "If they learn right, these kids are gonna make us obsolete one day, huh, Amelia?"

She turned back to the painting and replied, "Yes, I'd like to retire."

Osric then patted Lucian and helped him stand up. "That was great resistance, both of you. A common man would be on his knees, pissing all over right about now."

"Thanks, Master," moaned Lucian, his face a little pale, and Vern settled on a simple nod. He was still trying to match his previous understanding of Kingsmen with what was in front of him.

Looking at both of them in a new light, Lord Osric picked up the previous thread. "So, yes. The answer to the empire's rise was blood. Not many people know this because our emperor's a coward, so let me tell you our history a little. When Milady Sinatra uncovered a chthonic ruin under this very city, the whole destiny of the empire changed."

"Many of our predecessors explored it by sacrificing their lives, each unexplored path resulting in hundreds of deaths. However, after bartering thousands of our comrade's souls for years on end, they finally found it . . ."

He held his palm and nicked a finger with another one's nail. A dark maroon drop came oozing out, and he proclaimed, "The old blood." Just looking at it made Vern a touch dizzy.

But before Vern knew it, the cut was gone, and the Kingsman proclaimed, "The blood of beings from the genesis era. The blood that ran through the veins of those who later became gods. The old blood."

C H A P T E R **14**

CHOICE

As all four of them walked farther down the connected corridor of the training grounds, Lord Osric continued narrating the tale, "In the early years of its discovery, the royal court overruled Her Majesty's precautions and pumped hundreds of soldiers full of the old blood."

His eyes seemed to darken with the memory, his voice growing more intense. "The common foot soldier became better than the enemies' generals while the commanders became war gods—conquering one city after another. No matter the tactics, weaponry, or charms, no one withstood their might. After all, what could one do about men who could dodge a bullet with just their reflexes or crush bones into powder with a single hit?"

Glancing at an old portrait that seemed to illustrate a battle, Lord Osric shook his head slightly in a mix of awe and regret. "Villages, counties, cities, kingdoms—everything became a footnote as soldiers of old blood conquered whatever came in their path."

Then he paused for a while before speaking again. "Until one day. The day when the royal court couldn't contain their greed anymore. The day they decided to make battalions of blooded soldiers."

There was a noticeable shift in his demeanor, his voice turning graver. "All it took was a single man. No one knows why, but when the blood was injected into one certain soldier, it mutated. And then began the hell.

"Everyone who came in contact with that soldier lost control of their blood, and before anyone knew it, the city of Arisa, the second largest in the empire, became a land of death. Mutated abominations drunk on the blood roamed the city, and we barely had a solution."

When Lord Osric didn't continue right away and looked forward with complex emotion, Vern asked, intrigued, "How did you manage to bring an end to something like that? If a whole city was infected, did . . ."

Mistress Amelia replied without a hint of emotion in her voice, "Yes. We killed them and burned down the whole city."

A shudder went down Vern's spine. Simply imagining the horror of such a thing made his guts churn.

With a sigh, Lord Osric interjected, "It wasn't that simple. When the infection first spread in Arisa, the royal court couldn't handle it, so they went back to the empress for counsel. Some blamed her, some begged her, but as always, she managed to come up with a way forward."

Then he pointed at Vern and continued, "That's where your kind came in. Fundamentalists used to be considered even greater heretics than us users of old blood back then, but Milady Empress invited them in and gave them a chance."

"In a mere few months, they came up with a cure. However, it wasn't much of an option for Arisa because there was never enough of the vaccines to go around for ourselves, much less for a city full of people."

Then his eyes gleamed sharply. "But their next discovery was what turned the tide. They developed a more systematic approach to exploiting and infusing the old blood, called blood-borne subjugation art."

"It minimized the risks posed by the old blood while allowing one to acclimate to its power slowly. It was named as such to signify the subjugation of the inherent blood-borne disease in the old blood."

Both the Kingsmen halted in front of an array of rooms, and Lord Osric said, "That's when the empress handed down the old blood and its infusion technique to a group of trusted individuals, and the kings' parity court was established.

"This court was forged from enigmatic figures and individuals beyond the control of the royal court's nobles. The empress imposed stringent criteria for membership in the kings' parity court, decisively excluding nobility from ever joining its ranks, including the royal blood."

A light of realization illuminated Vern's mind. This was why Kingsmen didn't want the nobles. He finally got a proper answer to the question he'd asked Captain Shinsei not long ago.

It was evident that reading up Kingsmen's history was no longer necessary. The books couldn't possibly contain accounts of such heretical events, especially not in such meticulous detail.

Lord Osric continued his tale, "The court exists to overrule the emperor or nobility's excessive use of old blood if deemed necessary. However, we have to listen to his order otherwise."

He shook his head. "Anyway. Ever since then, Kingsmen have acted as sword and shield of the empire, and now that the threats have evolved so . . . radically, we need to step up too."

Lucian seemed to have turned into a yes-man and nodded at Lord Osric's every word, but Vern wanted to understand the dynamics better. So he asked, "No offense, my lord, but why not become observers yourselves?"

The leather-garbed man chuckled at the question and answered, "We tried. A lot of us tried. But any . . . What do you call those things?"

"Observation records," Vern suggested.

"Yes, those. They're just . . . too different from our usual mindsets. I obviously haven't given up yet, but your Vigil's leader told me that the older a person is, the more challenging it becomes for them to achieve enlightenment. That because my life's viewpoint and ideology have solidified; it is difficult for me to adapt to the radical ideas suggested by those records."

More gears clicked into place in Vern's mind, and he understood a lot of occurrences he'd passed over as coincidence up until now. This was the reason all those candidates above the tower were mostly in their late teens to mid-twenties, like himself.

Too young, and it's hard to form a viewpoint. Too old, and it's hard to adapt. An interesting balance.

"But apparently, it's worse for us Kingsmen. Each of us has led a very . . . bloody life and was trained to see life from a very specific . . . perspective. None of those records or whatever are a good match. So, either we find something that fits our particular ideology or do what we're doing right now. Train some new blood who can do both."

Vern nodded and thanked the man for answering. He now had a worry of his own. He didn't have an Observation Record either. How far could he go without the guidance of one?

After a deep breath, lord Osric gestured toward one of the rooms with a tilt of his head, and Lucian moved toward it instantly. Now that Vern looked around, these were all personal training rooms.

Mistress Amelia walked toward an opposite room, and Vern made to follow without hesitation. That's when he heard a final remark from Lord Osric, who stood beyond his room's door. "Remember, young one. The blood makes us human, makes us more than human, makes us human no more."

Thump.

And with that, he closed the door. Mistress Amelia, who had halted for a second, resumed her steps and entered their training room. Vern followed her in, but his mind was still stuck on that phrase.

Human . . . more than human . . . human no more.

The interior was more function than form. Weapons hung on the wall, fastened with mechanical latches, while training dummies, pads, and other equipment filled the rest of the room.

His eyes, however, were drawn straight to a golden case sitting on the table at the far end of the room. It was a little too long. However, before he could scrutinize it further, Mistress Amelia stood square and faced him.

He gave up his random curiosity, and his brain suddenly remembered to turn anxious. His heart filled with apprehension, coming in all parts from his lack of experience in combat training.

Five days of home exercises were nothing but a drop in the ocean. The only reason he wasn't sweating buckets from tension right now was the inherent changes that had happened to his physical body after shading his perception.

These changes were nothing to write home about, but they were . . . convenient. Breathing, eating, drinking—all these urges had become less frequent while his body had become more vigorous. His eyesight was better, he didn't get exhausted as quickly, and he felt more active.

He had conjectures as to why this was happening, but he didn't bother thinking too much about it because he was sure that this was a common side effect and that Vigil's library—or actually Vena's archive—would have an answer to that.

So, with a deep breath, he looked into Mistress's eyes and awaited instructions. After scrutinizing him for a short while, she began, "What are your expectations for yourself, Vern?"

A simple question. And she was nice about it, too. He answered earnestly, "To become a fighter who can hold his own against any kind of opponent and won't be held back by his lacking physical prowess."

Mistress nodded and pulled out a small silver case from her pocket. She opened it and presented it to Vern, who accepted it, focusing on its contents. It had a metallic syringe and a brassy vial filled with red fluid.

Maybe the vial suppressed that dizzying effect, but Vern knew exactly what it was. The old blood. After that conversation, he had expected to encounter it sooner or later, but not immediately.

"This is the first infusion of blood-borne subjugation art," she said, and an excited gleam appeared in his eyes. This blood could allow him to become a better fighter than he ever had been. His body, which was a bottleneck right now, would become his most deadly aspect.

But he recalled the fluid's origin and ruthlessly quashed any dangerous ideas. This was something that turned men into unparalleled warriors even before objectivity was shattered. This wasn't a simple thing. How could infusing some unknown species' blood ever be safe?

His apprehension soon turned into full-blown paranoia.

Was that why the other Kingsman had told him the story? To trick him into readily accepting it as safe? So Vern would feel the pressure and do their bidding as an observer? Would she refuse to teach him if he disagreed to make use of this?

But his skeptical musings were cut short as Mistress elaborated, "Now you have a choice. Since you don't plan on walking far down the path of a melee combatant, you don't really need to follow the blood-borne subjugation art to achieve your goals."

Vern furrowed his brows. If his suspicions were real, why would she give him a choice? Was she saying he had to pick either training under her and using the blood or losing the opportunity? Hesitant in his own conclusions, he asked, "So, would I have to leave if I . . . chose not to infuse the blood?"

She shook her head, her hat following suit. "As long as you fight for the city, I don't really mind. I will just have to find another candidate to train alongside you because our end goal is to nurture an observer who has the physical capabilities of a Kingsman."

Vern stared at Mistress, dumbfounded. Was she saying he could choose not to take on a Kingsman's responsibilities but still learn from one? Had he been too mistrustful of Kingsmen?

Maybe noticing his confusion, she elaborated, "Prince Akira asked me to train you before the parity court and Vigil even concocted this plan. So if you decide not to use the blood in the end, just keep the discussion we've had today to yourself and return the infusion kit."

She unlatched her scythe and deposited her equipment on a table. Soon Vern found another point of doubt and followed up by asking, "But didn't Lord Osric mention that Kingsly Court already expects a lot from me and Lucian?"

Taking off her hat, she replied without turning toward him, "Yes. But old blood is not something I'll force upon anyone, no matter the circumstances. As much as it's a blessing, it's a curse, too."

Her head full of white-blonde hair, which merged into a neat ponytail at her back, came in his full view, and she glanced back, an air of profound solemnity oozing from her every word. "Old blood can become an addiction. A vice that's near impossible to resist if one revels in it."

She paused, an unexplainable emotion in her voice. "Every year, we have to put down ten or so court members because they let the thirst consume them. And that's after the blood fundamentalists have refined the subjugation art for decades."

Vern had never heard of such an occurrence before, but this was indeed more in line with what he expected from some mysterious blood. This triggered his curiosity, and he said, "What happens if they get addicted?"

She turned around, leaned on the table, and folded her arms before replying, "They get drunk on it. The old blood amplifies not just one's strengths but also one's instincts, and without control, one risks becoming a slave to their baser impulses. So they must be put down before they tear through the civilians to sate their thirst."

Vern wiped the sweat off his face. He was standing in close proximity of one such person. If she were to be drunk on blood, he wouldn't have the slimmest chance of coming out of this alive. He remembered watching her fight on that bridge, and the coldness and detachment with which she harvested those lives was still vividly etched in his memories.

He was no match.

Luckily, he seemed to be in good hands. If so many Kingsmen got addicted every year, and she had survived ever since the plague of Arisa, surely she wouldn't lose herself to the urges now.

However, this information helped him relax quite a lot. This blood wasn't some sweet honey trap with incomprehensible repercussions down the line. It was a balanced system with its own benefits and drawbacks.

He even felt foolish about his recent thoughts. Why the hell would two powerful Kingsmen bother lying to him?

As he chided himself for his unbalanced response to the situation, Mistress examined him intently and spoke up, "However, if you have faith in your self-control, its benefits are just as immense. It acts as a catalyst for your body's innate capabilities. It heightens your physical attributes to levels beyond normal human capacity. Your strength, agility, reflexes, and even your body's healing capabilities will be significantly enhanced.

"Muscles become more robust and responsive, and your senses sharpen, allowing you to perceive threats and react quicker. It's like every part of you is awakened, fine-tuned for combat and survival. It essentially makes you into one of the most potent weapons known to mankind. At least, that was the case until observers resurfaced."

This point intrigued him greatly, so he asked, "No offense, Mistress, but how do you think Kingsmen would fare against observers? Given the wide scope of visions that observers have at their disposal, is old blood really enough to level the playing field?"

At the mention, her eyes curved like crescent moons, and a chilling aura swept through the room. "You think they will make us obsolete?" A smile formed under that face cover as she tipped her chin and declared, "I'd like to see them try."

A cold, numbing terror gripped him, and his heart stopped instantly.

CHAPTER 15

DUALITY

Not wasting a single moment, Vern sent a pulse of stability inducement through himself, but that didn't seem to alleviate much of that primal urge. His knees felt weak.

Right as he was about to buckle over, Mistress let out a gasp. "Oh . . ." and the unreal pressure disappeared almost instantly. Vern took the opportunity to reorient himself and barely avoided the fall.

After a dozen or so seconds, his eyes focused again, and his heart resumed its usual rhythm. But cold sweat formed on his forehead, and he still tried to process the terror from that single instant.

It was leagues above what Osric had done to him and far . . . sharper? Mistress had her hand outstretched, a clear look of distress in her eyes. After watching him stand straighter, she retracted her arm and asked, "Vern, are you okay?"

He tried to reassure her, "Yes, Mistress, it's no big deal," but his mind was in turmoil, feeling the exact opposite. How was this even possible? Even observers couldn't just "reach" into his heart and stop it.

But before he could ask himself more rhetorical questions, she sighed. "I am sorry. It's just that . . ."

She paused longer than made sense and stared at the ceiling before continuing, "It's just that we Kingsmen are finally advancing again, and I've yet to get used to my new powers."

He asked back almost instinctively, "New powers?"

She closed her eyes, and a rueful smile appeared behind her face cover as she responded, "When Emperor Aldric took the throne, he terminated all expeditions deeper into the ruins. This led to stagnation in our ranks when many of us reached the third infusion of the art. The old blood we procured from those depths couldn't push us any higher."

Vern also remembered the rumors he had heard about the empire's borders being pushed back and whatnot. Was that related to this? Other empires continued to advance while the emperor forcefully stagnated the Kingsmen? Not that he blamed the man for it. Clearly, this old blood wasn't an easy thing to control.

Then her eyes snapped open, and she declared, "Until that day. When dusk fell, each and every one of us in the kings' parity court felt it. It was as if the shattering of objectivity which Prince Akira mentioned had unlocked latent potential within us, a potential that we never knew existed."

Oh. More pieces of the puzzle clicked together in his mind. So Kingsmen were powerful before the duskfall, but this utterly inhumane strength was only unshackled after it.

His mind instantly conjured up a few theories as to why that was the case, and one of them terrified him a little. What if whoever this blood belonged to had become more prominent after duskfall, increasing their stake in the representation of reality and hence making the blood more powerful?

However, it was also possible that objectivity inherently suppressed the strength of old blood, and its shattering led to the unfettering of those limitations. Maybe these so-called blood fundamentalists would know.

Not knowing his thoughts, she carried on, "And that is not all. Right after Prince Akira proposed the formation of Vigil, the emperor convened the Kingsly Court and ordered us to restart the exploration of the chthonic ruins."

"It's only been a week, yet our newfound powers have propelled our exploration of the ruins significantly. We've made rapid progress and have already uncovered a purer source of old blood."

Then she stared him dead in the eye and proclaimed, "So, as much as I respect observers for what they are, they're not the only ones advancing rapidly. The path of blood, as it stands, will allow for a fourth infusion as soon as the blood fundamentalists figure out how to harness this new purity."

And before he could form a response, she added with a hidden smile, "And I don't mind the competition."

Hah. He didn't need any more signs to see that she was a battle junkie. And it . . . made sense? To a degree. Surely, not any random person can control their blood addiction for decades on end. Not that she looked a day older than thirty. Was that an effect of the old blood, too?

Surprised by the frankness she'd shown him throughout this conversation, he nodded with a look of gratitude and said, "Fair enough. That was very informative. I just wanted to understand how these paths differ from each other and if it's worth pursuing one over the other."

She nodded. "Our blood fundamentalists—or what's left of them—had a long discussion about it with members of Vigil, including Prince Akira, and the preliminary conclusion was that both paths can complement each other quite a bit."

Vern asked, a little hesitant at the mention of the man, "Do you know why?"

"Mm-hmm. I didn't take on this responsibility without understanding both sides of the coin. Each advancement for you observers alters your physical form slightly to align with your viewpoint. However, it's your consciousness that undergoes a far more profound transformation, leaving your body significantly lagging behind."

Vern's ears perked up, and he wished he could write this down without looking stupid. This was new information! If he understood it correctly, this was the reason behind the recent changes in his body, and it made perfect sense.

His body was more . . . balanced.

"Conversely, the main challenge in harnessing the old blood's strength lies in the necessity for the host to possess a robust consciousness, strong enough to subdue the inherent blood-borne disease in it."

Vern tapped his fist on his other palm, a look of realization on his face as he completed her sentence. "And observers like me and Lucian already have that from shading our perceptions."

She nodded. "Exactly."

That was interesting. No, it was far more than just interesting. It was almost like cheating. He reflexively wanted to ask why everyone wasn't doing this, but he could guess the answer.

This was an experiment.

They didn't know if the blood could further mutate down the line or something, so it was safer to start with only a select few individuals and observe how their bodies reacted to it.

He turned to the case containing the syringe and vial in his hands. It gave rise to repulsion as well as greed in his mind.

"You now understand the advantages and disadvantages of infusing the old blood. Now it's your choice. Don't rush to decide; sleep on it. If that's not enough, get opinions from uninvolved parties and make up your mind."

He nodded solemnly. "I will. Thank you very much, Mistress."

She then turned around and strode up to the table at the far end of the room, picking up that long golden case he'd seen when he entered. Carrying it in both her arms, she walked toward him.

Intrigued, Vern watched her every move, his curiosity piqued. What could the case contain? It had been sitting there even before they came in. Such formality and care in its handling suggested something of importance. His gaze followed the case as she carried it, a growing sense of anticipation building within him.

She extended the golden item toward him. "For now, let's start our training." Vern closed the case containing the syringe, pocketing it in his coat before extending both his hands to take hold of the bigger one.

It wasn't heavy but still had a solid weight to it. Many possibilities ran through his mind, but with its shape, size, and weight, there was only one answer to what was inside it. His heart thumped faster, and an excited gleam appeared in his eyes.

Once it was firmly resting in his arms, Mistress brought her palm to the front of the case and unlatched the tiny clasps with several clicks. Her soft fingers traced along its metallic edge before she flipped the lid open with a smile.

He let out a cold breath, feasting his eyes upon the beauty. He would be whistling right about now if he knew how to do it.

Inside lay a sleek, beautifully crafted longsword. Its elegant dark silver blade, longer than his torso, shone with a deadly sheen. Intricate designs ran along its edge as well as its raised core. It was a masterwork of craftsmanship and grace, a fine balance of lethality and art.

The golden hilt enhanced the overall design with its striking radiance, two eyes etched vertically where the blade met the hilt. But this was where it got interesting. The hilt was straight at its top, offering a traditional grip for wielding it with both hands. However, nestled beneath this austere facade were two additional symmetrically curved grips instead of a pommel, elegantly forged, giving the whole weapon a unique look.

Vern didn't understand the design choices here. Why two types of hilts? However, that's when Mistress broke the silence. "This is a custom design made by the workshop of the Finnesse family, tailored to your strengths. The fundamentalist craftsman who worked on it named it—Duality."

He looked up at Mistress, more puzzled than ever. "My strengths?" Did he have strengths? Why did he not know? Also, that was such a beautiful name for a sword. Ambrose's family clearly knew what they were doing.

Mistress Amelia gestured with her eyes to pick up the sword, and he did just that. He had worked on hundreds of blades before this, so he wasn't really nervous, but damn was he nervous!

Gripping the straight hilt with his right hand, he exerted a little effort to lift the sword out of its velvet casing. Mistress took the case from under his hands and put it elsewhere while Vern took the opportunity to set the sword tip down and fling his coat away.

He then held the sword in the only style that made sense to him with both his hands gripping the hilt one above the other closer to his chest. But that sharp edge seemed a tad too close to his own body, so he extended his arms a little.

He got the hang of its weight in just a few seconds, but his swings were as awkward as they came. Mistress Amelia watched him fiddle with the sword without a word, and instead of giving him directions, she asked him, "What do you think is the most important aspect of a weapon?"

Vern pondered, slowing down his hazardous swings, but he found himself faced with many correct ideas—or maybe all the wrong ones. What was the important thing about a weapon?

It's type? Size? Design? Material? Balance? Craftsmanship?

Not really sure, he answered hesitantly, knowing in his gut he was wrong. "Balance?"

She shook her head. "It's the synergy."

Tucking her hair behind her ears, she continued, "The better a weapon suits one's needs and combat style, the deadlier it gets. Doesn't matter if it's a scythe, sword, spear, or whatever. It's the compatibility that matters."

"But given that you've obviously never used a weapon before, you don't have a combat style."

The *obviously* made him sulk in his heart a bit, but she was right.

"So, I asked Prince Akira about your strengths, and he told me you can fortify and disrupt objects at will. Is that right?"

Vern sucked in a cold breath. He had never revealed to anyone the precise nature of his visions. How did Captain Akira pinpoint their exact workings with such an accuracy? Was it all just from the reports of Captain Shinsei and Ambrose? Or was there more to it?

That was disgusting!

For now, however, he suppressed his agitation and replied with a sharp nod. "Indeed."

She smiled. "Great. Then go ahead, grab those curved handles, and pull them apart. You'll see why it's tailored to your strengths."

C H A P T E R 16

TRAINING (POINT CLOUDS)

Vern knitted his brows, puzzled by her instructions. Nonetheless, he decided to follow her words. Positioning the sword upright with a firm grip, he placed his other hand on the right curved handle and gently pulled in the opposite direction.

Tch-tching.

As he pulled, it was as if a whole new world opened in front of him. The right hilt . . . disconnected from the left, and the blade followed suit. A seam he didn't know existed appeared on the blade, and the sword split cleanly into two separate pieces.

Two swords.

It split apart into two swords!

A surge of excitement flooded Vern's mind. With an enthusiastic flick, he tossed the other half of the sword into the air and caught it by its curved grip. Emulating the swordsmen he had seen countless times before, he instinctively spread his arms wide, a sword in each hand. Then, he launched into a reverse slash, albeit a clumsy one, feeling a rush of adrenaline with the movement.

His heart wanted to dissect the fundamentals at play here and forget everything else. However, his rational mind steered him back, reminding him of what truly mattered. He needed to concentrate on what the mistress had emphasized—his unique strength, his visions.

Without another prompting from her, he opened his perception and first focused on his left blade. Each one was made of a core that covered two-thirds of the blade's surface, and the rest was the edge. They were made of two distinct materials, and he couldn't pinpoint either one.

But Vern almost instinctively realized the purpose of each material. It was as if the idea of stability and instability were baked into the very design itself.

Turning the stability of the core all the way up, he felt the sword become heavier, and its sheen was replaced with dullness. However, when he ended his vision, it slowly turned back to the way it was before, gleaming sharply.

He looked at his hands, his brows knitted tightly. That wasn't supposed to happen. How did the sword "heal" back to its prior state? Vern didn't see any energy source that would've supported the change.

However, his curiosity didn't let him linger on that for too long. If this is what happened with stability, how would it handle the instability?

Again, it only made sense to use instability inducement on the outer edge of the blade, not the core. And like a kid pushing the crank of his new toy, he destabilized it.

Zing.

"Whoa." He couldn't hold in his surprise this time.

His hand trembled, and the edge of the blade began vibrating at an insane frequency. In a few seconds, it even began glowing with a sharp purple gleam, the particles heating up in unexpected ways due to his destabilization.

One part apprehensive and ninety-nine parts excited, he walked up to a dummy, a sword in each hand. He gently rested the gleaming edge against the dummy's wooden side. Surprisingly, even this light contact left a noticeable nick in the wood.

Whoa whoa whoa whoa.

His heart beating faster than ever, he put some strength on his hand and executed a sloppy slash. So sloppy it chopped the thing neatly in half with minimal effort.

He involuntarily turned toward Mistress Amelia, wondering for a second if these swords were this sharp by default. But she was staring at that edge herself, an intrigued light in her eyes.

She doesn't know, either?

He took his other sword, the one that was neither stabilized nor destabilized, and tried running it through what was left of the dummy. It got stuck in the hardwood almost instantly.

That was more like the reality in which he lived and understood. Stopping his vision, he fixated on the blade, and just like with stability, the edge soon settled back to its base state.

This . . . this is game-changing! The possibilities excited him to no end. He tried reimagining that fight in the relay station with this weapon in his hand.

He would've been able to cut down those zealots in a mere instant with that edge while using the other blade to defend himself from those ranged attacks—assuming he had the motor skills to back it up, of course.

He brought both swords close to each other, holding them with the outer curve of the grip. Then, when he pressed the hilt of one onto the other, the blades rushed each other at a terrifying speed, merging with the most satisfying *tang* sound ever.

Oh, my lady!

One second, he had a longsword, but in the next, sparks came out of the seam, and with a crisp *tch-tching*, it would split into two light swords.

The implications excited him to no end. He could use the left to receive attacks while doling out attacks with the right one, or he could combine the whole thing and use it as one great offensive or defensive weapon. The possibilities—

"Alright, Vern, let's pause for a minute," she interjected.

He stopped, a blush creeping up his cheeks. *That must have been embarrassing to watch.*

But right now, he was willing to listen to anything she said. How the hell did she manage to think of something so . . . compatible with himself?

Leaning on a wall, she asked, "Tell me, how do you feel about the synergy of Duality with your observational powers?"

He didn't even have to think twice before speaking. "It's a great match. I can't think of a better way to turn my abstract set of visions into something so . . . practical and useful." Those words came from his heart, too. It had never even crossed his mind to employ the dichotomy of his visions onto a physical weapon.

One reason was that instability inducement was supposed to . . . destabilize things. Yet, in this case, it seemed to have an effect that amplified the deadliness of the sword manifold.

Mistress nodded, maybe a little pleased with herself? It was hard to tell exactly with that face cover still in the way. Did she ever take it off?

"Then let's get the real training going. Your stance is horrible, the swings are pathetic, and your footing is as rough as it gets."

He winced at those remarks but moved to stand opposite her without dragging his feet. He knew where he stood, and the view from down there wasn't pretty.

Mistress unlatched a blunt longsword hanging on the wall and walked toward him, looking equal parts beautiful and terrifying. She extended it toward him while her empty hand reached forward, clearly expecting Duality in return.

He had only used the weapon for a couple minutes, but he already felt like it was wrong to give it away. But he didn't let such a stupid notion hamper his training.

After switching weapons, she stood in front of him, her hands atop the hilt of Duality, its tip in the ground. He followed suit, and she started, "I know how you fundamentalists think. So, let me first lay it out in a way that will make most sense to you."

"Swordplay is made up of multiple fundamentals—there's posture, grip, footwork, blade work, attacks, defense, breathing, and finally focus. Today, our goal is to give you a basic understanding of the first few. Later, if we have time, we can also practice integrating your visions in the combat."

Vern became a yes-man and nodded.

She held Duality up to her chest, and her aura changed almost instantly. In a tone that brooked no argument, she commanded, "Use your eyes, and observe me." He cleared his mind, his focus solely on her. Although he couldn't quite identify the reason, he instinctively knew that it was not the time to take her lightly.

However, as Vern locked eyes with her icy gaze, his heart missed a beat, and a wave of intense fear washed over him almost instantly. She repeated firmly, "Observe. Me. I don't know exactly what you can see with those eyes, but if it can help, use it!"

Oh! It dawned on Vern that she was instructing him to use his viewpoint to observe her. The thought hadn't even crossed his mind because Captain Shinsei told him that Kingsmen were elusive to one's perception, just like other observers.

But he had no plans of making her repeat herself another time. Vern pushed aside his burgeoning anxiety and the flurry of questions in his mind, unveiling his perception.

Instantly, the world shifted into stark shades of gray, and within this monochrome vista, her form stood out with clarity.

Maybe she could control when to allow one to observe her and when not to? He believed it might be related to the fact that she wasn't using the strength of the old blood right now.

Still, he wasn't sure how to focus his grays just yet. Stability in itself wasn't really the most practical lens for learning.

She noticed his glowing eyes and began, "Consider the human body as a sophisticated system of levers and fulcrums." Her tone was flaccid, reflecting a blend of logic and art. "Each joint, from your ankles to your wrists, plays a crucial role in your stance and movement. They work in unison, creating a fluid yet controlled flow of energy."

She was going out of her way to explain the mechanics in a jargon that better suited his field of study, but this gave him an idea.

Vern immediately adjusted his perception to target the fulcrums of the "structure." Suddenly, hundreds of bright spots materialized around him—within the mistress, in Duality, his own sword, his hands, the room, and countless other things. The world transformed into a canvas dotted with these luminous points.

Deciding to concentrate solely on the mistress and Duality, Vern narrowed his focus. As he did, the surrounding clutter vanished from his perception. What remained were just a dozen or so luminous points, loosely outlining a human shape, resembling a constellation scattered across the night sky.

As she subtly shifted her weight around, the movement resonated through her network of joints, and the dots in Vern's perception adjusted accordingly. "Balance and center of gravity are determined by how these nodes align and interact," she explained. "Your feet, the foundational nodes, establish your stability. The knees, adaptable and responsive, modulate your center of gravity. And the spine, serving as the central axis, upholds the balance within this network."

She transitioned through various poses, elucidating how each affected stability. Vern concentrated on the shifting dots that represented the structure of her body.

However, there was more to it. Surprisingly, or unsurprisingly, this observation caused new insights to blossom in his thought space, just like they did whenever he analyzed new structures.

Vern observed, captivated, as she performed more than a half dozen stances, each with its unique advantages and drawbacks. Every stance represented a distinct arrangement of those luminous dots, with the angles and distances between them defining the subtleties of each pose.

But then he suddenly had an even better idea.

C H A P T E R **17**

TRAINING (STABILITY HAZE)

Wait. What if...
Vern improvised at the speed of light and augmented the dots in his sight with a haze around Mistress's body, its shade signifying the stability of the stance. He was hoping to make use of the new insights that had just blossomed in his thought space.

So when the haze that he had conjured around the dots turned darker as she transitioned from one stance to the other, a surge of excitement washed over him. Its turning darker signified that she wasn't stable when going from one stance to the other, which was obviously the case.

But the moment she stopped and settled into a proper stance, the haze turned bright white while she verbally explained the intricacies of that particular stance.

Listening to her attentively, he studied the dots and haze with a singular focus. Soon he could even differentiate which stance was better in stability compared to the others, but as Mistress said, it was all a trade-off. If one stance had worse stability, it made for better mobility.

He even pulled out his notepad and pen, drawing diagrams and writing notes to better internalize the stances. Mistress was at first confused by his antics but ignored him soon after.

Seconds turned into minutes, and before he knew it, the mesmerizing dance came to an end.

She then looked him in the eye and said, "It's your turn."

Vern nodded solemnly, snapping the notepad shut before throwing it to the side. All the point structures of different stances were now imprinted in his memory—something he didn't really trust. So it was time to etch it into his muscle memory instead.

His brain was now in awe of her teaching skills and further muddled by the comprehensive trance, and he asked dumbly, "Can I first try them out in front of a mirror?"

She shrugged, not seeming to care one way or the other. He picked up the blunt longsword and stood in front of the mirror. He looked at the posture of his reflection with disgust. It was outright horrific compared to Mistress's.

So he closed his eyes but unveiled his perception, discarding everything but his own fulcrums and the sword.

Soon, however, he realized how stupid he had been to come and stand in front of a mirror. He could "feel" where each of the dots representing his joints were. He didn't need to "see" it, and his perception didn't really "reflect" from the mirror anyway.

Shaking his head, he recalled the diagrams of each stance and moved his body to match them as closely as possible. The dots representing his joints aligned one after another, and the dark haze around them—signifying the overall stability of his pose—turned brighter.

Then he focused on individual points and nudged the equivalent body parts in directions that caused the haze to grow whiter. Neck a little leaned back, three joints of central spine a little straighter, elbows farther stretched, and feet turned a bit more inward.

The haze around him lightened with every little adjustment, and he soon found a nice equilibrium.

Now moving even a little seemed to cause the haze to grow shadowy. It shouldn't have happened in this stance though. This one was called ox guard and was supposed to be the most stable one. So the haze should be as close to white as possible.

That's when he felt a subtle touch on his elbow, pushing it higher. The stability actually became darker with this movement, but this was only the start. A nudge came on his wrist, rotating it a little farther.

He maintained his rigid posture, only letting those gentle prods shift the joints in that area. Each change fluctuated the haze around him, and before it could settle came a dozen more subtle changes, including a touch on his back, a sliding force on his feet, and a push of fingers on his chin.

When the touches finally stopped, he felt it. The haze was the brightest it had ever been, and he did his best to engrave this state of joints into his muscle memory, trying to get a feel for every body part.

"Okay, stop," came Mistress's voice, and he opened his eyes. She stood right next to him, critically judging his figure in the mirror.

Vern stood tall, his sword raised to the side of his head, its point menacingly aimed toward himself in the mirror. His leading hand was positioned near the hilt just under his eyeline, while his other hand clutched right above the curved grips near the back of his head.

He looked . . . intimidating.

Making eye contact with his figure in the mirror, she said, "That took you three minutes." There was a menacing edge in her voice.

"Break stance."

Vern relaxed his grip and rested the sword on the ground. His arms were feeling a little sore already. The sword wasn't too heavy, but three minutes in that posture wasn't great for his wrists.

Before his forearms could even stop throbbing, she commanded, "Take stance. You have ten seconds this time."

Ignoring his almost screaming arms, he closed his eyes and focused on the positioning of the points. He didn't have much luxury for trial and error this time around, so he scrambled to align everything the way it had been a moment ago.

The haze around him quickly fluctuated before settling on a bright white, and he locked all his joints in position, knowing he couldn't do better in the allotted time.

Two hands ran along different parts of his body, nudging them to better positions almost instantly. He couldn't even fathom how her hands moved so fast, much less with this much precision.

In another few seconds, he was back in perfect stance.

"Break stance."

He did.

"Take stance, eight seconds."

He rushed again, a little better and faster than last time—finding an equilibrium in only six seconds. She fixed a few things still, and he tried to engrave each of the adjustments in his body.

"Break stance.

"Take stance; five seconds.

". . . four seconds.

". . . three seconds.

". . . two seconds.

"Two seconds.

"Two seconds.

"Two seconds.

"Two seconds.

"Break stance."

Vern huffed, gasping for breath. His arms screamed at him while his heart raced as if it were on fire. Then came Mistress's voice, "Three minutes. Grab some water and rest."

He nodded, not frustrated in the least bit. This was heaven. He had never had such a great teacher in his life. Not even Master back in Nvoria had such a dynamic method of tutoring.

She explained things in analogies that made perfect sense. She adapted to his pace but still compelled him to push harder at every step. It was bliss.

He had met great fundamentalists who would rank among the most knowledgeable in the world, yet they were some of the worst teachers in existence. A random professor in some institute could explain theories better than them.

Experience and skill were almost never proportional to one's ability to impart that knowledge unto others. Yet, in this case, she seemed to have all three.

Walking over to the bench, he placed the blunt sword next to him and massaged his forearms. He wasn't very keen on using stability inducement if he didn't need it. Not when the whole point of training was to extract the body's potential.

How was he going to get better if he kept using shortcuts and never let his body exhaust itself?

Chugging the water from a flask, he reflected on the session up until now. Notably, he hadn't really used a vision during the training. It was just the passive use of his eyes to isolate a singular concept and streamline his learning based on that.

He wondered if he could use his visions to "stabilize" his posture and envision his body into a fixed stance. But he discarded that thought as soon as it came to his mind. He wanted to build muscle memory, not make extra work for himself.

He wouldn't have the time or mind in an actual fight to correct his stances every step of the way. That would be a pathetic way of fighting. It might be worth looking into once he had all the basics down, but it would only be detrimental for now.

Mistress stood in the corner, her blonde hair a little more ruffled than before and her eyes distant, not really focused on anything. He wondered what was on her mind.

She was quite . . . complicated. He recalled she had mentioned that she wanted to retire, but there was also that blood-crazed look in her eyes every time she talked about fighting or advancing further.

Weren't these two ideas contradictory?

He shook his head, and his eyes fell on the small case peeking from his coat pocket. Within it was the first infusion of old blood. He wondered what exactly this blood-borne subjugation art was.

What exactly did those fundamentalists do to "subjugate" the blood-borne disease within the old blood? What did they mean by different tiers of infusions?

His personal understanding of human anatomy was quite minimal. Diseases, cures, and blood were not even in the same vein as his field of research. Still, everything originated from the insight sphere, so he could surely find a common ground if he tried hard enough.

Trying and failing to come up with any legible working theory behind the sub-jugation art for now, he let it be and switched the arm he was massaging.

Soon came the voice, "Take stance. Longpoint guard this time, fifty seconds."

Vern took a deep breath, grabbed the sword, and stood. Walking over to the mirror again, he closed his eyes and focused. Longpoint guard was all about a more open approach.

The nodes representing his hands and wrists stretched directly in front of him, the tip of the sword aimed at the chest of an imaginary opponent. His feet were spaced comfortably apart, one leading slightly, offering a balance between mobility and stability.

This one was far simpler. The first trial and error adjustments barely took him half a minute, and Mistress only had to nudge him a couple times before it was perfect.

"Break stance.

"Take stance; five seconds."

He did it in four, except for the fact that she still had to correct a bunch of things.

". . . three seconds.

". . . two seconds.

". . . two seconds."

She never really went below that number.

"Rest.

"Take stance. High guard.

". . . five seconds.

". . . three seconds.

". . . two seconds.

"Rest. Two minutes.

"Take stance. High guard.

"Take stance. Fool's guard.

"Take stance. Tail guard."

Every session for the particular guard became shorter and shorter, and he even adapted to one of them almost perfectly in a mere ten tries.

Mistress paced along the room, Duality hanging from her fingers that looped into that curved grip at the bottom.

She spoke without a hint of a hurry. "Next is to transition from one stance to another. Idea is to keep unnecessary movements to a minimum." She swung the longsword around until it was back in her hands, firmly secured in a long point guard.

Vern observed her with his eyes as well as his perception, and she changed from a long point to an ox guard stance in a very efficient motion. It was like watching a well-oiled machine going from one phase to another.

Not waiting for her to tell him to begin, he stood right next to her and began mimicking her every motion. He didn't even need to look to his right. He just focused on how those floating points evolved and moved around.

But that wasn't all. Anytime he wasn't doing it right, the difference in the shade of haze around himself and Mistress allowed him to realize it almost instantly, and he corrected those mistakes.

It was simple. Make the movements in a way that smoothly shifts the haze of stability from one pattern to another.

It *was* simple. Until she upped the ante, transitioning faster and faster.

It was almost like a mesmerizing dance where Vern was an eager yet untrained apprentice trying to match steps with the master. Each movement she made was fluid and assured, oozing with an innate grace.

Vern, in contrast, tried his best and remained diligent but lacked her finesse and rhythm. His steps were hesitant, often a beat behind as he tried to mirror her intricate footwork and swift movements.

She soon included other stances in the mix. From high guard to roof guard. Fool's guard to tail guard. Ox guard to plow guard.

Mistress Amelia continued to lead the dance without missing a single beat. Each transition was seamless, her mastery over the forms evident in the way she flowed from one guard to the next with elegance and precision. The dance of swords became more complex, more demanding, yet she made it look almost effortless.

Then came three stances in a cycle.

Vern struggled to keep up, his movements less graceful, more mechanical. The haze around him fluctuated wildly with each transition, signaling his faltering alignment with the fluid patterns. But he persisted, driven by a growing understanding and an unwavering focus.

Then four stances at a time.

As they cycled through the guards, Vern's movements became smoother, his timing improved, and the haze around him stabilized, mirroring Mistress Amelia's consistency. He was no longer just mimicking; he was learning, adapting, and evolving.

Then all stances at the same time.

The dance reached its crescendo when they seamlessly integrated all the stances in a continuous flow. Now moving with more confidence, Vern found himself not just following but anticipating the next move, the gap in their expertise levels narrowing with each synchronized step.

After who knew how long, the constellation of Mistress Amelia came to a smooth halt, and his body almost couldn't stop the momentum it had stored to shift into the next anticipated stance.

He opened his eyes to find Mistress's gaze upon him, her eyebrows slightly furrowed, a faint crease on her forehead, and the shape of her lips slightly curved down. Not sure what that meant, he stared back in anticipation.

She said, "Rest."

Yet, that one simple word seemed to shatter all his concentration, and he felt the weight of his mortal body bearing down on him.

His perception dissolved, and his head throbbed, the veins around his eyes pulsing rapidly. Sweat covered him from head to toe while every joint screamed in agony. His arms were red from the exertion, and his wrists felt weak.

Using the sword as support, he barely managed to keep himself from tumbling down. Taking deep breaths in huge mouthfuls, he made his way toward the wall and plopped down on the ground without a care for his image.

Resting his head on the wall, he took huge gulps of water from the flask. He had to revitalize for the next session as soon as possible.

The stances were done . . .

His eyes snapped shut on their own, but he kept wondering.

What . . .

His heart slowed, and it was hard to think, but he tried.

What . . . is . . .

His grip relaxed, and all noises disappeared.

What . . . is . . . next?

And the world turned black.

Chapter 18

Vena's Archive

Mommy, it's not fair! Big Brother broke my toy again!"

Vern scrambled to shut the door and ran back to her, shaking his head rapidly with a pleading look on his face. "Ari, please stop. Don't tell Mom; I'll fix it right away. Just give me a few minutes."

She calmed down a little, but her eyes were already wet with tears, and it looked like one wrong move on his part and the dam would burst right open.

"Ari, please trust me. I wrote down everything, so I won't forget anything this time," he said, showing her the crude diagrams and words on a yellowing page.

Grabbing the hem of her green dress, she sniffled, her lips trembling violently. Vern walked up to her, bent down on his knees, and pulled out the handkerchief Mom washed yesterday, dabbing it on her eyes.

"It's okay, Ari. Trust me this time, please?"

But soon, the handkerchief in his hands turned wet. He kept switching its sides, but her tears wouldn't stop.

He pulled back and looked at her eyes, and the tears continued to flow ceaselessly. Her arm was outstretched, and so was her finger. Soon, a ball of light appeared on the tip of her finger.

His expression scrunched up, and he embraced her in his arms instantly. But his . . . his body didn't move, and words slipped out of his mouth.

"I am sorry."

She was up in the air, the ball of light growing exponentially. He tried to reach out and dab the handkerchief at those eyes that shone with tears. Tears that wouldn't stop.

Tears that didn't stop.

He kept trying, but his body was frozen, and she continued to cry. Her body burned and cracked, but all he could do was watch and mumble, "I am sorry.

"I am sorry.

"I am sorry."

Then the ball of light exploded, and the world turned bright—

"I am sorry!" he shouted, his hands launching toward . . .

Toward . . . what?

Toward empty air in the training room. Vern blinked groggily, taking one short breath after another.

Thud..

The door to his right slammed opened, and bright light entered the otherwise dark room. He could make out a blurry outline that seemed to be saying something.

He blinked rapidly and shook his head to clear the drowsiness.

He tried again and soon heard, "Master Vern . . . are you okay? Do you need something? Is something the matter?"

Vern tilted his head, trying to match the voice with a face. He first thought it was De Flanc, but it wasn't him, so he replied to the man in a butler's dress, "I am sorry. Just give me a minute. I'll be right outside."

The man nodded and walked out, leaving the door open, which illuminated the room. Wiping at his eyes, Vern yawned. It seemed like he had been sleeping.

In the training room?

Sleeping?

He was sleeping in the training room!

His eyes suddenly snapped wide open, and his mind turned alert.

Where's Mistress Amelia?

He looked around, but the room was empty. All the candles and lights were extinguished, clearly out of fuel. He tried pushing himself up, only to feel his entire body scream at him.

Still, he gritted his teeth and lifted himself. This was not as bad as the first morning after he had worked out. He wasn't feeling refreshed by any means, but the sleep seemed to have done quite some good.

When he finally stood, his coat fell down, and he barely caught it. He scrutinized his navy blue coat and tilted his head. *I don't remember draping it over myself.*

Then . . . was it Mistress Amelia? Vern covered his face, glad that the butler wasn't here to watch him being stupid.

What would she think? he wondered. He wanted to pull out his hairs. He passed out on the very first day of the training. The first fucking day!

What the hell was wrong with him? He had been doing pretty good, too.

He stood there for a while, trying to sort out his thoughts. But all that did was remind him of the dream, only worsening his mood.

Soon, however, he shook his head. Mistress Amelia took the time to cover him with his coat—that had to count for something. It should mean she wasn't precisely angry with him, right?

Taking a deep breath, he surveyed the room and soon found what he was looking for. It was actually right there, just beneath him. Nestled next to where he had been sitting, or more accurately, sleeping, lay a golden case.

A smile gradually formed on his face as he recalled all the progress he made today. *Wait, was it today or technically yesterday?* he mused. The short window in the room made way for nothing but darkness, so it was probably still midnight or something.

He picked up Duality's case with one hand and used the other to retrieve the pocket watch from his coat.

It is three in the morning. Ugh, I even kept that butler waiting for me until so late.

But soon, his attention was focused on the small piece of paper that was tucked beneath the case. Shoving the pocket watch back in the coat, he picked up the paper and read it.

Tomorrow, same time.
Decide on what to do about the blood infusion.
Impressive work today.
    —Amelia

He kept reading it again and again, trying to make sure he wasn't hallucinating. His lips soon curved into a smile, and he pocketed the note, walking toward the exit with all his belongings.

The weight in the case assured him that Duality was still inside it. He had a lot of ideas and plans for the weapon.

Like how to make it easy to carry on his person, or better integrate it with his visions, and obviously—to figure out how the heck it worked.

How it split so smoothly and managed to merge back without any seams. And what was up with its edge? Why did stabilizing or destabilizing it cause such a peculiar effect?

The moment he stepped out, a voice said, "I hope you had a wonderful sleep, Master Vern."

Feeling slightly embarrassed, Vern replied, "Considering I was sitting through it, it was pretty good, I guess. Also, I apologize for making you wait." It was apparent that the man had been waiting outside the room for who knows how long. Vern couldn't recall when the training had ended or how much time had passed since then.

The whole training session was so surreal.

The butler began walking in a particular direction and replied with a smile, "Please don't worry, Master Vern, I am De Vere, the head night butler of the castle. Flanc has told me all about you, and it is our duty to make sure our observers don't have to worry about the mundane aspects of life."

Vern looked at the man, amused. Were they brothers? Even their demeanors were similar. They soon crossed past the central training grounds and then a couple of other landmarks that he remembered. But obviously, it was mostly quiet.

Everyone was sleeping. De Vere then guided him to some room, giving him the combination for its lock. He also told Vern he'd send someone with food soon after.

That was indeed a good idea because he was starving. It had been more than twelve hours since he had eaten anything. He might have been fine if all he had done was sit around, but his body needed nutrition to recover from the exhausting day.

So he quickly took a bath and changed into a fresh set of clothes. He really needed it, too. That training was intensive as hell.

Someone else came in with a cart of food, and he made quick work of the meal, not leaving anything unfinished.

Finally feeling right in all places, he lay down on the bed and stared at the ceiling. He wondered whether he should go back to sleep or find something better to do.

He did feel sore but not really tired. However, he didn't want to dream again so soon. So he grabbed his coat, left Duality in its case on a table in the room, and walked out, locking the door behind him.

His destination was obvious. Vena's archive.

How could he resist the allure of knowledge any longer? The fact that he was more learned about Kingsman history than the observer irked him to no end. *Here's hoping it's not locked at night.*

Maybe he could ask De Vere to open it if it was closed?

After getting lost due to the repeating architectural design of the castle, he finally found his way to Vena's archive. As he walked up to the entrance, the blue glow radiating from the windows gave him hope.

Why would the lights be on if one couldn't go in? He was more than ready for it, his heart racing with anticipation. But he still kept his calm and pushed open the large door slowly, not wanting to make any unnecessary noise.

Luckily, it wasn't locked.

The moment he laid his eyes on the elegant yet grandiose interior, his heart calmed down. Libraries always managed to do that to him, except maybe the sister library to this one. That hadn't been calming at all.

Vern shook his head and walked in only to hear a stirring behind him. Glancing back, he noticed two green, indifferent eyes opening on the rack above the door's arch. However, they only fixed on him for a moment before closing once more.

Luna was here!

But he gritted his teeth and held himself back from trying out something creative to get the kitten to come down. He had enough sense to not disturb the little one's sleep. He wasn't Lucian, after all.

He wondered what came of Lucian. Did he accept the blood infusion? *He most probably did.*

Closing the door behind him while making as little noise as possible, he walked farther into the library. Captain Shinsei told him that books and texts of importance were only available based on clearance level.

And that would require him to have a shaded gem on his badge—one he didn't have right now. So he planned on exploring the library and finding something worthwhile until people woke up so he could finally go about his business.

It was a new library we were talking about. There was no way he wouldn't find something to waste a couple of hours on. And if nothing else, he could even do some testing with the convergence note. The ambiance of this library was perfect for that, anyway.

So he weaved through one shelf after another, mesmerized by all the works on display. Picking a thin book on the empire's history, he perused through it, mainly focusing on the images as he continued to traverse into uncharted territories.

When this whole floor was mapped mentally, he returned the book and gladly ascended the stairs. He tried to find something, anything related to observation, but as luck would have it, or the maintainers of this library, there was nothing.

However, he had no plans to settle down and read that book about Kingsmen's gear and Von Industries unless he was sure there was nothing else left to check.

Gladly, his eyesight had gotten better, or he would have to find a ladder and slowly go through each row one by one. It would have been a nightmare, given that some of the shelves were two stories high.

So he perused through what was left of this floor, too, and left for even higher stairs. But there was just one small problem. There was a heavy metal door blocking the stairs. It was made up of multiple panels, the gaps between each of them teasing the path ahead.

Feeling more than a little disappointed, he walked up to the door. He wondered if there was some automated mechanism that could detect the shades on a gem and let the holder pass.

Interestingly, there was indeed something like that. Or maybe it was just a decoration and didn't actually work? Not that he could test it even if he wanted to—his badge didn't have a gem.

Still, for curiosity's sake, he bent down and ran his hand along the curved surface of the aperture that seemed like a cast for an eye. But the moment he touched the cold metal, its hinges creaked, and the whole door swung wide open.

Vern stood there, his hand outstretched, unable to process what had just happened. There was no way he broke it. It was clearly not his fault.

No. It was already open. That was the only possibility. He pondered what to do, and his mind unanimously came to a single conclusion.

Go up.

It wasn't his fault that the door was open, right? And if someone else left it open, they would be to blame, not him.

Acting as nonchalantly as ever, he walked up the stairs, latching the door behind him. Funnily enough, the thing actually locked, so he couldn't go back even if he wanted to. Surely, no one could blame him for perusing the third floor now, right?

With a smug smile plastered on his face, he ascended to the third floor that didn't have any of those blue lights. Still, it didn't even take him a moment to survey the bindings of the books on display, and his eyes shone with greed.

Many didn't even have titles, and that only made him more curious. He decided to first check out all the items on display before settling on something to read.

Rubbing his hands together, he made toward the leftmost shelf. He had to be formulaic about his approach. He couldn't just jump at this sacred task like some base beast without logic, after all.

Swish swish.

But the moment he was about to touch the shelf, it . . . disappeared. Vern staggered back, a flustered look on his face. He had heard something, too, but he couldn't put his finger on it.

Not entirely sure, he turned vigilant and moved toward the source of that sound. Maybe it was some kind of protective measure that worked against "intruders"? Not that he was one.

However, he didn't overreact like last time with Luna and decided to figure it out calmly first. He had been paranoid twice today, and both were in vain. Vigil was a safe space, he had to get that thing in his mind.

He recalled Captain Shinsei's chiding when he had scared Luna away. He wasn't about to make a fool of himself another time. So he regulated his breathing and walked toward the far end of the library.

He didn't move to touch any other shelves, and they didn't disappear. Step-by-step, he got closer to the other end, and when he weaved past a horizontal shelf blocking his path, his sight opened up.

Moonlight pierced through the stained-glass window on the left wall, illuminating the solitary figure that sat on a high stool in the center of the wide open hall—a brush in her hand. She cast a long shadow on the floor, but longer yet, was her hair—paler than the moonlight itself.

Chapter 19

PAINT ME?

A towering canvas stood before her, each stroke of her brush gracing it with elegance. She intermittently dipped the bristles into the palette next to her, a dance of color and creation unfolding. Half of her lit face had a picturesque beauty to it—thin lips, a sculpted nose, a sleek chin, and eyes that seemed tender yet detached.

Adorned in a beret, baggy pants, and a poncho, she was a canvas herself, splashed with myriad colors and vivid splotches of paint marking her attire.

Perched atop a stool towering over two men in height, she reached the upper echelons of the tall canvas. Her hair cascaded gracefully, nearly brushing the ground.

One leg rested on the stool's platform while the other swung rhythmically in the air, mirroring the sway of her body. It was as though she moved to an inaudible melody, her every motion in harmony with the music only she could hear.

A heap of smaller canvases lay at her side, all of them depicting a slight variation of what she was painting right now. Vern didn't understand art as much as he would have wanted to, but admiring it was always a pleasure.

He was having a hard time understanding this one though. He could almost make out a face and an opulent interior in the background, but there were these red and white strokes that seemed to cover up the face.

The general art style was mesmerizing, but it was hard to figure out what was actually going on in the scene.

She gripped the platform of the stool with one hand and leaned forward, making some intricate changes in the painting. That's when her lips moved, and a soft sound entered his ears. "What do you wanna read?"

Vern shook his head and snapped himself out of the reverie. The ambiance had captivated him, leaving him spellbound for a while.

But her straightforwardness threw him off a little. Hadn't they skipped a few steps there? Still, clearing his throat, he answered, "I was hoping to start with the very basics of observation."

She didn't even look back and replied, "Shelf C, fourth row, *The Axioms of Observation*. Bring it back and read it where I can see you."

Vern opened his mouth to say something but turned right around and walked to the mentioned shelf, which was made obvious by the lettering on its side. He easily spotted said book in the fourth row.

It was a thin one, which was sad. He was hoping it would be something with enough content to last him for a while. But if she recommended it, there must have been a reason.

So he grabbed the book and walked back to her, only to notice something peculiar. She was holding up the papers of the canvas, and a different painting peeked out from underneath it.

She swiftly added a few strokes to the painting underneath, and Vern watched in amazement as a second stool just . . . appeared between her and the window out of thin air.

He glanced at the small section of the painting that peeked from behind her hand and then at the stool. She had just added a similar shape to the painting! But before he could scrutinize it further, she dropped the hand that was holding up the pages on the canvas, and all he could see was that red-white scene again.

There was nowhere else to sit, so it was clear she had drawn it for him. Vern didn't mind. He would sit on a painted stool over a normal one any day.

Is this how she rendered that shelf invisible? he wondered, making his way toward the small stool wordlessly. If she could "paint" changes onto reality, what exactly was she trying to do by drawing that red-white thing?

Going by the thickness of the "sketchbook," there were at least a hundred other pages in it. *What other things can she "manipulate" like this?* he mused. But not like she would tell him, and he had no interest in prying for the sake of it.

He sat on the wooden stool, and unfortunately, it felt exactly the same as a normal one. He had hoped it would dissolve into paint or something. He chuckled at the thought and let it be.

She didn't really pay him any mind and focused on her painting, but he was curious, so he went ahead and asked a little hesitantly, "Are you Lady Irene?"

"Just Irene is fine," she replied, biting the brush's handle with a contemplative look.

His guess was on point, it seemed. Captain Shinsei was looking to introduce them to her during the tour, but she wasn't around last evening. So he made his usual introduction. "Nice to meet you, Irene. I am Vern."

"I know," she quipped back. After a couple new strokes on the painting, she added, "I also know that you just waltzed up here."

Vern almost dropped the book from his hands before scrambling to find the best way to vocalize his innocence. He began, "It's-it's not like that. The door was open. I was checking to see how it worked, and it just swung wide open—"

But then he heard low giggles and looked back up, only to see her lips trembling as she did her best to hold back a laugh.

Oh. Vern's cheeks heated up almost instantly as he realized he'd been had. She was making fun of him.

"I opened the door, hahaha." She tipped her head back and let loose, her soft laughter echoing through the library.

Vern didn't know how to react. Between her short fits of giggles, she added, "You should've seen your face when I painted the shelf away."

Vern opened the book and hid his face behind it, his cheeks flushed. But it was hard to hold back, and her laugh was infectious.

It spread through the room and soon caught up to him, and he joined with light chuckles of his own. That one might have indeed been a little funny to watch from an outsider's perspective.

But then, out of the blue, her soft laughter died down, and she yelled, pointing her brush at him, "Wow! Hold that pose!" Vern involuntarily froze in that exact position.

He was settled on the stool, one foot anchored on the footrest, the other extended slightly forward. The open book obscured the lower half of his face, concealing a hint of his smile, and the hand holding it relaxed upon his knee. Bathed in moonlight filtering through the stained-glass window, he was enveloped in a shadowy interplay of light and dark, creating an almost mystical aura around him.

Standing atop her own tall stool, she picked the next upturned page of her massive sketchbook and flipped it over. A new empty white canvas now waited for her, and she excitedly mixed colors on her palette. Doing so, she said, "Don't move. Please!"

Vern didn't know what to do about this situation. Trying to avoid a helpless look from creeping onto his face, he spoke, holding the pose strong, "Miss Irene, I am not sure if I am a worthy subject for your art—"

"First lady, now miss—can you drop the formality already? It's so . . . awkward," she interjected, picking up different colored vials from the bracket in front of the canvas and mixing them.

Vern sighed. "Okay, Irene. Can I go back to reading?"

She shook her head, a slow rippling wave propagating through her long hair. "No. It's your fault for looking so good in that pose."

". . ." He was speechless. Luckily, the book hid the blush.

It had been a while since someone had given him a sincere compliment about his looks. Fundamentalists didn't care much about faces, while most nobles he interacted with were all about wealth, status, and bloodlines—of which he had none.

Swish swish.

Dipping her brush in the newly mixed colors, she began with wide strokes that weren't really all that clear from this angle. She looked at him every few seconds before adding a couple new strokes to the canvas.

Swish swish.

Soon, however, his paranoia won over his shyness. But since it had done him nothing but a disservice today, he asked about his fears veiled as a joke. "Irene, are you drawing me so you can make me disappear, too?"

Swapping the thick brush for a thin one, she retorted, "Tell me you're joking. You can't be clueless enough to think I am some witch who can break the axioms of observation."

His hand wanted so bad to go up and scratch his head. What did she mean by breaking an axiom of observation? How did that work?

But he didn't get to ponder that for long because she chided him, "No, no, no! Go back to the previous expression. Don't bring your eyebrows together, and smile a little!"

But how? She was demanding too much of him. He was no model. Closing his eyes for a while, he tried to do as she suggested.

Without his prompting, she began again, a smirk etched on her face. "But obviously, you don't know the axioms." She stopped her strokes to laugh before speaking again. "You wouldn't be holding that book if you did, after all."

That is indeed true. Which is why I came here in the first place!

Taking a deep breath, he began his counterattack. "Well, at least I am not going through an artist's block," he chimed, his eyes focused on the heap of similar drawings next to her.

She stopped, clearly taken aback. She first looked at him, then at the heap, before she wordlessly grabbed the first few pages of her canvas like some curtain and then drew a few more strokes on the drawing at the page underneath.

Swish swish.

Vern watched in stupefaction as the heap of paintings was erased from reality as if it were some line drawing. She then dropped the canvas papers and looked back at him with a cheeky expression. "What artist's block? Where's the evidence?"

Vern stared back silently before shaking his head but soon broke out into another chuckle, and she followed him with a giggle of her own.

Then suddenly, she stopped, ready to chide him again for breaking the pose. But he didn't let her speak and declared, "Sorry, but this sketch model demands compensation for sitting here. I came here to read, but I can't do that now, can I?"

She opened her mouth to speak but then stopped. Then after a while, she looked at him as if she were making the biggest compromise of her life and asked, "I can read it to you?"

Vern shook his head and quipped back, "That sounds like reading it myself—but worse."

Her eyebrows shot up, lips pressing into a thin line. Then, as if she weren't going to back down any further, she replied, "I . . . I will answer your questions regarding observation."

Well, that was a little too easy, almost suspicious even. He hadn't even mentioned that's what he wanted, but he wasn't one to look a gift horse in the mouth. He smiled to himself and asked, "Are you well versed in the complexities of observation?"

She narrowed her eyes and leaned toward him on that stool dangerously. "I own this library! I am more learned than five copies of you combined! And I am starting to rethink my offer, the way you're ruining the pose right now."

Vern shrank back. *I guess that question was somewhat rhetorical anyway. Obviously, she knows more than me.*

He offered her a smile and applied the technique he had mastered during training, seamlessly readjusting himself into the previous pose with near-perfect precision. It was all just points, anyway.

Her expression went from exasperated to awed and then mesmerized real quick, and she grabbed the brush and began painting right away. Soon she spoke, the moonlight reflecting off her beautiful face. "Anyway, what do you wanna know?"

Vern reeled back his mind from her elegant features and pondered on where to start. The obvious choice was asking about these axioms, but honestly, he'd heard about them before from Esther, and he didn't think they were the "fundamentals" of observation.

If someone was willing to answer his questions, he'd rather start from the very basics. He was missing so many little details that any higher concept would just go right over his head.

So, he thickened his skin and braced himself for potential ridicule before asking, "Can we start from the start? Could you explain precisely what observation is and how it functions?"

Chapter 20

WHAT IS OBSERVATION?

She stopped her routine of looking at him before adding a few more strokes, clearly taken aback. Then she tilted her head for a while before finally speaking up, "It's not often I get such a stupid question, so I had to organize my thoughts."

Vern rolled his eyes before gesturing with them for her to continue, and she did. "For understanding's sake, let's think of reality as one big painting. Then observation is the process with which you can change the details of that painting."

Vern blinked his eyes to convey that he was following her train of thought, and she gladly went on—with her drawing and the explanation. "However, observation in itself is divided into two steps, 'perceiving' and 'envisioning' respectively. The first is to perceive or interpret the world according to a specific viewpoint. But this is where complications begin."

Dipping a smaller brush into the palette, she carried on, "The painting that is our world is made up of colors that one can never replicate, no matter the material used or the colors mixed. But we still have to perceive it, right? So what should one do?"

Vern began, "Paint—"

"*Paint* it with the colors you have," she interjected, answering the question herself. A menacing look emerged in her eyes, threatening him not to move or speak unnecessarily.

Vern blinked again for confirmation, and that was all it took for her smile to return. She continued, "That is the first step done. Now that you have the world painted with a limited color palette, you can make changes to it however you'd like. After all, you still have all the colors needed to paint the world, right?"

Vern wanted to frown at these words, but her dead stare and still-moving lips deterred him from doing just that.

"Wrong!" she declared, pointing the tip of her brush toward him as if he were in the wrong here.

Hey, I didn't even get to say anything! But he kept the complaint in his heart.

"In one sense, yes, you can alter that picture however you'd like, but what was our end goal again? It was to change the details of the painting with myriad colors that was reality and not our personal painting with limited colors."

Vern blinked. It made sense. This was all according to his own understanding of observation as well.

Picking an even finer brush, she began detailing what seemed like the eyebrows of his portrait and resumed. "So now we come to the second step of observation, which is to envision the changes we'd like to happen. The catch here is to only alter the painting with the colors that should be used to paint it in reality."

Vern had something to say again, but she waved her arm and overruled him. "I know, I know. I just said reality has infinite colors, and they can never be recreated. But we, as observers, only have to do our best in guessing the colors of reality. Rest is handled by those lenses in your eyes as long as it's molded properly."

Vern clicked his tongue. She had indeed put it very nicely. He also had to change the shades of grays to manipulate reality instead of messing with it directly. He first "perceived" the world as grays of balance and then "envisioned" them getting lighter or darker before they finally changed the world.

A few questions had already emerged in his mind from this condensed explanation, but she wasn't done yet, so he let her have the stage and decided to enjoy the show. Her take on the matter was quite interesting to listen to.

She cleaned the tip of her brush on her poncho and began again. "Now that was a very broad and surface-level explanation of how observation essentially works, but it misses out on a dozen nuances."

Vern let out a dry laugh when she wasn't looking. *You're not kidding about that. Those nuances are a bit too . . . nuanced.* He had worried over them so much he might have already aged by a year in ten days.

Before she could intimidate him, he was already back in the required posture, though his expression was quite hard to maintain. Now working on replicating his coat, she elaborated, "The most significant challenges with observation are the . . . whispers, viewpoints, and the visions."

He blinked, and she carried on, "Viewpoint is the palette of colors you have to make your personal painting, whereas visions define the colors you can paint back into reality."

Then her expression suddenly turned serious, and she added, "Then there's the whispers."

She even placed her brush back in the bracket for a while and turned toward him. "Whispers are our reminder that we shouldn't be trying to mess with the painting of reality in the first place."

Vern relaxed his stiff posture and tried to figure out what she meant. She didn't seem to mind him getting out of that pose and kept going, "They've given it such a simple name that it undermines the gravity of what they signify.

"They signify our mistakes."

With her hands behind her body, she leaned back and looked at the roof and said, "If your personal palette—viewpoint, and reality's palette of what you alter—visions don't mesh well, the whispers will tear your psyche apart, one color at a time."

She then looked at him from that tilted angle, her blue eyes glistening in the moonlight. "They leave nothing but an empty husk that knows nothing but to rave and echo the whispers until they lose themselves."

"They leave nothing . . ."

Then her voice turned into a soft mutter, and he only heard a small part of it. ". . . not even m . . ."

Soon, however, she leaned forward in a swift motion, a somber gleam in her eyes. "Any mistake you make in your progress to find the best colors, know that the whispers will be keeping toll."

Her voice rose with her every word. "Try to use a vision that makes no sense for your viewpoint, and congratulations, you've cut your mental lifespan short by a month if you stop in time."

"Do that ten times without recovering, and the whispers will be there with you every step of the way, eroding your sanity until nothing but shillings remain."

Then as if letting out her personal grievances, her words picked up speed, and she rattled, "Want to see if you've progressed and can envision this new change you've been working toward? No, too bad, you've instead killed ten innocent people because you lost your head and didn't even know.

"Well, maybe it would get better once you shade your perception, right? Haha, no! It only gets worse and worse the higher you go! Honestly, everyone should just reach the peak of their current shade and never advance again!

"It's just . . . stupid!" she yelled.

Vern received the outpouring of emotions and reassessed his thoughts on the matter. He hadn't really been worried about the whispers too much. He essentially only encountered them once due to an observational mistake. And that was when he knew pretty much nothing about observation in Eleanora's library.

The only other time was when he'd gazed at the gash in the sky, but he attributed it to his bad luck rather than lack of caution. Who could have expected the ravings of madness just from looking at the sky?

But her words painted a very different picture. It appeared as though these whispers were an intrinsic part of being an observer, and the consequences of any mistake might very well be the erosion of one's psyche.

He wanted to console her, but anything he said would come out as shallow. Their positions and experiences were too different for him to conjure the right words.

But she was clearly not one to stay down for too long. Before he could muster up the courage to get up and physically comfort her, she picked up the brush and pointed at him with an angry shout, "Agh! Get back to that stupid pose . . . please."

Vern didn't say anything and obliged. What else was he supposed to do? Give a fake assurance that everything would be alright? He didn't even know what exactly she was upset about.

He hadn't even known that whispers were this big of an issue before today. How was he supposed to sympathize with it?

So he chose to remain silent and allowed her to paint in quietude, making sure to remove any hint of judgment and awkwardness from his expression.

After a while, she bit the tip of her brush again and looked at the half-finished painting with a dubious expression. She then turned toward him sheepishly and asked, "Can you move to the right?"

Vern stared back, not sure what she meant.

She pointed at the stained-glass window behind him and said, "The moon has shifted a bit too much."

He nodded, picking up his stool and moving to match the shadow's angle as best as possible. He plopped the wooden article back down and heard, "Sorry about that. Do you wanna ask anything else?"

He let out a sigh of relief. He thought her mood wasn't going to get better any time soon. Readjusting into that specific pose, he asked, keeping an eye on her expression to make sure she was stable, "What exactly is an observation record, and how is it different from a viewpoint?"

Going back to her previous routine of looking at him with a merry gaze and then painting a couple of strokes (and almost as if that outburst hadn't happened), she answered, "Well, it is quite complicated, but let me try to stick to my previous analogy and see if I can explain it that way.

"Visions, in essence, take an altered painting with limited colors and revert it back to one with infinite colors. And we, as observers, imprint these visions into our perceptions, making them an inherent property of ourselves."

Then she narrowed her eyes. "But the catch here comes from the first axiom of observation, which states that all viewpoints are unique. That is to say, the color palette of each person is their own and distinct from everyone else's in the world."

Ah. A look of realization dawned on his face before he quickly buried it after a pointed look from her. Vern saw the problem. Though it might be better to not come to conclusions until she was done. So he listened with rapt attention.

"I guess you see the problem, eh?" She nodded with a pleased smile. "The visions can only take a painting made from a very specific color palette and turn it back to the one with an infinite palette of reality. That is to say, visions can't do the magic for your unique colors."

Vern nodded vigorously with each of her words in his mind. They slowly took off the shroud of mystery that had been settled on some of these ideas for too long. His brain was already leaping ahead, trying to figure out what this meant for him.

Then she took an even smaller brush to draw his eyes, its bristles barely visible. "So the problem is that there are actually three palettes of colors, not two. One for reality, one uniquely for you, and then one that the vision expects.

"So what we lowly humans have to do is try to bend and reshape our unique viewpoint or color palette to match what the vision expects. And that is what observation records are for. They describe the methods, ways, and ideologies to help one mold their viewpoint in a specific direction."

Vern really couldn't hold it in this time, and his eyes widened in understanding.

Maybe pitying his unlearned soul, she cut him some slack this time and carried on, "For example, there might be hundreds of ways to view reality as fire, but there are only two or three observation records in existence that define a stable path, or a shade sequence to progress in that domain."

Then her eyes took on that somber edge again. "And I think I've already hammered it home on what happens if you don't follow these paths properly."

Vern nodded gravely. Things finally started to make sense. Except he had one big question that was still unclear.

So he first bribed her by retaking her desired pose and waited until she was back in a good mood before asking, "What exactly is the measure of progress of an observer? What do shades of perception signify?"

CHAPTER 21

OBSERVATION RECORDS

Irene looked at him with suspicious eyes. Was that too basic of a question?

No. I am obviously asking all this to "consolidate" my knowledge.

She kept looking at him with those narrowed eyes before replying, "I guess I can give you another broad overview."

Vern nodded with great vigor, only to return to his original pose every time she looked at him to paint.

She started, "So I just told you that observation records describe methods to mold your viewpoint in a particular direction, right? And that it's mainly so you can use the visions in that record safely."

"Mm-hmm."

"Well, these records are usually divided into a sequence of shades. Think of each shade as a gradual method of molding your viewpoint into the direction of that record. However, that's not all.

"A higher shade means you're further removed from objectivity." She then said matter-of-factly, "Even though everyone's viewpoint is unique right from the start, they're still derivations of what's objective. So, the larger the number of shades in your perception, the more singular of an entity you become."

She carried on, "Each shade—"

"Sorry, Irene, wait," Vern interjected, his face a mask of confusion. He couldn't hold himself from noticing something glaringly contradictory about that statement.

"Didn't you just say that there are only a few observation records? How could anyone be 'singular' if they're molding their viewpoint in the same direction that many others have done so before?"

Irene looked at him with a puzzled look of her own.

Was that not clear enough?

He added, "Maybe they'll be unique if they're not following a record properly. But let's say two observers follow the same record all the way to the end. Are their viewpoints still unique? Are they still singular?"

Irene narrowed her eyes. "Getting semantical, are we?"

Vern clicked his tongue. "Ah, my bad, then. If it's just a semantics thing, then it makes sense. I thought I was missing something."

Irene chuckled. "Hey, I didn't say being semantical is bad because it seems you are indeed missing something."

"Oh?"

"Are you forgetting about the construct of isolation? Even if two people follow exactly the same path, the way they chose to isolate their viewpoint makes the world of difference."

A what? Vern's mind whirled, and he soon came up with a couple of conjectures on what that phrase meant. It had a very distinct choice of words that suggested an inherent meaning.

His best guess was that she was talking about the idea that he chose to perceive balance as shades of gray. It was the method or a psychological construct with which he isolated the balance.

"You know Ambrose and Antonia, right?"

He nodded.

"So even if two dancers like the Finnesse siblings followed the record down to the letter, they could still choose to isolate the rhythm differently. For all we know, it's possible that Ambrose isolates rhythm as talking squirrels that tell him the directions."

Vern chuckled at the thought. He wouldn't put it past the guy to do something like that. Still, it seemed that the shades of gray were his isolation construct.

"Anyway, the point is that constructs of isolation define what you can perceive, whereas visions define what you can change. *And* before you cut in again and ask the stupid question, yes."

She shrugged dramatically. "Yes, what one can perceive is still mostly gathered from insights learned by following the observation record, but trust me that this variation is enough to make them singular, okay?"

". . . okay," Vern replied, indeed a little dissatisfied with that answer.

Ignoring him, she asked, "Anyway, where was I?"

"The more the shades, the more removed from objectivity you become," Vern chimed back.

"Right! So, in each shade you engrave the colors of infinity—which is just the vision in your perception. Or, more accurately, in your thought space." She then stopped and gave him the side-eye. "I don't have to explain what a thought space is, now, do I?"

Vern wanted to say yes, but it was clear that she was getting impatient with him. Plus, he knew quite enough about thought space already. So he shook his head with an innocent look.

"That is so sad. Here I thought Shinsei had found us a miracle. Do you know how rare a non-vegetative observer with a shade in his perception is? Especially one who knows . . . so much about observation," she said with faux reverence.

It was Vern's turn to ignore the jab, and he managed it with barely a twitch of his lips. That was progress, if someone asked him.

Her face turned mischievous at his impassive response, and she asked, "Oh, am I wrong? Then why don't you tell me how many visions a second-shade observer can envision?"

Damn. That put him on the spot. The way she phrased it made it seem like two wasn't the correct answer. But then what was it? Can one imprint multiple visions in each higher shade?

As in one vision for the first shade, two for the second, three for the third, and so on?

But what if she was just doing some reverse psychology?

Ugh. It doesn't matter. She was fucking around with him anyway. So he hesitantly answered, "Three . . . ?"

Her lips curved upward, and she brandished her brush toward him before declaring, "Wrong!"

That might have elicited more than just a twitch of his lips.

"It's not that simple. It's neither one-for-one nor is it incremental. You can actually engrave multiple visions without shading your perception again. Take Ambrose, for example."

Well, he couldn't have guessed that.

"So, he imprinted two visions in his thought space in the span of a single shade. He first shaded his perception with his family's famous rhythm resonance that allows him to move with the rhythm, but then he went ahead and also learned an acceleration vision from another similar record that uses the concept of flow."

Vern's mind whirled at the implications. Did that mean one could mix and match the observation records? She did say *similar* though. What was similar?

Also, by this logic, could he engrave instability inducement on his thought space, too? According to his prior conjectures, it was the third rune that allowed him to use that vision.

Which meant that he was essentially borrowing it from the rune. But according to his own understanding of visions as well as what Irene had just told him, he should be able to imprint it properly in his own thought space without any whispers.

His viewpoint should already have been molded to understand the intricacies of instability. On top of that, his own testing in the land of dark sun told him it was the "experience" of having used a vision in multiple scenarios that was the most important.

He had loads of that. He had clearly destabilized more things than he'd ever stabilized.

He didn't know if having it in both his thought space and third rune would change anything, but it was definitely not a great idea to be reliant on an outsider rune to perform one of his vital visions.

Not when someone like Hensen might have a way to strip it out of my mind. I should look into getting that sorted out soon.

This also reminded him that he should stop being a wuss and send a message to Esther. If not for his own reasons, he should do it to ask more about her sister, Livia, and Hensen Vehen.

But his thought process was cut short as Irene continued, "So, it should be clear from that example that a shade isn't just about the visions you imprint in your perception. It's about taking a significant step forward in molding your viewpoint and your removal from objectivity, all the while exerting greater control over reality."

Vern opened his mouth only to shut it right back again as she started, "Now I know what you want to ask. 'But how significant of a step, Lady Miss Goddess Irene?'" She mimicked him in a deeper voice.

Hey, I don't sound like that! And where did goddess *come from?*

She was on a roll. "And I will reply to that, 'Nobody knows.'"

Before he could even part his lips, she drew another long stroke and persisted, "Then you will ask again, terrified, 'How could that be, milady miss goddess!?'"

I wasn't going to ask that.

"And I will reply, 'Because nobody knows.' Hahaha . . ." She giggled to herself, and Vern rolled his eyes.

After taking her sweet time to calm down from laughing at her own joke, she resumed, "All in all, my point is that we don't know. It is different for everyone."

Then she stopped.

Hey, that's only half the answer!

Vern waited for her to continue, but she smiled and went on with her work. He could already see his own image clearly coming out in the painting. She was really fast.

But he still had a lot he wanted to know.

He let out a sigh and asked, "How exactly is it—"

"Different for everyone?" she interjected with that fake deep voice. And before Vern could say anything, she burst into another fit of laughter.

"Hahaha. I knew it! Couldn't hold it in anymore, huh?"

Vern hid behind the book again, hoping the lady from beyond would take him away right this instant. She was reading him like an open book, for steam's sake.

Maybe he was thinking about it all wrong. If this was the price of learning the esoteric secrets and concepts about observation, it was a small one.

I guess it's time to embrace it.

He dropped the book and laughed with her. Soon she finally stopped, wiping at the corners of her eyes. Not waiting for her to trap him in some other word game, he pressed, "So, what is it? Or do you just not know?"

She snapped her head toward him, and that glare alone sent him back to the standard pose, but that was it. He wasn't going to back down any further.

She continued to stare him down, and so he stared right back. *If you want a staring competition, you got one.*

She seemed like she wanted a fight, too.

After what felt like a minute, it started to become awkward, and she suddenly turned away, mixing more colors, her long hair hiding her face.

The atmosphere seemed to have changed a little, and he wasn't sure if he should continue with the same line of questions anymore.

But she began of her own volition, "The reason it's different for everyone is because most observers have a limit on how far they can bend their unique viewpoint into these set paths. Think of it as the more compatible your viewpoint is with an observation record, the more easily you can achieve higher shades in that sequence."

Vern would kill to be able to write all this down. He wasn't going to forget it, but it would be so much easier to link ideas if he had it down on paper.

"It essentially boils down to synergy with one's viewpoint. If your viewpoint is already very similar to the observation record you follow, then you won't have to put as much effort as others following the same record."

Then she gave a dry chuckle. "While, on the other hand, if you choose to follow an observation record that goes against your viewpoint, prepare yourself a spot in a mental asylum because that's what happens when you try to mold a painter into a singer."

But then she ground the brush into the palette and bemoaned, "Ugh. I lost my train of thought again. What was your overarching question?"

Vern rephrased the question in his mind, excluding what she had already covered, and answered, "What is the measure of progress within a shade itself?"

She looked at him suspiciously. "Hmm, that wasn't it, but anyway, the answer to that piggybacks off the last one. It is different for everyone too. However, you can feel it. Whenever you successfully mold your unique viewpoint closer to the chosen record, you'll feel it.

"It's a very fascinating feeling, almost like a sense of . . . alignment within yourself. Similarly, when your perception is finally ready to accept the deeper colors of reality, you'll feel it."

A sense of alignment, huh? Wasn't that exactly how he felt after scrutinizing Captain Akira's plan? It was as if he'd gotten a better understanding of balance itself.

At least this time he had an idea of what she was talking about. So he asked about another key phrase. "Deeper colors?"

She shrugged. "Yeah. I just said you can imprint multiple visions in a single shade. If all you do is imprint visions that are of similar strength as your previous ones, what exactly would be the point of becoming more singular or whatever?"

He embraced the persona of one who asked stupid questions. "How is the strength of a vision defined?"

She also took that question in stride. "It is some combination of the size of reality transformed, by how much, in what manner, and some other factors that no one knows."

Vern happily continued the rapid-fire questioning. "How does representation factor in with the power of vision?"

"The amount of representation used increases directly with all the factors I just mentioned, except for one thing. The less your viewpoint is aligned to your shade sequence, the more representation it costs."

Vern's face was almost bursting with glee. This was a freaking treasure trove. He'd have had to read who knows how many different texts to formulate such a straightforward understanding of all these concepts.

He remembered a question he'd asked Esther a while ago. "What happens if one tries to shade their perception twice, one after the other?"

"Whoever gave you that idea is stupid and is courting death. You're asking me what would happen if you engraved deeper colors of reality on your perception without acclimating to the shallower ones?" She shook her head. "I am not even gonna answer that."

Ah. Vern realized what she meant. One would lose themselves to the whispers if they didn't let their perception slowly adapt to deeper and deeper colors of reality. To him, deeper colors pretty much meant higher reality and more complicated rules.

The thought sent shivers down his spine. He was quite keen on trying to shade his perception multiple times when he was in the land of dark sun. If that eye in the sky hadn't taken notice of him and burned the whole realm, he had planned to try to shade his perception again.

Maybe the whispers wouldn't have hindered him in that realm, but what would've happened when he came back to Elmhurst? Would his perception have handled interacting with higher reality?

It seemed unlikely. He might have dodged a bullet on that one.

Irene, on the other hand, got faster and faster, drawing broad strokes on the canvas one after another. She might be done with the painting soon.

Vern calmed his thumping heart and wondered what to ask next.

His primary goal was to figure out what all this meant for his own progress. He now understood the basics of observation, but he didn't have an observation record of his own to follow.

Should he try to find the record containing Cryptic Constructor's next shade sequence?

According to his understanding, the *Observation Record of Subjectivity*, which should now be in Ari's hands, wasn't exactly the same as the observation records that Irene talked about.

That book didn't suggest any particular direction for him to mold his viewpoint into but instead gave him free rein on whatever he wanted to pick. Which he did—balance.

On the other hand, the paper with the Cryptic Constructor's symbol, which was sitting inside a drawer in his hotel room, more closely fit the description of an observation record. So if he found its record of the next shade sequence, he should have a good synergy with it, right?

However, it was still up in the air if it would be any help since he hadn't shaded his perception with instability inducement but rather a vision of his own. How was that supposed to work?

So many questions, and I can't even ask about these. He couldn't really tell anyone that he had created his own vision, after all. Maybe he could tell Esther, but he wasn't sure how good of an idea that was.

I can only know her attitude once we talk.

On top of that, he was in the library that clearly had so many things for him to read through. Maybe he could come to some conclusion regarding his own progress by reading how other observation records worked?

That was assuming he had the clearance to read them.

But this reminded him of an important point. Did the world know about the link between fundamentalism and observation? If they did, how did it work? Was that the similarity between observation records that Irene was talking about?

So he phrased his question a little differently. "Irene, you said that Ambrose used a 'similar' observation record to learn his acceleration-related vision. Are there many that share this similarity?"

CHAPTER 22

ANOTHER RESEARCHER?

Irene replied, "Yes. There are quite a few."

That's all? But Vern had already given up on keeping any face, so he pushed harder. "Which ones?"

She wagged the index finger of her free hand, "Uh-uh, can't tell you. Even after what you've done at that station, your clearance is not high enough to learn secrets like these."

Vern tilted his head. "Secrets?"

"Mm-hmm. Observers have to risk their lives to find visions that might have synergy with some observation record. Most people aren't stupid enough to randomly imprint the vision of a completely different record on their perception. It's like trying to split your perception into two."

Interesting. That means they go through trial and error to figure out what works and what doesn't? That suggests they didn't know about the underlying link.

"Some similarities are readily apparent, especially those grounded in the same underlying concept. Consider fire, for instance. However, most aren't so obvious. Whenever someone uncovers visions that can be mixed and matched from various records, these insights are typically guarded as top-tier secrets within their organizations."

Vern nodded slowly. "Does Vigil have any that I can see? If not, how high of a clearance do I need?" He would have to analyze at least a couple visions to verify his conjecture about this "shareability" being related to the octants of fundamentalism.

She shrugged. "I don't really know your exact clearance. You'll have to go get a gemstone from the resource allocation hall, but I'm guessing it isn't high enough.

"To see anything with clearance higher than a third shade, you'd need to go through the confidentiality ritual. So if you haven't performed it already, you aren't getting anything from Vigil that can be called a real secret."

Vern clicked his tongue. That was unfortunate. What was this confidentiality ritual? Why a "ritual"? Right as he parted his lips to ask that, her glare came back in full force.

"Don't you dare! I know what you're going to ask, but you better save it for the right people." She then swept back her hair and added in a haughty tone, "I know I am the most knowledgeable person around, but that doesn't mean I'll answer everything."

Vern restrained his words, observing the wave cascade through her lengthy tresses. He had never really seen such long hair in his life. Driven by curiosity and aiming to alleviate her irritation, he instead inquired, "Irene . . . how do you walk around with such long hair?"

The edges of her ruby lips curled upward. "Guess."

He squinted. "Braid them, then bunch them into a bun?"

She scoffed. "You lack creativity, Vern." She moved her hand to the edge of her sketchbook and grabbed all the pages. Without any effort, she held all of them up and drew something on the canvas underneath.

Those silky white strands began shrinking from their edges as she rocked her head right and left. Dropping the stack of pages back, she eyed him with that cheeky look.

Vern shook his head, disappointment etched across his features. *As expected of her, I guess?*

She ignored his look and started putting what could only be called the final touches on the painting. It looked like she had finished with the form and his outline, no longer needing her so-called art model as frequently.

Vern felt a weird sense of urgency. He still had a few burning questions. There was no way he could let her go just like this.

So he asked in his most innocent voice, "Irene . . . I am a fundamentalist, so I was hoping to do some comparative analysis between observation records. Do you think I can be allowed to view some of them?"

She flapped her dangling feet and wailed loudly, "Agh! That old man didn't pay me enough for this!"

Did I go too far? he thought, scratching his head. But then he noticed something off with her words.

"Old man? Paid you? Not me?"

She halted almost instantly and turned toward him with a guilty face that was also three parts smug.

"Oops . . ."

Vern squinted, quickly coming to a damning conclusion. "Captain Shinsei bribed you?"

She gave him a bright smile. "What do you mean 'bribe'? It was the tuition fee!"

He knew something had been off when she offered to answer his questions without him needing to beg. *So Captain Shinsei really felt guilty about not being able to answer us, huh?*

Vern gave her the side-eye. "Isn't me sitting here also part of the 'tuition fee'?"

"Yes. I am expensive." She nodded repeatedly with a mischievous grin.

". . ."

Vern just bore down with his scrutinizing gaze until she started fidgeting, not daring to make eye contact.

"Argh. Okay. Okay. I'll answer this one question. That's it!"

"Five," he demanded in a deep voice.

"Two! No more than that!"

"Four.

". . ."

"Three! I'll fight you if you can't accept this compromise!"

"Sounds good." Vern nodded with a smile, his menacing expression changing instantly.

He could see she liked being dramatic and wasn't all that frustrated, or there was no way he would have pushed her this hard.

Pouting, she turned back to the painting and answered, "Yeah, you should be able to check out the first sequence of the low clearance records that we have. Don't ask me which ones. Your gem will make sure it all works out."

Vern rejoiced. As long as he could figure out the fundamental core reasoning behind how observation records helped one mold their viewpoints, he should be in a better position to make judgments for his own case.

So he moved on to the question that had been gnawing at him for quite a while. "Irene . . . what are your thoughts on the Kingsmen's blood-borne subjugation art? Do you think an observer should risk transfusing the old blood?"

Her hand, which worked the magic of the brush, stopped, and she replied after a while, "I would've done it if I'd had the option."

What is that phrasing? Is that to say she can't have it even if she wanted to? That could only mean one thing. She must be a noble. Not that it wasn't quite obvious already.

And Kingsmen can't pass on their art to nobles.

Vern waited for her to continue, and this time, she did. "You'll have another guillotine of thirst for blood hanging over your head besides the whispers, but the new improvements that have appeared in their bodies since duskfall are very much worth it."

Then she dropped her shoulders and scolded him, "I told you I'd only answer three questions, but you had to go and ask something that needs extra context to make sense. You filthy man!"

Vern scratched his head. *How was I supposed to know?*

She sighed and took off her poncho. Not sure what she was doing, he watched on. "Well, you see, we observers have this stupid situation where if we're not careful, we can permanently alter our bodies to match our viewpoints in an awkward way."

Beneath that splattered poncho, she wore a pure white nightgown. Pulling up a sleeve, she revealed her smooth pale white arm and turned it toward him. Under the moonlight, it appeared ordinary, but she kept pulling the sleeve until Vern saw something . . . disturbing.

Starting from her elbow, a twisted multicolored pattern ran up to her shoulder, the tints underneath blending and swirling like a living palette. Her upper arm seemed to be a waxy canvas of vibrant hues, each stroke creating an ethereal shade.

Vern asked in a low voice, horrified, "Does it hurt? Are you . . . okay?"

"Mm-hmm. I don't feel much of . . . anything," she whispered. "Another drawback of being too hasty, I guess."

She pulled the sleeve down and donned the poncho again before continuing, "Well, if I had the infusion of something as potent as old blood, there's no way my body would have turned this subjective."

So the physical body becoming too much like one's viewpoint could be an issue, too? One has to strike a balance in something like this as well, it seems. That is another pitfall to look out for in the future.

Vern voiced hesitatingly, "Can Kingsmen not make exceptions to the rule?"

She rested her head on her shoulder and replied while looking at the stained-glass window, "They can't. The blood fundamentalists who pioneered the art collected the blood of all major noble families and did something to the infusion liquid that nullifies its effect in our bodies."

Vern furrowed his brows. That was some dedication to prohibit the nobility from infusing the blood.

The only solution in this case would be to collect the old blood from its source and reverse engineer the infusion art. Which won't just be treasonous but also impossibly hard without those fundamentalists.

Not a viable path at all.

"Anyway, it doesn't matter. The point is that the blood could be very beneficial to observers the way it has developed."

But Vern remained unconvinced. "Don't you find it . . . frightening? The thought of transfusing blood from some mysterious being? There's got to be a reason it became so powerful after duskfall, right? What if that being just decides to drain us dry on a whim someday?"

He was reminded of that scene during duskfall. The blood of all humans around him flowed toward something beyond the sky, turning the corpses into shriveled husks.

She tilted her head to the other shoulder. "You're making so many assumptions right now."

Am I?

"Old blood doesn't belong to a singular being. It belongs to a race. But if your argument is that their progenitor—if there's one—can manipulate your very body, what makes you think that that can't happen right now?"

Vern rubbed his chin. She was right. Wasn't that what killed a third of humanity in one sense? So, who was to say that one blood was better than another?

"Also, you're forgetting an important point."

"Huh?"

"We're observers. If you so choose, you can get rid of the old blood in your body. They made a cure long ago, after all."

Vern continued to look at her with a puzzled expression, knowing she'd guess his question. Because if it was possible to do so, why did Mistress Amelia have to kill her colleagues? Couldn't they just "cure" them instead?

"I know. I know. You really want to go all the way down the rabbit hole, don't you? The Kingsmen can't do it because they've gone far down the path of infusion, and they're mentally . . . weak without the blood."

Ah, right. Mistress Amelia said something along these lines, too.

Irene exhaled deeply. "Look, you don't have to take my word for it. You're not the only researcher around, you know? Some rash observer, a fundamentalist too, who's already experimented with infusing and extracting this blood from his body, claims it's totally feasible to ditch the old blood."

Vern straightened up on the stool, his interest piqued. The idea that others were also chasing this knowledge was stimulating. He pressed on, "And everything went smoothly for him?"

"Well, if being chained to your bed for a night while raving like a parched lunatic is nothing, then yes. But that was about it. According to the article he shared with all observer organizations yesterday, there are no lingering effects after a week."

She then chuckled. "The funny part is his reason for flushing out the old blood—he wanted 'consistent experimental conditions' before he infused a higher tier of old blood directly into his system."

That sounded like someone with a death wish—even more so than himself. Yet, it was somewhat comforting to realize he and Lucian weren't the first to experiment with old blood.

Surely, this researcher had to have been an observer before the duskfall while also being a fundamentalist.

"Who is it?" he asked, his voice tinged with fascination.

Irene narrowed her eyes as if trying hard to remember, but then she gave up and lifted the sketchbook page to draw something.

A file soon appeared on her lap, and she opened it before responding, "Someone named Arlan Carter. Do you know him?"

Vern gasped as he tried to process the words. Soon he nodded thoughtfully. "He is one of the few surviving primal fundamentalists. Those who are said to have first parsed the insight sphere under the guidance of Lady Lennix herself."

She squinted. "I don't think he looks that old. But whatever." She clapped loudly. "I am done. You ask me one more question, and I will throw this paint on you."

However, Vern's eyes were glued on that file in her hands. *But I can't ask her any more questions.*

So he got up and walked toward Irene. She kept an eye on him but continued painting. When he could almost smell her fragrance mixed with that of colors, she quipped, "Hey, I still need to look at you occasionally. I will start charging interest if you don't pay the tuition fee."

Vern rolled his eyes and extended his hand toward the file sitting next to her. "I'll be taking this."

"Wow, so rude. What if you don't have the clearance?"

"You'll have to stop me. I can't ask you any more questions, after all." He smirked.

She seemed torn for a moment but replied, "Hmm, I guess I can make an exception for this case. Just go back and sit on the stool."

"Whatever you say, miss milady goddess," he chirped, snatching the file.

He could hear her mumbling something behind his back, but he waved it off and began perusing the article as he sat back on the stool.

A while later, Irene picked up a very wide brush and applied what could only be varnish on the painting as she declared, "Alright! I need to go to sleep. Get the hell out of here and get the clearance gem for your badge. I can't babysit you all day."

Vern extricated himself from his ruminations as he grabbed the file and the book—both of which he'd finished reading. Surprisingly, she took quite a long time to finish the painting. There was already a hint of sunlight seeping in from the window. What took her so long?

But instead of admiring the final result, he retreated and hid behind a large shelf before asking, "So I can still come back here and read what I have clearance for, right?"

She weighed the palette in her hand for a bit before sighing. "Obviously. I am not some watchman who sits here all day controlling who reads what. I only did it for you because your presence here without a gem would have been a violation." Then she folded her arms and gazed upward. "At least I managed to draw such a neat piece!"

This reminded Vern of why he'd been sitting without back support for so long. Stretching his back a little, he curiously walked toward Irene.

He had seen the painting at many stages during the process, so he was already aware of its direction. She had a beautiful and realistic art style. So, the end result was going to be lovely as well.

But when he stood behind her tall stool, his breath caught in his throat, a mix of disbelief and awe washing over him. His gaze, initially casual, transformed into an intense, riveted stare as he looked at . . . himself.

It was as if he were seeing himself for the first time through a new, surreal lens. The vividness of the portrait, the intricate details that captured not just his likeness but the very essence of his being, left him momentarily rooted to the spot, utterly spellbound.

It was that same pose—his face, partially veiled by the book, revealing a subtle yet enchanting smile. Moonlight streamed through the stained-glass window, casting a blend of light and shadows around him.

But that was only the start. It was as if . . . as if he could touch it. When he brought his palm closer to the canvas, the painted dust particles shifted away while his hand blocked the moonlight within, casting further shadows on his painted self.

Vern looked at Irene, who was projecting the smuggest smile, and then back at the painting.

He spent a few minutes just taking in the beauty of it, and all he could say at the end was, "It is beautiful."

Chapter 23

AXIOMS AND GEMS

Vern meandered toward the resource allocation hall that the captain had pointed out yesterday. But why the hell was it so hard to locate? This castle seemed more like a labyrinth than anything else.

I should ask De Flanc for a map or something, he thought, passing through one corridor after another. His pocket watch showed it was around eight in the morning.

He hadn't really felt the time flow by as he read that article and then the book of axioms. That article was very . . . enlightening, to say the least.

Everyone had put far more thought into this whole deal than he'd assumed. Kingsmen had given away the blood-borne subjugation art to more than a couple observers the very next day after duskfall.

However, Professor Arlan Carter was the only one to have produced tangible results already.

According to the article, there wasn't much in the name of risk for an observer to transfuse the old blood, at least not in the first infusion. The rest were yet to be tested thoroughly.

Vern hadn't made up his mind as of yet, but he wondered if he could strike a balance in this situation. If Mistress Amelia was okay with it, he was leaning toward accepting the first infusion as long as he could stop right there if desired.

If Mistress didn't mind him never infusing it a second time, it might actually be a steal. He could always perceive the blood's effects step-by-step and judge whether it was worth going further down the path.

He was hoping to wait at least until there was more study on the topic. He'd been focused on the negatives of the blood all this while, but its benefits were really not to be dismissed.

It would boost him in every aspect where he currently fell short. Honestly, he might even be the fortunate one here. If the trend of the old blood being purely advantageous continued, it wouldn't be long before there was competition over who got the chance to infuse it.

Surely, there wasn't an unlimited amount of it.

Anyway. He shook his head and stopped a servant to ask for directions yet another time, and the man was happy to help.

"So, second corridor, then left and another left, huh?"

"Yes, sir."

Vern let out a deep breath and eyed the second turn. It was just like in that book about axioms. It had two axioms as well.

However, he was still salty over the fact that the whole book was full of speculations and explanations from random observers. Worse, half the pages were conjectures on the Institute's origins and history of the ones who uncovered these nuggets of wisdom.

The axioms themselves were nothing but two simple lines. He retrieved his notepad, where he had jotted them down.

The first axiom: Every viewpoint is unique.

The second axiom: Comprehension of an object's representation is necessary to perceive it.

From what Vern could gather, there should be more axioms than just these, but it seemed even these two were dug out only after a maddening amount of archeology.

He had known about the former for a while and already understood its implications, but the latter was quite peculiar.

It had far-reaching consequences. When he asked Irene the paranoid question of whether she was drawing his portrait to paint him out of existence, she rebutted him by referring to this second axiom.

That is to say she couldn't have used a vision on him even if she wanted to. But that wasn't it. He'd actually seen this in play in many situations already. He just didn't know it was such a ubiquitous nature of reality.

In essence, it meant that one cannot perceive or envision changes to anything that wasn't primarily objective.

This was why one observer couldn't directly use their visions inside another of their kind. This was the logic as to why so many things appeared as black holes in his perception.

Every time he couldn't perceive things, it was because their representations were in forms he didn't understand.

If he were to extend Irene's analogy, his eyes only knew how to draw a personal painting from the objective reality that had infinite colors. It couldn't paint it for him based on someone else's personal painting.

Thus, as objects became more subjective, his vision faltered—unsure how to interpret them. This was why Irene was focusing on an observer's singularity so much. After shading his perception, he became more subjective, or singular and hence able to avoid appearing in others' perceptions.

But this was where it got interesting. The axiom didn't say that one could never perceive these things. One just needed the "comprehension" of that object's state to do so.

It gave rise to terrifying thoughts in his mind, suggesting that someone could use their visions within his body rampantly as long as they "comprehended" his viewpoint.

Vern had been quite surprised by the fact that no one asked him about his viewpoint. That was the first thing he made up many excuses for. He had planned to pass himself off as someone who viewed everything as a sword and a shield—something who justified his visions using a different logic.

But no one asked him. Not even Mistress Amelia. She told him to use his viewpoint to help with the training but didn't ask what it was—as one would have otherwise expected from a mentor.

Beyond that, neither Ambrose nor Captain Shinsei had asked him about it explicitly. He was always on guard about someone doing so because he knew his enlightenment wasn't straightforward like others.

But it all made sense now.

One could even say it was an observer's closest secret. It was beyond rude to ask anyone how they viewed the world. It's what made them singular. It's what gave them a sense of stability in this world full of dangers.

This also hammered home how desperate Esther must've been back at the station to allow him into her very thoughts, going as far as to personally explain her viewpoint. The risk she took in doing so was immense.

She probably understands my viewpoint to an extent as well, he mused, trying to figure out if it could potentially be a problem.

But as with all things in life, nothing was black and white. Comprehension of another's viewpoint wasn't some switch that one could just flip and turn their innards into paint, rhythm, veins, or whatever.

The higher one's comprehension of another's viewpoint, the greater the control one could assert over their adversary.

It's a mutual risk, and she has far more to lose than I do. He smiled ruefully. *I don't even know where I'm headed just yet.*

In that sense, the observers following the same shade sequence were the greatest threat to each other. He didn't know exactly how bad their interactions could get, given Irene said that the construct of isolation also contributed to singularity, but it was something to keep in mind.

Then he flipped over to that page from the convergence note. The axiom had implications for using this, too.

The underlying method of communication was the "trace" of one's viewpoint. Which was pretty much the same thing as understanding someone's viewpoint, just on a very surface level. Still bad news, all in all.

He resolved, *I shouldn't give away my trace to others casually.* But this reminded him of the grave problem, and he sighed. *How should I start the conversation with Esther?*

There were no more excuses. It would be killing two birds with one stone. He wanted to continue his analysis of those golden lists, and it was about time he found some leads on what to do about Hensen.

That man wasn't on his back just yet, but who the heck was to say it wouldn't happen the very next moment? He'd been subconsciously avoiding the problem to an extent, blaming it on Esther.

But if he procrastinated any more than this, he wouldn't even have the right to regret it later when things came crashing down. *Another reason to infuse the old blood, I guess.*

Before he could overthink this, he miraculously found that stupid resource hall. The same woman from yesterday sat behind the counter, three newspapers spread out before her. Each one was open to a page featuring the same striking couple.

Bathed in the sunlight streaming through the window, her sky-blue sweater complemented her olive skin and soft features. She leaned over the images, her face mere inches from the paper, almost as if ready to devour them just with her eyes.

Vern tapped on the counter with his knuckles, pretending to look somewhere else. "Ah . . ."

She sat back up with a straighter back and asked in a bubbly voice, "Good morning, sir. How may I help you?"

"A great morning to you as well. I was hoping to get my clearance gem so I can read in the library."

With a bob of her head, she inquired, "Sure, sir. What is your name?"

"Vern Lockwood."

"Hmm, give me a minute, please."

Vern nodded, and she began rifling through the drawers behind the desk. He idled around and found his eyes drawn to the picture of the couple. People took photos for granted nowadays.

They only developed a mass-producible version of the camera a few years ago. Before that, photography was an exclusive luxury reserved for the highest echelons of nobility. *Well, such are the benefits of fundamentalism.*

The headline above one of those large black-and-white images read "Garmen family heir Marquess Caspian proposes to Lady Marianne from Fairborn family." Beneath it, the first line was "The betrothal has been blessed by the stars, and the wedding ceremony's date has been set for Luminar tenth."

That's fast. Not just the speed with which the nobles resumed their romantic escapades after the world almost ended, but also the brief gap between the betrothal and the wedding. *How long is that? Barely nine days.*

Vern shook his head. He couldn't care less what others did with their time. There would always be those who found happiness even as the world teetered on the brink. In his view, it wasn't the worst way to live.

The lady across the desk finally retrieved a file, opened it, and then looked between Vern's face and its contents. Once satisfied, she set the file back down and said, "I'll be right back."

Vern nodded again.

She went into the room behind the counter and came back out after a few minutes, a small box in her hands. Setting it down on the desk, she turned it toward him before unlocking its latches.

"Umm, so, according to your past record, someone with far more brains than me has decided to award you a second-shade gem," she said, pointing at a red and orange gem sitting in a small compartment in the box.

As expected. Not a third shade gem.

"Other than that, there's also this royal insignia, which you can use to make your life in the city easier. It allows you to exit and enter freely into districts controlled by the Crown. On top of that, any transit that's publicly funded can be used without a charge. And . . . umm . . . ahem."

Vern waited for her to continue, but she patted her hands around the desk before opening some drawer and pulling out a dossier with a flustered look on her face.

Is she new as well? He chuckled to himself.

"Ahh . . . right. You can also use it to overrule the police constables and squad leaders. Umm . . . there are a couple more things, but I seem to have forgotten my notes back at home. But I am pretty sure they were mundane benefits," she finished, looking at him apologetically.

"Oh, that's okay. But do you remember if there was something about free food?" Vern asked, a little hopeful. Restaurants in the inner district could get expensive real quick, and he wasn't going to be in this castle all the time.

She pondered for a while before shaking her head.

"Bummer." He sighed.

"Sorry about that, but there's also this." She enthusiastically pointed at the last item in the box. "Your current determined salary is about twenty sovereigns a month, and the first check is right here."

A salary, huh? He wondered if this was a thing only for him and Lucian. Did all these nobles really need a salary to cover their expenses?

Still, it was actually quite a competitive salary compared to what he used to get as a fundamentalist. Not that he cared too much about it. He didn't need to pay for Ari's tuition anymore, after all. It was just . . . him.

But one can never have enough money! He pumped himself up. What if there was some way to buy observation records that weren't in the Vigil?

Vern closed the box and dumped it into one of his many pockets before asking, "Anything else I should know?"

She looked at the dossier again and recited, "Please feel free to lodge claims about your expenses incurred during the duties. We can usually reimburse anything from money to bullets to weapons to perceptual artifacts. That last one needs a detailed report and witnesses though."

Vern narrowed his eyes, feeling a little pinch at having bought all those bullets from Beaumont at the hotel. He hadn't even used half of them.

He nodded for the umpteenth time and thanked the lady, who smiled back. The moment he was out of the hall's boundary, she went right back to her newspaper.

He somehow remembered the path from there to the dining hall, and as he walked, he fit the two-toned gem in the eye badge, which settled in there snugly.

After devouring a healthy amount of breakfast, he grabbed a small piece of cooked fish and wrapped it in a tissue before heading back to the library.

It was time to get work done.

There were a couple of people sitting around in the silence, so he didn't dare to be too loud, but he couldn't find Luna in her usual place above the arch of the door. He tried looking around but eventually gave up with a defeated shrug.

With his eyes firmly peeled on every nook and cranny, looking for the feline, he made his way back up the door to the third floor. It was firmly locked this time. So, he took out his badge and slotted it into the opening.

Ka-cha.

As expected, the door clicked open without effort. He was of the mind that it was a result of fundamentalism rather than observation, but there was no way they would let him take the lock apart to figure out how it worked.

So he quashed his curiosity and ascended the stairs, only to halt at the top.

Why are the shelves empty? he wondered, his brows furrowed. It was as if a thief had ransacked everything, leaving the full shelves barebone. There was nothing to be seen.

However, before he could make a fool of himself, he saw some noble kid from yesterday point the badge in the direction of a shelf before grabbing at thin air. The very next moment, a book appeared in his hand, and he nonchalantly walked away.

Vern stood there, dumbfounded. *Yeah, this one isn't a product of fundamentalism.*

He followed in the boy's steps and quickly realized that pointing the badge toward the shelves illuminated their contents into existence. However, they were few and far between.

Compared to last night, this was barely a tenth of what had been available. *This is how the clearance works, eh?* he lampooned.

Weaving through all the shelves, he noted down the names of the books and bundled pages available to him. Except for the one that noble kid was reading, there were a total of twenty-three documents available to him, including the one about axioms he had read earlier.

However, there were only a few proper books. Most of them were just a couple of pages bunched together.

He didn't know what he had expected. One part of him hoped for the observation records to be these tomes of knowledge that could drill an ideology into someone. *It was too much to ask for, I guess.*

Shaking his head, he grabbed the three sets of papers that clearly seemed like observation records and found himself a corner table in front of a floor-to-ceiling window.

Stacking the documents to his right, he opened the notepad. He took a deep breath and dialed in. *It has to be done!* He pumped himself up a couple more times and flipped over to the page with the fancy runes.

Ignoring the boldly written *Shut the fuck up!* and *aaaaaaaaaaaaaaa*, he wrote down his planned conversation starter: *Hello, Esther.*

A HERALD OF FLAMES THAT CHAINS MEMORIES

It was very hard for Vern to try to communicate like this. After all, one couldn't send a letter just to say two words. Usually, any kind of communication included a complete purpose, intent, and expectations from the receiver.

But I have to adapt. It would seem unnecessarily formal of him to send a page full of words when the communication was almost real time.

At least, that's what he assumed. He didn't know how long it took a message to arrive to its recipient. But the way Esther and her mother talked about it, there was no way it was as slow as other means.

A couple seconds after his pen stopped, the golden runes converged into a singular pattern before being shuttled off into a list that appeared for a fraction of a second.

Even though he had done this a couple times, his heartbeat still rose in anticipation. How would she react? What exactly would be the focus of the conversation? *And how the hell do I ask about her sister without making it seem weird?*

He rubbed his forehead. He didn't know. Talking face-to-face was far easier than this. Body language spoke so much for a person, and he had become adept at listening to these unspoken voices. But how was he to do something similar in this context?

Confounding was the fact that she hadn't messaged him for all these days, when she had seemed eager to do so last they met. And even worse was the sad reality that the documents De Flanc alluded to regarding the experiments on convergence notes weren't available at his clearance level.

Vern tapped his foot repeatedly, waiting for something to happen. It had been a few minutes already, and he hadn't felt a notion in his mind or anything of the sort.

Is it not real time, then? He sighed, sliding over the stack of observation records. He knew something like this could happen, so he had prepared himself.

But then he remembered an important point. The notion produced due to sending messages was fleeting. What if Esther couldn't get to a convergence note and pen down the message in time? Because if she could, wouldn't she have replied right back, assuming it was actually received in real time?

This created another problem. *When should I try again?* If she couldn't pen it down, how was she supposed to even reply back?

He pondered the question for a couple breaths before deciding. *Once every half an hour should be a good balance. It shouldn't come off as too pushy in case she's intentionally ignoring me.*

Having made up his mind on that front, he nodded and focused on the stack again. All of them were quite thin, but the one in the middle was at least twice as thick as compared to the others. So he picked it out and assessed it.

The sheets were bound together using some kind of reddish string that weaved through the holes punched on its edge. On the brownish surface was the title, *Flame Herald*, in bold red.

Vern took a deep breath and focused shutting out the distracting and destructive thoughts over Esther's lack of response. He flipped open the sheet that acted as the cover and quickly found himself faced with an intriguing first page.

Archivist's insights: Flame herald, a renowned shade sequence, has perpetually meandered through the annals of the observer's society and is often hailed as one of the most versatile paths to power.

It guides one to the path of flames and destruction, allowing them to wield fire in its myriad forms, from the gentlest of embers to the most ferocious infernos. The sequence not only empowers one with control over the element of fire but also imparts a deeper understanding of its essence.

As observers progress through the shades, they gain the ability to create, manipulate, sculpt, infuse, and sense fire, making it into a tool for both creation and destruction. This path is known for its duality, offering the power to protect or devastate, making it a sought-after but challenging journey for those who dare to walk it.

Prior to embarking upon the scrutiny of this record, several considerations merit attention. This sequence encompasses no fewer than five shades. Superior shades, should they reside in obscurity, remain unfound. The honorifics for each of the five shades are enumerated as follows:

Kindling
Blaze shaper
Fire sculptor
Flame infuser
Pyro seer

However, I'd like to forewarn those excited beyond measure to find such a robust path that merely the first and second records are found publicly. The rest are tightly guarded by the firekeepers of the Hirul familia.

Some even conjecture that the firekeepers haven't gone out of their way to remove the records of the first two shades so they can find the future generation that will guard the fire. However, this notion is naught but a foolish hope, for only a solitary keeper is chosen every decade.

Nevertheless, aspiring to attain and ascend to the third shade is an ambition overly ambitious for most, and these initial two shades alone may illuminate one's journey for this lifetime and beyond.

To one such dear reader, all I have to say is—may the clarity guide your path.

Vern's eyes narrowed as he reread the pages yet another time. *This is . . . interesting.* There was no other way to put it. It seemed the only reason he could read this at his clearance level was because it was a widely circulated observation record.

Something to note was that each shade in the sequence had a name designated to it. It seemed quite telling of their abilities. Besides that, he chuckled at the idea of an "archivist's insights."

It got him curious, too. Did all the records have similar insights? So instead of burning through this record, he closed it and shoved it to one side—picking the next one in the stack.

It was only a dozen or so pages. This time, the cover declared *The Chain of Memories.* The name alone had him interested, not to mention the intriguing words presented when he flipped the record open.

Archivist's insights: Dear reader, this is a highly dangerous, experimental, and incomplete observation record. We have decided to archive it, not for the sake of usage by an individual, but as a cautionary tale and learning experience.

Vern leaned back in his chair, a curious glint shining in his eyes. *So this archivist's insight is a running theme for these records, huh? Wonder if they're the archivist of this library or someone from beyond this place.*

It was definitely not Irene. He was willing to wager a hundred crowns that she could never write like this.

However, that aside, his interest was thoroughly captured by the introductory words. What was in this record that called for so many warnings? With that question in mind, he read on.

This record is said to have come from a genius scholar of the Institute who embarked on a path never seen before. However, it isn't the creation of a vision that's so miraculous or heretical about this record. It's the nature of what it entails.

Vern furrowed his brows. *Created a vision, eh? Someone really managed to do that without a whisper-free realm like the land of dark sun?*

This record proposes the idea of viewing the world as a chain of memories. That everything that was, is, and can be, is made up of memories linked to one another.

As fantastic and almost plausible as it sounds, the author of this record is said to have died a terrible death trailblazing the path to the next vision for this unfinished sequence.

There is no designated name for the only shade in this sequence, but the author calls the vision associated with it Rewrite.

It is said to allow one to be able to rewrite the memories of reality, essentially suggesting that one could change any aspect of reality as one wished.

Many have tried and brought upon themselves a terrible death by following in the footsteps of this genius. Not one in the hundreds who have tried to attain resonance with this uncanny vision managed to succeed.

All they ever reached were disturbing contradictions and whispers that broke their mind. As mentioned, it guides one to view the world as a chain of memories, but the path that the author suggests to achieve resonance is beyond illogical. It's nothing short of a miracle that he survived long enough to finish writing this record.

It's documented that this brilliant scholar vanished shortly after penning down this alluring yet paradoxical shade sequence. It is widely conjectured that the man's first real attempt at Rewrite erased himself from the memory of reality.

So my dear reader, beware that this is not a path to be embarked upon. It exists solely to depict the words of a genius who created his own vision but also one that lost himself to the very thing he toiled for.

It is a cautionary piece to learn from. To know that even though we observers bend reality to our will, we shouldn't be too eager to try to achieve everything with a single vision.

Many consider the biggest folly of this vision is that it attempts too much right from the beginning. If the genius author had taken his time to slowly create a suit of visions for each shade, building up to such a potent idea of rewriting, things might not have gone down such a damning path.

Other geniuses have tried their hand at furthering this work, only to give up soon after or find themselves lost to the whispers.

And that's where I must let you be, dear reader. For I know, nothing I say can stop you from reading on. May the clarity guide your path.

Vern had planned to move on to the next observation record and also read its archivist's notes before digging deeper into the Flame one, but this . . . this was too damn fascinating.

It was the record of someone who created his own vision! And not just that, it was such a disturbing idea, too. It was as the archivist said—if this vision could be achieved, it would allow one to rewrite not just current reality but past, present, and future.

Such a vision had the potential to destroy the whole world's balance. But how did that play with the idea of objectivity healing the pollution? Wouldn't the memories of the world want to revert to their prior state?

Maybe that was what happened when the author of the vision disappeared?

Shaking his head, Vern dug in. He would go through this "failed experiment" to see how it compared to his own.

He only took a break to send the next message to Esther before diving back in. It was only a dozen or so pages, but he had to reread multiple sections of the esoteric wordings and incomprehensible concepts. What was worse was that it was written in Old Celestine.

Many analogies that the author tried to better portray the already elusive idea of considering the world as memory were made worse by the internal translation Vern was doing to modern Celestine.

The old rendition of this widely adopted language used complex grammar compared to the current times, and Vern was no linguist. Still, it was all so interesting he marched on.

A couple of things jumped out to him, which he promptly jotted down on the notepad—like the concept of vision resonance and catalysts to further this resonance.

But he was pretty sure this convoluted record wasn't a benchmark for him to learn and understand necessary concepts, so he'd first cross-reference the other two before jumping to conclusions on how exactly visions worked for others.

Right as he was at the final page of the sheaf, he felt something. An idea appeared in his mind, a notion. Vern's heart tensed instantly. *That's Esther, isn't it?*

Putting down the cryptic record, he flipped his notepad to that special page—not wanting to waste the "real estate" of the convergence note's pages.

He let the thought in his mind guide him, and the words formed on the paper.

They were three simple words . . .

CHAPTER 25

TRACE THE RUNE

Vern was far more focused on the golden lists that appeared, however, instead of Esther's three simple words. Unlike last time, the "fate list" was not in the center. That spot was instead taken by a list of twelve different runes—the rest of the page's height was empty.

The fate list on its left looked the same as ever, while the one next to it, which should logically be the list that displayed traces of people around him, was quite static.

Yet before he could analyze it too much, the golden lists disintegrated into nothingness, and his eyes landed on the words *Who is this?*

Vern stared at the words, puzzled. *Why does she...*

Oh...

He facepalmed. *How the hell is she supposed to know who sent the note when there's no context at all?* If there were multiple people who could send her a note, she couldn't magically figure out the message was from Vern.

Can I act like this never happened? he wondered, feeling queasy for making such a simple mistake. It must have been all the million new things he was learning.

If he didn't reply today and just sent another note a couple days later, she would be none the wiser, right?

However, he gave up on being a coward after some more thought. Given that someone's trace was such a guarded secret, she might get anxious not knowing who had sent her the note.

Also, he had something important he wanted to try out with those lists.

Taking a deep breath, he recalled those veins of her viewpoint as well as her visage—that vibrant ruby hair and the striking mechanical wings—before writing *Hello, Esther. This is Vern.*

He braced himself for ridicule but deserved it this time for being careless. *It is what it is.*

Soon, he felt another notion. *That was quite fast! This must mean that the conversation is actually real time.*

His pen didn't wait for long and flowed. *Argh! I wasted so much time and materials setting up the ritual to reply to this undirected note. That scared the hell out of me, Vern! Always end your first note for the conversation with a signature like this! —Esther*

He winced. It seemed he had caused her a lot of trouble because of his ignorance. Given that she didn't know it was him who sent that note, it was already unexpected that she managed to reply. Was that what the ritual was for?

This wasn't how he expected the conversation to start. So, he racked his brain and soon wrote *I... um, didn't know. I am really sorry about that.*

Before he could write another apology, his hand moved on its own once again, and particles flowed out of the first rune of the twelve on the list. *Hah! I should've expected it. Who else would be unlearned enough to not know the basic etiquette of note exchange? It's really my fault for not teaching you beforehand.*

Vern put down his pen on the paper to apologize another time, but he suddenly halted, a pensive look on his face. Instead of imagining her face and viewpoint this time, he tried to recall the three-dimensional symbol from the list that he believed to be the runic representation of her trace.

He wanted to see if he could send notes based on the runic trace rather than his own knowledge of her viewpoint. Because if he could . . .

He tried to visualize the almost impossible shape. He had seen it just a moment ago, but it was already hard to remember its exact features.

It reminded him of Cryptic Constructor's rune a little, but that one was at least a lot of straight lines—very much in character for an Elden One who was all about structures.

Suppressing these distracting thoughts, he focused on mentally envisioning that rune, its atypical design, and the unexpected angles. With his best attempt at the ready, he wrote *It was really my bad. I should have put more thought into it before reaching out.*

Then he waited, his heart beating with anticipation. *Will it work?*

Soon his headspace buzzed again, and he let out a little cheer for himself. *It really worked!?*

Word by word, his hand moved, and it wrote *Huh? Did the cat get your tongue?* He furrowed his brows, and she continued *I was just joking. It's understandable that you didn't know. When did you become so thin-skinned, eh?*

After finishing the line, Vern tapped the nib on the pad repeatedly as he sighed. *It didn't work.* Well, how could things be so simple, after all?

All things considered, she was being quite understanding of his predicament. Going about it the right way this time by visualizing her face, he rushed to clear up the misunderstanding.

Hah, no. I am still getting used to how this works. I am really sorry about the scare. I didn't think it would have implications like that. —Still pretty new to all this.

Shortly, he received, *Are you saying it's hard to imagine my face? Wow. Here I thought you lost your humor bone.* Vern relaxed a little. She didn't seem very upset about this as she continued, *Anyway, there's something you should know.*

This isn't my convergence note, so I have to give away its ownership every day for a while, and they need to keep a record of everything that gets written down on these pages.

That's where she stopped. But Vern looked at the latter part of the note with puzzlement. Why tell him that? However, it took him but a minute before a flicker of recognition crossed his face.

There is another implication behind those words! She was essentially saying that this conversation wasn't private and he shouldn't broach any topic that was supposed to be a secret. Like the third rune.

He nodded. That was a clever way to warn him without giving away the gravity of their secrets to future onlookers.

He replied, trying to play along. *No problem. I was just . . . you know, hoping to check in and see how you're doing.* That was more than one part true.

He didn't know if this was the right move, but this was him trying to nudge the conversation back in the proper direction. However, this time, he didn't wait for her to reply and grabbed another pen from the holder on the next table.

Rotating his notepad upside down, he gripped one pen in his left hand and the new one in his right. The page from the convergence note was now under the nib of his left-hand pen.

Since the notion in my head already guides it, I don't need to be able to write with that hand. That was to say, even though he wasn't ambidextrous, it wouldn't be a problem to legibly write down her responses with his left hand.

So this time, when the list appeared, somehow still from top to bottom, he drew the runic symbol of her trace with his right hand while his left moved on its own. *I am . . .* And his hand stopped for a while before a single word was added *. . . fine.*

Vern couldn't help but notice the pause, but soon his hand moved again. *Hah, you know, it's the usual. Our emperor died during the duskfall, so many prefectures have broken the chain of command, and what's left of the royals are dropping like flies.*

I suggested they better hide like rats instead of buzzing like bees, but well, they don't listen. Anyway, forget about this sad sop of a city. How are you holding up? Did those religious assholes try to mess with you again?

She had deflected his question. Not just that, the situation concerning the Senn Empire seemed far worse than that of the Calidian Empire. After seeing the prospering state of Ferrovane Heights, one part of him hoped that things would soon go back to the way they used to be.

All these were signs that he might be getting a little delusional.

If an empire as great as the Senn was already on its knees, what did that mean for smaller autonomous countries and cities like Nvoria?

Switching back to his right hand, he wrote *I hope you don't try to overextend yourself for the sake of the empire. Besides that, I haven't had any contact with the members of the Eternal Directorate.'*

However, this was a good opportunity to reroute the conversation in the direction he hoped.

So he continued writing. *But I am indeed quite worried about their actions, and I was wondering if you came across some new information regarding the believers of Asea? Or about that Quentin guy and the girl who tried to spare us?*

His right hand continued to further perfect the shape of the rune, while his left hand soon began writing. *Well, Mom's yet to be back from her chase, but it's very hard to pinpoint the exact perpetrators because of how widespread the belief in Mother Asea is in these new times.*

Vern furrowed his brows. Was there nothing, then?

But she continued. *Which makes no sense given their power and members.* Vern nodded. *However, we've found these people calling themselves the Kin, and that's led us to quite a few radical believers of Asea—some who even know about Quentin.*

But hey, I am not going to drag you into this anymore. You've already suffered enough at their hands. If they're happy to let you be, I'd suggest we keep it that way.

Vern narrowed his eyes, and he thought, *Yes, but I have no plans of letting them be.*

So he shifted his approach a little. *Hah, calm down, Esther, I have no intentions of engaging with them. I just want to be aware of the circumstances in case they indeed end up bothering me once I am no longer in the safety of the Vigil.*

Quite a while passed by this time before he felt the notion in his head. *Well, it's not like I can't tell you, but many of our . . . members died to get this information to us, and I can't just . . . give it away right now.*

His forehead creased in thought at this one. He hadn't expected to run into a wall like this. But her words were quite peculiar. She said *right now.* Was it because these words might be scrutinized by her family members later?

Vern soon nodded. The more he thought about it, the more it made sense. In that case, he had two options—either wait until she had her own private convergence note or not.

Hmm, Esther, if I remember correctly, Lady Andrea offered to remunerate me further for the event at the station. Could I use a part of that in exchange for this information?

Hey, what's the hurry? It's not like the Kin is going anywhere. Wait awhile or something.

Hah, she was clearly trying to dissuade him from wasting his "credit." She probably would've just told him if she wasn't in this peculiar situation. However, he cared far more about comprehending the way this Kin organization worked.

The more he knew about them, the better he could plan his future steps on how to extricate Ari from all this. Favors and currency existed to be used anyway.

Uh-uh, it's okay, Esther. Don't worry about it. I prefer not to stress too much about unknown variables. So, knowing more about them would really set my mind at ease.

He continued switching his hands back and forth as drawings from different angles of the rune became clearer and clearer. She wrote *Hah.* He could almost feel her sigh through the words.

Then, listen well. The Kin use a pyramid structure where a group of a dozen or so followers will be led by a first-shade wrath guardian. They usually handle preaching in small neighborhoods.

After that are sanctuary defenders who handle multiple wrath guardians to defend the territory and set up the atmosphere for proselytization. Beyond them are aegis wardens, who preserve the sanctity of all the sanctuaries in a city.

Finally, the last one we know is the name of the shade sequence of that bastard himself. It is called form sentinel, apparently giving him the power to form all those bizarre shapes. The Kin we captured mentioned that they usually handle the affairs related to the religion in a whole empire.

Vern actually stopped drawing the rune for a second to note all these titles. The names of all these sequences clearly held a lot of value. Maybe they could come in handy when he was cleaning up trash on his own.

Then his hand moved, and she wrote *Hmm, maybe one final thing I can add is that the Kin, as an organization, is said to originate from the birth grounds of their mother.*

Vern bit back almost instantly. *And where is that?*

Can't tell you. Why? Because I don't know either. Most of the ones we captured had no clue about the place except a firm belief that it existed.

Well, that sounded like a dead end. If Esther and her mother couldn't get it out of them with their resources, what could he do?

Not wanting to devolve into destructive thoughts of self-reproach, he instead wrote *I wonder how Lady Andrea is planning to deal with this?*

Vern's left hand moved slowly as it glided over the paper in circle after circle before transitioning into words. *I . . . don't know. She doesn't tell me much. I knew all this only because some of the Kin were captors in our estate.*

Vern sensed a hint of . . . loneliness in those words? He slowly inscribed *Esther, are you really okay?*

No reply came for a while, and right when he decided to follow up, his hand moved. *Yes, I'm fine. Mom is just a little . . . distressed because she lost someone.*

Another deflection. She really didn't want to talk about whatever was causing her discomfort.

Giving in, he changed the topic a little *She probably still has a plan. After all, she has handled a situation like this before, right . . . ?*

This time, when the list showed up again, he couldn't find any flaws in his drawn representation of it, so he focused on the words instead. *Well, the Aetheric Collective is very different from these Kin people who do nothing but shady business. They even ask . . .*

But his hands abruptly stopped moving, and right when he felt something was off, it started again. *Ah, umm, it seems I'll have to run. Duty calls, you know! Cultists to capture and sacrificial lambs to save. It was nice chatting with you, Vern, but please wait a few weeks. This is . . . really inconvenient.*

Damn. He cursed his poor luck. Things were just beginning to get interesting. At least the name *Aetheric Collective* should help him figure out more himself.

Hmm, it seems like she's got a lot on her plate. Did something go wrong within her family when she went missing for three days?

Because it made little sense for her to not be allowed a few pages of the note for herself as the heiress of the family.

She also mentioned that her mother had lost someone. Did that cause her position in the family to change or something?

So many questions, yet such limited information to work with. Sighing, he prepared to bid farewell but then suddenly halted.

Shifting his gaze over to the diagrams of the runes from many different angles, he visualized it in his mind and penned *Esther, please take care out there.*

But it didn't seem . . . enough.

So he took a deep breath, and right before the runes merged into a single symbol—ready to be sent, he gritted his teeth and added *I might not have a way with the words, but I want you to know that I'm here to listen, truly listen, whenever you need it. So drop me a note if you've got something on your mind.*

That felt better.

If her response seemed to not acknowledge his words, he was prepared to write them again swiftly. So when his hand moved, and the words *You as well* took shape, a somewhat sad smile formed on his face. She finished with *I will . . . try.*

His eyes lingered on those last three words for a while as he kept the nib held against the paper. Yet seconds turned into minutes, but his hand didn't move anymore.

She was really gone.

Dropping the pen, he rubbed his temple, trying to soothe the headache that was threatening to emerge. That took a lot of concentration on his part.

He'd figured out a great deal today. A bypass method of communication, the hierarchy of the Kin, the name of the organization to which Hensen belonged, and finally, there was Esther's situation—

However, that's when his thoughts were cut short. "Master Vern, there's a mission waiting for you."

C H A P T E R 26

VISIONS, PROGRESS, AND PLANS

Vern hadn't felt the butler creep up to him, but there he was, standing a proper distance away in his well-fitting tuxedo and side-parted hair.

Vern's gaze shifted at the two unread records on his table with longing, then back at De Flanc before he eked out, "What kind of mission is it?" This was his job now. He couldn't just deny such requests without proper cause.

One hand resting straight across his waist, De Flanc replied, "It's another site of minor pollution, and you'll be paired with Master Cedric for the task. It's essentially to help you get some experience with our line of work."

That sounded straightforward. So he asked, "How long is the carriage ride to get there?"

"A little under an hour."

Vern's smile returned, and he asked with an innocent expression, "Then, can I check out these two records to read during the ride?"

"Hahaha, please do, Master Vern. They're not higher than clearance level three. Just return them to Master Cedric before exiting the carriage. I'll inform him about the rest."

Vern replaced the record about chaining memories but picked up the other two, including his notepad, as he followed the butler. He glanced at his pocket watch, which displayed around ten in the morning, and another question popped up in his mind.

"Do you have any idea how long missions like these generally take? I have a training session with Lady Amelia around four."

De Flanc replied as he led the way, "They can take anywhere from a couple minutes after you're on the scene to a dozen hours. It depends on the complexity of the problem, really."

Vern nodded. That indeed made sense. "So what happens if I am late?"

"Please don't worry about it. If anything of the sort happens, I'll let Lady Amelia know about it beforehand. She won't hold it against you. The city is above everything for her, after all."

Vern thanked the man and descended one floor after another in tow. Soon, his eyes caught a shadow flitting behind shelves and casings, and a sharp glint appeared in his eyes.

It was Luna.

So when he caught her slinking around a chandelier and their eyes met, Vern waved around the piece of fish he'd wrapped in a tissue for her.

The little thing gazed at him with a disinterested look for a second before turning away.

Vern didn't mind the arrogance and found a spot away from the books to place the fish. Her large pupils seemed to follow him when he wasn't looking, but otherwise, she acted like she had no interest.

When they exited the door of the library, Vern sneaked his head back in for a second and saw a shadow jump down before grabbing the tissue and dashing away, rattling a couple things in its wake.

A sly grin crossed his face.

Vern sat across from the narrow-hatted gentleman, Cedric, who hadn't taken it off even now, making it so he couldn't lean back on the carriage seats. The man's fingers held a small book, his eyes focused on it intensely.

Vern was quite happy about such company. He got a chance to read in peace and quiet, and the other party appreciated the same.

He had just finished reading up on the methods of advancement from a kindling to blaze shaper in the flame herald shade sequence. It was . . . quite interesting the way it worked.

In the beginning, everyone started as an enlightened individual with no shades in their perception. To become a kindling, the record suggested the individual should go and work in smelting factories, forges, or anything of the sort. The point was to gain resonance with the concept of kindling fires.

Once the individual believed they had enough resonance with the concept, they just needed a suitable catalyst to have a shot at imprinting the first vision of flame herald and shading their perception with it.

The first vision of that sequence was called ignition. A simple idea. It didn't create fire from nothing. Instead, it transmuted objects into fire. What was fascinating, however, was that it did so without the intent to raise the temperature of the object but to simply turn it into . . . fire.

Not how reality worked, but well . . . observation was all about skewed realities. He then also realized that the vision primarily belonged to the lower northeastern octant of the insight sphere. The section that mainly embodied the ideas of transformation.

This made him wonder if anyone who was apt at transforming things into fire would have a much easier time transforming other elements or concepts too. It would make sense if they could.

Anyway, that was how the first vision was imprinted. The actual method of acclimating your viewpoint with it to progress toward the second shade was to try to ignite everything the kindling came across.

The record mentioned that the chances of how easy or hard it would be to do such a feat depended on the talent of the kindling, which was just a pseudonym for the synergy of underlying viewpoint with the concept.

Once the kindling had ignited enough objects to an extent that their perception felt acclimated, they would be ready to shade it again and advance to become a blaze shaper.

They could try resonating with the next shade on their own merit by using brute force to learn how to shape the fire. However, doing so ran the risk of inviting the whispers and ravings of madness. So, most preferred finding themselves a resonance catalyst.

Each vision had its own idea of what could be used as a catalyst.

Vern flipped to the page dedicated to potential catalysts for the two visions. Ignition favored simple, everyday sources such as burning fires and smoldering heat. Blaze shapers, however, necessitated more complex elements like steam cores and chemical fires, seeking out the most potent sources of flame.

And then, finally, right after the list of catalysts were some very odd instructions.

Create an untainted space around you with as much objectivity as possible. Then, write the name of the vision and the shade you wish to pursue in the ancient Elysian script on paper and clutch it in one hand.

Next, take a catalyst that belongs to no one and pray to the everflux. If you wish, you can also pray to other higher beings you believe in, but remember, this carries the usual risks and rewards of such a mystical endeavor.

If your perspective resonates well enough with the shade sequence, your mental realm will grow, and new, profound insights will emerge from the void itself and etch them into your thought space.

That was it.

That was what facilitated the imprinting process. There were no special bloodied words that passed on some deep insight into one's mind, nor was there some spell.

But upon further scrutiny, it was apparent that some of the requirements were quite odd. Why was it necessary to put down the sequence's names in an old script? Not to mention he hadn't even heard of it before. Also, wasn't everflux where the whispers came from?

And even with these specific instructions in the mix, there were some core discrepancies of reality with his understanding of visions. The record had mostly given vague directions and dubious ideas on what one should do to resonate better with the shade sequence.

How could that alone be enough to foster such complex visions in one's mind? Where did the "data" or "experience" needed to perform these visions come from? Was that the point of this almost ritualistic imprinting?

He remembered his own process of creating a vision back in the land of dark sun. He had to get a lot of experience stabilizing different objects by shifting their grays of stability before he could imprint it in his perception.

However, none of the directions in the records helped one gain experience in using the next vision. They only helped acclimate to the current shade.

But this was how it worked. He'd even asked De Flanc if flame herald was really a famous shade sequence, and the man had confirmed it. So everything written in there was practically and factually true.

Vern scratched his head, jotting down all these various points to figure out how they mapped over to his current situation.

The same was the case for the other record at hand. He shuffled the bundles of paper around, and the next cover read *Liar*. Opening it, the archivist's insights unfortunately told him that it was a broken shade sequence.

That was to say, it once used to exist as a complete path, but now, only its initial shade remained. The rest of the sequence had been lost to the passage of time.

The first and sole surviving shade detailed in the records bore the name socialite. The title for the second, now-lost shade was fabricator.

It was an intriguing shade sequence, exactly as the name suggested. According to Vern, the first vision's effects loosely belonged to the upper northeastern octant, also famous for all the cognition-related concepts.

This wasn't the same as the cognition necessary for observation, but rather a concept that was shallower and deeper at the same time. It delved into how one interprets the world around them, guided by their emotions and underlying psychological framework.

Regardless, the point remained that even this observation record described a similar method of imprinting the vision, allowing one to manifest something as complex as veil. It was a vision that allowed one to be subconsciously ignored by the others.

The catalyst for veil was an illusionist mirror, but there were no further limitations. Any kind of illusionist mirror worked. Which suggested the vision's experience couldn't be embedded into these items, either. They were there just to increase the user's resonance.

Then is everflux some kind of entity that can respond to prayers?

He ruminated over it for a while before his pen suddenly halted, and a pensive glint streaked past his eyes. He turned to his notes on the convoluted theory of the memory chain from the unfinished observation record from before.

It suggested viewing the world as memories, which was generally a bogus idea, but what if visions were actually something like that?

As in they existed in the memory of the world or everflux, and the resonance with the viewpoint they were created in supplemented by the prayer allowed one to imprint and use that vision personally?

After looking at it from a few more angles, Vern nodded. That did make some sense. He couldn't really be sure since it was based on the theory of a failed experiment, but it had a certain logical feel to it.

After jotting all this down in neat diagrams, he returned the records to Cedric and focused solely on the notepad.

Both men sat on opposite seats inside the carriage as the scenery beyond the windows reeled back ceaselessly.

When it was about the forty-minute mark in the ride, Vern dropped the notepad back in his pocket and stared out the window.

He had come up with a few plans for himself. Imprinting a vision had three prerequisites: synergy of shade sequence with the viewpoint, resonance with the particular vision, and finally, the prayer to everflux.

He believed he had the first two in place for imprinting instability inducement in his own perception. He just needed to study more on the third one.

However, he had no plans of imprinting instability inducement to ascend to the second shade, but just as another vision on the current shade on his perception—like Ambrose had. He was hoping to ascend with a vision not from the structure fundamental.

This was only his conjecture, but he believed that the nature of the vision imprinted to ascend to the next shade played an important role in determining the fundamentals one could learn and master throughout the span of acclimating to that vision.

Like, right now, he would have to gain a better understanding of structures to acclimate himself to stability or instability inducement. So, he would essentially be wasting an opportunity to learn an entirely different kind of vision if he ascended with instability.

Not that I have any clue how to go about doing that. He had no real shade sequence to follow, after all. *Also, I can't right now even if I had the means to do so.*

He was still quite a ways away from that threshold—his viewpoint was far from being aligned. So, his chief concern right now should be acclimating his viewpoint to the imprinted vision—stability inducement.

His primary goal had been to decipher an underlying logic in the progression—the very reason he had delved into these records. Now, he believed he might be onto something.

From his analysis, it seemed that the key to advancing as an observer within the shade lay in adapting one's viewpoint to align more closely with the vision's ideal.

So, if kindlings had to create fires and socialites had to weave lies, didn't that mean he just had to create . . . stability and balance?

It was just how Ambrose, a dancer—danced. Or Irene, who was probably a painter—painted.

Just yesterday, he'd felt a small sense of alignment within himself from comprehending the balance that Captain Akira struck in the political landscape with his single move.

But wouldn't he make far greater progress if he could strike such a balance himself rather than just analyzing it?

He nodded. That's what he would attempt with his every action in the following mission. To strike a balance between stability and instability wherever possible.

So he broke the spell of silence in the carriage and asked, "Sir Cedric, can you shed some light on the specifics of this mission?"

The man closed his eyes for a second before sighing. "You know, I liked you a lot better three seconds ago?"

". . ."

"Well, it's some mirror gone rogue. We need to contain it and cleanse it. Simple."

Mirror gone rogue? Vern stared at the man with an askance gaze, but he didn't elaborate further. So Vern pressed, "Is there any methodology on how to go about this? Should I be performing a specific role to assist you?"

Cedric pushed his book even higher, almost touching the rim of his hat as he replied, "First, we need to gather information about the anomaly from the locals. Since you're so keen on talking anyway, I'll leave that part to you."

Vern wanted to pry more, but the man's actions were a clear indication of his disinclination on the matter. So Vern let it go, and silence once again enveloped the carriage.

A short while later, it came to a gradual halt in the Ironhart district.

Chapter 27

INTERROGATION

Tucking in the collar of his trench coat, Vern sauntered down Foundry Lane in the Ironhart district with Cedric. Soot and snow mixed in the air, blowing to and fro along the heavy wind gusts.

Multiple lattices of slender wrought iron beams stood tall and resolute, forming triangular frameworks that ascended skyward. These graceful girders intertwined like intricate lacework, creating a mesmerizing pattern that cradled the railway tracks above.

However, these tracks internal to the district were broken down and tattered in many places. Some had obvious signs of melting, while others were . . . slashed through by weapons?

Not wanting to get too distracted, Vern focused on his destination. Fire flared from his right, but both men walked on, unfazed.

This is the only running forge in the whole street that was supposed to be full of them. I guess the demand for weapons hasn't gone up enough. Or maybe there are just not enough skilled forgers left.

This reminded him of Duality for a second. Before leaving the Vigil, he'd debated whether he should grab it or not. The answer was evident.

Even though he'd learned a couple of stances, he was nowhere near proficient enough to bring it along with him on missions. The way things were right now, he'd be too tired from simply carrying the damn thing for half an hour.

They passed a couple more forges, a vacant tavern, and arrived at the residential block of Foundry Lane. About thirty houses lined each side of the street, culminating in a dead end about two hundred meters from their current position.

Since Cedric hadn't given him much in the name of information, Vern decided to do things his way.

Retrieving the king's insignia, he curved toward the first house of the street and rapped on the door. He raised his arm to display the badge at the peephole but, unexpectedly, found it stuffed with cloth instead of glass.

Knock knock!

"Special Investigation Unit, open up!" he shouted in a deep voice.

He'd already confirmed with Cedric, who was walking right behind him—all his attention on the book—if doing this was okay. The man had nodded with a shrug.

After just a second, the door slowly creaked open, and a gaunt man stared back at him, heavy dark circles under his eyes. He was wrapped in a bundle of clothes. And not just him, but also the two other men who were sitting right behind him.

Vern narrowed his eyes. Why were they sitting at the door? The place had enough space for all of them.

The gaunt man spoke hesitantly, "Have you . . . have you . . . come to save us, milord?" One of the other two men turned his gaze toward Vern, hopeful, while the last one's lips curled in disdain.

Before Vern could respond, the second one exclaimed, "Please, lordship. You must do something."

The first man said, "Yes, milord, please! We haven't caught a wink of sleep in two days! It is after us, milord. If we nod off, it'll snatch our souls. Please, you must help!"

"Lordship, it took my Siri, it did. Please, you have to save her! I'm beggin' you, sir, save her," implored the second, suddenly rising and seizing Vern's hands.

"Heh, you expect the shameless Crown to help us? What fools—"

"Shut up, Yami! They're here to save us—"

Vern's forehead creased at this unexpected reaction. However, this wasn't the time to let them blabber on unintelligibly. He had to strike the perfect balance of stability and instability, even in his interactions.

So he took a deep breath, and a stern look crossed his face. The man holding his hands flinched back instantly, and the bickering stopped. Vern then responded in a tone of authority, "Calm down and tell me exactly what is going on here from the start."

Right when all three men opened their mouths to start rambling again, Vern interjected, "One by one."

The last one harrumphed and looked to the side while the obsequious one's gaze shifted toward the gaunt man, who gulped nervously before speaking. "Beg pardon, milord, but there's a nefarious spirit in the mirrors of this street."

Vern masked his thoughts on the matter, and the man continued, his hands flailing for emphasis, "I'm telling you the truth, milord. I saw it with me own two eyes. Wasn't only me, sir. It comes out from the mirror, and each time you dare to blink, it lurks ever closer. Ask them if me word ain't enough, milord.

"Upon me life, I ain't lying. You gotta believe me. It halts when yer looking at it—almost mocking ye for noticing it. But the moment yer gaze falters, it rushes you, pulling you back. Believe me, milord. I . . . I ain't wrong in the head."

Not letting the man devolve into unstable thoughts, Vern cut in, gripping the man's shoulders. "Don't worry, I believe you. I need you to calm down and tell me how it began."

"Y-yes, milord. 'Twas the day before yesterday. I just got back from smithin' at the forge over yonder, and I put on some food for eatin' before bed. But then when I entered me hall . . ."

The man visibly shuddered as he glanced at the dark corridor behind him. "Somethin' . . . somethin' was gazin' back at me from me late wife's mirror." He shook his head vigorously. "I swear on her grave, I've never run away so fast. Blessed be the eternal keeper, that that cursed thing didn't chase me out the house."

He then pointed at the second man, whose eyes were earnestly fixed on Vern. "I legged it straight to Jesec's. Thought his place, with him and his missus, would be safer than mine.

"But no, milord. He didn't open the door. He couldn't open the door. Not until I broke it."

The man named Jesec joined in with a quivering voice. "Lordship, it preys on you when your guard is down. Siri . . . she just glanced away for a split second. That was all it took. I turned to flee, but Siri was closer to it, right in its path.

"It snatched her, milord, in the blink of an eye.

"If you lose sight of it, even for a moment, that's when it strikes. You can't escape, can't hide. Once it marks you, you're its prey."

Vern gave another heavy nod. "Is that why all of you are sitting by the door?"

The first two nodded while the third one continued to grumble to himself. The gaunt one added, "It still comes sometimes . . . right beyond that wall. So we run out whenever that happens.

"We even broke all the mirrors, milord, but it keeps coming back. We . . . we don't know what to do. We will die like this, milord."

Vern quipped back almost instantly, "Why not just wait outside?"

"Milord, it's . . . cold."

Vern winced internally. That was a dumb question. There had actually been a blizzard last night. But he tried to save the shoddy line of thinking. "I mean, why wait for it to come and get you? There are so many empty houses in the city where you could go until this is resolved, right?"

A guilty look overtook the gaunt one's face, and the other two didn't speak either. Vern cleared his throat and bore down on them until the third one finally chuckled. "We all knew, that's why. The Crown has given up on this district. The only one who can save us is the eternal keeper. Not the dogs of the Crown. We have already lost our families. You want us to give up on our houses too? Hah!"

Vern didn't care much about the venom in the man's words as it was rightfully directed toward the Crown. Still, he looked back at Cedric to see if the man had any response to this. But as usual, there was nothing.

So Vern replied, "Well, we are from Vigil of Duskfall, so not exactly the Crown, but I see your point."

He sighed internally. The Ironhart district used to be one of the most prosperous in the city. But the huge chemical explosions had blown away a big chunk of it, and the Crown had yet to initiate any expeditions to reintegrate this district.

It made sense that the citizens of the district had given up.

So, Vern turned to the other two and spoke in his most assuring voice, "However, don't worry. Now that we're here, the problem should be solved in no time. We are trained to handle situations just like this." Well, at least one of them was.

Soon after, he continued the previous line of questioning, "Are there other people living in this block?"

"Yes, milord."

"Then why don't all of you just sit together in one place? Easier to catch sleep that way, no?"

"We . . . tried, milord. But when all of us gathered in one house, the cold seeped into our very bones. Even with all these clothes, it only got worse the longer we stayed together."

He squinted. What the hell was going on?

"I see. Anyway, when you say *it*, what exactly do you mean?"

"I . . . I don't really know, milord. Never seen it properly, not in the light. It's always just shadows, vague and formless, lurking in the mirror.

"Lordship, the lights dim, and the world shakes when it appears, making it beyond impossible to keep yer sights on it at all times."

The third one interjected, "I told you all, it's a curse. We've fallen from grace. That is why this is happening to us. We should be praying, not pinning our hopes on fools like these!"

Vern ignored the rambling man and replied solemnly, "Okay, give us a minute."

Walking back to Cedric, he relayed the information in a concise manner, painting a clear picture of the whole situation.

Cedric nodded with an unchanging expression and pulled out a pen from somewhere. Vern looked on in puzzlement as the man wrote in the empty margin of the book: *The mirror shadow is in this neighborhood.*

Vern waited, his eyes focused on the elegant handwriting. *What is supposed to happen?* But soon, Cedric's eye glowed a reddish-brown, and his pupils rippled, almost as if pages were flitting within them.

When the lakes of his eyes calmed down, the words he'd written on the margin twisted and turned before settling into *The mirror shadow is in the first house.*

Shifting his hat, he said, "It's in there now. Let's finish this." Vern stared at the man in disbelief. Did he really just forcefully relocate the entity?

But his next words broke Vern's train of thought. "Talk to them so they don't try to bother me when I go inside," he said in a low voice, tipping his chin toward the three men.

Vern wanted to shake his head, but he was too much in awe right now to care about the man's eccentricities. He turned toward the three men and spoke gravely, "I need all three of you to step out for a while. We would like to conduct a cleansing."

He then pointed at Cedric. "Also, don't disturb the commander. He's chanting a very important mantra right now. Breaking his concentration could very well spell our doom."

Everyone's faces turned pale, and the gaunt one asked, "Is it . . . is it in there right now?"

Vern nodded, and all three of them scurried out of the house at a breakneck speed—even the skeptical one—donning their gloves and boots outside.

Cedric took his time, waiting for everyone to clear a path, so Vern assumed the lead. He believed his actions had been quite balancing in terms of stability and instability, but he had felt nothing at all from within his perception.

He didn't expect every little thing to give him feedback, but then how was he to know if this was the right way to go about acclimating the perception to his vision?

Gotta keep trying, I guess.

But the moment he set foot inside the door, a chill washed over him, and his mind sobered up instantly. *Something is indeed wrong.* He could feel it.

He wondered if he should let Cedric take the charge. He wasn't an expert in dealing with situations like this. That experience atop the tower had been terrifying enough for him.

But he steeled himself and took another step, entering the house proper. Hiding behind Cedric in this situation wasn't the right balance. If something were to go wrong, there was enough time for Cedric to jump in.

Vern pushed his trench coat aside and lit the lamp latched to his waist hook. Purple light spilled around him, illuminating a narrow corridor that led to the kitchen, a small bathroom to the right, a hall to the left, and a staircase with very narrow steps leading down into the dark.

Ssss.

He had only moved a couple of steps in when he heard something from deep inside the house. His heart began racing, and he didn't take any random chances, unveiling his perception from the get-go.

A world of grays depicting the simple stability of the environment overlaid his vision as he ventured deeper into the house.

He considered his surroundings with great detail—that unnerving smell, the rough texture of the walls, the cracked pieces of glass littered across the floor. All of it supplemented his perception, causing the more chaotic grays to settle into stable shades.

The windows were smashed from the outside, evident from the spread of glass chunks on the floor. Ragtag clothes blocked the wind, barely enough to keep the interior from freezing over.

Ting.

Sounds continued to emanate from the far end of the house, and his perception that had yet to observe the interior of the kitchen firsthand was unable to extrapolate the details.

But that wasn't his destination. The man had told him the culprit mirror was in the hall. So he steadied his breathing and heightened his vigilance.

With measured steps, Vern walked in, looking back at Cedric, who was slowly walking around the group of men in a wide arc toward the entrance.

So Vern continued. The balance had yet to tip in favor of instability. He couldn't back out just yet.

One step.

Two steps.

Three steps.

Soon, he was in the hall. In the center of the room was a table set for four laden with rotten food. The room's only other piece of furniture, a dressing table, was positioned in the far corner. Its mirror was facing at an angle from Vern, completely unharmed.

Why couldn't they shatter this one?

He turned toward it, pointing the light straight at the reflective surface.

Nothing out of the norm.

But he furrowed his brows. He could feel it. The colors of stability around him were fluctuating rapidly, especially in the shards of glass.

He surveyed the room further. Discarded toys, dirty clothes, bloodstains. But then, abruptly, a chill slithered up his spine, prompting him to whirl around, his heart pounding.

An ominous darkness began to seep into the bottom left corner of the mirror.

It was a subtle shift, almost imperceptible to the eye, yet his senses screamed at the unnatural alteration in the mirror's stability.

Skitter.

Vern remained on the move, sensing a ripple of instability unfurling behind him, and in the moment he took to glance back, the eerie patch of instability on the undamaged mirror exploded into a circle of darkness.

When Vern found nothing behind him, he snapped his eyes back to the mirror, and a cold shiver raced down his spine.

Fingers materialized out of the reflection, oozing a transparent, viscous liquid that pooled on the floor. They clutched the edge of the dressing table, still and silent.

Chapter 28

CONFRONTATION

Goose bumps erupted across Vern's skin, but he dared not take his eyes away from the hand. He didn't forget that the entity couldn't advance as long as he was looking at it.

He pulled out the revolver and took aim. There was no way he'd miss the shot when it wasn't moving at all.

However, he didn't know how it would react to being shot, so he held back and focused on the structure of the dressing table's mirror instead, ready to destabilize it at a moment's notice.

Unfortunately, he couldn't perceive the fingers of the entity directly. They were subjective and appeared darker than black. The second axiom of observation was at play here.

With all this prepared, he stared daggers at the uncanny fingers, his mouth going dry just looking at that drenched pale flesh.

Cedric should be here any moment. And his ears indeed affirmed the fact as the footsteps grew closer.

As the seconds ticked by, his eyes began to feel unnaturally dry, the urge to blink growing irresistible. Finally, he gave in, but the moment his eyelids shut, he felt sharp pinpricks within his eyes, and his lids became impossibly heavy.

Panic surged through him. *It's doing something to my eyes!* Struggling to open them, Vern realized with horror that it felt like small hooks were physically keeping his eyelids closed.

His heart pounded in terror as the entity, a sinister shape darker than black, seemed to stretch out toward him within his blurred perception.

What the hell do I do?!

The blink that was supposed to last for a mere instant turned into seconds as Vern failed to cope with the disturbing situation.

His steps faltered, and he backed away, the shape closing in at an uncanny speed.

Focus!

A deep, unsettling chill coursed through him as the corrupting outline in his perception pounced at him.

Focus! Vern!

This finally snapped his mind in place, and he did what should have been obvious. Obvious, if he hadn't let the cold terror of losing control overwhelm him.

Vern rubbed his sleeve against his eyes, prying his eyelids open just in time to recoil from the advancing entity, feeling a brief gust of wind brush against his leg.

"Damn it, Cedric, hurry up!" he shouted, the adrenaline coursing through him.

He managed to fix his gaze on the entity's dark, liquid-drenched eyes, the droplets shimmering menacingly. It finally halted its unrelenting advance.

It stared at him from behind the shadow of the wall—unmoving itself, but there was a frantic cadence to the vibration of its black pupils.

Vern strained the muscles in his eyes as hard as possible, trying to figure out what the hell went wrong. What exactly did it do to his eyes?

However, at that moment, besides the heavy dread, he felt a weird sense of discordance within his thought space. A peculiar imbalance.

Yet, before he could analyze it further, Cedric rushed in and gasped, "Oh my lady!"

He peeked over Vern's shoulder, a serious expression emerging on his face.

He penned down something in the book in his hand and said in a heavy tone, "Do not let it get closer to us! I need a few seconds to set up the cleansing."

Vern followed the words to the letter, his eyes zeroed in at the head even though his heart pounded like crazy.

"Be careful," Vern warned, his voice tense. "It just did something to my eyes, forcing them shut after I blinked. I had to physically pry them open."

Cedric continued scribbling as he replied after a short pause, "Hmm, it probably has something to do with the fact that eyes can also reflect. However, everything has to follow the second axiom."

"Then how? And what else can it do to our eyes?" Vern shouted back, not feeling safe at all.

"It's probably just a minor control over the reflection itself and not your eyes. If it could control your eyes, you would be blind right now."

Vern's fingers clenched hard on the grip of the vapor blaster as he nodded after a while. That was right.

If he thought about it, this tactic worked so well on him because it was a surprise. If he had been prepared for it, it wouldn't have been a problem at all.

He could just use his hands to open his eyes instantly.

Also, the fact that the entity had to go through these weird hoops just to not be seen for a couple seconds spoke volumes about its powers.

It was bound by some rules and limitations.

So Vern took a deep breath and focused on the task at hand.

In every second that passed in this disturbing atmosphere, his heightened senses picked up more and more sinister details.

The sound of liquid dripping on the floor, the vibrating pupils, the indirectly illuminated face of the entity.

Maybe if he moved just a little to the right, his light would even hit it directly.

But he didn't take any chances and simply stared at that pale forehead that shook side to side at a maddening pace.

His every instinct screamed at him to get the fuck out of here, but it might actually be the worst choice in these circumstances.

He took short, deep breaths, keeping his eyes peeled and open, and finally, it came.

"It's ready!"

Cedric had written something in his book, but Vern didn't make the mistake of taking his eyes away to read what it said.

The scholar then pulled at something on his neck and brandished it toward the hall.

A brown glow appeared in Vern's peripheral, and the moment it did—

Screech!

An ear-piercing scream thundered in his ears, and it took all his grit to not drop the gun and clamp his ears to block out this fiendish shriek.

He felt a scream of his own rise within him, but he tamped it down and focused on tracking the squealing entity as its barely visible body twisted and turned into grotesque angles.

That's when Cedric said with a smug tone, "Good. Another one down for—"

But before he could even finish the sentence, a cold terror gripped Vern as a patch of darkness appeared in his perception around his legs.

A sense of panic fluttered within him, and his eyes involuntarily shifted toward his waist.

His eyes bulged as he barely made out the contour of a hand wrapping around the flame inside the lamp, and the very next moment, everything turned dark.

"It's trying something!" he yelled.

Bang!

This was his only opportunity to make use of the weapon. The muzzle's flash sparked a momentary brightness into the scene, but that alone was enough for him to be sure that he'd missed the shot.

The entity had disappeared from its place. The light that should've been coming in from the door and windows was entirely gone, too.

His gaze darted frantically, trying to focus on the entity to stop it, while his other hand took hold of the lamp's latch and yanked it, throwing it far away. Something was inside it right now!

He could make out nothing with his physical eyes. After trying and failing, he realized that all he had to work with was a chaotic world of grays in his perception.

He sensed a bright white in front of the pendant in Cedric's hands, contrasted by a patch of utter darkness that skittered across the floor straight back toward the mirror.

"It's running away!" Vern shouted.

His words prompted a sigh from his companion. "Too bad. I can't accelerate the cleansing at this moment. I guess we'll have to set up a trap and try again later."

What? Is he giving up already?

Vern frowned. He had no plans of letting this abomination leave just like that. It had already consumed someone's wife, and who knew how many more people.

What could it not do in that extra time? On top of all that, a part of him was furious at the entity for destroying his composure and scaring him like that.

So he shouted back, "Don't stop the cleansing! I might be able to do something about it."

He turned to that gray semi-reflective mirror in his perception with a singular focus and commanded internally, *instability inducement.*

Crack.

Sounds of glass shattering filled the room, followed by a frightening screech threatening to burst his ears.

"Oh," gasped Cedric before Vern heard him scribble something.

The patch of darkness skittered toward the hall's other exit, corrupting his perception. Vern felt a tinge of excitement amid the chaos. His simple intervention had thrown a wrench in the entity's plans.

But what is it doing right now? Are there any other mirrors of its size in this house?

However, Vern sucked in a cold breath when a mouthlike outline appeared around the entity, which tore at its own body and threw a chunk toward the shattered glass.

Screech!

It hissed in what seemed like pain, but Vern was having none of it.

A white ring flashed in his eyes, and he focused on the very shard, imagining it to become as unstable as possible.

It was about destabilizing a structure to the most fundamental degree, and he knew all there was to know about the composition of glass.

So right when the chunk of darkness was about to disappear into the shard . . .

Crinkle.

The somewhat triangular gray shard exploded into black particles, and the dark lump that was like a black hole in his perception hit the floor with a thud.

Skreeee.

A blood-curdling wail came from the entity, and its shape turned toward Vern, sending him into utter panic for a moment.

What do I do if it comes for me?! But as if the entity were eavesdropping on his thoughts, it did just that, and jumped toward them with a ferocious momentum.

"It's coming for us!" Vern shouted and took cover behind the kitchen wall.

But right as it was about to pounce at the unmoving Cedric, the brown glow flared again.

An illusory eye formed from the radiance, and the imperceptible entity recoiled.

The very next moment, a hundred jagged edges appeared on its dark outline, and soon, many pieces of this corruption flung themselves toward other shards of glass scattered around the room.

Vern clenched his fists and decided to go all out.

Focusing on the shape of each and every shard of glass in his perception, he imagined their demise . . .

Crinkle.

Crack.

Chime.

Hundreds of such tiny sounds reverberated in his ears, and his perception was saturated in dark particles that exploded everywhere.

Numerous terrifying wails followed this sound, but the eye in front of Cedric only grew brighter and brighter, corroding the dozens of little black holes in his perception with something akin to ropes constricting the lumps.

Blood pumped through Vern's heart with intense thumping as he gazed at the happenings with a tense mind.

He had shattered everything in his perception, but there was too much "noise" in what he could perceive because of the entity corrupting the shades of gray with its presence.

So he wasn't sure if he had accounted for everything.

His pulse continued to race, each beat a loud echo in his ears. As seconds stretched into minutes, the darkness shrouding the distant lamp finally receded, allowing light to break through.

The oppressive darkness enveloping them also faded away, slowly but surely. When the purple light filled the corridor, white powder laid scattered everywhere—a result of his vision.

However, there were no traces of that abominable entity anywhere.

His shades of gray settled down into stable states, and all the chilling sounds vanished into silence.

That seemed to have done it.

Regardless, Vern continued to focus on the patches on the ground where those lumps of the entity had been lying a while ago.

He had to be sure.

But then, suddenly, something gripped his shoulders, and his nerves exploded. His body moved on its own, and he pointed his gun at the movement.

A voice said, "Calm down, kid. Calm down," stopping him from mashing the trigger.

Fuck! Vern cursed under his breath. That had scared the hell out of him. It was just Cedric, his book held between two fingers.

"It's over," he added with a steady tone.

Vern gradually lowered his arms, scolding himself for letting this situation overwhelm him. After a while, he leaned on the wall behind him and sighed.

Wiping away the cold sweat that had built up on his forehead, he asked, "So, that was it?"

The man nodded. "Yep, that's it. Didn't really expect you to pull that off though," he said, sounding a little impressed.

Vern's heart slowly calmed down, and he nodded back. "Thanks for saving my ass there."

Cedric didn't reply but instead tipped his chin toward the exit. The three men were slowly closing back in toward the entrance, terrified looks on their faces.

The skeptical one had some kind of talisman in his hand, while the other two huddled around him as they advanced.

He wants me to get them out of the way, doesn't he? Vern shook his head and instead asked Cedric, "Don't we need to clean up for any lingering traces or something? Can they come back here just like that?"

He shrugged. "No need, and don't worry, they don't expect us to clean up their house for them."

Right.

So Vern walked toward the exit, still trying to get his heart rate back to normal. Glimpses of that scene still lingered in his mind, and his skin prickled at the mere thought.

But it was over.

He picked up his lamp, which had a small dent on its top, and took a deep breath, trying his best to wipe away the terrified look.

When he stepped out of the house, the fresh air cleared his mind, and he saw many people standing on their doorsteps.

The gaunt one soon walked up to him and asked, "Milord, is it—dead?"

Vern announced, "It's done. This mirror spirit will haunt you no more."

An elated look flashed past his eyes, but the second man looked at Vern with confusion before asking, "But lordship, my Siri. My Siri . . . ?"

Vern winced. He had no idea. Was that being the amalgamation of all the spirits it had captured? If it was, they had already evaporated it out of existence.

Siri was most probably gone.

Not that she could be considered alive if she was assimilated within that entity, anyway.

All the eyes around him looked at him with awe. Even the skeptical one looked on with a mixed expression. Everyone except Jesec, who stared vacantly at nothing in particular.

Conflicting feelings washed over Vern as he tried to figure out how to clear the path for Cedric without coming off as insensitive.

But right at that moment—

Argh!

CHAPTER 29

COMPLICATIONS

Screams rang throughout the residential block, and a hubbub arose in the whole neighborhood.

Vern snapped his neck to the right, a deep frown etched on his face. *What is . . .*

The anxiety he'd just suppressed came flaring right back as the possibilities whirled in his mind. *Did it really manage to escape?*

Cedric came rushing out, using Vern as a shield against the three men before beelining toward the house numbered 3-31—the closest home where someone had screamed.

Some inhabitants standing on their doorsteps jumped out on the streets, probably scared of the spirit coming for them. Others rushed to their neighbors' houses, shouting their names.

Cedric banged on the door, and when there was no response, he pulled at the latch with all his might. Failing to budge it, he took out his pen and flipped the book to a free page.

"Let me take care of this," Vern interjected as he sprinted up to 3-31, the cries of help from within growing more desperate by the second.

Cedric eyed him suspiciously but still moved aside, not dillydallying.

Vern put his hands on the doorknob and considered the same balance he'd used back in the Ascendant Council for a similar use case: *integrity.*

Ka-cha.

The door clicked open, swinging ajar on its own, and Cedric rushed in with a nod. Vern took a deep breath and made to step in, only to suddenly halt as he remembered something.

He looked at his lamp and debated on whether to leave it out here. That entity had probably used the glass around the metal structure to materialize within the lamp.

What if it used the same tactic again? That was what threw them into disarray last time. He wasn't about to repeat the same mistake.

"Help!"

Vern gritted his teeth. Every moment he wasted on this decision might very well cost the woman in there her life.

So he focused, rapidly analyzed his options, and soon landed on a good one.

He took a deep breath, a white glow spilled from his eyes, and—

Crinkle.

The glass around the lamp shattered into the finest particles, which blew away in the cold wind.

However, that wasn't all. The wick inside the lamp began swaying, too. So he quickly chained it with a stabilizing sphere around the fire.

It would be constant work to keep it up, but it was a minor hassle, and his thought space was doing most of the heavy lifting anyway.

The flame steadied, casting a firm pool of light around him. With a renewed sense of assurance, he wielded the lamp and hastened inside.

The layout of this house mirrored that of the previous one, though everything was reversed. Maybe the entire block followed a uniform design.

Yet as he ventured deeper, the reach of the lamp's light dwindled, surrendering the surroundings to an enveloping darkness.

It's that unnatural darkness again. He realized the entity was manipulating the shadows right from the start, making it hard to see and limiting their ability to track its movements and consequently restrict its movements.

So it really escaped, huh? He cursed under his breath.

As he eyeballed the environment, suddenly the scream took on an even shriller pitch. "Please save me, mister!" Vern chased its sound, reaching the brown glow of Cedric's pendant.

The man was already writing something in his book.

But when Vern turned to look inside the hall, his heart thumped loudly, and he involuntarily clutched the lamp harder.

An outline of arms, legs, torso, and a mouth formed through gleaming droplets just beyond the light. It brutally clenched the screaming woman's face, pulling her back toward the mirror.

Her tearful face and convulsing body disappeared into the dark void beyond his lamp's light, second by second.

Fuck! Vern's body, however, worked faster than his brain for once, and he leaped forward almost instantly, gripping the woman's flailing wrist.

Agh! She clutched back with a ferocious grip that was followed by a terrifying wail from the entity.

Dropping the lamp, his left hand clutched at the wall's edge while his right did its darndest to pull the woman back out.

"Cedric, how long?!"

"Almost there . . ."

Vern dared not let go as the brown glow intensified. However, right that instant, something completely unexpected transpired, and his breath caught in his throat.

The drenched arms that held on to the woman suddenly switched targets, and an uncanny force gripped his left leg.

He lost his balance and the grip on the woman, and only the arm holding on to the wall saved him from instant doom. His gaze darted frantically as things started slipping out of control.

"Cedric, what the hell?!" he cried out, his head almost hitting the floor.

"It's suddenly become more powerful out of the blue. I need a few more seconds! What did you do?!"

Fuck! I didn't do shit! He cursed under his breath as he tried to focus on his perception.

Ehh!

The drenched entity gave another bloodcurdling screech and pulled at him harder. His tibia felt like it was about to be ground down to powder while the tendons of his arm were ready to unravel at any instant.

A viscous liquid seeped into his skin, and the mere contact sent a cold shiver racing through him. But the adrenaline was real, and he kicked the entity with his other leg, shouting, "Leave me the fuck alone!"

Gritting his teeth, he focused on the mirror on the wall in his perception and soon executed a mental command—

Crack.

The whole surface of the mirror exploded in a burst of particles, and Vern stared at it with a hopeful look, only for the force yanking him to suddenly turn sharper.

It didn't work! And he quickly realized the problem too. Not all the glass had shattered.

That entity was already halfway inside the mirror, and being invisible to his perception, that part of the mirror wasn't destabilized at all.

DAMN!

It continued to pull him harder with another screech, going as far as to bring out another hand from inside the mirror to pull on his right leg.

Screech!

Fuck! Fuck! Fuck!

He shoved his other flailing arm into the holster and pulled out the vapor blaster. Aiming it toward his assailant, he shot it point blank . . .

Bang!

Bang!

Bang!

Bang!

The entity squealed louder with every hit, but its grip only seemed to grow tenser. Liquid burst out of the entity's body, but it barely helped the situation.

The vapor chamber glowed, steam bursting out of it. It was overheating. These were heated shots, after all.

If only I had mastered duality, he thought, envisioning how differently the battle would have unfolded. That destabilized purple edge would've easily severed the monstrous arms that were inexorably dragging him closer to doom.

But the intense pain racking his body caused him to cut off this line of thought. There was no point in thinking about what-ifs right now.

He couldn't have mastered the weapon, no matter what. Not even if he'd infused the old blood already.

However, before the vapor chamber could cool down for another barrage of shots—

Thud.

The entity let go of him for a second, and in the moment, his body relaxed involuntarily, but the next instant, it pulled him again, harder than ever.

The unexpected jerk messed with his grip, and the force behind him didn't miss the chance, dragging him toward the mirror. "Ah!" he roared, barely getting an arm in place to cushion his head's fall.

He scratched at the floor, trying to grab anything to stop the momentum. Unfortunately for him, there was nothing to perch on.

The woman had retreated all the way to the back of the room. She was looking at the ground vacantly, her arms holding on to her head as her body trembled violently.

She was in no condition to help him, and Cedric was completely focused on the pendant. Why the hell did the brown light still not cleanse this monstrosity?

Fuck! He continued to flail around, but his body didn't have the strength to extricate himself directly.

For some reason, however, he felt a weird sense of discordance within his thought space like before, and he didn't understand it. What the fuck did it even mean?

But he knew one thing for sure. *It's nothing that can help me right now!* So he threw it out of his mind and racked his brain for a solution.

What else can I do?!

His mind flitted past all the myriad objects in his perception, and he soon had an insane idea.

He focused on the wall behind the mirror. Even though it was dark for his eyes, he extrapolated the shades of objects according to the layout of the previous house.

With a ferocious look, he took the fulcrums of the wall above the entity and destabilized the damned things.

Thud.

Crumble.

Crash.

Furniture, windowsill, mirror frame—everything came crashing down, exploding into chunks that fell around him.

It didn't crumble the whole house, but a big chunk of the wall and ceiling were destroyed—some of the debris hitting the entity straight in its extended torso.

And there, for the briefest of moments, the grip on his legs came loose.

But that was all he needed.

Yes!

He kicked hard at the entity and extricated his legs, rolling out of its immediate range and falling debris.

However, his perception depicted a horrifying future. The entity that was darker than black in his shades of gray was already pouncing back at him—its claws reaching out for him.

Vern debated going ahead and destabilizing everything around him.

That won't do! he hissed. Doing so might very well destroy the whole house. He would be buried in the rubble alongside everything else.

Desperate, he looked toward Cedric, and unbelievably, the man was rushing toward him, book in one hand and a pendant in the other.

Is this . . . His thoughts were cut short, and a thunderclap went off in his mind, followed by the flare of the brown light.

Eaahhh!

The terrifying entity squealed, and all Vern saw in his perception was ropes constricting around the imperceptible mass of darkness, searing through its mass at a terrifying pace.

Vern backed away, his heart thumping madly. The drenched outline being corroded away by the brown light became a little clearer.

His leg throbbed in pain, and his heart rammed into his chest faster than a runaway carriage as he tried to come to terms with what had just happened. *That was too close!*

From the half-torn parts he could make out, it was . . . humanoid, except it had utterly pale flesh, drenched in something like water—but thicker.

Its burning eye sockets were pure black, yet the features on its face were otherwise very . . . humanlike.

Taking one deep breath after another, Vern stared at the horrifying entity disintegrating into nothingness as he massaged his shin and pulled out small chunks of glass stuck to his coat.

The last minute or so played in his mind on a loop, the possibilities sending him into a panic. What would have happened if that entity managed to drag him back into the mirror?

Would he have turned into one of them? He shuddered at the thought.

After a few more seconds, the brown light died down. Correcting the angle of his hat, Cedric dusted off his coat and turned toward Vern with sharp eyes.

"You need to calm down, kid! Don't ever jump in like that without a plan. I'd be nothing but bones if Prince found out I let you commit suicide on your very first mission."

Vern opened his mouth to speak but swallowed his words right after.

He knew.

It was his fault for jumping in like that. Still, what else was he supposed to have done? That woman would've surely been dragged back into the mirror if he hadn't stepped in.

Cedric had a point, but things weren't as black and white as they seemed in this situation. When Vern came in, Cedric didn't even try to help the woman physically.

If she were to be dragged in, he would have said something along the lines of "We have to try again and capture it later." But she'd be dead! Why bother at all, then?

The middle-aged scholar shook his head after a while and asked, "Can you get up, or do you need to rest?" He then glanced at his book for a second before adding with a distressed look, "There's at least nine more of these in other houses."

"We need to do something about them right now. If we dally for too long, people will keep turning."

Nine more?!

Pushing himself off the ground, Vern countered, "Didn't you say we were done back in that first house?"

Cedric walked toward the woman and huffed, "Well, you saw what I saw. We cleansed everything, didn't we? I would have divined it to be sure, but I never had the chance. It went right back on the offensive the moment it escaped."

". . ."

Vern slowly nodded. That was indeed the case. They barely had any time before the screams rang throughout the neighborhood.

"Anyway, I just checked. There were nine a minute ago, but their numbers might grow if we let them snatch any more people."

Grabbing his lamp again, Vern asked with a frown, "Are all of them as powerful as these two?"

Cedric shook his head. "No. I think they have a shared representation. We took care of most of it in the first confrontation, but then it bolstered itself from the other people it consumed while we were stuck here."

Shared representation? Things started to make more and more sense. Still, why didn't it share that representation until Vern was in its grasp?

"Is that how it suddenly became more powerful?" Vern asked.

Cedric's long hat tail bobbed up and down as he gestured at the woman to get out before saying to Vern, "Seems like it."

Vern was speechless. Nine people had died. Just like that.

Would have been ten if I hadn't pulled her back, he thought, his eyes falling on the woman. And as if noticing his gaze, the woman stood up and rushed right toward Vern, bursting into tears.

Out of the blue, she prostrated on the ground and exclaimed, "Thank you very much, mister!"

She joined her hands in prayer and rubbed her head on the ground. "You . . . you almost died saving me, mister. It's my . . . my fault. Thank you. Thank you.

"Please, good sir, I owe you my life, but I-I ran away. Sir, I don't know what happened. I-I was scared. I apologize. I am sorry. I thank you. I am sorry."

Vern stared at her, dumbfounded and unsure how to handle this. His mind was already juggling so many things it failed to catch up with her words for a while.

When he came to, he swooped down and stopped the woman. She was rubbing her head on the floor full of chunks of glass. That wasn't good.

He was unsure of how he felt about the process of saving her, but he knew this was the right outcome.

So, he stood her up and guided her toward the exit, replying, "It's . . . okay. It's not your fault, really. You're the victim here, so don't blame yourself."

That's what he actually felt too.

Most people might permanently be traumatized after such an experience. The fact that she was already back in her senses was the real shocker here.

Yes, he'd felt a little betrayed in the heat of the moment that she had run away instead of helping him, but that was his desperation speaking. How could a normal civilian have the mind to handle that?

Dropping the tearful woman outside her house, he warned her to not go back in, and then he followed Cedric.

The man seemed to know exactly where these entities were.

They rushed toward 3-07 on the other side of the street, wading through the crowd that had broken the door but dared not go in.

The throng of people parted at Vern and Cedric's arrival, their eyes fearful and terrified.

Vern ignored them and followed Cedric into this house with an identical interior, the darkness quickly enveloping them.

But this time, Cedric was preparing beforehand. The pendant already radiated with a brown glow.

The scream from this house had long died down, but the fact that the forced darkness still lingered meant that the entity hadn't left just yet.

Vern decided to remain composed this time no matter what. He couldn't save everyone, especially not when it had been active this long. He had to balance the risks to some degree.

A part of him wanted nothing to do with any of this, but even he understood this was life and death for the ones living here.

Maybe Cedric could end this without him, but who was to say the man wouldn't let another dozen die before he could wrap things up?

Ugh! He gritted his teeth and walked on. This was more than just about himself right now, and the balance had yet to tip over to an impossible degree.

Also, this entity shouldn't be as powerful as the previous two. They had already culled their representation twice, so it should be running on fumes right now.

The thought put him further at ease.

Tap.

Tap.

This time, Cedric headed toward the kitchen instead of the main hall. Vern's stomach churned, but he continued anyway.

But then the scholar suddenly halted in his steps, and Vern followed suit. Right as he opened his mouth to ask why, he noticed the problem.

The darkness enveloping them was fading away rapidly, and soon the uncanny chill was completely gone too.

Cedric frowned and peeked into the kitchen. There was nothing inside. Except for a few scratch marks on the floor, everything seemed normal.

After a dozen seconds, Vern asked the obvious, "Did it . . . escape?"

Cedric flipped the page of his book and wrote *There's another mirror spirit in 3-01.*

Vern peeked at the statement with puzzlement. Wasn't 3-01 the first house we cleansed? How could it be—

But soon, the room number morphed and settled into 3-04.

"Shit!" cried Cedric. "There was no spirit in that house a couple minutes ago. It fled there instead—"

However, before the man could even finish his conjecture, a scream confirmed it. "Papa!"

CHAPTER 30

POWERLESS

Vern bolted out of the house and rushed toward 3-04 without any prompting. *This isn't looking too good.* He analyzed the situation. They couldn't just keep running around all these houses, hoping to get there in time.

He destabilized the lock long before he was close to the house and rammed right in.

His eyes darted frantically to find the source of the anomaly this time, and he didn't have to look for long.

A tall, muscular man was precariously holding on to the railing of the basement stairs with one hand while the other held on to the body of an unconscious young kid.

Gripped firmly around the child's dangling legs was a drenched, pale hand, relentlessly pulling him into the basement's darkness. Despite the man's efforts, the ghostly hand was steadily gaining ground.

"Help, mister! It's . . . it's taking my child away!" yelled the burly man, his voice hoarse.

Vern, however, wasn't sure what to do in this situation. He hadn't been to any of these basements before, so he couldn't exactly extrapolate the position of the mirror to destabilize it.

But I have to do something!

So he jumped down on the staircase and pulled out his gun. This entity wasn't as powerful as the previous two, so bullets should have some sort of effect.

Yet, just as he aimed it toward the shadowy depths beyond the basement door, a surge of brown light infiltrated the house, triggering an unforeseen turn of events.

The soaked arm clutching the unconscious child abruptly released its grip and recoiled, vanishing into the basement's darkness.

Vern turned toward Cedric, and a dark look appeared on the scholar's face as he hissed, "They're intentionally avoiding me."

"Save me!" Another shout came from somewhere on the block, and Cedric turned toward it with a frown. The spirits were clearly switching targets on the fly.

A frantic civilian darted from the street toward Cedric, eyes wide with panic. "Please, save him, milords! Quickly!" he pleaded, his voice trembling with urgency.

"It's my nephew, Oliver. He is only sixteen. His pa is out for work, and he is all alone there, milord. Only you can save him now." Desperation etched his every word, his plea a stark echo of fear and helplessness.

Cedric recoiled from the man and instead rushed in this new direction.

Vern's hand twitched, an impulse to smack it against the wall surging within him, yet he restrained himself. Showing weakness was not an option. These people were already terrified enough.

Still, how were they supposed to end this for good if the spirits continued to escape Cedric's grasp—preying on so many people at the same time?

With a composed demeanor, Vern turned to reassure the burly man, ensuring the kid was safe. Then with a sense of urgency, he dashed out of the house toward the end of the street.

However, halfway to the next destination, he stopped, and a thoughtful expression emerged on his face.

He had an idea.

Ironing out the details, he turned around and sprinted over to the crowd of a dozen or so residents who were following his and Cedric's every move.

A few backed away, keeping their distance from him, but he didn't mind it and declared, "I need everyone's help."

That was the only way.

Otherwise, many more would die in this battle of attrition between Cedric and the mirror spirits.

The gaunt man from the first house as well as the woman from the second rushed forward.

"Please tell us what to do, milord."

"How can we help, mister?"

Vern addressed the group and spoke firmly, "I need all of you to help me get everyone in this block out of their houses. Shout their names, bang on their doors, and do anything you need to get them out on the streets. Everything except going inside the houses yourselves."

Some looked unsure, while others had terrified expressions. But Vern maintained his faux authoritative demeanor and pressed, "Understood?"

The gaunt one shouted, "Y-yes, milord!"

Vern nodded, and the man ran off to his neighboring house while the woman from before also followed suit. After hesitating for a few seconds, most others agreed and ran off, too.

With that handled, Vern turned to the end of the street.

Cedric was already walking back out of the house by the dead end, but his expression was even darker than before.

Vern met up with him, and the scholar jogged in another direction as he spoke with an edge to his voice, "This is stupid."

Holding up the glowing pendant, he added, "I've even charged the amulet of restoration to its maximum capacity. I just need to come in contact with them for a second. For a damned second!"

Amulet of restoration. That's what it's called, huh?

Also, Vern might have judged the man a little too harshly. He was clearly trying. Maybe he just didn't like to put himself in harm's way while helping others?

So Vern asked, hoping to figure something out, "Can't you force them into a house of your choice once again?"

"Well, that's not how my vision works. It only amplifies probabilities. But even if I could, it'd only be one of them. There's actually sixteen of them roaming around right now."

Sixteen!?

The implications of the increase in this number sent a shudder down Vern's spine. Seven more people were gone—just like that.

Their incompetence had led to this result.

Cedric eyed the shouting civilians and asked, "What the hell are they doing now?"

"I asked them to get everyone out on the streets. That way, we won't have casualties as we try to figure out a solution to this problem."

Cedric shut up for a while before replying amid his ragged breaths, "It's a good idea, but if the spirits don't have any more victims, they might just escape this neighborhood."

Vern frowned. "That's possible?"

Cedric nodded. "Given their uncanny tactics and how shrewdly they're dealing with us, it's very much a possibility. Our attempts at eradicating them have clearly sent them into a frenzy, and it might not be long before they decide to ditch the place for good."

With his voice turning deeper, he added, "This is a product of prolonged objectivity pollution. Even though most of them start off rooted to a place or object, they can escape those bounds once they're intelligent enough."

Vern clicked his tongue. That indeed made his current strategy just a temporary stopgap. If they didn't come up with a real solution, they might even lose track of these spirits. Who knew where they would end up wreaking havoc if left unchecked?

Vern asked with hope, "Then do you have any plans for how to capture these spirits? Surely, Vigil has dealt with something like this already."

Cedric chuckled with mirth. "You're overestimating the experience we have with all this, kid. We latent observers mostly went against others of our kind before the shattering. It's been merely ten or so days since we've had to find ways to use our visions in scenarios like . . . this."

"Usually, pollution cases are straightforward. But this one?" His expression twisted into a scowl, and with a click of his tongue, he muttered, "Tch . . . seems like the numbers are not in my favor today."

Cedric outpaced Vern as he slowed his steps and tried to process the situation. The way things were unfolding right now, he wasn't of much use to Cedric anyway.

It would be wrong to say Vern wasn't disappointed by that answer. Yet, it also . . . made sense. Everyone was adapting and evolving to this rapidly changing situation.

There were no guidelines or standard procedures. One had to play it by ear and figure out the solution to each specific case.

But people were dying here! Yes, they had saved a few, but many more had lost their lives right under Vern's and Cedric's noses.

Maybe if they had prepared a better trap right from the start, things wouldn't have come to this?

He wasn't technically responsible for any of it. In fact, one might argue that he had already gone above and beyond for the woman in the second house.

Yet as one of the few capable of intervening before more lives were claimed, he felt a compelling duty to act. *These people are already dealing with death, loss, and starvation. They don't deserve this.*

Even though his plan of enacting a balance of stability and instability in all his actions to progress wasn't bearing any fruit, he had to keep trying.

But what exactly?

Getting people out of their houses was the priority. Cedric just had to keep scaring the spirits away until everyone was out on the streets.

Then, they would have to do something about it before the spirits decided to leave the neighborhood for good.

Cedric rushed from one house to another, and sometimes, there weren't even any screams. Sweat pooled on the man's forehead, even in this chilling cold, as his steps grew slower and heavier.

The gaunt man came rushing and addressed Vern, who was writing something on his notepad. He looked up from the web of details on the page and eyed the man with an askance gaze.

"Milord, it's done."

Vern raised his eyes and noticed a crowd of over sixty people huddled together in several groups. There were all kinds of looks in their eyes, ranging from excited and terrified to mournful and hateful.

Vern closed his notepad and gripped the man's shoulder before walking past him. "Good work."

He made straight for Cedric. He had an idea, but he needed to clarify a few things with the man.

Now that all the potential victims were already in a safer position, the middle-aged scholar didn't have to continue running around haplessly among the houses. He sat on the stairs of one, breathing rapidly, the hat still perched on his head.

Before Vern could say anything, Cedric said, "Kid, I get that you can't do much to help me with the mirror spirits, but are you really okay seeing me become miserable like this?"

Vern opened his mouth to say something, but the man continued to vent, "Seven people! That's how many have tried to talk to me. If nothing else, can't you handle them, please?"

For a second, he didn't know what to say. But looking at that helpless face with a hint of wrinkles, Vern sighed before replying, "I apologize. I will take care of it from now on."

The man clearly had some form of extreme social anxiety.

Cedric let out a deep breath and slumped in on himself—exhausted. However, Vern was here for a reason, so he started, "I have a plan."

Chapter 31

ENACTING THE PLAN

Vern's words prompted the scholar to push up his hat and look at him dubiously.

Vern took this as a sign to continue, "However, before I get ahead of myself, I'd like you to help me understand a couple things."

Cedric nodded.

"How does the amulet of restoration work?"

The scholar closed the book in his hands and pulled out the amulet, which looked like an eye—a little like the badge of Vigil. "It does exactly what you would think. It restores the objectivity of the space around it."

Vern frowned. That seemed contradictory. So he countered, "Then why doesn't it harm us observers? I didn't find myself turning objective under its light."

Cedric shrugged. "It's simple, really. This thing has limited capabilities. We observers are far more singular than these mirror spirits. Leagues above, even. It is pollution, after all—a mix of unstable thoughts that don't conform with our reality."

"We have a proper system to nurture our singularity whereas these things are just an amalgamation of random ideas and subjective notions."

A look of realization crossed Vern's face as he took this new information in. That was indeed a very reasonable argument.

"So, what do you think is causing the spirits to run away from you?"

They weren't running away from Vern, after all.

Cedric's expression turned for the worse, and he spat, "The disgusting things can sense my power. What else?"

Exactly my thoughts. However, he had to be certain. "Are you sure it isn't the amulet that's scaring them away?"

"No." His hat turned side to side. "It's just a tool."

Good.

"So, do you think I can also use this amulet to cleanse these spirits?"

"..."

Cedric stared at him with narrowed eyes for longer than it made sense before asking, "You want to face them by . . . yourself?"

Vern nodded heavily.

That was the only viable idea he could think of. Time was a luxury they couldn't afford. Returning to Vigil to devise a better strategy risked the spirits escaping, threatening more innocent lives.

Moreover, there was no assurance that anyone else would be more capable of handling this situation. If Cedric's "power" was what made the spirits evade him, then introducing someone more powerful would likely cause them to flee even more swiftly.

They'd have to be incredibly lucky to have someone just sitting in the Vigil right now who could counter these spirits.

Noticing the disapproval in Cedric's eyes, Vern explained his rationale, "If I can use the amulet of restoration by myself, I should be able to dent their numbers somewhat. They don't come near you, but they have no qualms about pouncing on me."

The spirit in 3-04 probably would have given up on the kid to get a piece of him, too.

These words seemed to send Cedric into a thoughtful trance, and after a while, he probed, "You said you had a plan. What is it?"

Vern met the man's eyes and explained his findings regarding these spirits, "I believe I can use the rules governing their behavior to my advantage.

"We know they can't move when they are actively being watched by someone. However, this limitation doesn't apply if a part of them is still attached to the mirror. In that state, they can even share representation.

"So, to counter that, my first step would be to separate them from the mirror. All I need to do is keep my distance and let them come to me. The crucial part here is that I can charge the amulet's light in advance and just have to wait for the right moment to use it.

"If I can execute all that properly, it should nullify their advantages and help us wrap this up."

It was obviously not going to be that simple, but how was he to convince the man if he didn't hold back a little?

Moments after Vern finished, Cedric's expression darkened before he chided, "And what if it's not that straightforward? What if you don't even get the opportunity to use the amulet?"

Vern knew where the man was going, and he'd already considered this point, so he interjected, "I've thought of that. That's why I need you nearby, ready to intervene at my signal or if you sense any trouble."

That stopped Cedric's next word in its tracks. Vern didn't miss this chance and added, "If they're afraid of your power, your mere presence should be enough to nip any complications in the bud."

Cedric started to reply, then paused, his gaze dropping to the ground as he furrowed his brows in contemplation.

After a while, he opened his book, took out a pen, and spoke while scribbling something. "We can try this, but only in a house of my choosing. If the probabilities aren't high enough, you are not going anywhere."

That's possible?

Vern nodded enthusiastically, walking closer to get a look at what the scholar was writing. *The spirit of sixteen-year-old Oliver is in house 3-58.*

He gasped. *Isn't this the name of the nephew that someone begged Cedric to save?*

Vern had been puzzled when Cedric left that house all by himself. Now it made sense. Maybe the distance from one end of the street to the other had been too long?

Still . . .

It ended with the death of a teenager.

An inexplicable feeling surged within Vern, and he turned his eyes back to the crowd that kept their distance from both of them.

Many among them allowed the gently falling snowflakes to settle on their bodies, their eyes shimmering with unspoken intensity.

A group, clasping hands, hummed a melancholic hymn, their pleading melody resonating in Vern's ears while another settled on their knees, praying to some god.

Most had drained their wells of tears, yet a handful still grappled with grief. One woman even had to be sedated as blood began to weep from her eyes.

In such a moment, five or six men exited the forge—their equipment still in their hands. Maybe they had finally noticed all the commotion.

While most blended seamlessly into the existing groups, one man darted around, frantically engaging with everyone on the street.

Suddenly, he broke away from the crowd, charging toward a house. Vern's brow furrowed, instinctively moving to intercept him.

Yet, before he could even take a step, someone tackled the man to the ground, and another group of people held him down.

Vern couldn't hear exactly what was being said. But he knew.

That man had lost someone.

They had failed him.

In another minute, the man stood, and the crowd whispered before someone pointed in Vern and Cedric's direction.

The man stared at them for a while before collapsing on his knees—the hurt in his eyes strong enough to plunge a dagger into Vern's chest.

He bit his tongue and looked away.

"It is very simple to use the amulet of restoration. You simply have to try to observe it in your own perception. It'll suck away your thoughts and representation to restore objectivity."

"Kinda like insight spheres, then?" Vern asked.

"Well, I haven't personally used an insight sphere to store my thoughts, but yeah, I guess it should be the same feeling." He then shook his head. "Anyway. It has this knob, which you can use to control the release of restorative light.

"Be aware that it has a finite capacity for sustaining the representation you infuse into it. Generally, mine can maintain it for up to ten minutes, whereas most single-shaded observers last about a couple of minutes."

Vern nodded, taking the silver pendant in his hand. It was surprisingly heavier than it appeared. The design closely resembled the symbol of Vigil, distinguished by intricate, vein-like brown patterns sprawling across its surface and notably lacking a slot for a gem.

Vern coiled the chain around his fingers and, without further delay, attempted to perceive it through his unique shades of gray.

Just like an insight sphere, it absorbed his thoughts entirely, and light began to leak out of the knob.

Cedric interrupted him after a dozen seconds. "That should be enough for a single spirit. Go on. Quickly."

Vern took a deep breath and turned toward the door of house 3-58. He could feel the gazes of the people behind them boring into him.

Vern hadn't explained his plan to the crowd, but his actions were indication enough. The silence was heavy with unspoken expectation, placing an odd pressure on him.

No matter how he rationalized it, with each step he took, he was shaping their future. Failure meant the spirits could flee, looming over the residents like an ever-present guillotine.

They might even have to find a new home if I don't get it right. They could—

At that moment, a hand gripped his shoulder and he heard, "Remember, this isn't more important than your life.

"Additionally, I will monitor the probability of the spirits sharing their strength every few seconds. If the numbers go above thirty for whatever reason, I am rushing in. No matter what."

". . ."

That helped. Nodding, he pushed the door and entered the house. The clock was already ticking—the restoration light couldn't be sustained indefinitely.

According to Cedric, the teenage kid named Oliver was already inside this house. However, Vern had no stupid hopes of trying to save him.

He'd seen what these entities could do once they had turned into mirror spirits. He needed no reminders.

When the door clicked shut behind him, he was left to the mercy of his lamp's purple light.

It latched on to his belt, a metal sheet wrapped around its inner half to ensure it didn't set Vern's clothes on fire. He'd asked one of the forgers to do this patch job for him. After all, it didn't have the glass encasing anymore.

Tap tap.

He greedily observed his surroundings, ensuring he didn't miss any chunks of glass this time. He'd come to realize that his perception was like an odd combination of all his senses.

However, he was sure it went deeper than that. It didn't use just his eyes to help him shade the environment into grays.

It seemed to use knowledge.

Anything he could infer based on his senses, logic, small changes, or past insights could be used to extrapolate the grays of his surroundings.

So whatever knowledge he had could be used to help him supplement the grays of his perception. There was definitely more to it, but according to his experiments, these were the primary contributors.

In the current situation, he didn't really care about the stability aspect of his perception as much. It was mainly to see what the entity could be doing without using his eyes.

So when he felt confident enough in the gray representation of the corridor, he delved deeper, his first stop being the hall.

Creak.

The floorboards groaned, and the tiniest of sounds had him turning around—didn't matter if he could also see behind him using his grays.

As he turned into the hall, the shadows cast by the purple light lengthened, presenting amid them a hall with a table for four and a dresser crowned with a mirror.

Exactly like the other houses.

Yet, it was empty.

Oliver wasn't here.

He shoved open the bathroom door with a kick and leaped back.

Luckily, nothing jumped out at him.

Closing the bathroom door behind him, he headed toward the second to last possibility in this house. The kitchen.

However, as he waded through this eerily silent house, a weird notion emerged in his mind.

No . . . it was his thought space. It was as if something wasn't right. He felt . . . discordant, unbalanced.

The feeling wasn't overwhelming or anything, but it was growing.

What even is this?

He'd felt it in previous confrontations, too, but he didn't have the opportunity to analyze it.

And maybe he wouldn't be able to this time either—

Snap!

He didn't even cross the threshold of the kitchen before a sound echoed from ahead, and he clutched the pendant harder, his fingers resting on the knob.

He swallowed hard and widened his eyes, trying to force in as much light as possible. He had to make sure the entity was far enough from him before committing to this.

Cold sweat trickled down his spine despite the stagnant air as he took in the poor state of the kitchen.

Utensils were scattered on the floor, and transparent liquid pooled at random spots. A rusty smell mixed with something putrid assaulted his nose.

However, he found something even more uncanny—a trail of that transparent liquid. Goose bumps erupted across his skin from the implications.

He followed it with his eyes, and it led him to a slanted wooden frame leaning in the small gap between the kitchen counter and the wall.

Vern frowned as he cleared the rest of the room and walked in for a better angle.

However, he only took a few steps when—

CHAPTER 32

FACING ALONE

R*attle.*
The wooden frame shook, and a drenched pale hand clutched at its edge—mere inches away from the wall.

A sense of déjà vu washed over him as he stared at the ghostly fingers. It was pretty much the same situation as it had been in the first house, 3-01.

However, this sense of familiarity instead helped him calm down his fraying nerves. A known quantity was always better than unknown. He'd dealt with a similar situation already.

What was also better was that he held all the cards this time, and the enemy was far weaker.

Vern pinned his gaze on the hand and made sure his perception had already accounted for everything in this room.

Once that was ready, he did it.

Closed his eyes.

And the moment he did, that feeling of imbalance within his thought space grew rapidly. The floorboards creaked with the weight as something walked atop them.

Plip plop.

Tiny droplets fell one after another, flooding his ears with their macabre melody.

His heartbeat also joined in the symphony, pounding in his ears, but all of this served a contrasting purpose instead. They calmed him down.

Things were panning out exactly as he'd planned.

Yet, his thought space felt more and more skewed.

No. This is working! He couldn't let this novel feeling mess with his judgment.

His perception depicted a figure of corrupting darkness in a world of grays as it emerged out of the mirror, the limbs twisting at uncanny angles to squeeze through that small gap.

It then moved on all fours, skittering toward him. The sight caused Vern to grit his teeth, making him falter just a little.

But it was okay. This was expected.

Turning the knob and the expulsion itself could take a few seconds. So he had to account for that and make sure the entity couldn't run back to the mirror within that time frame.

Srrr.

Its limbs crept up to some object in the room, its body tilting to match its angle. The corrupting outline of half its body bent to grip the sink's top while the other half prowled on the cupboard door.

Vern's spine chilled, observing all these uncanny movements, and his imbalanced thought space wasn't helping his concentration.

Any moment now! he reminded himself.

Surprisingly, the entity made little sound as its massive body crawled all over the utensils and furniture. If not for his perception, he'd never have guessed that something like this was coming for him from the dripping liquid's noise alone.

Just a bit more.

Before Vern knew it, it crossed the sink. Then the stool. Then the chair.

Just a little farther.

It was very close to the halfway point between Vern's position and the mirror.

Almost . . .

His thought space made him feel awfully inharmonious, but he endured it. This was the key moment. He couldn't fuck it up.

Vern held his breath, and the entity continued to slither forward. The moment it crossed the imaginary line representing a perfectly balanced position, Vern snapped his eyes open.

It was . . . dark.

The purple light of his lamp barely made it to the entity, its drenched hair and soaking hands painting a disturbing picture in Vern's mind.

But that didn't matter. He was staring right at it!

That was all he needed to shackle the entity to that position. Rolling the knob with his fingers, he unclenched his fist and brandished the amulet with a flourish.

The eyelid of the amulet seemed to pull up slowly as the brown radiance spilled out of it. And the moment it did—

Screech!

The scream rattled his very being as a sharp chill coursed through his bones. In that instant, the face of the entity rotated around, giving Vern a clear view.

He backed away out of instinct, but when he stared for longer, pity instead of terror welled up within him. A perpetually scared expression hung on the pale face that had yet to lose its baby fat.

Its hair stuck to its skin, and bones protruded at disturbing angles. Its neck was rotated a full circle at the wrong angle, but those eyes.

Those pupilless eyes.

They were frozen with a look of terror.

Vern let out a sharp breath. *It's okay . . . This is the only way. This is the only way.*

Brown radiance continued to explode out of the amulet, visible gashes appearing on its pale face.

Sreee!

The entity convulsed and quivered in place as the gashes turned to ropes within his perception.

A mixed feeling washed over him as his imagination superimposed this scene onto how this teenager might have been nabbed—resisting just like this.

Still. The kid wasn't in there.

Maybe out there, somewhere in the world, there was an observer who could turn these poor souls back to the way they were. But it would be too late for everyone else.

This was the only way.

So he kept the amulet brandished, his palm heating up alongside its radiance.

Like fire to paper, it burned him raw.

It almost felt a little too easy. He'd stuck to his simple plan, and all of it just fell into place so perfectly.

However, on further thought, it was only natural. The distinct advantages he had as an observer of balance weren't really to be shortchanged. His perception alone acted as another unfettered eye, something even Cedric didn't have.

On top of that, they had isolated the entity and used the rules of its existence against it. It was a proper ambush.

It would've instead been surprising if Vern failed.

Right. This can work. He nodded to himself, a tad more confident in his plans and his path as an observer.

The screeches grew louder, but all that it amounted to was faster evaporation of the entity's skin.

He could only be thankful it wasn't conventional burning, or the stench alone would have made him nauseous.

Instead of a brain or skull, grainy liquid appeared behind the skin, but at that moment, the entity tried something.

Its skin burned faster, but the darkness surrounding Vern became heavier, restricting the space where the light reached.

The disintegrating figure in his perception took this moment to jump back. However, its limbs were already half gone.

Vern didn't let up and chased it in its direction, quickly forcing it back within his sight.

There was nothing it could do. Not anymore.

This teenager survived the greatest genocide known to mankind only to be wrapped up in such an unfortunate event.

But that wasn't the end. It had to go through something like . . . this.

Ah!

Its mouth soon fully evaporated, and Vern looked on with revulsion. He found no pleasure in doing this.

As if showing its proof of existence to the world, it extended its hand toward Vern.

When all traces of the entity disappeared from his perception and sight, he closed his eyes, trying to control his shaking will.

But that's when a euphoric feeling washed over his thought space, and the lights of his insights seemed to bloom.

It was a distinct sense of . . . correctness?

Vern shook his head, trying to reconcile the contradictory emotions swirling within his mind and thought space.

The situation made no sense. He was acutely aware of his revulsion toward the horrific transformation of these innocents, their inability to coexist with the living, and the heavy burden on his shoulders to put an end to it.

Yet, within his thought space, a completely contradictory feeling surged, running counter to his current mental state.

This led to another sense of déjà vu. He was reminded of that realization atop the tower after having understood Captain Akira's unique balancing act.

It was the same sensation of correctness.

However, it didn't stop there. He could "see" the strands of insights within his thought space rearranging. Some that were blindingly bright dimmed, while others that were barely lit found a higher radiance.

Like a sewing needle piercing through fabric—or, in this case, the surface of his spherical thought space—the strands reemerged in a slightly altered position.

The change wasn't as dramatic compared to a few minutes ago, but it was undeniably there. Just yesterday, when he experienced a similar feeling, he hadn't noticed any such shifts.

But what does this mean?

If he had to infer from his understanding of how observation worked, he'd guess that he had better acclimated his viewpoint to his vision, which meant it should be slightly easier for him to use his visions now.

Closing his eyes, Vern leaned on the wall behind him, focusing on the question that stumped him the most. *What triggered this?*

Since the start of this mission, he'd tried to be very deliberate with all his actions and instill a sense of balance in them, yet it hadn't produced any results.

It was by no means a thorough attempt at balancing the stability and instability of the conversation, but it hadn't induced even an iota of change within his thought space.

However, now that he'd almost given up on this train of thought and simply followed the plan, it suddenly worked. How? What changed?

Well, there's one thing that's been out of the norm today. That feeling of imbalance.

Indeed. It had happened more than a couple of times on this mission alone.

What could it signify? An imbalance in my state of mind? Did me stressing cause that imbalance?

Vern brushed his fingers through his hair, trying to straighten it one section at a time as his brain churned.

Reflecting on this, he quickly identified a flaw in his previous reasoning. *If that feeling resurfaces whenever I'm mentally unbalanced, it shouldn't have dissipated just yet.*

His current state was far from stable. The loathing he felt, the weight of responsibility, and a pervasive sense of despondence significantly burdened his mental equilibrium.

Didn't seem very balanced to him.

So what is it?

This led him to wonder about the specific situations whenever this feeling of imbalance was triggered in him.

And there he noticed a pattern.

This feeling had triggered every time he'd willingly thrust himself into danger. Be that when he walked ahead of Cedric into 3-01, or when he was being dragged into the mirror in 3-07, or even a few minutes ago when he walked into danger of unknown quantity.

Yet only the last one had given him this sense of acclimatization.

He pulled at some of the pesky strands of his hair, trying to get them back in line. They simply liked to go against the general flow of his hairstyle.

Then suddenly, he stood up straight. *Right! That has to be it.*

Each time that feeling of imbalance arose within him, it vanished just as abruptly, dissipating the moment the danger had passed.

However, the last case was different. It was—

Thump.

Suddenly, the door slammed open, and footsteps resounded in his ears.

Tap tap.

Cedric was here.

Vern quickly filed these incredibly valuable findings in his mind and got serious again.

He had to plan his next steps. First was to worry about the representation he had left. There were about sixteen more of these spirits. Assuming the amulet always required this meager amount of representation to cleanse one entity, then given his remaining representation, he should easily be able to handle another fifty or so of these.

But that's not how it works. He shook his head with a wry smile. There was overhead and other expenditures.

Every second that he made use of his perception ate away at his reserves. He'd already used it a bit too much for the day.

Not only that, but using visions also cost representation, and it wasn't negligible at all. Destabilizing that wall had cost him gravely, devouring almost an eighth of the total in one go.

Maybe he could try and regenerate it, but he didn't know if the urgency of the situation allowed for that. Neither did his mental state, for that matter.

The hat's tip entered the room before the man, and he asked in a raspy voice, "Did it manage to escape?"

Vern shook his head. "He died." A smile bloomed on the middle-aged man's face, but Vern added, "In pain."

That instantly put a damper on Cedric's voice, and he settled on simply patting Vern's back. "Let's go. There's a lot of work to do."

Vern walked past Cedric and hastened out of the house. He needed some air.

However, the moment he exited back to the light snowfall outside, his eyes fell straight on the building on the opposite side of the street.

It took the space of over three houses all by itself, but it was the title that irked him to no end.

The sign said MIRROR EMPORIUM.

CHAPTER 33

TENET

When Cedric followed Vern outside, Vern pointed at the building and asked with a whisper, "Do you think their source is in there somewhere?"

It was how it typically went, right? It only made sense for mirror spirits to originate from a mirror emporium.

Cedric shook his head. "That's not how it works, kid. This place might be their origin, but they're not tethered to it anymore. Each one is an independent entity now, so even burning down the whole store wouldn't make a difference."

Vern sighed. *Obviously, it can't be that simple.*

Barely stopping himself from appearing disappointed in front of all the gazes filled with hope and expectations, he turned and asked, "Which one's next?"

Cedric pulled out his book and pen. "Lemme see. Are you ready?"

Vern nodded.

Vern charged the amulet of restoration a little more than last time and wrapped it around his fingers as he waltzed into 3-51, the gun in his other hand.

He only needed a couple of glances to supplement his perception and paint it in grays that were an accurate representation of the corridor.

His thoughts were constantly occupied by more than just a few concerns. First was obviously to figure out where the entity was hiding this time around.

Second, he focused on his own thought space. He theorized that his sense of imbalance stemmed not from personal mental discord but rather from being in an inherently unstable situation.

Therefore, if he could maintain his mental composure this time yet still experience that sense of imbalance in his thought space, it would partially validate his theory.

He had further ideas he wished to explore, but putting the cart before the horse wasn't how one experimented.

One thing at a time.

He went through his usual order of scouring these houses. The hall was the first destination, but distinctly, there was no dressing table to be seen.

Maybe they never had the dresser to begin with? He shrugged off the oddity and moved on.

Surprisingly, he felt quite a bit at ease this time. The little noises didn't make him look around anxiously, nor did the creaking of the floorboards get him all jittery.

Experience and routine were one hell of a thing. On top of that, the similar design of each house helped his perception in mapping it out far more conveniently, also putting his mind at ease.

Following the exact same pattern, he kicked down the door of the bathroom, and when nothing jumped out of that small face mirror from inside, he closed it and moved on to the kitchen.

Tap tap.

His finger on the trigger of his gun, he sneaked in.

"..."

It was quite . . . ordinary, and there were no portable mirrors lying around this time. Letting out a breath he didn't know he had been holding, he checked every corner of the place.

There were no mirrors in here at all. Vern frowned as he lampooned, *That only leaves one place. Hah.* He sighed. *They always want to keep me on my toes, eh?*

Making sure the energy within the amulet was still at its peak, he made his way back to the entrance of the house to go downstairs.

The basement was the only spot he hadn't checked, after all. Given that Cedric was more than 80 percent certain that a spirit was inside this house, it could only be down there.

He avoided the awkward moment of having to confront all those piercing gazes once again when he retraced his steps because he always closed the door behind him.

It wasn't really locked. He did it so the spirits weren't unnecessarily scared away by Cedric, who was standing just a little distance away.

Sticking close to the railing, he focused on his senses and descended one step at a time.

There was no need to be afraid. He was okay. He could do this. These spirits weren't all that scary as long as they came at him one by one anyway.

Surprisingly, or unsurprisingly, the moment he began his descent, that feeling of imbalance, which was nothing but a mere flicker until now, began exploding again.

One part of him almost wanted to consider this some kind of warning mechanism, but that wasn't a good idea. The sense of imbalance wasn't proportional to the threat in the last house.

So it was a bad indicator.

Hah, he chuckled. He was going to be face-to-face with some terrifying and inexplicable thing in a moment, but here he was, nitpicking his theories.

At least it helped with the nervousness.

However, only a few steps later, a strong, unpleasant odor hit him, and he sobered up.

One step.

Two steps.

Three—

He stopped at the landing at the bottom of the stairs and prodded open the door before peering at the interior illuminated by the light of his lamp.

Pipes ran along the short ceiling of the chamber, extending beyond the barely plastered walls. Bricks seeped with moisture, and moss glowed in the purple light.

A dusty handloom of the old design collected spiderwebs in one corner while heaps of discarded daily items littered the rest of the floor.

Vern, however, had little time to assess their nuances, for his eyes were drawn to the dressing table that was half covered by an old cloth.

Why the hell is it down here? Did they not have the heart to throw it out or something?

Anyway, that didn't matter either. It was hard to see in this dim light, but he could make out a trail of something red and shiny on the floor.

Is that . . . blood?

Vern's heart clutched. The cloth on the table was ripped and torn, also with blood dripping from its frayed hem.

What could have happened for this—

No. Vern stopped himself right there. It didn't matter. He just had to finish his job and get out of there.

There were at least twenty more of these. He couldn't waste his time unnecessarily analyzing each one of them.

So he took a deep breath and waltzed in. The moment he did, darkness began taking hold of his surroundings.

The limited information he'd managed to gather before entering painted a world of grays in his perception, allowing him to "see" beyond the reaches of his lamp.

The entity is here.

Vern waited with bated breath when suddenly, the cloth draped over the dressing table fluttered. He sucked in a deep breath, and soon, a corrupting darkness materialized in his gray perception.

Closing his eyes, he embraced the instability that bloomed within himself.

Adrenaline was going strong, and blood surged through his body with intense thumping, but he wasn't terrified, really.

Does this imply that the imbalance in my thought space is a result of placing myself in these precarious situations and not because of some mental instability?

He mulled over this idea while waiting as the darkness drew nearer, seemingly emboldened by his evident vulnerability.

For a moment, he pondered why they hadn't adopted new strategies like last time or simply avoided him altogether.

Am I really not as intimidating as Cedric, even though I already eliminated one of them easily? They should be fleeing from me as well.

Could this be the extent of their adaptive capabilities?

He didn't know. The presence of the entity here meant they had already made their stance clear.

In reality, this was the optimal scenario. If he could really finish them one by one, he wouldn't ask for more.

The dark shape slinked closer, and this time, the window for a balanced position to begin his attack was pretty small.

So Vern poured a little more representation into the amulet, and it began to heat in his hands, aggravating him just like the skewed feeling within his thought space.

The feeling resembled the sensation of spotting a flaw in what was otherwise flawless. Imagine ten nearly straight lines on a sheet, with just one askew, disrupting the uniformity.

With each passing second, the discomfort intensified, and his desire to correct the misaligned line did so too.

At that instant, the entity stopped and made to pounce toward him. Vern's muscles tensed, and the random thoughts running through his head evaporated almost instantly.

Steady!

Vern couldn't show his hand before it lunged, or it might just jump backward into the mirror using its momentum.

If something like that happened, he would have wasted a golden opportunity.

Can't have that.

Eahhh!

The entity finally shrieked, going feral and giving up on the silent approach, knowing its prey couldn't run anymore.

And then it attacked.

Vern was ready for it. He snapped open his eyes, brandished the amulet, and retracted one leg, stepping to the side—perfectly avoiding the assault.

Watching it with his physical eyes didn't cause the entity to freeze in the air as he'd hoped, but when it crash-landed, it became immobile.

Skriiii—

It thrashed and convulsed, its skin evaporating as Vern backed away just enough to make sure it couldn't tear at him even if it gained a sudden burst of power.

He looked down at the thing and reveled in the feeling that blossomed within him.

He had already somewhat come to terms with the fact that these entities had to die and he had to be the one to judge them.

There was no point in second-guessing himself at every step. There would be time for that later.

But in this moment? He savored the sensation of the crooked line straightening out. The irritation in his thought space, which had been a constant annoyance since he was on the basement stairs, felt alleviated.

Yet, that wasn't it. It was as though every line had become slightly more aligned. Of course, these weren't literal lines in his thought space, but he didn't know how to put it in a better way.

It was another step forward toward that illusory goal of acclimating his viewpoint to his vision.

This time, however, he might have uncovered the fundamental cause behind this phenomenon. The concept linking all three occasions where the shade on his perception became deeper.

The core tenet that propelled him further down his path as an observer.

Looking at the evaporating . . . corpse of the pale entity, he spoke to no one in particular, "It's about finding stability within instability."

That sounded vague, but one had to take every word of the sentence literally—even the word order.

In essence, always maintaining a constant balance and perfect stability wasn't the right answer.

He needed to embrace the chaos first—precisely what he did by stepping into these houses shrouded in uncertainty.

Only when things had spiraled to their most chaotic, to the brink of collapse, was it time to restore balance.

That's exactly what he achieved by turning the tables on these entities at the end moment—even if unintentionally.

Vern nodded. *So I do have to find an optimal balance of stability and instability in my actions, but their order and gravity matter too.*

Thus, the more significant his intervention to restore balance, the more profound the impact on his perception, and the closer he moved toward fully embodying his vision.

This ran very much counter to his prior idea of always maintaining a perfect balance.

It was like a weighing scale. He could only make a bigger change in the balance when the scale was tipped to one side.

Should the scale remain evenly balanced, only minor tweaks were possible to maintain its stability, which offered little in terms of personal growth.

He would need more testing to figure out the exact details, but this was definitely the gist of it.

He shook his head. *Just how is this so . . . nuanced?*

He knew that was a stupid question to ask, but he wished to know. He really did. Observation was such a complex framework with intricate setups like this that constantly blew his mind.

Vern tilted his head upward, almost wishing to see past the ceiling and the light of day to gaze at that gash in the sky.

Things like these reminded him of his meager place in the vast cosmos.

In this ruminative trance, he waited for the convulsing entity to run out of energy. Soon, liquid began pooling underneath it as the screams began to die down.

Crash!

Suddenly, the gate upstairs slammed open.

"Vern! Get out of there!"

CHAPTER 34

FIRST STEP

A sinking feeling crept up within Vern as something appeared in his perception at the same time as this shout.

Fuck!

He bolted out of the basement, dipping to avoid the doorframe from hitting his head. Cedric came rushing down, and Vern tossed the amulet to the man without hesitation.

Catching it, he joined Vern on the platform at the bottom of the stairs and peered inside the basement.

Right in front of their eyes, something bizarre transpired.

Dark spots of corruption appeared in his loose depiction of grays inside the room.

Not one or two, but at least half a dozen.

Vern conveyed this information immediately. "Six of them might come here soon. Get ready."

Cedric nodded, instilling the mostly spent amulet with his own strength.

Vern's heart beat rapidly. He didn't know what the hell was going on. This induced another sense of imbalance in his thought space, but it wasn't anything significant.

He held on to the revolver, one foot on the higher step—ready to get the fuck out of there if things went south.

However, in the next moment, the half-evaporated corpse of the entity lit up.

Vern frowned, and Cedric focused on charging the amulet, but soon, the pale light surrounding the corpse burst into motes of light.

The patches of darkness within his perception extended into uncanny shapes.

It didn't even make sense. There were no mirrors where these patches of darkness appeared.

No!

He remembered. There was blood pooling in some of these spots, while others had moisture from leaking pipes.

They were using these as small portals of reflection to materialize here! And because these openings were so small, they couldn't appear fully—just odd fingers and limbs.

But why?

The motes of light didn't wait for Cedric to be done, and they floated toward these patches of darkness around the room.

Everything was happening so fast Vern didn't have the time to investigate it deeply, so he blurted the only thing that made sense, "They're trying to reclaim the lost representation!"

Cedric looked up in shock—unmoving. So when Vern snatched the amulet from his hands, the man didn't resist.

With a blinding brown light spilling out of the amulet, Vern brandished it all throughout the room.

But it was too late.

The motes of light seemed to merge into the pale things that jutted out of the ceiling, walls, and blood, and before the amulet could have much effect, they retreated.

They were still "connected" to their source of power, after all—the reflective surfaces.

"Damn!" Vern shouted, turning around and smacking his fist on the wall.

These things were adapting too fast! He'd thought they had hit the limits of their intelligence, and hence the reason they didn't learn from the last encounter.

But they did!

Even though Cedric's probability amplification played a big part in letting that happen, he'd still underestimated them.

These things were too smart. Too fucking smart.

Since they'd run out of victims, they carefully chose their targets. They avoided Cedric because he was too powerful, but Vern seemed to hit that sweet spot of being just weak enough that they thought it was worth the risk.

However, they hadn't repeated their mistakes even once. Vern shouldn't have underestimated them! How could they let him get away with the same tactic another time? He was foolish for thinking like that.

Noticing that he first had lured them into a position where they couldn't reclaim or share the representation, they found a way to still reclaim a big portion of it.

Maybe it was just them preying on their own kind after it had lost. He didn't know. Maybe he was being too paranoid, thinking it all an elaborate plan, but damn, did it look like they were always one step ahead.

Cedric walked up to him with a dark look on his face and said, "Now they won't even let you do the job, huh?"

The scholar then patted his back and sighed. "It's time to let it go, kid. We should ask all these people to find different places to stay for a while. We can't deal with a situation like this. We need a specialist."

Vern tried to protest. "But—"

Cedric stopped him right there. "No. This is getting riskier and riskier every time we try something. Next time you go in there, they might just have some kind of ambush ready."

"Yes, but you're giving up too soon!" Vern rebuked sharply. "We haven't tried everything within our means. Heck, all we've done is chase them around and play in their hands."

"So what?!" he countered, an edge to his voice. "What does it matter when there isn't anything we can do without being suicidal?"

"If you're so afraid of death, then why the hell are you even doing this job?!" Vern vented, finally speaking his mind.

Cedric's eyes narrowed, and he spoke with a lethal inflection, "Everyone has their reasons, kid. But mine isn't to throw myself or those around me into certain death."

"Why the hell are you calling this certain death? It's risky, but nowhere near to the point you're exaggerating it."

"Well, you don't know how the numbers change. I've seen the probability of danger go from negligible to certain in a mere second."

Then Cedric pulled down his hat and added, "And all I've come to understand in my long time with these numbers is that if the probabilities have a trend of going upward, they will converge to certainty."

Vern shook his head, a baffled look in his eyes. "That's not even remotely related to our conversation. What are you even talking about?"

Cedric's lips curled up with mirth, and he held his book up to the wall and wrote in the margin of a page *It is dangerous to confront mirror spirits 0.*

Vern furrowed his brows and stared at the words that soon morphed. The zero suddenly became 31.34.

Then every other second, the number kept changing . . .

31.36

31.37

31.49

31.50

31.51

Looking at them, Vern slammed his hand onto the wall yet again. "Yes, this is why we need to take care of them right now! The longer we delay, the worse it gets. Not just for us, but for everyone."

Cedric rubbed his temples. "Did you hear nothing I just said?" He snapped his book shut and prodded Vern with it before demanding, "Okay, tell me. Tell me what we can do to solve this."

Vern, who had lost control of his emotions for a second, dialed back at these words and slowed down.

Completely serious, he pulled out his own notepad and responded, "Give me a few minutes."

He needed to think.

"Make sure to get it through your skull, kid. I am completely against this madness!" yelled Cedric as they walked out of the mirror emporium that they'd just surveyed. "You're courting death."

Vern, however, stared back with an intense gaze—completely unmoved. He wasn't going to let the man cow him anymore. "But your numbers just agreed with me, didn't they?"

"Yes, but they will only get worse!"

Vern didn't bother replying.

Cedric was a complex man. He wasn't inherently a coward, but he had come to revere his viewpoint and its indications to the degree that rivaled reverence and fear.

Instead of digging deep into why the numbers of his probabilities represented what they did, he treated them as a black box or revelation from some higher entity.

Something that could guide his decisions, and this was where it became a slippery slope. Where did these revelations come from? Was it from a broader understanding of reality or his paranoid viewpoint that saw everything as more dangerous than it was?

That wasn't something he could ask the man, for it was an observer's secret, but Vern believed he wasn't too far off the mark in his understanding.

It would be akin to Vern closing his eyes, ears, and insight, then relying solely on his world of grays to make important decisions. It would be disastrous. He would miss out on so many nuances.

Still, he saw the allure. If the grays of his perception represented the balance across time and depicted the future, he might be tempted to rely on it, too.

"A stubborn fool!" Cedric hissed. "Sure, you might save a few today, but at what cost? You're gambling with the future, risking countless lives that you would have saved if not for this foolishness of yours. Believe me, it's a risk too steep."

Vern's mind wavered at this one. That was actually a solid argument.

But, no. This isn't just about saving everyone.

Indeed, it wasn't. Ever since that last surge of insight into the order of instability and stability, he felt something within himself. It was as if he were standing on a precipice.

Of what? He wasn't sure. It definitely wasn't the leap that would propel him to the point of being able to shade his perception again, but it was bound to bring forth a significant change.

His thought space screamed that at him. Even if it didn't, he was sure this was a unique opportunity of growth he shouldn't miss.

If he managed to execute the plan he'd devised properly, he would be able to reenact the core tenet of his vision, but on a much grander scale, deepening the shade on his perception as a result.

Was it a stupid risk? Yes.

Would he take it? Also, yes.

He didn't let the brutal reality affect his daily thoughts because otherwise, the pressure alone would crush him, but he had to get stronger.

Strong enough to handle this oppressive and uncaring world.

Because if not, he was well on his way to being in the same position as all these civilians—terrified, uncertain, and helpless.

And that last one was one thing he'd come to loathe from his very being. It reminded him of that day. Of that minute. Of that instant. When he stood there . . . helpless as that bastard messed with Ari.

It reminded him of the compromise he'd had to make with Hensen. It reminded him of the time he ran away from the Ascendant Council. It reminded him of every damned time he had to escape from a confrontation.

Not anymore. Not when he had a reasonable path to victory. Not when running away meant death for at least a dozen other unsuspecting civilians.

Still, that alone wasn't his reason for being reckless. This society, this world, it was only going downhill. He had come to care for many things, but all of it was turning for the worse every day.

As an individual, the odds were stacked against him so hard in this indifferent universe that he had to seize every little opportunity to tip the balance in his favor.

So, as long as he saw an opening to advance as an observer with favorable odds, he would jump at it. Just like this one.

Cedric may like to look at things with a pessimistic view, but Vern preferred to be . . . objective.

Were the mirror spirits terrifying as a whole? Yes.

But Vern had found many rules that governed their powers and had a solid plan on how to deal with them.

So when he didn't respond for so long, Cedric gritted his teeth and hissed, "Damn you, kid. Damn you. If you die, I will find someone to raise your soul back and explain to Prince that I tried my darned best to stop you!

"That you wouldn't listen to me. That you were so keen on playing the hero, you died a stupid death."

" . . . "

Vern still didn't say anything and just stared at the man's wavering eyes.

" . . . "

"Argh! Curse you, kid!" He slammed the emporium's door closed. "The probabilities will only turn for the worse if we waste any more time. If we're doing this, we better do it right!"

Vern broke into a wide smile as he sighed internally. He was putting up a strong front, but his plan had no chance of working if Cedric decided to back out.

"Argh! I'll try to guide their probabilities to converge over here, but you'll have to create a factor that will drive the change and reduce probabilities of their existence everywhere else."

Exiting the unnecessarily large emporium that also had a conjoined forge, Vern nodded with a confident look. "I got this."

He calmly walked all the way to the start of the residential block—toward 3-01. His eyes fell on the throng of people that followed them, barely holding themselves from shouting their thousand questions at Vern and Cedric.

The scholar's stern rejection to speak all this time probably made them so hesitant.

Inhaling the sharp, freezing air, he shouted at the top of his lungs, "I need all of you to get away from the houses!"

This instantly caused the crowd to break out in discussions, but most still followed his words like law, and those who didn't were forced by their peers.

Cedric then stopped a little behind him and nodded, scribbling something on his book.

It's happening.

Once Vern was standing at the border of where this residential block started, he holstered his gun, unbuttoned his shirt at the neck, and cleared his mind.

This was the first phase of his plan.

The whole world stilled, and—

He unleashed his perception.

A world of grays unfolded in front of him, and he intentionally ignored everything on the streets, focusing solely on the houses and their structure.

Edge after edge, room after room, mirror after mirror, myriad shades of gray colored his perception, becoming more precise by the second.

First 3-01, then 3-03 next to it, then 3-05. The same was true for the houses on the left, ranging in an even pattern of 3-02, 3-04, and so on.

The veins around his eyes bulged, yet he strained them even harder. He had to capture as much detail as possible. After all, his perception was a construct of knowledge and understanding.

All the time he'd spent scrambling in and out of these houses gave him insights into how they were structured and where all the mirrors large enough to house the spirits may reside.

It helped immensely that all the houses in this society were built precisely the same, and most residents didn't bother changing up the interior too much.

With all those factors working together, his perception now showed a world of grays that barely resembled the houses but with their roofs and walls stripped off.

They painted a diluted picture of the interiors with some objects constantly in flux as his thought space attempted to assign shades, but they probably didn't make sense.

However, it didn't matter. He didn't have to be perfect. He just had to provide a driving factor for Cedric to drive the probabilities in one direction.

A surge of excitement as well as apprehension coursed through him as his lips moved and he muttered to himself, "Instability inducement."

Rosie watched on with bated breath as the kind yet powerful mister walked to the front of the street.

She didn't understand their intentions behind asking everyone to get away from the houses, but she wasn't one to presume. Surely, there must be a reason.

Mollie, Lizzie, and even Jesec were skeptical of these great men's capabilities, but she believed. No, she knew!

So when the mister who saved her from that . . . that thing entirely stilled, clearly preparing for something big, her mind churned in anticipation.

Everyone talked loudly, thinking they could guess the thoughts and gifts of such powerful beings. They didn't see it, but she did.

These had to be the apostles of the god. The eternal keeper had finally sent someone to end their misery.

They weren't ordinary mortals.

So she shook her head and drowned out the noise, focusing solely on every movement of the mister.

What is going to happen?

Suddenly, a chill coursed through her body, and the entire crowd turned silent. Many forgot to breathe—including herself—as the falling snow seemed to slow.

The tall mister who saved her . . . no, the chosen one, opened their eyes, and it was as if the eternal keeper himself had descended into them. Their eyes shone like beacons as they extended their arms to either side and took a step—

Crack!

Crunch!

Thrum!

Crash!

Everyone around her jumped and screamed, scurrying away from the houses as their windows exploded into small fragments.

"Oh, the eternal one . . ." she gasped, her eyes glued to the face that appeared more ethereal than the deacons of the keeper himself.

It is real! How could a mortal man do something like this? she gushed, filled with a reverence she had thought lost forever.

All the glass in their surroundings shattered with their mere gaze as they walked toward the crowd like a god among men.

Crunch!

Their every step brought forth another wave of destruction as they sauntered past one house after another. Their heavenly eyes sparkled akin to a lighthouse in a stormy ocean, offering solace in the darkness.

"What . . . what is he doing?!" blurted Latham, and many others who were just as lost perked their ears.

Then before she could clue them in to the plan of the divine mister, Charlie, who also seemed to understand the chosen one's will, interjected, "Milord is crushing the devils of the mirror!"

His gaunt face lit up with zeal, and he continued, "If there's no mirror left, obviously, the devils would have nowhere to go!"

Everyone listened in, and many even tore their gazes away from those angelic eyes as they realized the plans of the chosen one.

Crunch!

Crash!

Soon, the hubbub died down as the world-shattering steps of the mister brought them closer to the throng, and even the chunks flying around them further grounded into powder.

The older companion of the mister then turned to everyone with his terrifying look and pointed behind the chosen one.

Ah . . . Rosie understood in an instant and ran behind the harbinger of destruction. Soon, others followed her steps and parted down the middle, making way for the chosen one.

The crowd dispersed and reemerged behind the envoy of the eternal one as the divine one continued on their path, destroying every mirror in their wake.

She watched on in fascination and adoration, and so did many others, as the envoy's steps brought forth destruction and hope.

She had all but made up her mind to leave this place for good. The last vestiges of her late husband and child were etched in every corner of that house, but what else was she supposed to do?

If it wasn't . . . if it wasn't for the mister . . . she might actually be on the other end of his fury. A demon—a spirit that devours men.

She shuddered at the mere thought, and goose bumps raised all over her body. However, she soon shook her head and reveled in the miracle taking place in front of her eyes.

They crossed house 3-30 . . . 3-40, then 3-50, and when they approached the end of the street, they gently let their hands back down.

As if on cue, a shock wave traveled through the whole block, and another surge of shattering ensued, the grounded powder of the glass mixing with snow.

There was so much of it that it blocked her sight of the chosen one as it blew in their direction.

Yet, there they stood, a dark silhouette with shining eyes against the fog of powdered glass as their coat billowed in the wind.

Chapter 35

SECOND PHASE

Vern stood entirely still amid the tide of powdered glass as thoughts not his own assaulted his psyche. Soft murmurs played in his head, and whispers he couldn't make out seeped into his very being.

His perception seemed to flutter into many states, a hint of color slipping into the grays. However, he clenched his fists and ignored the oddities, focusing solely on suppressing the invading thoughts.

This was the result of forcefully using instability inducement when he didn't have a proper interpretation of the manipulated objects.

It started as a simple ringing in his head, but he'd chosen not to stop partway. If he did, that would've messed with Cedric's probability amplification, essentially dooming his plan before it even started.

Hngh! He gritted his teeth and thought, *Even I am not immune to these whispers, huh?*

But it was okay. They were far from overwhelming him. He just needed to focus for a while and assert his singularity.

Seconds ticked by as he stood there, dizzy, gusts after gusts of powdered glass and snow blowing past him. Cedric soon emerged from the dissipating fog and walked up to him.

Maybe not noticing Vern's situation, he eyed his book with a suspicious look and relayed, "The numbers are looking good, but I am warning you again, kid, the increasing trend is never a good sign."

Vern finally managed to have enough spare thoughts to rub his temples, and he replied, "I am not changing my mind."

It was getting better. The whispers that seemed to peel at the insights within his thought space calmed down, and the flow of invasive notions ebbed by a lot.

Breath after breath, he inhaled the sharp, cold air, and his mind became clearer. Cedric shook his head and sighed. "Then get in there and finish it before the probability of danger converges to certainty. Just remember, even if I rush in, I might not be able to get to you in time. So . . . don't be stupid and be sure to escape if the failure is guaranteed."

Vern nodded. Time was of the essence. Most of the glass in their vicinity had been destroyed, so with Cedric's guidance, all the spirits had converged in the only place with intact mirrors.

Luckily, this district was sparsely populated, and on top of that, this block had a metal scrapyard on one side and a rail track on the other—neither known for being good mirrors. Otherwise, he'd have had to account for many more reflective surfaces.

After all, it appeared that Cedric's vision worked more as a suggestion than a strict binding. Hopefully, the vast distance to the next intact mirror and Cedric's guidance would make it so the spirits wouldn't bother wasting their energy to relocate until after Vern was ready.

"All of them are in there, right?"

"All fourteen of them," confirmed Cedric.

"Good."

Soon all the lingering whispers in his head died down, and he was back in complete control.

Closing his eyes, he wholly cleared his perception—discarding the grays, fluctuations, and odd colors, leaving nothing but a blank canvas.

Time for the second phase.

His plan hinged on a simple yet bold strategy—to corral all the spirits within his sight at once. By doing so, he could immobilize them, setting the stage for the amulet's power to take effect.

This was what he'd come up with after racking his brain hard. He'd realized that trying to cleanse them one by one was nothing but a fanciful dream. They would keep finding ways to counter his tactics, and his bag of tricks would become empty sooner or later.

So he had to make a single move that would end it once and for all. This was why he had to bring all of them together into a single venue.

Yet herding the spirits was easier said than done. Shattering the glasses of the whole block was a straightforward process, even if mentally taxing and fraught with the danger of whispers.

This, however, was a direct confrontation, where he'd have to adapt to any deviations from the plan in an instant. He would be in their close vicinity at all times, and a single mistake would see him swarmed from all angles.

Vern took a deep breath. *I got this.*

He unleashed his perception again, this time focusing on the emporium's interior. From his prior survey, it was a two-story storefront hiding a glass forge full of apparatuses needed to melt, shape, and store the special sand.

Generally, a store without an owner in the outer districts was an invitation for looters to hop in and steal everything of value, but clearly, the terror of the spirits had ensured no one dared to try their luck.

So the display hall was still full of hundreds of glass trinkets—jewelry, showcases, jars, cutlery, and anything one could think of producing from this construct of molten sand.

In this situation, with all the spirits concentrated in this building, they were akin to time bombs, potentially granting his enemies unrestricted teleportation access throughout the building.

Or were they?

What if he could instead leverage all these glass constructs as variables for a controlled experiment? An experiment where these apparent liabilities could be transformed into a tactical advantage.

Vern recalled the Second Axiom: *Comprehension of an object's representation is necessary to perceive it.*

The axioms had earned their names for a reason. They didn't apply just to him; the spirits were also bound to the same rules. It was a universal restriction.

His lips extended. *Time to turn this emporium into a controlled testing ground using the side effects of axioms.*

Bracing himself, he held the store's lock and unleashed a pulse of stability that surged outward from him as the epicenter, radiating a force of calm control.

He observed the gray depiction of every glassy object he had meticulously mapped beforehand, turning them a shade brighter, essentially making them subjective.

Glancing at Cedric one final time, he asked, "Still in there?"

The man stared at his book for a while before nodding heavily.

It worked!

In his experience, the spirits were almost always "behind the mirror" unless he caught them in the middle of the act.

This meant they had to "come out" if they wanted to confront him. But what if he denied them the opportunity?

That's what this active stabilization hoped to accomplish. By constantly envisioning every reflective construct within the emporium, he'd essentially trapped them behind the mirror.

Yes, they weren't behind the glass in a literal sense. Still, they surely used some kind of twisted form of observational vision to emerge into reality—using the reflective surfaces as the point of entrance.

By stabilizing these entrances, he changed their underlying representation, making them unable to be observed by the spirits and hence blocking them out of reality.

That by itself didn't achieve his intended goal of cleansing the spirits, but this was a necessary step to bring his overall plan to fruition.

What was even better was that the spirits hadn't left the emporium even after he'd blocked their entry points.

A sharp look crossed Vern's eyes. *Now, all that's left is to bring them together in a controlled fashion.*

Vern's initial apprehension about the plan started to fade as he witnessed two of its most uncertain elements fall into place flawlessly. The relief was immediate and significant, eroding his earlier doubts and bolstering his confidence.

This turn of events shifted his mindset, readying him for the next steps with a renewed sense of purpose.

He still had to physically verify whether the spirits were really blocked from entering reality or not, but he was quite confident because of the weight the word *axiom* held.

He would be out of his depth if they could exit even after all this. *No shame in backing out if things turn out to be like that.*

Swinging the door open, the dusky ambiance of the storefront greeted him, all the lights and candles long since dimmed or out of fuel.

Nevertheless, it didn't matter. The picture he had in his perception of the place was so crisp he could create a lifelike drawing of it if needed.

He squared his shoulders, ready to face the challenge ahead. *This is it.*

Ignoring the reproach in Cedric's eyes, Vern coiled the amulet of restoration around his fingers and walked in, shutting the door behind him.

Long counters ran on either side of the door, showcasing jewelry and ornaments encased within glassy walls, reflecting the purple light of his lamp.

Yet, there was something different about their reflections. He was actively stabilizing all these trinkets, and it seemed to have some effect on them—one he couldn't pinpoint.

Well, it doesn't matter.

He didn't go farther in and waited close to the entrance—his heartbeat echoing in this dark silence. When a minute passed by and no pale entities jumped him, he clicked his tongue. "It seems they aren't called axioms for nothing."

The spirits really couldn't come out of all these mirrors. This meant he was ready for the next part of the plan.

Focusing on the stockroom at the far back of the emporium, he stopped stabilizing one of the tall mirrors. The white rectangle turned back to its gray shade, and Vern waited in eager anticipation.

Tick.

Tock.

Tick.

Tock.

His pocket watch cut through the heavy silence, but nothing happened.

Vern frowned. *Why aren't they coming out?*

He'd finally gifted them a chance to emerge out of the mirrors and come at him. Given how they hadn't missed a single opportunity to hunt their prey, this didn't make sense.

Even if Vern was far from the entrance, this should have roused them to take action, right?

He pulled at the strands of his hair and looked around him. Did they leave the emporium?

No. Cedric would've rushed in.

Then what happened? Did they suddenly become pacifists?

However, a peculiar possibility crossed his mind. "Can they not . . . sense me?"

The more he thought about it, the more it made sense. Surely, they had some kind of method to detect their targets and threats.

However, he'd "blocked off" all the mirrors around him, which could mean that they were essentially blind right now and didn't know where Vern was in this whole emporium.

Well, this is easy enough to test.

He directed his perception to one of the small rings sitting inside the showcase and stopped stabilizing it.

This action triggered a sense of imbalance within his thoughts, a sensation Vern anticipated and eagerly welcomed.

It was a calculated risk that acted as a second layer to his strategy—embodying the core tenet of his vision—instability before stability.

Hnnng.

The moment the ring became ordinary, corrupting darkness appeared on the accessory as well as the tall mirror running across many walls in the stockroom.

The darkness on the ring retreated soon after, failing to emerge from that small opening, but the corruption around the tall mirror at the back only grew larger and larger.

Vern ignored the rest of the grays for a second, and his perception made it seem like he was watching a grayed-out painting of the happenings in that room from a short distance.

He leaned his elbows on the counter, a thoughtful expression on his face. *That worked. And not just that, they seem pretty eager, too.*

Vern "watched" these happenings with sharp focus, and the moment the dark shape was completely out in reality, he quickly stabilized the mirror as well as the ring again.

It was a little taxing, given how the grays depicting them had been corrupted to an extent, but it was well worth the cost.

He couldn't have more of them coming out of the same mirror. How could he maintain control over the experimental setup if he allowed the test subjects to act unrestrained?

Vern swiftly ascended the stairs to the second floor, tracking the corrupt entity's movement. It prowled steadily toward the entrance hall he had just vacated.

It can't see me, huh?

Because if it could, the entity should have rerouted to take the stairs that directly connected the second floor to the stockroom.

This . . .

A rush of adrenaline flooded his veins, sending shivers down his spine. *This is better than I thought!*

With a quick mental recalibration, he reassessed all potential entry points, integrating this pivotal discovery into his strategy.

His plan, now refined with precision, promised a more controlled experiment.

Vern's grin widened, eyes alight with the thrill of the imminent challenge. "Time to play hide-and-seek."

CHAPTER 36

HIDE AND SEEK

Subject Number One soon reached the entrance hall and halted, maybe even confused, having lost its target. After a while, it started circling Vern's last position endlessly in a loop.

Vern watched all of this from behind a shelf on the second floor. His physical eyes were mostly useless, given how it was so dark, and he had long switched off his lamp.

He didn't want to attract any unwanted attention to himself. Yes, he called them experiment subjects, but he didn't mistake them as harmless for even one second.

The terminology was just his way of giving himself a semblance of control where there was little.

Shaking his head, Vern focused back on the situation at hand. *It seems they have a tendency to wait for their prey to come back instead of going out to search for it.*

That could work in his favor. However, before he was ready to introduce more subjects within this experimental environment, he wanted to test the limits of their senses.

He picked up a small glassy toy sitting on the shelf and threw it in an arc, aiming for it to land on the other side of the room from Number One.

Crunch.

The trinket shattered the moment it landed on the floor, its sound echoing everywhere. Yet Number One didn't react to it at all.

Vern furrowed his brows and picked up a bottle of perfume, aiming it right in the middle of the last throw and Number One.

Clink.

The shape in his perception seemed to shift its head a little, but it didn't stop circling his last position on all fours.

Hmm, their hearing is only so-so.

Having a controlled environment really allowed him to find their limitations like this. He didn't expect they would have so many.

When they were rushing at him like monsters, they didn't give him much time to think, but right now, he was slowly peeling back their inner workings—layer by layer.

Picking a small makeup mirror, he aimed it as close as possible to Number One. He didn't need to be an ace shot to do this. He just had to get close enough.

He launched it with a *whoosh.*

Grrrr.

However, before it could even hit the ground, the entity jumped and opened its mouth—

Crunch.

The mirror shattered into small chunks, which Vern had to work even harder to stabilize, making sure not to let his enemies gain any semblance of omniscient sight from the fragments.

He stopped his hand from moving to his notepad to write this down. It "saw" the trinket just a second before it would have fallen on its body.

Is their sight subpar as well?

There was some logic to that. He'd seen the insides of their heads. It was a pale imitation of the human body filled with that weird liquid, and there weren't any nerves either. The eyes seemed more for form than function.

The best way to confirm this would be to inch closer to the entity step-by-step and pinpoint where it had started noticing him.

No. That would be too risky.

He couldn't confront it prematurely. If he did, he might be forced to cleanse it to save his own hide, which might as well become a tipping factor that made the other spirits avoid Cedric's suggestion and just leave this place for good.

For now, it's good enough to know that they do have physical sight, but it's nothing to write home about.

Vern stopped messing with number one for now. Sound was essentially the only sense he could test without wasting too much time or effort.

Smell wasn't worth worrying over too much because if they were good at it, he should've already been found out. Also, he didn't have any practical ideas on how to go about testing that.

Vern rested his forehead on the counter's edge and processed all this, further refining his plan. Soon, his already glowing eyes narrowed as he stood.

Time for Subject Number Two.

He was ready.

Vern walked to the other end of the second floor, taking the stairs that led down to the stockroom where Number One had emerged from.

While he was standing in the corridor, just looking at that mirror completely removed any corruption that had appeared when Number One had emerged.

Taking a deep breath, he stopped stabilizing another large mirror a few rooms ahead of him alongside a small piece of the big mirror inside the stockroom.

One to show them where he was and another to let Subject Number Two out.

Srrr.

As if a sigil branded on the iron, the small section of the mirror in front of him became riddled with inky noise, and at the same time, a bigger shape emerged out of the other room.

The moment the corruption retreated after failing to materialize from the small opening in front of him, he stabilized it again and left the room for good, heading back upstairs.

He stood behind the door atop the stairs and waited until another full humanoid shape of darkness fully surfaced out of the other mirror.

However, Vern didn't even wait for its legs to be fully out before he started forcefully stabilizing the mirror. He didn't want to leave anything up to chance.

What if the spirits learned from the last time and were prepared to jump out the second this one was done? It'd be too late by then.

Yeah, no.

The entity still managed to pull out his feet, but the mirror's shade became a perfect white the instant it was out on the ground.

Not bothering with anything else, Subject Number Two crept out, heading straight for Vern's last position in the corridor connecting this room to the stockroom.

When it got there and didn't find Vern, it repeated the same routine as Number One—circling around it like some predator. Yet the disproportional form of this one made it far more eerie to look at.

Interesting. Vern ran his hands through his hair.

One hadn't moved at all from the entrance hall and was still circling the same point around and around.

This meant the spirits that were already out of the mirrors couldn't communicate with their peers. Because if they could, Number One should have headed for Vern's latest position in the corridor too.

Maybe they needed to be inside a mirror to communicate?

"This is good. Really good," Vern muttered to himself, cracking his neck. He could see it all coming together.

The sense of imbalance within his thought space hadn't gone up by much, but that was okay. He had time to engineer that too.

Vern took a deep breath and descended to the ground floor yet again. These stairs ran from the room to the left of the entrance hall, allowing him to avoid getting too close to Number One.

He strategically planned to drop each new subject in a fashion that maximized the distance between each of them and himself.

Starting two rooms away from the far end of the left-side corridor of the emporium, Vern repeated the same method.

One big mirror as an entry point, and one for them to peek at his current position.

The moment Subject Number Three was out of the mirror, Vern quickly retreated two rooms back. When Three moved out into the corridor, Vern ceased to stabilize the same mirror once again.

Using a small part of the glass lamp on his left to give them a peek at his new position, he continued retreating.

Four came out right behind Three, who was slowly making its way toward the first spot Vern stopped at.

Vern then escaped from the corridor back to the second floor, focusing on the interaction between Three and Four.

Vern's last known position for Three was closer to the room it'd come out of, whereas, for Four, it was farther ahead.

That meant Four would have to cross past Three to get to the desired position. Vern wanted to know how they would react to each other's presence.

Soon, Three halted and started circling, the shape of its head trembling violently. This little detail reminded Vern of how disturbing they looked up close.

Luckily, everything was so dark, and he wasn't using his physical eyes anyway. He couldn't have relied on them even if he wanted to—not when these spirits had the ability to darken their surroundings.

Shaking away the disturbing imagery from his mind, Vern focused. As if on cue, Four reached right behind Three, ready to run into it any moment.

However, as if with some tacit understanding, Four pressed its right limbs onto the wall and skittered past Three without even a thought, soon stopping and circling around—its limbs still rotated awkwardly.

Hmm, so they avoid each other, huh?

That was fine too.

Averting his focus from the two new subjects, Vern massaged his forehead and veins around his eyes. Every second of doing this was taking quite a toll on him.

There were just too many glassy objects in this emporium, and he was starting to feel the fatigue of keeping all of them stabilized. Luckily, his representation was still doing fine.

He even wondered if he had too much of it. Compared to when he used to go out of commission after a single use of his vision, this was insane.

He still had about a third of his total representation, and that's when he was also slowly pouring some of it into the amulet gripped within his fists.

I can't keep this up for too long.

Clenching his fists tighter, he made up his mind and said, "Time to speed this up."

He only had a few more zones where he could safely access the first floor and be able to retreat to the second in time.

The second floor had four sets of stairs connecting it to the ground floor. One on either side of the entrance hall through adjacent rooms, the third one led to the stockroom, while the last one linked it to the forge.

Unfortunately, there was no basement for him to farther spread his enemies. However it just hit him that, even if there was one, it might not be the best idea to use it.

It would mess with the next and most important aspect of the plan—bringing them all together.

With silent steps, he crossed to the other side of the second floor and descended from the right-side staircase. The emporium had a symmetric design, this corridor exactly the same as the one where Numbers Three and Four were prowling.

The positions of items were a little different, but he easily improvised. Deciding to go bigger this time, he started just one room away.

He stopped stabilizing the largest mirror and small chunk around him. However, this time, he didn't close the "portal" after just one entity.

Backing away from the last known position, he perceived Number Five coming out of the mirror.

Then Six. Then Seven—

All his focus was on these entities, so when his leg hit something, it was too late.

Thump.

Vern's heart tensed before he remembered that sounds didn't matter much—

Grrrrr.

However, Subjects Number Five, Six, and Seven turned the shape of their heads straight toward him, scrambling out of the room.

Vern's heart dropped, and he bit on his tongue, barely swallowing his scream. "What the fuck!?"

CHAPTER 37

SHEPHERD

Subject Five leaped out of the room, its limbs hacking away at the floor in a mad dash toward him. Six was the same, and Seven, who had just fully emerged out of the mirror, didn't waste a moment either.

Yet Vern didn't lose his head. Before any more of them could slip in, he snapped the entrance shut.

His instinct told him to forget everything and run like hell.

No.

Adrenaline wanted to take over, but doing so would ruin everything. These new subjects hadn't reacted to him taking a couple steps back, they only reacted to this louder sound.

That must mean their hearing has improved, but not by too much.

Retreating as fast as possible while making not even the slightest sound, he watched the noisy shapes of all three newcomers rush toward him.

They're coming straight for me!

However, he gritted his teeth and continued to backpedal slowly, not giving in to his fear.

Grrrrr.

Rrrr.

All three of them kept scurrying toward him, and soon his waving hands caught hold of the railing of the stairs.

Hghhrrr.

He tightly held one of his palms over his mouth and slowly turned, getting onto the stairs with muffled steps.

At that moment, Five pounced in the air, Six prowled on the wall, and Seven just lunged with the outline of its jaws opened wide, landing in empty air a little distance away from Vern.

Crack.

Thump.

Grrrrrrrr.

Their disturbing noises of falling, growling, and whatnot filled his ears, and he mentally let out a sigh, gripping the railing harder.

Fuck! Almost gave me a heart attack. He wanted to yell and lodge his grievances at something.

What changed? Why did their hearing suddenly get better?

One hushed step after another, he continued to fall back to the second floor. Once safely there, he moved to a spot that was farther away from all the subjects and let out a silent hiss.

His eyes narrowed as he ran through many conjectures and landed on the most probable one.

The more of them that are out simultaneously, the sharper their senses become.

That had to be it. Because most other ideas contradicted the basic rules of these spirits. Leaning on the wall, Vern reassessed his plan, every idle second making it harder to keep all the glass in the emporium stabilized.

His knuckles turned white as his grip on the amulet tightened—light leaking out of it.

He still had to get seven more of them out of the mirror without engaging in direct combat and then find some way to herd all of them into one place.

The imbalance within his thought space had finally begun to shoot higher, giving him another constant source of annoyance—also motivation.

This imbalance was something he had to maximize, too. However, he knew his priorities. First came survival, then finishing up these spirits, and finally, his own advancement.

He wanted things to work in that order, but the complexity of the situation was messing it up by the second.

He clapped his hands to his face lightly, then opened his eyes wide, absorbing this mostly dark environment. The light that had been seeping in through the windows was entirely gone—surely a result of the mirror spirits radiating their domain of darkness.

Vern moved again, not keen on wasting too much time thinking. It would be catastrophic to come so close to finishing them off only to lose control of the emporium's stability in the final moments.

He walked toward the staircase that connected it to the forge at the back. There weren't many other options. He didn't want to spawn any of them to the second floor, or he would be entirely out of places to fall back to.

He took care to not make more sound than necessary as he pushed the door of the forge open. He walked amid a world of grays that depicted an outline of sand stores, casts, drain channels, tongs, and a dozen other tools to help mold glass into various shapes.

He left the door wide open for his retreat and closed all the smaller ones down here, creating as many obstructions as possible between himself and the portals he was going to unlock.

Doing so would give him enough time and leverage to retreat in case something went south. He couldn't start too close to the stairs, or that would become the "last known" position.

Standing in the center of the forge, he mentally selected seven different mirrors around him and deliberated. *I should unseal all of them at once.*

If he waited for the ninth to the fourteenth subjects to come out of a single mirror one by one, the first few would have long had their way with his corpse.

That won't do.

So, with a mental command, he focused on the stabilized frames—some leaning slanted by molds, some stacked high while others hung on the wall.

Then he did it.

The sense of imbalance within him exploded, and seven of the dazzling white shapes in his perception, alongside a small trinket on the ground, lost their radiance.

A bony hand stretched out of one while a frazzled head peeked out of another. Three of them gripped either edge of their mirrors and pushed themselves, and finally, the last two came out with their limbs rotated awkwardly.

Vern sucked in a cold breath as goose bumps erupted all over his body. Retreating with as light footsteps as possible, he focused.

He had to stabilize everything again as soon as they were out.

His mouth went dry as his thought space seemed to pulse with imbalance—like an echo of his inner dread.

He retreated one step after another but then he noticed a big problem.

He hadn't thought about this before, but if all fourteen of the spirits were already emerging from these mirrors, then how the fuck were they peeking at him using that small trinket?

The thought sent his mind reeling, and then suddenly, his footsteps halted, his pulse racing rapidly.

The corruption on the trinket refused to disappear.

He couldn't stabilize the trinket anymore! Every time until now, the corruption had retreated after a short while when it realized it couldn't use such a small opening to emerge.

But then, what went wrong now?

Grrrrrrrrr.

Thump!

Growls echoed from all around him as one spirit after another jumped out of their openings. The ones stacked between multiple mirrors sent everything flying, while the rest wreaked havoc on everything in their path as they rushed toward Vern.

A shiver ran down his spine, and his backpedaling footsteps grew hasty and unfocused.

There was no point in being silent if he couldn't stabilize that trinket again. They were still "looking" at him, updating his "last position" every second.

Fuck!

What the hell was going on!? Cedric had confirmed that there were only fourteen of them left. Then what was this?

The shapes in front of him clawed and raked at anything obstructing their paths. Doors were savagely thrashed apart while containers burst open as if struck by invisible forces.

He fumbled for a few seconds, and his balance grew worse. "FUCK!" he shouted, then finally turned around, bolting toward the stairs.

Crash!

Thump!

Panic coursed through him as his mind worked at top gear to figure out what the hell to do. This was a direct confrontation; if he used the amulet right now, that would resolve nothing.

All his preparation would be for naught.

However, that's when the spirit closest to him—the one he wanted to call ninth boosted its strides apathetically with its eerily long hands—launching toward Vern at a terrifying pace.

A cold, numbing terror seized Vern as the entity contaminated everything in its path, its trajectory set to collide with him in a deadly arc.

No! Fuck! Vern preemptively turned his feet, barely shifting his momentum to an angle. There was little time for him to do anything else.

Skriiiiii!

His feet stumbled, and a coarse presence brushed past him, sending chilling droplets splattering across his skin. Cold sweat broke out on his forehead, yet he righted his faltering posture and surged past the entity.

Despite his efforts, his keen perception mercilessly highlighted the futility of his actions in any contest of physical strength.

Having narrowly missed him, Nine dug its nails into the ground, coming to a screeching halt with a grating noise that pierced the air.

It wheeled around to face Vern—its intent murderous. The other six spirits, mirroring its determination, bulldozed through obstacles in their path, relentless in their pursuit.

Badump badump.

His heart pounded like a drum in his chest, loud and frantic—the staircase almost within his reach.

Clatter clatter clatter.

His footfalls merged with the cacophony of destruction as he pushed himself to his limits. That door was the only thing that could save him.

He needed mere seconds—a sliver of time! A rough plan to shepherd them all together flickered in his mind, yet events were unfolding at a breakneck pace, giving him little chance to think.

He had to improvise and somehow herd his other subjects in one place right now. He'd planned to corral them one step at a time, but these bastards never stayed within his calculations.

What the fuck went wrong this time?! he asked himself, only to ruthlessly suppress the pointless inquiry as he lunged for it.

Yet as he moved, a heavy sense of impending doom enveloped him, the focused gaze of Number Nine burning into his back.

Vern clenched his teeth, shaking off the ominous feeling, and seized the door's edge as he landed on the platform—

Tang!

The door bucked under the impact, a deep dent marking where the entity on the other side had slammed against it. Quickly regaining his footing, Vern vaulted up the stairs three at a time, mentally affirming the door's stability.

This should stop them for a few seconds.

Thump!

Clank!

Bam!

All seven of them converged on the door, hammering against it with ferocious strength. Vern strained hard to keep it from falling apart, the veins around his eyes bulging in protest.

But he had to split his focus with more things. Yes, his thought space subconsciously handled most of it, but the sheer volume of things he had to control was overwhelming.

Shaking his head, he focused. *There's one in the entrance hall, three in the right corridor, two in the left, one in the stockroom, and finally, seven behind me.*

With this inventory in mind, his pace quickened even as the door endured more brutal assaults. Narrowing his eyes, he mentally tracked the positions of all the spirits aside from the relentless seven at his heels.

First, I need to deal with Subject Number Two. It's too far.

So Vern selected a trinket right next to the prowling Two and shattered it with instability inducement. The entity whipped its head around in a grotesquely unnatural motion, drawn to the noise, its maw agape.

But this was just the beginning. Vern caused another piece of glass to explode toward the entrance hall, and like a predator drawn to the scent of blood, Two lunged toward the new disturbance.

In tandem, Vern orchestrated a series of similar disruptions for Subjects Three and Four in the left corridor, compelling their forms to advance with intent toward the entrance.

Clank.

Crunch.

Without pausing, Vern shifted his focus to the trio in the right corridor, setting off another sequence of deliberate noises, when suddenly—

Bam!

As if someone had clobbered him on the head, his perception of the door he'd been barricading cracked, and shadows made manifest surged upstairs, their mouths emitting nightmarish sounds.

Gritting his teeth, Vern veered into one of the rooms, initiating a cascade of destruction among the displayed items on this upper floor.

Clink.

Crunch!

The ensuing cacophony was so overwhelming that, despite their proximity to Vern, there was no way they could discern his exact location.

That's all that matters for now.

Yet, when all seven of them split and stormed into various rooms—including his own—Vern crushed a few more objects in sheer panic.

Just a few more seconds!

Krichh!

Two was the farthest from the entrance hall, and luring him was taking longer than Vern had expected. *Why didn't I think of this beforehand!*

He wanted to curse at himself but didn't have the mental capacity for even that. Shards and chunks of exploding glass flew all around him, some cutting his exposed skin without mercy.

He might have managed the situation better if he wasn't preoccupied with resta-bilizing every piece of exploding glass, preventing them from using it to track his movements.

Number Thirteen was hot on his trail—tracing his route closely. The moment Vern dashed out the room's opposite door, it seemed to notice the sound and turned toward him—

Skriii!

A shiver coursed through Vern as he attempted to block out the ghastly visage of the entity from his mind, his steps crunching over glass shards.

Vern's thought space pulsated with the discomfort of imbalance, yet he pushed these sensations aside, strategizing a path that would afford him the precious seconds needed to align all elements of this "experiment" perfectly.

One of them was mere steps behind him, with the remaining six wreaking havoc on the same floor, tearing through the contents of other rooms as they converged toward the entrance hall.

That was the result of a calculated move on his part. He orchestrated the destruc-tion of glass objects in a deliberate wave that rippled from the rear to the front.

Vern's hair whipped around wildly as he gripped a shelf, propelling himself toward the emporium's center and running alongside the railing that offered a view of the entrance hall below.

Down there, Number One darted in random directions, confused by the cacoph-ony of sounds, its erratic movements making it even harder for Vern to focus.

Redirecting his attention, Vern spotted two entities emerging from a nearby room, swiftly joined by three more from the opposite side.

Almost there! Only Subject Number Two was left to corral!

The amulet in his grasp trembled, radiating intense heat as he funneled vast amounts of energy into the artifact, preparing for what was to come.

A profound, disconcerting cold swept through Vern as the other six entities on his floor burst through walls, panels, and shelves, converging into the same corridor he was in—their heads whipping in his direction instantly.

Two more besides his pursuer emerged behind him while the rest rushed at him from the front.

Feeling exposed, vulnerable, and imbalanced, a torrent of fears threatened to overpower him. Yet he compelled himself to keep a steady pace, determined not to falter in these critical moments.

The end was nigh.

Thirteen, the entity that had been doggedly pursuing him, also emerged from a room and turned toward him, choosing to defy the laws of physics by crawling along the balustrades of the railing.

It then propelled itself toward Vern with unprecedented speed, intent on closing the gap.

"Hah!" Vern's shout pierced the charged air as he rapidly calculated the dwindling seconds before the entity would be upon him.

It was at that moment he saw it—Subject Number Two was nearly at its intended position.

This is it!

It was time.

There was nowhere to escape.

No mercy to be found.

Nowhere to hide.

For his enemies.

Taking account of every piece of intact glass on this floor and underneath, Vern finalized the details.

He let out a grunt and, leveraging all his momentum, jumped, his front foot finding precarious purchase on the railing. Controlling his muscles precisely, he somehow managed to hoist his other foot up too.

The railing was perilously narrow, and Vern teetered on the brink of losing his balance, his upper body lurching from the sudden shift in momentum.

Eventually, his frenetic steps stilled, and there he stood, poised on the edge, back turned to the entrance below, as malevolent spirits surged toward him from both directions, their presence intensifying by the second.

A sense of impending doom settled over him like a dark cloud.

Yet . . . there was also an inexplicable thrill.

A crackling energy surged through him, igniting his fatigued senses with a fiery anticipation.

Three seconds . . .

The amulet in his grip crackled, its heat threatening to sear his flesh.

Two . . .

With every leap, the gaping maw of Thirteen stretched impossibly wide, shattering any semblance of human anatomy.

One . . .

The mass of pursuing spirits swarmed onto the railing as well, their collective force vibrating the whole floor and unsettling Vern's precarious balance.

"Zero," he whispered, propelling himself from the ledge with a determined kick. As he twisted the amulet's knob, he spread his arms wide.

Chapter 38

FALLING APART

Spirits surged toward him into the air, their jaws and limbs closing in on Vern mere inches away.

Suddenly, a brilliant sun burst from his hands, its light eclipsing the lone white ring glowing in his eyes amid the darkness.

Within that ring, energy thrummed, culminating in a forceful shock wave—

Bam!

Glass panels shattered into a hailstorm of shards, blasting backward with a symphony of destruction and chaos.

Chunks and fragmented crystals rained everywhere as the emporium became brighter than even a burning forge.

Spirits caught in the maelstrom howled, their voices lost in the cacophony of ruin as the sharp splinters sheared through their pale skin—bursting out the other end.

In this spectacular yet terrifying blend, Vern fell through the air—unharmed. A profoundly soothing sense of balance rippled through his thought space, a massive contrast from mere seconds ago.

Uncanny pale faces marred by terrifying, inhuman expressions overlapped in the noisy darkness in his perception.

Seven pale faces in all the tiny reflections and seven in front of him—all of them utterly rooted in position, except the ones falling with him.

Vern preemptively ground all fragments of glass beneath him into powder. It was one thing to break a bone while pulling off this stunt but completely another to land on a bed of sharp fragments.

This was all he could do to minimize the injuries from this . . . landing. It was a calculated risk—a jump. Not a fall.

He might break a couple bones, including some ribs, but that was fine given the healing methods available in Vigil. They could treat this much.

Hah . . .

The way he'd orchestrated the glassy explosions, he still had a few mirrors underneath that'd let him "see" the reflection of the other seven from his landing spot.

Eehhhhhhhh! Raw, guttural cries of pain echoed through the emporium, a sound of pure anguish as the purifying light seared their forms.

Scriiiiiiichhhh! A high-pitched, ear-splitting screech reverberated as the spirits writhed and convulsed, their dark forms blistering and burning away under the relentless assault of purity.

However, right before he hit the floor—

Zzeeeeeeeeeiiiinnn! The screams suddenly turned shrill and thin, piercing through his very thoughts.

Splash!

Confusion flooded Vern as he landed in . . . something cold? Liquid enveloped his body in an instant, and the fall he braced for never came.

"Wout bwis . . ." Words failed him, turning into a confused yelp underwater as the liquid rushed into his lungs.

The equilibrium that just took shape in his thought space flipped on its head and reversed its course entirely.

He thrashed violently, the sudden shift of environment disorienting him to no end. Yet soon his back met what must be the seafloor.

The water wasn't too deep.

This gave him purchase to reorient himself and not feel like being in some fever dream. Pushing against the ground, he sat up, his head now out of the water, and took deep breaths that quickly turned into violent coughing.

"What the hell is going on?" he groaned, getting back on his feet. "Where—"

His words left him the moment his eyes processed the harrowing scenery in front of him. Murky cyan water rose and fell around him beneath a fog so heavy, he couldn't see a few meters ahead of him.

Except for one thing—the bloody hue that pierced through the dense mist. A giant red moon hung high in the sky, blocked only by the occasional gnarled foliage in its path.

Vern's eyes widened as he took in the sight. *That's not how the moon's supposed to look.*

Simply peering at the cosmic body led to new insights blossoming in his head. His almost empty representation began to recharge as new thoughts sparked in his mind.

However, the moon was the least of his worries. A shiver raced down his spine as he fought to control his nerves.

How did I get here?!

Just how?

"It doesn't make any sense!" he yelled, his voice drowned out by the churning water. He didn't need someone to lay it out for him. He realized what this place was.

It was the world behind the mirror.

But how in Lady's name had he landed himself here? Didn't he just turn the tables on the spirits—finding stability in an utterly unstable situation? Then, how did they force him in here?

He'd won, hadn't he?

What went wrong?

His damp hair stuck to his face as his soaked coat became a few shades deeper and heavier because of the water.

"New . . . play. Come! with me!"

Vern snapped his head in the direction of this sudden childlike voice, but the fog was so thick, he didn't even see a shadow. *Who is this?!*

Yet, his breath caught in his throat when his eyes shifted down into the water. Something was moving under the surface!

Scriiichhhh! Garbled yells from all around him.

This is bad! He eyed the amulet in his hand, and for some dastardly reason, the thing was completely out of energy.

What? How?! It should still have two-thirds of the total energy I charged before being forced here. What happened?!

He involuntarily raised his hand, ready to smash the damned thing into the ground.

However, he took short, rapid breaths as droplets fell from his eyes, forcefully calming his thumping heart. Breaking it would be a stupid decision.

With a dark look, he gritted his teeth and poured his representation that had refilled a little by peering at the moon into the amulet again. Now wasn't the time for questions. They were coming for him!

Holding the vapor blaster in the other hand, he stood at the ready, his mind flitting through possible solutions.

Tch! The only useful conclusion he arrived at was the fact that he'd already damaged the spirits to some extent.

I can still survive this. Surely, they must have wasted a ton of representation to force me in here.

Clamp!

Suddenly, something grabbed his feet, and the ground slipped from under him. In a primal reaction, he brought his elbows together and took a deep breath before his head plunged into the water again.

"Ahaha. Come . . . play!" came that voice again, and its seeming innocence sent a chill down his spine—

Splash!

Bubbles formed due to exertion as he kicked away at whatever was grabbing his feet. No, his eyes could actually see down there. Pale, charred hands emerged out of nothingness, grabbing at his legs.

Vern flailed around, trying to get out of their grip. However, more such hands emerged out of the water, grabbing his knees, thighs, and even torso.

Shit! Shit! Shit!

He rested the muzzle on one of these hands and pulled the trigger—

Bwmm!

A muffled shot rang through the water as the hand fell limp on the surface underneath. But that barely helped. There were more than ten of these.

This won't do, and the amulet isn't ready either! he realized, pouring more energy into the trinket.

Simultaneously, he stopped bothering with the gun and instead unleashed his perception.

For some reason, he still perceived the grayed structural depiction of the emporium. The shades conflicted disastrously with the reality around him, and a bout of mad ravings invaded his psyche almost instantly.

Argh! He bit his tongue. *Why the hell is everything going wrong at the same time?!*

He forcefully wiped his mind clean, turning it into a blank slate. He didn't have the time to resolve these perception conflicts right now.

"New . . . uncle. Play. Big uncle!" *Clap! Splash! Clap!*

That juvenile voice continued to reverberate all around him, audible even underwater. Yet the words and the implied actions raised the hair on his neck on end.

Since when were these spirits able to communicate? *And why is it a . . . kid?*

But he chucked that question to the back of his mind and struggled hard against the bindings, while mentally repopulating his perception. Hopefully, one of his visions would be able to do something about this bullshit situation.

However, his face turned aghast when he tried to perceive the water around him. It didn't work!

No! He screamed internally, What the hell?! Why isn't my perception assigning the grays to water by itself?!

He suppressed the ugly possibilities and kept kicking around underwater as he processed this new departure from the norm.

How could his perception not know how to interpret some stupid water? He'd surely perceived water more than a hundred times since the day he got this power. How—

Wait . . . That's when it hit him. *It's not really water, is it?!*

Bwam!

He shot at another arm that was going for his neck into smithereens, barely keeping up with the situation as the lack of oxygen started to mess with his thoughts.

The rest of the pale hands continued to constrict around his body, threatening to squeeze him into a pulp.

No. I can't back down! he hissed internally. This was it. No one was coming to save him. If Cedric could, he would be in here already.

So he bit his tongue and braced himself mentally. He'd never done this before, and the repercussions were going to suck, but he had no choice.

With a thought, he assigned the liquid around him to exactly the same shades as he would water.

The exact shade of gray wasn't the point, it was the knowledge of how water reacted to his fundamental concept of balance. He had experience with that.

Not waiting for the soft whispers to slowly corrode his mind, he activated stability inducement all around himself in one swift blow.

Chik . . .

His vision bled red, and a scream escaped his mouth that came off as nothing but gurgles.

Yet the weight pulling him onto the seafloor reduced substantially, and his body became utterly stiff. The water around him lost all its motion and almost became solid, encasing him alongside those macabre hands.

He didn't expect it to be this successful, even if the whispers assaulting his psyche were messing him up in the head.

Double down!

He expertly controlled the shades just around the silhouette of his own body to loosen up, and he promptly pulled himself away from the stiff hands that tried to push against the almost solid "water" but failed.

Hah!

With a kick, he finally pulled back out of the water and took a deep breath. Inexplicable particles started appearing within the space he was stabilizing, and they induced a sense of unease within him.

It's more pollution, isn't it? He frowned, but there were no other options. Even if misinterpreting the liquid around him as water resulted in pollution, he could do nothing about it.

Sprinting away from the grasp of those hands, Vern stopped stabilizing the large area and instead focused solely on his legs that were submerged in water.

This would make sure they can't just appear around me once again. I should have done this from the start. But well, I didn't expect them to be able to teleport a small chunk of themselves.

"Plorvix quinzorflar phantosynx . . ."

The whispers in his head grew worse, but that was only because of the accumulated damage. It was instead becoming easier to stabilize the small surroundings.

He could feel it. The more he observed this patch of liquid underneath him, the less burden it became to shade it into a gray.

"Uncle! Big. Big! Play!"

Splash. Plop.

His frown grew deeper as something appeared at the edge of the fog alongside that tender voice that felt wrong.

Keeping one eye on the newcomer, he suddenly jumped to his right.

Skriii!

Bang!

His explosive shot rang true, blowing the head off the already half-scorched Number Seven. Its body flipped a few times in the air and disappeared into the water with a huge splash.

Yes! he cheered. That was very much an instinctual move on his part, but if it worked, it worked. He still couldn't believe that a single shot could do so much damage.

They're probably far weaker because of the assault of the amulet. Also, pulling me in here must have had a cost, too, he theorized. All good news for him.

If he could just—

"No! Bad! Uncle bad!" shouted the shadow that seemed nothing like a child as its splashes on the water grew faster and faster, the shape breaking out in a sprint.

The discordant combination of these two aspects threw Vern off-kilter as his pulse raced. He was no match for these things physically.

That's when the body that had just plopped turned into dim motes of light and rushed toward the shadow that cut through the fog.

"Uncle bad! You no play!" it shouted, jumping high as its grotesque body emerged from the fog, coiling to strike Vern into nothingness.

CHAPTER 39

LULLABY

The creature's disproportionately towering silhouette loomed against the backdrop of the blood moon, its skeletal limbs elongated, imitating the gnarled branches of a tree.

Sinewy and dripping with pus, its skin was a patchwork of shadows and oozing sores, some of them reflecting oddly in the red light.

Infused within the chest of this macabre monstrosity was a small face with closed eyes—enswathed by the writhing masses. Fair skin peeked through the sinews, mangled and torn.

Yet Vern ruthlessly quashed his disgust and puzzlement, jumping haphazardly and diving headfirst into the water.

His pupils dilated as this amalgamation raised both its elongated arms high and plunged toward him with terrifying momentum.

Bam!

Splash!

Water exploded at Vern's last position and the creature's other macabre hand—stripped of all flesh—landed mere inches from Vern's head.

The adrenaline kicked in hard, and he didn't dare come back up for breath from the same spot. Waving his hands and knees, he backstroked underwater.

Fortunately, he wasn't useless enough to not know how to swim while living on a continent that regularly faced floods.

Wave after wave rippled around him as the entity threw a tantrum, repeatedly smashing the surface with its limbs.

At least it isn't the most persistent attacker. However, suddenly, a dark shadow appeared in his periphery. Vern switched the gun's mode with his thumb and swiveled around—

Bwanmmg!

Schwaa . . .

His shot missed. *Damn!*

It dodged. Here he'd thought his aim had improved, but apparently, that wasn't true underwater.

Pwah!

He took a deep breath as he emerged from the water and frantically jogged in the opposite direction from his enemies.

Jamming his hand in his drenched pocket, he grabbed a couple of ammo cartridges. They were all soaked, too, but fortunately, vapor blasters' cartridges didn't spoil from water.

Thank the lady that Cera gifted me this! If it wasn't for her, he'd probably still be using that old ironsong and would've met his end by now.

Popping open the compartment, he tilted the gun, and old cartridges plopped down into the water.

Click.

His blaster ready and loaded, he assessed the situation.

And once again, the answer was the same.

"I'm doomed." he muttered, his eyes landing on the child-monster hybrid, a hand jutting out of its disfigured stomach that doubled as a head.

A thick tar-like substance coated its body as it continued to flail around his last position. *Where the hell did this thing even come from?*

This wasn't one of the fourteen mirror spirits that Cedric calculated. And Vern was sure this wasn't one of the subjects from the emporium. *Then . . . ?*

Oh!

He almost fumbled as his footsteps grew even quicker from the realization. *It's always been there. It's the second and the fifteenth!*

Vern and Cedric hadn't let the spirit run away in that first house. It never escaped! They had finished it right then and there. However, this second one hadn't emerged from behind the mirror and survived!

So, this is the force that spawned more victims the moment it witnessed its kin fall into our trap.

Also, it's the fifteenth because it was the same entity that spied on him from within the trinket in the forge at the emporium. He'd been puzzled as to who was behind the mirror when all fourteen subjects were out in the reality.

But now it made sense. It was likely even the cunning architect behind various schemes and plans to one-up Cedric and him.

This was what kidnapped that kid Oliver and became the cause of his death. This was what turned the lives of the whole neighborhood into a nightmare.

"Uncle!" It turned toward him, a harrowing smile on the writhing head, but a peaceful one on the small face underneath.

It was this . . . child . . . entity that committed all those horrors?

"Please. Play! Sorry. I'm sorry!" it plead, and a shiver raced down Vern's spine as he suddenly ducked, plunging back into the water.

Whoosh!

"Eahhhhhh!" A screech traveled right over his head. From beneath the surface, Vern saw a monstrous jaw snap shut, missing him by mere inches, its owner carried by sheer momentum past him.

Number Three crashed with a crunch into what looked like a rigid pile of mirrors just beyond the edge of the fog—its body was skewered by the glassy fragments.

The child-monster had thrown it at Vern with its flailing arms, and if he hadn't dodged in time, the collision alone would have rendered him unconscious.

Not that surviving the crash would've mattered. Getting skewered by those pieces of glass would've punctured his body anyway.

A shiver ran down his spine as he continued his frantic mad dash, changing directions.

He tried to let his thought space assign grays to the pile of shattered glass, but it was as he'd feared. The "glass" wasn't pure glass.

He even wondered for a second if he should forcefully perceive the glass, given how he'd used it so well in the emporium.

However, he soon shook his head, shooting another bullet that grazed the shoulder of Number Eleven swimming up to him.

I can only handle the whispers from one source of conflict at a time.

If he added this glass into the mix as well, he would be long mad before that "kid" came for him. The risk outweighed the reward.

He didn't know if the third rune would help him against the whispers this time or not. The uncertainty alone made it not worth the risk.

Not when he couldn't give up on stabilizing the water for even a second. Doing so would mean all of them teleporting their hands all over him and slowly battering him to death.

This is fucked!

The bleakness of the situation slowly dawned up on him. There were still thirteen enemies left for him to deal with, and one of them was this abnormally large child-monster hybrid.

How the hell am I supposed to handle this?

There were no limitations on his enemies in here. Looking at them didn't immobilize them like on the outside.

He had no advantages to speak of. Not the environment. Not the strategy. Not the numbers.

His gaze landed on the amulet in his other arm. He still poured some of his representation into the thing, but it wasn't going to be as effective of a tool when his enemies could move around as they pleased.

His breaths turned ragged as he squeezed through the only large obstacles in this primarily barren swamp.

Yet when he looked closely, his expression turned puzzled. *A toy train and a . . . music box?*

Vern hid behind the giant-sized "toys"—mostly corroded and rotten—collecting his breath.

However, before he could even get his heart rate down, a shrill scream came from that thing. "Get away! Toy! My!" The ground rumbled.

The monster lunged toward Vern, each of its jumps crossing dozens of meters. "Kill Uncle! He kill mother!"

And as if obeying the orders of their liege, the rest of the spirits went into a frenzy.

Ever since Vern started stabilizing his immediate surroundings, they had stopped using teleportation, as it was not worth the cost.

However, this time they seemed to let go of all their inhibitions and emerged around Vern, encircling the large toys from outside.

Badump! Badump!

Words failed him, and panic gripped him as the blood pumping within him picked up to an explosive pace. His eyes darted all around as the monster jumped higher and higher, its silhouette getting closer with each lunge.

So Vern instead rested his hand on his chest and took a deep breath.

Hah . . .

I guess I'll have to start expanding my scope of stability. That was the only card available to him. There was no easy escape this time.

Instability inducement would most probably just evaporate the water. Not useful at all.

With this bit of energy in it, the amulet would do scrapshit in the mere seconds it would take them to maul him to death.

So, stabilizing a longer space around him was the only option. Now the question remained whether he'd understood this "water" enough to be able to pull that off without being consumed by the whispers.

"Well, I can only try," he muttered, cracking his neck.

So he waited.

The spirits rushed toward him with reckless abandon, and suddenly his eyes turned cold as he extended his arm and—*Bang!*—blew off the head of Number Twelve that had pounced at him from behind the toy.

It had gotten too keen—jumping at him way before the others. Vern wasn't in the habit of missing his shots at point-blank range.

If he actually wanted to use this last resort stabilization to struggle further, he had to find the perfect moment—that exact balance. *Just a few more seconds.*

Because if he activated it too soon, he wouldn't be able to keep it up without losing himself to those mad ravings. So, the only valid strategy was to use it at the last moment.

Thump! Thump! Leap after leap, the "kid" kept rushing toward him, a disturbed expression on its little humanoid face.

Vern couldn't help but feel miffed. That thing acted like it was the one being mobbed to death by eleven monsters, not him.

Clatt!

Vern dodged to one side as a pair of jaws clamped shut right next to him. But he'd felt this one above him beforehand. His perception had no issues interpreting the air, after all.

However, before he could use this perfect opportunity to further reduce their numbers, he jumped, grabbing hold of some lever on the box.

He barely avoided a dark shadow that swam and aimed right for his leg.

"Hah!" he wheezed. This was too much. He was handling it well for now because his mind was quite calm, but his body had limits.

Just a bit longer! The towering child-monster was almost here.

But that's when the lever he'd been holding on to slid down. Vern gripped it harder, but that only increased the speed of its descent.

Tch. He clicked his tongue. Pushing his legs off the face of the music box, he jumped, barely avoiding the open maw waiting for him to land right inside it.

Clamp! Another one clutched at his leg right as he landed in the water.

"Fuck off!" he yelled, following it up with a *bang!*

Number Eight's head burst into a white mass as the explosive shot rang true, leaving the vapor blaster overheated.

Pushing off against the seabed, he stood up for the umpteenth time, his breaths coming out in ragged gasps.

Yet there was no rest for the wicked.

The putrid monster that was raging toward him like a train slowed down, even slipping and falling to one side as it barely avoided smashing into the toys.

It wants to . . . safeguard them?

"Eaahaaaaa! Mommy! He kill kill you kill!" came a distressed voice from the small mouth, then augmented by the larger and grotesque mouth into an eerie screech.

Vern's eyes twitched as he looked at the monster, its bony arm stretching toward the gigantic toys almost as if in longing.

Thump!

It smashed that hand on the ground and stood right back up, staring at Vern with an expression that was combined hatred and disgust.

The hand lunged straight for him, and so did ten more spirits around him.

Vern took a deep breath and—

Mm-hmm, mm-hmm . . .
In moon's embrace, you find your rest, my dear
While stars above in silent watch do keep,

". . ." Vern lost all his momentum as a soft humming played from behind him alongside this sweet voice.

Dreams crystal clear in night's soft cradle here,
In tranquil seas, beneath the whisper deep.

All the spirits halted in their place, and so did the tall monster, looking . . . guilty? It moved with tiny steps and hid itself behind the edge of the toy train, peering at the music box behind Vern.

As much as Vern was perplexed, he didn't waste this golden opportunity and squeezed past Numbers Eleven and Twelve, listening to the words of the lullaby.

The music box actually works? How did it even start— Oh!

He looked at it again and realized the lever he'd used as a ledge wasn't just some decoration. It was the switch of the box. He'd accidentally flipped it on with his weight.

When night's dome sparkles with each twinkling light,
The mirror's grace reflects your smile so bright,
Mm-hm . . . mm-hmm
In every star's glow, in every loving face,
My love for you, the sands of time can't trace.

The whole world seemed to brighten as the redness of the moon gave way for some purity. The fog seemed to lift, and the sights beyond it slowly revealed themselves.

Did he get lucky for once? Vern shook his head and went underwater to avoid the next three spirits in his path. Yet, the melody continued . . .

So drift, my child, in dreams of sweet embrace,
Through silver streams that time cannot erase,
In clouds that carry you to love's soft space,
Our bond, a mirror of eternal grace.

The melancholic song resounded throughout the whole swamp as he sprinted farther away from the gathering of the entities, panting heavily.

Cracks appeared in the sky around him as if a chunk of glass had fallen off a large mirror. Vern's mind involuntarily fixated on some of the words in the lullaby—

Moon . . . Cradle . . . Seas . . . Mirrors . . . Sweet child . . .

It didn't take long for him to piece together the context of the situation. A solemn expression appeared on his face as he earnestly glanced back at the . . . child.

The face encased within the grotesque monstrosity looked barely older than four or five. Many questions ran through Vern's mind.

How did it come to this? What went wrong? Where was his mother? Why did he turn into this . . . ?

Then, as if sung in soft whispers mirroring the onset of light sleep, the words slowly came to an end . . .

In every gleam, in every gentle face,
My love for you, time's hands will never trace.

All that was left was her soft humming, and the skies seemed to grow bright every second it continued.

Vern's head buzzed with a thousand emotions, not sure how to process any of this. This entity didn't just sound like a child.

It was indeed a child. Yet, he was different from Oliver. Oliver had lost all his mental faculties and was nothing but a husk.

But this . . . ? Was he in there? If he was, how was Vern supposed to handle this?

The distinct sense of imbalance within his thought space grew worse at the mere thought, yet he continued running.

What else was there to do? There was no guarantee that the spirits would have remained still if he'd used the amulet then and there.

Mm-hmm . . . mm-hmm

The lullaby's humming continued to morph the world around him as he saw more toys and mirrors that reflected two silhouettes.

In one large mirror within the heap, the outlines seemed to depict the interior of mirror emporium. It was the forge room.

Mm-hmm . . . mm-hmm

Then there was another one where the silhouettes were even darker. A small shadow held the hands of a taller, thin one.

One after another, the scenes became more vivid as colors were breathed into the darkness, when—

Goodnight . . . my little one . . . Mm-hmm . . .

And the music stopped.

Suddenly, an intense trepidation pulsed through Vern as he looked back with a slow turn of his head.

"Mommy . . . please . . .

"Don't go . . ."

The small head cradled in the writhing mass that had kept its eyes closed until now, opened them with a snap.

The very world changed around Vern; it was as if someone ran a razor down his body, only to then crush and mush him into a small box.

His legs felt like lead, and he naturally slipped, falling into the water without mercy. Before he could force himself back up, a terrifying reality transpired in front of his eyes.

A grotesque thing materialized in the water right in front of him, emerging from it to stand tall before raising both its arms high—right over Vern's head.

"No one . . . takes . . . my . . . mommy away!" shrieked the small face, and the arms smashed down toward Vern.

CHAPTER 40

1 V 9

Vern's eyes widened as the fists became larger in his vision. He commanded everything in his body to move—to back away, to escape, to dodge. All was in vain; something was constricting him.

So he narrowed his eyes, and they flared a bright white when—

Thump . . .

One of the spirits that had teleported perilously close surged toward Vern with relentless speed, only to collide with the leg of the towering monster instead.

Splash!

Caught in the terrifyingly narrow space between two massive hands crashing together, Vern felt the intense pressure threaten to crush him. His heart raced, teetering on the edge of bursting.

But he wasn't dead. The monster had somehow missed perfectly!

The ground and water trembled beneath him, and the odd constriction that plagued his body disappeared. Seizing the moment, Vern propelled himself forward, squeezing through the tiny opening left by the giant fists.

How . . . Just . . . What? Vern's mind failed to process how he'd managed to escape certain death—or an uncertain death were he forced to escape to the third rune.

However, he set these queries aside momentarily and focused on fleeing this death trap. He knew he stood no chance against such ferocity.

Moments later, a few meters from where disaster had nearly struck, Vern resurfaced. He caught sight of the childlike monster, staring down at its hands in bewildered dismay. Could such a creature even feel confusion?

Then, with a turn, it reached for the spirit whose misstep had spared Vern, picking it up with a sense of what seemed like perplexed frustration.

The thought of those hands crushing him sent a shiver down his spine. So when the monster showed his back—ignoring Vern—an idea surfaced in his mind. An unseemly, yet practical one.

He gritted his teeth and flipped the blaster's mode to charged shot. Pulling the trigger, he held it taut.

Sssssiiiii.

Red glow and steam began to radiate out of its chamber, and his hands trembled.

Drenched, battered, and shaken to his core, he justified to himself, *I have to do this. Now!*

As much as he loathed to hurt a child, his conscience wasn't more important than his life. At least not in this situation. The child was clearly too far gone, and Vern didn't have much in the name of options.

His hands involuntarily dropped down a little, aiming away from the most fatal spot. *No!* He reminded himself of all that he'd experienced and pulled them back up.

It was either dying under the fury of a child who had lost himself to pollution or—

Bang!

A fiery bullet burst out of the vapor blaster as it shot straight toward the back of the large monster—exactly where the head of the little one should be.

Yes, he'd gone straight for the head.

If he was going to shoot at a child anyway, it would be hypocritical to not go for the most fatal spot and end it in one go. Yet his hands continued to tremble even after the shot, and he didn't let go of the overheated grip as he watched intently.

The child-monster that was pummeling the already crushed Subject Number Fourteen like some toy didn't even turn around until the last moment—

Boom!

"Eeeaaaghhh!" it screeched as the bullet exploded inside its back in a burst of gore and sinews.

It fell face first into the water and thrashed, the convulsions similar to the dying throes of an animal, but Vern's heart sank instead.

Motes of light emerged from Fourteen, and then another one of the spirits that had slinked up to them, heading toward the child-monster.

No. I can't let this happen! Vern dashed toward the convulsing monster only to suddenly dodge to one side—

Chomp!

"Fuck!" he yelled, almost slipping into the water.

This won't do! His heart palpitated, going mad from the frustrating realization. *They're not going to give me a chance to end him!*

Another choice. Another fucking choice!

Closing his eyes for the briefest of moments, he took a deep breath and came up with a new plan.

Switching his gun back to simple shots, he focused on its stability, forcefully cooling down its overheated frame.

Doing so left the chamber expanded and would probably cause issues down the line. *But that's all I can do for now.* He needed the gun immediately.

Ignoring the shrieks and cries of the thrashing monster behind him, Vern turned back, and his heart that he'd just pacified broke into loud thumps again.

Three gruesome humanoids rushed at him from his right, their bodies charred and scarred, their maws so wide his skin prickled with fear.

Four on his left displaced the water, their trembling heads and eyeballs reminding him of their uncanny nature. Finally, two more came at him from the front, a maddening fervor in their deadened expressions.

He felt exposed and vulnerable, like prey in the sights of a predator. Still, he'd chosen this. He had no one but himself to blame.

Or to be proud if he survived.

The imbalance within his thought space that he'd come to ignore was firing at full force, too. Opening and closing his free palm, Vern waited.

Soon, the six from his front and left somewhat clustered together as they got closer.

Now!

His eyes flared with a white ring in each, and the six spirits halted in their tracks—their bodies resisting a water that turned as rigid as ice.

With a swift step, he dodged to the right and tightened his grip on the gun, trying his best to suppress the whispers in his mind.

Chomp!

The three from his right came at him, all at the same time. He ducked from one and shot at the second, but the third took this chance to swipe at his legs.

"Agh!" He screamed, not forgetting to kick the spirit back in its mouth while also using this chance to land a shot on the first one that was coming for round two.

Like ink dipping into the water, red blood blended into the cyan liquid, and his leg burned like hell.

With a sharp hiss, he jumped back and spent more of his rapidly dwindling representation and mental focus to close the wound.

To offset the expenditure, he reined in his perception and stuck it very close to himself, the grays only depicting the things that he actively stabilized.

Running out of representation just because he was wasteful with it would be a terrible mistake.

An acute pain surged through him as he felt the skin around the bite marks stretch and try to cover the flesh underneath.

Bang!

One shot. One down. More glass-like chunks fell from the sky and shattered in the air as the whole world unraveled.

While dodging and weaving, he speculated, *Killing these spirits is also affecting the stability of this realm.* Which made sense, given this world was probably a twisted representation of reality—propped up by the thoughts of all the spirits in here.

Not keen on wasting even an ounce of extra representation, Vern cut the size of the cluster he'd been stabilizing in half, and three more spirits rushed toward him as he finally nailed a bullet in the head of the one that had bit his leg.

Turning to face this new wave of enemies, Vern remained on the move and reloaded the ammo chamber of the gun another time, making the first bullet count.

Bang!

The pale maw that had opened wide enough to fit his whole head burst into gory bits and pieces with so much force it sent Vern's damp hair fluttering.

However, that's when two dangling arms wrapped around him, and a sharp pain exploded on his shoulder as his body was weighed down by something on his back.

Shit! He'd reined in his perception, so he wasn't able to "see" behind himself.

"Get the fuck off me!" he cried, barely keeping himself from falling over as he switched the gun to his other hand and pulled the trigger—its muzzle facing the head above his right shoulder.

Eahhh! It screeched, and the arms holding on to him fell limp. Yet before he could stop the bleeding or reorient himself, another one pounced.

Splash.

It opened its maw wide and chomped at his arm. Vern barely managed to stabilize the liquid wrapping around his hand in time, even missing a bit as sharp a few teeth punctured his skin.

His gun was still in the wrong hand, so he punched it instead. The boneless entity's charred face dented inward, yet it opened its maw again, aiming for Vern's head.

That's when he had an idea.

He narrowed his eyes and imagined a small knifelike shape in the water between his head and the entity. The light seemed to curve around the floating knife made out of stability, but the spirit didn't care and plunged right in.

The sheer momentum skewered the spirit's maw as the stably floating knife pierced right through its pale mouth.

His right hand snatched the gun back and rested its muzzle against the pale head as it still tried to bite Vern.

Bang!

He clenched his fist and stopped stabilizing the last cluster of enemies. Only three were left.

Hmm, they aren't very smart when their leader isn't in the mix. Their ferocity, on the other hand? He didn't even want to imagine what would've happened if all nine of them had attacked him at once.

This started with fourteen of them, but he'd slowly cut their numbers down.

He killed one right at the start, and then the child-monster "broke" another by throwing it at Vern. He'd managed one more before being surrounded. Then the monster had cannibalized two more, leaving these nine for him.

Six of which he'd already downed.

A determined light burned in his eyes as he stood back up and looked at the final three charging at him.

His leg was screaming in pain while his right shoulder burned. Blood flowed out of his left arm, but he let the wounds be and deepened his focus.

He was running dangerously low on representation. He had to save every ounce to go against the big one later. It clearly wasn't dead.

Eehhheeh!

Another bout of screams rang out as all three of them came at him from different angles, almost at the same time.

A little bit of trajectory calculation, and he moved his hand to follow the leftmost almost intuitively.

Bang!

And the shadow halted in its path. More chunks of glass dropped from the skies with another spirit's death, and the world became hollower.

That did it! However, he didn't have the energy or mind to rejoice as he dodged to one side, barely escaping the lunge of the second one.

This time, he expected the last one coming at him from the front and jumped, landing back with all his might.

He almost crushed its arms and a leg in the process, but that wouldn't end it. So he tamped down his foot on its neck and shot it right in the head.

Bang!

In that instant, however, a primal terror surged within him, and his body constricted just like last time.

A shadow loomed over him, and he felt a pressure build in the air as the hand above him raised high, primed to pummel Vern's head.

C H A P T E R 41

GOODNIGHT

Vern's knees felt weak, and the sense of impending doom settled over him. *What do I do?!*

He'd completely missed all the movement in the tussle, and his reined-in perception didn't help either.

If it was in the water, I could maybe stop it, but . . . this?

A sense of helplessness washed over him as he piled up contingencies after contingencies, even sparking the third rune in his mind. An uncertain death in that land was better than a certain death here.

Still, he wasn't about to give up just like that. He didn't bank on getting lucky like last time, but he'd found new ways to apply stability inducement—like that knife in the water.

Maybe the same would work in the air?

He instantly unleashed his perception, imagining layer after layer of sheets of stability above his head and beneath the corrupting, taut fist charged with too much tension.

And before he could do anything else, it launched—

"UNCLE! DIE!"

Sssss.

Vern hyper-focused and scrutinized every little change in stability as a muffled ripping sound came from above him.

They clearly slowed down the hammer-like fist to a degree, but his barricades were as flimsy as cloth in front of that menacing momentum. It wasn't enough. That fist would still turn him into pulp with a mere touch.

He sighed. Sending a wave of thoughts into the third rune, he looked at this world one last time—

Thump!

An unexpected sideward momentum launched him into the water—away from that rippling fist of death. His physical faculties came back to him almost instantly as the last mirror spirit prepared to devour his arm.

Unable to process how this could happen, Vern almost let the spirit rip him apart. In that last moment, his instincts kicked in, and he coated his arms with a layer of stability, followed by a quick shot to its head.

This . . .

A frown etched itself on his face as he frantically swam away. *What the hell is happening?* He didn't believe such timely interruptions by the spirits made any sense.

Not when the child-monster could command them as he pleased. Then what happened? Was he really just lucky?

Or...

His face gleamed in realization as he found a very satisfying answer to this conundrum. *It is Cedric! He's messing with the probabilities to help me out!*

That had to be it. Most other observational visions couldn't directly affect subjective entities like the mirror spirits. However, Cedric's visions worked on a higher concept that bound everything indirectly.

Was that music box situation also a side effect of his positive manipulation? But his joy at this revelation receded quickly as the ground trembled and the water rippled behind him.

"Mommy! Don't go!"

A conflicted feeling arose within him as those words seemed to resonate somewhere inside him. But he had to quash it.

His personal priority list put self-preservation above the well-being of a boy who was tainted by the subjectivity pollution to such a degree.

As much as he wanted to save everyone and everything in the world, he knew that he didn't have the capability to pull that off. *Not yet, at least.*

This also made him realize that he probably wasn't going to get any more help. Both times, Cedric had messed with the spirits, not the child-monster itself.

Given that all the spirits were finally out of the equation, it was just him and the boy.

Emerging from the water, he continued to sprint in this crumbling swamp as he cobbled together a plan to fight this monstrosity. *I need to watch out for that constriction.* That one ability almost led him to his demise not once but twice before.

Hmm, it walked up to me both times before using that skill. That was a pattern. There must be a range limitation.

He nodded. He just had to keep a little distance from the thing and he should be fine. *What else...?* He racked his brain, accounting for all the possible uses of his two visions.

"Come back!" it yelled, and Vern dodged out of instinct. A pale hand still struck him on the back as the headless body of a mirror spirit whizzed past him.

Vern's gait became unstable for a second, which he soon stabilized.

Wait!

This gave him an idea. *Instability before stability.* That was the tenet or rule or axiom that allowed him to deepen the shade of his perception.

Yet who said there were no more insights to be gleaned from that idea.

A plan soon shaped up in his head, and an excited gleam thrummed in his eyes. Yet when it was time to stop and fight the creature, a small part of him protested.

He was no fighter. Fundamentalists weren't made for battlegrounds. He wasn't supposed to be doing this.

If he escaped to the third rune, surely Vigil would come back sooner or later and clean this up, right?

Hah... he chuckled. That was a small part of him, a really tiny one. And he had to work, had to crush it into smithereens.

So he used his back leg to pivot around his front leg and transferred all the momentum elegantly, firing a shot in the general direction of the monster as he shouted, "Can you hear me, kid?"

It halted and used both its giant gnarly arms to shield the small boy inside its carcass. Vern's breath hitched when he saw the mangled skin of the child. His explosive shot had done a number on him.

"Mommy! Good. Uncle! Bad!"

He completely ignored Vern's words and came charging in again. Vern rapidly imagined a solid block in the path of one of its legs.

Yet his eyes twitched in pain as that giant leg smashed through his blockade without too much effort. Though it halted its advance and made the creature stumble, it was not enough for him to get a shot in.

Vern backpedaled as he rapidly adjusted his strategy. He had a very limited amount of representation left. If he kept wasting it on pointless ideas like this, he'd have no one but himself to blame when he ran out.

After running through all the scenarios in his mind, he narrowed his eyes, and a flame of determination burned within them. *Time to go all out.*

Completely ignoring the creature, he closed his eyes and perceived the liquid in front of him—something he could now assign grays to without any whispers.

"Instability inducement," he muttered.

The water in front of him stilled for the briefest of moments before a small ripple emanated throughout it. Then another . . . and another. Tens, hundreds, thousands of ripples soon turned into chaotic vibrations.

The water seemed to boil, but there was no heat. The height of the surface in front of him waned, yet more water surrounding it instantly claimed the lost land.

The speed at which the water disappeared far outpaced what filled the gaps. Soon the rugged ground underneath became visible, and a whirlpool formed around it.

Droplets floated in the air as steam churned all around Vern, who was standing in this world of glass that shattered more and more by the second.

Thump!

The world didn't stop for his visions. The creature rushed toward him, slamming its fist into the ground with each step, shouting, "Bad! Bad! Bad! Bad!"

The sense of instability within him exploded, and his primal instincts screamed at him to get the fuck out of there. But he held his ground and continued destabilizing the water.

More of it boiled without heat, and the cloud of steam became denser.

Just a bit more . . .

"Bad! Uncle! Mommy! Help! Please! Bad!"

The monster soon entered the periphery of his mist, but as if it knew Vern hadn't moved, it ran straight for him.

The tremors from the movement of the creature sent repeated pulses of terror coursing through him, but a smile stretched on his lips.

His actions had caused his insights in thought space to leap far, far ahead of the mental precipice he was standing on. Now, he just had to maximize the distance and land back safely.

Vern didn't budge, and the creature's grin widened when Vern didn't move at all. Excited like a child, it jumped and hopped, slowly approaching him like a predator did prey.

It was completely within Vern's range of attack, but he held on. *Instability before stability.* The worse it was, the better the results.

It completely ignored the lacking water underneath itself and happily grinned one final time, not even bothering to forcefully constrict Vern as it stretched its arms taut to crush Vern into a pulp.

Vern zoned in.

No care, no thoughts, no remorse—that was how an unattended child would act. Yet the consequences were real as the fists plummeted like twin meteors, ready to disintegrate him into nothingness.

Sigh . . .

"Stability inducement."

Whoosh!

A terrifying force manifested around Vern as all the steam surged in one direction, pulled toward the center by the pressure differential.

Steam condensed into droplets, and soon, a floating mass of cyan liquid encased everything in front of Vern, binding it with a terrifying force.

"Bwwad! Blub! Mwommiee! Help!" came muffled yelps as Vern finally opened his eyes.

Uncoiling the amulet of restoration on his palm, he rotated its knob, and a brilliant light shone out of it.

He brandished it toward the sinewy monster stuck inside the highly compressed ball of water. A small part of its body was still touching the ground, but there was almost a boundary between the water and the stabilized prison.

He'd destabilized way more water than this, but it seemed the stabilization had squashed it more densely when all the steam rushed back, making it more rigid than if he'd just stabilized the water in a straightforward manner.

Instability before stability. An interesting methodology, indeed. He nodded in understanding. It opened a new world of possibilities for his visions.

Something he'd have to experiment with later.

The rotten hands of the carcass enswathing the boy attempted to build momentum and break itself out of prison, but the encasement didn't budge one bit.

The light from the amulet of restoration mercilessly did its job—it burned away the rotten flesh as the carcass thrashed harder. Whenever it managed to break a small chunk, Vern forcefully stabilized it right back up.

"This is it," he whispered. Pulse after pulse of soothing stability surged within him, moving toward a crescendo, and his mind drifted away.

However, he soon shook his head, focusing single-mindedly on the monster. He would analyze the situation within his thought space later. He first had to ensure this was really over.

Veins bulged around his eyes, and a terrible throbbing wormed its way up to his head. Yet, his mind was somewhere else.

"Please . . ."

Vern shifted his gaze to the chest of that melting husk. The mangled torso of the boy, barely attached to its sinews, looked at Vern with his blue eyes, fear and innocence rippling within them.

He took his tiny, rotten, mangled hands and wrapped them around himself, curling into a ball.

Vern found it impossible to tear his eyes away, and something broke inside him. The sense of pity overwhelmed him, but he gritted his teeth and stopped his hand that was reaching to turn off the amulet.

However, he wasn't an extremist. It didn't have to be either utterly cold cruelty or naive kindness. He could balance this better.

Extending his perception in a straight line far beyond this entire mess, it reached the huge toy train and a music box. Spending what was left of his meager representation while leaving enough to maintain the bubble for a bit, he destabilized the music box's mechanism.

And in the next moment, that sweet humming began once again.

Mm-hmm, mm-hmm . . .
In moon's embrace, you find your rest, my dear
While stars above in silent watch do keep,
Dreams crystal clear in night's soft cradle here,
In tranquil seas, beneath the whisper deep.

Soon most of the grotesque carcass turned into red ash, spreading inside the water prison, and the boy floated in there, his corrupted skin slowly but surely evaporating due to the light of restoration.

"Mommy . . . please . . . help . . . please . . . please . . . please . . ."

Vern silently rested his head on the cold prison wall for a dozen more seconds, trying and failing to block out the pleas.

When the polluted carcass was completely gone, he couldn't handle it anymore and imagined a path inside the prison. Taking a deep breath, he entered with unfocused steps, his eyes tethered to the trembling boy.

Mm-hmm . . . mm-hmm

Each hum seemed to soothe the shivering child, and his eyes became clearer.

When night's dome sparkles with each twinkling light,
The mirror's grace reflects your smile so bright,

Vern's chest tightened with each syllable as he walked through the cold prison, ash filtering down on him as new cracks appeared in the otherwise stable sphere.

And as his slow steps led him underneath the boy, his thought space gave up—he was all out of representation.

Crack!

The prison shattered, and water rained down on him as the tiny figure fell amid the shower, still curled into a ball. Vern rapidly holstered his gun and spread his arms wide.

Catching the light body, he cradled it as the downpour soaked them thoroughly. The little thing shivered and gazed at Vern, its left body nothing but a mass of blackness that evaporated in the bright light.

Mm-hm . . . mm-hmm
In every star's glow, in every loving face,
My love for you, the sands of time can't trace.

Vern parted his lips to speak, but no words came out. The child looked up, his expression clearly etched in a mix of confusion and fear. His cheeks, once plump with youth, seemed to hollow out as the shadows crept over his skin, giving him a gaunt, almost ghostly appearance.

What was left of his left arm tried to struggle and claw at Vern, but the tiny right arm wrapped itself around his back as the boy leaned into his embrace.

"Pl . . . please. Don't . . . don't go," came a whisper, launching Vern's emotions into a whirlwind of conflict. As if to rain on his parade, the shattering mirrors in the skies reflected more scenarios.

So drift, my child, on dreams of sweet embrace,
Through silver streams that time cannot erase,

All of the mirrors shone the silhouette of a woman cradling a small baby, singing under the moonlight in myriads of situations.

In clouds that carry you to love's soft space,
Our bond, a mirror of eternal grace.

Winter, spring, summer, autumn, she never stopped, and the small baby in her arms almost always slept by the end of it with a smile.

With every syllable, the small thing in Vern's arms trembled, muffled sobs filling his ears. He tried. No, he was trying. He was trying so damn hard.

He could see it. No, he knew it. There was no coming back for this boy. With the negligible amount of representation left within himself, he perceived it.

The boy's right body—the uncorrupted half was porous, almost transparent in his perception. It was as if the boy had lost his innate representation.

That grotesque husk was what kept him alive in such a horrid state. The child didn't have an anchor to reality on the most fundamental level. So even if there was something that could heal his decaying body, it wouldn't keep him alive.

Even knowing all that, Vern's hand moved, and he rotated the knob of the amulet of restoration—turning it off.

In every gleam, in every gentle face,
My love for you, time's hands will never trace.

Yet as if noticing the change, the tiny hand clutched at his coat. "Unc . . . le, I . . . wanna—go . . . go to Mommy."

As if to convey his feelings, the falling mirrors all showed a single scene . . .

Mm-hmm . . . mm-hmm

A woman stood against the backdrop of a red moon by the river, holding the boy in her arms, when suddenly, the whole world shook, and he fell into the water.

When the small thing found its bearings, it turned around, only to find the woman missing—greeted with nothing but her clothes and a pendant floating in the water.

Mm-hmm . . . mm-hmm

The images shattered, and the child in his embrace hugged him tighter, those light sobs laying over top of the rhythmic melody.

"Wanna go to Mommy . . ." he repeated again and again.

When the sobs soaked his already drenched coat, Vern finally couldn't take it and gave in.

Turning the knob of the amulet again, he held the boy close, ignoring his left body's onslaught as the light rapidly ate at the corruption—reducing the child's agony but also his meager lifespan.

"Wanna go to Mommy."

Gently caressing the boy's frail back, he was reminded of how Mom used to do the same for him and Ari. Unsure and unfocused, he whispered, "Me, too."

Mm-hmm . . . mm-hmm
Mm-hmm . . . mm-hmm

The world continued to shatter, collapsing in and on itself as the mirrors passed right through Vern, and everything turned more illusory by the second.

The weight in his hands got lighter and lighter, and no matter how much he tried to wrap the tiny body in his embrace, he couldn't stop it from leaving.

Mm-hmm . . . mm-hmm

Thousands of jumbled memories played in the last of the mirrors, and all of them stopped reflecting her silhouette in a slow transition.

Like eyelids closing when heavy with sleep, the world turned dark, and his hands felt weightless as she whispered one final time.

Goodnight . . . my little one.

Chapter 42

AFTERMATH

A dizzying sense of vertigo claimed Vern as the darkness receded, and the glass continued to shatter around him.

The emporium's walls and interior came into his view, and his pupils quickly adjusted to the new light. The crackling of glass continued around him for a while longer as his body became whole with each crack, as if emerging out of that realm in steps.

"Huh . . . ? Vern . . . ? Kid?" Came a voice from his right.

Vern wiped away the water from his eyes before turning toward Cedric with what should pass as a smile on his face. "Thanks for your help in there, old man."

If Cedric could call him by a nickname, doing the same back to him should be fine, right?

Cedric stood there in his long, narrow hat, the nib of his pen resting on his book. His expression was frozen, and his forehead creased as he ignored Vern's words and asked, "Is it . . . over?"

Vern glanced down at his hands, cradling the only tangible proof of that child's existence—or was it his mother's? Lifting a pendant that dangled a small mirror on its end, he offered a more genuine smile. "It's over."

"Wahhhhh!"

"He's done it! By the eternal keeper, he's truly done it!"

Vern flinched as a tidal wave of clamor surged from behind, and when he turned, a sea of faces peered at him through the shattered remains of the emporium's glass walls. He didn't remember shattering them of his own will, but who knew what happened in reality while he was fighting in there?

The crowd erupted into an ecstatic frenzy, their cheers and shouts of gratitude merging into a harmonious cacophony that filled the air. "Savior! Savior!" they cried, their voices laced with reverence. Faces young and old beamed with a mixture of awe and relief as if witnessing the dawn after a prolonged night of darkness.

As he absorbed the joy and relief radiating from the crowd, the despondency that he was unable to shake toned down a tad. His mind, strung tight with tension, found a moment's peace, though a wave of weakness threatened to overtake him.

The feeling of emptiness coursed through his body, but the attention of so many people seemed to keep him aloft. He'd acted strong for so long, it would be such a waste to let it go now.

Thump,.

Cedric patted his back and sighed, shaking his head. "When the emporium went quiet, I really thought you were gone, kid. For good." Turning his gaze to the book, he added, "Even the numbers converged to infinity."

Vern didn't respond and just shook his head.

"Hah. Young'uns these days. You know it's gonna be hell to write a report for this, right?"

Vern shook his head. "I'm a little too young to know anything about reports, sorry."

"Our saviors! The chosen ones! We're indebted to ye, lordships."

That's when Cedric realized they were also cheering for him, and his face turned pale. He stumbled and inched behind Vern bit by bit, seemingly terrified. This reminded Vern of the situation, and his face heated up, too. What was going on?

Could he also back away like Cedric? Would that be a bad idea? The largest crowds he'd ever handled were at conferences, and even there, people indirectly cheered for his master, not for him. After all, most of the credit of an apprentice's invention went to their master. Yet all of these people were addressing him right now.

"Thank you, milords! Thank you!"

Umm . . . should I respond? After a bout of hesitation and indecision, he sighed. *I should handle them like any other crowd.*

Resting one hand on his chest, he pulled the tail of his coat high with the other and bent his rear leg before executing a gentleman's bow. "It was my honor to serve you good people. May Lady keep you all from harm's way."

"Oh my god! He's a believer too!"

"Lady bless us! May the keeper bless us!"

The crowd cheered another time, and Vern barely held his facial muscles from twitching. Cedric used Vern as a shield and hid behind him due to the lack of other furniture in close vicinity.

But that's when he felt another sensation in his thought space, and it seemed this final act on his part had concluded the changes it was undergoing. The feeling of alignment within himself was so soothing.

As he was lost trying to understand the change, someone in the crowd shouted, "Shut up, everyone! Don't you see milord is hurt?! You and you—go get some tinctures and bandages. You go bring back Simi from the bridge."

"Stop wasting time! Go!"

The shouts quickly turned into gasps as the crowd dissolved, and many ran back to their houses.

Cedric then whispered, "How bad are these injuries?"

He'd almost forgotten all about them due to the adrenaline. Almost. His shoulder was soaked with blood, and his arm was still leaking a profuse amount of blood. However, this reminder seemed to flare back all his pains.

Ugh.

"It's . . . manageable." But then he finally remembered to ask, "Hey, Cedric, is there something wrong with using my visions on myself?"

He didn't have the representation to do so right now, but he should soon have enough to patch up the wounds at least. However, he didn't know if it would be any better than normal medicine.

"Hmm, it's . . . complicated and differs on a case-by-case basis. However, a general rule is to only use visions that temporarily affect your body. Permanent ones can alter it in unintended ways."

Darn! His visions leaned more toward creating permanent changes in objects. *Fuck! I knew I shouldn't have used it too much.*

After giving a nod that acknowledged the crowd one final time, Vern limped over to a stool by the counter, put pressure on his arm, and asked, "What about healing visions, then? How do they work?"

Cedric pulled out a handkerchief and very carefully pushed on Vern's shoulder—adjusting its position based on Vern's reaction. Once settled, he answered, "Hmm, do you know about the famed Asea's Tears?"

Well, he more than just knew about it. He'd fought more than a couple of addicts who overdosed on it. So he nodded.

"Right. That's an example of why one shouldn't ingest materials that permanently alter one's body. They're a product of some high-shade vision that reconstructs the body based on the whims of the observer who materialized those tears."

"This is why most healing methods we've approved at Vigil temporarily alter your body's healing capabilities, not heal it directly. So it's the body that's doing the mending itself, not the vision."

"Ugh," he grunted. That made a lot of sense. A sinking feeling emerged as he recalled all the times he'd "stabilized" himself. *Did I mess up big-time, then?*

Gritting his teeth, he pulled up the right leg of his pants and pointed at the injury. "I used my vision to patch up this wound. Do you think I've permanently messed it up?"

Vigil already knew about his skills to a certain extent, and Cedric had seen all of them today. There was no point in hiding his skills for the sake of it. What if things got worse because he didn't seek help and wasted more time?

Cedric looked at his shin intently. Jagged teeth marks were clear to see, the skin around them a little purple. The old scholar rubbed his thumb at the sensitive skin, and Vern winced. The pain in the flesh underneath wasn't stabilized at all.

After a while, he answered, "It seems you've only patched up the skin. The flesh underneath is still torn and not forcefully healed. It should be fine if you're just suturing your skin with it. Especially if you aren't creating anything new and bringing together existing tissues."

Vern sighed in relief. His paranoia hadn't really been unfounded then. He'd been holding back because of similar suspicions, and it seemed he was right to do so.

It seemed he hadn't gone too far, and should be fine as long as he didn't "create" the flesh or skin. That was to say, as long as he closely stuck to using the fundamentals of structure and not creation, it should be okay.

It would limit him to only fixing minor wounds, but it was such an important tactic in the heat of the battle that he couldn't not use it.

Vern then asked, "Are we good to go back? I'd like to get it looked at by a professional at the Vigil." He remembered Captain Shinsei had mentioned an infirmary.

However, Cedric's face suddenly turned apprehensive. "Oh no. We still have to cleanse all the civilians of any remnant pollution."

"Couldn't you have done it a minute ago?"

"M-me?" He pointed at himself, but before Vern could nod, he continued, "No. No. that's not how it works. The protocol is to cleanse them individually. It has something to do with the amulet's effectiveness on mostly objective people."

"Soo . . . we have to stay here for a while?"

Cedric nodded amid heavy breaths. "I-I will have to. You should . . . you should go. You need rest. You've already done too much in my place today. I-I can't put this on you."

Vern struggled to keep himself from laughing. Social anxiety was one thing, but this was entirely something else. It looked like the man was getting ready to sacrifice himself for the cause or something.

After a while, Vern sighed. "I will be okay. I just need some time to regenerate my representation. Just handle them until then, okay?"

Cedric shook his head. "No. This is wrong. I will not listen to you another time. I can do this—"

"Milord," came the voice of the man from the first house, "Please let us help with your wounds. Simi right here used to be a nurse, and Hanni once fought in the war. He knows all about wounds."

Cedric stumbled back, his face only growing paler as the crowd reconvened with odd trinkets in their hands.

Vern smiled wryly and thanked the man who'd helped him since the start. However, he had more for him to do. "Can you help me with something else as well?"

He'd have to facilitate the individual cleansing of all the residents.

Vern bit the cherry cake that one of the residents had gifted him as the carriage towed them across one bridge after another. He eyed the bag full of these little trinkets they'd given him with a smile.

It felt . . . good.

Cedric was also curiously eyeing the pocket watch that someone had gifted him. And even that only happened because Vern was there to accept it on his behalf. The man was ready to escape the moment someone tried to talk to him.

Anyway . . .

Vern's body still hurt all over, but he finally couldn't hold back anymore. With some food in his system, he relaxed and peered inside his spherical thought space.

All it took was a single glance for him to realize that many new insights had populated his otherwise sparse octant of structure and a few more in upper southeastern—the one usually related to force. Yet, that wasn't the extent of the changes. All the insights seemed . . . more aligned.

He didn't need to hunt far to understand what these new insights could do. He just focused on the new islands of lights, and his perception unveiled itself.

He almost jerked back when the gradients he was so used to were taken over by something else. Many lines appeared in his surroundings, ranging in colors between black and white.

For a while now, he'd directly been using the balance between stability and instability to assign the grays to the objects around him. However, its biggest advantage was acting as a second vision rather than giving him some actionable information.

Other than that, he'd been able to see a vague harmony or discordance in the objects as well as fulcrums—both of which were far more useful than a plain balance of stability and instability. But this . . .

Vern brought his palms up to his eyes out of habit, even though he was perceiving them through his perception, not his eyes. Inside the hazy transparent outline of his hands ran lines that seemed to represent nerves—but were markedly different.

When he clenched and unclenched his fist, the shades of the lines at the joints brightened. Vern knitted his eyebrows as he tried to figure out what this could mean.

He brought up his other palm and compared both side to side—one clenched and the other unclenched. He swapped between these states for a while.

This actually reminded him of something. *I think I saw these lines back when I first shaded my perception in the land of dark sun.* Back then, they'd appeared for a while before fizzling away.

He shifted his focus to the carriage around him. It was also a transparent husk with varying colors adorning its surface. Lines ran along its edges, most of which didn't change their shades by much.

However, he noticed something interesting when he extended his perception to the wheels. Whenever the carriage ran over some ditch or uneven terrain, the curved lines representing the coiled springs of suspension turned brighter.

He looked at them for another minute and . . . Oh! A spark of realization jolted through his mind, and he understood what was going on. These are the stress lines of the structure!

That had to be it. A simpler way to put it would be tension in the structure, but stress lines were a more comprehensive look at this ability.

Feeling a little adventurous, he focused on the suspensions of the carriage, closed the bag of trinkets, held on to the handle overhead, and . . .

Stability inducement.

The coiled springs' lines turned dark as they released all the tension and became rigid.

Thud.

"Ah, what the hell!" yelped Cedric as he was jerked back onto the seat, crumpling his hat. He looked on in puzzlement and then shoved his head outside the window to see what caused the carriage to lurch so hard.

"What in the name of nine gods was that?" he asked, turning toward Vern.

"Yeah, that was weird," replied Vern with an innocent look.

Cedric side-eyed him for a while, but Vern acted nonchalantly, looking outside the carriage. Suddenly, his eyes saw something peculiar—a set of purple spherical lamps. He pointed at the building before asking, "Hey, Cedric, do you know this palace?"

The man grumbled under his breath for a bit before following Vern's finger. Narrowing his eyes, he answered, "That's one of the manors where no one survived the duskfall—an anomaly. Last I heard, Prince Akira had petitioned to cleanse it. It seems they have yet to get the permission to do so."

The moment the words hit Vern's ears, they triggered a cascade of thoughts, each more alarming than the last. *Wait, no. That can't be!*

CHAPTER 43

THE CONSPIRACY

Unlit purple lamps hung everywhere in that manor, the same ones that burned down Eleonora's archive. He didn't need to be up close to identify that peculiar frame—perfect for cyclical condensation.

His heart began to race, pounding against his chest as the pieces of the puzzle fell into place with chilling precision. The signs he had overlooked, the subtle hints that he had dismissed as mere coincidences, all pointed to a singular, terrifying truth.

This is how they targeted the people they wanted dead during duskfall!

The thought sent a shudder down his spine, the mere scope and insidiousness of the plot making him feel weak. It was a perfect crime with no evidence—all of it burnt down and buried beyond time itself.

The masterminds had to know everything about duskfall beforehand, including the reversal of time and that the dead remained dead forever, to plan such a targeted mass murder.

However, he soon snapped out of the panic. *No. I am being too hasty.* Yeah. It could be a coincidence that both these establishments used the same set of lamps. It didn't need to be a trend.

"Huh, is something the matter, kid?" asked Cedric, waving his hand in front of him.

"Oh, hah, nothing. I just saw some contraptions I thought were outdated long ago." Vern made excuses. He had no plans of speaking up about this matter directly.

Under no circumstances could he let it slip that he'd survived duskfall. It may seem like a thing of the past already, but if someone had indeed orchestrated this mass murder and Vern brought it to the light—

Another cold shiver ran down his spine, and he shook his head. *No. I can't let such a notion take root in my mind.*

Hensen's words back in the library suggested that his mistress had noticed him breaking the decree by trying to enlighten himself during the duskfall.

Who was to say they wouldn't get the wind of it this time? On top of that, the all-seeing surveillance method they used on Esther only further fueled his paranoia.

This is too big for me.

Luckily, Cedric wasn't the best at judging faces, or this would've become a problem. He wiped the cold sweat on his face and tried to ask something related instead. "Hah, how does one even flag these places as anomalies?"

"Well, it's just places where an unusual number of people died."

"Then, did Vigil ever find out what went wrong with them?" It was only natural to be curious about that, right? Not asking about it would be the odd thing.

Cedric shook his head. "Early on, we spent quite a lot of resources to try to figure this out, but after multiple failures, most of us came to an agreement that it wasn't worth the effort to solve a mystery about dead people. Not when so many more would die if we didn't spend that time more productively."

Vern couldn't argue with that logic. Yet, he wanted something more, so he pushed, "I see. Then, are we completely clueless?"

"I wouldn't say that. We have multiple theories based on the circumstantial evidence." Then he narrowed his eyes and added, "However, I can't share them with you. Not unless your clearance reaches the fifth shade."

Oh? Vern's expression sank as he rested his head on the window. "I . . . see."

Cedric extended both his arms. "Don't blame me, kid. These rules exist for your safety. Higher clearance information generally involves high-shade sequence observers, and you really don't want to be mixed with them."

Vern sighed and nodded. "I was just curious; don't worry about it."

The man spent a minute or so straightening his crumpled hat without taking it off before speaking up again. "However . . . the locations of these places are public information. So, if you're really interested, we can stop by some of them right now."

Vern's eyes shone. *I guess dealing with all those residents on his behalf wasn't in vain.* Not letting all his excitement creep into his expression, Vern replied with a balanced amount of enthusiasm, "Yes, that would be great. We don't even need to stop by, I just wanna see them from afar."

"Hmm, we can always go some other time, you know?" He eyed Vern's bandaged shoulder, which had a bit of red seeping into it. "Your wounds aren't completely healed."

Vern shrugged. "It's fine. The pain's almost gone, anyway." It wasn't.

Repositioning his hat, Cedric shouted, "Mr. Driver, can we pass through the intersection of Marshal Street and Agatha Road?"

"Yes, sir!"

Vern entered the Vigil alongside Cedric, a solemn expression on his face. He was right. He was more than fucking right!

They passed by ten different locations—a couple of them cleansed, but those that weren't all had Rupert's sphere as their primary source of light. Not one or two, but each and every one of the locations.

The implications were more than obvious to Vern. Someone had popularized and supplied Rupert's spheres to the demographic they wanted dead during the duskfall. If he remembered correctly, fundamentalists and modern nobles were the earliest adopters of that mechanical wonder.

Fundamentalists were simple creatures, really. They adored efficiency, and this sphere was the very pinnacle of the notion. Even his master had ordered a dozen for their lab. He wondered if it was good luck that there weren't enough in stock back then. That was the reason he tried to steal one from Eleonora's archive—for research.

This . . . Is this why most fundamentalists died during the duskfall? The mere thought disgusted him. But he knew it made sense.

Most of the establishments they'd been to were hosting parties and gatherings for the fundamentalists who had congregated in Elmhurst from all around the world for the annual conference.

After all, nobles were the primary employers of fundamentalists. Some, like his master, performed independent research that sent waves throughout the world.

But most of his kind were dependent on nobles to fund their projects and help them make a name for themselves. Many fundamentalists even joked about aristocracy being their banks and whores.

Obviously, these nobles were also the ones who'd benefitted the most from such a relationship. If they bet on the right person at the right time, they might become shareholders of a technology that could make them more money than kings of some small countries.

Yet all that is now gone. He sighed.

So many great minds—dead because someone decided to play god. *No, play devil, really.* At least the "god" gave them a chance to survive the duskfall. This devil, however, snatched even that opportunity and stabbed them in the back. Killed those who had the highest odds of surviving this nightmare.

He'd analyzed this against all the information he had. Hensen's Aetheric Collective was a potential culprit, but there was no solid evidence to back up that claim. Yes, they'd come for him, but it wasn't because he was a fundamentalist. They wanted him dead because he'd managed to enlighten himself through objectivity.

In his subtle attempts to highlight these parallels to Cedric, he was met with no response. Why? Because there were dozens of other minor similarities.

Most of these villas and banquet halls also have other common features like heating systems, pipes, grills, chimneys, and whatnot. They were such mundane aspects of architecture that no one would think twice about them, at least not as the scythe of a cunning reaper.

This only hammered home the treacherousness of this large-scale scheme in Vern's mind. It was hidden in plain sight, yet it had stripped the planet of its sharpest minds.

As far as he remembered, Sterling Rupert, a famed fundamentalist, made these spheres. Someone who was supposed to present on this sphere's intricacies at that fateful conference. He didn't know much about the man.

Guess it's time to dig up all there is about him while being discreet. It would be risky to chase the direct leads, but information about a fundamentalist should be mundane enough to find in unmonitored archives.

"Kid."

"Oh, yes?"

"Remember to submit that perceptual artifact for inspection as soon as possible."

Vern looked back in puzzlement. "What perceptual artifact?"

Cedric looked at him like he was some idiot. "The pendant. The pendant you brought back from behind the mirror."

"Oh? That's an artifact?" he blurted, excitement coloring his voice.

Cedric opened his mouth only to stop and shake his head. "Just go and submit it right away. You can collect it later if it is safe and doesn't need to be suppressed in the whispering repository. If not, you'll be compensated equally."

Whoa! Why didn't Cedric tell him this during their ride?

He pulled out the pendant with a small mirror hanging on its end. However, that's when he remembered something important. His eyes snapped toward the clock hanging by the wall, and his mind whirled.

"Fuck! It's already half past three. My training starts at four!" he blurted. He was tired as hell, but he wasn't going to miss even a single day of the training if possible!

So he looked at that pendant with a gaze of longing before thrusting it into Cedric's hand. "Can you please submit this on my behalf? I need to drop by the infirmary quickly before my training session starts."

"Wait—" Cedric couldn't even respond before Vern shouted while running off.

"I'll check it out later!"

"No, Master Vern, you'll have to rest for the day."

"But—"

"I'll go inform Lady Amelia. She was with Master Akira last I saw." And before Vern could protest any further, De Flanc left with a bow and closed the door on him.

Vern sighed. Not knowing where the infirmary was, he found De Flanc instead, only for the man to send him back to his room while he handled everything.

"Ow," he cried as a doctor in a plague mask and black robe shone a green lamp on his leg. He felt something squirm in his wound, but he held on.

Soon, the doctor moved over the green light to his shoulder, his right arm, and finally above his head.

Whoa . . . a sense of serenity washed over Vern as the dull heaviness that had settled down in his head was slowly soothed away. And then, right before the drowsiness was about to claim him, the doctor turned off the lamp and walked away.

Huh? That's it?

"Wait, Doctor." They stopped. "Am I healed? Then can I go for the training?"

The doctor latched the lamp to their belt and rummaged through a pouch hanging on the same strap before pulling out a small device. Vern squinted to figure out what it was, but suddenly, out came a deep booming sound. "No!"

Vern involuntarily picked up the pillow next to him in defense. *What the hell is that?* Soon, however, he shook his head and tried to communicate another time. "So am I healed or not?"

The doctor clicked on the contraption again. "No!"

Vern recoiled, almost wanting to plug his ears. It was too freaking loud. Yet he attempted one final time, "I see, doctor. Then can I train tomorrow?"

The doctor rummaged through the pouch once again, only to pull out another tiny thing. "Yes!" it boomed.

Not letting the bewilderment show on his face, Vern smiled and responded, "I . . . see. Thank you, then. Have a great day."

They pulled out a third contraption. "Okay!" They walked out of the room, closing the door behind them.

"What the hell was that?" he murmured, adjusting into a better posture. De Flanc really pulled through for him by arranging all this.

Soon his eyes landed on the clock, and he let out a sigh. It was already ten minutes past four. *I wonder how Mistress Amelia feels about this.*

His eyes felt heavy, and before he knew it, everything was dark.

Knock knock.

Chapter 44

A CAUTIOUS PROPOSAL

Huh?" Vern rapidly blinked and noticed it was already seven in the evening. Shaking his head, he pushed himself up on the bed only to feel a jolt of pain in his shoulder.

Ignoring it, he shouted, "Please come in. The door's open."

Click.

Light seeped in from the doorframe as the figure of a woman entered the room. He rubbed his bleary eyes and realized who it was. He greeted her first, not burdening her to start the conversation. "Good evening, Mistress. My apologies for skipping class today. I wanted to come in, but—"

She waved her hands, and Vern took the cue to stop. Pulling the chair from the desk, she sat, folding one leg over the other. Finally, pulling down her face shield, she asked, "How're you feeling?"

A part of him wanted to continue spouting boastful nothings. However, he disregarded any such notions and answered honestly, "Tired." Sighing, he continued, "Far more tired than I initially thought I'd be. It really drained me far too much."

Mistress nodded. "Mm-hmm, rest. Your injuries seem to be healing quite well already." However, she shook her head. "Besides that, did you commit any grave mistakes today? Something that could've gotten you killed?"

Hmm . . . Vern slipped into a thoughtful silence, seriously reflecting on the whole process. He didn't expect her to ask that. After rubbing his chin for a while, he responded with measured words, "Many, actually."

Vern recounted all his mistakes in a concise manner, including every time he was unable to adapt to the ever-changing nature of his enemies and both the times in the mirror world when he could have died if not for Cedric.

Mistress ran her fingers on the flat of her scythe's blade as she sat there in silence, listening to Vern ramble.

Obviously, he didn't talk about any of his contingencies. Not that it would be a good idea to reflect on his mistakes with those in mind anyway.

Once he was done speaking, she sat up straighter and looked him in the eyes. "What you described aren't mistakes, but indicators and consequences."

She then raised one of her index fingers. "Your first oversight was the lack of a lethal and surefire countermeasure against multiple enemies. I can't help you with your visions for this, but I can definitely teach you better crowd control."

Vern nodded seriously.

"Second," she said, raising another finger, "you rely too much on your perception to inform you of your surroundings. Which is to say your situational awareness is quite poor. You've already seen how you're essentially blind once you're low on your representation."

Vern winced but still agreed. These comments were true. This wound on his shoulder was essentially a product of just that—not anticipating the enemy behind him.

Raising another finger, she said, "Third and final. You don't have enough combat experience. What you managed is already a miracle, and you should be proud of yourself. Yet don't forget that your enemies will always be ever-changing. The only surefire method to increase your odds of winning is to have more experience under your belt."

The words resonated deeply with Vern, and he nodded, already a little fired up. *Should I ask for more lessons right away?*

Mistress Amelia stood. "We can fix that over the next week." But then, suddenly, the aura around her turned impenetrable, and she asked in a calm tone, "Now, have you made a decision?"

Ah, right. She's talking about the infusion of old blood. He knew this was coming, yet he was still a little hesitant.

Vern collected his thoughts and took a deep breath. With rehearsed precision, he began, "After considerable thought, Mistress, I've come to a decision, albeit a complex one. So please pardon my unlearned self if I'm overstepping my boundaries, but I would like to make a request." He trailed off, seeking any hint of reaction.

She stared at him with one of her eyebrows raised for a couple of seconds before giving an almost imperceptible nod.

Hah, reasonable as always!

Wetting his lips, he spoke, "If I may, I'd like to humbly suggest a cautious progression with the blood transfusion process. Given my deep commitment as an observer and the significant strides I've made on my viewpoint—a path not chosen lightly and one fraught with too many trials—it's paramount for me to integrate this new experience with utmost care."

His heart jumped with every word, and he had to work hard not to cower due to her lack of reaction. *But I can't stop either. This is important.*

So he added, "This way, I hope to safely navigate any potential conflicts with the insights I've developed. Would it be possible to tailor our approach, allowing me the flexibility to pause or discontinue the infusions if they seem to move me away from my core values and the hard-earned progress in my journey?"

With all that out of his system, he exhaled deeply and waited.

Seconds turned into minutes, and his nervousness began to shoot through the roof. *Did I ask something taboo? Was I too blunt? Damn. Should I try again?*

However, before he could gather the courage to speak up again, she sighed, latching her scythe back into the holster. "Sorry, Vern, but it's not something I can decide for you. The court handles all decisions on subjugation art as a collective. Especially something that may require them to make an exception to the recruitment rules."

Vern fidgeted under the sheets. "Am I asking for too much?"

"Hmm, there's precedence of something similar being approved, but the personage in question was quite a character. Anyway, I'll try to summon the court as soon as possible. The last one was just yesterday, so it'll be a while before I have an answer for you."

"..."

Vern didn't know what to say. If possible, he'd have liked a solid answer right away to plan accordingly. But, well, he was the one making demands here. It was already a miracle that she didn't outright disown him for favoring her competitors.

So he rested his hand on his chest and bowed his head. "My thanks, Mistress. I hope I am not wasting your time by having you train a candidate who may or may not be able to help the Kingsly Court."

Adjusting her hat, she turned and added, "Don't worry about it. I'm first a citizen of this empire, then a court member. It's your first day, and you've already done more good than most others with power. Keep it up, and I'll find someone else to train for the court on the side if need be."

Click.

"I will . . ." Vern said to empty air as he fell back on the bed.

She is so nice! He had difficulty reconciling her behavior just now with the reaper he'd seen on the bridge.

He held his palm high in the air and reflected on his recent experiences. A serene feeling washed over him, and for once, he felt . . . at ease with himself.

He'd finally made progress in so many aspects of his life. His understanding of observation had deepened significantly, and it wouldn't be an exaggeration to say he had figured out his own path forward. He now even had certain leads on Ari's and Hensen's whereabouts. To top this all off, he had a great teacher, an organization backing him, and driven people all around him.

Most important of all, he felt alive again. Five days by himself in the hotel hadn't done him much good. Not when he'd had so much rage and questions bubbling within him. This . . . however, was what he wanted with life. For now, at least.

To continue working toward that ethereal balance.

Hah! He heaved, getting up and heading for the bathroom. He needed a shower. The water back in the mirror realm wasn't even real, after all.

As hot water pelted his body, the soreness of his muscles slowly fizzled away, but he was more focused on the lines all around him. A plethora of straight paths depicted the water pipe and how its structure ran beneath the floor tiles, too.

However, it cut off a little distance away, and his knowledge of the piping routes in the Vigil was nowhere near enough to extrapolate it with high confidence. Yet the shades and distribution of just these lines were very interesting.

The stream inside the pipes was a line of its own, but the moment it split into droplets at the showerhead, they disappeared from his perception. *Almost as if there's a threshold of how much tension a structure should have before it can be perceived at all.*

When he turned off the faucet, the stream inside the pipe turned brighter, signifying more tension stored within it. *Hah . . .*

Wrapping a towel around himself, he exited the steamy bathroom and looked at the lines on his arms. They were the same. Clutching his fists or straining for a punch, they all turned the veins inside his body brighter.

Hmm, what if— His eyes narrowed as an interesting idea blossomed in his head.

He took on a fighting pose, a mix of the footwork he'd learned yesterday and stances from pictures he'd seen in high-society magazines. With his fists and arms held in front of him, he flexed his muscles, and the lines in his perception at those points brightened.

He drew back his left arm for a punch, straining as much as possible while ensuring it didn't hurt. Then he took these bright lines and imagined . . . *instability inducement.*

Oof. He flinched, his hand jerking closer to his body on its own as a powerful force surged within his hand. He remembered Cedric's words. It was generally acceptable to use visions that temporarily affected the body.

As he'd seen throughout the day while testing it on other objects—including the carriage's suspension—stabilizing or destabilizing the tension of these stress lines was a temporary affair. He had to actively spend representation if he wished to keep them tenser.

So with his left hand held taut using the vision, Vern ripped a paper with his right hand and flicked it upward in the air. His eyes glowing with white rings, he zoned in on the paper like a hawk, and the moment it dropped down to shoulder height—

Whish.

His hand shot from his side in a blur. He paired it with the stability inducement when it was mere inches away from the paper, instantly releasing all the tension.

Paaa.

Unable to dodge Vern's attack because of its inertia, the paper fronted his attack directly, and the fist tore a huge hole as the hollowed sheet ran up his arm like a shackle.

"Ow!" he yelped, supporting his left arm with the other. *That hurt, damnit.* It was almost as if he'd sprained his otherwise healthy left shoulder. But then he caressed the paper wrapping around his hand, almost all its edges folded in the direction of his attack.

That was clearly a lot of force.

"Hahaha . . ."

Vern froze on the spot, unable to comprehend this sudden laughter. It wasn't him. He hadn't laughed. Still, it didn't seem to come from outside the door, either. He walked up to the room's small window and looked beyond the glass, only to find nothing.

Frowning, he murmured, "No way I hallucinated that, right?" He narrowed his gaze and looked around before rubbing his left shoulder and switching his perception to the simple balance of stability and instability.

He unleashed it all around him, and grays exploded out with him as the center, mapping the shape of the walls, tables, carpet, and whatnot when suddenly, it failed to map the large mirror in the room.

His expression instantly turned grave as his hand reached for Duality sitting atop the closest table. Barely holding it upright with his somewhat injured hands, he slowly approached the exit.

As much as he denied it, he needed all that rest. He was in no shape to fight right now. *Why the hell are these mirrors not leaving me alone?*

However, the moment he reached in the line of sight of the mirror—

CHAPTER 45

VOYEUR

A face looked back at Vern, and he yelled, "What the fuck, Irene!?"

"Hahaha." Her eyes curved like crescent moons as her giggles rippled in his room. "Eh?" But her movements suddenly turned stiff, and she demanded after a pause, "Hey, stop looking at me."

Vern stared at her, dumbfounded. She wanted him to do what? Not sure if he should be angry or laugh at this, he responded, "What are you even saying? *You* stop looking at me! What the hell are you doing inside a mirror?"

"That's the thing! I can't stop looking?"

"W-why?"

"I can't move."

"Why?"

"Argh! Stop asking questions and just look away for a second."

"No! This is my room. You tell me what the hell is going on."

"Hey, I was just testing out this artifact you brought back today. How am I supposed to figure out what it does if I don't use it?"

"What's that got to do with peeping on me?"

"That's what it does! And it seems the user's frozen if someone looks back at their image." Then her face flushed red. "Now look away! I am getting embarrassed here."

"Hey, I am the one that should be embarr—" Then it suddenly clicked, and Vern looked down. A horrified expression emerged on his face as he bolted toward the bathroom, dropping Duality outside.

"Hahaha."

After combing his damp hair back, he folded the cuffs of his shirt and walked out of the bathroom. He first looked into the mirror only to find it reflective as usual—no woman with silver hair laughed at him this time. Soon, however . . .

Knock knock.

Vern walked up to the door and opened it with a deadpan expression, towering over the tiny Irene, who was dressed in a delicate white dress with a high lace collar and puff sleeves that kissed her wrists.

A neatly tied bow accentuated her waist while the ruched and laced bodice hugged her figure softly. Above this ensemble, her frost hair—short this time—cascaded along either side of her face, her ears adorned by the same thin earrings he'd seen before.

She looked back at him like a guilty child, tapping her index fingers against each other. Vern tried hard not to let it show on his face, but he was quite taken aback by the massive shift in her overall aesthetic.

Compared to her messy poncho and artistic look last time, this felt . . . noble? He'd seen her in the mirror just a second ago but was far too occupied to notice any of her beauty.

Still, he narrowed his eyes and harrumphed. "Here, I thought you didn't know how to knock."

Her fingers tapped each other faster and faster as she wet her lips and replied, "I-I was going to knock back then, you know. You were just so . . . focused. I didn't want to break your concentration."

Vern raised his chin and continued to look down on her. "No, you shouldn't have even attempted to peek through my mirror without asking for permission beforehand."

She pouted. "Hey! I didn't know what this pendant did either, okay? It just showed me a bunch of mirrors, and I picked yours. How am I supposed to know that fire burns if I don't touch it?!"

Vern wanted to point out the flaw in that argument, but he shut up and sighed. It did seem like a string of honest accidents.

After half a minute of his intense glare meeting those seemingly innocent eyes, he shook his head and opened the door, welcoming her in.

"Heh. So easy . . ." she mumbled.

"Did you say something?" Vern countered, blocking her path. She walked right into him, headbutting his shoulder.

She struggled not to laugh. "No. No. Must be the wind."

"Thought so . . ."

Not locking the door to avoid any misunderstandings, he turned back. That's when she suddenly ran up to his bed and ducked down, picking up a circular paper cutout from the ground.

Caressing it gently, she lamented, "Poor thing. How much must it hurt to be punched by a naked brute." She placed it tenderly on the bed, crouched down, and rested her chin close to the paper, cooing, "There, there . . . It's going to be okay."

Vern's face flushed red, but he knew this would become a one-sided beating if he didn't counter swiftly. He approached the mirror with exaggerated tenderness. "Oh, the horror you've endured today. Assaulted by a voyeur, and not just any, but a shamelessly perverse one. How deeply I wish I could make it better."

"Hey! I am not perverse."

"Yes, you are."

"No—"

"You didn't need to break my concentration there. Instead of watching me unannounced, you could have just backed out."

She suddenly stood upright and countered, "Did you know it snowed today? I forgot to bring my cardigan for the tea party, and they decided to host it outside under an umbrella."

" . . . "

She wrapped her hands around herself and shivered in an exaggerated fashion. "I was so cold the whole time! You know what they did? Tried to offer me a red shawl. Red! I'm wearing white, for Lady's sake."

Vern opened his mouth to speak, but she shut him down. "Not just that. Now that I am back, I have more work to do. Make it make sense!"

He sighed. He may have won the battle but lost the war. She was too good at controlling the flow.

"And, now that we're talking about work, here you go." She threw the mirrored pendant toward him out of the blue, and Vern rushed to catch it.

"You already know what it does—peep—and its limitations—can't move if you get caught. However, there's another aspect. At first, it consumes your representation, but if you use it for too long, it chomps away at your very singularity." She smiled innocently. "So, don't. Peep. For. Too. Long."

Vern rubbed at the cracked glass and rebutted after she was done with her innuendos, "Just how long did you watch me to have figured that out?"

"Haha, you're so funny, Vern." She faux laughed, hiding the smile behind her gloved hand. "We're talking about work, okay? Work. You've got to act more professional around me."

Not wishing to be swept up by her pace, he settled down on the other end of the bed and asked something unrelated, "Did you even get enough sleep today?"

If he remembered correctly, she hadn't slept the whole night and only went to bed around eight in the morning. If she had already been to a party and back at eight in the evening, how long did that leave her?

"Huh? Is it that obvious?" She walked up to the mirror and watched her face from all angles, especially the eyes. "Ugh! It's not. Don't try to be cheeky, you towel boxer!"

Hah. A piece of him died hearing her call him that. Yet, he remained impassive, for showing her even a smidgen of vulnerability right now might please her too much. Then what if she decided to always call him by that name?

No . . . He shuddered internally.

"Okay, Irene. You win. I will make sure not to tell anyone that you watch naked men alone in their rooms. Now, what else did you want to talk about?"

"Ugh, I guess I also have to inform you about a couple more things. So, the pendant you brought back is a second-shade perceptual artifact. Which means you fought and won against an enemy equivalent to a second-shade observer."

Then she rested her hands on the wide mirror's counter and leaned back. "You know what that means?"

Vern just tilted his head.

"It means you probably won the fight by boxing in a towel *and* already have enough contribution to apply for the confidentiality ritual. Ugh, it even sounds weird as I am saying it. You've only been on two missions, and one of them wasn't even assigned to you. How can you already be fit for the ritual? What a broken scammy system."

Oh? That sounded good. His simple brain was more than happy to see the number of shades in his gem go up. *Better my gemstone than nothing, I guess.*

"Great. When can we get it done? Also, why does it sound like you're jealous? Bet you only defeated a second-shade enemy when you were third or something."

"I see, I see. Injured one-shade amateurs who didn't even know about observation records until yesterday really think they're the best, huh? Come fight me when you're third shade so I can bully you as a fourth-shade observer."

Vern's eyes glinted with curiosity, and he leaned forward. "You already have four shades in your perception?"

"Not yet." Her lips curved upward. "But soon."

However, at the next moment, her eyes narrowed to slits. "Anyway, we're not buying cabbages from a farmer's market, okay? The ritual only takes place on certain dates. You can go check out the schedule for the next one."

Vern shrugged. He already had many directions to work toward at the moment. He didn't mind if this ritual would be a while.

"Alright." she dusted her hands and walked toward the exit. "Final thing. If you don't like this artifact, you can try to replace it with something more suitable at the resource allocation hall."

"Mm-hmm . . ."

She then slumped her shoulders and whined, "There's moreee work."

"Hope it drowns you," replied Vern with a sweet smile.

From outside the door, she pouted and gave him a sharp stare. "Mean."

"Goodnight, Irene. Do get some sleep today."

Her face instantly lit up, but he couldn't watch it for long as she slammed the door closed. Then from outside, he heard, "Goodnight, Vern. Get better soon."

The room turned dark, and Vern relaxed. Hoisting his legs up the bed, he mindlessly fiddled with the pendant with a smile etched on his face. Chuckling to himself after a while, he shook his head and perceived the pendant in his hand.

The moment he did so, vague, blurry, and frozen images showed up in his mind. They were all around him, including one right in front of him—his own room's mirror.

However, he quickly stopped perceiving the artifact and backed out of its world. He had no intention of trapping himself in a loop where he saw himself through the mirror using the artifact, but his eyes were also looking back at it.

Would he be stuck forever, then? Maybe not. But at least until someone else helped him out of it. *Yeah, no. I am good.* He also didn't want to be like Irene and peep into random people's rooms without permission.

He'd rather not be known in the Vigil as a voyeur. So he would try later with a more controlled situation.

Shaking his head, he rested the artifact on the table next to the bed and opened its drawer to pull out his insight sphere.

It had been a while since he delved into the fundamentals. Unfortunately, doing so didn't induce new insights to blossom in his thought space.

Hmm, maybe it's because I am not pushing into uncharted aspects?

Holding the sphere on his chest like some corpse gripping a seraph effigy inside a coffin, he lay down and closed his eyes.

From inside the void of initiation, he felt all around before picking a direction and letting his mind flow.

Vern cracked his neck another time as he put together many parts laid out on the workbench. The lamp's light spilled down on gears, brackets, and cranksteel stripes as he compared the measurements with his diagram occasionally.

He was no seamster, so he'd decided to make the sheath he'd use to strap Duality on his back out of cranksteel rather than some random metal or fabric. This ground-up approach to making a contraption was his style as a mechanical artist.

And was it going to be a fine piece. He'd planned the design to maximize Duality's synergy with him. It might not turn out better than something the Finnesse workshop could produce, but it would definitely be leagues above riffraff sheaths.

Unfortunately, he had to spend a big chunk of his saved-up contribution points for all this cranksteel. *Well, it's worth it.*

Every once in a while, he used stability and instability inducement, trying to incorporate them into his routine wherever possible.

Being able to see the fulcrums and stress lines made his job far more effortless, avoiding a lot of iterative fixes he usually had to perform to get his contraptions functioning right.

Minutes turned into hours as he assembled one puzzle piece after another for the contraption. It was directly inspired by the sheath used for the ember edge by Kingsmen. Except it didn't include any heating capabilities, not that he needed them anyway.

The side-release mechanism would allow him to slide Duality out from either hand—combined or one blade at a time instead of pulling it upward like a barbarian.

One couldn't forget about the magnetic locks and aligners. Then there were the straps that would distribute the weight on his back as evenly as possible without hindering his movements too much. He'd used some of the blueprints lying in Vigil's workshop to make things easy for himself, but with a little work, it became a perfect match for his needs.

Grabbing the welding mask and blowtorch, he got to assembling all the little pieces together.

Phew . . .

Wiping the sweat off his face, Vern quickly cleaned up the workbench and picked up the sheath—making sure it wasn't hot anymore. It didn't look very aesthetic since he had yet to polish and paint it, but damn, was he running low on time.

The pocket watch showed three. *Only an hour before today's training.*

Yeah, he could make it look better next time. It didn't matter as long as it was functional anyway. Because of Duality's crazy length, he really needed the sheath as soon as possible. It would be a nightmare to carry it around otherwise.

This was the only way for him to have Duality with him in dire situations without being stupidly awkward the rest of the time. One reason he didn't take it with him on the mission yesterday was inconvenience, after all. Such annoying factors had to be taken care of as soon as possible.

The final product was more like a sheath attached to a harness. The scabbard itself was engineered as a semi-open containment unit for a longsword, featuring a unique frame structure on one of its planar surfaces.

This frame was integrated with a series of inward-tilting, one-way latches that facilitated a rapid, secure sword placement mechanism. Upon contact, the blade would automatically align and lock into position by these precision-engineered latches.

Furthermore, the sheath incorporated the side extraction mechanical art similar to Kingsmen's. This was achieved through strategically positioned, elongated extrusions operating on a one-way slide mechanism designed for lateral sword release.

Donning both straps of the harness and tightening them around his healed shoulders, he picked up Duality. He simply held it by the merged hilt behind himself, hovering it around the scabbard's opening.

The moment he nudged it inside the sheath, he felt the sword pulled by the magnetic force, only to snap in with a satisfying *click*. Its weight was evenly distributed around his torso as he stretched while wearing it.

Hmm, maybe I can modify the straps to be more rigid next time. Jotting down possible improvements in his notepad, he checked the room one final time before heading out of the mini workshop.

Unfortunately, it was mostly empty, and no one was there to keep it maintained anymore. Clearly, Vigil had no Fundamentalists around to make full use of the facility.

Sighing, he walked out, trying to get used to the weight and always seeing Duality's handle in his periphery.

After a while, however, his steps became light, and he was more than just gratified by this contraption. *It's incredible, really!*

Then, suddenly, came a voice. "Hey, man, what's with that little sword you got there?"

C H A P T E R 4 6

GOSSIP

Vern looked back only to clamp his eyes shut. *Why?! Why would anyone willingly wear such an abomination of an outfit?*

Vern let out a deep sigh and did his best not to cringe. Lucian carried a majestic great sword on his shoulders, which somehow didn't seem off alongside his thin frame. But those clothes? Yeah, they disgraced that great sword's elegance and the man's otherwise handsome face.

He wore a vibrant green-and-yellow-checkered coat adorned by purple accessories that made Vern want to never open his eyes again.

Lucian noticed Vern's stare, and a smiled blossomed on his face. "Hey, you're literally dripping jealousy. It's okay. You can stop. If you really want one, I can have my tailor make another one for you."

Vern smirked, held back the scathing remarks that were dancing on his tongue, and shook his head before switching this terrifying topic. "Imagine having a sword so long you can't even sheathe it."

Lucian matched his strides and rebutted, "Hey! I asked Master Osric about it. There are a couple scabbards for this one in the market. I just . . . don't have the money."

Vern quirked his eyebrows. "Didn't you get the salary yesterday alongside the gem?"

Lucian scratched his blonde hair awkwardly. "Eh, that was yesterday."

"So?"

"It's gone."

"How?"

"Beauty doesn't come cheap now, does it?"

No. I can't! It's rude! Vern chided himself, but his hand didn't listen, and he facepalmed. *Ugh!* However, he managed to play it off as wiping his forehead, and he chuckled nervously. "Haha, right. Good for you." Not waiting for the man to start again, Vern pushed on, "Anyway, how are you carrying that thing around so easily? Is it a replica or something?"

Lucian replied, a frown on his face, "What do you mean? Aren't you feeling stronger too?"

Ah. Realization flashed across Vern's face as he nodded. "So you accepted the first infusion already?"

"Heh?" Lucian looked at him like he'd seen a dead rat. "You didn't?"

Vern shook his head.

"Why?"

"I am still weighing the options."

"Yeah, but why?"

Then suddenly came another voice, saving Vern from having to explain his rationale to the brute who had wasted all his money on such an outfit.

"Hey, how're you doing, Lucian?" said a tall man wearing a sophisticated white vest that suited his slim frame and intelligent eyes as he patted the brute on the shoulder.

Hmm, I have seen him before. Vern stressed his memory and quickly realized he was one of the people he'd eavesdropped on before Captain Akira's speech. This was the one who didn't want to miss out on being one of the founders of the Vigil.

If Vern remembered correctly, his viewpoint was related to weaving lights or something. He'd seen the man playing with glowing lights on his fingers.

As they walked through the gilded corridor toward the dining hall, Vern was content to listen in on their perfunctory conversation.

Soon, however, he got pulled into it, too, as the light-weaver looked at him and asked, "And how might I address you, gentleman?"

Vern followed the etiquette of greeting between equals by dipping his head a notch and responded with a smile, "Name's Vern. How about you?"

"Ah, right." He clicked his tongue. "Nice to meet you, Vern. I am Arthur. Arthur Machen. I remember you from back on the rooftop. I thought I did great by not losing consciousness in that hell, but I heard you didn't even flinch."

Vern smiled politely and recycled the excuse Captain Akira had made for him. "Haha, don't be too impressed. I'm also a fundamentalist, so you can say I cheated a bit. After all, we're used to sights like that."

"Don't sell yourself short, Vern. Most of us nobles were also trained for situations like that. But you saw what came of it—a mere tenth of us managed to even get back up in time."

Vern kept smiling as the waiter grabbed their attention. All three communicated their wants to the man and found themselves a table. Vern only asked for something light to snack on—no training on a full stomach.

Grabbing the hilt of Duality, he rigidly pushed it to the right, and the whole sheath rotated on his back step-by-step with a clicking sound, allowing him to sit with the sheath not poking a hole through the chair. Such were the advantages of making something yourself.

Not wanting to seem unnecessarily pompous, Vern started the conversation this time. "Did you two go on any missions yesterday?"

Lucian hoisted that massive sword off his shoulder and leaned it on his chair's edge as it creaked in agony. "Hah, that's where I met Arthur, actually, but it was anticlimactic."

The black-haired Arthur nodded with a smile of his own and added, "Indeed. That's how we got acquainted with each other. Though, I didn't expect him to be so good at handling that massive sword already."

"Well, not like I got to use it much. It's meant for cracking open skulls, not doors."

Their food soon arrived, and Vern chuckled. "Sounds like you all had a fun time. Was it a simple cleansing mission?"

Arthur shook his head, sipping what looked like wine. "Not really. We were sent to investigate a string of murders in the high society."

Vern raised his eyebrows. "Isn't that something better left to Kingsmen and police?"

Lucian was too busy with his pastry to reply, so Arthur leaned in close, whispering, "Not in this case. Apparently, the ones who died were observers too."

Vern frowned. "So the murderer is an observer?"

"We . . . aren't sure. Even Lady Antonia, who was overlooking the mission yesterday, hasn't reached a conclusion. The witnesses claimed that the victims suddenly started mumbling incoherently and flailing around before they fell dead soon after."

Hmm, this is only getting more baffling. "Aren't those just the signs of losing oneself to the whispers?"

Arthur's face brightened. "Exactly! That's what I pointed out too. But Lady Antonia believes there's more to this than meets the eye. So we ended up scouting the prior cases too. To no avail, unfortunately."

Lucian jumped in, grumbling as he finished his plate. "I still don't know why we wasted so much time chasing dead nobles."

Vern sighed exaggeratedly. "Now even brutes think they know better than Captain Akira."

"Eh, haha, I didn't mean to slander Captain, really," Lucian stuttered, looking all around him. "He's very good."

"Mm-hmm," Arthur hummed in assent and leaned back before taking another small sip. "Prince Akira has a clear picture of everything that's going on in the city. So, I definitely trust him more than myself in these situations. Also, he's the last person who would favor nobility over the well-being of the city itself."

Lucian agreed to Arthur's words with repeated nods.

Weren't you the one who was just grumbling about it?

Soon, however, Arthur placed his glass on the table and rested his chin on his palms—fingers intertwined like a mastermind's—before he eyed Vern. "I suppose you had a far more exciting day than either of us? I've been hearing interesting things since this morning."

Vern finished his own plate of biscuits and settled back, trying to adjust to the discomfort of sitting with the sheath on his back. "Hmm, what did you hear?"

"Hmm, let's see. It was something along the lines of you defeating an amalgamation of subjectivity pollution that's equivalent in power to an observer with two shades, all by yourself."

Vern replied, taken aback, "That's a bit too detailed. Who told you that?"

Lucian interjected, "He . . . what?"

However, Arthur didn't respond to either of them and fell into an introspective trance. "So it is true . . . ?"

Lucian looked back and forth between Vern and Arthur. "Hey, what's going on? You really defeated something like that?"

Vern didn't want to boast, but he had no qualms about bashing Lucian. The man deserved any amount of hurt to his ego for the torture he inflicted on Vern's eyes. So Vern shrugged. "Well, I managed it without this "short" sword right here. Imagine what I could do with it. Your great sword should be scared."

Lucian's eyes suddenly turned wild, and he stood up, a fierce aura all around him. "Fight me! Right now!" he implored, excitement and anticipation clear on his face as his veins bulged. "Come on, man! I really need to fight someone of my own strength. Master Osric beats me up one-sidedly, and it doesn't help me gauge my strength."

Arthur looked at them both, an intrigued glint in his eyes. Vern, however, stared at Lucian like he was stupid. "Our training starts in a few minutes. You really want to go in there half dead?"

"Haha, very cocky! Very cocky."

"But not wrong."

"Ugh! I just wanna fight something!"

"Hmm, well, how about we ask our mentors and see what they think about fighting each other?"

Vern nodded farewell to Lucian as he pushed open the door to the training hall from the day before yesterday. Or was it yesterday, since he had slept here past midnight?

"Good eveni—" Vern choked on his greeting as he looked on in awe at the spectacle in front of him.

A red glow shone like a beacon in the center of the hall, emanating from Mistress Amelia herself. Her palms gripped the handle of her scythe behind her—one close to the blade, the other close to the faux pommel.

However, like a string being pulled taut to the extremes, her upper body was twisting forward while her legs stretched back alongside the gleaming crimson blade, primed with so much energy it seemed the scythe would break at any moment.

As her cape and ponytail billowed wildly, gusts of air rippled out of her body. Looking at this, Vern's chest tightened, but he couldn't tear his eyes away.

Rows of armored mannequins stood in front of her, filling a good third of the room, but she continued to pull the ends of the string tighter. So much so Vern's hair stood on end just imagining the terrifying strength charged in that attack.

If that hit him, forget the energy in the mix; the sheer physical energy alone would turn him into mincemeat. And in that moment—

Snap!

The hand keeping the blade's end taut let go, and pivoting around her other palm, the scythe shot out like a blur, swinging in a wide arc. The saturated crimson on the blade's end released like a gash, in reality, itself, staining everything bloodred.

It was so bright he almost missed the carnage it would wreak on the mannequins.

Sizzle. The metal disintegrated at the mere touch of that reddish hue that advanced at a relentless pace. *Srrrrr.* It burned and churned. However, that's when something bizarre transpired.

Mistress turned around with all that momentum, and the scythe suddenly extended beyond its usual length before she hooked back at the arc of energy that had disintegrated the first row in that mere instant.

What? Vern looked on in puzzlement, but she hooked the blade of the mechanical scythe into the red energy, and bafflingly, she managed to . . . tug the energy back?

Paaah!

Like a balloon, the energy suddenly burst as red droplets exploded everywhere, burning the very ground like some acid, but not as potent as before. Soon, it evaporated like water under the sun, and Mistress's sigh echoed throughout the room.

She contracted the scythe and latched it on her back before sitting on the raised platform, supporting herself with her hands.

Vern finally walked up to her and said, "Hello, Mistress. Is that a new attack you're working on?" That's what it looked like to him.

"Mm-hmm." She nodded, wiping the bloody droplets off her face. "I am having a little trouble at the last step. Anyway, it has direct implications for you as well."

Vern swallowed his follow-up questions and tilted his head with a questioning gaze.

She answered him in kind. "I'll be practicing for the next seven days myself to harness the power of my recent infusion. So, I went ahead and asked Akira to exempt you from participating in any missions for the week."

"Oh . . ." Vern gasped, feeling a bit of apprehension but also excitement as he tried to figure out how that changed his plans.

"If you have anything important to attend to, you're free to finish it today. Tomorrow onward, I want you here twelve hours a day."

". . ." Vern was dumbfounded. His mind quickly whirled through the implications, and he rapidly assessed it from all angles, including the opportunity cost of training day and night.

Soon, however, he arrived at a singular answer. This was a rare opportunity. Yes, he had ten other things to focus on, but none of them were going anywhere, and nor were they urgent.

Balance wasn't about never being extreme. As *never* was extreme in and of itself. It was about knowing when to embrace the extremes. This situation was it.

He was sorely lacking in everything related to physical combat, including intuition, form, coordination, and experience. For an average human, seven days could never be enough to comprehensively learn the art of combat.

They wouldn't be enough for him either, but his perception offered him a tool of learning unlike anything else. He didn't want to become a master anyway. He just wanted to not be held back by his frailness in this terrifying world.

I need this! Everything seemed to clear up, and he rested his hands on his chest and bowed deeply. "Then I will be in your care, Mistress."

Chapter 47

METAMORPHOSIS

Mistress Amelia held two straight blades, one in each hand, their tips ominously pointing to the ground and mirroring the heavy stillness of the air around her. In a fluid, almost serpentine motion, she raised both swords, the gleam of the polished metal catching the hall's light.

Her eyes, fierce and unyielding, locked onto the mannequin with a predator's intent. Vern, however, watched it with more than just his eyes. The moment her arms coiled behind her like a spring, the stress lines grew brighter as the fulcrums moved into a very specific arrangement.

With a sudden burst of energy, she lunged forward, her left foot leading into a slide that closed the gap between her and the metal hunk in a heartbeat.

He perceived the fulcrums of her body moving in a three-dimensional space augmented by the stress lines all around them. And as her arms came descending like a guillotine, the lines of her arms turned from bright to dark, signifying an imminent release of tension.

Clang!

Two deep slashes on the armored thing expanded into massive cuts that chopped the whole thing into three neat parts.

Her movements were like a dance, and Vern saw it in full glory as those lines forming the shape of her body recovered to their default states in a smooth shift of gradients. She wasn't doing any of that actively. Her innate movements were so perfect that this property emerged independently.

He studied the form, the states, the angles, and the changes over time, jotting them down on the paper whenever necessary to make the links in his stupid brain.

Scratching his head at one of the subsections of the maneuver, he asked, "Hmm, Mistress, I can't seem to get this right."

She walked over and looked at his notes, somehow understanding what he was getting at. Pointing at the fourth diagram, she said, "Hmm, it's not about the specificity of the movement here. I get that you're trying to replicate the exact form, but where possible, try to understand the why behind each movement."

"For this one . . ."

Tch-tching.

Vern split Duality into two singularities—a name he'd decided on—and pointed their tips downward. He recalled the arrangement of fulcrums of Mistress's body and slipped into exactly that stance. It was complicated because he had to mentally rotate them to match how he was standing.

However, static stances were useless in real combat. It was how one quickly adapted and reacted to changes that mattered. That was where seams started to show in his arrangement learning approach.

For static stances, he just had to replicate the three-dimensional arrangement of the fulcrums. However, for myriad maneuvers that Mistress had demonstrated, another dimension was added to the mix—time. With each little movement, the fulcrums moved to new positions, and stress lines changed their shades.

He could memorize the static state of fulcrums and stress lines, but trying to cram all the continuously changing variables' states was a fool's errand. *Yet that's exactly how everyone learns to fight*, Mistress had said.

She definitely had a point. Most people brute-forced these moves and attack patterns into their muscle memory, spending days or even years on the task. And there was nothing wrong with it.

However, Vern didn't want to give up on his unique method so quickly. So he settled on a compromise—a balance. He had gotten the idea from how he'd ended the training on his first day. Transitioning from one stance to another.

Vern looked back up at Mistress. A dozen bloody tendrils shot out of her back as she controlled them with the precision of a master, using them to pick up mundane objects. His heart still lurched every time he saw her in this state, but this was how she trained her new powers.

None of it was aimed at him, and she wasn't using even a tenth of her full strength, but despite all that, a primal terror arose from within the depth of his very being every time the tendrils first emerged out of her.

Taking an idle stance that perfectly mirrored Mistress's from back then, he first started by destabilizing the edge of his singularities, gripping them harder to reduce the vibration coursing through them.

Purple glow bathed him for an instant before dimming as he imagined the position of fulcrums and shades of stress lines for when she had raised both the blades above her.

Unfortunately, he couldn't keep the edges destabilized for long as the blades soon recovered on their own, and he didn't have enough mental capacity to juggle these exhausting tasks simultaneously.

Hopefully, it'll get better, he thought, focusing back on the new cloud of points he'd imagined.

Now that he had two possible states—the current one and the next one—in his mind, he just had to transition between these two. Exactly like one would between two stances.

He breathed out and prepared himself. A part of him wished to close his eyes for concentration, but Mistress said that was a terrible habit.

So with his eyes wide open, he thought, *Idle to . . . rise.* With a speed that couldn't match his thoughts, he manipulated the fulcrums of his arms and upper body to shoot toward the risen stance.

Tch. It wasn't perfect. He overshot a little, but now wasn't the time to stop. This was just the start.

Rise to coil.

Not waiting for the last movement to finish all the way, he adapted his body to match this next state and flexed his muscles. Coiling his upper body like a spring, he connected this surge to end the next stage of fulcrums and stress lines.

Coil to lunge.

He streamlined his body a tad and loaded his legs for a pounce, his perception of himself looking an exact mirror of what it did for Mistress.

Lunge to dash.

Thump! His body rushed through the air toward Mistress. Two of the ten or so tendrils held gleaming swords in a cross-guard, their blades reinforced by a bloody haze.

Dash to strike.

He lashed out his arms, an exact replica of what she had done.

Clang!

The crimson tendrils didn't even flinch, but the swords visibly bent, signifying the insane amount of strength he conjured by simply following the maneuver's intricacies closely.

Triumphant, Vern smiled and continued. *Strike to recover.*

With a simple tap of his leg, he retreated.

Panting, he allowed the tip of the singularities to rest gently on the ground. *Each attempt, each maneuver . . . I feel them slowly becoming a part of me.* He gasped, seeking approval in Mistress Amelia's inscrutable gaze.

However, her expression was buried beneath the layers covering her face, and soon, she spoke in a matter-of-fact tone, "It was barely above an utter failure. Your movements are too mechanical. It's as if you're a puppet dancing on the strings controlled by a fumbling child."

Vern flinched. *Oof . . . I thought I did well there.* He dipped his head and ran through his movements mentally, and he quickly realized the stark difference between her version of the maneuver and his own. As much as he tried to make the motions fluid he was just moving through checkpoints.

He snapped into those points, but everything else didn't flow too well. *Is this not the right balance, then? Should I focus more on the feel and flow of the movement?*

Vern sighed. "Then what do you suggest I do, Mistress?"

The moment he finished those words, an oppressive aura suddenly enveloped him, and his instincts screamed at him to hide. "Frustration is a luxury, Vern. Focus!"

He snapped back and stood straighter as she continued, "Even though it won't make the cut in its current state, this learning method of yours has great potential. Stop second-guessing yourself and work harder. Remember that practice isn't your enemy. What you're doing doesn't have to be mutually exclusive with typical methods. They should work in tandem."

That one sentence sent his mind into a whirlwind of thoughts, and he quickly realized how he'd been subconsciously trying to find loopholes and methods to sidestep the usual tactics. And he'd be damned to not recognize that it was foolish. Standing on the shoulders of giants was how the world moved forward.

Reinventing the wheel was for those with unlimited time.

"Get started," came her sharp command. "Now!"

Grabbing the singularities, he merged them into one with a clang and shouted, "Yes, Mistress!"

Once . . . twice . . . thrice . . . a dozen . . . a hundred . . . a thousand? He lost count on the very first day as he repeated the simple movements with a maddening fervor. However, it was far from a mindless repetition.

The fulcrums and stress lines were like an artist's muse, allowing him to adjust the painting at every step of the way.

Mistress was showing him no mercy, and he loved it. Heck, he needed it. When he repeatedly messed up attack patterns, she didn't hesitate to take the chance and knock him into the dirt.

She walked a fine line between being understanding and strict. She corrected genuine mistakes but made sure to punish the repetitions.

Vern studied, mimicked, fought, resisted, got smacked, and then got smacked again before getting thrashed even harder until he finally managed to dislocate his shoulder and had to revisit the plague doctor, only to come back stronger the day after and get fucked once more.

On the fourth morning, she decided to change the pace a little.

"Now that you have a basic understanding of footwork, combat stances, and offensive and defensive maneuvers, it's time for you to start incorporating your visions into combat. Better to start early than graft them on later."

Vern, still sore from yesterday's grueling session, instantly snapped to attention.

"However, before we can get to that, we need to talk about battle instincts."

He pulled out his notepad and began writing the key points as usual.

Mistress simply rolled her eyes and continued, "Combat against intelligent opponents is more than just about who has flashier skills or bigger weapons. It's as much psychological warfare as it's physical. Outmaneuvering and outthinking your opponent often proves more lethal than brute force."

Vern picked up the speed, and Mistress added, "Manipulating the battlefield, diverting the enemy's attention at the right moment, disrupting their moves, finding flaws in their defense—all are examples of this."

"I've fought about twenty or so observers these past couple weeks, and they're generally most effective in this department."

That makes sense. Very few visions were about raw power or strength. Most of them bent the reality in odd ways to shift the tide in one's advantage.

"So this begs the question, what can your visions do to put you in these advantageous situations?" Then she turned around. "Take some time and think it through. I can show you some examples that depend on burning the old blood and help you refine what you can perform. But you'll still have to figure out the possibilities by yourself."

Vern nodded solemnly. "That would be great help. Thanks as usual, Mistress."

"Mm-hmm . . ."

He watched her perform a myriad of little things, and it was nothing short of eye-opening how those negligible alterations could completely disrupt the flow of the battle and change its course.

Once she stopped and busied herself, Vern stood in a corner to try to dig out the petty potential of his visions.

According to his understanding of his own viewpoint, his visions were best at manipulating the "structure" or "composition" of objects with a tad of "force" aspect that had begun to bleed in ever since he could see the stress lines.

Back in the mirror realm, he'd used the battlefield to his advantage to a great extent, and now the question was whether he could find a more general way of doing so because most battles weren't fought in knee-deep water.

Hmm, in terms of the battlefield, I'll almost always have access to ground and air. When he followed that train of thought to its logical conclusion, he realized that his viewpoint was ripe for little tricks. Simple instability at the right place at the right time could work wonders.

He jotted down every dumb idea he had and soon ran them by Mistress—demonstrating them to the best of his abilities. Some failed, but many were doable.

She further shortened the list to a mere few because of the impracticality of others. When she elaborated on the ones still in the running, he quickly found himself dumbfounded by his lack of creativity.

"Alright, time to practice these."

Vern nodded and stood square, quite a bit pumped to see how it would go. However, she suddenly stopped and stared at him with narrowed eyes.

Vern fidgeted and quickly realized the mistake—his hands were empty. Reaching back to the sheath, he pulled out Duality with a *shwing.*

His arms weren't going to get any kind of rest, it seemed.

She then grudgingly turned her eyes away and commanded, "Show me what you got."

Not willing to waste even a second of Mistress's precious time, he completely cut down on all unnecessary activities, including socialization with his peers. Even though she spent most of that time practicing her own techniques, mere offhand remarks from her had proved more than enough to save him days of trial and error.

Even while eating, he cycled through the myriad offensive moves she'd demanded he learn, mentally simulating their optimizations in his unique method of learning. What helped him stay on track was the variety of problems at hand.

It wasn't just about jumpstarting his muscle memory to become a better fighter but also learning new and creative ways to integrate his visions and perception into his every move. Unsurprisingly, he was having a far easier time working with visions than physical combat.

One evening, his body gave out somewhere along the line, so when he got back up after midnight, he didn't bother going back to his room. Yet, he was surprised to find he wasn't alone in the training hall. Mistress was there, tirelessly following one of her enigmatic routines. It was as if she never slept.

No matter if it was early morning or deep in the night, she never much left that hall. Heck, he didn't see her go out even for food. And whenever he brought her snacks, she always politely refused. He was curious, but for some reason it didn't seem right to ask.

In this blend of day and night, exhaustion and rejuvenation, learning and failing, his sense of time blurred, anchored in this training hall, leaving room for nothing but his training.

Thump!

Mistress stood, a network of crimson tendrils unfurling from her back like a macabre crown, each coalescing in a crimson blade that gleamed with lethal promise. With a casual flick of her wrist, she launched a barrage of bloody projectiles toward Vern.

Slice! Swipe! Swish!

Vern waited all the way until the last moment, embodying the tenet of his viewpoint as he suddenly burst into movement.

He weaved through the onslaught with grace, his movements fluid and assured. The purple glow around his blades now pulsated in sync with his thoughts, a visual echo of his efficient use of destabilization.

Each slice through the air met its target precisely, disintegrating the bloody arrows into harmless mist before they grazed his skin.

"Better." Mistress's voice cut through the silence, a note of approval in her tone that was far rarer than he could have hoped. Almost as rare as his master's back in Nvoria.

Vern's response was a nod, his focus unbroken. The barrage intensified, the projectiles coming faster, some curving in unpredictable arcs designed to test his limits.

Yet he stood unyielding, his singularities weaving a protective dance around him, their edges a blur of destabilizing energy.

Minutes stretched on, the air thick with the tension of this one-sided assault.

But where once fatigue might have claimed him, Vern's resolve now burned brighter. His arms screamed, and his lungs caught on figurative fire, but he held on.

The rhythm of his movements hadn't become second nature just yet, but he was leagues above the fumbling fool who moved worse than a puppet.

"Your strikes have improved," she said, her gaze assessing him. "But strikes are only one aspect of control. Remember, true mastery lies in knowing what to control and when to do it."

Suddenly, the assault ceased. Mistress's tendrils retracted save for one that she extended toward him in beckoning.

"Be that the enemy, battlefield, yourself, or reality itself."

Vern absorbed her words, understanding that each step forward was a step toward a horizon that never receded, inviting him to chase it.

"Show me again," she commanded, "the transition from defense to offense. Use what you've learned."

Thump! Vern's stance shifted, the idle position he once mirrored now imbued with a dynamic tension. He visualized the path ahead, the fulcrums of his body not a rigid state but a soft cloud that allowed for room to breathe for some of them.

Idle to . . . rise. His body responded, the transition seamless, a testament to the countless hours of repetition and refinement. His singularities, now extensions of his intent, prepared to strike.

Rise to coil. He didn't wait for completion—or hitting the checkpoint; the momentum carried him forward, his muscles coiling in anticipation.

Coil to lunge. A deliberate streamline of his body, every muscle aligned for the pounce.

Lunge to dash. His advance was a blur, closing the distance with a speed that matched his determination.

Dash to strike. The singularities lashed out, not just mirroring Mistress's technique but adding his own flair, a twist in the trajectory that spoke of his unique understanding.

Clang!

The contact was met not with resistance but a sharp chorus of metal as the reinforced blades held within those tendrils were sent flying in the air—leaving nothing but incomplete stumps behind.

Strike to recover. He fell back, but not as a retreat. It was a reset, a preparation for the next step in their endless dance of learning and mastery.

Panting, Vern allowed himself a moment to reflect. The movements, once disjointed in his mind, now flowed like the force in a well-oiled engine.

Mistress nodded, her expression hidden behind that fabric. "You've come far, Vern. Farther than I had anticipated."

Those words sent a wave of relief pulsing through his body, followed by his knees buckling from the lack of energy, and he fell back without any care.

Hah-hah. He breathed large mouthfuls of air as he closed his eyes and discarded his perception, not keen at all on using any of his senses. Yet his mind continued to whirl—analyzing, dissecting the changes he'd made throughout these sessions of madness.

His largest leap of improvement in this visualization technique came from finding a better balance of rigidity. One issue with mimicking Mistress was that it didn't account for the difference between both bodies.

To remedy that, he'd slowly figured out which nodes could have a greater margin of error and didn't need to be mirrored perfectly. Then, from there, he had spent a big chunk of the time figuring this out for each sub-state in the fifty or so maneuvers she'd demanded him to learn.

He wasn't this good with most of them, but that's what one practiced for. What was funnier was that he didn't even need to follow the mental nodes for most of these moves anymore. His muscle memory had long since kicked in.

Now it helped him overcome the flaws or pick up new movements. *I guess that's for the best anyway.* This unique visualization method wasn't meant as a combat art but more of a learning aid.

"Let's end early today." Those words suddenly jolted him back up, and he stared at her with intense puzzlement.

She shook her head and replied, "It's been a week, Vern."

What? When . . . ? Fuck!

It was . . . over? Already? How? "But, Mistress, I've barely figured out how to incorporate my visions into the combat style. I need at least another month. No, maybe just another week? How am I supposed to—"

She raised her hand, and Vern instantly shut up. Sliding her arm into the coat, she sighed. "The city needs us, Vern. I have spent enough time with my new powers. If I don't use them for a good cause right about now, it might be a little too late for many."

He opened his mouth to say something but didn't know where to start. She was right.

She walked through the wreckage that was the training hall, cutting a graceful yet deadly figure as she added, "The plague's getting worse, and one of the teams in the ruin has been involved in an accident. I suppose the Vigil needs you too. We can't just stay cooped up in here."

Walking past his sorry ass, she added, "Rest well, Vern. I look forward to watching you fight tomorrow."

The mere mention of the fight sent his blood pumping again, and the despondency at having to stop progressing at this speed faded away a bit.

Well, Master Osric had also spent a big chunk of time with Lucian, almost as if to compete with Mistress, and had proposed a "friendly" dual on Lucian's behalf.

A confident smile blossomed on his face, and he declared, "I have no plans to let you down, Mistress."

When she was about to exit the door, she sighed. "Be warned that Lucian has already subjugated the first infusion of old blood. As much as I want you to win, you should temper your expectations and know when to back down. Your combat prowess may not be enough to overcome the raw strength that comes with the old blood."

Vern didn't speak unnecessarily and just nodded. He would let his actions do the talking.

"Goodnight, Mistress Amelia. Thank you very much for this last week. I wish there were some way for me to show my gratitude."

She walked out and left words in the air in a tone barely above a whisper, "Just do your best for the city. That's all the thanks I need."

Slam.

C H A P T E R **48**

UNEXPECTED SPECTATORS

Hey, Arthur, can you put in a good word for me with your uncle? I've been trying to get my hands on the first vision of the shadewalker sequence, but it is impossible to get in touch with nightshades directly."

Arthur weighed Gareth's words for a while before replying, "Hmm, I can try, but there's no guarantee my uncle would bother tapping into his network for outsiders."

"Hey, man, just try, okay? I am slowing down my team a bit too much right now. Worse, I am assigned to the same team as Victoria. She's outperforming me in every department. Dad's not happy that a new family like hers can produce someone as talented as Victoria—"

Arthur suddenly gripped Gareth's shoulder and gave him a menacing look before light footsteps approached them.

A girl almost as tall as Arthur himself, clad in tight black leather and red velvet inners, walked toward them, knives floating all around her. Arthur's face quickly turned all smiles, and he greeted her first. "Hey, Victoria."

Gareth cowered for a bit, but Arthur pushed him, and the man turned around, greeting her with a sheepish smile. She smiled back at both of them—her way of acknowledgment probably—but she didn't stop and walked past them, her black cape with golden etchings of an eye fluttering behind her.

Gareth was happy to see her go, but Arthur wasn't about to squander another opportunity to network with this powerful girl. Not just that, she was also a member of the new nobility—the ones who filled in the vacancies created by those who were eradicated by the anomalies of duskfall.

So Arthur tugged at Gareth and tried to match her stride while keeping away from those knives before speaking. "Are you heading out for another mission?"

She shook her head slightly before replying in a clear voice, "The Kingsmen candidates are about to go against each other."

Arthur almost stopped in his tracks before realizing what she meant. He recalled that conversation between Vern and Lucian. *They were going to fight, weren't they?*

He hadn't seen them for a while, so he assumed they were too busy with their training or something. But this? An excited gleam flashed across his eyes as his steps quickened, and he inquired, "How do you know? Also, where are they fighting and when?"

"Next to the central garden in a few minutes."

Hmm, she completely ignored the first part of my question. Well, it didn't matter for now. However, it was an odd choice for a fighting arena. Why not just fight indoors? The former royal palace even had a dueling arena.

His mind whirled, and he tried to figure out how to turn this into an opportunity for himself. Everything was an opportunity if one was willing to put in the work. So he unveiled his perception, and hundreds of light streams flowed around him like wind.

Hmm, there's indeed a congregation around the central garden. It wasn't much, but who cared? He stopped wasting time and turned to Gareth. "Quickly spread the news around! The sole wielder of both old blood and subjectivity is about to showcase his combat prowess. Tell them to spread it further."

Gareth stopped in place, and it soon dawned on him. He gasped and spoke out in protest, "But I don't wanna miss it! Can't I just join you guys?"

Arthur narrowed his eyes. "I was thinking about meeting my uncle tomorrow . . ."

Gareth shut up and gritted his teeth before turning around and sprinting away, the Vigil's cape billowing behind him.

Arthur continued to think about how to get more people to watch this so he could gauge their reactions and understand their stances on mixing these two power systems.

Suddenly, Victoria interrupted him, "Hmm, you didn't say anything about the other fighter. Is he not good?"

Arthur liked this question. It told him that she didn't know Vern or Lucian personally. Not letting any of that show on his face, he expressed his genuine opinions. "Hmm, I wouldn't say that. The man's cleansed a second-shade polluted abomination all by himself."

Victoria gasped, her thin lips parting to say something but didn't. Soon, her pretty eyebrows scrunched together. "How . . . did he? Is he a latent observer? Or was the tainted monster he fought a very weak second shade?"

Yeah, she knew nothing about Vern. Arthur shook his head. "You see, this is why I didn't ask Gareth to advertise the fight with that information. It's people's first instinct to assume that he was cheating or didn't defeat the monster on his own merit."

Her knives became a little unstable, and she demanded, "Did he?"

Arthur smirked. She seemed competitive. He spilled the beans to get her invested and glean more about her by association. "Well, the guy has no sense for normal. What he did was outright madness. The subjectivity pollutant he fought was sapient enough to escape in dire circumstances, resourceful enough to infect and assimilate civilians, and powerful enough to have its own domain."

Victoria gasped, holding her hand in front of her mouth. She walked on without giving leeway to anyone in her path from her knives like she usually did. "A domain? You mean it was strong enough to assert its own viewpoint out in the real world?!"

Arthur remembered all her inclinations and nodded sharply. "And that's not even all. He fought the monster alone, in its own realm, because it only preyed on the weak and escaped every time his team's captain was around. Also, remember that we're talking about someone who shaded their perception literally two weeks ago."

She caressed one of her knives in stunned silence, and Arthur didn't pause. "I thought I did well clearing that tunnel alone, but this guy didn't just fight the monstrosity—he took on dozens of its puppets too and came out victorious."

Arthur was skeptical when his friend in the resource allocation department shared tidbits from that mission's report. So, he had someone verify the information with the civilians involved. Their accounts painted the guy as achieving far more than the reports suggested.

Definitely someone to befriend. He had intended to reach out to Vern since then, but the guy was cooped up in that training hall like the world was about to end for real this time.

Victoria didn't say much, and Arthur let the gravity of his words sink in. That alone told him about her personality. Soon they reached the balcony with a clear view of the central garden, and in but a few minutes, many more came sprinting from all around.

Seems like Gareth filled in the ears of the right people.

First it was just the ones he knew, but maybe noticing the commotion, more observers joined in. Even the sightless servants stopped their work, trying to figure out what was going on.

Victoria ended up storing her knives in their pouch as the balcony began to crowd. Some people appeared on the opposite tower, while noises came from above them too.

A dozen people looked down from the walkways high above the garden while windows of the rooms in the central tower opened up in droves.

As the name suggested, the central garden was an open garden surrounded from all sides by the towers of this former royal palace, linking outer halls with all these sections of castle under open skies—almost.

Almost because architects liked to complicate things. There were also walkways high in the air, connecting these towers, allowing one to cross without ever touching the ground.

Beneath these bridges, there was a clearing as large as some minor noble's manor. Though no one tended to it anymore—there weren't enough people around to do chores like that. Also, winters weren't great for gardens anyway.

Tap tap tap.

That's when a familiar noise came, and Arthur's perception became a mess. *Wait. No!*

"What's up, kiddos?!" resonated a voice, and Arthur shuddered.

Damn, why is he here?!

"Come on, make some space for this distinguished gentleman."

Tap tap tap.

"Hey, be careful with your drink. That cane's worth three of you."

Arthur tried to slip away, but—*tap*—a hand wrapped around his shoulder. "Wait! Aren't you the friend of that little twat who ran away from his first mission?"

Arthur bit his tongue and stood rooted on the spot. When everyone turned to look at him, he sighed. "Indeed, young Master Finnesse, though I must let you know that Captain Akira has forgiven him since then, and he's doing his best to repent."

Well, that guy wasn't really his friend, but he couldn't say that in front of so many people now, could he? And why was Ambrose like this? It was impossible to figure out this man. This is why Arthur liked keeping his distance from him.

He was stuck now.

"Eh, whatever, then. Tell me, kiddos, what's all this commotion about?"

Some girl from the crowd chimed in before Arthur could speak, "Young master, it's the Kingsmen candidates fighting each other." Ambrose continued looking at his nails with a bored expression.

But then a short guy in a terrible outfit interrupted, "Hey, only one of them is a candidate now. Mr. Lucian has already subjugated the first infusion of old blood. But the other guy? Hmph. I heard he's too scared."

Ambrose started filing his nails with the flat of the segments of his cane and spoke in the dullest voice in all Elmhurst, "Lucian, who?"

However, Arthur suddenly remembered some information. *Weren't Vern and Ambrose together during that explosion in Starfall Heights and the following scandal involving Asea's church?*

So he found a moment when the crowd was distracted and whispered, "The other fighter is Vern."

Ambrose, who was berating others, pointing his cane at them, suddenly stopped and looked back at Arthur, the grip on his shoulder tightening.

Arthur understood the question in that gaze and nodded.

As if he'd unleashed a plague, a devious smile appeared on Ambrose's face.

"Ladies and gentleman."

Tap!

That simple hit of his cane broke the flooring but also shut up the heating crowd. Then Ambrose smiled sincerely and shouted, "How about we place bets on who's going to win today."

The crowd seemed amenable to the idea, but Arthur could see they were skeptical. That's when Ambrose pulled out one note from his pocket, and everyone's eyes lit up. "I feel adventurous today. So, I will bet this regalia against the Kingsman guy for the sake of it."

Wah.

The crowd erupted in murmurs, and Arthur sucked in a deep breath. That was equivalent to a hundred sovereigns—the greatest denomination signed by the emperor. Not just that, Ambrose was sneaky about it, too, acting like he was being reckless with the bet.

Arthur took this chance to slip away from the madman's grasp and backed away from the crowd, focusing on everyone's choices. He wasn't going to take part in the bet himself, or how would he remain neutral otherwise?

"Hah, I hope you take no offense, young master." Out came an effeminate man with a regalia of his own. "If you really don't like it, I'll have to take that money from you."

Hmm, that's Simon from the Dexter family. It seems like he's sour toward Finnesse in general. Which made sense, given that both these families followed the same shade sequence but had very different interpretations of it, leading to a natural rivalry between them. However, the consensus among the nobles was that the Finnesse family was simply superior.

"Hah, would you good sirs mind if I joined in on the bet, too?"

"Yes, me too! Me too! I'll bet on whatever Master Ambrose does."

"Heh, no, kid. Rhythm guides me alone. Don't follow me, flow against me. Bet on the other guy, I win more that way."

After a while, Victoria suddenly looked up.

Tiny snowflakes that missed the bridges above filtered down into the garden. In this chilly ambiance appeared a figure at the far end of this graveyard of flowers.

A shout erupted from behind her, "Hey, look. Someone's coming. It's about to start!" The crowd surged forward, each person vying for a better view. Victoria cast a sidelong glance, and the man directly behind her backed away.

The figure approaching from the distance was striking. Tall and lean, but not thin. Sharp eyes and a handsome face, but not weak. An imposing gait and excellent posture, but not overly so.

An eerie sense of correctness assailed her as she looked at the man, and others around her quietened down too.

Victoria scrutinized him, trying to figure out what was so unique about him. Lucian was powerful because he infused the old blood, but what about him? A lost shade sequence? A terrifying perceptual artifact? Some illogical vision?

That high collar hid his face, but with that outfit and the sword on his back, he seemed more menacing and mysterious than even the highest of the Kingsmen.

His long strides quickly landed him smack in the middle of the garden, where he stood alone, exuding a confidence that made even Victoria feel small.

The crowd around her seemed to match his ebb and flow, as some even switched their bets after simply looking at him for a few seconds.

However, that's when a booming sound came from somewhere high up. "Oi, Vern."

The handsome guy on the ground looked up, and everyone followed the voice to the source, only to see a shadow standing on the eave of a connecting walkway high up, a broken hilt in its hand.

The crowd suddenly started pointing and murmuring, but the shadow did something disturbing the next moment.

It said, "I didn't expect this many spectators . . ." and jumped.

"Whoa!" the crowd gathered all around the garden shouted in unison, some even cursing the man's stupidity. However, Victoria wasn't lost enough to not know what was going to happen.

Whir.

A gleaming string released from the man's gear on his waist and deftly latched on to some structures down the way.

Landing on one of the lower walkways—albeit roughly—the shadow became clear. It was a blonde-haired guy in an ominous suit of armor. Its plates were layered like the scales of some ancient, dark leviathan, each segment interlocking to provide formidable protection.

That has to be Lucian, right? Victoria thought.

Suddenly, a guy beside her chuckled. "Hah, look guys, he's not wearing that terrible outfit today?"

Victoria frowned but ignored the remark as the crowd around her continued to go wild, when suddenly Lucian said, "Tell me, Vern . . ." He jumped down to another eave on the third floor.

"Are." Another descent with a jump.

"You." Another rush through the air.

With a *thump,* he landed on the roof of the first floor of the central tower and pointed his hilt toward Vern, shouting with a wide grin, "Ready!?"

And as if to match the ferocity of his challenge, the broken hilt flared with a purple light. Like a ghost materializing into reality, a massive blade emerged out of nothingness, aimed at the tall figure on the ground.

"Oh, my lord! How can someone even wield that massive sword?"

"Hahaha! What did I tell you all? Mr. Lucian will win this one. What does it matter if the other guy seems calm and composed? Do you think he can win against someone with the strength of a Kingsman and visions of an observer with just their calmness? Heh."

"Lucian can just go airborne, but this guy will always be stuck on the ground. Haha, what a loser."

Many others quickly chimed in, echoing this opinion, and the participation in the bet became more ferocious. However, this really made her wonder. *Who will win?* Both of them had solid reasons as to why they should be able to beat the other. *But only one can win.*

She had no clue, honestly.

Whir.

Suddenly, more reeling sounds echoed around them, and two shadows appeared high up on the walkways. The crowd went even wilder.

"Hey! It's official. It's official. Those are the best Kingsmen in the city up there. If they're here, we can't back out from the bets later, okay?"

"Right. Right. This is going to be good."

"Haha, I don't know. Seems like Lucian will end this in just a few seconds."

Victoria looked up and saw it was indeed Lady Amelia and Sir Osric speaking. *Vern is her disciple, right?*

Shaking her head, she ignored all the mundane talking behind her and geared herself up for the upcoming fight. These were her peers—her competition. This was her chance to analyze their strengths and possibly learn something new. It wasn't some mindless entertainment for her.

Everything was ready. The participants were here. The spectators were here. And the judges were here. The air quickly became charged with passion as people began cheering for their pick.

Amid this electric atmosphere, snowflakes danced wildly around Vern, yet mysteriously, none dared touch him. However, In a move that caught everyone off guard, he chose not to draw his sword and just pulled at his gloves.

With a confident smile, Vern extended his hand toward Lucian, who had his massive sword pointed at Vern, and beckoned him.

"As ready as you'll never be."

Chapter 49

DUEL

Vern took a deep breath as he internally chuckled at Lucian's display. Clearly, the man was playing to the crowd, embracing the theatrics.

Yet, as Mistress had relentlessly drilled into him, the prelude to any battle was a mind game.

Someone like Lucian naturally wielded his confidence and presence like a weapon, subtly undermining his opponents, making them doubt their own strength before the fight even began.

Vern had no plans of surrendering the psychological edge before they'd even crossed swords. Not that he was very keen on going head-on against that massive thing anyway.

The conditions were made clear to them beforehand. Anything but instant death was fair game. Their masters would intervene if things looked unnecessarily hairy for either of them.

With all that in mind, Vern focused.

His last words and gesture sparked something in Lucian as his smile grew wider, and he bellowed, "Give me your fucking best, then!" Resting his sword on his shoulder, he burst into a sprint.

"Wah! It's on!"

The crowd's roar intensified as Lucian dove from the rooftop's edge, launching himself toward Vern as two gleaming cables shot from his waist, propelling him forward with explosive speed.

Vern's outstretched hand fell to the side, his heart pounded like a drum, and his mind churned with myriad possibilities as it plotted his strategy for the fight.

He had deliberately entered this fight with minimal knowledge about Lucian's fighting style, aiming to replicate a battle with unpredictable foes he might face in the future.

His hand involuntarily reached for Duality's hilt, but he forced it back. *Not yet.*

He was going to wait until the last second. He had been trying to embody the tenet of *instability before stability* in his every action. This was how he progressed as an observer, and it would be foolish not to maximize his gains whenever possible.

It didn't always work, but whenever there were stakes, following this tenet helped him understand his viewpoint better.

His coat fluttered as the cold wind buffeted him, but he stood there amid the snowflakes as Lucian came hurling toward him, the ropecaster's strings latching onto one structure after another as he closed the gap.

Vern followed every anchor Lucian used for those wires in his perception while his fleshly eyes reflected all the people who were bewildered by his lack of action.

Jumping off a wall, Lucian twirled up in the air, building a terrifying momentum as he coiled for a downward slash, and Vern looked on with naked jealousy.

My body's not tough enough to handle even a single accident while using a rope-caster. Mistress had denied him even coming close to the contraption without infusing the old blood. The dynamics of this fight would have been so different otherwise.

With a dreadful amount of inertia stored in that massive blade, Lucian soared even higher, his silhouette bright against the setting sun.

Finally, the strings launched and clamped on to a pillar above and behind Vern, sending Lucian hurling toward him like a meteor.

Vern's blood pumped hard, and he took conscious control of his posture, all his muscles tightening in anticipation. *Almost . . .*

He couldn't directly influence Lucian's gears because all observers had the habit of keeping the subjective ownership of their gears—including himself.

Yet, there was no need for him to be direct. Lucian was careless. Or maybe he didn't know how Vern's vision worked.

The crowd gasped, and a rush like never before claimed Vern as his thought space pulsed with instability.

Yet, he didn't move.

With every instant, the shadow loomed larger and the crowd held their breath. The whole garden turned as silent as a graveyard, but Vern was living it. Feeling it.

Lucian had a puzzled expression, but there was no hesitation in his actions as the downward slash aimed to claim Vern's head.

Vern watched it all with intense focus, and he counted three beats of his heart when—
Now!

Each of his eyes flared with a white ring, and a sharp *snap* echoed as cranksteel wires recoiled toward Lucian. Debris fell behind him, and the chunk of the pillar where the ropecaster's clamps were anchored ground into fine dust.

"Wha—" Lucian's immaculate posture and form quickly crumbled as his controlled descent turned into a free fall, and Vern could see there was no way for Lucian to recover from that mid-air, much less release all that momentum without opening up even bigger gaps in his defense.

Vern pulled back his leg as his hands shot toward Duality; his eyes zeroed in on the sides of the uncontrollable force of nature that was Lucian.

The battle was on. Vern had snatched the upper hand in the opening, and it was time to exploit it.

The combined blade flared violet with instability in his hand, and he executed a slanted slash beat to beat, cutting across Lucian's abductors as he rocketed past him.

But the moment Vern's blade kissed Lucian's armor, a *zwang* echoed ominously. His blade sharpened with instability, managing only to carve a tiny gash in the metal before the chance slipped away.

Crash!

Snow and dust erupted into the air as Lucian, barely managing to arrest his charge, drove his sword into the ground. The earth split beneath the blade's might, halting his advance with brute force.

Vern had been ready to hold back the moment his sword drew blood, but what the fuck was this? He knew the armor wasn't for show, but instability inducement, when applied to Duality, was no joke either.

"Holy fuck, man. That was dirty! I like it!" Lucian coughed.

Vern, however, narrowed his eyes and bolted toward the blonde, his sword gleaming with deadly light.

Tang.

Lucian barely managed to put up his guard, hoisting the massive sword's flat toward Vern.

"Whoa—" Lucian gasped as that simple exchange wedged a nick in that inch-thick blade.

Vern kept up the pressure, slashing once, twice—crisscrossing nicks on the darned thing before Lucian managed to stand back up.

A wire shot out of his hand, and the gears reeled back the string, pulling him out of the downward slash aimed for his head.

Vern expanded his perception, chasing the new destination of this ropecaster. However, his perception was met with emptiness he couldn't perceive.

Vern clicked his tongue. *Tch. Lucian wasn't as dumb as he'd thought. He now knows to observe the immediate area around his anchor points.*

That wasn't to say Vern couldn't destabilize the whole thing, but he didn't want to pay the cost for the cascading effects of smashing a whole pillar—or worse, the whole tower.

That would mean the end of the battle for him.

He debated chasing Lucian on foot but quickly gave up the idea. *He could just keep running away like this.* Vern would spend his stamina while Lucian would just use some steam.

I'll let him come to me, then.

So Vern relaxed and eyed Lucian, who held his abdomen, a small hint of red dripping from the chink in his armor.

Yet, the wound inside healed right back up in mere moments. *Fuck. This is some bullshit level of cheating.*

"That was good, man. But don't think you can get me twice with the same thing." Lucian dusted himself off and rested the sword's tip on the ground with a *thump* as he took rapid, deep breaths.

Damn. Did that excite him instead? Was he feeling no psychological pressure from this? Hmm, no. Lucian's just a little wrong in the head.

So Vern took the time to reorient himself and smiled before replying, "Sounds like someone's got excuses today."

"Hahaha, I like it. I like it. I really hope you can keep this up. Trust me. This is what I want."

As Vern waited for Lucian, Ambrose shouted, "Ahem. Simon, are you seeing this? Didn't know you were one to bet all your money on a mindless brute. Here I thought the rhythm guided you to do that."

Then he chuckled to himself. "Oops, my bad. Forgot you can sense fuck all kind of rhythm."

Simon remained silent, his hand on his chin.

However, some other guy spoke up, "Just you wait, young master. Now that Mr. Lucian is prepared for that trick, things will go down for that guy real quick."

Ambrose simply snorted and continued watching with interest. At least the newbies knew how to put on a show.

Lucian used this leeway to reattach the ropecaster's rerouting contraption before cracking his neck and aiming his sword toward Vern another time. "Let's go for round two."

Vern remained in his usual calm headspace. To him, this was exactly like Mistress had put it, a complex game of chess, and he appreciated every second of it.

Real-life encounters wouldn't give him the safety net he had here. With his mind ready for the next bout, he nodded and said, "Round two it is."

"Hi-yah!" Lucian stomped and let out a battle cry before rushing at Vern, his massive sword primed behind him for an overhead slam.

Stability Vern thought, and his glowing Duality instead devoured light, turning heavier in his hand as he shifted to his most practiced ox guard stance—leveling the sword's blade with his eyes.

However, he knew that alone wouldn't be enough. So right as Lucian was upon him, he perceived the air around the blonde's ears and—*pop.*

It was nothing but the most minor of distractions, but Lucian's attack trajectory shifted just a tad.

To exacerbate this inaccuracy, Vern shuffled to the right and received it with his blade's length, redirecting all the force in one direction.

Bam! The giant sword slammed into the ground, and the moment the weight was lifted off Duality, he connected it into an upward slash.

Rip. Tang.

He barely managed another shallow cut before Lucian blocked it. *Damn! How the hell did he get such a big hunk of metal back up so fast?*

However, his peripheral vision gave him the answer in the next instant. Half the blade had turned ethereal, and Vern understood what just happened.

He can control the exact part of his sword to materialize. A practical application of his visions for sure. It essentially negated the poor mobility that came with a great sword.

Another variable for him to consider.

However, Lucian had no plans of letting Vern breathe. The gigantic blade disappeared again, leaving nothing but the hilt as he pulled his hand taut for another attack.

It was so fast, there was no time to retreat. Vern's heart thumped wildly, but he somehow managed to transition that last attack into a guarding stance. An empty hilt came for his chest with a terrifying promise.

As expected, in the last moment, a ginormous mass manifested on the hilt out of nowhere, creating a whirlwind as Vern flailed to angle Duality against it.

Clang.

A tremor spread through Vern's body, and he tasted copper as he took the full brunt of that attack, almost losing his footing. *Fuck!*

That was bad. It packed a lot of punch. Negating all that force wasn't going to be easy.

Giving Vern no chance to counter, Lucian continued his flurry of attacks, imbuing the hilt with momentum, which magically then transferred over to that hulking block of steel.

Bam.

One parry after another, Vern stepped back, trying to get out of the range of the attacks, but failing to do so.

However, with every exchange, he found ways to better nullify or redirect the force. Next when the sword came for a skull crusher, he perceived the ground beneath his feet and timed a destabilization to synchronize with the hit received by Duality.

Clang. The moment the blades made contact, the ground cracked beneath his feet, channeling some of that force like a lightning rod catching thunder.

Sweat trickled down his brow as he continued to block one hit after another, his arms starting to feel numb from the havoc that giant sword wreaked on him.

This can't go on . . .

And he switched up his tactics right away.

As the colossal blade materialized just beyond his arms for the umpteenth time, a purple glow flared on the edge of Duality at the last moment.

Instead of trying to redirect the attack like earlier, he slashed toward the massive blade, aiming for a frontal clash that should come out with victory for his destabilized edge.

Swish! However, when Duality made contact with metal, a blue flare erupted from Lucian's eyes, his blade turned ethereal, and the purple edge cut nothing but air.

Tch. He clicked his tongue. *It worked out differently in my head.*

"Hahaha! I knew it. I knew you could push me harder!" Lucian stared Vern down as he made for another attack.

Vern didn't have the capacity to conversate with the crazed Lucian as he took this opportunity to back out of the massive weapon's range, perceiving the ground around him as he did so.

Lucian smirked. "Don't run away, now. It's only starting to get fun," he said and pursued him.

Crack.

However, the moment Lucian took his next step, the ground beneath his feet caved, and he stumbled. *Hah. It worked?!* Vern assumed Lucian would be able to suss out such a blatant trap.

Seems not. But this was good.

He synchronized small bursts on the ground with each footfall, allowing him to leap farther and run faster as he rapidly covered the distance he'd just retreated.

Whizz.

Lucian tried to run away again, but Vern was also ready this time and in a perfect position.

The moment strings shot out of his hand, Vern chopped down. It didn't cut the wire but managed to throw it off wildly, pulling Lucian in an unexpected direction. When Lucian managed to halt the gears, Vern had circled around to get a clear shot at his back.

A smile appeared on Vern's face, and he didn't let such an opportunity go—thrusting his sword with all the might.

However, Lucian did something entirely unexpected. He took that hilt and . . . stabbed himself?

The massive blade protruded from his own back, and since Vern's instincts had sharpened over the past week, he narrowly saved himself from being impaled by the unexpected assault. And all he managed in return was a minor slash on Lucian's armor.

"You've got some tricks up your sleeve, too, eh?" Vern conceded, acknowledging the surprise with a nod. It completely caught him off guard.

But he didn't allow the shock to paralyze him. Adrenaline surged through his veins as he launched back into the fray, determined not to offer Lucian even a moment of respite.

Clang-shh.

His purple edge struck the giant sword, only for it to disappear as Lucian tried trick after trick to regain his footing.

It was exactly like a minute ago, but Lucian was the one caught off-balance this time. The crowd cheered and jeered, but each thump of Vern's heart drowned it all out.

Thump! Thump! Thump!

Amid a whirlwind of feints and strikes, Vern pushed through the pain, his body hurting everywhere—the aftermath of the previous defensive moves. Lucian, however, fared worse, his body gradually marked by an increasing number of wounds.

Once again, Vern had decisively claimed the upper hand.

That's when Lucian suddenly did something wholly unexpected. Instead of dodging or blocking Vern's thrust, he rushed right into him.

Vern's instinct nearly made him retract his hands, yet he held firm, his sword piercing the armor as they collided.

However, instead of the anticipated resistance from skewering flesh, his hands felt . . . nothing.

An ominous premonition welled up in his mind, but it was too late.

"Seems I can't beat you without using all my visions, after all," Lucian declared as he completely ignored both the swords and rammed right into Vern with his formidable physique.

Before Vern could react, a knee crashed into his abdomen. Bone met bone, and a loud *crack* cut through the pounding in his ears as he was sent flying.

Blood erupted from Vern's mouth as he tumbled, finally slamming against a pillar with a heavy *thump.*

Yet, the ground trembled beneath him the next instant, and a monster with blue eyes jumped high in the air, the colossal sword gripped in both his arms, poised to split Vern in two.

CHAPTER 50

DUEL II

Vern's head was a mess of pain and fog. His eyes reflected a blurry, dizzy world, but the grays of his perception made it clear that he would be proverbially dead if he didn't do something quick.

He assessed his meager options and realized he had close to none. Running away was the only valid choice, but he was a little too late to start now. However, the pain in his back reminded him of the pillar, and it clicked in his head.

Gritting his teeth, he gripped the sword hard and slashed behind him at an angle—the purple edge vibrating as it cut through the pillar like a hot knife through butter.

A fissure appeared in his perception at the point of impact, and he mentally grabbed hold of it with maddening fervor as Lucian reached the peak, on the verge of descending to obliterate everything in his path.

Creak—the pillar groaned, yet Vern realized this single slice wasn't going to cut it.

Ah, damn this! Vern bit his tongue, funneling an overwhelming surge of energy into the effort, focusing much of it on creating another fissure at the top to hasten the fall.

His eyes burned with intensity, but the payoff was immediate and dramatic. *Crack* after *crack* extended around the pillar's circumference, severing it from both top and bottom with definitive thumps.

The middle segment began its sliding descent due to the smooth cuts, and he pushed back at its base as if his life depended on it. Predictably, the top started to tilt, with Vern becoming the unwitting pivot for the pillar's demise.

Glancing back, he caught Lucian's gaze, now wilder with frenzy, as a gigantic marble slab appeared right in his path.

Yet, the man didn't care and smashed right through it with his sword.

Bam.

A tinge of fear washed through Vern as a web of cracks ran down the height of the pillar before exploding into debris and stone.

Vern swallowed the blood that his internal organs couldn't seem to keep contained and took this chance to leap out of the way. Disintegrating everything that came flying in his direction with either his sword or eyes, he cleared out of the area.

Dust swirled everywhere, and the crowd went wild with their cheers. However, Vern paid little mind to it as he barely found his footing and focused on the balance within his body—hoping to heal some of the damage.

Just need to make sure I don't create anything new. With Cedric's warning clear in his mind, he assessed his own skeletal frame and quickly noticed many broken ribs.

Stability. And the moment it activated, it was as if worms crawled inside his body, shearing at his flesh and organs. He let out a sharp breath, distracting himself by focusing on the surroundings.

"Haha-Hahaha! You're full of surprises, man. Thought I had you there for a second." Lucian huffed, veins pulsing near his glowing blue eyes amid the settling dust and rubble.

Vern didn't know why Lucian wasn't using this chance to rush him and finish him off for good. Because if he did, Vern wouldn't be able to resist much with his innards in such a tangled mess.

Maybe it's because of that last vision? Seems like it didn't come cheap. Which made sense because it was a disgusting ability—being able to pass through objects selectively.

Vern simply kept his mouth shut. He realized he wasn't a big fan of talking during combat. It wasn't optimal because he was missing out on the psychological warfare that came with it. *Well, only so much I can do in my first real fight.*

However, Lucian wasn't like that. "I'm quite mad at myself," he chuckled. "I should clearly have the advantage in this fight, but you're still standing there, almost unscathed."

My ribs would like to disagree, Vern grumbled internally but maintained an outward front of strength, brushing off his coat as if shedding the fight's weight. At least he had managed to stabilize his viscera a bit.

"Guess I underestimated you," Lucian admitted with a forceful *thump* as his sword cleaved the earth effortlessly. Locking eyes with Vern, he declared with a deliberate pause between each word, "Not . . . anymore." His eyes flared like stars before a blue radiance blinded Vern momentarily.

"Wha! He disappeared! Wait, did you all see that?"

"What kinda vision is that?! Do you know his shade sequence?"

The volatile crowd continued to shout, and Vern's slowly relaxing heart suddenly ramped up as his perception faced something entirely new.

A haze of darkness settled over his grays, making him work twice as hard to perceive them. However, they weren't entirely gone like usual.

It was as if Lucian had taken subjective ownership of everything around him, but only partly. What was worse was that he couldn't sense where Lucian was at all.

Usually, observers were like beacons of darkness in a world of light—like the mirror spirits. But right now, everything was dull, and there were no gaping holes to guide him.

Vern furrowed his brows and gripped Duality harder as he stood there, trying to pick up the most minute of the changes.

Suddenly, the air rippled behind him.

Clang.

He barely managed to turn around in time, deflecting the thrust that was about to impale his back.

Fuck! He sliced back at the elusive figure, but the silhouette was gone before he could even graze its flesh.

Vern's heart fell as all his mental simulations pointed to a similar result of such passive back-and-forth. Lucian's combat style forced him to be defensive.

First, he couldn't chase the guy because of the ropecaster and had to wait for him to come to him. Now, it was worse than that—Lucian held all the initiative.

This is bad—a nonoptimal balance, really. I need to find ways to shift it.

So Vern pivoted unpredictably, using quick surges of instability beneath his feet to alternately hasten and decelerate his movements.

He could just focus harder on his perception and try to suss out Lucian, but then he would be going down the same path as Cedric—and be blindsided by that limited perspective.

Also, Mistress pointed out that too much dependence on his perception, which just depicted stability, wasn't enough for a real fight.

So he kept a sharp eye on every little thing around him—the rustle of the wind, the pathing of the snowflakes, the tremors of instability.

That's when he felt tiny signs of disturbance at nine o'clock, and a sharp glint crossed his eyes.

An opportunity! He whipped his left hand to intercept the incoming assault, and intercept it he did with a resonant *tang*. However, another sound mingled with all this.

Tch-tching. Sparks flew as his right hand sprang into action, the tendons in his left straining under the effort to counteract the formidable force.

"Huh?!" A surprised yelp escaped the shadowed figure before Vern, but it was already too late. One blade, black as night, parried the blow while its purple counterpart gleamed fiercely, slicing a deep gash through the gear strapped to his adversary's belt.

Yes! Vern silently cheered, pressing his advantage, but his quarry vanished once more, leaving behind a cascade of cogs and gears that tumbled to the ground.

"Whoa, he managed to take out the Kingsman's gadget. Lucian's fucked."

"Lucian didn't need it anyway. Are you not seeing how he's playing him like a fiddle?"

"Damn. This sneaky guy is really playing dirty, huh? Come on, Lucian, show him!"

"Whoa, he's wielding dual blades?! Wait. It's from the Finnesse workshop, isn't it?! Only they make stuff like that! Holy! Another—"

Vern drowned out all the yelling and cursing, tuning back into the heightened sense of his surroundings.

But this is good. He'd managed to cut off Lucian's primary method of escape. *Now, I just need to figure out what to do about this overpowered vision.*

Vern's left hand was numbing fast. The impact of those strikes was more damaging than anticipated, far beyond a mere scratch he could mend with stability.

Fixing such damage without somehow also making it worse was beyond his current understanding.

Hmm, he has to be spending a lot of representation to pull this off. Clearly, keeping the subjective ownership of their environments, even if partly, had to be draining.

How did this even work? Is it kind of like me back in the mirror realm at the start, where I only somewhat understood the water?

Hmm, maybe I can still control this. He imagined a wave of instability spreading all around him, turning the dull world a notch brighter.

His eyes flared bright, but all that appeared was a tiny wave of radiance that got swallowed by the darkness in no time.

Tch. He clicked his tongue. *What is going on? Something happened, but not enough to drive any change. But doesn't this run counter to the second axiom of observation?*

How could he "somewhat" observe it? That's when another change appeared in his surroundings, and he preempted a slash.

Rustle.

His sword hit nothing.

A feint?

Swoosh. Something else moved behind him, and he jumped away, but again, there was nothing.

Oof, he's being smart about it. Lucian was trying to confuse him with all these feints.

Once, twice, thrice . . . Each of them forced him to react to the best of his capabilities without being able to figure out anything new.

Suddenly, a massive blade materialized, looming ominously above Vern. With no time to spare, he switched both swords to their most stable form, crossing them overhead in a desperate guard—

Bam.

The impact sent shock waves through his body, the earth beneath him shattering, his knees buckling under the unprecedented assault. This direct hit was more than just brutal—it was crippling.

Barely deflecting the force, Vern gritted his teeth, his vision blurring with pain as he ducked and staggered forward, targeting the shadowy figure. Yet, the moment their steel disengaged, Lucian faded out of existence once more.

Fuck. I need to do something.

He scrambled for any solution, trying one failed strategy after another, but to no avail.

Each attempt left him more vulnerable, the situation growing increasingly grim.

Everything somewhat worked but not enough to break the cycle of relentless damage and evasion.

"Hey, who do you think is going to win?"

"I gotta say, the guy with the dual swords is putting up a fierce fight, but my money's on the big guy."

"Man, the old blood's strength is unreal. Did you see him shatter the ground like it was nothing? I've only seen observers from the monster shade sequence pull off something like that."

"Seriously, with old blood this strong, do you think we're about to see a surge in powerhouses? It's outside help, after all. I even heard rumors about some ancient ruin's discovery, so they found more, right?"

"Forget it. Those hoarders at Kingsly Court have it all under lock and key, especially the good stuff. They're just throwing away scraps at these pathetic lowborns."

"Hey, shut up, man! We're in the Vigil, and for heaven's sake, the Eclipsed Reaper's right above us. I'd like to keep my head, thank you very much."

"Hmph. Whatever."

Arthur weaved through the crowd, gathering snippets of conversations as he went. Each opinion added a layer to his understanding, a mosaic of perspectives that fascinated him.

However, he was most interested in the opinions of the Kingsmen. *What do they feel about this?*

So he climbed one floor after another and reached the walkway above the roof where Sir Osric and Lady Amelia stood.

Luckily, there were only a few people watching from up here, leaning on the railings. He conspicuously pulled an orange dagger from his pocket, chanted the name of Seraphine the Omniscient, and lightly nicked himself on the skin.

A sudden rush of terrifying thoughts burst into his mind, but he'd long gotten used to their onslaught. After a while, his pulse calmed down, and the sounds around him amplified significantly.

His ears began to pick up every little thing, but Arthur tuned out the ambient distractions, concentrating on the conversation unfolding beneath him. As Sir Osric made emphatic gestures toward the arena, Arthur's heightened senses caught the words clearly.

"What is wrong with that fool? Seems like I didn't beat the lesson into him hard enough."

What? Arthur hadn't expected that.

"I instructed him to cut the theatrics and go all out right from the start. Now look at him, barely holding his own."

Lady Amelia nodded, a slight smile on her face.

"And these rich brats? Watching as if they're some monkeys fighting in a circus. Tch. We should've gone for a place far from these prying eyes, like I said."

Lady Amelia's gaze then drifted back to the central tower. After a moment, Arthur's followed suit, sweeping across the building's height until it settled on the pinnacle.

There, a blindfolded figure and another smaller person stood behind the window, both silhouettes casting a foreboding presence.

Arthur instantly looked away. *Fuck me! It's Captain Akira.* He shrunk into himself, trying to disappear into the background, pretending he hadn't seen a thing. The collective insights of the crowd meant nothing if it risked drawing the prince's attention his way.

Yet the remnants of the perceptivity ritual lingered, betraying him as Lady Amelia's words floated to him, "The prince must have his reasons. He was insistent on Vern and Lucian clashing here in the Vigil, aiming for the grandest display possible."

Hmm, here I thought Gareth alone tricked all these people into watching this. Another reason for Arthur to keep a low profile. Clearly, the prince was orchestrating something, and Arthur had no desire to become a pawn in his game.

Or at least not one that was captured.

"Yeah, but my idiot apprentice is dragging the Kingsmen's name through the mud. How can it take someone with twice the power and gear this long to win? It'd be one thing if Vern were one of the old blood, but this? It's a stain on our honor."

Mistress Amelia simply shrugged. "Should have taught him better."

"Pff . . ." Arthur struggled to stifle a laugh. Lady Amelia was straightforward, it seemed.

"Teach how though? The kid's head is denser than a night beast's hide. He has the instincts of a grandmaster but the common sense of a fool."

Arthur nodded. *That's Lucian, alright.*

Just then, a collective gasp from the others on the walkway drew their attention back to the garden below, and Arthur's eyes snapped to the unfolding fight.

Oh . . . His eyes lit up. Something was going on with the environment around the arena, and before he could figure it out, Lady Amelia's words cut into his thoughts, resonating with him.

"The fight's nearing its climax. Be prepared to step in."

CHAPTER 51

DUEL III

Vern swallowed the blood that rose from his insides as he blocked another hit. This was tough. A bit too much for him, really, who barely had a week of training under his belt.

How the fuck was he supposed to nullify such an absurd amount of force with just his body and swords reinforced by indirect visions? *Maybe I overestimated myself. I should have prepared better.*

Even Lucian wore armor instead of those horrible clothes to the battle, but Vern had chosen to come with bare minimum gear—even forgoing the vapor blaster. It was coming back to bite him now.

He had clear reasons for doing so, but Lucian's combined advantage of gear, weapon, strength, and this disgusting vision turned out to be too much to handle. His mind was perfectly fine. But his body? *Ugh!*

He still had more than two-thirds of his representation, but what did it matter if his hands went limp long before he could use any of it?

In a real battle, he might just say fuck it and collapse the whole building or something, but even that wasn't an option right now. There were people in there, and it felt a bit too much like flipping the table because he couldn't win.

Swish.

He ducked, barely avoiding the swing that crossed overhead, and sent another flare of instability around him, hoping to wrest the ownership from Lucian.

Sizzle . . .

Yet all that obeyed his command were the tiny snowflakes that evaporated in an instant. Yet they were so sparse they couldn't do much to the man nor help him wrench ownership of subjectivity indirectly.

He slashed, but Lucian faded into nothingness once again. *Tch.* He gnashed his teeth.

This was bullshit. His visions worked, but they didn't do anything useful.

Hah. Let's calm down.

Seems like I can't control the surrounding air that well. Hmm, or maybe Lucian's doing it better than me?

The latter conjecture seemed more and more plausible by the second as he dodged and performed some devastating blocks.

That's when an idea crossed his mind, and he had to force his body not to jerk to a halt and get chopped as he thought, *Yes! It might just work.*

He focused within his perception once again, but instead of trying to mess with his immediate surroundings that were covered by a haze due to interference from Lucian, he zeroed in on the area above it.

Stability, he thought, imagining a white dome right above them, beyond the demarcation of the haze Lucian had a hold of.

"Wait, what's that?" someone shouted.

"You're seeing that, too, right?"

"Huh? Why is the snow gathering in the air?"

"Hmph. It must be another one of Lucian's tricks. Seems like he's got more to show us."

Nope, it's me, and it's working as well as I'd imagined, thank you very much.

However, these offhanded comments seemed to spark something in Lucian. Right in the next moment, a clearly noticeable ripple spread behind Vern, and he avoided it with a simple dash to the side.

Bam!

Good. Fear it. Lucian might not understand what Vern was going for with this roof made of air, but just like anyone with common sense, he probably feared the unknown, wishing to end things before this inexplicable guillotine executed him.

Vern continued to prop up the heaven of stability above their heads as holes began to appear in the dome. Air's structure was not an optimal choice for stabilization.

It inherently didn't have the bonds needed to hold much weight, at least not when spread around like this.

The white rings in his black pupils continued to shine as more and more snowflakes accumulated above them, and Lucian hurled one attack after another at a pace that was increasingly becoming deadly for Vern.

Clang.

Sweat dripped down Vern's forehead while blood flowed out of his midsection as he somehow continued to hold on, almost getting impaled a couple of times.

However, while doing all this, he recalled the penultimate day of his training. He'd spent the whole morning perfecting one move and that move alone.

It wasn't the most devastating attack, but it was definitely close to the top. With the snow overhead almost done piling, he focused on the edge of his left blade.

Stability inducement.

Stability inducement.

Stability inducement.

One after another, he unleashed the vision around the edge, and the air surrounding it condensed into a visible mass. That's when—*thump.*

The flat of that massive blade caught him right in the hips, and he bit down a scream, trying to flow in the direction of the attack to minimize its impact.

He barely managed his footing, but his instincts screamed at him, and he leaped away once more.

With another *thump*, the ethereal blade emerged out of nothingness and shattered the ground where he stood a moment ago.

Shit. He's getting restless.

Vern looked up at the snow accumulated and came to a decision. *Fuck it. This is good enough.*

With his mind made up, his eyes flared, and the roof that kept the snow eroded to an extent. This made sure the snow didn't just plop down in large chunks. That would mess with the subsequent part of his plan.

When the fake heaven rained, the sight turned reminiscent of a snowstorm, and a copious amount of flakes filled his perception. Vern repeated to himself, *stability before instability.* Inverse of his usual tenet.

Sizzle.

Whir.

Almost all the snowflakes around him instantly turned into water and then steam. Except that wasn't all; something weird happened in parallel, and he quickly noticed an odd disturbance in his mind at six o'clock.

It was clear even for his eyes as the air flickered, showing glimpses of black-scaled armor, and the veil of invisibility became a torn mess.

This had gone far better than he hoped. A smile bloomed on Vern's face, and he mouthed, *Found you.*

With a precise aim, he whipped his left blade in that figure's direction, syncing his hand's motion with a tiny bit of instability on the surface of the edge to release the condensed air.

Whoosh!

A white blade of air shaped like the crescent of his right singularity blitzed through the space and struck true. "Agh! Fuc—" came a panicked cry, and a vertical slash tore through the armor, even drawing blood before it fizzled away.

The crowd erupted into collective gasps as Lucian stumbled, his body jerked out of the invisible state one flicker at a time.

This sent the haze covering Vern's perception into disarray, and he didn't miss this opportunity and pressed his advantage.

Instability.

The ground sunk underneath Lucian's already tumbling figure, and Vern rushed forward, his singularities poised on either side.

Clang.

Tang.

"Bloody hell, man. How did you do that?" groaned Lucian, parrying almost all his attacks even with that horrible posture. And the ones that did hit were far from being fatal.

Heh. Vern smirked back in response, but his heart was filled with worry. *Damn it! What should I do? All his attacks failed to bring the fight closer to an end. Just what would it take to finish this for good?*

He had another trump card in his arsenal, but there was no way he would be able to pull it off amid this hectic back-and-forth.

This time, when singularities hit the massive blade with a *clang*, Lucian suddenly disappeared, and Vern released the deluge of snow that had yet to be dumped down in kind, hoping to counter his invisibility as soon as possible.

He still hacked at the spots where Lucian might have rolled over, but it was as if the man's vision made him detached from reality, not invisible.

Ugh... Vern groaned as one of his right arm's tendons threatened to snap. He backed away, and when snow filled their vicinity once again, he repeated *instability.*

Crackle, zzzt, and myriad sharp noises boomed out from behind Vern, and he dodged easily as Lucian was thrown out of that realm once again.

Vern turned around and caved the ground beneath Lucian's feet for the umpteenth time, but the man seemed to anticipate it and only lost his balance a bit.

However, something far more interesting happened to Lucian. He gripped the side of his head with one hand, and his sword wobbled in the other. Bloody trails ran down his eyes, and the veins were swollen to an unnatural degree.

Vern didn't know what to do for a second, but the excited look behind those eyes helped him make the decision.

He pulled both his arms back and slashed. The right one made a clean cut, but Lucian still somehow managed to dodge the other one.

Is this even doing anything to this monster? It was hard to figure out because of that armor. Yet, he gritted his teeth and continued his relentless assault.

And completely out of his expectations, it became a slog of a battle as both sides repeated their tricks, only to be countered in the same fashion.

Vern breathed in large mouthfuls of air, trying to douse the fire that burned in his lungs. But it was for naught as the battle of attrition continued with each side countering the other somehow.

Then suddenly, Lucian slammed his sword down on the empty ground, and Vern backed away with a frown. Lucian bellowed before he could enter the fray again, "Wait a second!"

The adrenaline and the losing vigor of Vern's body suggested he ignore this remark and push the guy until the end—surely he was on his last leg too. However, the brain still prevailed, and he halted, taking this opportunity to regulate his terrible breathing.

"This is stupid, man. We're getting fucking nowhere. We did this to get some real combat experience and test out the practicality of our kits. Not this stupid cycle of back-and-forth."

Before Vern could say anything, the people watching from balconies and windows above them shouted, their words suddenly scathing.

"Hey, what's going on? Was that the end?"

"Ah, no. Who won, then? What happens to the bets? Are they nullified?"

"I know, right? Looks like they're done."

Lucian turned back and snarled, "Shut up! I am not fucking done. Just you wait."

He turned back to Vern and asked, "Do you feel the same?"

Hmm, This is indeed getting us nowhere. If we kept on like this, both of us would drop down from exhaustion sooner or later.

Vern physically and Lucian because of his eyes.

After a quick thought, Vern sighed and nodded. "What do you suggest?"

A smile formed on Lucian's bloody face framed by his matted blonde hair as his words boomed, "A final exchange. One attack to settle it all."

The crowd erupted at those words, their mood as unpredictable as the weather of this city.

Vern pondered this for a while, and his eyes involuntarily turned toward Mistress Amelia, who was standing high above them.

And as if noticing the question in his gaze, she nodded.

Does that mean she wants me to agree? What if we go too hard? Can they really stop such an attack in time? And if they'll stop it anyway, what's the point?

"Ah, fuck this." Vern grunted and stared back into Lucian's bloody eyes. "Let's do it." He wouldn't have many chances to go all out like this. It'd be a pity to waste it.

"That's my man!" Lucian cheered, stabbing his sword into the ground with excitement. "On ten?"

Vern nodded in understanding. "On ten." That would be enough time for Vern to prepare his best move. The one he'd only practiced a couple of times because of how destructive it was to his body.

Lucian's eyes suddenly became inert, and his veins calmed down, but a more primal aura surged out of him the next instant, and his demeanor changed entirely.

However, Vern ignored this transformation and focused on himself. *Time to use everything.* He sheathed the singularities on his back as they settled into their housing with a *click*.

This was the first step. His palms were still holding on to the individual hilts of the singularities, and he took a deep breath and focused.

Bending one knee forward, he slid the other one back. His posture turned leaner, and he dipped low, priming himself to launch forward.

Indistinct grays gave way to stress lines, and he focused on the ones within his body as well as on the sheath.

His hands pulled the two swords in opposite directions, but he kept them locked in there, forcefully stabilizing the latches, denying exit to his blades.

The stress in there accumulated with every breath that passed, and when the count fell to six, the springs groaned furiously.

Taking this as a cue, he moved on to the next part of his preparation—*instability*—and a purple glow flashed on the edges. That was just the start though.

Instability inducement.

Instability inducement.

Instability inducement.

It worked the same way as that stability wind slash but for instability. Not to anyone's surprise, this move was relatively harder to prepare because of what it fundamentally entailed to destabilize things.

An odd air differential formed within the sheath as the reality became more and more unstable around the edge of his blades. It was as if they were voids that consumed that air, but he knew better.

It was still condensing air around the blades, just with a different underlying assumption.

His sheath continued to work as a cauldron, where multiple aspects of his visions combined, and his eyes fell on Lucian, who was busy with his own preparations.

The blonde ran his palm over the edge of his blade, and it sliced through it without any inhibitions. Blood dripped on the length of that metal hunk, and the moment it came in contact with air, it seemed to ignite.

In a couple of seconds, the blade gleamed red, and in the next, it shone hotter than lava, sending chills down Vern's spine.

"Hngaah!" Lucian yelled, and a red aura exploded out of him, sending his hair and cape flying from the momentum alone. But the man ignored it all and leaned into a pouncing position.

Three. Vern focused on the stress lines of his arm and destabilized them, allowing him to store a terrifying amount of tension within his muscles.

Two. Even the casing made of cranksteel, which wasn't in direct contact with the blades, sheared and lost its shape, a *weng* sound emanating from his back.

One. His heart raced with a maddening fervor, and his hands shook from the sheer force they were holding back. Giving his legs the same treatment of tension, he zeroed in on the enemy.

The excited crowd suddenly lost their collective voice as if they had counted alongside Vern and knew what was coming.

In this oppressive silence, both men shouted at the same time, "Zero!"

Chapter 52

COLLISION OF FLOWS

Three!"

Someone shouted behind Victoria, and she felt the urge to pepper them with her knives if it meant they'd shut up and let her focus.

There was so much disparity in how Lucian and Vern built up their final attacks, and she was running out of time to dissect it.

A literal sea raged within her eyes as the fluids she saw curved and bent around Vern—swirling, twirling, focusing on that sheath on his back.

She could generally figure out far more detail than just that, but Vern clearly had better command over the surroundings than she did, suppressing her perception.

How can a first shade like him distort reality to such an extent? she wondered, frowning and watching him compress all that force and reality.

What was even more bizarre was how his eyes looked perfectly unharmed. Almost as if doing all this didn't empty his representation reserves at all.

Lucian had forcefully taken ownership of that space for a couple of minutes, and he was almost about to lose his eyes for good.

Yet Vern had also used his visions nonstop since the start. *Why, then, is he not even fazed?*

She tried imagining herself going against Lucian, and the only path to victory for her was to overwhelm him right from the start. Allowing him even a single opportunity to use that sword on her would mean the end of the fight for her.

It was a miracle Vern endured all those attacks head on. Even when reinforced by wave barriers, her knives would stand no chance against that much pure strength.

"Two. Just two seconds. It's about to happen, boys!"

Shut up! she almost screamed, but knew that would mean this fleeting moment would be lost in meaningless argument.

Somehow ignoring the ticking clock, she turned toward Lucian, and her heart began thumping in fear.

If Vern was like a sharp and deadly flow, Lucian was more of a raging torrent, one made of magma. Simply looking at him hurt her eyes. *The Kingsmen are wild cards.*

A bloody sea gushed out of Lucian, smoldering the crimson fire around the man as he soaked up more and more of it—channeling it all into his sword.

Her family's archon had told her not to make enemies of the Kingsmen even before duskfall, and she could see why. *Would they deny me if I asked for an infusion of the old blood?* After all, she was from the newer wave of nobles.

The blood-borne art had restrictions baked into it for the last generation nobles only, not the new ones like her.

"One."

Ugh! What the hell am I even thinking?

Victoria snapped out of her daydreams and gripped the edge of the railing, her knuckles turning white from the sheer force.

Her heart raced to a zenith in anticipation as their flow solidified almost like the calm before the storm.

The terrifying aura from both the monsters condensed into an even sharper wave as the ground cracked and the wind ebbed.

The morons behind her finally shut up, and both men down in the ruined garden leaned forward.

Above her, two more destructive ripples emerged in the sea of reality, surely the famed Kingsmen getting ready to defend their pupils.

She unconsciously held on to the cravat around her neck, crumpling it to try to release some of the pressure surrounding her.

That's when the silence shattered and two shouts came in unison.

"Zero!"

Bang.

Waves parted behind them in her perception, and like bullets bursting out of the chamber, both the men disappeared from their initial positions.

She etched every minute movement in her memory—the way Vern broke the ground and launched himself forward, how Lucian brute-forced even more power than that out of thin air, and how their flows exploded.

They parted the fluid that made up the reality like two ships on a collision course. Right as their bows were about to smash into each other, their masts unfurled and they released the terrifying might in their arsenal.

Clang!

A purple glow exploded from Vern's sheath as it suddenly opened up from its sides and two blades darker than the night itself whipped out of them in a cross arc.

Lucian, on the other hand, stomped right before Vern, and his bloody longsword launched into an upward arc.

That's when someone shouted behind her, "Shit! Move aside, girl, and let me watch."

"Fuck off," she yelled without turning and created a small *wavebash* with her hand, launching the man out of the crowd.

Forgetting about that untimely disturbance almost instantly, she savored the final moments of this battle.

Blade met blade—one red and two purple—in the most satisfying *clang* ever as her own blood boiled in this display of utter madness, the crowd exploding with excitement.

Lucian seemed to be entirely out of representation, for his sword didn't turn illusory and met a gruesome fate as the purple ones sheared right through the metal.

Not that it changed the course of the fight, for a vertical bloody arc had already sprayed out of that massive hunk of metal, corroding even the air itself as it landed on Vern's body.

In that very instant, something magical happened.

Two even deeper crimson auras exploded from both their chests, instantly expanding and swirling as they draped over their bodies like some skin.

Victoria sneaked a glance upward and saw that the two master Kingsmen had their hands outstretched, a red haze flowing around their fingers.

What is this trickery?! Were they creating something akin to a shield with the power of blood? No one had told her they could do such a thing.

Suddenly, the people all around her who'd been holding their breath threw their fists in the air, screaming their excitement in one way or the other.

"Wahh! their combined voice was so loud she felt the vibrations in the flow of the whole palace.

"Aghhh! Motherfucker—"

"Hahhh!"

Almost drowned by these cheers came a guttural scream followed by a yelp as she almost lost her grip when the destructive attacks interacted with the red aura of their opponent.

Vern's cross slash physically razed the dual armor on Lucian's body—blood and scales alike—as they failed to hold the corrosion back. The red one stretched inside his body as the slices created deep wounds, blood spurting out of them in droves.

Fascinating!

When the blades finished their arcs, purple energy remained—wreaking havoc on Lucian's flesh. The red armor didn't allow the energy to invade his innards, but it didn't entirely stop it either.

Is that intentional? To give them the taste of pain they'd face, had they received these attacks in real life?

Because Vern was undergoing the same process. An upward slash of a bloody arc wanted to split him down the middle, but the only part of his body that remained unharmed was his head.

The rest met the same gruesome fate as Lucian. The red skin protected him just enough to not exacerbate the wounds, but it was clear it pointedly relayed every ounce of pain he was owed.

Victoria shuddered imagining herself on the receiving end of these attacks.

No . . . no. This is madness. The terrible sea of fluid colored by their personal perspectives raged around them with a fury so potent it disintegrated the waves time and again, just like the ones crashing in her heart.

Thump. The chopped heavy blade fell to the side, but the two men were already on their knees, clutching at their abdomens. Yet, that first scream was their only expression of pain.

Almost as if they'd agreed to decide the winner and loser based on who screamed first—neither opened their mouth.

"Oh my god, oh my god, oh my god! I feel like I'm in love. Why is it over?! This is crazy! Who are these people?! Where can I meet them? How can I date them? They're so cool!"

"That was fucking beautiful! This is how real men should fight! Fuck, I want to duel someone right now."

"Hey, I am on Lucian's team, you know? If you guys have something to ask, I can relay your questions to him for a small fee."

"Shut up, man. Lemme replay that in my mind a couple times."

"A marvelous display of skills indeed. The finesse and the control they showed is breathtaking. We should—"

"Hey, forget all that. Look there!" someone yelled, pointing behind Lucian, and the combusting crowd turned their attention.

Gasps echoed all around her when she noticed that the purple arcs that hadn't landed directly on Lucian's body continued to whiz through the air, disintegrating everything they touched.

"Fuck! Someone stop it. Looks like that thing has no plans of halting on its own. It'll enter the central tower and cut through who knows what."

Victoria suddenly felt an impulse to test herself against that attack. So she narrowed her eyes as the sea within them raged.

With a deep breath, she used the second vision of her shade sequence, *wave barrier.*

The reality folded in front of the path of the purple hues and—

"Ahh," a cry escaped her mouth as her sight suddenly turned bloody. She'd definitely burst a vein there. *Wh-what?* She tried to get hold of the railing, almost keeling over.

But when that guy who'd been eyeing her like some piece of candy since the start tried to touch her, she recoiled, finding her footing as she politely warned him, "Sorry. I am good. Just lost my balance there for a second."

He backed away with a scowl, and she couldn't help but wonder what the hell these nobles were doing here. She remembered that they weren't her colleagues, just random people of influence.

This guy specifically belonged to the trifecta of top noble families of the city. Vigil almost never had unnecessary people around.

What were they doing here again?

"Ahh, fuck." The guy who'd first warned everyone screamed, "Lady above and beyond, what the hell is this attack? It ripped through my aegis like nothing."

"You dumb logs, keep trying, or someone will get hurt."

"Shouldn't the Kingsmen be the one to handle these wayward attacks?"

"Yeah, you want to show them we can't do anything by ourselves, don't you? Shut up and try again."

Victoria massaged her head as she eyed the perpetrator of this attack down in the garden. She wasn't about to try to stop it again. It wasn't her problem; she had already reduced its potency enough. *And it's far too much for me anyway.*

Both men were sprawled on the ground as the vicious attacks continued to sunder their bodies—the light snow falling and evaporating instantly.

Her heart, which had been boiling all this time, failed to calm down as she tried to imagine the damage these bloody armors had to negate.

Strings flew through the air as the two Kingsmen landed next to the two stars of this show.

She wanted to hear what the masters said to their writhing apprentices, but the ruckus behind her grew in intensity once again.

"Alrighty! Now that you kids got that attack under control, me says I won this bet," shouted Ambrose with a wide grin, his hand reaching to scoop the piled money.

"No. No, how can you say such a thing, esteemed lord? Clearly, Mr. Lucian didn't lose. That other guy would be just as dead if this were a real battle."

"Yes, but that's not what we bet on, did we? You do see that only one of them lost their sword, right? Clearly, Vern won the ego competition here."

"No, sir, that's just semantics."

The heir from the Dexter family on the other side of the room simply shook his head and exited, leaving his money in the pile.

Even he agrees that Vern won? This made her wonder. Who was the winner? Did any of them really win? That Lucian fanatic had a point that both would be just as dead in a real fight.

"Okay, tell me. Who do you think will win if they were to get up and continue fighting right now?"

Well, that was a good point, too. This shut up the naysayers as Ambrose greedily swooped in on all the cash, only letting the others who'd bet on Vern take their winnings.

"Hey, are you guys really okay with this?!"

"Whatever, man. Just take the loss. I say this shit was rigged anyway. How the heck were we supposed to guess at the power of these two monsters?"

"Yeah, no shit. These are first-shade observers? Got to be some kind of funny joke. What the hell kind of training did the Kingsmen and Vigil give them to produce these disgusting creatures?"

That had to be the sentence that resonated with Victoria the most from their rubbish discussion. For Vern, it wasn't his physical combat prowess that set him apart but the ingenious use of his visions.

Just how many of them did he have? There was no way one or two visions could be this versatile, right? He controlled air, ground, marble, and snow. Then there was also the wind and corrosive blades.

It was possible his viewpoint worked on a higher concept than those individual elements, but then hadn't he shaded his perception just a couple weeks ago?

How could he already control a higher order viewpoint with such finesse? And what was that endurance? Given the veins around his eyes hadn't swollen at all, he might not have spent even half of his total representation.

And Lucian wasn't a slouch either. He had clearly mastered the first infusion of the old blood completely. In one week! She remembered that only those with a bloodthirsty nature could pull off such a feat.

But that kind of mentality usually clashed with the shade sequences available in their society—or the Kingsmen would have no need for new recruits. How had he juggled both his progress as an observer and Kingsman so well?

Victoria felt the pressure of waves of reality breathing down her neck. People said she was talented. Then what about these two? What would she have to do to catch up to them?

"Hey, you, girl." Someone was bothering her again. *What's wrong with people today?!*

She turned around, but a guy in disarrayed clothes looked at her with a wronged expression. "Why did you blast me like that? I was just trying to get a better look."

Oh. Umm, oops. That was indeed rude, wasn't it?

Shaking her head, she slipped into her noble persona and left it on autopilot to deal with the man as she tried to figure out how to use the experience of this battle to better herself.

Maybe she could ask the involved parties directly? No, that would be too much. No one's going to give away their secrets like that.

Hmm, I can try and do some missions with them and see how they think. That was usually what set observers apart—their perspectives on life.

That might just be the only way to not fall behind in this race to the top.

Vern's eyelids felt heavy.

Something gouged at his chest and abdomen relentlessly. It didn't go away no matter what. He tried to clutch at it but failed at even that when his hands didn't respond.

Fuck!

His eyes soon opened for a second, and he noticed people. A lot of them. Cheering, jeering, and shouting. Soon, Mistress Amelia's face entered his sight, and he relaxed.

Some grumbling words from . . . Lord Osric? "Ugh, what is this attack? It's still not done."

Mistress said something, but his mind was too dull to follow. Soon the cold ground stopped embracing him, and warm hands replaced it.

Whose? He didn't know. All he heard was, "Good job," and the world turned dark.

"H-hello, Mr. Plague doc-doctor."

That's all Vern managed to say before the green light of that lamp lulled him into another deep sleep.

How long had it been? He didn't know. There were many dreams, but nothing in particular that stuck out.

His consciousness slowly awakened, but his body refused to cooperate.

At some point in time, golden tendrils appeared in this unerring darkness, and he geared up for the start of a lucid dream.

The tendrils soon whirled and twirled into tiny knots before they exploded. Following this light show, a monotonous voice resounded in his head.

O, visionary of thine realm, trails from antiquity and futures yet born shall meet within the sanctum beyond the gaze of the first observer's. Arm thyself in spirit and flesh; for on the morrow, thou shalt be summoned to the epoch's confluence . . .

Vern didn't have the mind to be stunned by the absurdity of these words or the meaning behind them, for something far more bizarre went on with the threads that had just exploded.

Right when they were on the cusp of disappearing, they suddenly shone with an even brighter energy and started morphing into . . . runes—similar to the ones in the convergence note.

However, as they settled toward their final shapes, a terrifying notion appeared in his mind.

In parallel to this, the voice in his mind continued, *This council, ordained by the threads of existence, seeks thy insight. For as the realm teeters on the brink of despair, we, the convened, shall dictate its salvation or its doom.*

And with that, the voice was gone. Yet in this numbing silence, the runes persisted, and the unease in his mind reached a crescendo when the glowing tendrils finally fell into a stable shape.

He couldn't help but shudder, for the notion in his mind solidified, and he realized he could . . . comprehend what the runes meant. They said . . .

Help.

C H A P T E R 53

MORE QUESTIONS, MORE ANSWERS

Vern trailed behind Captain Shinsei as he explained some details about swordsmanship to the third member of their party. Generally, Vern would be listening attentively, but his eyes were glued to his notepad.

That's gotta be a Hir, *and that one should be* keu. *He tried to see if anything else made sense, but it didn't. So, he flipped to another page. Hmm, that should be* dea, *and that . . . dxl? Dlx? No. That's not right. Ugh.*

It wasn't working out as well as he'd hoped. He was trying to see if what happened this morning—or was it last night—had been just a dream or not.

It wasn't, and he didn't know if this was a good thing.

What confluence? What council? What visionary, and what summoning?

What even is happening? What was that plea for help?

Was it from the same people who were trying to summon him? If so, why not just add it to that intrusive monologue?

And if it was someone or something else, then who and what did they want from him?

Most mystifying of all—he could suddenly comprehend the runes! Well, at least some of them. The pages of the convergence notes sprinkled throughout his notepad that used to be full of random glowing shapes now held meaning.

Not much, but it's something.

However, it wasn't like the usual understanding of a language. He had no clue about the letters, nor did he find any patterns or grammar in them. Even worse, things he now understood didn't look one bit like the *Help* rune he'd seen last night. So his understanding wasn't visual.

It was more of an instinctual thing than anything, and that irked him quite a bit. He couldn't dissect instincts. He didn't know for sure what governed his comprehension of this "language," though he did have conjectures.

It could be about making contact. The simple act of being contacted by whatever higher entity delivered that message could have given him new insights that helped him comprehend the runes.

Or . . .

He rubbed his forehead. He didn't want to believe himself special after what the aqua-skinned god—Yharl Ballin's avatar—had told him.

Him getting the *Observation Record of Subjectivity* was just a "seed" the entity had sown—one among many. Not something Vern alone was chosen for.

Yet if he looked at this new situation from an outsider's perspective, then someone asking for help in runes that were only visible to him clearly meant something. How would others help if they couldn't even see the plea?

So maybe their need for him to understand could have been why he was gifted an inkling of comprehension of this runic system.

Hmm, could this also be a broadcasted plea for help? Because the message discussed a "confluence" and a "council." Then others had to have received the same message, right?

Yet, just how many people could really see these runes?

He flipped to another page that had conjectures regarding this written down in a complex cipher his master used for trade secrets.

He still made sure not to put down any damning information on paper because observers were hacks and cheats who could skirt basic common sense, but there was enough to jog his memory.

Enlightenment through objectivity and surviving duskfall: These were the two conditions he believed were necessary to see the runes. He was sure that many would have passed the first stage.

That's because a big chunk of Yharl Ballin's other seeds should have managed it too—much less others with their own luck. But surviving duskfall was where things got tricky.

He'd managed to slip out of that one by the sheer luck of having Hensen as his hitman—someone with means and reason to leave him alive. If they'd assassinated all such people throughout the world, what were the odds that they'd survived too?

Yeah, that's impossible to guess based on the current information at my disposal.

So, assuming I am one of the very few who met both these conditions, something or someone is asking for my help. But for what? How am I supposed to help them if I don't even know what is happening?

He didn't know.

Though he had an inkling he would have a better idea about that soon.

Hah, it's sometime tonight. The oral message said he should prepare his *spirit and flesh* to be summoned on the *morrow.* He just hoped that *morrow* meant one full day, not just any time. Because he had to make a couple of preparations. Like—

"My friend, are you ready?" said the swordsman as he stopped in front of what looked like a burnt-down row of houses. The new addition to the team for today, a girl in red and black overalls—Victoria—also looked back at him.

Oh . . .

Vern reeled back his thoughts and closed the notepad shut. He was on another mission today. This was supposedly a "simple one" too.

However, when he looked around, he felt a weird sense of déjà vu. Yet he didn't let the confusion show on his face and nodded to the captain.

Captain Shinsei then pointed at the charred remains of the houses. "I'll take the leftmost house, Vern will take second, and Victoria, you can take third. From there, we skip the already cleared houses and move down the row."

So, second, fifth, and eighth. Simple enough.

Victoria nodded solemnly, and Vern looked on in amazement as she opened the pouch hanging on her waist. Knives came floating out of it before arranging around her.

"Well, you might not need them today, my friend. We're simply here to suppress the subjectivity pollution. There's little to no risk."

"Sorry, yes. I just like to keep them around me whenever possible," she said sweetly.

"No worries. Then let's be quick because once we're done here, we have four more sites to cleanse. Pollution here is minor, so you don't need an amulet of restoration. Just observe it from your viewpoint, and things should fix themselves after a while."

Kind of like how Ambrose did back in the steamscript relay station? That was in far worse condition though.

Vern shook his head and followed the other two to the beginning of the burnt houses. That's when his gaze landed on the street sign. It said Hartley Street.

A shiver went down his spine, and he asked, trying and failing not to jump to conclusions, "Sorry, but what district is this again?"

"Hah. I knew your mind was somewhere else." Captain chuckled.

It indeed was.

But then Victoria answered without turning back, "We're in the Athenaeum district. The next site is—"

Vern zoned out the rest of her words as his mind whirled. Hartley St. Athenaeum district. Hartley St. Athenaeum district. This . . .

This is Ari's dormitory!

"Ah, thank you, Victoria." And before the captain could enter, he followed up by asking, "My bad, but did you also explain what happened to these houses? Is this one of the anomalous places that Vigil burnt down?"

"Hmm, not really, my friend. Yes, we did burn down a bunch of places, but this wasn't us. If I remember correctly, this was reported the same night as the incident in Starfall Heights alongside a hundred other similar reports."

Once the captain stopped, Victoria added in her plain voice, "Probably just some cultists using this place as their grounds for rituals. I think we had a couple of similar cases around my family's mansion too."

"Mm-hmm, that's what our investigators think too. Other similar cases had signs of them everywhere."

"Ahh . . ." Vern nodded.

He counted the houses from the left and realized that the fifth was actually Ari's place. *Even I can be lucky sometimes.*

Thanking them another time, he entered the second house.

He quickly moved through the burnt-down first floor and observed it using stability. The pollution was so minor that all the black particles in the vicinity disappeared with a single glance.

The wooden stairs to the second floor were in pretty bad shape and would clearly crumble at the lightest of touches. However, his eyes flared, and the stability supported the stair's structure as he ascended to the second floor and made quick work of it.

Indeed an easy job.

Not wasting any time, he exited and walked to the fifth house, nodding to Victoria, who had also just left the house assigned to her.

The moment he set foot inside, his memory flashed, and he contrasted what lay in front of his eyes with what he'd seen back then.

It was . . . gone.

This house was markedly in worse shape than the other one. Heck, the whole ceiling had collapsed, and he could clearly see what used to be Ari's room.

It was . . . empty. There was nothing inside it except soot and ash.

A fierce tug pulled at his heart. He'd come here just a couple weeks ago, hadn't he? Then what the hell happened?

He hadn't come back for fear of raising suspicions about his relationship with someone in the building, but who would have thought something like this could happen?

This was the last sign of Ari in his life.

This reminded him: *What happened to . . . Ari's friend?* He remembered her name rhyming with some cathedral. Did she survive this? Were people involved in this accident?

He didn't see any blood, but fire was a cruel mistress and gluttonous for everything human.

The thought of that innocent girl getting caught up in this further weighed on him.

He wanted to continue staring at it. Hoping . . . wishing to see it all go back.

It didn't.

Thump. Someone knocked on the door, and he shouted, "Sorry, one second. I was writing something down."

He stood there in silence for another dozen seconds before he cleansed it all with one glance and walked out.

Nothing was going to happen by standing there.

The eighth house wasn't much either.

The trend continued at the second and third sites for the day. It really was a simple mission this time. However, the fourth site had him stumped again.

It was the Chamber of Astromancers from Elmhurst's Institute of Higher Education—where Ari used to study.

It was a high observatory with a gigantic telescope at the top. However, most of it was in shambles with clear signs of destruction—some of it even burnt. Winter-resistant moss and vines had started to lay their claim on the building, but Captain and Victoria entered it without much thought.

It was a massive tower of many floors, and going up after cleansing each of them became quite a chore. However, Victoria hadn't complained about it even once. It'd be weird if he did.

So he shut up and kept at his job. Many questions whirled in his mind as he breezed through his allotted floors with ease.

Why would rituals burn the places down? He found it hard to believe these were the work of some cult.

So, he grabbed on to a different thread. He'd been wondering why Vigil hadn't figured out the vessel's identity when she had lived here for so many years.

Now it started to make sense. *Someone actively wiped away the evidence of her existence.* It'd be one thing if duskfall hadn't made it impossible to figure out who was alive and who wasn't, but in the current state of the city's infrastructure, it would be foolish to trust any identity documents.

Not that the members of Asea's church couldn't have wiped any information about her from there too.

Wonder why they didn't come after me, given they'd probably perused through all the documents. They surely knew I was her brother.

After cleansing a dozen more halls, he had a weird answer to that. *Did Ari register me as dead?* A wry smile formed on his face. Was there a gravestone with his name in the city somewhere?

After all, he was dead for all intents and purposes for the first three days post-duskfall. Maybe that threw them offtrack, and their premeditated cleaning tactics kicked in when she had to leave the city?

Or Ari had a hand in this. She wasn't as slow as it seemed. Especially when she had time to think through things. She probably understood that involving him would be nothing but trouble.

The mere thought disgusted him. His incompetence was why he was here cleansing the remnants of her passing rather than being with her as she struggled to retain her being against a literal god.

Tch. The only good that came from these Asea's grunts, it seems. They had inadvertently helped him by destroying all the evidence of her existence. It actually eased a lot of the worries on his mind regarding this secret.

Once they were all the way at the top, Vern looked at it all one final time. *Did she spend a lot of time here?* She liked telescopes, didn't she?

The thought reminded him of that gash in the sky, and he quickly sobered up. Things were larger than just him and Ari. He had to think bigger or he'd be always stuck one step behind her.

I have to get a grip.

Once they were done there, their carriage escorted them to Fulham borough for the last cleansing site, and all three of them finished it right when the sun was setting.

"I have something to take care of back at my place, so I shall take my leave here. See you both tomorrow," Vern said as he bowed to his team members. He didn't want to risk being summoned for this confluence or whatever inside Vigil.

He still didn't know what to feel about the whole thing. But it was coming soon, and he had to take precautions. He wanted to avoid it if he could, but something told him he couldn't just back out from this.

Not when they claim to be something of a secret hand behind the world itself.

In almost perfectly noble etiquette, Victoria bowed back, her slender fingers resting on her cravat. Captain Shinsei just nodded and held his sword before taking off himself, leaving Victoria alone in the carriage.

Vern chose to walk. Hotel Inkwell was nearby, and he had a few things he wanted to buy in preparation for tonight. He quickly found what he was looking for, albeit at absurd prices.

Grabbing at the heavy knocker, he rapped twice.

"Welcome, Master Vern. Nice to have you back," greeted Beaumont with that familiar serious yet kind face.

Vern smiled and returned his greet.

"Could you please send some food upstairs?"

"You have some mail, too, Master Vern."

"I will look at it tomorrow."

Beaumont nodded, and Vern didn't dally. He ascended the stairs and entered his room by inputting the lock's passcode.

The smell of parchment and old wood hit him, and he instantly felt at ease.

Loosening the straps of Duality's sheath, he rested it in a corner and slumped onto the bed. It wasn't as physically comfortable as the one in Vigil, but it definitely made him feel at peace.

Once the food arrived, he brought it all to the table and slowly nibbled through it as he read his notes and solidified his plans for the following day and week and onward.

Minutes turned into hours as he waited. Soon, the tower next to the hotel chimed eleven times, and as if synchronized with the clock, golden tendrils suddenly appeared all around him.

It is happening. Fuck!

A mixture of disbelief, excitement, and nervousness coursed through him as he grabbed his notepad, the mask he'd bought, and a couple of other items before his vision exploded with gold.

CHAPTER 54

HIJACKED

The golden threads rushed into him, heating up his body. In another moment, the grays in his perception saturated beyond measure, and then came a sudden jerk.

"Whoa!" he screamed, and something pulled at his mind. He braced for pain, yet none came. Instead, it felt like he was floating in a river and letting the stream whisk him away.

The golden flare disappeared, and . . .

Wait, is that . . . me? For an instant, his perception populated with the surroundings of the room, but it was as if the origin of his perception was behind his back. And that tug pulled again—

Schwaa.

The world remained oversaturated, but he finally calmed down. *I swear, that was me. Wasn't my "flesh" going to be pulled, too?* Before he could make any more judgments, his white reality faded into a bright hue.

This repeated a dozen times with different colors before their rate of change sped up, and all of them began blending together, making sounds that were nothing but hollow echoes.

Vern just watched on in awe.

The colors were so brilliant he couldn't believe he was "seeing" them. *It has to be my perception, right?* There was no way the human eye could sense this much vividness. He tried "looking" around, but everything was more of the same.

Seconds passed, or was it minutes, before something changed.

One of the hues making this tunnel came off like a thread from a sweater. As if blown by an inexplicable wind, it billowed opposite to the direction of his perceived motion—stretching off eternally into the canvas of colors.

Huh . . . ? Is this normal? The thought of a failed travel terrified him. That would be a pitiful death.

His surroundings sheared and distorted as more strands came off the walls, and the tunnel became sparse. He tried to flail, but he had no limbs to move. He was just that—a ball of consciousness.

In some time, the far ends of these threads attracted one another and began assembling into shapes. Shapes he'd seen. Shapes he knew. Shapes he understood— the runes.

It's happening again! His fear swiftly turned into excitement, but mixed within was an unhealthy amount of uncertainty. *Are these runes really not from the people organizing this confluence, then?*

It was still hard to say. What if these runes were the underlying concept that facilitated this consciousness travel? *Yeah, anything is possible.*

The more he perceived them, the more they encompassed his perception. As if those runes held more than just verbal meaning, new sight began to overlay on the former, and it transitioned into . . .

Darkness.

No. More like nothingness.

Darkness had an intonation of the color black to it. This? This was nothing. *After all, perception is more than just colors or sight.*

In this endless void, he waited.

Until something spoke. *Words? No, sounds.* They bored through his skull or whatever equivalent of it existed in this realm. *But they are so faint.*

Yet these voices were the only ripple in this still lake. So he thought of moving toward them, and his origin of perception obliged. He'd already waited for quite a while, and nothing had changed.

Soon the voices got louder, and the distant noises became echoes. Echoes became cacophonies, and before he knew it, they gripped his psyche and whispered into his mind.

"Will thz gld tea ivela mih."

"Cetare cerate eracte etraec creeta."

He willed his hands to grab hold of his skull to soothe this bludgeoning headache; didn't do much. His flesh wasn't really there.

Feeling unsure about his decision to proceed, he looked back, and an infinite void greeted him. *Fuck. My only choices are to move forward or wait here for who knows how long.*

He chose the former.

The whispers were nasty, but they had yet to reach the point of overwhelming him. However, the more he moved toward the source of these whispers, the worse they became.

"Pleh llep hllp eee llsha sdg."

"Em rrifam."

Vern did his best to ignore all the ramblings as he waded through more of this all-consuming darkness. Yet as terrible as the voices were, they were still a solace when null was all that surrounded him.

He gritted his proverbial teeth and kept chugging along. *There's surely a source of all this.*

The cacophonies continued to meld and amplify, becoming an incoherent mess once again, and when doubt and regret colored every inch of his mind, he saw something.

A line.

Vern somehow sped up as he finally found a change in this monotony. The sole line continued to grow, stretching from his left all the way to the right.

He continued to shorten the distance, for the whispers were eternal, and he would only do his psyche a favor by arriving at his destination—if there was one—quickly.

That's when another line joined in. Then a couple more, and then a dozen, but they floated and flickered aimlessly. *Hmm . . .* Vern decided to touch the fire to see if it burned by observing the line closely under his viewpoint.

Whoosh. As if something clicked in place, the floating lines suddenly rushed toward that singular point of his focus, and a vague outline formed there. Was that a . . . strip? A bandage? A plank?

It was just an outline, so it was pretty hard to tell.

Soon, however, a new wave of whispers threatened his focus, and the strip exploded into aimless floating lines yet again.

This . . .

For some reason, he felt his heart beating faster. Maybe not the physical rhythm of its beats, but the adrenaline that came with it.

He steeled his mind and continued pushing farther. More lines sprung forth from the void and soon came the point where thousands—no, millions—gathered around in a small space, out in the distance.

These edges of white in nothingness hovered all around him, and as if to tax him for standing here, the assault of whispers grew heavier.

Ugh. This is annoying.

Whatever had corralled him into this realm wanted him to come precisely here, didn't they? Something within him wanted to rebel and go against this choice forced upon him.

Yet his rational mind weighed the pros and cons and realized waiting around for whispers to end him wasn't a good idea either.

Hah . . .

He sighed. Really, the only choice here was to observe these lines. Doing so caused them to come together and reveal the underlying structure of reality. He eyed the cluster in the middle. It was obvious what he was supposed to do.

So he started from the fringes instead. Always paid to be cautious, after all. He focused on the most significant cluster after the one in the center, and random lines floating around it quickly came together, forming another strip.

Vern didn't waver and followed this strip's length to the center of it all. Pain thrummed in his head, and he could practically feel his representation escaping him.

Hnggh. He sharpened his intent and sped up. The farther he moved, the blurrier and more distorted the lines back at the fringes became. They exploded back into their initial chaotic state when he focused too far away.

It's as if they had so much inherent chaos within them that they'd only remain whole when actively observed.

Faster, then. Stability! The speed of lines coming together upped by a notch, and surprisingly, nothing untoward happened. So he skipped a bunch of smaller clusters to reach that central one with millions of lines.

When he did, a jolt of energy crackled through him, and he practically felt the representation separate from his thought space. *Fuck! Why is this so expensive?*

His massive reservoir of representation emptied like a steam chamber, leaving him in droves. Yet he furrowed his brows and kept at it. *If I lose focus now, the whispers will make it impossible to try again.*

Argh . . . Fortunately, his efforts bore instant fruit. The chaotic ensemble of lines slowly came together, and a shape found form in chaos.

The more he focused on it, the clearer it became. Thousands of lines combined to first form the outline of hundreds of those twisted strips—one on each side of a hollow center.

Myriads of lines culminated into this twirl, but from within their sublime curving mass dangled . . . fingers? The more the shape solidified, the deeper his frown grew.

More lines emerged, and shapes that seemed like arms materialized on the hoops' other ends, tied by those twisting strips. That's when he noticed something odd. The strips weren't just wrapping around the skin; they . . . pierced through it—impaling the wrists.

The central outline of a body began to take shape in the cluster—limping downward, held only by the two wrists as the anchors.

He felt his brain fogging up, almost as if his fleshly body had forgotten to breathe. A mix of perplexity and fear washed over him. He knew this whole ordeal was uncanny right from the start. But this just made it worse.

What is a human doing here?

He'd be less surprised if something alien like what he'd seen during the duskfall formed from the process. But this . . . ? The conjectures in his mind were going wild.

Hundreds more strips manifested out of a dark void all around the body, seeming to wrap around those hands.

Perturbed, Vern flared his eyes harder, and almost all his representation left him in a single instant.

Snap.

That's when his mind froze as something else entered his skull. Something other than the destructive ravings.

"Thou . . . came?" resounded a whisper within his mind—standing out among the ravings without even trying to. Myriad feelings projected into him from those words, and his similar past experience with Esther only hammered home the sorrow and . . . pain within them.

Yet he didn't have the luxury to feel it. A shiver went down his spine, and the words scraped at his very psyche—worse than any of the other whispers. He instantly lost the focus out of sheer panic.

Fuck. It'll all break—

It didn't.

Nothing happened. As if his observation didn't matter anymore, the ensemble of lines retained their shape.

When he had enough brainpower to perceive things again, he got a full view of what had become of that cluster.

The outline vaguely resembled that of a woman. *They— Uh, she?* He didn't know if gender was even a thing for this entity, but the feelings enveloping him, as well as their outline, made him think of them as a woman.

Hundreds of strips emerged from nothingness, merging into her upturned arms and dangling legs. It almost seemed as if they were nailed on a cross, except he knew it was two heaps of strips wrapping and piercing through her wrists.

It was all just outlines, so it was hard to make out anything concrete, but there was something wrong about this image. It was like he was seeing life for the first time ever; it was too . . . raw? Too . . . pitiful.

Worse were the words—for they still ravaged his mind. He commanded his body to take rapid, deep breaths, and dozens of seconds passed before he had the mind to process it all.

Snap!

Vern suddenly focused and noticed one of the strips breaking off her body was fizzling away into nothingness.

However, before he could try something, the outlines of that face moved. The change of expression helped him realize she wasn't bundled in a cocoon of those strips, but almost as if they were a part of her body.

Then came a whisper even tinier than last, "We thank thee."

Vern braced himself for pain. Yet, it was nothing compared to the last time. Almost as if he'd gotten accustomed to hearing the voice—or the entity had found ways to make them hurt less. It was so mild it didn't even make him want to scream.

As if knowing when he was ready to receive the next set of words, the voice continued, "For thine gaze . . . is all we have." An intense pang of loneliness burst within him.

Wh-what?

When he was back to not shaking like a leaf, he wondered, *Thank . . . me? My gaze is all they have? What?*

He ran those words through his mind again and again, unsure what the fuck was going on. He understood the words and their implication but not the logic.

Who the fuck was he in the grand scheme? Nothing.

Someone who could hijack his passage to a council of the planet's "visionaries," the "secret hand," shouldn't have any reason to rely on him or his gaze or whatever.

Was that his paranoia speaking? Maybe. But it was more so the intense emotions that exuded from each of their words. It just . . . didn't agree with his worldview of balance, of equivalent exchange.

So he bit his tongue and willed to speak the same question he'd asked Yharl Ballin—the question whose answer had shattered any delusions he had of a higher being watching over him.

It had broken something within him—for the good and for good.

It was probably a stupid question to ask a being like this. Yet, she wanted his help. He couldn't not find it suspicious. What would they even stand to gain from praising or relying on someone as insignificant as him?

He wanted to know.

He knew he had zero control of his life and death the moment he was pulled out of his body. It wasn't a pleasant feeling, but such disparity in strength and means only awakened one sentiment within him.

Indifference.

Toward death and the outcome. He would strike a fine balance of cautiousness and rationality, but that was about it. The rest would be left to the whims of his mind.

When he searched it, what came to him weren't words but shapes. So he imposed them onto reality with his perception, and some runes formed using the lines.

The runes asked, "Why me?"

CHAPTER 55

THY GAZE

The strips constricting her arms tightened at his words, and an aura of melancholy emanated from her. When he observed the very runes he'd made, he cursed himself.

They weren't just words; they were intent. His paranoia, suspicion, fear toward this being—all of it was imbued within them, and this was her reaction to those terrible feelings.

For a moment, he wanted to retract the harshness within them, but what was done was done.

As much as observing this entity in such a pitiful state—chained on a proverbial stake all alone in a void—saddened him, he just didn't feel worthy to pity them.

Soon, the softest of the whispers emerged—coherent among the ravings, and myriad emotions assaulted him.

"Boundless One," she began, and an inexplicable sorrow gripped him from simply hearing that title.

"Thou fail to observe thy own singularity.

"Thou witnessed the origin—the dissolution of the first." There was pain in those words. Pain he had a hard time understanding for how vast and all-encompassing it was.

What first? The first observer? The invitation last night said that the confluence would be held beyond the gaze of this first observer. What does she mean by dissolution, then? Is the first observer dead?

Yet she kept going, "Thou bear the mark of an Elden as well as everflux itself."

He understood the mark of Elden, but what was a mark of everflux? Each of her words implied so much he had a hard time keeping up.

"Thou studied the ethos of the First and molded thy thoughts to their ideal."

Now he was just lost. When did he study anyone's ethos? Much less first observer's.

"Thou alone engaged with mine own weft—seeking an understanding of our perspective."

A what? Weft? A weaving of threads?

But a realization struck him in the next instant when he searched his mind for things he'd tried to understand. Only one of them really aligned with the idea of a network.

The convergence note. It definitely created some form of connection between people, allowing them to communicate. She said that was her "own" perspective.

This . . .

Things began coming together. He was growing baffled over how she knew so much without intrusively rifling through his mind as Yharl Ballin had.

If she was the weft of convergence itself—

However, that's when the intensity of her voice amplified significantly. The emotions pierced through his very soul, and the lines forming her body shivered as she declared, "Thy perspective, thy intent, thy ideology, thy kindness—thy singularity rivals the first."

She stopped, and one of those strips wrapping around her arms unfurled before floating toward him. He had no form in this realm, yet when the outline neared, something magical happened.

The random slew of lines floating all around him rushed toward the origin of his perception, constructing a very crude, almost smoothed outline of his body.

A novel sensation washed over him. It was like finding sunlight after a lifetime of freezing. Like being recognized by someone you'd always longed for. And soon came a touch, an imperceptible caress of that strip, and his mind blanked.

She whispered, "Thou alone sensed mine plea.

"Thou alone affirmed mine existence.

"Yet thou wonders why we long for thy gaze?"

He was speechless.

Perplexity washed over him, and he did his very best to digest all this. It was— hard. She seemed to know more about him than he did himself.

The silence stretched between them, as deep as the darkness of the void itself, before she shattered it again.

"Whence the First lost its singularity, we had prepared ourselves to never be observed again."

His thoughts wavered. It almost felt like she was talking about life and death. As if never being observed signified an end.

His focus lingered on the outline of her eyes, and the void seemed to cage him as he felt the weight of those words press on him.

Before he could muster up the courage to finally reply, she continued in a voice that became softer and more intimate with every sentence.

"Not unless we allowed the objectivity record to fall in the hands of those who seek to retread the old paths—the ones foredoomed to failure.

"So, we held on—seeking, wishing, hoping to let our realm stand to see the morrow. Yet mine weft and record combined are naught but a cheap imitation of first's gaze."

Vern's mind reeled, and his thoughts turned chaotic. She was talking about the cause and effects of duskfall, wasn't she? *Fuck! Just who is she? And what is this objectivity record?*

The name suggested some kind of account that kept a log of objectivity itself. Not that it made much sense to him. What he did understand was that she was replacing first's gaze using her weft and this record.

I-I . . .

Words reached his tongue many times, but he failed to will them into reality. It was just too . . . absurd. He didn't know how to process this. Were they like the architect of reality itself?

This is too fucking surreal.

If he understood her correctly, it wasn't that he was the only one who could have "affirmed" her existence, but rather that she would have to give up the objectivity record had she asked for aid from others who met the criterion.

Hmm, is it because she's not strong enough to contend against those observers? Maybe she could, but not while sustaining reality at the same time? *And I am acceptable because I am weak?*

She didn't outright say this, but it seemed . . . plausible.

Ironically, this line of thought made him feel far better than anything else she'd said. It made this whole situation make sense. It grounded things back to a semblance of equivalent exchange. A sensible balance.

He liked that.

What he didn't like was being asked for help by an entity of immeasurable insight and knowledge under the premise of being lucky or the chosen one, for there were no free lunches in this world.

This, he could work with.

That's when her whisper echoed in his conscious one more time, "So, Boundless One. Wouldst thou think of us? Help us?

"Gaze at us like the first did. Gaze at us like the first wished."

Vern stood there, incapable of responding. The idea of balance he'd just conjured shattered into fragments, and his mind failed to catch up. Those words held so much . . . longing, pain, and hope; he just didn't know how to reciprocate.

He didn't feel his heartbeat, but if he could, he was sure it'd be trying to rush out of his chest right about now. His emotions, which were already in turmoil, had oil poured on them, and those words lit them on fire as if they were a spark.

It was pure chaos. In that instant, the whispers of everflux that should've been stripping him of his sanity felt more like the words of wisdom instead.

When he managed to calm down, he realized the silence had stretched for far too long. He had enough sense to know when to stop being ungrateful. If he understood this right, she was the one holding the reality together ever since duskfall.

He owed her his very existence, not to mention a gaze of affirmation.

So he willed the only words he could conjure and said, "What shall I do to help you, Eminence?" He imbued each letter of the rune with his regret and silent apology.

The overwhelming amount of grief in her every sentence had done a number on him. He regretted his selfish question and was hoping his true sentiments would do something to mend the hurt he might've caused.

Soon a jumble of emotions erupted from her. They were far too . . . raw and unfiltered for a being with such insight and means.

Or maybe they're like this exactly because of what she is?

He didn't know.

Her fingers moved, but the moment they did, the straps around them tightened, and she grimaced before whispering, "We only wish for thy affirmation. Thou tread the path of first's ideal—the eight fundamentals, and we seek nothing more than such a gaze."

A thunderclap went off in Vern's mind, and he gasped. That's what she was talking about earlier!? The fundamentals? So first's ethos is fundamentalism?

Wait, wait, does that mean the insight sphere, which combines these fundamentals, is the first's ideal? Like an ideal viewpoint?

Wow! It all started to make sense. When she had said his thoughts matched the first's ideal, she was referring to his thought space, wasn't she?

A sigh left her mouth. "First spent ages nurturing, grooming, stealing, destining, and whatever thou can imagine in hopes of finding one who can embody the ideal, yet perspectives are a fickle thing. Even the greatest sins first trained only ever managed to embody seven out of eight fundamentals."

This . . .

"Yet, we've observed thee. Thou art yet to walk far, but thy perspective of balance is all-encompassing, all-harmonizing. If thou wished, and put in effort, thou could form any ideal in existence.

"Yet, we'd wish you not to stray from thy current path. For even though first's ideal may be far from perfect, it's the closest we've ever reached."

Rustle.

Another strip unfurled from her arms and moved toward him. He stood there, confused by the excitement bubbling within him to feel more of her—be observed by her.

"And we wish thou wouldst gaze at us through each one of these fundamentals." Both the straps held the outline of his face, and he felt like he would melt.

"So, Boundless One, affirm us with such a gaze. Affirm that we're alive still. Affirm that we've not lost ourselves to the whispers. Affirm us that there's yet a world to see.

"For thou art all we have."

As much as her words encouraged him, an inexplicable pressure also settled on his shoulders. The . . . eight fundamentals . . . That had to be the core concept of each of the octants of the insight sphere.

Ever since reading how others advanced down their shade sequence, he'd indeed been perplexed about how to handle his ascension to the next shade. After all, he had no sequence to follow.

Her words implied he go for a wider approach.

That's when something jerked him back. *Wait, no!* He knew this feeling. It was the same pull as before. Shit. *I barely understand anything.*

The outline of her eyes drooped, but there was also acceptance. She farther extended those strips to keep his face within their cradle, but they did nothing to stop the pull.

A sense of urgency welled up within him, and he scribbled out, "Does Eminence propose I tread down a different fundamental for each shade?"

However, against his expectation, she shook her head. "Thou mustn't consider any of our insights but mere passing thoughts, for doing otherwise would taint thy path forever. Even one as desperate as us couldn't bear to commit such a heinous crime."

Ahh . . . ? Vern lost his train of thought. That sounded severe. *How exactly am I supposed to help her, then?* Not letting the bliss from that gentle caress numb his mind, he pushed himself to fall into his usual calculative headspace.

He wasn't about to give up this opportunity just like that. *So assuming my last conclusion was right . . .*

"Then Eminence, how would I shade my perception with these varied fundamentals? I have no shade sequence to follow."

She wasted not a breath and responded, "Thou art more than equipped to forge thy own path, Boundless One."

Am I though? He vehemently shook his head. *I know how visions work under the hood, but that's about it. I don't even know if I can replicate that without the land of dark sun.*

Another tug, and he was pulled farther away. Vern smiled bitterly, willing for runes to form.

"Eminence, I am flattered by your trust, yet I must remind you that I am but a mere speck of dust in this vast cosmos. My strength amounts to nothing even if my perspective is unique."

She remained silent for a breath, but his origin continued to be flung back into the void, away from her sight.

Then came her words, full of sorrow. "It shames us to no end, yet we haven't much else to offer thee, for thy path is thine own, and we aren't fit to guide thee. However . . ."

The force pulling his whole consciousness doubled, but luckily, the mad ravings had also quietened down, allowing him to focus on what she said next.

"Mine weft is thine to peruse and utilize as thou see fit. We shan't taint thy perspective by helping thou comprehend it, yet neither will we bar thee from doing so. Thine next destination is a nexus of our weft, and if thee attempts, it may support thee in thy endeavors."

Oh? Umm . . . I . . . Okay. That was great, but he had more things to ask!

"Farewell, Boundless One. We await thy return—thy gaze."

Ugh, damn it! He willed all his imagination, but his focus was in tatters, and the runes came out incomplete, "Who a-e y-u, Eminence? H-w w—ld I g-ze at y-u in fut-re?"

She smiled, and her form destabilized, exploding into lines preceded by her final whisper, "Sylphina." Then the pull came, hurling him off to his original destination.

CHAPTER 56

DISTILLING FUNDAMENTALS AND COMMENCEMENT

Vern gnashed his teeth as the tunnel of oversaturated colors surrounded him, morphing into myriad fractals. *Fuck. How did I fumble it so bad?!*

He had barely asked her any questions. Yes, she wasn't answering anything that could mess with his path as an observer, but there were thousands of other things she could've clarified for him.

Like, what's the deal with the first observer? Is it really . . . ? Because the conjecture had terrified even him—a nonbeliever. Every fundamentalist knew who gifted the insight sphere to humans.

Lady Lennix.

If he connected the dots from Lady Sylphina's words about the insight sphere being the first observer's ideal to Lady Lennix being the origin of the contraption, alongside the "first's dissolution," then . . .

A shudder went down his spine. *Lady Lennix is dead?*

Again, he wasn't a devout worshipper, but her name had helped him through many dark times. Her sharing of the fundamentals was what allowed him to become the person he was today. It just felt . . . surreal that someone as omniscient and worshipped as her might not be around anymore.

Ugh . . .

He shook himself out of it. This wasn't the time to worry about any of that. His real problem was that he could've asked what would happen in this meeting. She . . . um, Lady Sylphina, seemed to know exactly where he was going. Who's to say she didn't know what would happen in there?

Damn, me!

As Vern tried and failed to expel the frustration, something finally changed. Dust detached from the tunnel and rushed toward him. *Huh?*

More and more such particles floated all around him, but he soon realized exactly what was happening. First, the dust coalesced to form his head, then his arms, then his torso, and finally his legs.

However, it was entirely different from the experience he had had when Lady Sylphina . . . caressed him with her strips. This felt . . . mechanical, for it even reconstructed his clothes alongside shoes and everything.

Well, he wasn't going to complain about that. Meeting the "visionaries" and deciding the world's fate naked sounded like a terrible idea.

In another dozen seconds, the colors began to fade, and he regained control of his body. He clenched and unclenched his fists, and his body reoriented itself. Before he knew it, he was standing on . . . a silver floor?

In front of him was a giant archway, bubbling with fog and blocking his view of beyond. Soon a monotonous voice resounded in his head, "Dear visionary, wouldst thou wish to conceal thy identity?"

Ugh, why is everyone using Old Celestine? He had to remind himself that *thou, thy,* and *thine* all essentially meant *you.* Could it be some form of broken translation to Celestine?

That was a possibility.

However, the question it had asked was important, so he nodded seriously. Heck, he stopped gripping the mask in his coat and sighed in relief. His biggest fear coming for this confluence was being noticed by the wrong people.

He knew the effectiveness of such a mundane measure was next to nothing in front of the realm's observer, but he had to try something, right? This was why he didn't wear anything highly personal or bring Duality with him.

He even had plans of faking injuries and scars if need be.

Seems I won't need to mutilate myself. They've got measures for that. Which made some sense in a meeting of people from all over the planet. It would help them avoid political bias and unnecessary conflicts.

The fog in front of him suddenly turned into a reflective mirror, and he noticed that his facial features flickered ever so slightly, and he frowned.

He asked, "Is this it? Would this be enough?"

That voice resounded once again, "Please be assured that any and all form of scrying is prohibited in the nexus. Anyone attempting to breach the veil would have to contest with the nexus itself."

"I . . . see." He nodded. That indeed soothed quite a bit of his worries.

Vern waited, and when minutes passed by without the door in front of him unlocking, he asked, confused, "Are we waiting for something? What's the hold-up?"

The wait was torturous to say the least. His anxieties were piling up as his brain conjured scenarios. His experience with Lady Sylphina contributed to him feeling still on edge for some reason.

"Confluence necessitates preparations. Please practice patience."

Vern grumbled under his breath, tapping his foot repeatedly. *Why did you pull me away from Lady Sylphina if you were going to make me wait here anyway?*

He rubbed his forehead. The havoc wreaked by the whispers had done a number on him, and this wait wasn't doing him any favors.

He sighed and retrieved the notepad from his perfectly reconstructed coat. Better to spend the time productively than worrying over things outside his control.

Lady Sylphina's words gave him a newfound motivation to better analyze the relationship between fundamentals, observation, and reality.

Hmm, I think I should first find a more systematic way to categorize visions and viewpoints into different octants. He already had a concrete word to categorize his own vision—structure—the domain of Cryptic Constructor. However, as things stood, he needed the rest of the picture.

Hmm, It might also help me partially "comprehend" someone's vision. If that was possible, he might just be able to counter others' visions to an extent.

Fuck. Why didn't I think of that before? he groaned.

Except he soon remembered that he'd only learned about the partial comprehension in the fight with Lucian yesterday and had been busy with work and anxiety over this meeting ever since.

He shook his head. *Let's see. I need to find one word to describe each octant.*

For now, he ignored all the glowing runes that beckoned him on pages that belonged to the convergence note because he liked to tackle one problem at a time.

He perused through his notes that detailed his experience with each octant. In some of them, he had ventured farther himself; in others, he used his colleagues' and seniors'.

Hmm, lower northwestern is where I found those foreign thoughts of preservation, which accelerated the rate of my thinking.

If I remember correctly, most research on creation from thin air comes from the lower southeastern octant.

Right . . . Force related discoveries—including gravity, torque, and steam propulsion almost all were found in the upper southeastern octant.

Ugh, how the fuck am I supposed to condense all the facets of this octant into one word?

Should I just do a sentence for each of them?

Nah, fuck that.

After who knows how long, he headbutted the wall with a thrum, a grin plastered on his face. He had all but forgotten about this meeting. If not for his immense self-control, he'd have written everything down on the notepad just to feel better about it.

Yet unwilling to pen down his hard work, he focused on the eight keywords that revolved in his mind: dissolution, creation, and preservation. Transformation, cognition, structure, force, and finally relationships.

This was his masterpiece attempt at distilling the primary essence of each octant of the insight sphere into a single word.

He was already quite familiar with some of these, like structure—the primary fundamental of stability inducement—or preservation or even force. The other five, however, made him wish he had three more brains.

It's done now! He sighed. Even though he missed out on a lot of nuances by condensing them into a single word, he could now use them to dissect complex ideas far more efficiently.

He massaged his glabella and marveled at the brilliance of fundamentals for the millionth time. *This is such a well-thought-out system! If one simply mixed and matched these core fundamentals, they could explain almost any phenomenon in reality.*

Such was the beauty of fundamentals. They were like the building blocks of the universe itself. *At least in an objective world.*

That's when the fog door in front of him bubbled—turning translucent. *Hah, finally!*

However, he soon lost his train of thought, his eyes opening wide. His free hand reached forward involuntarily but was stopped by the see-through wall that this prior foggy mirror had become.

Before Vern lay a vast chamber whose sweeping architecture was sculpted entirely from glass. It was as if the very essence of sight had been frozen, its crystalline expanse catching the light in myriad reflections.

Directly ahead, a series of steps led to a circular platform, elevated and austere in its simplicity. Encircling it, eight tiers of seats rose in a meticulously designed slope, each row higher than the last, directing all focus to the center where a singular, distinguished seat commanded the space.

Above, an expansive dome mirrored the heavens themselves, stars and distant galaxies glistening within its clear surface as if holding the universe captive within its span.

That can't be real, can it?! Ari would've gone mad over something like this. Yet, he stopped that thought right there. He had to avoid fixating on her—for that would be an extreme, and he would get nothing done.

So he returned to appreciate the beauty of it all. At the heart of the dome, a luminescent column of light showered down upon the central seat as though it were the recipient of some celestial favor.

Around him, the air was still, the chamber's atmosphere imbued with a silent expectation. Though devoid of presence, the room whispered of watchfulness, each glassy contour and angle designed to observe and be observed, a silent sentinel over the exchange of visions and ideals that would soon unfold.

Vern made to push at the glassy wall barring his advance, but it didn't budge.

"Please wait. For the order of each visionary's entrance is preordained for thy own safety."

Vern creased his brows. *My safety?*

That's when one of the chambers on the far right of this circular entrance of many halls glowed with incandescent light before fizzling away into particles of light, and someone walked out.

Vern's pupils dilated, and he held on to the pillar on his archway to keep himself from losing his balance.

The whole amphitheater flashed red, and the silky curtains hanging from the high ceiling soaked with blood as horrifying screeches echoed to match his entrance.

Vern's whole body trembled, and for some reason, the case containing the blood infusion syringes, which he'd never bothered to take out from his coat, vibrated intensely.

He shoved his notepad back and gripped the case tight, the frown on his forehead deepening. *Why does the blood react to him—*

Yet before he could overthink it, the man stepped on the stairs, and suddenly, the whole anomaly surrounding him was brought down a peg. Howls and screams grew muffled, almost as if someone had caged him inside a giant beaker.

The bloody curtains fluttered, and they were spotless once again after a blink. *Even the decorations aren't normal, huh?* The domain of blood around the man followed him up, but it had clearly shrunk quite a bit.

As he ascended each step, the red aura compressed farther and farther. Right when he reached the seventh set of seats from the bottom, where his aura was naught but entirely suppressed, he slowed down.

A clear look of exertion appeared on the man's devilishly handsome yet pale face, and his red coat fluttered as if blown by an unseen wind.

The man grunted and stabbed one of his fingernails into the opposite arm. A clear gash opened, and as blood leaked out of it, he pushed higher, reaching the set of seats right underneath the mantle.

Oh . . . Vern watched on in a mix of awe, fascination, and fear. *It seems the higher stairs brutally suppress one's subjectivity.*

More gears clicked together in his mind, and realization dawned on his face. *Now I see what the voice meant when it said this order of entrance is for my safety.* Observers with potent subjective influence were made to take the seat first, suppressing themselves so the weaker observers wouldn't have to bear their pressure.

Not just that, it almost looked like the man was trying to go higher to show off his prowess. Which made sense. Undoubtedly, many others like Vern were watching this display, and being able to sit higher was clearly a status symbol.

Sheesh.

Suddenly, many more chambers unlocked simultaneously, and men and women in gorgeous and uncanny attires poured out—all kinds of phenomena following their trails.

A soft pulse radiated with every step of a woman who tapped in the air, her dress flowing behind her like some ghost—only to be brought back down to the ground when she floated over the fifth set of stairs. For another, every one of his steps transformed the floor into shapes as they rose and fell around him.

That's when he remembered his prior line of thought. *Ah, damn! I didn't spend all those brain juices for nothing. I should try and figure out the primary fundamentals of each of their visions.*

That was definitely a good plan.

So he refocused, hoping to figure out the primary fundamentals that might fuel their viewpoint. He tried but honestly had no clue about the ones who had already settled down.

So his eyes sparkled when another person ambled up the stairs, and he had an idea of what it might be.

Lines grew with every step of this man, and the moment they became long enough, they cracked the floor. Hmm . . . it could just be dissolution, but there's also a pattern in which the cracks expand.

They seemed to follow the structural lines on the floor. He smacked his fist on the other palm. Right, it's got to be structure—for the lines, and dissolution—for the damage.

He didn't know how far off he was from reality, but he liked being able to dissect what someone might be fundamentally doing with their viewpoints and visions.

This person managed to ascend to the sixth stair set from the bottom but didn't try too hard like the bloody man.

Vern's eyes sharpened, and he quickly found his next prey. A ravishing woman in a flowing white cloak with hair of the same color and donning a pointy hat, stepped through the auditorium like some diva, each of her steps turning heads.

However, Vern's eyes were focused on the ground. Flowers blossomed wherever she passed, and his mind whirled. That's primarily creation, isn't it? Vern closed in, his eyes mere inches from the glass door.

That's when a man in white robes entered the same area as her, and the flowers that were happily swaying due to all the movement in the hall suddenly froze. It almost seemed like they were statues.

The white-haired lady frowned, and the man sported a smug smile. Vern, however, narrowed his eyes—anger rising from within him. This attire and the powers of this man reminded him of a motherfucker. A cunt who would do well to die before Vern got his hands on him.

He's using preservation, Vern hissed to himself.

His eyes turned cold, and he carved each inch of this man into his memories, never to be forgotten. His gut told him that this man also deserved to die under his hands someday.

However, that's when another person walked up to the center, and his breath hitched in his throat.

Is that . . .

Fuck!

Chapter 57

WORST FEAR AND HIERARCHY

An indigo velvet frock coat billowed with each of the man's steps as air combusted on his right, only for it to freeze over on his left. It looked like his legs were moving backward, but his body glided forward.

In this confusing paradoxical display, he held on to his top hat, flashing a smile that graced his sleek jaw and sharp features, raising goose bumps all over Vern's body.

Fuck me!

It's Hensen! Hensen Vehen. Vern screamed internally, his body trembling from the implications alone.

He involuntarily hid behind the pillar next to him as one destructive scenario after another flitted through his mind, reminding him of all the brutalities this man had inflicted on him.

The vicious promise he'd made; an unconditional pursuit through the ends of the world. This was one case where even escaping to the death trap that was the land of dark sun wouldn't work. Hensen might just chase him down there.

Fuck! Fuck!! Fuck! This is bad. Beads of sweat formed on his forehead, and his knees felt weak. He hadn't planned for this at all. Yes, he had high expectations coming in here, but this was too much even for his imagination.

He was nowhere near ready to face this man. . . . With every step he took, Vern feared he'd suddenly snap his head in his direction and tear him apart in an instant. Vern continued to watch with bated breath, his heart beating so loud it trumped the hubbub of the people outside.

No. No. No. Calm. I need to calm down. He hasn't even glanced at me a single time.

Hope growing in Vern's chest, he watched the man stroll up the stairs.

One step.

Two.

With every step he ascended, Vern's chest tightened. He didn't need someone to tell him what these stairs represented. It definitely had something to do with the number of shades in one's perception.

Maybe they weren't perfect quantifications of the shades because that first man had managed to leap higher with some extra effort, but it was clearly a measure of strength.

Three.

Four.

Fuck you. Just stop, man! The more powerful Hensen was, the lower Vern's chances were of surviving an assault.

Five.

Vern gritted his teeth, zeroing in on the man's indigo shoes, which didn't do anything paradoxical after the third step. . . . A lump formed in Vern's throat when they raised another time, but instead of heading up, they turned, and Hensen ambled inside the semicircular row of lavish mini thrones.

Vern finally exhaled. *He's probably a fifth-shade observer.*

On one hand, Vern was glad that Hensen wasn't more powerful than Esther's mom, but on the other, it terrified him that he was supposed to survive the pursuit of someone as powerful as her—the Puppeteer of Crimson Court.

Vern's eyes continued to follow Hensen without blinking. The man skipped past the observer already sitting by the aisle before stopping in the middle of the whole row, flopping down without a care in the world.

He even tipped his hat to a couple observers above him, and to Vern's surprise, the seats of said observers rotated on some invisible axis—almost floating to facilitate this otherwise awkward interaction.

Vern suddenly had the urge to check under these chairs that looked like mini thrones to see what kind of machinery hid beneath it all. *Hmm, what if it isn't a mechanical art but some weird vision?*

Heh. It was an absurd thought to have in this situation, but this distraction went a long way in helping him slow down and analyze this properly. *It seems like he really doesn't know I'm here.*

Which logically made sense, given the man had never even met him—at least not since the time turned back. However, Vern most feared their shared connection with the third rune. What if there was some way for rune bearers to sense each other?

He rubbed his chin. *Hmm, my rune's supposed to be derivative of his. If I remember correctly, he said he'll sense it whenever I use the rune.* He rapped his fingers on the glass in a wave and kept staring at Hensen's chilling smile for a while.

Soon, he came to a conclusion. *As long as I don't activate the rune in Hensen's vicinity, he shouldn't be able to sense me.*

There was obviously no guarantee that this was the case, but the evidence was right in front of him. The man was merely meters away from him but hadn't given Vern a second of his life.

Could the identity interference by this place be messing up with his senses too?

Hah . . . Vern deflated as his heart finally calmed down. These were all half-baked ideas, but it looked like he might be in the clear and survive this unexpected meeting.

"Damn."

This had really given him the shock of his life. Hensen had haunted him like a reaper every time he was forced to rely on the third rune. Heck, the visions this man had used were still some of the most bizarre Vern had ever experienced. Now that he'd appeared so suddenly, it would instead be abnormal not to be scared.

Vern shook his head.

Hope things stay the same once I get out there.

This reminded him of something odd, and he surveyed the faces of people who had already taken a seat. Very few of them had hidden their identities. *Do they not fear for their personal safety? Or maybe they have some kind of backing?*

This launched him into a cascade of thoughts. He hadn't noticed it until now, but their reaction to all this was pretty tame. No one had even expressed their curiosity aloud. Unlike him, who was still unsure what the hell was going on, they were patient.

So, they already know what's going to happen? Vern nodded to himself. That made sense. Yes, a few seemed lost while a couple others had hidden their faces, but most were clearly prepared for this. This gave him quite a lot of insight into the overall structure of this event.

Surely, these people knew about this confluence beforehand. . . . His mind, now somewhat relaxed, quickly fell into his previous ponderings. One after another, more gates unlocked, and new observers joined the fray while Vern tried to figure out the fundamentals they used.

There was a wide variety, actually. He even didn't doubt that some observers embodied multiple fundamentals, not just one. There was an obvious one where icicles formed in the air behind a lady and then floated still. Vern believed she was some combination of creation, transformation, preservation, or force.

Icicles could have been formed either by way of pure creation, or by transforming the moisture in the air into solid ice particles. Once they were formed by either of these methods, they could then be suspended in the air by applying an inverse force or preserving the whole space around them.

There was a mix of possibilities, but it was straightforward.

However, Hensen's case, for example, was a troublesome one. His visions weren't directly about heat or cold, which would've put them in the same fundamentals of creation or transformation as before.

They were deeper. As per Vern's experience from back in the library, he believed there was a higher concept at play here than simple temperature. *Hmm, contradiction, maybe? Or paradox?* Which brought him back to the same question: What fundamentals?

Or it might be more nuanced like mine. I use balance on structure right now, but there's a possibility I could implement balance on other fundamentals in the future.

That was to say, each of Hensen's visions encompassed different fundamentals. The heat and ice could be using the ones like the last example, but that paradoxical movement of his body might be related to the fundamental of cognition—creating the illusion of paradox.

That might be it. Vern nodded to himself. . . . More and more people filled the hall, and Vern's excitement multiplied. *Just what the hell is about to happen here?* He was beyond stoked to figure out why such an impressive ensemble was gathered.

True to the order the voice had implied—those who came out later sat lower than those who came before. Given Vern had yet to be allowed out, it meant that he would be sitting beneath all these people.

Hah. I'm probably the weakest here. It sucked, but what could he do?

He impatiently rapped on the glass wall again, analyzing the neat little hierarchy that came together out there as more and more observers found their seats.

Surprisingly, there were only two people in the top row—the man who invigorated old blood and someone who had hidden their identity. The row beneath it—seventh—had four observers.

The one underneath it, however, had a significant jump—almost all twenty seats were occupied. The fifth row was about the same, including Hensen.

Yet, after that came another sharp drop in numbers. Fourth row only had seven people, while third had four, and the second only had two observers, with none in the bottom row.

Vern furrowed his brows, staring at this odd arrangement. The pattern didn't make much sense to him. Why would they invite such a weird distribution of observers? What were the criteria? It'd be one thing if they only invited people of higher shades, but that wasn't the case.

Because if they invited all the world's fifth-shade observers, why wasn't Esther's mother here?

There is some logic to all of it. I just can't see it.

On some other day, he wouldn't have tried too hard, but when he'd compiled the keywords of each fundamental a while ago, he hadn't glossed over his own. Structure wasn't just about buildings or physical compositions.

It's about societal structures and hierarchies, too. . . . Snap. The moment he acknowledged that fact, it was as if something clicked in his mind and the fog covering it faded away, and new ideas popped up like candy.

Huh. What? Why? Vern had the mind to write down this weird phenomenon to analyze it, but he already had an inkling from his prior analyses. His tenet of instability before stability also only helped him deepen the shade on his perception if he intentionally restored the balance.

If he just performed the tenet's actions without conscious effort, their effect would be dampened significantly.

So, in the same vein, now that I acknowledged that this specific pattern of people signifies a structure, I can see it better? Vern nodded. Observation never failed to mesmerize him with its consistent yet sometimes obtuse logic.

Ahh, fuck. I did get sidetracked.

He focused back on the hierarchy, and his sharpened insight seemed to form the image of a diamond-shaped structure in his mind. He hadn't bothered trying to observe them using his perception, and it seemed he wouldn't need to. Clearly, the balance affected more than just his perception, it evolved his very thoughts to an extent.

After a dozen seconds, his best conjecture was that this pattern had something to do with an observational concept he had read up on in Vena's archive last week when he couldn't cram the fighting stances anymore.

Shackles of subjectivity.

It was somewhat of a loose idea that determined the upper limit of complexity of concepts that one's viewpoint could capture in lower shades. The more shocking and eye-opening one's enlightenment, the more thoroughly the shackles would be broken.

That was to say, if he had a simpler enlightenment, he might have been unable to properly form his viewpoint of balance because of how high and encompassing of a concept it was. In Hensen's own words, Vern had broken the shackles entirely.

In simpler words, the ruder the awakening, the better.

A part of him even believed that most of the things he could see but others couldn't—like the gash in the sky and runes—were also a result of differences in the extent to which one's shackles were broken.

However, most weren't as fortunate—or unfortunate, depending on how one looked—as him. Everyone only had one real opportunity to shatter the shackles significantly, and that was enlightenment.

However, it wasn't that straightforward. A higher enlightenment came with its own difficulties.

If one was mentally weak, they would become a vegetable long before they could consolidate their viewpoint from too rude of an awakening to the subjective reality.

Another problem was finding sources of a higher enlightenment. Many lineages had their secrets for doing so, and they guarded them as tightly as their observation records. Heck, he'd even found a list of noble houses in Elmhurst where the strength of their enlightenment methods was ranked.

The only way to further loosen one's shackles after initial enlightenment was to experience events shocking enough to rattle one's whole worldview. They were opportunities that could only be grasped with power or luck.

Most people didn't have either.

It might seem odd to try to connect this concept to the seating arrangement of the observers in the hall outside, but Vern was getting more confident by the second that the criteria had something to do with these shackles.

He believed that the "visionaries" invited here were just observers who had crossed some threshold of how much they'd broken out of these shackles—and a high one at that. So it made sense that there were little to no people in the lower seats since they'd have to have survived a brutal enlightenment.

Whereas people with five or six shades in their perception were powerful enough to capture the said opportunities for another awakening.

However, this idea, if considered in isolation, couldn't explain why there were only five or so observers in the seventh and eighth rows. *But that can be explained by something even simpler—the harsh reality of progressing as an observer.*

It was clear that ascending to the seventh or eighth shade was a monumentally difficult task. So much so that the whole planet only had two such people.

Vern interrupted himself. *Well, maybe more than two, but then their shackles of subjectivity must be tighter than everyone here. Given how intricately linked one's power is to the shackles of subjectivity, there probably still aren't many of that shade.*

Which went to show that the path of an observer was a bleak one. Billions of people on the planet, yet only a couple who managed to reach close to the top.

Vern felt a pressure settle on his shoulder. Lady Sylphina hadn't explicitly said it, but if he was to shade his perception with all eight of the fundamentals, he would have to beat the same—no, worse—odds than the two sitting up there.

If he wanted to rescue Ari from those disgusting leeches, he would have to become stronger than that priest in white in the sixth row.

If he wanted to achieve his ideal of a more balanced world, he would have to rise above billions.

"..."

His chest tightened at the thought. He knew he had many advantages unique to himself, but if only vague powers that didn't directly strengthen him were enough to reach the higher shades, there would have been at least a dozen more observers on that top row.

And this is why the throne above all these rows is empty. Just how strong would one have to be to stand up there? Surely, the pressure alone would be so terrifying it would be impossible to mount.

Even though he tried his best to not let the weight of this monumental task crush him, the anxiety still took root in his heart.

That's when the world suddenly turned silent.

Vern looked up and saw that everyone from top to bottom had their chairs turned to face the newcomer on the stairs. After a short second, the hall exploded in murmurs.

Vern's eyes quickly found the target and widened as one of his prior assumptions came crashing down without any regard.

How is this even possible?

CHAPTER 58

ETERNA

With her black hair cascading down her back, she ascended the stairs in a backless rouge tea-length dress, complemented by matching earrings and high heels. However, her face, phasing like Vern's, remained obscured behind an impenetrable veil.

Pity. He didn't know why he felt that way, though he quickly forgot all about it as she continued to ascend. *She is on the third step already!*

"Huh, what is going on here?" asked a man in the second row with an unnaturally deep voice. "She just came out, right? Ain't no way she got more shades than me. Why would she be ordered behind me otherwise?"

Those words embodied the incredulous looks on everyone's faces, but the lady in question didn't even glance at the naysayer and continued onward with unmatched poise and elegance.

Four steps.

Five.

"Oh, the primal one, could something have gone wrong with the nexus itself?" spoke the icicle lady from before, sitting in the fifth row and presenting a perfect ostentatious faux surprised expression.

"Has to be, right?" chimed another man with a large beard a few seats next to her. "Do you think there's something wrong with the order in which the nexus assigned her entry, or the nexus's forced objectivity isn't working?"

"Haha," she giggled. "The latter option doesn't really make much sense now, does it? Do you not feel your singularity being caged this very instant?"

The long-bearded man shook his head. "Well, then, the omniscient one's warnings were indeed true. The Weft of Elyndor is losing its grip on reality. Never before has such a mistake been allowed."

Vern's ears perked up at that name. *Weft of Elyndor? Is that the real name of Lady Sylphina's network?*

Had to be. After all, Lady Sylphina had said this was a nexus of her weft, and this man could only be blaming the same thing for the issues with the nexus.

Vern wondered where they got their hands on that information. Lady Sylphina clearly hadn't engaged with anyone but him since the dissolution of the first observer.

Whoa.

Suddenly, the whole crowd gasped, and Vern refocused. That lady was already on the . . . seventh step. Though, to be fair, he didn't understand why people were overreacting after already concluding that she was just ordered incorrectly.

"Milord Elysian, what is going on? Has another one of your angels really graced our gathering?! We have another seventh-shade visionary!" shouted someone who'd hidden his identity while all the ones who hadn't shut up their mouths, a solemn expression on his face.

Yet, the lady didn't waver even a single bit and continued her march.

"Milord, she isn't stopping! It can't be!?"

Tap.

Her feet landed on the eighth step, and as if she had dropped a match in a pit of combustion fuel, the whole crowd exploded.

Whoa!

Even the two sitting at the very top looked surprised, especially the man in the bloody outfit. He turned to face the lady with interest and asked, "How may I address you, milady eterna?"

And at the same time everyone else erupted too. "An eterna! Our realm has birthed another eterna! And a visionary, at that! Lord is watching over us!"

"Damn this. Now we have another big player eating the pie. Fuck!"

Vern simply filed away that moniker in his memory. It seemed someone with that many shades was called an eterna. However, he was far busier watching new little insights blossom in his thought space as he understood more and more about the structure here.

Hmm, so those people on the right in the fifth row think that the birth of a new eterna is a joyous event, whereas those with scowls are clearly more self-minded and annoyed at having more competition at the top.

"But who is this? She couldn't have become an eterna in a couple weeks, right? Surely, she must be the leader of one of the hidden societies, yes? Could she be the famed sage of Visandra, the Great Resolver? Or maybe Maelbeth's Silent Schemer?"

"No. What if she's someone from the Institute?"

"Haha, that's the craziest idea I've heard today."

Among all these wild speculations and exclamations, the lady at the top executed a shallow curtsy before speaking in a musical voice, "Glad to make your acquaintance, lord of primordial blood, but I wish to keep my secrets."

She didn't even wait for a response and sat on the throne farthest from the other two.

"Darn. Who the hell is she?"

Only those who'd hidden their identities spoke now. Clearly, the ones out in the open didn't wish to badmouth a powerful being.

"I think—"

Sheesh!

A blue glow exploded in front of Vern, who was heavily focused on trying to figure out the allegiances and stances of everyone.

Ah, fuck. It's my turn!

He dusted his outfit and stood straighter. He was about to become the complimentary joke, after all. Someone had just settled on the top row, and now he was about to sit alone in the lowest one.

Ugh. Pushing away the gloom, he strode forward the moment the glass door was all gone.

Crisp, cold air entered his nostrils, and his mind rejuvenated instantly. Since he didn't have any intention of showing off his visions, he just beelined toward the seat closest to him.

"Hey, do you think the nexus has really gone haywire? Could this person also be an eterna?"

Umm, no, please. I am not. Vern groaned inwardly, and his steps grew quicker. Many continued to conversate about the eterna, but he still felt dozens of gazes boring into him.

This was one time when he was annoyed by this weird instinct of his to sense gazes. *I don't need to know this.* He hoped to keep as low of a profile as possible, and that lady coming right before him had messed it all up.

Hah. At least they can't see my face.

"Haha, yes. If this guy is also an eterna, we are doomed."

Vern was of a mind to continue grumbling about this miserable situation, but he lost his words when he took in all the scenery that had been blocked from his little box before.

Colorful stars dotted the heavens beyond the transparent dome of this nexus, their ethereal beauty capturing him instantly. His eyes also took in the stunning yet unique design of the pillars, the cool and uncluttered architectural style of this whole hall, and every little reflective gem that dotted his surroundings.

This whole nexus was like a giant semicircle, with doors of titanic proportions on the far right and left, leading to dark and untold corridors. In front was the amphitheater, but reversed in the sense that he was making his way to the seats from where a performer would've otherwise stood.

He tried, but the unfiltered view of the cosmos was like a magnet and his eyes were unwieldy iron. Swirling stars, nebulous planets, overly saturated asteroid belts— all that Ari would've paid a million to admire. In the middle of it all stood the lotus-shaped pillar of light connected to the empty throne at the podium.

And before people could conjure more conspiracy theories, Vern reached the stairs.

He took a deep breath, braced himself for the onslaught of the terrifying pressure, and stepped forward.

Huh?

Vern's eyes widened instantly, and his feet halted.

What the hell?

" . . . "

Is the nexus really broken?

He felt . . . nothing. Not even a single ounce of resistance.

However, the gazes drilling a hole into him instantly doubled, and all the sounds came to an abrupt halt. His heart began thumping violently as possibilities crossed his mind.

Fuck. What should I do?

Remembering how the lady before him had stepped through everyone like a god among mortals induced a sense of excitement within him.

His mind whirled, and he realized he had two options in front of him. Either use this opportunity to fake more power than he had, which might benefit him for whatever was to come in this meeting. Or simply stop at his rightful place and keep this card hidden for the future.

Damn. I need more time to think about the implications of both! If I had known this was going to happen, I'd have thought about it beforehand!

Unfortunately, he didn't have the luxury of time. Everyone had their gazes pinned on him, and standing here was only making him seem all the more suspicious.

Vern closed his eyes for an instant before snapping them back open. *One of these options is clearly superior.*

His mind made, Vern fluidly connected his prior motion to move to his right and settled down on the small throne by the aisle.

Once done, the world stopped holding its breath, and someone chuckled, "Hah. A first-shade visionary? That's some talent right there. Should I try and recruit him?"

Yes. Exactly. I'm just a first-shade observer. Vern praised himself for his quick decision.

"Uh-uh. Don't do it. You'll somehow end up crossing the clause of mutual respect in the codex of confluence. Coercing or pushing those who hide their identity might just get you kicked."

Oh . . . is that why that lord of whatever blood didn't push the eterna lady for more information? He'd been wondering about that.

"Yeah, Yeah, I get it. Stop being so right all the time. I was just kidding."

Ignoring the remarks, Vern settled down snugly in the chair that was more comfortable than it looked and sighed internally. *Glad I didn't rush up.*

Fooling the world's most influential and powerful people for the sake of it sounded like one quick way to hell. Cons like this demanded proper planning, backstory, and motive. Doing so without all of them was nothing but foolish.

And it's not like I've lost the chance. If the situation demanded he go up, he could still do it. Whereas if he had stepped higher, he couldn't just take it back and go sit down on the bottommost row.

Mm-hmm. This is indeed the right decision. What would even be the point of pretending to be more powerful? Not like I can just start ordering people around to do my bidding. If they asked me even simple questions about higher shade observation, I'd be fucked.

Yeah. Go me! Good choice.

Everyone soon turned away and ignored Vern, passionately discussing the advent of the new eterna. Vern even wondered if she was in the same situation as him—the pressure didn't apply to her.

Though he doubted it. She had been far too smooth and flawless with her steps, answers, and mannerisms. She hadn't stalled for even a second like Vern did.

There was not one ounce of hesitation in her ascent.

I still can't rule it out though. Not that it mattered much to him. *Also, why exactly do I feel no pressure?*

Soon, he landed on the same answer—shackles of subjectivity. It really was such a fascinating concept now that he thought about it. If that was indeed the case, then the tightness of shackles almost acted like a priority ranking where Vern was close to the top.

It didn't equate to pure power but something more ethereal. He didn't understand the exact logic, assuming there was one, but he knew it was one of his most significant advantages in indirect confrontations.

Vern looked back and quickly grew annoyed to see that there was no one behind him. He was dead last.

Ugh. Whatever.

Before he had time to settle into his prior state of mind, heavy thuds resounded from the far-right corridor. *Looks like it's starting!* Vern sat straighter. He was finally going to get answers as to what the hell he was doing here.

A bulky man walked out of the darkness in a long black and gold blazer decorated with epaulets that matched the dark vambraces and gloves he donned. His bun of fiery red hair and a beard that was better called a mane matched his solemn demeanor as he made his way down to the center of it all.

A sudden burst of nostalgia washed over Vern, reminding him of the days he used to attend lectures of famous fundamentalists just like this, in a hall full of curious students, waiting for the lecturer to begin their enlightening session.

In essence, it was the same situation, just that the stakes were a million times higher and the material of study was a subject more arcane than even fundamentals.

Soon, the bulky man stopped and rested his arms behind himself. Most observers above Vern turned their chairs around to face the man, and he followed suit. *I'm sitting in the first row too—almost as if this were a lecture.*

"Visionaries of this realm," spoke the burly man in a naturally loud voice, "I, Horace Estefan, welcome each and every one of you to the first confluence of visionaries of this era."

First of "this" era, huh? Vern remembered Captain Akira had said something like this, too. He took out his notepad and started taking notes—just like at a lecture.

A small hubbub arose behind him, and his peripheral vision told him everyone was nodding. Vern matched their beat to blend in nicely, and Horace continued, "I suppose there's no need for me to rehash the state of our realm—each and every one of you've already witnessed its misery, so let me cut straight to the chase."

The crowd's expressions turned solemn, and Vern perked up his ears.

"Duskfall was a nightmare that has left our civilization in tatters, and to this day, we have no clue what went wrong. The worst outcome of it all was that our prayers and attempts to make contact with the first observer—the supreme one—have all been in vain."

Haw.

Whoa.

The hall suddenly felt far more downcast and solemn.

"So the rumors were true!"

"Then . . . are we really all by ourselves?"

Hmm, it looks like they don't know the exact details of what went down. Not that Vern knew much himself.

Horace raised his hand, and everyone quietened down.

"I know it's a tough pill to swallow, but it only gets worse from here. Many of you may not know or understand this, but our realm as we know it should've ceased to exist the day the first observer went missing."

"Each and every sapient being contributes to keeping our reality stable, but some of us play a larger role than others. The first observer was the principal contributor. Given the difficulty of enlightenment before duskfall, our greatest seers had conjectured that four-fifths of our realm's representation was concentrated in the gaze of the supreme one."

There was such a thing? Though it did make some sense given the context of how Lady Sylphina had talked about the first observer.

"It wasn't."

The whole hall exploded into another round of murmurs, and Vern sat there all by himself, matching it in his head with Lady Sylphina's words. He jotted all this down using his unique cipher. This was some information he would never have come across in his day-to-day life.

Regardless of the crowd's reaction, Horace continued, "For, if such was the case, only we observers would have survived the duskfall, and even our days would be numbered, for not many of us possess viewpoints that could sustain themselves perpetually."

Ah, is he suggesting all observers would have had their own little biomes? That was an interesting thought experiment, but Vern kept his impulses in check and focused on listening.

"So my fellow visionaries, that leads us to the question: Who or what is keeping our reality stable if the first observer is gone?"

Vern's pen suddenly halted. He didn't like the direction where this was going.

"So in an investigation jointly conducted by all our societies, we have narrowed down the list of possible large contributors to a few. Yet one among them stands out like a sore thumb . . ."

A chilling inkling suddenly crept up Vern's spine, but Horace pushed on, "It's the Weft of Elyndor."

They're onto Lady Sylphina!

C H A P T E R 59

CRITICAL CONSENSUS

Horace paced through the hall, his hands behind his back. "As of last week, the Weft of Elyndor is the only vision that encompasses every inch of our realm. As some of you may know, it is the backbone of convergence notes, allowing us to communicate across our planet, albeit on strange rules."

"Until duskfall, everyone believed the records of past eras, which suggested that the supreme one created this weft by assimilating the viewpoint of every observer from Elyndor—the underground city."

Vern frowned. *Assimilate? What does that even mean practically? Did the first observer just eat them or something?*

Horace then stopped and scanned the hall. "But as you might have guessed, we were obviously wrong. The source of the weft isn't the first observer. It never was. For, if that were the case, the weft should've disappeared alongside the supreme one."

Vern stole a quick glance around him, and while some of the expressions were entirely impossible to read, the rest were either worried or concerned.

Vern wasn't sure what to feel about this. He didn't even know about the first observer an hour ago, so all of this was like a tale far removed from himself.

On one hand, the fact that they assumed the first observer to be the owner of the weft meant they didn't know about Lady Sylphina. On the other, Horace was just setting up the context to make a point, which might as well be related to her.

What should I do?

From his understanding of the matter, Lady Sylphina didn't want to be noticed by others. But then again, if these people already knew all about her, there wasn't much he could do.

Hmm, let's just listen for now.

"That is to say, our friends and families are still alive because of the existence of this very weft—the last gift of the supreme one. If not for this realm-encompassing vision, we would've blinked and the entire world would've slipped through our fingers when the dusk fell."

Vern nodded internally. *Yes, we should all be grateful.*

"Unfortunately"—he stopped pacing and shook his head—"if everything was working as intended, there would've been no reason for us to pay the astronomical costs needed to arrange for this confluence."

Checking the crowd's reaction to his words, Horace continued, "The reason we're all gathered here is simple: even this second lifeline, as unexpected as it may be, is failing."

Ah, crap. They know. Vern finally understood where this was going.

"It isn't a secret that the rate at which the world is healing the subjectivity pollution is horrible, and like I said, even that is a miracle. Yet, every day that passes by, those healing capabilities are dwindling at an unsustainable pace."

The burly man's face suddenly gleamed with . . . sadness, and he said, "So ten days ago, my father"—Horace pointed at a handsome-looking man with shoulder-length red hair in the seventh row—"the ruler of Estefan, invoked the fate."

"And as your family's and organization's leaders may have told you before coming for this confluence," he said, his expression turning grim, "we have naught but a couple weeks before the weft loses its grip on reality."

Whaa.

"Master really wasn't kidding, then?"

"Damn! Only two weeks?!"

"Why the hell did you wait so long to tell us? We're wasting time sitting here. I should be spending these last days with my wife."

The whole hall became a mess of accusations, conspiracies, and a fair bit of denial. Vern ignored the chatter and pondered the man's words. *So Lady Sylphina only had a few weeks before she had to make a decision?*

However, he suddenly realized something. *Wait. Haven't I already solved this problem, then? Lady Sylphina was getting weak because of not being observed at all.*

Yet his unique circumstances allowed him to alleviate that. Not permanently, but it definitely wasn't as bad as they were making it out to be. Vern gave his pen a rest and leaned back. This was getting interesting.

Horace's brows furrowed as he watched the devolving crowd, and he stomped his foot with a loud *thump,* then said in a booming voice, "Stop! This is no time to panic! I need all of you to act your station and maintain your composure."

This indeed slowed down the discussion, and he continued, "In light of the graveness of our situation, my father, a former eterna, paid the heaviest price to steal more from fate."

Oh?

Horace closed his eyes, almost as if containing the words that threatened to burst out. Vern looked back at the said former eterna, who was sitting in the seventh row. Unlike his son, the man's face was bursting with pride, and he accepted others' gratitude with a smile.

Soon the burly man up front managed to control himself and spoke in a wavering voice, "Through his sacrifice, he learned something of immense value." He paused.

But soon continued with a hint of regret in his tone, "We learned the Weft of Elyndor is borne not of an observer, but a perceptual artifact, one that used to be part of first observer, one that is keeping us afloat, one that is losing its steam this very moment."

Huh? No. That's straight-up wrong.

But then he remembered Lady Sylphina's words. *Mine weft and record combined are naught but a cheap imitation of first's gaze. Hmm, could Horace be talking about the objectivity record? It sounded like an artifact, after all.*

The more Vern thought about it, the more it made sense. He had no clue how fate or divinations worked, but it was possible that the objectivity record and Lady

Sylphina's fate were so intertwined they confused the two during their divinations.

So, they really don't know about Lady Sylphina. A wave of relief washed over him. He didn't quite understand her reasons for wanting to stay hidden, but she'd made her stance quite clear.

That's when he remembered something. *Wait, I know.*

More dots connected in his mind, and he lampooned, *She probably doesn't want a repeat of what happened with the first observer.* Given how even someone strong enough to affirm the whole of Prima all by themselves went "missing," who was to say she wouldn't meet the same fate if her presence was revealed?

Vern's expression turned solemn. *That would be disastrous. I hope they don't plan on seeking her out.*

"Ever since Royal Father figured out this truth, the wisest observers of the Estefan kingdom and the Coven of Truth have been working tirelessly to find a solution. And find a solution they did."

Wait, what? Vern wasn't sure he hadn't just imagined that. *Did he just say Coven of Truth?* Vern fished into his pockets, and his hands felt the shape of the hourglass on his emblem from the coven.

He can't be talking about the same coven, right? That . . . that would make no sense, right? The Coven of Truth Vern belonged to was just a big congregation of fundamentalists.

Or am I just not in the know? He was unsure.

"So, visionaries, we've gathered all of you here for one simple reason."

The whole crowd suddenly turned silent.

"To arrive at a consensus and affirm the rules and ideas of the said artifact. To rejuvenate its drying source of inspiration and ideas with our own, and to not give up on our world without a fight."

Ah?

As if mirroring Vern's confusion, someone from the crowd chuckled and said, "Are you pulling our legs, Lord Estefan? I know we observers like to pretend our gazes can change the world, but it's in no one's interest to overplay our abilities. We can't just will something into existence that we don't even understand."

"Hah. This is the solution that the 'wisest of the observers' came up with? Disappointing."

However, Horace raised his hand in the air once again, forcefully culling all the commotion and said, "I understand everyone's skepticism. So let me explain the rationale."

He pointed at the lotus dome above them all and continued, "According to our research, this nexus, as its name suggests, is where all the threads of the Weft of Elyndor come together. And as we've already established, the weft is borne out of the aforementioned artifact. So we're essentially inside the artifact right now.

"Yet that's but a single reason. Don't forget that we're the visionaries of this realm who can envision the highest of the concepts—so even if this artifact is a piece of the first observer themself, no aspect of it would be left unobserved if we all come to a consensus.

"That's not even all. Remember that this artifact doesn't have much representation left to its name, so its defenses to outside influence aren't much. Finally, since not many know about its existence, the unified perspective has no memory that we'll need to erase first."

Okay, what the fuck? This was some mind-fuckery. This was precisely what he feared one could do the first time he encountered observation.

"And like I said, we've done our research." Horace smiled and plucked at empty air. Right when Vern began to wonder if the man had gone senile, the space in front of him split, and a sheaf of parchment materialized out of thin air.

Vern looked on with his mouth agape. *What kind of vision is this? Can I also use it if I master the underlying fundamentals?*

A thick stack in his hand, Horace moved toward the crowd, surely with the intent to distribute the pages physically. "This is why we needed these ten days. Most of it was spent reverse engineering the clues of fate to figure out the best blueprint of the artifact we could provide all of you. The kind that will supplement the artifact's abilities and rejuvenate its aura if affirmed by everyone."

Vern extended his arm forward to accept the paper, eager to see the design. As much as he feared such an idea—of reality itself being so malleable—it was exciting too. It seemed they planned to use the imagination of the best observers on the planet to envision what was defined within the blueprint to affirm the rules and essence of the objectivity record.

Hmm, this might actually be a good thing. As long as the blueprint is indeed supplemental in nature, this will really benefit the stability of Prima.

He almost wondered if Lady Sylphina had been a bit too mistrustful.

That's when a voice boomed behind Vern, "That's enough, young Estefan. It's not a good habit to impose your viewpoint and ideals on others."

On the highest row, the third and final eterna other than the lady in the rouge dress and the lord of blood stood up, grabbing his regal-looking cane from his throne.

Tap. Tap.

"And it's certainly worse to present a nuanced situation as if there's only one solution to it."

CHAPTER 60

REBIRTH

The third eterna, whose face was hidden behind a veil, walked toward the center of the highest row, his cane tapping on the ground rhythmically.

The haze shifted, and out came an unnaturally deep voice, "I see that the Estefans don't plan on giving everyone the time to chew on this information and make their own decisions." He shook his head and added with a tone that slowly became more natural, "An unsightly state of affairs, really."

Tap. Tap.

Horace stopped in his tracks, and the parchment that was almost in Vern's grasp remained out of reach. Everyone turned toward the voice, intrigued. However, Vern's sense for the structure of this hierarchy allowed him to notice more.

Some were surprised by this chain of events, but many clearly expected it. He couldn't pinpoint why because it was a more intuitive understanding of this whole structure than concrete ideas, so he put his eyes to work where he sensed anomalies and instantly found evidence for his suspicions.

That priest from Asea's church is clearly smiling, and so is that teenager in the fourth row. Vern quickly found many more with similar expressions. *What is going on here?*

Within a few seconds, the haze receded, and the man stood at the top, an anomaly in human guise, commanding an inexplicable reverence without a crown on his head. Clad in the finest of black clothing in existence with layer after layer of fashionable elements, each embroidered with golden patterns, he stopped everyone in their tracks. Draped over this masterful fashion was a black cloak, its gold-etched tall collar framing his hazy face.

Haze that continued receding by the second. Even Vern held his breath as the fog slowly lifted and the man's face appeared . . . The crowd lulled for a second before it erupted.

"It's the omniscient one!" shouted the guy sitting ahead of Vern.

Many stood up from their seats and bowed in elaborate gestures.

"Greetings, omniscient one!"

"Junior pays his respects to the coven master," yelled a man in the fourth row whose whole body was fitted with hundreds of contraptions, each serving a function Vern couldn't even begin to fathom.

To Vern's surprise, Hensen was glaring at the man. However, that expression was gone as quickly as it came.

"An eterna of the gazebinder sequence here? We're fucked!" rasped a man who'd obscured his identity as he quickly hid his face under a scarf.

"He knows who we are, doesn't he?" chimed in another one of the kind, his unnatural deep voice trembling.

That's when an ancient-looking man who was clearly from the eastern continents commented, "Hah, don't worry, children, I am pretty sure even eternas can't overrule the nexus's veil."

The scrawny man sitting next to him snapped his neck toward the old one, his face a mask of terror. "What the fuck is wrong with you? Are you trying to provoke a literal god?"

The ancient one just laughed it off. "Haha, don't worry, son. It's not like the omniscient one can descend the stairs until we in the lower rows exit the nexus."

However, their discourse quickly got suppressed as more voices joined in. "We thought the omniscient one won't have time for meetings like these . . ."

"Please help the city of Kerinza, lord omniscient one. We're stuck . . ."

"What is the coven working on next? Can we . . ."

Similar exclamations rose from all over, but Vern didn't have the mind to focus on them any longer. A terrible sense of unease arose within him as he took in the sight of the "omniscient one."

Thin, angular features on pale skin with a sharp nose and sleek brows. Bulbous green earrings and backcombed dark wavy hair. However, they were all but backdrops.

His most striking feature was those eyes.

Black threads sutured his eyelids to the skin underneath, crisscrossing in a macabre fashion that contrasted with the pure white light spilling out from the gaps between the lids. The threads looked strained beyond measure, almost as if they couldn't rein in the immeasurable power oozing from the eyes sealed behind them.

A shudder went down Vern's spine. Yet there was more.

A third eye.

A tattoo of a cross with four points on its end graced the center of his forehead, framing the pearl-shaped crease that sat in the middle of it all. It wasn't apparent, but Vern was more than sure that another pupil, one more terrifying than his normal ones, was hidden underneath.

Vern's pulse raced the longer he looked at it.

However, the omniscient one in question raised his hand, and the chatter died down. But before he could say anything, the Estefan ruler from the seventh row frowned and interrupted, "What are you doing here, coven master? We came to an agreement that Master Seras will be attending the confluence, not you."

The coven master held the staff with both his hands and leaned on it before his lips parted. "Plans change, Your Majesty Keras, the one who stole fate, and I'm glad they did. Seems like you were planning on foul play. Not explaining the full range of options available to us—possibly even stripping us of our only chance at a comeback as a species? That's low, even for you."

Hohh? Vern set aside the agitation borne from the man's appearance and focused. It seemed like there was more to this than met the eye.

"Hah," King Keras scoffed. "That's defamation, and you know it. Horace was going to get to that in a bit."

The coven master smiled, and his sutured eyes curved without any problem to match the expression. "Yes, but that'd be too late."

Then he shifted his torso and addressed the whole crowd with a broad gesture. "You see, my fellow visionaries, observing that parchment they're handing out would have permanently tainted your opinions, incepting a bias on how the artifact should behave, preemptively rendering the other option a worse choice."

Ah. That's a thing? Vern retracted his outstretched arm and frowned. *Seems like the lack of prior knowledge is also crucial for pulling off a proper "consensus."*

"Haha," the coven master laughed lightly and shook his head. "Do any of you really believe that a dozen stupid observers can figure out the inner workings of what is literally a piece of god in a mere ten days?"

"Don't do this, coven master. Please!" shouted Horace from behind Vern, a pleading tone marking his words. "We picked this method of delivery after intense deliberation and debate with our seers and your fundamentalists. This is the only surefire way to assure the continued existence of our realm. We cannot leave it up to your whims. What you propose will result in nothing but chaos and doom. It is—"

"Shut up," interjected the man at the top sharply, his eyebrows growing fierce.

Thump.

The parchments in his hand scattered on the ground as the burly man fell on his knees, a trickle of blood leaking from his eye.

King Keras suddenly shot up and barked, "Rupert! What the hell do you think you're doing?!"

Vern's mind reeled when he heard that name, but Rupert pointed his cane at the king and said, "You shut up, too."

"Rupert!" yelled back the king, "End this charade right now! What you're trying to accomplish will do nothing but dampen the effect of the eventual consensus using the insights we gathered."

Rupert dropped his smile and leaned forward, enunciating each word with a dangerous tone, "I . . ."

An invisible barrier tried stopping his descent to the seventh row, but that third eye on his forehead flashed red. "Said . . ."

Rupert's face crossed the threshold for the briefest of the instants, and he demanded, "Shut up!"

Keras's expression grew horrified, but it was too late." Argh!" he shrieked, followed by his body turning limp. The woman sitting next to Keras, who supported him in time, was the only reason he didn't hit his head on the floor.

Rupert smirked, the small gap of that vertical eye closing like it had never been disturbed. "You're lucky I'm under the nexus's restrictions, or . . ."

The dead silence that followed that threat was more than enough to prove its effect.

He pulled his face back and dug his heel in further. "Mere seventh-shade regressed rabble thinks they can stop me from telling everyone the truth? Deprive our species the greatest and possibly only opportunity to make a comeback from this utter disaster? You aren't an eterna anymore, Keras, and it'll be in your best interest to act like it."

After a while, he scoffed. "What a joke!"

The whole hall remained silent, and even that ancient man from before was trembling in his seat. Clearly, he had realized that the restrictions of nexus only went so far, and if this half-god wanted him dead, it wasn't out of the question.

Vern, however, flipped through his notes like some demon had possessed him.

No . . . no . . . no. Fuck!

It's him. It's him!

Multiple pages' worth of notes detailed all his conjectures and the little information he had managed to dig up from Vigil's library on that name.

Sterling Rupert.

The mastermind behind the targeted mass murder of fundamentalists during the duskfall.

Public information regarding this man was close to none.

Before he created the spheres that revolutionized the interior lighting industry, he was said to hail from the Artez continent. Vern had no means to look further into his origins because Artez was literally on the other side of the planet compared to Quartzford.

Besides that, the man had neither many prior publications nor given any famous lectures. Which wasn't too out of the norm for fundamentalists, given their reclusive and research-focused tendencies.

However, there was one problem, even with this limited information. Those purple lighting spheres—his first publication was featured on the front page of the coven's journal for this year, eclipsing even the inventions with far more significant impact on society innovated during the same period.

Yes, his spheres had major practical applications. Still, they weren't nearly important enough to overshadow the breakthrough in steam velocity engines that halved the cost of passenger airships for intracontinental trips.

Vern remembered there was some drama regarding this unfairness detailed in a couple newspapers and gossip journals, but the coven never issued an official statement or explanation regarding their choices. Soon, it all blew over, and no one remembered it.

Now, however, it all made sense. Until today, Vern didn't know that *coven master* was a thing. But if such a master existed and they wanted to push something on the front page for themselves or under an alias, it'd be child's play.

Given the context, motives, and power of this man, it all just made sense.

Vern closed his notepad and stared at him with cold eyes, a seething rage bubbling within him. *He's the one who orchestrated the deaths of all fundamentalists.*

There were some assumptions and leaps of logic here, but Vern was pretty sure that even if this man hadn't been the mastermind, he'd undoubtedly played a part. It'd make no sense for an "omniscient gazebinder" to not know about such a massive conspiracy within his own coven.

Ironic that the leader of a fundamentalist coven would be the one who sentenced those very people to damnation.

This quickly changed Vern's views on the current situation. Just a second ago, he was inclined to agree that it was insidious of the Estefans to partially reveal the matter as per their narrative.

Now? He felt King Keras and Horace might have had good reasons to do so. At least better than Rupert's.

He rubbed his forehead. *What the hell is he up to now?*

This whole thing reminded him of Captain Akira. Heck, both of them even kept their eyes hidden by one means or the other. And that man genuinely scared Vern to some degree.

Tap.

Suddenly, Rupert shattered the silence with the rapping of his cane and he spoke, "Now that we've dealt with the obstructions, let me present you the real choices."

He extended his arm in a vague artistic expression and eloquently relayed, "What the Estefans propose is rejuvenation. A continuation of the misery that each and every one of our cities, countries, and continents are facing this very instant. A clear path to doom, destruction, and eventual madness."

No one spoke, but their demeanors had clearly become a notch more solemn, and Vern was no exception. He was taking each of Rupert's words with a mountain of salt, but it would be foolish to preemptively disregard him without hearing his side of the story.

"It is a proposal that will further prolong our suffering but would do nothing to ward off the cosmic menace that looms over our realm. I dare not speak their names, but the influence of Elden Ones among the mortals and observers alike is multiplying, and it won't be long before outsiders will be sitting up here in our places."

Passion filled each of his words, and he gesticulated to supplement his thoughts, but it had the opposite effect on Vern with those mutilated eyes and the trembling King Keras. "Now given the opportunity to rewrite the very laws of reality itself, if all we do is mindlessly parrot and reinforce the ancient ones, how would things ever turn for the better?

"If our species is so cowardly, we might as well just give in to whispers and stop resisting. Why bother fighting against these horrors? Why risk our lives daily if we're just going to pass up the opportunity to turn the tide on a global scale?"

Tap!

"All for . . . what?"

He scanned the crowd and snickered. "Our safety?

"Assurance?

"Hope?

"Hahaha. Let me tell you, nothing they've got on that parchment is guaranteeing success. There's no assurance that affirming what it says will actually give us a new lease on life. It's nothing less than a gamble.

"A big fucking one at that."

He raised his cane high and slammed it back down with a loud *tap.*

"So, for those who still don't understand what I'm getting at, let me make it simple for you.

"Instead of rejuvenation, I propose . . ." He paused, and his smile widened.

"Rebirth."

C H A P T E R 61

MANDATE OF OMNISCIENCE

Rupert let his words hang in the air, and almost everyone was captivated by his little speech.

Vern chewed on them. Unfortunately, this plan didn't sound as outright villainous as he'd hoped. That would have made it easier for him to mentally cast Rupert as an asshole.

However, he did have a reason to disagree with his plan. Lady Sylphina had explained her reasons for not beckoning these eternas.

She'd said, *We had prepared ourselves to never be observed again . . . Not unless we allowed the objectivity record to fall into the hands of those who seek to retread the old paths—the ones foredoomed to failure.*

That clearly suggested that what Rupert proposed was bound to fail. However, as much as Vern felt disposed to blindly trust Lady Sylphina, he couldn't bring himself to stop thinking about it critically.

Yes, Rupert's suggestion might be doomed to failure in the long term, but if things are as dire as everyone's suggesting here, there might not be a "long term" at all.

He'd loathe for anyone to harm Lady Sylphina, but if they were just changing the content of the objectivity record, it might not affect her at all. Even if that meant a failure after millennia, it might still be a better option than having the whole civilization routed by the nightmares of subjectivity.

Horrors like the one that resided inside that child or the one he'd seen from the terrace of Vigil, or worse, the one who'd caused the duskfall, the entity who'd enlightened Vern.

If even these people who were supposedly at the top of the food chain were so pessimistic about the future, did he really know better?

Argh. Vern groaned. *What exactly was the scope of her proclamation?! What if she meant any other ideas could cause an instant failure of reality at a microscopic level, and everything would end with only the slightest change?*

That's not all. What sort of rewriting of rules is Rupert suggesting? That was the most important question.

Fortunately, Vern didn't have to wait for long, as the sweet voice of the eterna lady pierced the oppressive silence as she asked what was on everyone's mind. "What kind of rebirth are you proposing, then, Rupert?"

Vern didn't miss how she called the eterna of blood with his moniker but resorted to using Rupert's name directly. *Interesting.*

The bulges on Rupert's eyelids shifted in her direction, and he nodded. "Indeed. The devil is in the details, as they say."

Turning back to the crowd, he said, "Let's start with the problem rather than the solution." He extended his hands outward and requested from the crowd, "Tell me, fellow visionaries. What are the gravest of the problems that plague our society right now?"

Chatter erupted again, and people discussed fervently, yet no one dared to speak their conclusions out loud. Vern also had an answer, but he wasn't going to stand out for something like this. Not to Rupert.

Maybe noticing this trend, the man in black smiled. "It seems I have made a bad impression on everyone here. But I am sure most of you would agree with me once you realize how big of an opportunity the Estefans would have stolen had I not intervened.

"It may have seemed cruel, but it was for the welfare of whole humanity."

His words had a clear effect, and a blonde from the fifth row eventually took the bait. "Omniscient one, I surmise the worst problem right now are the sightless. They suffer from the pollution, propagate it, and taint the unified perspective."

Thump thump. Rupert repeatedly smacked the head of his cane with one hand, almost like a clap. "Very much on point, Miss Firekeeper, as expected from one of your lineage—straight to the point. That's indeed problem number one."

Turning back to the crowd, he prodded them again like a teacher asking questions to his students. "Anyone else?"

This time, a bunch of people exclaimed simultaneously, and Vern could never have prepared himself for this.

"We all know that the real problem is our mortal coil. If only we could become machines with numerical minds, we would never have to face the whispers ever again."

"The world has too much entropy. We need to further cull it. I suggest we end everyone who's infected and restart the society."

"It's the observers other than us visionaries. We should wipe them all!"

"The problem lies in the emotions. We should prune emotions from humanity. If there's no fear, there will be no madness to succumb to."

"The chaos we witness is the result of its nightmares. Our only salvation lies in awakening the dreamer or, failing that, lulling it into a dreamless sleep. Only then can we find peace."

"We at Veiled Sovereigns believe it's the lack of education about subjectivity. If the public understood it properly, they wouldn't be as susceptible to pollution."

"It's obviously the gods, the Elden Ones, and irresponsible observers. We need to somehow restrict their influence on reality. They're messing with our lives too much."

Uh . . . what? Vern doubted his own ears by the end. He thought he had a wild imagination, but this was . . . enlightening. It made him reevaluate the people surrounding him. They all looked human, but their minds were clearly very far from that.

"Hah, some of you are really amusing. Well, I suppose it's only for the good that consensus is necessary, and any one of us can't just enforce such . . . outlandish ideas.

"Anyway, Mr. Schaummer from Elysian Circle is onto something. Gods, Elden Ones, and unruly observers are the second, third, and rest of the problems, rapidly hurling our civilization toward doom."

Tap!

"These issues have already wreaked too much havoc on our planet." Pointing at a woman wearing a silky black veil in the fifth row, he continued, "Take Lady Amaira from Darkmoor—the underwater city, for example. Her whole habitat, which existed peacefully for seven centuries and survived even the duskfall, was ruined in but a single day. The day when the Great Resolver, one whose name shan't be evoked, decided the dark sea was his."

The woman in question bit her lip and didn't comment.

Vern felt his horizons broadening. He had never heard of an underwater city, nor could he fathom the logistics of such an arrangement. So he did what any other sane man would—he wrote down everything about it. These were things he could research in the future.

Heck, he went ahead and jotted down those bizarre suggestions from a minute ago alongside slim descriptions of their speakers. He wasn't sure about it, but he felt like these assertions could give him a window into their minds and viewpoints.

Even if it wasn't anything useful in the long term, those words were still worth dissecting.

Also, who is this Great Resolver? An Elden One? Or a god? Are these two different entities or just synonyms?

Rupert obviously didn't answer any of Vern's unspoken questions and instead pointed at someone who looked like a samurai and said, "The Satsuma clan used to be the sole owner of the blademancer shade sequence, but the corruption of their retainers and outer members led to a terrible mutiny, which ended with the whole clan burned to the ground, including the observation records for said sequence."

The samurai slowly shook his head, bitterness clear on his face.

"Many of you may not know of it, but a group of unknown observers massacred Artemis, the airborne legion of Westminster. They went as far as to derail the floating city from their orbit, and it's bound to fall to its death in a couple of months if what's left of their observers can't do anything about it. That's the reason we're missing at least three visionaries today."

A . . . what? Floating city? How even?

Vern's pen flowed nonstop, greedily feeding on all this free information about the observers of the planet. This was terrible news, but it would be a disservice for it not to be immortalized in his notepad.

After a couple more examples along the same line, Rupert tapped his cane for the umpteenth time and said, "As is clear from all these cases, the core problems are indeed the masses, the gods, the Elden Ones, and psychopathic observers."

The skeptical expressions in the crowd were all but gone; what remained was curiosity.

"Now that we understand the problem, we can finally worry about the solution." He paused and coughed lightly. "Before I tell you about the mandate of omniscience—my solution to these dilemmas—know that I'm open to practical ideas that are strictly better than mine."

He then turned his mutilated eyes toward one of the observers who'd answered him before, and his voice suddenly turned cold. "However, make sure not to waste everyone's time with stupid notions like wanting to turn everything into machines or anything that upends the fundamentals of perception. If the seriousness of our situation hasn't fully sunk in yet, then you're not fit to contribute to this consensus. Consider yourself out."

No one answered him, but the light smiles hanging on a couple of faces disappeared, and the whole hall turned solemn. Vern also perked up. He had yet to find any flaws in the man's argument, and that irked him. He didn't like being of the same mind as the person who'd committed genocide.

Taking the silence as their agreement, Rupert sighed and took a deep breath. "Let's set the record straight: the mandate of omniscience doesn't aim to dismantle the core pillars of our existence. To do so would court catastrophe, not progress. I envision the introduction of innovative principles that build upon, rather than dismantle, the scaffoldings of our reality.

"I'm not here to advocate for turning the constants of our universe into variables, nor am I interested in altering the fundamental forces that bind our existence. To meddle with the constants of time's flow, or to warp the very fabric of space itself, is a folly I wish to avoid. Our reality, maintained by a delicate equipoise, cannot endure such fundamental upheavals without cascading into chaos beyond our command."

Vern was further depressed. The man was talking so much reason, it was clear he'd given it more than just some serious thought. However, those words quickly caused many in the crowd to be displeased, almost as if some legitimately considered that as a viable reality.

Pointing at his sutured eyes, Rupert continued, "I am a man who likes to see. Being able to see and critically analyze the information available is the greatest advantage humans have over the rest of the intelligent species.

"Now, everyone calls me omniscient, but I indeed can't see everything that's happening in our realm, nor can I analyze it.

"However . . ." He paused just long enough for the crowd to get intrigued, and then asked, "What if I could?"

Vern frowned.

"Imagine, if you will, a reality where I could see every sightless across our planet and monitor their psyche moment by moment, determining their level of corruption and catch it before it breaches the dam of their sanity."

Huh?

"A reality where I could determine destructive thoughts long before one has the chance to act upon them.

"In this envisioned world, the very notion of consorting with the lurking horrors that gnaw at our reality's edges would be rendered impossible—erased before such perilous thoughts could even take root."

That . . .

"Disruptive observers would be found out before they would have the chance to ruin any more lives.

"Armored with such boundless insight, we would foresee the gods' watchful eyes upon us, orchestrating preemptive defenses with unparalleled speed and precision.

"The whole world could work in concert to push back the uninvited guests.

"It would—"

"Wait, wait." The lord of primordial blood sitting next to Rupert raised his hand.

Vern caught the hint of displeasure on Rupert's face, which was gone in the next instant as he turned toward the other eterna.

The man in the red outfit continued with a sharp voice, "I don't have a thousand lab rats in my backyard like you do, but my experience tells me your plan is flawed."

He sat wider on his throne and checked his nails before continuing, "You're essentially trying to create a vision to calculate the future perfectly, and surely you know the fifth axiom better than me."

Without looking away from his nails, he shouted, "Someone remind Mr. Rupert here of the fifth axiom of observation."

Most in the crowd hesitated and fumbled, probably not wanting to get caught in the middle of an argument between two eternas. But then, the lady who was holding on to trembling King Keras spoke with a defiant gaze, "Fifth axiom says that everflux is the state of infinite change, and any attempts to calculate the next state of chaos will result in nothing but destruction."

Vern was still disturbed by Rupert's idea, but he wasn't about to ignore such an unexpected windfall and penned down the fifth axiom. It seemed quite an enigmatic one too.

The lord of blood clapped his hands. "Exactly!" Pointing his other set of nails at the man in the center of it all, he added, "Well, Rupert, it'd be one thing if you were planning this for a city or something. But on this scale, you're essentially trying to predict the everflux, and nothing good comes out of that." He then scoffed. "Surely, you know that better than me, too."

Rupert nodded. "Valid points, one and all."

"Except"—he smiled—"I don't mean to calculate the future at all."

The lord of blood retracted his extended arm and looked at Rupert suspiciously. Silence fell in the hall, and people shifted in their seats.

After a while, the only dissenter slowly nodded and said, "Well, go on, then."

The smug Rupert took the stage back. "Indeed. What I wish to analyze has nothing to do with the future. All I need is the present. I just need a window to everyone's minds to catch those thoughts that would be the cause of our eventual doom.

"The mandate seeks to seize the present in my gaze, wielding my wisdom to excise any future that threatens our society."

The man continued with increased bravado, "What I propose will neither interfere with the current state of society nor will it even be known by the people. For the masses, it will be like nothing ever changed. Except their lives would suddenly be free of disasters caused by madness."

His voice grew in intensity. "The gods wouldn't be able to kill hundreds of thousands on their whims like in Darkmoor. The information exchange wouldn't be limited by stupid factors like our viewpoint's trace that we're too paranoid to share. We could all communicate and prepare for such tragedies on a world scale as necessary."

Passion oozed from his every word, and he stressed, "The unruly observers won't even be able to lift a finger to hurt the innocent before they're found out and punished.

"This world, currently fractured and self-absorbed, will weave itself into a tapestry of unity and altruism." He gazed in turn at all the people he'd given as examples of tragedies and poured his heart out, "When I can see all of the world in a single glance, I could efficiently manage and assign resources to the battlefronts that would need it the most."

He looked up at the cosmos. "No one would be left unheard. Everyone would have equal opportunity to be seen and to receive help, unlike the gods who show favor only to their worshippers."

He extended his arms and exclaimed, "It will be a world that's free of chaos, for it will be culled before it has any chance to grow."

A fervor beyond anything radiated from him, and he bellowed, "It will allow us to tide over this unprecedented cosmic catastrophe and come out stronger!

"The whole world would become an efficient clockwork—each cog and wheel dialed precisely to rout the unknown. To maximize sanity and minimize madness.

"When everything can be seen, nothing is unknown.

"It will be the dawn of a new age.

"An epoch of subjectivity unlike any other."

He shouted at the top of his lungs, "An era of omniscience!"

Oh my lady . . . Vern stopped his pen, and his heart dropped. *This is worse than I thought.*

CHAPTER 62

ALTERNATIVE APPROACHES

Rupert stood tall and proud, his aura fierce, daring the whole crowd to challenge his mandate.

He's finally showing his true colors, Vern mused. A single sweat bead formed, then made its reluctant journey down the side of his forehead. He'd been expecting Rupert to suggest something insidious just like this, but now that the man had actually gone and done it, Vern was more than a little scared.

In the company of ordinary people, such a proposal would be nothing but a farcical joke. But here? In a place where some believed that humanity would be better off as machines or that society needed restarting, who was to say they wouldn't support such an absurd mandate?

No. Please. God, no! The mandate essentially anointed an omniscient overseer who had direct access to everyone's thoughts on the planet.

Vern took the idea and ran with it, simulating his future in such a world.

I'll be dead within a minute of this mandate's universalization in almost all scenarios.

The only method of survival would be for him to find ways to prune his memories and never think about his uniqueness ever again. He'd also have to somehow forget that Rupert was the perpetrator of the fundamentalists' genocide, for there was no way such a devious man would ever let Vern live with knowledge of his wrongdoings.

The more Vern dug deeper, the more he realized how fucked up he'd be if such a reality came to pass. He'd have liked to believe that his singularity as an observer would give him immunity against visions, but Rupert suggested he could read the minds of even "rogue observers" to cull them before they did something he deemed "dangerous."

As uneasy as he was, he still couldn't help but notice this oddity. What happened to observers needing to understand their foe's viewpoint before they could use visions on them?

What factor decided that one could be envisioned by another? What was the priority order of observers?

In this numbing silence, it didn't take him long to arrive at a couple of conjectures. *Hmm, it seems like this property of observation doesn't work in blacks and whites as I've assumed for a while.*

Tapping the pen on the notepad repeatedly, he lampooned, *Could someone of higher shades take control of others' viewpoint by brute force? So the number of shades determines the priority?*

He furrowed his brows and followed that train of thought to its root. *Ah, right! That doesn't always have to be the case. There's actually a more fundamental reasoning at play here.*

He nodded. *It's the insights.*

That's to say, if two observers decided to fight over the subjective control of an object, the one with more comprehensive insights into said object would come out on top. It was just like how he'd wrested control of the surrounding air from Lucian when the man had turned invisible.

Generally, someone with more shades in their perception would have more comprehensive insights than a lower-shade observer. So brute force was still possible, but it may not work if the lower-shade competitor specialized in the particular domain.

And one would be infinitely specialized in their own viewpoint, making it very hard for higher-shade observers to envision changes directly inside one's body.

Hmm, but it isn't exactly impossible either, he mused.

After a while, he scratched his head, thinking, *Wow, I am stupid. Why didn't I notice this earlier? I already had all the clues needed to figure this out.*

Soon, he gave a mental shrug. *Anyway. Does that mean Rupert has comprehensive insights regarding all observers so that he can use his vision within their minds?*

After only a second, a realization dawned on his face, and his expression worsened. *No. It's the objectivity record that has the comprehensive insights, not Rupert. If he did, he wouldn't need the artifact at all.*

Inferring from how everyone, including Lady Sylphina, talked about the artifact, he came to another realization. *The objectivity record is essentially the compendium of the most comprehensive insights regarding our world.*

Fuck. This is downright terrible! If someone of Rupert's caliber gets access to infinite insight, what couldn't he do?

With every second, the gravity of this "consensus" sank in like never before. The mandate of omniscience essentially handed over full control of the planet to Rupert. He would practically be no less than a god.

What was worse was that Vern wasn't the only one who'd lose his freedom to think in such a world—everyone would. Anyone who simply even thought of rebelling would be found out and dealt with swiftly.

That's when the heavy silence cultivated over the past couple of minutes shattered, and a cold voice emerged, "Rupert, are you listening to yourself?"

Vern extricated himself from his thoughts and looked up. It was that lady eterna in the rouge dress.

She rapped her fingers on her throne's armrest and reprimanded with a dangerous tone, "You really think all humans in the world should give up their freedom and privacy and open their minds to someone like you?"

Exactly my thoughts!

"Have you considered that none of us here would like you to be inside our heads, passing judgment on everything we should and shouldn't do?" She then shook her head. "Just how narcissistic does one have to be to think they are fit to decide what's right and wrong for every human on the planet?"

Wow. Vern couldn't help but feel that he'd finally met another kindred soul in here. *You tell him!* he cheered.

No one in the crowd dared to agree with her verbally, but Vern's intuition for structure told him that many had similar thoughts.

Phew . . . He let out a sigh. *Yeah. There's no way any of these selfish people would agree to such a power imbalance.* Rupert had shot for the stars, only to have his ambitions mocked and shredded.

Tap.

Rupert didn't let the crowd read into her words too much and responded back in kind with a scathing tone. "Heh. Just how ignorant does one have to be to think they can sit around doing nothing with all this power as the world goes to hell? Surely, all the problems will solve themselves if we just twiddle our thumbs, right?"

Vern felt like punching something. As much as he hated this man, he had to agree with most of the points he raised. These people didn't know that Vern had already delayed the end, so they should be doing everything in their power to fix the reality.

On that note, how am I supposed to convey this information? He had no proof, after all. No one would believe him if he just stood up and told them that the former eterna, King Keras, had raised a false alarm. Not unless he explained his encounter with Lady Sylphina, and it'd be the height of foolishness to even bring that up here.

Hah . . . I don't know.

Rupert continued in the same tone as hers, "Have you considered the toll it'd take on my singularity to stretch across the whole planet? After the critical consensus propagates the mandate of omniscience, I doubt I'll ever be myself again. You think I revel in the idea of losing my singularity and merging with an artifact?"

The lady rebutted without a pause, "Portray it as you will, Rupert, but it doesn't change the fact that you plan on controlling the denizens of the whole world like puppets on your strings. If that's what survival means, I don't want it, and I'm sure most would agree with me."

"I see." He sighed. "It's a shame you put your individual self above our civilization's continued existence." With a shake of his head, he turned back to the crowd, "My fellow visionaries, I am sure there's more of us who believe the world can be a better place and don't think that it starts and ends with them."

The lady snorted but didn't respond.

Rupert continued, "Tell me your thoughts. If you disapprove of my mandate, give me a better proposition. Doing nothing is not an option!"

Vern frowned. *What is he playing at?* He found it hard to believe this man would give up on his grand plan just like this.

An impassive man in the seventh row jumped at the opportunity. "Lord omniscient one, our doom is not a matter of flesh or spirit, but of emotion. Fear, despair, rage—these are the true contagions. I propose we engineer a new kind of existence, one devoid of these destructive emotions. A society of beings who cannot feel fear cannot succumb to madness or the whispers."

It's this guy again.

Rupert didn't even turn his head and rebuked the man, "A poorly thought out idea. Emotions are a complex amalgamation of many fundamental assumptions of our reality. Removing them would mean, in part, removing those fundamentals—essentially destroying the nature of reality."

Vern's pen stopped in its tracks, and he looked back up at Rupert, his eyes wide. *Did he just . . . mention fundamentals?*

Clearly, most only processed those words at surface level, but if Vern understood this right, Rupert just claimed that emotions were a combination of some of the eight fundamentals.

Does that mean he knows? Knows that fundamentals, observation, and subjectivity are undeniably entangled.

Has to be, right?

A mixed feeling arose within Vern. It made sense that the leader of a coven of fundamentalists and an observer with so many shades in his perception knew about the link between those concepts.

He sighed. It wasn't a pleasant feeling to realize he wasn't the only person to have figured it out.

I guess I'll have to find peace in the fact that fundamentals suit my viewpoint better than everyone else, and that no one here seems to understand the profound insight behind that rebuttal.

This also had its logic. All these visionaries had their own observation records that guided their paths and experiences that shaped their insights. Many would laugh at and disagree with fundamentals that categorized reality into eight separate domains.

After all, Lady Sylphina had told him that even though eight fundamentals were the closest they'd come to perfection, there were other answers to abstract reality, too. This was just one of the better ones.

He had to chew more on this, but the impassive man backed down, and a dark-skinned man in the sixth row stood up in his place and bowed. "I wonder if the omniscient one could grant us an opportunity to speak."

Rupert nodded, and the man began, "We at Veiled Sovereigns propose a minor adjustment to reality that may solve the problems that the lord mentioned. We suggest injecting knowledge of subjectivity into the minds of everyone."

Vern listened closely, and so did others, as the proponent continued, "If everyone, including the sightless, understands the drawbacks of making deals with the devils, the terrors that await them if they lose their minds, and the consequences of their actions, we believe that the world will heal itself on its own."

That was . . . interesting. But it's a flawed idea.

Instead of Rupert, a woman on the far right of the row rebuked the speaker, "Hah, naive." She scoffed. "Have you considered that many would rush to enlighten themselves, even knowing the terror of the whispers? I don't know about you, but I have no wish to compete with such leeches for the world's representation."

Aha. Vern clicked his tongue. *There are gatekeepers in here, too?* Such people existed in all professions, and observation was no exception, it seemed.

Soon, more people chimed in. One said, "Doing so will be a terrible idea and would achieve nothing more than blowing up the already ever-increasing entropy."

"Are you stupid? Do you think the minds of sightless are ready to accept the knowledge about Elden Ones? Billions more would succumb to madness or lose themselves to such knowledge in mere days."

Vern mostly agreed with their points too. He knew better than most. Secrets were secret for a reason. Exposing them willy-nilly was careless at best and disastrous at worst.

The dark-skinned man tried to argue, but after only a bit of back and forth, Rupert interjected, "I generally respect Veiled Sovereigns' public-minded approach, but this idea is impulsive and foolhardy. You seem to forget that spreading the knowledge of these horrors would further anchor them to our reality, strengthening their prowess. I'm sure I need not say more."

The proponent repeatedly opened his mouth to speak but eventually sighed and sat down.

That is indeed a good point. Rupert knows what the hell he's talking about.

"Next," Rupert declared, both his hands resting on the head of his cane.

A priest on the third row stood up. "Coven master, I suggest we attempt an exchange for this opportunity of critical consensus with the eternal keeper. As a firm believer of the eternal one and a preacher of their faith, I assure you that the lord will listen to me and offer us far greater benefits than we could ever extricate ourselves."

To this reasonable-sounding tactic, observers sitting in higher rows looked at the priest like they were eyeing a unique specimen. Before long, most shook their head, and Rupert shouted, "Next."

A little unsure what happened there, Vern debated whether he should finally speak up and join the fray.

CHAPTER 63

THE COUNCIL OF OVERSEERS

Even though Rupert was a sly fox, he genuinely seemed invested in finding solutions for the betterment of the world.

Vern thought, *Hmm, I don't know.*

After a short while, he decided not to engage. It wasn't out of fear of speaking in front of this group or an irrational need to stay hidden. No, it was more fundamental than that.

My vision for reality doesn't really align with these circumstances. As much as he loathed to accept it, his idea of aligning subtle balances of the world wouldn't be very effective in the current state of society. A relatively stable world was needed as a prerequisite for his balance to work well.

As things stood, a worldwide subtle balance would be shattered at the drop of a hat. There were too many disruptive elements that could tip the scale to the extremes.

Seems like I've quite some work ahead of myself. He sighed and focused on the discussion at hand.

One after another, visionaries proposed their ideas, only to be shot down promptly by others or Rupert himself. Someone even suggested they end the world once and for all, leaving nothing but these visionaries as the sole survivors. That person was promptly silenced using nexus's moderation methods.

After about an hour of heated discourse, sour expressions covered everyone's faces. Many were ready to lunge at the throats of others, and sub-structures had appeared in this overall hierarchy—factions of those with the same ideas.

The problem was that most plans had glaring flaws that either made them entirely unfeasible or outright destructive due to their side effects. There were definitely mild ones that advocated some form of peace, kind of like Vern's balance, but they were shot down on account of not wanting to waste this opportunity for potentially paltry results.

Vern still had no clue how to express that the world wasn't on as short of a lease as Rupert made it out to be, and they should be thinking a bit more long term.

Well, this proceeding isn't even about "rejuvenating" the weft anymore. He doubted that any of them would be satisfied with just rejuvenation now that Rupert had dangled such a tantalizing bait of infinite insight in front of everyone.

He scratched his head. This was a problem.

After another few of them argued to their heart's content, Rupert finally slammed down his cane and commanded, "Enough."

His three closed eyes bore down on everyone, and he spoke in a measured tone, "I believe this discussion has made it crystal clear that none of you have the vision required to steer our dying world in a better direction."

He tipped his chin up and said, "Some of the viewpoints presented today are as shallow as the arguments made for them and lack the boldness as well as subtlety needed to lead the civilization to its height."

His lips curved into a disdainful sneer. "Whereas others are too radical, hoping to upend and destroy the very fabric of existence."

Tap!

"As much as I enjoy hearing myriad opinions and absorbing them, we don't have the luxury to do so for much longer. The nexus has its limits, and we shall reach a consensus before we're all expelled.

"According to my superior judgment, only three viable solutions were proposed throughout this meeting." He first pointed at himself and said, "My mandate of omniscience." Then he indicated a group of people in dark veils and said, "Elysian Circle's interdimensional sanctuary edict." He pointed at a man in the fifth row. "And finally Mr. Kanin's blitzkrieg approach.

"We shall vote on which one to proceed with shortly. All these options have their own pros and cons."

"Agreeing on the interdimensional sanctuary edict would mean we essentially give up on billions of denizens and this realm itself as we relocate the weft to a smaller manmade dimension.

"Mr. Kanin's idea is a nuanced one. Forcefully erasing the memories of the horrors we faced in the past weeks from a unified perspective would indeed weaken all malicious beings for a short while. In that small span of time, all of us would have to take out the most egregious perpetrators."

He nodded. "It's a beautiful strategy with essentially no long-term negatives. However, that's its shortcoming too. New monstrosities that come our way would be entirely unaffected by this plan, and we wouldn't be able to execute another critical consensus with such effectiveness a second time.

"Finally"—he smiled—"there's my mandate of omniscience that perfectly solves all our problems with minimal sacrifices. Some suggest that it intrudes on one's autonomy, but that's as far from truth as possible.

"As I've explained, I don't intend to dictate how anyone lives their life. All that matters to me is one doesn't collude with outsiders or propagate the pollution."

The eterna lady interjected with a flat tone, "And we're supposed to take you on your word? Haven't you seen what happens to dictators once the power gets to their heads?"

A hint of anger flashed on Rupert's face, and he replied sharply, "A selfish woman who ignores the pleas of our realm has no right to censure me. Either stop speaking or propose a better solution. I am not a mere aspirant to tyranny, seeking power for power's sake. Every step I plan to take, every sacrifice I propose, is aimed at the future well-being of our people."

He pointed his cane at her and chided, "Desperate times require drastic measures. If you can't accept the burden of our reality, I will. Even if that means going against another eterna."

That's when the lord of primordial blood, who was filing his nails, cut in, "You are really falling over yourself to rule over us, aren't you, Rupert? Calm down a little, okay? Your eagerness is working against you here. Your mandate or whatever will solve the problems, sure. But the cost of giving up our autonomy is just too much."

With a tone of finality, he closed his eyes. "You will not get me on board with a plan that puts me under you. No matter what."

This actually gave Rupert a pause, and he gripped his cane tighter.

After a minute of silence, Rupert snapped his head back toward the crowd, showing unprecedented seriousness in all his actions. With a deep breath, he extended his arms forward and proclaimed, "If a monarchy is disagreeable, would an oligarchy fashion everyone's tastes?"

A sense of unease exploded in Vern. *What the fuck is he trying now?!*

With his voice rising, Rupert challenged the crowd, "If I alone am unfit to govern, would the visionaries of the realm join me in my quest to usher our civilization to its greatest heights?"

Softer but still filled with intensity, his voice echoed, "Indeed, the burden of our existence is too great for one alone. So I propose the council of overseers."

The crowd's skeptical expressions gave way to curiosity.

He paused for effect, then added, "As overseers, you shall gaze through my eyes and wield influence over the world's thoughts as I do, yet remain untouched by the very oversight you administer."

Eyes scanning the crowd, Rupert proclaimed, "It will be a government unlike any other, formed by the greatest of the minds, tirelessly seeking agreement on the minutest matters to bolster every corner of our domain."

His gaze fierce, he asserted, "We shall dictate the ebb and flow of all that exists. We shall be the sun that incinerates the dark forces to ash and the moon that freezes the waves of wicked thoughts right in their tracks."

With a voice brimming with promise, Rupert envisioned, "Under our guidance, countries teetering on the brink of disaster will find salvation in our council's wisdom as we knit the fabric of the cosmos closer, mending the tears wrought by lesser gods and misguided observers."

His tone turned solemn, "We shall stand as the guardians at the gates of infinity, the arbiters of fate itself."

With a final flourish, Rupert invited, "As the council of overseers, we shall forge our destiny, not from the whispers of capricious deities or the chaotic whims of Elden Ones, but from the strength of our collective resolve."

Then, boring directly into the eyes of his audience with his closed ones, he questioned pointedly, "So tell me, visionaries, do your visions extend beyond the mundane? Do you have what it takes to lead the realm, or are you nothing but selfish cowards who avoid responsibility?"

After a brief pause, with an invisible gaze that seemed to pierce through the very soul, Rupert asked, "Tell me, would you rather be satisfied with mediocrity or become overseers of the council that will change the very face of this world?"

With that, he lowered his arms, the intensity of his proclamation lingering in the air like a tangible force. The crowd was silent, not just in awe of the vision laid before them but in the realization of the monumental shift such a council could herald for the universe and for their very own lives.

Vern's thoughts spiraled, his every sense sharpened to an unbearable keenness. The revelation struck him like a bolt from the blue—this was Rupert's masterstroke.

The realization dawned on Vern that what he had previously dismissed as overly ambitious boasting and narcissism was, in fact, a deliberate feint. Rupert had floated a proposal so outlandish, so utterly against the grain, that rejection was the only possible response.

This maneuver, Vern understood, was not about the proposal itself but about manipulating perceptions—crafting an image of Rupert so ambitious, so power hungry, that dissenters would unite in their disdain. Yet the true genius lay in the aftermath: offering his critics a share in this newfound power, a chance to shape the world alongside him.

As Vern's realization deepened, a subtle tremor took hold of his hands. His breathing quickened, a physical testament to the alarm ringing silent and clear in his mind. *Fuck. This is bad.*

What was the difference between one power-hungry observer controlling the world versus fifty? In a world with billions of humans, such a small number of individuals, especially the ones as . . . crazy, polarizing, and self-serving as these visionaries, could never represent even a fraction of the population.

Heck, if such people were given the reins of this world to play god, there was no telling what kind of future was in store for everyone.

Damn.

His intuition for structure told him of a stability that suddenly permeated this otherwise volatile hierarchy made from many factions. It was as if everyone was of one mind and on board with this idea.

Vern surveyed the hall, and the shining eyes all around him were more than enough proof of the current tide.

A sense of instability exploded within his thought space. *If nothing is done about this, people all around the world will undoubtedly lose their autonomy.*

Rupert claimed he wouldn't interfere with one's regular thoughts, and Vern called bullshit. Rupert was a man of deception. Someone who cared for the planet wouldn't go out of his way to slaughter the world's fundamentalists—the people who'd have been invaluable in rebuilding the society post-duskfall.

Not just that, King Keras's words made it clear that Rupert had planned everything right from the start. He first acted like he would be sending someone else from the coven to make the Estefans lower their guard and then promptly took out the king—his biggest dissenter—at the first opportunity.

After that, he'd acted like he was open to others' opinions, but it was all just a sham. They were nothing but comparison points to prove to the crowd that his option was the best for everyone.

Heck, Vern didn't even doubt that Rupert had seeded people in the crowd to respond the way he wanted and push his narrative.

He rubbed his forehead. *What do I do?*

This was the real ingenuity of Rupert's open scheme. Even though Vern understood the dirty machinations behind it all, it would be a lie to say he wasn't swayed.

The clause *you shall remain untouched by the very oversight you administer* was sorely tempting. It would mean his secrets would remain his, while he would also get to play god alongside all these people.

On the other hand, not joining them would mean he would instead become a target of their surveillance—an ant under their watchful eyes, and it wouldn't be long before they'd dig their mandibles into his flesh.

Vern ignored the surrounding chatter and rested his head in his hands to sort out his thoughts.

Unsurprisingly, he soon found another angle to perceive this complicated situation.

There were two choices in front of him, both diametrical opposites of each other.

And to such terrible notions, he only had one response. *Fuck extremes!*

Eyeing his notepad, he reasoned, *I will strike a balance.*

CHAPTER 64

EMOTIONAL VAULT OF A LISTENER

Illeana closed her eyes and unleashed her perception. A noisy vista of tones rang in her ears, and she frowned. They were nowhere near the clarity, expression, and pitch she'd experienced back in free representation.

So she took a deep breath and focused harder, barely managing to activate the first vision of her shade sequence on top of the second one that was burning through her reserves already.

This one was called dominant emotion tuning—practical in its naming as well as usage.

While activated, she could, well . . . sense the dominant emotions of her targets. It didn't sound very awe-inspiring, but there was something special about all the visions of her shade sequence.

They worked on other observers without her needing to contest with their singularity.

At least to a far lesser extent than most other viewpoints. Emotion-related shade sequences weren't notorious for no reason. They worked and built upon cues exhibited by one's physicality and body language that couldn't really be masked well by their singularity.

And that was just their inherent property. Her insights into each emotion or person in question could still boost their potency.

Glad I didn't actually become a soul seer, she mused. Father had great intentions in setting her up with that sequence, and the silence of soulstrings was terrifyingly powerful, but its first three visions were nothing to write home about.

At least not when compared to the listener sequence—the one she'd ended up going with for her first and second shades. It matched not just her viewpoint but also her construct of isolation—it had a subjective interpretation of emotions isolated by a sound-like construct.

Also, she should still be able to imprint the silence of soulstrings once she reached the fourth shade.

This synergy of hers, paired with her nonexistent shackles to her subjectivity, allowed her to acclimate her viewpoint to the shade sequence as naturally as breathing air. So much so that she felt like she was already halfway through the second shade in a mere few days.

There was just one little problem.

She had no clue how to get her hands on the observation records or resonance catalysts for its higher shades. This was why Father had advised her against following down this path. Even with all his resources, he had only found the record for its first shade.

Luckily, duskfall had set too much into motion, and sequences that were considered broken were being dug up from myriads of ruins. She'd gotten her hands on its second shade—empath's catalyst a couple days ago from the black market vendor who owed her his life.

This advancement was the only reason she could sit up here without being caught in her preposterous lies. The lack of pressure from nexus was entirely unexpected, and as much as she liked to believe she could conduct her emotions perfectly, she knew it was impossible in that situation.

So she had done it. Vaulted her emotions. That was the other vision she'd kept on since the start of this confluence—emotional vault. It worked on the insights she had regarding her own emotions and tendencies.

The better she understood herself, the better the vision negated her emotions, pushing them into her psyche's vault. Yet, as the name suggested, these emotions weren't discarded; they were just muted temporarily.

The thought of backlash that awaited her for vaulting such strong emotions for so long was terrifying, but luckily, even her fear found itself stashed away, letting none of these silly notions mess with her judgment.

Her quick actions, nexus's restrictions, and people's wild imaginations had all come together, allowing her to pretend to be an eterna, close to what her father used to be.

Someone above all these deranged psychos and narcissists who thought they could treat the world that her father had sacrificed himself for like their plaything. And she didn't want to waste this.

Except she was having a hard time now that Rupert had dangled delicious meat in front of these hungry vultures. It sickened her, what they wanted to do. Sadly, even that feeling was elusive as the emotional vault stifled their tones.

She was surely raking in too much emotional debt because of how infuriating this Rupert guy was.

The man was essentially a devil in human skin. His plans and methods were far too elaborate. She remembered Father being annoyed by the scheming fundamentalists from the Coven of Truth, and now she understood his pain very well.

With a shake of her head, she focused on the tones around her. The muted, incoherent noise that wasn't very different from the whispers gave way to burning melodies and sharp sagas.

Which would be great, were it not for the dominant emotion they signified—greed. Due to a lack of insights, she could only tune in to two emotions as of right now: sorrow and greed. After all, these were the two emotions she had observed the most since duskfall.

These tones flooding her ears were no doubt greed.

This vision would generally make her feel the same emotion that she tuned into, but the vault captured even that, essentially negating the drawbacks of dominant emotional tuning. *At least for now.* She sighed. The backlash was going to be ugly.

Careful not to focus on the eternas in the top row, she wielded her perception like a weapon. She had no wish to antagonize the other eternas, especially when there was a possibility they would sense her vision.

The lord of primordial blood may not remember it, but he'd fought on the front-lines alongside her father beyond the time. At least from her understanding of the events. Father mentioned he would be up there with him, resisting the descent of the unseen one.

And as much as she wanted to tune in to the dominant emotions of Rupert, she knew that'd be stupid. Nexus's pressure on the eighth row was unable to restrict him completely, and she didn't want to take any chances.

So she focused on the rows beneath herself. Different pitches and tones of greed arose from the individuals. From the so-called visionaries who were supposed to wield the wisdom of the sun and the strength of the moon.

She had heard legends of them and even idolized some, but right now, there was little difference between them and petty, mundane politicians. Avarice took hold of their minds. The allure of becoming omniscient gods was evidently too much, even for these otherwise aloof and sophisticated individuals.

Illeana lamented the state of affairs when only King Keras and his wife's tone crooned with sorrow in all thirty or so high-shade observers. The rest of the tones came together in a chorus of insatiable greed, their tones harmonizing in a disgusting crescendo.

Pathetic. She'd hoped to see at least a few in higher rows who would rise against this terrible mandate. Alas, morality wasn't a requirement to become a visionary, and it showed.

This, however, was an unexpected note in her symphony. If even a few were ready to sing tunes of opposition, she would have dogged Rupert's choice and trashed his mandate, but this just felt like a song without a chorus.

Her forcefully pacified mind, devoid of any emotions, churned, hoping to figure out her next course of action. And soon, it arrived at the most logical conclusion.

Give in.

As much as she loathed the idea of working with these conniving bastards to foster what was essentially a hyper-surveilled society that aimed to kill all free thought, her mind told her that was her only choice.

Rupert already held all the notes, and she lacked the means to alter the tune.

There were risks of them finding out about her true strength—a mere second-shade observer, but she still had her father's artifacts with her. They had limited representation to their name, and she couldn't bring herself to use them unless absolutely necessary, but they would be more than enough to scare even Rupert and let her exist among them at her rightful position.

She feared this exact situation. For she had no other reason to hold her tongue against this sinister mandate, which aimed to rear humanity like sheep in a pen.

After all, a mind watched is a mind caged. It might tide them over this one hump in the road, but down the line, it would stifle innovation and evolution. Surely, all these people knew this in their inner hearts too. Yet it seemed their priorities were far too skewed.

Not like she was much different. After all, she couldn't allow them into her thoughts, no matter what. And the only way to guarantee that was to fall in line.

Her usual emotional self would disagree with such a callous decision, but the more she observed everyone's greed and tendencies, the clearer it became that there wasn't anything else she could do.

The other two options of relocating to a smaller dimension and waging an all-out world war against pollution were clearly inferior to this choice for the crowd.

Ah, she groaned. *I shouldn't vault my emotions unless absolutely necessary.* She couldn't stop now, for Rupert would surely notice something was off, but it was clear that vaulting emotions was a double-edged sword.

It allowed her purely rational thought, but it also made it easy for her to go against her own values. Running counter to one's viewpoint was a quick way to cut one's journey as an observer short. And it was worse for her.

Because of how well her shade sequence suited her, she had yet to dissociate her actions as an observer from her actions as Illeana. And Illeana would never choose to trust the world that Father saved with these despicable opportunists.

If she didn't sort out her thoughts soon, she would essentially be inviting the whispers to feast on the contradictions within her viewpoint and rend her from the inside out.

Ugh. She leaned on the back of her chair and tuned back into the emotions of the observers. Maybe the lower-shade ones were better?

She lost all hope when she reached the second row from the bottom. The chanting that spoke of greed for power was more intense here than even middle shades.

In between, she couldn't tune in to the dominant emotions of some people, but more than two-thirds were definitely full of greed for this opportunity. Alas, the lack of greed in middle-shade observers wasn't of much use given how some of them were already vetoed as overseers by the others.

A majority, she repeated, trying and failing to get it to sink in.

That's when her perception reached the lowest point of the hall, and a melody unlike any other assaulted her ears.

Huh . . . ? She opened her eyes and turned her head back. Her peripheral vision landed on the lone figure sitting in the bottommost row. He looked just like any other guy who'd hidden his identity.

She absentmindedly twirled a strand of hair around her finger and thought, *It's him.* She'd entertained the idea that he might be in the same situation as herself—someone unfettered by the pressure of the nexus. However, his actions made her doubt the conjecture.

Yes, he had hesitated quite a bit before settling down there, but many who faced this pressure for the first time were also disoriented just like him.

Soon, however, she lost that train of thought, and confusion overwhelmed her. She focused harder on perceiving his dominant emotion.

It's definitely greed, but—

Her eyebrows furrowed as she struggled to pinpoint the emotion each of his actions sang of so melodiously. It was no doubt another form of greed, but it was unlike others in the room.

As she tried and failed one time after another to figure out the exact emotion he was emitting, the power-hungry egotists around her used excuse after excuse to justify why this council of overseers was in everyone's best interests.

"I can't believe the coven master is so magnanimous as to share his grand visions with us lowly ones."

"Indeed, the world would be a far better place if we would come together and govern all its intricacies."

"It's a sacrifice, but one that must be made for the prosperity of our civilization."

Illeana sneered. *Weren't you vehemently denouncing this same mandate just minutes ago?* It was fascinating how their tunes changed the moment their interests were taken care of.

However, the thought that she'd have to say something along the same lines to show her acceptance of this mandate soured her mood quickly, only for even that to be vaulted away.

It was almost surreal, and annoyingly, her vaulted emotions made it so this insane and terrible chain of events felt utterly mundane—as if putting shackles on all of humanity's thoughts was just another day in the life.

Feeling her activation of the emotional vault faltering, she discontinued this line of thought and returned to impassively scrutinizing the unique emotion of that man in the bottom row.

It is set in stone, she reasoned. *There's no stopping this council of overseers now. I should aim to solidify my position instead.*

Slowly, she turned her chair in the direction of that man, not making her actions or gaze too obvious. That's when she noticed something peculiar, and her eyes almost widened in reaction.

Wait! Aren't those the glyphs of Elyndor? What is he doing with them? She sat straighter, her eyes glued to the golden sparks that found themselves pulled toward his quill as if it were some vortex.

She'd been able to see these glyphs since her enlightenment. Alas, she didn't have one whit of talent in their comprehension. Not even Father's artifacts helped her in that regard.

Her mind whirled. *Is he sending someone a note right now? What would be the point of that? Even if he notified observers outside this meeting of what was about to transpire, it wouldn't change a damned thing.*

Nexus was essentially cut off from reality, after all.

However, before she could become too sure of her conjecture, something changed, and a fully solid glyph floated above the man's convergence note.

She tilted her head, wondering, *This never happens to me.* Nor had she seen it happen when others used their convergence notes.

She was supposed to be impassive, but a hint of excitement somehow flared within her heart as she watched him write one glyph after another.

The crowd took this time to work themselves toward a faux consensus of words— as if their minds weren't already one.

Two, Three, Four, she counted as the number of glyphs surrounding the guy increased, new ones emerging and floating around him faster than the prior.

What is he doing? she questioned, only to be amazed by her own curiosity.

It looks like the vault can't contain all my emotions properly. Hmm, or maybe it's because I have never really analyzed my own curiosity deeply.

However, that's when someone in the fourth row smacked their chair with a loud *thump* and shouted, "Hah. Fuck this. I don't care anymore. Fuck you, Rupert!"

Chapter 65

ACCUSATIONS

The enraged man continued, "You think a serial killer and butcher like you deserves to rule the world? Become the uncontested dictator of the planet? Nah, go fuck yourself."

Illeana didn't miss the flicker of astonishment and . . . sorrow within her original target's melody as he snapped his head toward this new speaker—his quill coming to a pause.

She was caught unprepared as she wondered who to focus on, but she quickly found a solution to her predicament. Pinning her perception on the author of the glyphs, she turned her gaze toward this foul-mouthed newcomer.

Brown hair, unclear face, and a very . . . foreign fashion sense. He wore a formless white garment with a mysterious, oversized hood embellished with pointless cords. His legs were wrapped in indigo fabric, rugged and intentionally frayed, as if torn in a skirmish with an unseen adversary.

Rupert raised his arm, and all the visionaries stopped their chatter, looking down on the newcomer with derision, contempt, and schadenfreude. Illeana knew why. *No one cares.* Who here hadn't killed their fair share of people?

Anyone who'd shaded their perception a couple times was bound to have gone through mortal conflicts. The world had limited resources for observers, after all.

Heck, even she had a life to her name, much less these people who abandoned all pretenses at the drop of a hat and jumped at this chance to enslave all of humanity.

Illeana didn't even need to use her vision to figure out what was going on in the newcomer's head. His body language made it more than obvious he was befuddled by their nonchalance and disdain.

"You all don't get it, huh? I guess I need to give you sons of bitches more than just this." He then pointed at Rupert and yelled, "This motherfucker." Rupert stared back with a flat expression that hinted at a bubbling rage, but the newcomer doubled down. "Yes you, bitch."

With a flourish of his arms, he exclaimed, "This waste of human skin slaughtered the Lorendale clan down to their last cats and dogs."

Illeana frowned. She wasn't very versed in world politics, but even she'd heard legends of the Lorendales. They were supposed to be the spiritual successors of the Institute.

A priest from the sixth row snickered and said, "Just sit down, you uncouth beast. You can't defame the lord's title and make such grave accusations without any proof. No one even knows if the Lorendales are real. Yet you accuse the lord of slaughtering them? This is embarrassing."

Some teenager added right after, "Hmm, I don't think someone as hot-tempered as you is suitable to act as an overseer for the whole world." Turning toward the crowd, the teen added, "I vote for him to be stripped of the chance to join us as an overseer of the council."

Another visionary chimed in, "Indeed. Such a young man who doesn't understand subtlety or nuance shouldn't be allowed to decide what to pick for food, much less the world's fate. I vote for him to be excluded as well."

More voices echoed this sentiment, and Illeana couldn't help but chuckle at the absurdity of it all. The arrogance, gatekeeping, and elitism were already running rampant among them. And this was when they had yet to taste any tangible power. She could only imagine how big their heads would get once they actually wielded true control over the thoughts of the planet's denizens.

If only I were truly an eterna. She sighed. *I'd have called off this charade long ago.* This made her wonder why the lord of primordial blood wasn't saying something about it.

Maybe he has the same reservations as I do? She bit her lip. Her silent acceptance of this ruse as another "eterna" probably wasn't helping either. After all, he'd have to think of it as him against not just Rupert but also everyone else in the room. Especially when he had far more to gain by siding with their plan.

Should I try and get him on my side? However, she soon shook her head. She wasn't actually an eterna. If things really devolved into the worst case, it would already be a miracle if she could keep herself alive, much less actively fight others so many shades above herself.

She sighed for the umpteenth time. There wasn't much she could do to steer this situation toward a better outcome, and she knew it. All these deflections and misdirection were ways in which the "rational" Illeana coped with all of it.

She shook her head and returned her mind to the proceedings as well as to the author of those glyphs in the bottom row. He was doing something she didn't understand, and it was a good distraction.

A dozen or so glyphs floated around him as he occasionally checked back, as if curious how the newcomer would handle this lynching.

With a scornful posture of his own, the man in the spotlight snorted. "I wouldn't join your oppressive authoritarian orgy even if you begged me to. All of you who agree to this are sick fucks falling over each other to master an army of mindless puppets. Puppets of your own making."

Illeana's emotional vault, which had remained as still as a lake until now, rippled at hearing those words.

"As for proof?" He sneered and slid his hand into the pocket of his top, retrieving a contraption. It was a slim, rectangular object made of transparent glass, small enough to be grasped firmly in one hand. "Here's the proof of your lord savior ruthlessly obliterating an entire city."

He held it with an air of solemnity, and with a swift motion unfamiliar to Illeana, the surface came alive with colors and moving figures. She squinted, trying to make sense of the miniature tableau playing out in the palm of his hand.

It was as if he had captured a fragment of reality itself—a miniaturized film theater even—within the confines of this enigmatic device. The figures in the film ran haphazardly as a tall man in black with a bloody red eye in the middle of his forehead wreaked havoc and destruction, delivering despair without remorse.

The whole crowd quietened down, their eyes slowly turning toward Rupert. The man breathed heavily, almost as if genuinely enraged. After a deep breath, he hissed, "A slanderous bastard. My wife is a Lorendale herself. Are you insinuating I slaughtered my own in-laws?"

Right when the crowd made to gasp at this revelation, he smashed his cane hard, and the whole hall rumbled with a *Thump!* "Are you out of your fucking minds?!"

Following a wave of Rupert's hand, an image floated above it. The glowing scene depicted the nexus with the haughty newcomer in focus. However, soon red vines erupted from his body, and he exploded into bits of gore and blood.

Obviously, that just happened within that image. The newcomer was still standing there, hale and hearty, but a hint of defensiveness had definitely wormed its way into his body language.

Rupert didn't even need to elaborate, for one of his cronies spoke for him, "Hah, are we all looking at this slimy bastard? He wants to sow discord among us by showing us his conjured illusions. As sir Rupert just demonstrated, anyone can fabricate false illusions. They mean nothing. A vile creature, really."

"Blasphemy! This vulgar cretin is trying to smear the omniscient one's name by painting him as a slaughterer of the wise."

The newcomer in question snickered and said, "Well, sure, don't trust me. I'm nobody. But if there's even a sliver of chance that you'll be under such an insidious man who didn't think twice before killing his wife's family and refuses to show any remorse, it should give you all pause.

"It should make you reconsider this choice. Imagine what he wouldn't do once you all are ensnared in his trap and he's actually inside your heads. All in the name of this consensus or whatever."

Illeana mulled over this vulgar but deep advice.

She'd sensed genuine rage within Rupert's demeanor at this assertion, but these words indeed held quite some weight to them.

That's when Rupert slammed his cane down with full force and rebuked, "Enough! If you have any real evidence, bring it forward. If not, stop trying to get a reaction out of me. I've touched upon it already, but let me reiterate that none of us would be able to access each other's thoughts without consent while we're connected."

The newcomer raised his chin higher and sneered, "Hah. Real proof? Are you suggesting I let one of you motherfuckers rifle through my memories? Fuck off. Disgusting pig." A revulsed look in his eyes, he snarled, "I just want to remind that you should all be wary. What if he changed his mind one day and decided to collapse your minds from within?"

Rupert, who had been charged with fury until now, suddenly calmed down, and he spoke as if coaxing a child, "It's certainly in one's best interest to prepare for all eventualities. However, unnecessary fearmongering and hesitation only leads to one conclusion. Defeat."

He then turned toward the crowd and said, "Fellow visionaries, enough time has been wasted on these baseless accusations."

Leaning on the cane, he proclaimed, "I am sure everyone's concerned that I'm hiding some trick up my sleeve. However, what if I told you that no one even needs to lift the barrier of their singularities for the consensus to be achieved. Instead—"

He brought his hand to his chest and declared, "I'll be the one doing that. Giving you all a window inside my mind."

The whole crowd stopped dead in their tracks as the mild suspicion that had begun to creep up in the atmosphere fizzled away, giving way to astonishment. Even Illeana frowned. *What is he doing? Is he really that confident in his strength? Why would he go so far as to open up his viewpoint to others?*

The newcomer in the fourth row simply shrugged. "Your call, man. I tried. I just wanted to out this slaughtering wretch for who he really is. If all of you don't give a fuck, I give even less."

The teenager from before took this chance to pour on some venom. "A terrorist is what you are, you imbecile!" Shaking his head, he proposed, "I suggest we strip him of his right to speak up in the nexus at all, otherwise he'll continue to waste our time. I know people like him. They thrive on attention and revel in becoming a nuisance to the order."

The newcomer made to comment but was drowned in a few breaths as the crowd passed another quick vote to silence him under the laws of nexus itself. It just needed a majority vote, not a unanimous one.

After such vehement opposition, Illeana felt like voicing her own concerns, but something held her back. It seemed that being unfettered by her emotional shackles didn't suddenly make her a more decisive person.

She tried reasoning to herself, *Rupert is giving them too good of a deal. There's no way I can convince anyone otherwise.* She didn't even have some damning proof like the newcomer did.

Yes, she was pretending to be an eterna, but what if she opposed and still failed? All these men and women who pretended to respect her would flip sides at the drop of a hat. They'd vote her out of their council, and she'd lose her own autonomy as a direct result.

Ugh, a bit of light music would be perfect right about now. She'd love nothing more than to go back to her room and play something. This was . . . exhausting. She had no clue what this consensus really meant for the future of their world or if it'd even work.

She was just a lowly second-shade observer with her father's gifts. She wasn't someone who could go against these observers in a fair fight or even as the false king sitting on her rightful throne in Karthain.

After a while, she sighed. *It just . . . doesn't feel right.*

No more interruptions disturbed the proceedings anymore. And to their credit, some observers chose to voluntarily leave the nexus before this final step of the consensus.

However, most remained in their seats, including her annoyingly rational self, as well as the foul-mouthed newcomer as Rupert expounded on the methodology they'd follow to make it all work.

Sighing internally, she focused back to the author of the glyphs, who emanated that same flat tone of profound greed. Now, however, fifty or so glyphs floated all around him, and his quill had long stopped and was resting within his top pocket.

A curious light flashed through her eyes as she gazed at him. *What exactly is he doing?* It made no sense to her. At first, she'd thought he was sending notes to someone about this meeting, but that clearly wasn't the case.

Why would so many glyphs orbit him if all he did was send some stupid notes? *Then what?*

A tiny hope blossomed within the core of her mind. A hope for a change. A hope for a miracle. The unknown could be like that sometimes, no?

She knew it was stupid to expect anyone to go against the most terrifying observers of the planet, but a girl can dream, right?

She bit her lower lip. *Maybe these glyphs are like some kind of protection?* After all, they were in the nexus made by the observers of Elyndor. It would make sense that their glyphs would somehow interact with the nexus in some shape or form.

Then would he use them in a fight?

Before she could delude herself further, Rupert tapped his cane, and almost everyone voted yes for another proposal aimed toward reducing the pressure of the nexus a little bit.

With or without her consent, the matters continued to progress at a rapid pace. Soon the restrictive pressure in all rows reduced just enough for Rupert to set the next part of his plan into motion.

Small glassy vines materialized out of the ground as Illeana mulled over Rupert's latest speech on how it was all going to work. It was far more sophisticated than what the Estefans had proposed for sure.

Everyone would first link with each other using the essence strands of Lightveins, which Rupert had somehow managed to imprint in his own perception. This would allow him to act as a hub of sorts for all visionaries to share their insights and sync their ideas perfectly before they envision a shared reality.

Once that was done, he'd link himself to the core of nexus, allowing their shared vision to permeate the artifact behind it all. It was very well thought out.

It's almost as if he'd planned it all beforehand. She curled her lip. It was cute how he'd acted reluctant in the earlier parts of this meeting, playing out this whole situation as if he'd relented based on the feedback from the crowd.

Still, how did he manage to imprint the Lightvein legacy? she wondered. Father had mentioned of it in passing. It was supposed to be this brutally hard shade sequence that required a very specific personality and disposition to progress comfortably.

However, Rupert had gone a step beyond simple acclimation. He was already an eterna in his own shade sequence. Yet, he still somehow managed to imprint the essence strands into his perception.

Given that it was from such a wildly different shade sequence, it was a miracle he hadn't lost himself to the whispers. *Is the Lightvein shade sequence secretly interchangeable with the gazebinder sequence?*

If so, why had no one tried such a powerful combination before Rupert?

Well, not like it mattered anymore. Things were already in motion.

All Lightveins manifested a different form for their essence strands, but Rupert's rendition looked like a standard network of glassy vines, extending all around the nexus like a tough one, its segments further splitting to bloom into a flower in front of every observer.

Everyone hesitated to interact with it, and Illeana was only the second-worst offender. Next to herself, the lord of primordial blood didn't even glance at the peculiar thing and continued filing away at his unnecessarily sturdy nails.

With a curt bow, Rupert said, "I put my trust in all of you with this. I hope you will reciprocate."

No. she refuted the man in her mind. She wasn't going to interact with it until the last moment. If nothing, she wanted her displeasure with this whole charade made very clear. She didn't really buy the whole idea of restricting everyone's thoughts for some man's wild ambitions.

It was against the nature of humanity itself.

She very much wanted to rub her forehead, but it wouldn't be a good look for her to appear distressed. She couldn't show weakness. Not right now.

Given things were already at such a juncture, a sense of urgency welled up within her, held at bay by nothing other than the emotional vault.

It is really happening, she repeated to herself, hoping it'd somehow sink in and permeate through to her core.

Seconds passed in a silence of inaction. Right when she started cheering in the hope that everyone was getting cold feet, that priest in the sixth row closed his eyes and shouted, "For Mother!" He then plucked the flower from its stem.

CHAPTER 66

ASSASSINATION

Everyone waited with bated breath, and soon, the tense expression on the priest's face flattened, only to turn blissful the next moment. It flitted through many phases, and dozens of seconds passed by in this silence.

Just when people began to turn uneasy, the priest snapped his eyes open. "Marvellous!"

"Ese-nashii! I have seen the path! It is real! It is real!"

Before he could finish, a couple others who'd been exclusively speaking in Rupert's favor jumped in and plucked their flowers.

"Oh, the omniscient one! This is the most beautiful construct in existence!"

Illeana felt disgust rise within her chest, and even the vault refused to stash it away as if her perception was just as revulsed by this whole rigged ordeal.

In no time, people who were otherwise unaffiliated with Rupert joined in too. Not outside her expectations, things went exactly as she'd envisioned they would.

No one changed their minds. Instead, their fervor reached a new height.

It is inevitable, she repeated. Her eyes darted side to side, and a sense of panic broke past the vault. She repeatedly glanced at the author of the glyphs.

Yet he did nothing.

He sat there, his face in his palm, lazily watching the happenings as if all of this had nothing to do with him.

She bit her lip. *Did I really judge him wrong?* It was a late realization, but at this point, she was even willing to fight if it meant they could somehow stop this consensus. She didn't care if it was the lord of primordial blood or the author of glyphs who started it. *Someone just do it!*

The vault was clearly losing its grip on her, and she didn't care.

She tapped her legs faster and faster, but her unsung pleas fell on deaf ears. Nobody moved to stop this horrendous business. Instead, they reveled in it as more of them reached out to the essence strands and joined into the collective, coming out of it more convinced than ever.

Her heart beat rapidly, and she opened her palm to gaze at the pocket watch chained to her bracelet. Its second hand ticked with that same gentle rhythm, anchoring her back in reality.

As her facade of indifference crumbled, a suicidal plan instead took its place. Her vaulted emotions had stopped her from going down this destructive line of thought previously, but this was the only option available to her now.

What was left of her rationality told her that it was a stupid idea, but these psychos wanted to ruin the world her father had brought back from the jaws of death and decay, paying for it with his own life. It just didn't sit well with her that they got to pour oil all over it and watch it burn. She'd thought she could hold herself back, but it just wasn't working.

A part of her knew that she desperately needed to reenact the emotional vault right now, but that part was small. Too small.

Soon, more than a dozen observers had reveled in the essence strands.

Then twenty.

Fifty.

Before she knew it, other than the ones voted out by the council, only three people were left. Herself, the lord of primordial blood, and that nonchalant man at the bottom row with his useless glyphs.

However, that's when the eterna sitting next to her sighed, a bitter look on his face, and said, "I can't really stop this, can I?" He plucked the flower with a *snap*.

Illeana's hand moved to stop this irreversible action, but it was too late.

Rupert flashed a creepily encouraging smile and gazed at her, completely ignoring the author of glyphs in the bottom row. Even if no one had mentioned it, this made it clear that an eterna played a far more significant role in this consensus than a first-shade observer who was foolish enough to show them attitude.

A chilling realization took hold of Illeana, and a tremor rippled through her body. *This is it.* No one else will do anything. These lowly scums were hell-bent on plunging the whole world into a nightmare where even one's thoughts weren't their own.

The thought sickened her, and the fact that she'd been willing to go along with it up until a while ago only made it worse.

She gritted her teeth and eyed the source of all problems. *Rupert!* Her gaze shifted between her dagger, the pocket watch, and the man's neck.

She didn't know if the vault had really stopped working or if it was the backlash—releasing all the bottled emotions with double the intensity—but she couldn't ignore this crazy idea anymore.

No. It can really work, she hissed internally. *Rupert's singularity is all but suppressed up here while I still have access to my second shade's physical enhancements. If I activate Father's epoch keeper within Rupert's vicinity, he'll be frozen in time—helpless. Then, a single slash from my dagger should be more than enough to end him for good.*

Her mouth went dry at the absurd yet genius nature of this plan. The very peculiar circumstances of her being not pressured by the nexus and her decision to sit up here next to Rupert, made this mad idea an almost practical one.

The more she mulled it over in her head, the firmer her resolve became. Sweat ran down her neck, and the audacity of her plan settled in. *I am trying to assassinate the most powerful man on the whole planet.* She gulped, *And I actually have a shot!*

That's when the hated voice of that narcissist grated on her ears once again. "Milady eterna, I have duly noted your disapproval for my mandate, but it would be unwise to dally any longer."

With a faux politeness, he added, "The nexus has its limits, and we still have much to accomplish. I can understand the ignorant new observer, but I am sure you know better than to waste everyone's time. This is a chance of a lifetime. Surely, you wouldn't want to sit this one out."

Her eye twitched. *He's pressuring me to make a choice.* This, however, only made her actual decision easier. Fuck if it was just the emotional backlash speaking; she had a genuine shot at saving the world.

She thought, *Mm-hmm, ending him here would be like chopping a pianist's fingers right before a performance.* If there was no one who could wield the essence strands, a consensus where these paranoid leeches could implement something so radical would become nigh impossible.

It was perfect.

Closing her eyes, she first entirely blanketed her perception, stopping all the visions. Then with a deep breath and calm mind, she thought once again, *emotional vault.*

She funneled all her representation into that single thought. The vault had just shown its seams, but her next moves would really benefit from a cold, purely rational headspace. She couldn't afford any mistakes in the heat of the moment due to simple emotions.

The backlash of emotions that had just begun to burst out of the vault was pushed back in, but its resistance was fierce, and it grew in size while at it, promising a worse rebound next time it burst. Her stomach churned, and her mouth went dry, but she held on.

Soon a calm melody emanated from her very being, and her trembling fingers turned perfectly still—steady enough to play the most complex of the vibratos on her violin.

When she snapped her eyes back open, a dozen oscillating strings emerged from her pupils, and her whole irises radiated a green haze. Not that anyone could see the beautiful pattern, for her impassive gaze was focused on the icy flower by her knees.

With each moment, every inch of her body shifted oh so subtly, streamlining for action. All the while, her right palm moved toward the flower at a steady pace.

The whole crowd held their breath, knowing this would seal the deal for good and symbolize the beginning of something far more treacherous.

Her gaze flitted toward that man in the bottom row one final time.

He remained unbothered, facing her general direction with a calm aura. Illeana sighed. *I really misunderstood it, huh?*

"It's really up to me, I guess," she hummed with a sweet smile. Her index and middle fingers rested on the stem of the flower.

Snap!

She burst into action, her whole body flowing into the smoothest transition possible from sitting to spearheading toward Rupert.

The icy flower and vines shattered beneath her heels as she crossed the blood lord's seat before the crowd even had a chance to exclaim.

Rupert narrowed his eyes and jumped back, holding his cane from its center like some scepter.

However, Illeana was too quick. She covered the rest of the distance by the time Rupert landed.

Good, she affirmed emotionlessly as her free hand reached into her thigh belt through the opening in the sides of her dress, pulling out the sheathed dagger in an upward slash.

With a *schwing*, it hit Rupert's cane, failing to wedge even a nick in the damned thing. Not that it mattered. This wasn't her end game.

She ducked and invaded the man's personal space, all the while avoiding the knee he aimed to incapacitate her.

The veins around Rupert's eyes bulged, and a terrifying premonition gripped her. Alas, it was too late for Rupert. She was already mere inches away from him.

Her left thumb resting on the epoch keeper's dial applied force, and with a *click*, the world rippled.

A hum of victory permeated her very being as she reverse-gripped the dagger and thrust it toward Rupert's throat, roaring, "Rot in hell, you psycho."

The slow crowd exploded in cries, but Illeana waited for the feeling of her dagger ripping through flesh and coming out the other end through his nape.

She'd never reveled in physical violence, but something within her wished for this man to meet the most gruesome of deaths.

Except . . .

Chink.

The sound echoed in her ears, and her mind failed to register the implications. Instead of the expected resistance of the flesh, a solid metal deflected her attack, and before she knew it, the world flipped upside down.

"Argh!" she gasped as a terrifying smack of the cane on her chest knocked the wind out of her lungs.

However, her mind, mostly devoid of emotions, ignored the pain and latched on to her only hope. She didn't know what went wrong, but Father's epoch keeper was the only thing that could save her now.

"You vile woman! How dare you?!" Rupert thundered as he slammed his cane down once again like some barbarian.

Holding the dagger above herself in her right hand like some shield, her left palm repeatedly tapped the dial to activate the pocket watch. Reality rippled, and—

Nothing happened.

Thump.

The cane broke through her block, rending her tendons from the sheer force of it, but time wasn't on her side. Literally.

Yet she took this brief window of respite to internalize her error calmly. *Seems like the epoch keeper isn't working.* And it only took her a moment to realize where things had gone wrong.

It was stupid, really.

In a tone that one would use to speak of matters unrelated to themselves, she thought, *The nexus's pressure may not restrict me, but it's still restricting my perceptual artifacts with full strength.*

It's over.

I failed.

Her mind wavered, and she debated turning off her emotional vault but decided against it in the very next instant. She didn't want to give this bastard even one ounce of satisfaction now that things had come to this.

Rupert finally managed to crack open his middle eye, and a maniacal expression covered his face. Dusting his coat, he barked, "I respect your choice, woman. However, I expected more from an eterna. Did you really think you could kill me with nothing but a surprise factor? Hah. You aren't just selfish, but stupid too."

Did he not notice Father's pocket watch? It seemed even though he could exhibit so much power up here, there were still some tight restrictions.

Illeana stared back with a defiant, sharp gaze, still resisting the push of his cane.

However, suddenly, a red light blinded her perception, and a wave of terror coursed through her. Her limbs refused to obey her commands, and her mind fogged. Her pulse raced, and the facade of the vault began to crumble. The icy vines shackled both her wrists and pulled her up in the air.

Rupert turned his head toward the crowd and bellowed, "This despicable woman, an eterna, a supposed leader of the realm, is hell-bent on cutting the dreams of our council short.

"This vile creature couldn't bear the shame of her own selfish existence and wished to deny us the sacrifice that would usher our civilization into a new era."

Rupert shook his cane, and a red aura materialized around it. Simply staring at it was like being sucked into a void. A shudder went down her spine, but she pushed past it and chuckled, then said, "Remember. All of you are nothing but power-hungry psychopaths and deranged lunatics. Don't let anyone tell you otherwise."

Rupert ignored her remarks and smiled. "Now tell me, fellow overseers. Should such a creature not be punished?

"Should such a dissident not be put in her place?"

Those cronies of his yelled back with too much excitement, "Yes! She tried to assassinate our lord. It's only fair she's killed to compensate for her sins."

"We'd be doomed if such a deviant eterna roamed the lands. We should punish her right now!"

"Cull her!"

"Punish her!"

"Indeed." Rupert nodded. "A self-seeking observer has no place in a world envisioned by us overseers. We shall mark the beginning of a new era and restructuring of our realm with her sacrifice. So let us arrive at the first consensus as the council of overseers."

The cane's length turned a deeper shade of red, and he manifested an icy flower in his hands—an essence strand. With his eyes closed, he whispered, "Overseers, let the voting begin!"

Illeana eyed them with mirth. "Haha. Posturing and roleplaying won't lighten the burden of your sins, you sick fucks."

After just a couple seconds of silence, he shouted, "A two-thirds majority consensus has been achieved. As per the will of the overseers, this witch shall be burned on this proverbial stake for the sin of attempting to overthrow the council."

Illeana narrowed her eyes. Exiting the nexus and running away were out of the question. They would just hunt her down once they'd finished their little game here. And down in the material world, all they'd need to kill her was to steal her thoughts to eat, or worse, steal her thoughts of remorse—forcing her to kill and then be killed.

There were a thousand other ways in which they could end her, and she would be none the wiser.

Her eyes grew dangerous and she traced the edge of her pocket watch with her perception. It may have failed to activate fully under this much pressure, but she was more than certain that exploding it would injure even a god, much less this piece of shit in front of her.

With a terrifying grin of her own, she declared, "I will remember this. I'll remember all of you!" That gave Rupert a short pause, but he steeled himself, and the red aura around his cane warped the air further, vibrating violently.

Illeana sneered internally. *He still thinks I'm an eterna.* The amount of energy stored in that thing was enough to kill her a thousand times over.

"Opposing the council mustn't go unpunished."

"End this contrarian!"

"Off with her head!"

"Kill the witch!!"

"Burn her!"

"Cull her!"

"End her!"

In this charged atmosphere, Rupert's grin stretched from end to end, and he pulled back his cane one final time. He shouted, "For humanity!" and hurled the glowing cane toward her chest like some meteor.

Illeana's heart beat in defiance and desperation as she sharpened her intent, ready to pierce her pocket watch with her perception.

However, in that instant, the myriads of colorful lights—blue from the nexus, green from her own eyes, and red from Rupert's staff, all just . . . disappeared.

In this realm of utter darkness, a sigh echoed in the hall, "Disappointing."

Chapter 67

CONTRADICTIONS

Hensen bubbled with rage, so his smile grew softer. He wished to etch this disgrace in his memories, so it became nothing but a fleeting one. He wanted to scream, so his vocal cords stiffened.

Not that it mattered, for these wastes of skin had stolen his right to speak in the nexus anyway.

They all wanted a world that'd essentially end his life. What difference was there between dying and being unable to serve Mistress? None.

Apart from some complications due to the rune in his head, he'd been having the best time of his life. Could there even be anything more fulfilling than following Mistress's every order down to the letter—serving a purpose grander than himself?

Was there really any higher honor than watching Mistress illuminate this realm of gloom and despair with her unmatched radiance?

None.

However, if these intellectual barbarians were to have their way, the whole world would become Rupert's eyes. And there was no way Mistress would keep him around if it meant Rupert could glean her plans through him—not that he wouldn't kill himself before inflicting such harm upon Mistress.

Hensen clutched at his heart, an ecstatic grin covering his face as the thought of Mistress going against the world all by herself saddened him to no end. It minced his thought space and crushed at his singularity. And so he chuckled.

The idea of being denied to serve her was so disgusting it made him laugh out loud.

That's when someone shouted, "Burn her!"

Hensen snapped his head toward the voice and stared at the source with a murderous gaze. These wastes of skin were trying to justify killing an eterna for their whatever plan. An eterna! As if the birth of an eterna wasn't the result of cosmic alliance and the will of the world itself.

The muscles on his face twitched, and he opened his mouth, scathing insults churning on the tip of his tongue.

Which obviously ended up with him biting it instead.

"Off with her head!"

"Kill the witch!!"

"Burn her!"

"Cull her!"

Hensen ran his left hand through his hair, nodding his head side to side. It was infuriating. So infuriating he couldn't contain the joy at all.

He hissed, trying and failing to stay inconsistently inconsistent. However, the sly fox that was Rupert continued to rile the crowd, using the wishes of the masses to further suppress her. Others may not see it, but he knew. This was Rupert's method of killing an eterna.

After all, physical attacks alone weren't nearly enough to kill eternas. Blinking rapidly, he thought with a burning itch, *Rupert's trying to destroy her singularity. Just like he attempted with Mistress.*

This weak fuck had tried to assassinate Mistress after their temporary alliance post-duskfall ended in disaster. The vision he used was called the gaze of the fallen.

Hensen didn't know all the conditions required for Rupert to activate it, but the moral superiority and psychological victory of the user were the two known ones. Both of which he'd just achieved against this eterna.

Surely, he was doing something right now to fulfill other conditions.

Fuck! he chuckled, only to grimace in the next instant.

Frowning and actually succeeding this time, Hensen ignored the contradictions within himself and focused. This was a terrifyingly unique vision—one of the few that could permanently kill otherwise unkillable eternas.

It somehow wholly negated the resurrection artifacts from past eras, as well as visions that achieved a similar function. Obviously, Hensen didn't know the extent of this vision, but this was the reason almost no one fucked with Rupert.

It was already incredible that Rupert—no, no. It was terrible. Terrible that Rupert had managed to somehow rally everyone to agree with his mandate. Not that Hensen was against it personally either.

If he'd also become an overseer of the council, it would have significantly sped up Mistress's plans. He would have been of great use to her!

However, Rupert's men had vetoed him out from the council the first chance they got. After all, their prior animosity had yet to be settled. Worse, Hensen couldn't even argue against it right now.

Seething ice raged in his thought space as the fire froze every notion it touched. The raving noise breached his mental barrier, and he struggled to find some way out of it. He didn't want his days of servitude under Mistress to end like this.

He bit his knuckles, and only when his tongue tasted copper did a semblance of control wash over him.

"It's getting . . . worse," he murmured, his voice trembling. It . . . it was . . . it was bad.

He generally never let the contradictions pile up this high, but the suppression from the nexus made it so he couldn't untangle his fucked-up head.

Suddenly, his gaze shifted over to the intricately crafted lighter tucked into his coat's pocket, and he gulped. A ravenous smile emerged on his face, and his hand moved toward the contraption like a cart rushing downhill to its doom.

Yet, the moment his finger came in contact with the cool metal, his hand jerked away, and he jolted back in his seat.

A shudder went down his spine, and he chomped down on his knuckles, feeling the bone crunch under his teeth. Shivering, he pulled out his bloody hand and slapped himself in the face. *Paa!*

Finally, some clarity entered his mind, and he reasoned, *Not yet.*

Not yet.

Not yet.

Not yet.

Not yet.

Not yet.

He couldn't use Mistress's precious gift to merely help with these routine contradictions. No, that'd be a gigantic waste. He'd essentially kill all possibilities of serving Mistress if Rupert's plan really worked out.

No, he had to instead find the perfect moment to use it.

There was a reason he'd sat through this entire meeting in this terrible state of mind and hadn't just left the nexus.

The worse his mental state before the activation, the better the effect her light would have on his viewpoint.

It was the only light in the universe that helped him ignore the fog and whispers that eternally clouded his mind.

The light that allowed him to be . . . himself for a single moment.

A moment of pure lucidity.

A moment when he could unleash his unique vision.

A single moment where he'd flip the fucking table if they continued to try to separate him from Mistress.

A single moment that may very well result in the end of the world given how his vision—if it worked—would introduce contradictions in the consensus that'll decide the world's new rules.

As if I give a fuck about that. He laughed, wiping his handkerchief on his hands. All he cared about was continuing to serve Mistress.

And he would be dead to her for all intents and purposes if Rupert succeeded and he failed to worm his way into the ruling class. Which didn't seem very likely as things stood currently.

So why not take a chance and shake things up?

With all this running through his mind, he somehow managed to pull his attention back to the charade up high. His cane gleaming red, Rupert riled up the crowd one final time.

However, Hensen suddenly had a stupid urge to see it all by gouging out his eyes.

F-f-fuck. He groaned. This wasn't gonna work. His body was going against him. To figure out when to take that leap of faith and utilize Mistress's gift, he had to at least have full control over his faculties.

So he gritted his teeth and decided to take a safety measure. It'd mess his head up further in the long term, but he was really out of options right now.

His mind made up, he focused on the two dim inverted triangles inside his mind and channeled his thoughts toward them.

It was the rune of the Cryptic Constructor—his pride and burden. For reasons beyond his understanding, he'd been unable to make contact with it for a while.

So when a couple weeks ago, a distinct pull arose from within it, he'd left all his tasks unfinished and voyaged east across the lost cities and crumbling lands in a frenzy—leaving Mistress's side.

The scholars of his Aetheric Collective believed the pull could point them to the origin of Elden descent for the Cryptic One, and no way in seventeen hells those greedy old bastards would let such an opportunity slip by.

Sadly, the pull grew weaker over time, and he lost the trail before anything could come out of it.

It sounded like a dead end, but it wasn't. Before he'd left to chase this trail, the scholars had already predicted such a situation. So, following their advice, he'd found himself a local traveler from where the trail ended, bringing the man back to the collective.

This way, whenever this pull appeared next, he would teleport right back and be hot on its heels in just a few minutes. Not that he cared much. He just wanted to make sure Mistress would recognize him and . . .

Hensen shook his head. *Focus!*

Not allowing this momentary clarity to slip from his fingers, he created something akin to a loop of thoughts around the rune.

Almost instantly, a rigidness unlike any other permeated his thoughts, and his body, which had been a chaotic mess of adrenaline and hormones, slowed down.

Despite its drawbacks, using the burden to filter and screen his thoughts provided crucial relief for a head as fucked up as his. However, this method did inflict lasting damage on his psyche, with each use causing the permanent loss of some insights.

In but a few seconds, the effect permeated his entire being, and a jolt ran down his spine. Everything felt rigid at first, like his body only followed him if he performed the actions in a certain way. Well, such was the price of letting a construct filter his viewpoint.

However, he soon narrowed his eyes, intelligence shining within them. The conductorless orchestra that performed in his mind slowed down, and he breathed out.

That's when Rupert's cane flared with a demonic glow and he shouted, "For humanity!"

A hateful look crossed Hensen's face as the implications of this witch hunt dawned on him properly. Nothing was going to stop this council of overseers.

The cane made to impale the lady eterna's heart, and Hensen steeled himself for what was to come next. Once this charade was over, he had to be ready to use Mistress' lighter at the drop of a hat.

Sad that this lady eterna is about to die. He obviously wouldn't waste his single moment of lucidity on trying to save someone else. Things didn't work like that. Not that his vision was suitable for such a task anyway.

This was real life. It was her mistake for not understanding her own limits. It was her fault for failing. If he'd tried something stupid and failed, well . . . he'd deserve the punishment.

Why would it be any different for her?

It is over. He sighed. It'd have been great if she'd at least injured Rupert. Then maybe, just maybe, someone else would have taken over the stage, giving Hensen a chance to slip back into the council.

Sadly—

He frowned. "Huh?"

Thump!

Suddenly, the world went dark, and Hensen instinctively tapped into his perception, only to have it be suppressed ruthlessly.

What!? He gawked around himself, trying and failing to make out his surroundings, even with his impeccable eyesight. *What is going on?* he thought, an unease growing within him.

A voice cut through the alarmed cries in this eerie darkness and rose above all the distress, echoing deeply, "Disappointing."

Hensen snapped his head to the source of this voice, and his heart came to an abrupt stop.

Two rings that burned almost as bright as Mistress's light with another even deeper darkness within them were glowing from somewhere in the lower rows.

As if everyone else had also noticed that striking pair of eyes—not just rings—their agitated screams and dumb hollers came to an abrupt stop. With that, the whole hall, deficient of any light, drowned in a heavy silence too.

Hensen watched those rings with rapt attention as their owner began to walk.

Tap. Tap.

Each of their steps reverberated throughout the hall, and everyone held their breath. However, one of those steps was different than the others.

Tap.

They hit the floor another time, and the height of those soul-piercing rings changed.

"What is going on?!" some low-shade observer yelped. "Did . . . did he just ascend higher?"

Hensen turned his seat around completely, not caring about the darkness at all.

"Wait. Isn't he the guy who was sitting in the first row underneath us?! How could this be?"

The crowd gasped, surely making wild conjectures like he was. His spine tingled, and only one thought rang in his mind: *Could this be another eterna?*

Yet some moron shouted, "How dare you mess with the nexus?! Identify yourself!"

The bearer of those void-like rings didn't bother responding and continued his ascension, one step at a time.

Hensen's heart began to race faster. *A change!* he screamed. He'd take anything over Rupert's bullshit right now, much less someone who could bend the rules of nexus itself.

"Hey, I can't sense the essence strands at all! What is happening to the omniscient one? What happened to the execution?"

That last question forced the whole crowd into another lull of silence, and Hensen grinned when that sly bastard Rupert didn't respond to this at all. *He couldn't already be dead, could he?*

Hensen chuckled. The thought was amusing, but surely, things couldn't be that simple. He leaned forward, and his head shifted back as he watched the proceedings with great anticipation.

Following this silence came a voice of reason, "Something's wrong with nexus's lights. Did someone bring a mundane lighting contraption? If so, we should use it right now!"

Heh. Observers were so used to tapping into their perception and using myriads of visions for sights that being blinded like this—both in the perceptive realm and physical one—surely grated at the nerves of many.

Tap. Tap.

Soon, a small yellow light appeared on the far left corner of the hall, revealing a pale face that seemed straight out of some ghost story. She held but a little candle that barely illuminated anything.

Another one tried to light their cigarette with a flint, and someone complained, "Bah. This is nothing? Where are the fundamentalists when you need them? It is pertinent we sort this out quickly. We shouldn't waste any time."

Tap. Tap.

Sounds of tinkering and fiddling came from above Hensen while the ones beneath continued to count each of the steps.

"He's . . . he's already on the fourth row! What? How? The nexus should have made it impossible for him to suppress his singularity all the way down to first-shade observer. What is going on? Don't tell me . . ."

In the heart of an abyssal hall, where shadows draped every corner like velvet curtains, he ascended. The steps beneath his feet were the only sounds that dared to echo against the oppressive silence of the darkness. Each stride was measured, a slow cadence that seemed to command time itself to pay heed.

"Found it!" came another shout, and then a fickle beam of light—a traitor to the gloom—sliced through the void, a fleeting spotlight on the enigma who was the master of ceremonies.

A majestic figure dressed in rugged black overalls that suited him so well it made Hensen jealous, continued his march. However, when Hensen looked up, the sight caught him by surprise. In place of a hazy, veiled face that showed no features, there was a . . . mask.

Hensen frowned, and right when he narrowed his eyes to get a better look, the beam of light flickered and disappeared.

"Huh?" came the puzzled voice of the one who held the light source.

Thump. Thump.

He smacked the contraption, but the beam didn't stabilize—flickering endlessly.

Tap. Tap.

Hensen scrunched his nose and watched the figure ascend higher than his own row in the backdrop of darkness where the only light source trembled as if awed by the entity's strength.

That's when the light flickered to full strength for a fleeting moment once again, and the whole hall gasped.

Hensen furrowed his brows. The mask the entity wore was . . . interesting. It seemed to reveal a stark dichotomy, and Hensen knew from more than just experience that every little detail about an observer spoke volumes about their viewpoint and singularity.

Much less something so intentionally symbolic. On one side, a network of lines and geometric precision and order overlaid the white backdrop, while the other half was pitch black, an ode to entropy—an intricate collage of jagged edges and fractals that seemed to disintegrate and crumble away from the mask.

However, this was just how it looked at a glance. After a couple seconds, when the lightning struck true once again, the patterns renewed.

The order on the white side gave way to chaos, while the ashen particles on the dark side condensed back into pure mass, reintegrating with the mask.

Hensen watched on in fascination, and the stunned silence was more than enough to tell him that others were doing the same.

Even the man holding the light gave up and left it to its whims. This allowed Hensen to get a look at that mask every other second, a glimpse into the fascinating cycle that transpired.

Order bore chaos, while instability bred stability.

It was a perpetual cycle of creation and destruction. A seamless transition of one extreme into the other.

For a heartbeat that seemed to outlast time, the light lingered, and in that ephemeral glow, the mask covered all that was human, leaving only his eyes to be seen.

Hensen almost felt like he was back in the realm of Cryptic One, for the composition and structure had nigh-infinite wisdom behind it. That mask alone showcased insights beyond what most could conjure in their whole lives.

Hensen suddenly shuddered. *Could this be an eterna on the path of the Cryptic Constructor?! That'd be terrible for him.*

"Sixth . . . sixth row! Oh, no."

"No. No. No. Another eterna!?"

"Oh, god!"

That's when some lackey of Rupert's slammed his table down with a thump. "Stop wasting time, people. This is an eterna!

"He will use this unique opportunity to kill the omniscient one while he's recovering from this trickery. The council would crumble before it even begins. We should vote him out of nexus right now!"

CHAPTER 68

WHO ARE YOU?
WHAT EVEN ARE YOU?!

Hensen pulled down his top hat and sneered. *What a joke.* It was actually quite funny how everything around here needed a consensus. All the jokers who'd paid the cost to convene at nexus had prayed for it to run based on the majority's will.

However, it was different from the critical consensus that Rupert wanted for the world. That consensus made use of essence strands and complicated mind games, whereas the nexus had something of an impartial will that was supposed to listen to the majority.

Hensen had ideas on how this was going to play out, but he kept his mouth shut and scoffed internally, *If they want to make fools of themselves, who am I to stop them?*

The one who'd begun the topic shouted at the top of his lungs, "I vote for this person to be kicked out of nexus, and I implore the rest of you to follow quickly."

A palpable sense of contradiction spread all around the hall, and Hensen reveled in it. It was clear what was going on here. Many here knew it had to be done, but who in their right mind would verbally oppose an eterna?

However, Hensen slapped his forehead the very next moment, realizing the contradiction in that statement. *Yes. These dumb fucks will do it. They did just almost lynch an eterna, after all.* He shook his head. This was fun.

He was curious to see if they had the guts to do that again. Do it when neither the nexus's pressure contained the eterna nor was Rupert there to "serve the justice."

"This is worse than we thought, overseers. We need to kick this usurper out right now!" came the voice of that hateful teenager who'd started the motion for Hensen to be silenced. What was his deal? The kid was annoying as all hell and had one bad idea after another.

"What . . . what do you mean?" came an old hesitant voice.

The kid didn't die because of Hensen's focused hate and instead barked, "Think about it. The only reason someone can sit at the bottom of the nexus while being this powerful is that this . . . thing, this usurper, is not an observer! It probably doesn't even follow the same path to power as us at all."

Hensen raised his eyebrows. He'd been wondering how anyone would ever get all these slimy bastards to offend not one but two eternas, but as usual, he'd under-estimated the imagination of observers. This was actually quite an interesting excuse.

Well, Hensen gave zero fucks if this person was a god, an Elden One, some out-sider, pollution, or whatever, as long as it meant he could go back to Mistress after this. However, all these people obviously weren't of the same mind, and the hall instantly devolved into panicked cries.

"This . . . this can't be! How could the Nexus of Elyndor allow such a thing?! I support his removal."

"Blasphemy! Oust him!"

"Gods and heavens beyond. We need to stop him. This . . . usurper is getting closer to the weft's core. Oh, nexus. I vote him out! Kick him! Kick him!"

"Oh, no! That was his plan, wasn't it? He struck the omniscient one right at the worst moment to have free rein in here? That has to be it! I endorse the expulsion."

More and more of these hasty conjectures exploded in Hensen's ears, and he even began to feel a bit apprehensive. *What if this really worked?*

Well, he still had Mistress's light.

In but a few seconds, the mechanical voice of the nexus's will resounded. "The motion for removal of a member has been passed by a two-thirds majority. Removal imminent . . ."

The crowd suddenly turned silent, their ragged breaths acting as background music to the figure who walked between the shadows and lights.

However, the figure casually strolled higher, a hand in his pocket as if to show his disdain for such tactics.

In a few seconds, that mechanical voice boomed in the hall once again, "Motion for removal has been overruled. The meeting will continue as is."

"Hahaha ha ha ha! Get fucked," echoed the boisterous laugh from somewhere in the row right beneath Hensen's.

Isn't this the guy who was silenced, just like me? Hensen mused. But, well, he was far too ecstatic to care about any of that, and this other guy was definitely challenging him to a competition by laughing so hard.

Hensen's body shook. No. It fucking rocked. "Hah . . ." He was trying. He was trying so damned hard.

A palpable dread permeated the hall, and Hensen could hear their heartbeats over the disdainful laugh. This proclamation shattered any and all their vain hopes of resistance.

Hensen also stopped giving a fuck and leaned back, his chuckle escalating into a rapturous laugh, "Hah hah Hah hah! What a pathetic lot. Overseers? Can't even vote one person out. Hah hah hah."

To his surprise, people indeed turned toward him, and he reasoned, *Seems like the restrictions they piled on us are all gone. Did this newcomer overrule more than just his own removal?*

Who cared?

"Hah hah hah hah!"

"Hah hah hah hah."

Two laughs, one almost maniacal, the other unrestrained, echoed in the hall, and someone finally couldn't take it anymore.

"Stop this folly, you worms! Do you think this is going to end well for any of us? This is an outsider we're talking about! It could very well be the culmination of all that is uncanny, and he has come to usurp our foundations and ruin our realm from its very core."

Hensen snickered. If he was the usurper in question, he'd have taken this guy and made an example of him right about now.

However, before he could put this marvelous thought into words, his laughing buddy who'd called out Rupert for what he was—a bastard—and was silenced promptly, scoffed, "You're all really blinded by the prospects of becoming gods, aren't you?"

Only the footsteps of the usurper greeted his question as they crossed what seemed like the sixth row.

Tap. Tap.

"Hah," he chuckled, "Are we really believing any stupid conjecture now? Come on, guys. There could be a million other reasons why this being was able to sit down at the bottom. Where is this talk about him being an outsider coming from?"

"What the hell would you know?" rasped some new voice Hensen hadn't heard until now. "Who do you think you are?"

"Well, I worked with the Lorendales before your omniscient one slaughtered them. So I am definitely far more knowledgeable about the inner workings of the nexus than anyone else here."

That shut up the naysayer quickly, and the guy continued, "The answer is simple. You may or may not know this, but the vote of stronger observers counts more than us pathetic middle and low shades."

Sarcasm dripped through his voice, and he asked, "You know what that implies?"

Tap. Tap.

Someone gulped and replied, "They . . . they're far stronger than any of us? Strong enough to outweigh all our votes."

"Bingo! Here I thought Rupert had already muddled your brains. I mean, yeah, there could be a couple other reasons for this anomaly, but the assertion that they're an outsider has got to be the most absurd one."

The crowd chewed on his words, and in but a few seconds, the whole hall flickered, and the lotus pillar at the pinnacle that had been utterly dark, radiated pure light. Everyone stopped what they were doing and snapped their heads to the highest row.

The usurper, as expected, stepped into the eighth row without a hitch. People stood abruptly, their faces masks of anxiety and apprehension as they took in the aftermath of the previous proceedings.

Even Hensen stood, a hand on his top hat. When his brain comprehended the sight in front of his eyes, a shudder went down his spine followed by a rush of ecstasy.

Above all common observers were these four demigods. One sat on his throne, filing his nails with a frown, while another pulled herself out of icy vines. These two were expected.

It was the third figure—the kneeling one—that gave Hensen pause. A furious vertical eye shone with a red hue, doing its best to resist the pressure and unfurl.

Alas, every attempt was a miserable failure. Its owner had it worse as he trembled, trying his best to oppose a pressure so terrifying it warped the very air around him.

Finally, there was the usurper donning that unique mask, black and white debris swirling around him like a cosmic halo as he stood there, overlooking the kneeling Rupert.

"This . . . this . . . coven master. Resist! We can't give up like this!"

"How is he doing this?!"

"How do we help?! Should we try to vote again?"

"Shut up. You know the vote is rigged."

"Coven master, unleash the essence strands. We will support you!"

Hensen watched them all flounder like puppies without a master. *Tch.* He clicked his tongue.

If only I had my champagne to go with all this. This was too fucking entertaining.

Regardless, all these cries and prayers did nothing to faze the people in question. Rupert didn't have the luxury to respond, while the usurper didn't bother and instead walked toward the lady eterna.

He extended a hand toward her, and without showing even a hint of fear or gratitude, she accepted it. It was as if none of what had happened fazed her even a single bit.

What Hensen saw, however, was that Rupert was still on his knees. This meant that the usurper could selectively control the pressure and only apply it to Rupert. Hensen narrowed his eyes. This was good. It looked like there was finally someone who could keep Rupert in check.

Lady eterna cradled her right arm as she walked back to her throne, but there were no serious injuries. Her heart was entirely unharmed, and Hensen somehow felt better about it.

As much as he hated Rupert, too, he would loathe for the man to really be killed by anyone but himself or Mistress. Eternas were existences that deserved reverence for the feat they'd achieved, and dying in such a mundane ordeal was tantamount to disrespecting the cosmos that had supported their journeys.

Murmurs echoed around the hall as people watched the proceedings with bitter expressions on their faces.

In this otherwise terrible situation for the council, Rupert's lips moved, and he hissed through gritted teeth, "What are you playing at, usurper?"

The usurper in question slowly turned toward Rupert, his figure an enigma against the backdrop of the only light in this whole world—heck, even the stars from beyond were blocked by something. And after all this time, he broke his silence and said, "Usurper?" He shook his head, the particles of entropy orbiting him. "I'm just expressing my . . . disappointment toward the visionaries of this era."

The whole crowd quietened down as he focused his gaze on them.

Like an elder reprimanding children, he started, "As beings born from the flux, did everyone really just advocate for the execution of an observer for having an opposing perspective?

"Did everyone really agree to a drastic measure that would essentially run the first axiom of observation into the ground? A choice that would have severely limited the possibilities one's viewpoint could grow into."

In a crestfallen tone, he beseeched, "Have we really learned nothing on our journeys as observers? From the axioms that guide our path and our very singularity?"

Many in the crowd lowered their heads without a word. However, Rupert uttered through clenched teeth, his kneeling figure straightening bit by bit, "You can question the methods all you like, usurper, but we have limited time, and unlike the weak-minded, my fellow overseers and I decided to accept the burden and do something about it."

He rasped, "Go ahead, be disappointed in us. But that doesn't change the fact that our decisions are the best ones for the world in its dire circumstances."

The usurper narrowed his eyes and said, "God complex and tangible power don't mix well, coven master. They don't mix well." He sighed. "Why does each and every era have someone like you?"

Rupert frowned but soon responded, "I understand neither your strengths nor your means, usurper. However, I don't need to, for you're another one of millions who virtue signals without contemplating the consequences of inaction."

He stabbed his cane on the ground and used it to help himself back up little by little. "I allowed everyone to brainstorm and offer us a means out of this predicament. Yet what was your contribution? Nothing. Zero. Regardless, you now play this power game and come here, pass judgment on me and my fellow overseers willing to shoulder the burden?" He sneered. "What a saint."

Hensen rapped his fingers against each other. He had to give props to Rupert for not backing down one inch in front of such a figure. The man had strong ideals and beliefs, to the point that the possibility of provoking someone beyond his means didn't stop him at all.

As always, someone from Rupert's camp—a priest this time—jumped to agree with the man, "Yes, yes. You're nothing but a self-righteous wolf in sheep's clothing, usurper."

"A pretentious idealist," barked that teen once again.

Hensen felt like he should rebuke these guys, but he held his tongue. After all, he had no clue what this usurper's deal was. It would indeed not be ideal if he'd gone up there just to lecture everyone about morals.

At that moment, a low laugh permeated the hall, and everyone shut up once more.

"Who said I don't have a solution?"

Rupert parted his lips to speak but closed them with a confused expression. After a while, when he looked like a hunched old man using his stick to pick himself up, he challenged, "Then it was arrogant of you not to present it during the open debate. You do understand that all of us need to come to a consensus of ideals for this to work, right?"

The eyes behind the mask turned playful. "Do we?"

This offhanded declaration was like a spark in a barrel of oil, and people exploded into worried chatter. "What . . . what does he mean? How could there be a critical consensus without most of us being involved?"

"What is going on?"

"They were right. He's not human. He's something else!"

"Yes, he plans on killing us all and harvesting our viewpoints for consensus."

"Fuck. I am leaving. I don't want to be a part of this. This has gone far out of our hands."

"I am leaving too. This is wrong."

Tap!

Rupert smacked his cane and finally stood fully—this simple action pacifying the panicked ones. Clearly, the idea of more people leaving didn't sit right with Rupert. There were already many who didn't want or get to be an overseer. So the loss of even one more visionary would hurt their chances.

Hah. Hensen mused, *He's still trying to make this council of overseers work.*

Rupert then finally stood tall and matched gazes with his opposition before asking, "What do you mean, usurper?"

The enigma chuckled. "It seems humanity often expects the worst, even from its saviors." He shook his head. "No. I don't need any of you, nor do I plan on killing anyone. I can mend the weft all by myself. Feel free to leave the meeting at your leisure. I will take care of affirming this realm with my will alone."

The hall fell silent, the visionaries frozen mid-movement, their expressions etched in confusion.

Rupert was the same, his face rifling through myriad expressions before settling on a dark one. After a short silence, he asked with a suspicious look in his eyes, "Why would we leave our world's fate in the hands of someone like you? Who are you? What even are you?!"

The enigma sighed deeply, a sound that seemed to echo around the hall as he moved to center stage, his gaze sweeping over the crowd. His mask, which had been in a constant flux of darkness and light, suddenly calmed down, and he spoke, "Call me a usurper if you must. But know this: I am here not to destroy but to fulfill; to balance what has been tipped; to correct what has been skewed."

He paused, his voice then carrying a somber note as he said, "As much as I wished that things didn't have to come to this, everyone's poor decisions have forced my hand."

His eyes locked with those of his audience, compelling attention. "You wish to know who I am? What I am? Then listen. And listen well."

He extended his arms, his voice deepening. "I am indeed not a human. For I am the embodiment of something older, deeper—borne from laws that you have long forgotten or never truly comprehended."

He clasped his hands together as if embracing the weight of his words. "This world operates on fundamental truths—axioms—that govern all. Most of you recognize some as mere theories or principles. I live them, for they are part of me as much as I am part of them.

"I am the manifestation of those fundamental truths from which all else flows. I am the proof of the first axiom and the last, the one who strikes equilibrium between that which cannot be balanced."

His arms spread wide, he embraced the expanse of his declaration and proclaimed, "In a world divided into absolutes of light and dark, I arbitrate the path of grays.

"For I am the manifestation and harmonizer of the rules upon which our world runs.

"I represent the laws. For I am the law.

"For, I am . . .

"Axiom.

"The zeroth axiom: balance."

CHAPTER 69

MASQUERADE

Hensen's heart pounded like a drum in his chest, loud and frantic.

Ax . . . axiom? His knees felt weak, and a sense of panic fluttered in his chest. *From the . . . Ins . . . Institute?*

A cold, numbing terror gripped him, and he plopped back down on his seat, his hands trembling uncontrollably. *It . . . it still exists!*

His gaze darted frantically, seeking escape from the plethora of eyes that used to watch him all the time. *It's them. It's them. It's them!*

His hand clutched at his head, and he rocked back and forth. *No. No. No,* he chanted, his thoughts an utter mess.

How could someone from the Institute be here?

He shook his head. *No. They're not real! The Institute is not real! These feelings are not real!*

He'd been forced to inherit the third rune from his predecessor after she'd lost herself to the whispers, but there were hundreds before her. Hundreds that . . .

No! They're not mine!

He knew they were not his, but emotions flashed through his mind. Of terror, of a fear so primal, so innate, it surpassed his dread toward the Cryptic One.

Hensen gripped the contraption containing Mistress's light harder, his knuckles growing white from the sheer pressure.

That touch.

That simple touch seemed to mend something in his broken mind, and his shivering body calmed a little.

His hand moved to flick the lighter ablaze and let her light wash all over him. Yet, he somehow managed to keep his hands to himself.

This wasn't the first time this had happened to him. Every time the Institute came up, something stared at him from inside. He . . . he didn't understand it.

Lifting his top hat, he ran his hand through his hair and focused on the people around him. It would be stupid to spend more time within his mind. He couldn't afford a real episode here.

"This . . . this can't be real," a woman whispered, her voice trembling as her hands clutched at her chest, eyes wide in disbelief.

A young observer rifled through a heavy tome in his hands. "There's a zeroth axiom?" he murmured, his brows furrowing in confusion.

"Is this . . . is this really happening?" another exclaimed.

"Balance . . . ? A never before seen axiom called Balance?!" yelled a man who seemed like a scholar.

"The Institute actually existed, then? It isn't just a figment of the imaginations of the last generation of observers?" an older man asked, turning to his peers as if seeking confirmation.

"Didn't the records speak of them being lost to time? Are they resurfacing? Is the Institute coming back?" a paranoid voice called out from the back, each question louder than the last, injecting a note of fear into the growing cacophony of voices.

For the first time throughout this whole confluence, Hensen felt like he was of the same mind as these people. What was going on? A zeroth axiom had emerged, not as a line of text, but rather . . . as an observer?

He generally wouldn't care even if the sky fell down, but . . . this? His mind whirled as he tried to look past the horror that arose from within him from what the axioms signified.

Suddenly, an idea emerged in his mind like a bolt out of the blue. A shudder went down his spine, and the idea took further root.

Could they . . . Hensen gasped, wave after wave rocking his mind space.

It should be possible, right? He's from the Institute, after all. Hensen wondered, hope growing in his chest. If his conjecture was right, he might not have to give up this rune as well as his life anytime soon and continue to serve Mistress without being replaced.

His excitement was palpable, yet he knew such a request shouldn't be made lightly. Not if this . . . entity was really who they claimed to be. He wasn't one to believe in gods because he knew they couldn't help him. But this . . . ?

This was it. He didn't care if it was a false hope. He'd latch on to anything, not to mention such a tangible one.

So he adopted a posture of deep reverence. Setting his top hat gently upon his lap, he closed his eyes and clasped his hands before him.

After making sure he had the words at least close to being right, he infused them with his singularity, and in a hushed, reverent tone, he intoned, "O, Lord Axiom, arbiter of balance, I beseech thee—grant me insight to reconquer this third rune wrought forth by your esteemed disciples.

"For this burden is beyond mine talents and threatens my very being. Guide me through its tempest, that I might harness its power without succumbing to its whims."

Vern looked down at the visionaries from the highest spot in the nexus, a sharp look in his eyes.

Yet his nervousness was so far off the charts that his heart, which he'd forcefully caged inside a sphere of stability, was sending literal pulses of instability.

Cold sweat trickled down his brows behind the mask as he watched the audience devolve into chatters and some of the wildest conjectures he'd ever heard.

Luckily, his bet had paid off. Sighing internally, he reflected, *It seems like a zeroth axiom doesn't already exist.* This was his greatest fear when building up this fake identity. While he was waiting for Rupert to destabilize the hierarchical structure to the greatest extent, he'd given it a very serious thought.

He'd had to meet many self-imposed constraints to construct an identity that would stand under the scrutiny of these terrifyingly knowledgeable observers. So anyone who was very famous, like the first observer or something along those lines, was out of the question. After all, Vern knew very little about them.

Beyond that, it wouldn't work for this identity to be entirely unrecognizable as that would have little to no effect in calming the greed-driven minds of this crowd. Him being a "powerful eterna" who traversed nexus's highest step, would only go so far without actual power to back it up.

This had narrowed down his search quite a bit.

He'd even considered pretending to be an Elden One or a god but discarded such thoughts in mere moments. *I've already attracted enough attention from those beings as is.* He didn't even want to imagine the kinds of horrific situations that disrespecting such beings would land him in.

So he had to go for something that didn't really exist but still held enough weight to its name.

And hence, axioms. Yes, they weren't supposed to be living, breathing humans, but who was to say otherwise? Such were the wonders of this world of subjectivity.

Vern himself had considered the idea of "concept" like axioms being personified before today. Heck, he even had conjectures that some gods might very well have been make-believe at first but ended up becoming real gods over a period of sustained faith.

He didn't have any proof of this, but the idea was one of the best ones he could come up with in such a short time. Regardless, any worries he had about the matter were erased when these people made even wilder conjectures as to why he existed.

One seemingly unimportant but still a point of great indecision for him had been which axiom to masquerade as. Because he didn't really know the axioms or their numbers all that well. So instead of picking an existing axiom or one he didn't know, he'd chosen to reel back to zero.

There was a small chance that such an axiom already existed, but lady permitting, it didn't. At least the reactions of the crowd made it seem as such.

Vern watched this whole situation and hierarchical structure slowly fall back into a semblance of stability as his thought space gleamed with intense pulsation—further aligning his singularity to the viewpoint.

Instability before stability. This whole ordeal embodied his tenet so well that he still couldn't believe it. If Rupert hadn't decided to be a piece of shit and try to execute his fellow pretender, he might have been able to wait even longer—letting things destabilize further.

Yes, a pretender. That lady he'd just helped up was no eterna. At least, that's the feedback he got from the will of the nexus. He'd managed to contact the will in quite an unexpected manner.

Once he'd flipped to the pages belonging to convergence note—the ones connected to the weft and indirectly to nexus—he'd tried a few conjectures and failed miserably before realizing something important.

The nexus was an extension of Lady Sylphina. So he'd sent a note to her trace—at least, what he understood of it—asking to focus all the nexus's energy on restricting Rupert further.

Which worked! Except that meant he couldn't contact Lady Sylphina this way. Just nexus.

Beyond that, these visionaries weren't wrong when they said the nexus was low on representation. Simply containing Rupert's attack had caused the nexus to lose all its light, and the man was already recovering from it.

And that is where he realized that the lady who was daring enough to try to assassinate Rupert couldn't be controlled by Nexus at all—just like himself.

Yet she wasn't his concern right now. The real problem was that nexus was again losing its grip on Rupert, which meant Vern was essentially standing inside a lion's den. If he couldn't get Rupert and everyone else to back down quickly, and the man decided to turn it into another battle, he would be dead unless he somehow escaped— which would render it all useless anyway.

Did I go overboard? he wondered, eyeing the silent Rupert from the corner of his eyes. The man seemed lost in thought, his expression unreadable.

This is my chance.

He hadn't come up here without a plan. So when an appropriate lull appeared in the chaotic ramblings of the crowd, he raised his hand.

Wetting his lips, he began once again, pumping as much authority in his voice as possible, "I am certain all of you have myriads of questions. Alas, I deem you lot unworthy of further explanation."

He whirled around, one hand in his pocket, and said, "Since all of you still have some time in here, you might as well watch me affirm this realm." Then he glanced at the seventh row for a second, his mind patching together runes that should mean to reduce the pressure on the person of his choice.

His hand inside his coat moved on its own, imprinting this rune onto a torn piece of convergence note with the small pencil nib. He made sure the movements were minimal and just came off as him being eccentric.

This particular note was for the will of nexus once again. Once this was done, he said, "King Keras should be able to confirm the validity of my claim once I'm done."

The former eterna whom Rupert had attacked—his eyes bloody—suddenly perked up. He gasped, feeling the pressure on his singularity reduced, and his eyes widened.

After a few seconds of being filled in by the woman who looked like his wife, he suddenly stood tall and bowed. "Your wish is my command, Lord Axiom. I shall do everything in my power to predict our fate, even if it means I'll regress another time."

The visionaries hemmed and hawed, most of them unwilling witnesses to his actions yet too scared to do anything about it. Vern could only hurry it up. The longer this went on, the more loopholes would appear in his performance.

So he nodded to King Keras, actively cycling the stability of his mask to seem enigmatic, and he walked toward the pillar of light in the center of it all.

Tap. Tap.

The whole crowd turned silent, and he felt everyone's eyes boring down on him. A shiver ran down his spine, reminding him of the strength of these people outside this nexus. Any one of them could easily crush him like a bug.

They could—

Hah, let's not worry about that right now.

Just have to make it look flashy, he thought. There wasn't much else to do, after all. If he'd gotten the lay of the things right, then when King Keras divined the fate of the world again, it should come off as stable.

He just had to pretend to have done something to lay claim to it officially.

Well, I hope they can't figure out the exact time of the restoration, or I'll be caught. There's just so many moving parts, he grumbled.

Feeling all sorts of pressure weighing down on him, he walked farther, his left hand outstretched, his right one still inside his pocket in case he was in further need to communicate with nexus's will again.

"Stop," came a measured voice, and Vern's mind shuddered. *No! Don't do this, you ...*

Slowly letting his left palm drop back down, he looked back at Rupert, a cold expression in his eyes as he answered in the deadest voice, "What?"

"I have to ask you," Rupert began, holding his cane as he walked toward the center. "Does your method help us push back against the calamities we face today?"

Vern's expression turned dark. He knew where this was going. Acting unbothered and only succeeding because of his mask, he replied, "It doesn't need to. The world is sufficient as is."

Rupert nodded. "Then, I have one final question."

The crowd suddenly looked hopeful once again, their loyalties very clear. Vern had a bad feeling about this, so he didn't respond at all.

Rupert continued, tapping his cane repeatedly before stopping as he inquired, "Would you like to join the council of overseers?"

"The human greed knows no bounds. At least think over your words before spouting them out so carelessly." Vern chuckled out loud at this one. Rupert really was one stubborn bastard. Sneakily forming a new rune with his right hand, he prepared himself for anything.

Showing even a hint of weakness now would essentially doom his whole charade for good. Nexus should be able to give him at least enough time to forcefully kick everyone here. If Rupert tried to kill him or anything of the like, he wasn't about to go down easily.

For good measure, he even reformed the rune that would try to pressure Rupert again. Even if Nexus didn't have the energy for another full-on assault, there should be enough to help him plot his own escape.

Assuming nothing falls out of my calculation, that is. Which it almost always did for observers for some reason.

Feeling an odd mix of terrifying pressure and thrill coursing through his body, he stared back at Rupert, his stance challenging the man to try anything funny.

"Overseers!" Rupert shouted, and Vern narrowed his eyes, his fingers feeling jittery.

Bam! A sudden explosion erupted from Rupert's position, and Vern's pupils dilated as a red aura threatened to engulf him. *What the fuck?*

His mind raced, and his hand scribbled. Yet, something even more bizarre transpired before the runes could even take effect.

Vern watched, befuddled, as the small outward propulsion suddenly halted and reeled back toward the center. *The explosion . . . reversed?*

Nexus's suppression came a moment too late as the sole pillar of light in the hall faded, plunging everything into the darkness once again.

The red implosion settled down in this shadowy ambiance, and within it floated a man above even Vern himself. His body levitated in the air, disregarding the pressure of the Nexus as if he were standing in his own space.

The crowd shot back up and cheered, their shouts turning into a cacophony of celebration. Almost as if a literal god had come down to grant their wishes.

His middle eye drowned this otherwise dark hall a crimson red, and Rupert spoke, his voice ethereal, "Overseers. A ghost of the past that wishes to ignore the pleas of humanity has no right to decide its future."

He extended both his palms out in the air from the red void, and like lightning striking in the heavens, red vines shot out of them. In a blink of an eye, they were in front of everyone, and people rushed to connect themselves to the essence strands.

Vern, who was somehow left entirely unharmed, watched it all with narrowed eyes. *Ghost of the past, huh? An apt moniker.*

However, a sharp grin appeared on his face. Cracking his neck, he openly pulled out his notepad and eyed the golden runes floating around him.

Rupert had played the wrong hand. He should've gone straight for the kill.

Time for this ghost of the past to scare the fuck out of everyone.

CHAPTER 70

EDICT OF ERASURE

Illeana gritted her teeth as she tried to keep the rampaging emotions from bursting out and ruining things. The vault was at its limits once again, and at this instant, fear leaked out of it.

Red strands extended from Rupert's hands, and bloody flower stems appeared in front of everyone but her. Overlooking the hall with his single vertical eye, he proclaimed, "Extend thine hands and reach out, overseers. I shall bear the burden of keeping you safe as we strive to achieve the critical consensus."

A shiver ran down her spine as she gripped the armrest of her chair tighter. *It's not over? He really has another card up his sleeve? Can even Mr. Axiom not stop him for good?*

The mere thought sent her barely controlled emotions into another round of frenzy. Her eyes involuntarily flitted toward the unfathomable Mr. Axiom, and her heart ramped up. An ancient yet amiable feeling radiated out of him as he stood there, completely unbothered by Rupert's proclamations.

It had yet to sink in that she was rescued by a being so terrifying he could affirm the whole world all by himself.

Wait! she suddenly gasped as a surge of embarrassment replaced the fear that flowed from the vault. *I didn't even thank him for saving me!* A blush crept up her cheeks, and she hid her face in her trembling hands. *What is wrong with me?!*

Luckily, the stream of escaped emotion disappeared as quickly as it had come, and she somehow managed to make her odd actions look natural.

Her face in her hands, she reflected as paranoia rushed through her mind. *He knows.* Surely, Mr. Axiom had already figured her out—realized that she was faking the number of her shades. That piercing glance he'd given her when helping her back up felt like her whole existence was laid bare in front of him.

The vault acted up again, sending who knows what emotions this time as she murmured internally, *Yet there's something so . . . human about him.* His touch was even gentler than some of her dance partners.

After a few seconds, the stream of emotions trickling from the vault slowed down, and she shook her head. *Ugh. Why am I thinking about all this?*

It was hard to keep her thoughts straight now that the vault was overflowing with all these random emotions.

Somehow focusing on the matter at hand, she analyzed it as calmly as possible. The situation wasn't great. Rupert had begun his counterattack right when Mr. Axiom was about to fix the root cause himself.

This hateful bastard! she seethed, eyeing the floating Rupert. *Can Mr. Axiom not just affirm the world before them?*

Illeana quickly found a problem with that logic. *Applying two different ideologies for critical consensus at the same time might do more harm than good.* Yes, Mr. Axiom could affirm the realm himself, but that didn't mean he could negate others' effects as well.

She bit her lower lip. *This is bad.*

Turning her chair around, she stared at the crowd who plucked the red flowers in front of them without hesitation. The moment they did, their eyes closed, and their bodies emitted a crimson glow of their own before floating higher, matching Rupert's cadence.

She frowned. *He's actually isolating them from this space too.* This was problematic. A new idea had just begun to take shape in her mind, but it was already falling apart.

Given that her plan of assassinating Rupert had failed miserably and Mr. Axiom seemed to be in a bind, she was hoping to become the catalyst of change.

And she could've done that by removing these very observers from the equation.

As much as she wished to never part with Father's epoch keeper and loathed the idea of murder, she knew this was the right thing to do. If killing a few people here could save the world's freedom, so be it.

She was more than willing to explode the epoch keeper in the crowd behind her, essentially killing the pawns that Rupert wished to use to supplant his cancerous ideology.

The man was doing everything in his power to minimize the defectors. So, if she killed enough with her blast, surely he'd have to leave it all up to Mr. Axiom.

This wasn't an option before as these very people were essential to affirming the world. But things were different now that Mr. Axiom could do it all by himself.

Alas, it's not even an option anymore. She sighed. Rupert had expected Mr. Axiom to physically harm his herd of overseers and accounted for this eventuality. Yet it indirectly threw a wrench in her nascent plan too. He had done it so quickly she didn't get a chance to even think through it all.

It's because of the vault. She frowned. She might have acted faster if her mind wasn't going through all these random phases of emotions.

Her heart palpitated as the situation began slipping out of control once again. *What do I do?* Her eyes flitted around, monitoring what everyone was doing.

Most behind her had their eyes closed, almost as if their conversation didn't need words anymore. *Yes, it totally doesn't,* she quickly realized. They were connected using the essence strands—they didn't need words for private conversations.

Yet before too long, Mr. Axiom suddenly smiled and pulled out the notepad he was writing on back during the early stages of the confluence.

Illeana perked up. *Wait. Does he already have a plan to handle this situation too?* Her eyes lit up as she berated herself. *Obviously, he does! Why did I presume to understand the methods of the divine?*

These uncontrolled emotions seeping out of the vault had really muddled her mind.

That's when an unexpected but grating voice resonated in the hall, "Haha, what's wrong, the great zeroth axiom—the arbiter of balance? Can't do anything now?"

Illeana's eyebrows furrowed high as she eyed the speaker. It was that teenager again. He'd opened his eyes and extricated himself from the private conversation of consensus just to hurl taunts. What kind of backing was he leeching off to have so much confidence?

The guy had a big mouth and was a hard-line supporter of Rupert. So much so that he was willing to insult even someone as unfathomable as Mr. Axiom.

She couldn't wrap her head around the sheer recklessness of it. Even if Rupert had already won the exchange—which he hadn't—it was a universally agreed unspoken rule to respect the unknown.

And Mr. Axiom was probably one of the most mysterious entities to have surfaced since duskfall—on par with the Elden Ones. Yet this guy's arrogance had blinded him to the point he didn't even show a hint of cautiousness.

And this self-important leech wants to control how the world thinks? She looked down at him, disgust rising within her.

Not heeding her unspoken warnings, that leech sneered with a cold laugh and said, "Master Rupert has triggered the dimensional divide. We still dwell in the nexus but are elevated to a higher plane. We stand above you! Your efforts are futile—nothing you do can stop us now!"

Illeana's gaze sharpened as she studied Mr. Axiom, who appeared utterly unfazed by the exchange. *He really is different*, she realized. All he exuded was that same profound greed from before, even in the face of these vitriolic comments.

"Hah, what axiom? What balance?" the leech taunted with palpable contempt. "Know your place, outsider! You're merely a specter of bygone days, less than human. You have no standing to interfere with our affairs. Begone!"

In response, Mr. Axiom's eyes merely narrowed slightly, the ghost of a smirk playing at the corners.

Regrettably, only the mildest of feelings leaked out of her emotional vault at the moment, actively stifling her urge to speak up. Otherwise, she would've put this leech in his place.

However, the existing seed of doubt further expanded in her thoughts. *What exactly can Mr. Axiom do in this situation?* Yes, the leech put it disrespectfully, but he wasn't entirely wrong.

"Each era has its own leaders, and we're the chosen ones this time around. If you cannot keep pace, get out of our path." He poured more venom with a curl of his lip.

Illeana felt like breaking something. *This is too much.*

Mr. Axiom exhaled a weary sigh as if the ignorance before him was a burden too trivial to bear. "I suppose the terror of the Institute has really left everyone's minds," he remarked, his voice echoing with a charming magnetism.

Some in the crowd opened their eyes for a brief instant, but most maintained their connection to Rupert, surely debating on how to better raise humanity like some cattle in the pen.

"Very well, then."

He paused, his gaze sweeping over them with an air of finality. "Consider this both the first and last warning I will extend to each of you," he declared, his tone firm yet eerily calm.

Illeana sat straighter. *He's going to do something!*

Slowly, he unfurled the notepad in his hands. With a deliberate motion, he penned a single word in an elegant, flowing script. He then turned the notepad toward them, displaying the letters for all to see.

Cease.

However, Illeana saw more. Those dozens of runes hovering all around him suddenly shone with a brilliant glow. Unsure what to make of it, she continued to watch.

He flipped the page with a flick of his wrist and added another, even as the air around them seemed to grow heavier, charged with an unspoken threat.

Or be erased.

Illeana stared at the words in confusion, a crease forming between her brows. *What is Mr. Axiom doing . . . ?*

The crowd behind mirrored her reaction. Some had opened their eyes, probably afraid of the threat, but most didn't even bother.

The leech's laugh cut through the tension, loud and mocking. "Hahaha, what a farce! Is this meant to frighten us?" he scoffed, rolling his eyes dramatically. "Oh, no! He's written down a command—guess we all must scurry and comply now! Oh, the horror!

"I simply must abandon my convictions because he demands it, or else he'll be so very heartbroken. I should—" His voice choked off abruptly as his face paled, the mockery turning to a strangled gasp as if the words were physically snatched from his throat.

That was when Illeana felt it—a sharp, intrusive buzz in her mind. *Who's sending me a note at this time?* But then a thunderbolt struck in her mind, and a chilling realization dawned on her. *Could it be . . . ?*

Even Rupert, previously aloof, stiffened in midair, his expression darkening. Fumbling, he began to write frantically in a small notebook, his movements desperate.

The rest of the crowd, previously unengaged, suddenly snapped open their eyes. Many hurriedly pulled out pieces of parchment or devices, while those without a means to imprint the notion on a paper looked around in panic, their eyes wide with dread.

It . . . it's real, she realized. *Mr. Axiom just sent a note to everyone!*

She quickly reached for the piece of her own convergence note hidden in her thigh belt. With a rustle, she unfurled the paper and smeared some rouge on her index finger, letting the invasive notion guide her movements.

Before she knew it, the words had formed on her paper:

Cease.

Or be erased.

A cold shudder raced down her spine. *He . . . he knows my viewpoint's trace!*

She snapped her gaze back to the hall, which had descended into a palpable hush, the earlier air of defiance replaced by a suffocating pressure.

A simple thought repeated itself in her mind. *He knows everyone's trace!*

C H A P T E R 71

FALLING IN LINE

In this newly oppressive atmosphere, that leech's voice trembled, breaking the quiet. "This . . . this . . . can't be. How do you know my trace?! I've never shared it beyond my oath-bound clan members."

"No. It's not just you." Unexpectedly, the lord of primordial blood sitting next to her stopped filing his nails and uttered with a dark expression, "He knows each and every one of our traces."

Clutching his head, the leech cried out in terror, "How . . . how can this be? He knows my trace! He has the power to invade my body, manipulate my very being!"

To all this, Mr. Axiom had no reaction. The only change in his constant silhouette was his mask that roiled with a smoke that was light and dark, cycling through phases more rapidly.

A cold silence swept through the crowd as the teenager's bravado crumbled. Each person held their breath, the realization of Lord Axiom's power sinking in with terrifying clarity.

"I . . . I can't believe this," an elderly man whispered, his hands trembling as he clutched his own convergence note, the paper rustling softly in his shaking grip.

A young woman, her face stricken with fear, stared down at her note as if it might come alive. "How can he know our traces? They're our deepest secrets, our very essence!"

Whispers began to flutter around the room as others checked their parchments. Panic was evident in their eyes, and some dropped their notes as if burned by the revelation of their inner thoughts.

King Keras slowly nodded, his face a mask of resigned yet hopeful acceptance. "There's nowhere to hide," he muttered. "He can see into our very souls. He's Lord Axiom."

The heaviness was palpable, their earlier defiance dissolving into palpable dread. Those who had laughed at Axiom's words now trembled as their faces grew pale.

"I . . . I yield!" shouted a burly man in the sixth row, someone who'd been supportive of Rupert since the start. Turning toward the stunned man in the air, he exclaimed, "I am sorry, coven master, but I don't think I can be an overseer of the council anymore."

He brought his hands together in prayer and suddenly fell on his knees. "I apologize, Lord Axiom. I . . . I was swayed by the devils. I swear in the name of the eternal one, I will never associate myself with them again."

His eyes pleading, he smashed his head to the ground and begged, "Please. Please spare me. Please don't destroy me from the inside out. Please don't share my trace. I beg of you. Please."

Mr. Axiom, however, didn't even put this person in his eye, and before Illeana knew it, more people began expressing their regrets.

She felt an odd sense of satisfaction besides the creeping horror of having her trace exposed. She'd grappled with something similar just a few weeks ago, when some bizarre entity had either gotten hold of her trace or was her "default" note partner. So, this time, it didn't faze her as much as everyone else.

She narrowed her eyes and analyzed the situation. *Mr. Axiom hasn't distorted anyone's form even after having the knowledge of everyone's traces. That must mean this was exactly what he'd said—a warning.*

But why am I also being warned? She bit her lip. Surprisingly, she felt a little hurt that even she was a part of this warning. Hadn't she done everything in her means to resist this mandate of omniscience? The council?

As she grappled to reconcile her feelings, more people in the hall rushed to defect.

In the fifth row, a once-proud transparent woman with sharp features, stood abruptly, her eyes darting around as if seeking an escape from an invisible predator. "I, too, must step down," she announced in a quavering voice that shocked many around her.

"I cannot align with this council any longer." She looked directly at Rupert, her expression one of profound regret. "Forgive me, for I cannot endure the wrath of a higher power."

She bowed deeply toward the exalted figure, her voice breaking as she pleaded, "Lord Axiom, forgive my ignorance and my past transgressions. My allegiance is to the truth now, to the peace you promise. Spare me, and I will serve faithfully under your new order."

Once done, she shattered the flower and red vines in front of her with a wave of her hand.

A young couple, hands tightly clasped, stepped forward from the crowd, their faces etched with fear. "We, too, have been misled," the man said, his voice barely a whisper. "We renounce the old ways and seek mercy under your guidance, Lord Axiom."

The woman nodded vigorously beside him, tears streaming down her cheeks as they both knelt, their heads bowed low in submission.

Amid the cascading defections and pleas for mercy, that leech who had scoffed earlier stood again, his face flushed with defiance as he tried to rally his fading courage. "Wait, everyone, just wait!" he shouted, his voice cracking under the strain. "This is a scam—a manipulation! If he really had the strength, wouldn't he have stopped us long ago? There's no way—"

"Drake!" bellowed a man in a black hood in the seventh row. "You've lost your mind!" Then without a pause, he turned toward the exalted figure on the highest podium and fell down on one knee, bowing his head. "This young fool speaks out of turn, milord. He's fueled by ignorance and misguided bravery. We, the Duskborne clan, do not share his views. Please, allow me to prove our loyalty to you."

"But uncle," the leech who was aptly named Drake fumbled. "What do you mean? This is our enemy—"

"Enough!" The man raised his hand. Not turning to face Drake, he proclaimed, "From this moment forth, Duskborne clan has no son named Drake. Lord Axiom, we ask for your forgiveness and beseech you to punish the child as you see fit."

Drake's face went white as the blood drained from it. Around him, the room's earlier raucousness faded into a heavy silence, every pair of eyes fixed on the scene.

Drake looked around desperately, seeking an ally, but found none; even those who had earlier shared his skepticism now averted their gazes, fearful of attracting the wrath of Axiom.

Illeana sneered. All of this opened her eyes to the hypocrisy and sliminess of these people. One moment, they were doing everything in their power to worm their way into the council.

And now?

Haha. She couldn't help but chuckle. Now each and every one of them was scrambling to suck up to Mr. Axiom, going so far as to throw their own child prodigy—such a young visionary at fourth shade—under the cart if it meant a better image in front of Mr. Axiom.

What a shit show.

"Uncle. You . . . you can't do this to me."

The uncle in question completely ignored this plea and simply maintained his reverent posture.

Illeana turned her attention back toward Mr. Axiom. *What will he do now?* She had zero sympathy for Drake whatsoever. Anything that happened to him, he had it coming.

Heck, whatever happened to everyone here who'd planned to take over the world had it coming. However, she still hoped that Mr. Axiom would have mercy on those who were just going with the flow.

She massaged her head. She would never have expected this confluence of visionaries to have so many twists and turns.

After a while, when many more pleaded in their own ways, Mr. Axiom suddenly snapped his convergence note shut and shelved it.

With one hand casually in his pocket, he spoke in a clear, deliberate tone, "Your pleas and apologies mean nothing to me. I believe only in the balance. Save your breath. It's your deeds that will determine your fate, not your futile appeals for mercy.

"I have no faith in the characters of you visionaries except for a select few." Unexpectedly, his gaze shifted toward Illeana, his eyes briefly softening with a flicker of appreciation.

Illeana stiffened, and as always, the vault chose this critical moment to instill into her a pulse of an emotion she didn't want—fanaticism. Something it had suppressed for her since Mr. Axiom's appearance.

The memory of Mr. Axiom's earlier warning, a silent rebuke that had even included her despite her actions, now seemed to dissolve into the chaos of her emerging emotions.

Confusion swirled within her. The boundary between her genuine feelings and those forced upon her by the vault blurred, leaving her uncertain and vulnerable.

She mentally fought back. *No!* But her body betrayed her inner turmoil. Her eyes lit up with an uncontrollable zeal, and before she could stop herself, she clasped the hem of her dress and curtsied deeply.

Mr. Axiom nodded and turned his gaze to a few others. Illeana completely ignored that and settled back down, trying to calm her racing heart. *He appreciated my efforts!* she thought, her mind a battlefield of conflicting emotions.

As she wrapped her head around these tumultuous feelings, Mr. Axiom spoke again, his voice cutting through the silence like a knife. "Despite the treachery displayed today, understand this: I am an arbiter of balance, not a deliverer of mercy or brutality. I am not swayed by sentiment or deceit.

"Those of you who dared to disrupt the order have not merely bent the rules, you have broken them. As such, while I refrain from extremes, I also do not turn a blind eye to calculated betrayal. This is not about vengeance; it is about rectitude. It's time for you all to confront the chaos you've sown."

Despite the harshness of his words, there was a clear mercy within them. The dark pressure constricting everyone's minds suddenly gave way, and their expressions turned hopeful. Illeana managed to slow down and realized, *Mr. Axiom is going to forgive them.*

She didn't know how to feel about that. While forgiveness seemed right, some, like that inciteful teenager and the mastermind behind it all, surely deserved a harsher fate.

Turning his piercing gaze toward Rupert, Mr. Axiom commanded, "It's time to end this ruse." The message was clear, and Rupert, as if understanding his fate was sealed, began his descent.

The menacing red aura that had encircled him slowly dissipated as he returned to the ground.

Illeana's heart skipped a beat. *He's surrendering!* She almost couldn't believe this was happening. She had no idea how Mr. Axiom could know the trace of all these visionaries, but the proof was at hand, and there was no denying it.

Given his immense strength and intimate knowledge of their traces, he could reduce everyone in this hall to a mess of blood and gore with just a snap of his fingers.

Rupert turned toward Mr. Axiom, the voices of his emotions and reactions inaudible even to her—a listener.

The whole crowd stopped their reverent praises and waited with bated breath. Rupert, clutching the bulb of his cane, took a measured breath and locked eyes with Mr. Axiom. "I still believe your proposition will lead to a worse future, marked by significantly more deaths and a rampant loss of global representation to outsiders."

His voice was steady, almost unnervingly calm, belying the fierce emotions she knew must be roiling beneath his composed exterior. It was a masterful suppression of rage from a man who had just watched his chance at ruling the world dissolve before an audience of erstwhile followers.

"Do not test my limits, Rupert," rasped Mr. Axiom with a chilling coldness. "You've tipped the scale too far already. Back down now, or I will be forced to restore the equilibrium myself."

Rupert's fingers twitched imperceptibly, but his face remained an impassive mask. He closed his middle eye—a silent concession—and with a final, deliberate *tap* of his cane, he turned away.

As he walked back to his seat, a ghostly haze obscured his features, masking any hint of the turmoil within. He settled to the empty throne next to the lord of primordial blood, his movements slow.

This extinguished the faint glimmer of hope that had persisted in some faces around the room. Realization set in, and many who'd been heaping praises on Mr. Axiom, thinking it to just be a temporary loss of pride, lost their voices.

However, Illeana felt miffed. She understood that Mr. Axiom owed her nothing—heck, she owed him for saving her. But seeing Rupert walk away unscathed after everything he had done to her stung deeply.

It just . . .

She closed her eyes and took a deep, steadying breath. *No. It's not Mr. Axiom's role to act as jury, judge, and executioner. His purpose isn't to distribute personal justice but to maintain the cosmic balance.*

Realization dawned on her. She was being selfish, expecting a being like Mr. Axiom to avenge her personal grievances. Shaking her head, she fortified her resolve. *I need to rise above this.*

The failed assassination attempt was on her. If she had executed her part flawlessly, none of this would have escalated to such a crisis. Perhaps Mr. Axiom might have even commended her for independently resolving the issue.

Her resolve grew stronger, and she looked back. Mr. Axiom turned to the crowd and declared, "Consider this not just a rebuke but a final opportunity to realign with the principles that govern us all. While I am not omniscient like all of you hoped to be, know that if any of you disrupt the balance of the world too severely . . ."

Suddenly, as if his words were a physical force, everyone except for Illeana and a few others were violently pulled downward, their bodies strained under immense pressure.

Illeana watched, her eyes glued to his every action as her heart raced frantically.

In the shadowy room, where only Mr. Axiom's masked face was illuminated, he extended his hand decisively and declared, "For, there will be no further warnings."

C H A P T E R 72

DIVINATION

Vern beheld the crowd as myriads of thoughts ran through his mind. His heart raced faster than a train, but he somehow managed not to melt under the stares of everyone.

Fuck. It actually worked! He knew this method would scare the hell out of everyone, but it turned out to be far more effective than his wildest imagination. Even Rupert, a man of endless means, was clearly shaken to the core when Vern sent him that note.

This was something he'd prepared beforehand for such a situation. It was actually just an extension of what he'd tried out with Esther a while ago. He first sent a note to himself and then used the "proximity list"—as he'd come to call it—that subsequently appeared and slowly copied down the trace runes of people around him.

Unsurprisingly, now that he had a better intuitive understanding of this runic language, it didn't take him more than ten minutes to copy one rune as it had for Esther's test run.

And in the moment of truth, he'd simply used these traces he'd found on this proximity list to pretend to know their traces. A bead of sweat trickled down his face behind the mask. *Looks like no one's suspecting that I know their traces and understand their viewpoints.*

Because if he did, there was no way he'd leave Rupert unharmed or let these people go unpunished. He sighed internally. *Alas, my "knowledge" is fake, and I can't really do anything but send these people notes with these traces.*

However, there was a silver lining in all this. He'd learned something peculiar when he was slowly perfecting everyone's traces. Two of the traces from the proximity list overlapped with those in the fate list.

One was the trace beneath his own on the fate list—second—the "fated person," whereas the other was seventh on that list.

His eyes involuntarily landed on the lady who was pretending to be an eterna in front of him. *It has to be her,* he reasoned. His multiple data points and common sense told him she was the fated person he'd sent all those stupid notes to. He smiled. *Also, the one who asked me to shut the fuck up.*

There were a bunch of reasons for this assertion. From his understanding, the proximity list was generated with himself as its origin. So those farther away from him would appear lower down the list, while closer ones would be at the top.

When he was sitting at the bottom, the overlapping traces had appeared somewhere in the middle of the proximity list, making it impossible for him to associate with a real person in this room.

Well, maybe I could have done it if I had precise measurements of the room, the distance between each seat, row, and a couple of other metrics. As much as his eyes had improved, they sadly hadn't evolved to the point of making him a walking ruler.

So, he had another idea in mind. Triangulation. He could use multiple data points to figure out which trace belonged to what person based on the changes in the list. He already had a data point from the bottom. One from the top and one from either end of the hall would be enough.

Except, it was impossible with how things turned out. He couldn't just abandon his position and walk to either the right or left of the hall and whip out his notepad again with everyone staring at him like hawks.

That would be far too suspicious.

However, surprisingly, things still turned out in his favor with his second data point, the one he'd gotten just a couple minutes ago by sending that final warning to himself as well.

To his surprise, the second trace on the fate list happened to be third on the proximity list too. So, excluding himself, this person had to be situated very close to him.

Which narrowed it down to three people: Rupert, the pretender lady, and the lord of primordial blood.

He probably could have confirmed it further by moving a bit, but the fact that this lady could ignore the pressure of nexus just like himself clearly suggested she shared more qualities with him than the other two options.

Combining all this, there was only one conclusion to be had. *She's the one my notes default to.*

Unfortunately, he still couldn't connect a face with the seventh entry on the fate list. That one was still somewhere around the middle of the pack in his second data point. *And I'm definitely not getting the third data point.*

Shaking his head, he focused back on the situation. *My words should have sunk in by now.*

With a sharp turn, he announced, "It's time for me to fulfill my duty." Many eyes bore down on his back like the last time, and he chanted internally, *Don't interrupt me this time. Please don't stop me.*

He was out of cards to play. If Rupert stopped him again, he really didn't know how to salvage the situation.

He made his way toward the large pillar connected to the lotus dome and extended one hand toward it while the other furiously scribbled some instructions inside his pocket for the nexus to follow.

Just have to make it look flashy, he reminded himself.

In another few seconds, when no one dared to interrupt him, he exhaled a deep breath. His left hand resting on the pillar, he said, "Balance," keeping up with the theme of this axiom he'd built.

Suddenly, the dim pillar exploded with light extending outward from his touch. *Thump.*

A sharp, bassy pulse echoed from his position as the pillar flickered with different shades of light. The crowd's eyes finally left his back and focused on the anomaly surrounding him.

Gasps reverberated in his ears, but he paid them no mind and slowly reduced the flickering of the pillar, making it settle down on a particular shade of gray.

All this, however, depleted the already low reserves of nexus, and Vern felt the end of this confluence draw near. It was already barely keeping everyone in check. If he let it run for much longer, Rupert would be unbridled, and he might just figure out that Vern had no real strength.

Can't let that happen, he asserted. That would be terrible. So as soon as the pillar settled on that perfect shade of gray, he leisurely disengaged his hand from the pillar and turned back to the crowd.

His eyes landed on the seventh row, and without his prompting, King Keras stood up and asked in deference, "May I begin the divination, Lord Axiom?"

Vern nodded before adding, "Please be quick about it. We don't have much time left."

Keras's face turned solemn, and after what looked like an intense internal debate with himself, he asked with a hint of dread in his voice, "Lord, could you help me ascend to the throne of the first observer? That would allow me to divine the artifact's resilience directly."

Vern narrowed his eyes. Keras's face paled, and he explained further, "Oh, Arbiter of Balance, I have no nefarious intentions in proposing this. Direct access to the nexus's core will allow me to finish the divination in a few minutes.

"Whereas if I repeated my prior methods, I might really be forced to burn my insights and regress further, all the while having no guarantee of a successful divination. Obviously, it's understandable if such a thing is not possible."

Vern debated for a couple seconds. Keras didn't seem like the person who would take this opportunity to destroy the core of nexus, but he didn't fully trust him either. *Hmm, I can just increase the pressure if he tries something funny.*

Blinking, he replied, "Come."

Keras's face lit up, and he bowed before quickly making his way out of the row. His maroon hair and beard, paired with somewhat old yet sharp features, gave him a solemn look as he ascended the stairs.

Once at the top, his eyes briefly gravitated toward Rupert, a dark look within them, but he clenched his fist and walked toward the pillar, his gait strong.

Seems like what Rupert did to him only fueled his rage further rather than scaring him, Vern speculated.

Right before reaching out to the pillar, Keras turned toward Vern as if asking for permission. Vern didn't know what to feel about this and just nodded.

Keras's eyes suddenly shone orange, and an aura of similar color covered his hands.

Vern watched with interest, but someone from the crowd murmured, "It's His Majesty's hand of fate. We're seeing it in action!"

He was continually amazed by how quickly everyone double-crossed their beliefs. A couple of minutes ago, they would have gladly denounced "His Majesty." Now, they were more than happy to sing his praises.

He felt like there had to be some kind of explanation for this in his understanding of structure.

There wasn't. At least not yet.

This reminded him of the rapid integration that his thought space was about to undergo. The insight sphere within him felt so taut, warped by the immense instability he'd let things devolve into before taking action to stabilize them.

However, he knew this was the right course of action for himself. He would jump leaps and bounds ahead as a first-shade observer and get closer to the second shade.

However, he felt like he wouldn't be ready to shade his perception another time even after this giant leap in aligning his insights toward this vision's singularity.

The reason was simple. He'd had two major events where he'd embodied instability before stability—one in the mirror realm on his first mission and the second just now.

But beyond that, he barely had any insights into the structure fundamental. His foundational insights into the matter were sorely lacking.

Essentially, once this was over, he felt like he would have the bare minimum insights needed to advance, but he would be missing out on the maximum potential of this shade.

And given that this was a shade where he'd created his own vision from scratch, he had no plans of dropping the ball.

He suddenly felt like massaging his temples as he sighed internally. *It's not like I know what vision to shade my perception next with anyway.*

He clearly had many more bottlenecks to clear before he could even think about advancing to the next shade.

Closing his eyes for a second, he opened them back up and focused on Keras. The man went around the pillar and plucked at it with his glowing hand at one place after another.

He extracted shimmering orange light with each pluck and collected it in his other hand. Vern tried to figure out what fundamentals were at play here but quickly lost focus.

He was tired. Tired beyond measure. Adrenaline and the thrill of having overturned such a strong tide, all the while fooling the most knowledgeable people, were the only reasons he hadn't just passed out.

Copying all those runes required intense focus and mental strength, sapping him of almost all his representation. He was essentially running on fumes right now. Simply keeping up his mask's cycling stability and instability was getting harder.

So he simply watched Keras accumulate more light from the pillar as its shape became increasingly evident. It was condensing into a prism.

After a few more minutes filled with hushed whispers from the crowd, Keras perfected the orange prism in his other hand. Finally, after his seventh full circle around the pillar, King Keras stopped, his face pale as a sheet.

Heaving, he backed up a little and turned toward the crowd, the prism in his hands outstretched in the air. Vern had his eyes glued to the gleaming object, a hint of apprehension bubbling inside him.

What if this divination proclaims that the world is still on a short lease? He bit his lip. That would be terrible. Given the nature of these people, he didn't harbor any doubts that they would quickly turn on him once again.

Yes, he had the deterrent of knowing their traces, but they would still need some kind of solution for this massive problem, and as the debate prior had displayed, there weren't many good options.

Cold sweat trickled down his back as Keras lethargically opened his eyes and held the prism aloft, letting it catch the light from the surroundings. The orange glow refracted through the prism, scattering vibrant beams across the amphitheater, casting a warm light on the faces of the gathered visionaries.

After a deep breath, Keras began to speak, his voice shaky but carrying a weight that settled over the crowd. "The prism's steadiness speaks for itself," he said. "There is hope!"

The paranoid and cautious crowd murmured among themselves, their conversations shifting from whispers to explosive speculations in an instant.

Turning toward Vern, he added, "Lord Axiom was true to his words. Though I don't see an eternal rigidity within this prism, the Arbiter of Balance has bought us more than enough time."

Vern felt a surge of relief wash over him as his taut nerves began to ease bit by bit. *I didn't misunderstand it all, then. I really helped Lady Sylphina and, by implication, the whole world.*

It felt . . . surreal.

However, before he could ponder the effects of his actions any further, Keras waved his hands, and the prism dispersed into shimmering motes of light. He knelt before Vern, his regal robes sweeping the ground in reverence.

Keras spoke, his voice resolute, "I—no, the entire Estefan kingdom—are in your debt, Lord Axiom. You've granted us each a new lease on life. Without your intervention, the world would have lost something irreplaceable under the mandate of omniscience."

With a deep breath, Keras lowered his head farther, his voice swelling with fervor. "Praise be to the arbiter who embodies balance! Your hand alone holds the fabric of our existence together."

Vern again had no clue what to do about this. This was a seventh or a former eighth-shade observer and a king for fuck's sake. Who the hell was he to pretend to be better than him?

It has to be done anyway, he reasoned. So he nodded curtly as if it weren't a big deal.

However, that's when another shout came from the crowd. "Praise be to the arbiter who wields the axioms!"

Someone else chimed in, "Praise be to Lord Axiom!"

A bitter smile appeared on Vern's face as more voices joined in.

"Glory to Lord Axiom!"

"Exalt the axiom!"

"Honor to the Keeper of Balance!"

This unexpected feedback somehow made the assimilation of his vision into his thought space faster. He wondered, *Can this be because the structure is becoming more stable by this action?*

Yet, that didn't matter. As much as he was opposed to being too much in the limelight or being praised by these opportunists, he wouldn't put a stop to it if it meant he would advance further as an observer.

Regardless, the clock ticked, and suddenly, the flaccid voice of nexus's spirit intruded in this cacophony of glorifying yells. "The pact is complete. Insufficient flux for a graceful exit. Expulsion imminent."

Suddenly, the cheers stopped, and a buzz went through the crowd. The observers sitting on the second row shone with blue light, and before they could voice their disapproval, they disappeared.

Finally! Vern remained patient, not letting his fatigue show in these final moments.

However, in this charged atmosphere, an unexpected voice emerged once again. It was Rupert as he spoke with a tap of his cane, "Arbiter of Balance, would you be willing to share a proxy trace with all of us?"

Chapter 73

PRAYERS

In this situation where the members in the lowest row were already being expelled from the nexus and those in the middle rows were getting a bit restless, Rupert's question puzzled many.

Maybe noticing the question in Vern's and everyone else's gazes, he elaborated, "I can see that you're against the council of overseers, but I am sure even you can't deny the benefits of worldwide information exchange it would have brought with it."

Vern raised his brows, but Rupert continued, "My essence strands would have been the perfect solution, but as things stand, you already have access to all our traces."

It clicked, and Vern couldn't help but praise this man's quick wit. However, his request was going to be problematic.

"With such knowledge, you could emulate the same effect as my strands and act as an information exchange hub between the visionaries of this realm. However, as things stand, only you can contact us. It's a one-way street without much use to most of us."

"Right! So if we had Lord Axiom's proxy's trace, we could still cooperate with everyone else through him."

Vern remained silent, but he understood where Rupert was going with this.

But what is a proxy trace? he wondered. *Is that a fake trace one can form?* However, he instantly rejected that idea. If one could fake their trace, its knowledge wouldn't be a big deal at all.

Another idea soon came to him. *Maybe it is the trace of a subordinate or something?* It made more sense. That felt like a viable way to go about solving this problem. Except such a person's life would be fleeting, and why would anyone willingly agree to such a job?

Ugh. This complicated things for him. He didn't have anyone like that, nor did he want one.

Vern narrowed his eyes, and he thought, *Rupert must have deliberately waited until the last moment to ask this of me.* It put him in a difficult position: agreeing would aid Rupert's own interests, but refusing would paint Vern in a bad light.

It would make the zeroth axiom seem like someone who preached morals but wouldn't do even a simple favor.

Hmm, maybe he wants to test the limits of my abilities. Vern stared at those sutured eyes. There was no malice visible on the surface, but he felt like a hungry monster was lurking behind them, waiting for him to slip up.

Ugh, can't they just do what Esther did to reply to me without knowing my trace?

Hmm. I don't know. It's possible some restrictions in that method, which limit its long-term usage.

"Coven master is right," shouted someone from the third row. "Lord Axiom, if you could help arrange the rescue of our city—" The voice abruptly cut off as blue light enveloped him, and like a streaking star, he disappeared.

Vern bit his lip. *This is problematic. I have no logical reason to refuse this. But I can't act as this "information exchange hub" even if I wanted to.*

While he could broadcast messages, what Rupert and his people expected required precise control and detailed note-sharing—something he couldn't perform.

He furrowed his brows, rethinking it from all angles.

Yeah. I can't do it. He was only really sure of one person's trace in here, and that was his fellow pretender, and even that was because of additional information he had. For everyone else here, he couldn't really connect faces with their runic trace.

These runes were practically meaningless for pinpointing anyone in this crowd.

What was worse was that there would be terrific advantages if he could actually do what Rupert wanted. The whole world's vital information going through him could cement his position as one of the most influential figures of all time.

But again, there were cons to that, too. He'd already heard tales of people losing themselves to whispers because they came in contact with something they shouldn't have.

Who was to say these people wouldn't try to send something of the sort to him? And as a first-shade observer, he would be utterly defenseless against such attacks.

I'll have to deny it, he realized, feeling apprehensive and regretful about the decision.

It wasn't rational, and Rupert would definitely draw conclusions from his refusal, but there was no other way. If he agreed now but failed to do his job properly later, he'd only expose flaws in his disguise and get caught in his own lies.

Besides that, he didn't trust anything Rupert suggested. Who was to say this wasn't a trap? Nexus had restricted his prowess, but the methods at his disposal outside this setting would be beyond anything Vern could even imagine.

Yeah, no.

His mind made up, Vern looked up. "I—"

"Have some shame, Rupert," rasped King Keras, cutting him off. Vern swallowed the rest of his words. He turned to see Keras, who suddenly seemed uneasy about interrupting him.

Vern gave him a nod, and Keras thanked him with a gesture before turning back to Rupert. "You really expect Lord Axiom to take on such a demanding task without anything in return?" He sneered. "Worse, you expect him to have expendable observers around himself like you?

"What a joke! You think the lord doesn't have his own matters to attend to? That he has the time to play messenger for every little gossip all of you want to share with each other?"

Ah, well, that's one way to do it. This was a valid reason. Except it wouldn't have been as effective if he'd said it himself.

He finally realized how great of a job Rupert's own lackeys had done in this regard by helping him convey critical information without his own intervention.

Yes, keep going. Vern encouraged King Keras with his demeanor. The man clearly had more to say, and Vern was happy to take all the help he could get against Rupert. Especially from someone who was once on par with the man.

But the hazy-faced Rupert suddenly cut him off. "I would have gladly made the sacrifice if I had the means to do so. Lack of effort or remuneration are no excuses not to help millions in need.

"A being of laws—Lord Axiom should understand this too. It's not too much to ask to share a trace of a person close to him, is it? Surely one life isn't more important than all the ones that could be saved, right?"

What was left of the rapidly disappearing crowd nodded, their faces pleading and hopeful.

This fucker . . . He was ruthless with his words, seizing every chance to tarnish Lord Axiom's reputation.

Damn! I have to do something.

Seeing Keras at a loss for words, Vern ran through his options before settling on one. Shaking his head, he declared, "I don't owe any of you anything."

This silenced the entire crowd, guilt painted across their faces. Not the response he wanted, but it would have to do. With a chilling coldness in his voice, he continued, "My only loyalty is to balance. I won't meddle in worldly affairs unless the equilibrium is disrupted."

Rupert chuckled, and right when he was about to say something, Keras interrupted, "Show some humility, Rupert. You may be an eterna but don't forget what happened just moments ago. If you think you're in charge here, why aren't you standing where the lord is?"

This gave Rupert pause, but Keras continued, "And if there's really something that warrants Lord's attention . . ."

He paused, then shifted to a more reverent posture before continuing, "One could always follow the old ways and pray in the name of the arbiter of balance."

Vern had to summon all his willpower to hide his surprise at this revelation. *What? How would that even work?*

The impact of this proclamation was clear. The crowd grew thoughtful while Rupert snorted and looked away as if he found the idea distasteful.

Keras spoke again in a reverent tone, "Given the lord's actions today, it's clear they have carved their singularity deep on the unified perspective. Especially considering the unique audience they had for his resurgence—we visionaries who can imagine anything, their impact is bound to be even more profound."

Glancing at Rupert from the corner of his eye, he added, "As long as your prayers are sincere, they will reach the lord."

What the hell? Vern struggled to keep himself from asking that question audibly. He understood the words but felt they suggested something too grand. It didn't feel real to hear prayerlike words associated with himself.

So prayers are actually real, then? Ever since delving into fundamentals, he'd considered them to be nothing more than a means of self-consolation and a display of faith. *But this . . . ?*

He pondered these words in silence, just like the crowd.

Breaking down Keras's statement word by word, he began to understand. *So, prayers are another form of communication.* But from his limited understanding, they functioned differently than convergence notes.

It relied on him having "carved his singularity" onto the unified perspective, which was a fancy way of saying he was famous.

So, Keras thinks I've left an impression that's deep enough such that anyone can pray in my name directly and possibly reach me?

That was . . . intriguing, to say the least.

However, at that very moment, an incomprehensible raving suddenly echoed in his mind.

Vern frowned and focused on this sound, and it quickly became clear. They were . . . words. It said, *O, Lord Axiom, Arbiter of Balance, I beseech thee—grant me insight to reconquer this third rune wrought forth by your esteemed disciples.*

The voice continued, but Vern's mind halted right there.

What?!

His head snapped toward a peculiar man in a top hat and violet coat in the fifth row. The man had his arms crossed as he muttered something to himself with his eyes closed.

He gasped. *This . . .*

Refocusing his mind, Vern listened to the incomprehensible babbling again. It repeated the previous words and continued, *For this burden is beyond my talents and threatens my very being. Guide me through its tempest, that I might harness its power without succumbing to its whims.*

Gears whirled in Vern's mind as things rapidly began clicking into place.

Hensen is praying to me for help in mastering the third rune? What kind of joke was that? Hensen was supposed to be the one with all the information.

That had to be the craziest thing he'd heard today. Even more absurd than Rupert's mandate of omniscience.

Also, what was this timing? He heard a prayer the moment Keras explained it. *Or . . .*

It was like he'd analyzed beforehand, where he might have had the ability to do some new thing for a while, but becoming aware of it is what allowed him to finally "observe" it and interact with it.

Like his intuitive ability to feel structures.

However, suddenly, the raving in his mind disappeared, and he looked back up only to see a blue light enveloping Hensen.

Is the fifth row now expelled too? Things were happening too quickly.

Should I warn them one more time?

No,. he concluded after some deliberation. *I've already said my piece. I need to maintain this image.*

Surprisingly, however, King Keras wasn't done. He sighed. "I'd hoped we would have some time to chat among ourselves and catch up once the consensus was over. Many of you are my old friends, and while I can't say I am not disappointed by your choices today, I do understand them."

He shook his head. "But I suppose fate has its own plans." Blue light enveloped him alongside others on the seventh row, but it was slow to permeate.

In this haze, he lamented, "There's a lot that still needs to be done, but I guess we'll have to do it the old way—or pray to the arbiter to get our pleas across."

Standing taller, he nodded to everyone. "I wish we could convene like this again under better circumstances and brighter skies. Until then . . ." The radiance around his body exploded.

The glowing figure turned toward Vern and bowed another time before saying, "May the shades of your perception carve your path to singularity." His whole being dissolved into a cyan beam as his last words echoed in the air.

Many voices came together to respond in farewell but were cut off just as abruptly as the nexus threw out their owners.

Finally, blue light washed over Rupert. He stood up and dusted his coat, his fierce eyebrow and closed eyes aimed at Vern. But he didn't say anything.

Vern stared back, his eyes exuding an unmatched might, but internally, his head swirled with complicated thoughts. *This man is sophisticated and shrewd.* Everything he did had a purpose, and it would be wishful thinking on Vern's part to assume he was done playing his tricks.

However, he'd done enough for the day. They were leaving, and he could finally go back to his comfy bed back in Hotel Inkwell.

The lord of primordial blood didn't bother standing up and continued to file his nails without a care in the world.

Then there was the poser lady. Surprisingly or unsurprisingly, an aqueous radiance also began to swirl around her at this time.

The first one to go was the lord of primordial blood, then Rupert, who tapped his cane as if to assert dominance before he disappeared. Last of all was the lady.

Vern turned his gaze toward her, and she stared back.

One second.

Two.

Three.

Why's it taking so long? he mused. Right when things began to turn awkward, and she parted her lips to say something, the blue glow exploded.

Schwa.

This final burst of light snuffed out, and before he knew it, even the pillar with the lotus dome behind him lost its radiance.

"Everyone is gone," he muttered in relief after checking the feedback from the nexus.

His surroundings grew dark, and he waited for his own turn. When a dozen seconds passed and nothing happened, he frowned and murmured, "What's going on?"

He reached out to his face and removed the mask. He let out a deep breath and ran his fingers through his hair. "I need to get a better mask. Why the hell is this thing so heavy?"

Many things had to be addressed, but his head throbbed, and his body felt weak. *I just want to sleep.*

He massaged his temples for a while, but no blue light came to whisk him away.

"Did the nexus forget about me?" he wondered aloud.

C HAPTER **74**

REALIGNMENT OF THOUGHT SPACE

No way that nexus just forgot it had one more person to send back, right? Right?

He pulled out his notepad, hoping to ask the nexus's spirit itself what the hell was going on. Golden runes hovered around the pad, combining and disintegrating into shapes he still couldn't comprehend.

Furrowing his brow, he imagined the trace of Lady Sylphina and, by proxy, nexus's, and wrote, *Please send me back.*

He stopped moving his pen and, after that consistent delay of two and a half seconds, watched the inked words written in the runic alphabet morph into new blazing runes as they streamed into a new list that popped up.

Whirr.

He snapped his head toward the noise and noticed a tiny spark of light in the pillar behind him, which housed the throne of the first observer. Suddenly, an invisible force tugged on his body, moving it in a particular direction.

Ah, it was that simple? He chuckled.

Yet, just a second after he closed the notepad, the sound died down with a mechanical groan, and the unnatural pull halted in its tracks.

Huh?

He stood there, waiting for something to happen.

Nothing did.

"What the hell?" he asked the empty air, his hands spread apart. As if to mock him, the slight hint of light in the pillar behind him fizzled away.

An uneasy feeling washed over him, and he paced for a while, only to give in and open his notepad again. With a flourish, he rewrote the last request once again, all the while ignoring the plethora of runes that formed around his words even before he could send them. It said, *Please send me back to Hotel Inkwell in Elmhurst in Calidian Empire in Quartzford Continent.*

Whirr. Something buzzed again, and an even smaller blue light sparked around the bottom of the pillar only to die out instantly. However, this time, the force that was supposed to send him back couldn't even begin before everything shut down.

"Fuck me," he cried out. He was very familiar with such behaviors. Engines and contraptions that were out of steam or coal had a habit of groaning like this, too.

Uneasy, he tried one final time and sent another similar note to the nexus.

There wasn't even a peep, just like a machine with zero fuel.

"It's really out of power!" He groaned, stomping his foot. What were the odds? Fifty or so people managed to escape before him. How was he so unlucky?

Soon he grimaced and thought, *Did I overdo it with Rupert?* After all, he'd used nexus's energy to suppress him there. Pacing on the platform around the center dimly lit by nothing but the stars and nebulas beyond the tinted canopy, he racked his already fried brain.

What do I do? It was an absurd problem. Who the hell would expect such a facility to run out of energy just like that? Worse, his thought space was pulsing intensely, making it hard for him to think through the current situation.

Soon, however, the choice was taken from his hands.

His eyes blazed on their own, and the ring within each of them shone brightly. Feeling a sensation of rising through space wash over him, he gave up on any further investigation for now and settled down on one of the seats in the eighth row.

Looks like my thought space is further aligning the new insights I gained today. He'd now become quite familiar with this feeling and could identify it from miles away. This one felt quite significant. The conscious effort on his end to let the situation destabilize as far as possible before reversing it and striking the balance had been pivotal in this monumental result.

Taking a deep breath, he closed his eyes and delved into his thought space. A large, ethereal sphere with eight sharp boundaries on its surface covered his vision.

Caged by three such boundaries, the upper northwestern octant—the structural octant—was populated with swaying lights, more than two-thirds of it covered.

Surprised, he thought, *That's a big jump.* Last he remembered, only a bit over one-third of it was covered.

So I'm about 66 percent done aligning my viewpoint to the first shade? However, he knew not to rely too much on this kind of indicator.

First, it was hard to make out the scale of this sphere when there was no reference for size. Who was to say this sphere couldn't get bigger or smaller? That would make any absolute visual calculations entirely useless.

Not only that, insights were also a fickle thing. He'd often delved into his thought space and seen some odd things happening here. Kind of like what was transpiring right now.

A bunch of the lights closer to the sphere's north pole detached from their neighbors, the bright bonds between them dwindling into nothing as the whole thing displaced a bit to the west.

This happened everywhere in the octant as the "tiny islands" drifted away from their original location, breaking their previous bonds and making new ones in different territories.

Heck, one that veered around the boundary of this octant tugged and pulled for a while before completely snapping its bonds as it crossed into an adjacent octant.

Vern watched it with fascination as the feeling of "correctness" spread throughout him with every second that passed.

After a bit, some insights merged and grew taller—further making his previous visual estimation of two-thirds progress inaccurate—while others split and filled some of the gaps.

Yet this is where his biggest deficiency came to light—his lack of foundational insights. He already knew it to be the case based on his gut feeling, but it wasn't visually apparent before this restructuring of his insights.

After all, newly learned insights blossomed into random spots, filling the octant haphazardly without proper rhyme or reason. From his understanding, insight sifting sessions existed for this very reason—to help one align their insights to better fit with the rest of their viewpoint.

This was something he got for free thanks to embodying his tenet to such an extent and causing such a wave inside his thought space.

He would probably need to align them further, but that would have to wait for a truly introspective moment. And not just that, if he'd done it before today, the gains wouldn't have been massive since this new influx of insights would have thrown it all in a mess again.

So one had to pick between stability or speed, all the while juggling the redundancy of efforts.

Though he didn't really know how it worked for others. They might not have an organized thought space like he did.

Anyway, the point was that this realignment made the holes in his insights evident. Between and inside the islands of flowing lights were gaps. Not tens or hundreds, but thousands. Annoying little holes that signified his failure to comprehend the subtle nuances of structure.

Vern clicked his tongue and murmured, "This won't do." Embodying the tenet of instability before stability helped him gain huge influxes of insights, but these subtle gaps in his knowledge regarding structure were hard to fill by just experiencing big events like today's.

He needed to find some ways to better attune himself to this fundamental.

Until now, a big chunk of his time as a first-shade observer was spent training under Mistress Amelia, and while he wouldn't change that for the life of him, it was a trade-off.

He missed out on possible missions and situations where he could have gained and deepened the insights needed to plug these very holes.

"One step at a time," he murmured with a shake of his head.

Sitting in the silent nexus, he continued to observe all the transformations that happened inside him, and after what felt like half an hour, his thought space finally settled down, and all the changes halted.

His head felt lighter, and the throbbing ache from before gave way to flowing thoughts as he watched the beautiful symmetry of the new islands in this octant of the ethereal planetlike thought space.

They looked perfect, and he seemed to realize something new about structures.

However, the moment that thought registered, a couple of new insights blossomed out of thin air into the thought space and broke the perfect symmetry he was just admiring.

"No," he lamented, only for that insight to burn even brighter as if to mock him.

He sighed and opened his eyes.

The eerie sight of the dim nexus helped him forget all about his complaints with the ever-changing shape of his thought space.

He rubbed his eyes, and a clear *paah* sound echoed in the hall as he lightly smacked his face and stood. "Alright. Let's see what the hell is going on here."

Walking over to the giant pillar in the center, he ran his hands over the glassy surface and pressed his face against it to better see the throne nestled inside the pillar.

How is anyone even supposed to sit on it if this thing's closed off like this? The pillar had no gaps or openings. Who would design something impractical like that?

Anyone sitting on a throne inside a glass pillar would look more like an experimental subject than a god.

This reminded him of Lady Lennix. Unfortunately, when he imagined her likeness sitting inside this tube, the image wasn't as funny as he'd hoped. Instead, it seemed . . . regal and untouchable?

Shaking his head, he dismissed that image. Obviously, the first observer, whoever it was, wouldn't sit on the throne when it was in this state. A hand on his chin, he lampooned, *Maybe it is closed off to show that only the first observer deserves to sit on this throne. Anyone else can only dream of it.*

That made sense.

Except, why the hell am I even thinking about this question?

This sent the distracting thoughts packing as he circled the pillar and began his first attempt to actually solve the problem at hand—the obvious solution.

What did one do when a machine ran out of energy? He shrugged. *Give it some fuel.*

White rings shimmered in his eyes as he observed the pillar without any specific vision or change in mind. It was kind of like how he did with the amulet of Restoration with an intent to let the subject absorb his representation.

Luckily, many new insights had blossomed in his mind during the confluence, helping him regenerate his otherwise emptied representation. After all, he had almost nothing left after conversing with Lady Sylphina.

Keeping a close eye on his reserves, he began to channel some of his representation into the pillar. To his surprise, it was like an endless void that guzzled up everything Vern sent its way. Yet, it was . . . slow.

He backed away and stood with his arms folded as his eyes slowly channeled his representation into this deep pit. Doubt assaulted him as his stores began to dwindle, but nothing happened.

Until it did.

Whirr. A sound echoed from somewhere high up as a light sparked on the surface of the pillar's bottom like it did before.

Vern narrowed his eyes. *Is it doing the same thing as before? But I didn't ask to be sent out of the nexus this time.*

He monitored his body intently but felt no tug or pull that'd send him back to his humble abode even after a dozen seconds. "Interesting. This is different," he spoke aloud, mentally noting all the changes around him.

In the previous three attempts, he'd asked the Nexus to send him back, and it had caused the meager lights that shone to be snuffed out as quickly as they came.

This time, however, the light remained shining as if representing it was stored for future use.

A bit more optimistic, he poured more representation into it, and soon the light began to spread around the bottom of the pillar in a ring.

However, before he could fill even half a single ring, he was only left with one-third of his supposedly large reserves of representation.

Should I keep going? he debated, eyeing his notepad. He didn't know how much energy was needed to complete his return. What if the current amount wasn't enough, and he got stuck somewhere in the middle of his travels?

A gruesome image formed in his mind, and he wiped the sweat off his forehead. *That would be a terrible way to go out.*

However, he didn't want to use up all his representation either. The journey itself was to be covered as a ball of consciousness rather than his physical self. And while he was no expert, it wouldn't be a stretch to extrapolate that being completely "unrepresented" in such a situation would be a terrible idea.

After some deliberation, he slowed down the flow of energy and waited, his eyes glued to the end of the half-ring. He wanted to see if this storage was temporary or permanent. What if the nexus lost the energy soon after he poured it in?

That would make some of his ideas unviable.

If the ring depleted rapidly, then he might be in big trouble. It would mean he couldn't slowly regenerate his own representation and pour it into the nexus over time.

Heck, in that case, it might be better for him to just try to get out right now, assuming there was enough energy to even initiate the process.

Similar fears and thoughts swirled in his mind, but as seconds turned into minutes and the lowest ring of light remained lit without even flickering, his paranoia fizzled away.

He sighed in relief. "Wow, this ancient machine is more efficient than most stuff available in the market nowadays."

Thump. He settled back down on a chair and tried to wrap his head around these circumstances. He knew it had yet to sink in because of his prior excitement, but this situation was worse than it looked. What if he was really stuck in here?

Yes the nexus was inextricably linked to Lady Sylphina, who was . . . nice to him but said she wouldn't interfere with his life's path. Then who was to guarantee she wouldn't just watch voluntarily or involuntarily as he slowly lost himself to hunger and loneliness in here?

He wasn't inherently against the idea of being inside nexus, but he didn't want to remain here longer than necessary. After all, he had a life to get back to. And while hunger and sleep had yet to beckon him, they were sure to come knocking in due time.

It would be one thing if he had control over his entry and exit, but he didn't. And that gnawed at him.

Rapping his fingers on the armrest, he assessed his options. One was to try to explore this dark and ancient palace by himself in hopes of finding food and shelter.

He didn't like the sound of that. Who knew what the hell was hiding in the nexus of Elyndor that had housed an ancient family at some point in time?

Yeah, not my first choice.

The other option—the best one—was to stack enough representation inside the pillar to be able to leave safely, but it had its own complications.

Maybe getting a little desperate by these uncertain cases, he even thought of what to do if worse came to worst.

I can probably send a note to all visionaries, asking them to pay the costs to keep nexus running for a while longer, but I don't know what reasoning to give for such an absurd request.

Though it had to be the last resort since it would hurt the mighty image he'd just built after so much effort.

Shaking his head, he reasoned, *It looks like I'll need to slowly fill it up with my own representation and explore the nexus if it doesn't work out in a while.*

Something of a plan at hand, he dove deeper into the problems with this solution. *I don't know exactly how much energy is needed to send me back. One ring? Two? Twenty?*

That's when a sudden flash of inspiration struck him. "Oh, wait. I can just try asking the nexus's spirit."

Surely, such a simple idea had eluded him until now because of all the thousands of worries running through his mind.

With a quick flourish of his pen, he imagined Lady Sylphina's trace and began writing, *How much representation is . . .*

However, as his hands moved to pen all this in runic form—something he did intuitively rather than deliberately—the golden symbols that were floating aimlessly until now suddenly rushed toward the paper.

Vern furrowed his brows. This wasn't entirely something new. However, until today, he'd been unable to make sense of what these runes meant. And ever since he'd entered the nexus, he had little time or energy to spend on anything that didn't directly help him solve the issue at hand.

After that realignment, however, he felt it might be worth spending some of his brain power to focus on and decipher exactly what these specific runes said—the ones that congregated around his writing even before he finalized and sent the note.

Nodding, he concentrated on them.

Scratch. The pen's nib that had been flowing to his whims until now suddenly came to a halt as he stared at the congregation of the runes with wide eyes.

Beyond his own words, which read, *How much representation is . . .* appeared another set of glowing words in a handwriting not his own, which added, *inside a night beast's heart?*

"What the heck is this? I didn't mean to write that."

C H A P T E R 75

ECHOES OF THE PAST

The whole sentence read: *How much representation is inside a night beast's heart?* Vern held the nib of his pen, moving it just enough to ensure the note wasn't finalized and sent to nexus. After a few seconds, more runes converged beneath his query, which was written in two distinct handwritings.

It's uncanny that I can even tell the difference. After all, visually, both of them were just some symbols in this runic alphabet, but his mind comprehended more. *This language has too much nuance.*

As runes engraved themselves onto the paper one by one, new words soon emerged in a third, entirely new handwriting. He read on with great interest: *An acolyte like you doesn't have the right to access such valuable information. Work harder and become a trainee. We'll talk then. Until that day, be diligent and do your best.*

He looked at this odd . . . conversation with his mouth agape. *What the hell is going on? What even is this?*

Unsure what to make of it, he continued writing his original query. However, this time, he only reached *How much representation is needed to send . . .* when the runes ahead of his words rearranged themselves and completed the rest of his sentence in a new handwriting.

The whole thing now read, *How much representation is needed to send a fleet of barbarians across the oceans?* He stopped his pen once again as curiosity grabbed him. *I didn't ask that, but I'd like to know too.*

The prior set of runes scattered before slowly coming back together and boring into the paper.

This time, the new words, which looked like a response to the question about barbarians read, *We will need three seafarers of second shade. But I don't know where we're gonna get them. Aizek might have some clues about their hideout, but we'll need to pay—*

However, that's when a burning sensation sparked in his eyes and his mind, forcing him to stop. The runes beyond this last word remained fuzzy, floating there with a beckoning charm.

Hmm, so there's some kind of mental cost to reading this? Perturbed, he focused harder, and to his surprise, a few more runes consolidated into words. "*. . . but we'll need to pay the harbor master his commission—*"

After this, he really had to stop. The burn had turned into a sharp sting that tore at his mind. The more he read, the more it strained his mind and eyes.

His focus soon slipped, and only the initial conversation remained. He narrowed his eyes and thought, *Is this really what I think it is?* After a bit of deliberation, he decided to test it further.

To do so, he completely dismissed any notion of sending his words as a note to nexus's spirit, removing Her Eminence's trace from his mind as he continued the sentence *How much representation is needed to send someone . . .* and stopped.

The floating runes lost their prior shape before engraving back onto the paper word by word as they spelled *How much representation is needed to send someone hurling using gale blow?*

Gale blow? Is that some vision? How interesting, he mused as he waited for the reply to this question to show up.

The moment it did, he felt a light sting in his mind as he read the answer. It was somehow as straining as the last part of the previous answer.

Frowning, he pushed through and read the single line, *We believe an average first-shade observer should be able to dish out three of them before running out of representation.*

Fuck. It's really that! He bolted upright and muttered to himself, "These are the echoes of conversations from the past that start with the same words that I'm trying to write."

"This . . ."

This was insane!

His heart ramped up as he paced around the hall once more, the implications of such a . . . tool slowly taking root in his mind.

Before long, he asked himself, *Does that mean I have access to all conversations that happened using a convergence note?*

In the best case, that would mean he could snoop on some of the most private conversations that might have occurred between people of power worldwide since the note existed.

That can't be true, right?

His footsteps echoed in the hall as he digested this revelation and racked his brain to figure out how to best make use of such knowledge, forgetting all about his current predicament.

"First things first. I need to keep my expectations in check. There are some bizarre limitations."

He remembered the mental strain, which seemed dependent on two factors as of now. First was the length of the conversation, and second was the content. Length was straightforward. The more he wanted to read, the more he would have to focus. And the further the text from his key phrase, the more it cost.

The content, however, was far more interesting. When the note included any information of value, like the amount of representation needed to execute some vision called gale blow, he had to try much harder, almost as hard as the other condition's worst case.

Hmm, then what exactly decides the value of the information? That was the most important question because it wouldn't matter if he could stumble on the most earth-shattering secrets in these conversations if he were too mentally weak to read them.

Well, more like eavesdropping, he corrected himself. These conversations weren't really meant to be read by a third party like him. However, the ethical implications of reading someone's private conversations wasn't too high on his priority list right now.

Ethics were important in considering most decisions, but given he didn't know the people involved in these conversations, he just had to think of them as anonymized experimental data.

After all, knowledge was his one weakness—something he had a hard time giving up on. And to that end, knowledge was the highest power in this world of observers, making it even more alluring.

Feeling more assured about this, he made some mental terminology for the two important aspects of this process. He gave his convergence note a "key phrase," and it returned an "echo from the past."

Once these concepts became clear in his mind, he gripped the pen hard, a terrifying, almost scary gleam shining in his eyes. *Hmm, let's see . . . Where to start?*

With a quick thought, he penned, *Observation Record of Subjectivity . . .* and waited.

And to his utter surprise, the runes actually began to converge as they added to his sentence, . . . *by Cyrus L. Cartwright.*

Fuck. Could this really be in here? And on the first try, at that!?

Before he could think any further, the runes coalesced and reiterated words that began his journey as an observer: *The pursuit of objectivity is a necessary prerequisite to determine the facts about our cosmos. However, the acquisition of these facts is dependent upon the act of observation, but to observe is to shade reality with one's perception—*

Yet the words ended too soon. Vern clutched the pen harder, feeling waves of unknown emotions roiling within him. This . . . this was the start of it all.

This was what set him on his path as an observer. Not one day went by where he didn't lament losing access to the record.

So close . . .

Regrettably, he couldn't even read the first page here, much less the whole book. Simply trying to finish this paragraph was turning out to be impossible because of how many words it had.

After a few more seconds of wasting his mental strength, he let it go, and the runes split back into incomprehensible symbols, floating aimlessly.

This was very interesting, still. Just the fact that the *Observation Record of Subjectivity* was even accessible here raised many questions.

Is it possible I jumped to the conclusion of these echoes being the conversations held on this note? What if they're instead depictions of real-world events or something?

However, he soon shook his head. This was still the most sensible conclusion. It was very much possible that someone sent the whole text of this observation record to another person.

Adding to his conjecture was the fact that these words were written in beautiful handwriting, which had a bunch of typos in it. Real conversations didn't work like that.

Also, why could I read this paragraph without straining myself? There was no way the information about gale blow or whatever vision was more valuable than such an insightful introduction to the world of observation.

Looking at nothing in particular, he mused, *Maybe it's because I've already read it before. It's possible that might factor into the cost my perception has to pay to reach and listen to these echoes of the past.*

Not ready to jump to any more conclusions just yet, he decided to continue testing and wrote a single word, *Dear.* A very common greeting used to begin letters and the like.

Soon, the runes completed his words. *Dear Martha.*

This beautiful morning, I woke up and decided to smell some roses, and that reminded me of you—

Entirely uninterested in reading a vain love letter, Vern picked up the nib of his pen, making the runes disperse before writing *Dear* once more.

He wanted to check if repeating the word would land him back into the same conversation.

It didn't.

Dear Master, I humbly apologize for the folly of my children and assure you that they would never dare intrude upon your private chambers again. I hope—

Interesting. But next.

Dear, how could he do such a cruel thing? Looking at his face, no one would think that he has a mistress hidden behind his wife's back. Men can't really be trusted—

Why were people talking about mundane events via such an arcane mode of communication? He grumbled.

Next.

Dear sir, here's the transcription of words of wisdom from the Great Resolver's seventh symphony—

However, the words beyond these didn't form on their own and floated fuzzily. Intrigued by the premise of this query, he strained his mind, and runes came together. *Ethrex Nous Viz—*

"Fuck!" he cried and recoiled, his expression morphing from curiosity to anguish in an instant. Dropping the pen, he covered his eyes with his hand as blood seeped through his fingers.

After a few moments, he steadied his breathing, wiped his eyes with the back of his arm, and carefully regained his composure. Sitting back in his chair, he took several deep breaths, trying to steady the tremor in his hands.

The hall fell silent except for the soft whirring somewhere above him. Slowly, he lowered his hands and stared at the multiple *Dear* symbols that dotted the notepad before him. Luckily, the glowing runes had dispersed the moment he lost focus.

This is what I get for being too greedy, huh? he reprimanded himself.

He almost felt lucky that he got some sense knocked into him before he stumbled into something really forbidden. That might have actually made him lose his head in this godforsaken place where no one would even find his body.

Taking a deep breath, he made a simple rule for himself. *Don't read anything that demands too much focus. Especially when the context behind it is ominous.*

Wiping away the streak of blood from his eyes with his handkerchief, he waited a few more minutes before picking up the pen from the ground and wrote, *Third axiom . . .*

Runes combined and words formed. *Third Axiom of making steam engines: Air. Harness the elemental trio—water, fire, and air. Remember, Hatham, to control the true power of steam, one must control the three elements and especially air.*

Vern's lips twitched. *This is not what I meant.*

Exhaling, he restarted, this time adding more context. *Third axiom of observation . . .*

It gave him a window into another intriguing conversation. *Third axiom of observation suggests that you're not just wrong, but also foolish. Henceforth, any theory you propose will need to go through stricter checks and balances—*

This looked useful.

However, he was already at the limit of how many words he could read from this one. *Ugh, why can't I just start in the middle or something? Why do they have to start from these points?*

Then it hit him—start from the middle! *Yes! Who said I can't start from the middle?* After all, even the conversations he was reading right now were picked somewhere from the middle.

So if he just changed the key phrase to begin from the middle of the previous echo, he might just be able to pick up the conversation where the last one read and slowly figure out the whole thing one sentence at a time.

That'd be cheating . . . no?

Excitement bubbled in his chest, a feeling reminiscent of his childhood when he played with new puzzles and toys. Moving his hand, he wrote the last sentence of the previous echo. *Henceforth, any theory you propose will need to go through stricter checks and balances . . .*

If he was right, the echo to this key phrase should be the next sentence in the original conversation. Soon, the runes shuffled, and he waited with bated breath.

His face turned sour as he read, *. . . through stricter checks and balances ensuring our wives don't go out together. After all, they both think their husbands' friends are cheating.*

He deadpanned, *This is an entirely different conversation. It doesn't even have anything to do with the first part of my key phrase that talks about "theory."*

So he tried again and rewrote the last sentence. This time, the echo from the past was even weirder. *Henceforth, any theory you propose will need to go through stricter checks and balances. I will not tolerate my accountants being lazy.*

What the fuck? He scratched his head. This made no sense. It was almost as if the first part of his key phrase message was completely ignored. He'd understand if these conversations had totally new content but still somehow followed the full context of his key phrase, but they didn't.

The echoes seemed like a result of only a few words of the key phrase.

Which ones, though, and how do I test it?

After racking his brain for longer than he'd hoped, he had an idea.

What if I combine all the prior conversations and use the whole thing as a key phrase, then see which context the resulting echo makes sense for?

It seemed like a good idea. It would allow him to narrow down the window of what was considered and what wasn't.

Nodding, he wrote, *Dear Martha, this beautiful morning, in the light of recent revelations, how does the elemental trio—water, fire, and air—contribute to the folly of our actions? Can wisdom from the Great Resolver's seventh symphony . . ."*

And there, he stopped. If this whole message was being considered equally, there should be no echoes. There was almost a zero percent chance that someone before him wrote this exact string of words together, much less someone with access to a convergence note.

However, against all odds, the runes bunched together. And when Vern tried to focus, it wanted to strain his mental faculties to the limit.

He frowned.

Why is the value of this echo also so high? Could it be because my key phrase doesn't exist, and it's trying harder to find an echo?

However, that would be a nonoptimal way to go about it. If he understood this right, these echoes were just conversations others had using the note in the past. So an echo of the key phrase he'd just written shouldn't exist at all.

This actually made him even more curious. *What would the echo be when the key phrase is straight-up nonexistent? Or maybe it's like I thought, and it's only echoing based on part of the key phrase?*

He tried to reason with his brain for a while. Told it how he'd just burst some vein in his eye and made a rule not to read anything that needed too much focus.

He lost.

Taking a deep breath, he focused, and more of the runes came together, declaring, *Ethrex Nous Viz—*

"Argh!" he squealed. "Damn it! It's these whisper-like words again!" However, behind his wince, a smile bloomed as he pressed the handkerchief against his bleeding eyes and doubled over from pain.

The smile grew wider and wider. "Hahaha!" His unsettling laugh echoed in the hall as he proclaimed, "I see what's going on here."

C H A P T E R 76

PUTTING THEORY TO PRACTICE

Vern eyed the key phrase on the notepad that had tumbled to the ground and was tinted red by the blood oozing from the edges of his vision. However, he focused only on the end of the long paragraph.

Flipping around the handkerchief to a side that had yet to be bloodied, he dabbed it lightly against his eyes and thought, *Echoes are based only on the last few words of my key phrase.*

The results of this test, even if painful, were evident.

After a minute of heavy breathing, the pain in his eyes began to subside, but the one in his head lingered. It seemed that exposure to that seventh symphony of Visandra wasn't great for his mind.

Picking up the notepad and pen that had slipped out of his hand, he settled them in his lap and held the nib of the pen over the parchment. Adrenaline still coursed through his body, but a lingering fear had also wormed its way into his head. No, maybe it was more . . . respect rather than fear.

Every time he wrote something, an unknown echo awaited him. And while fearing such a thing had its own logic, he felt respecting it might be a better way to go about things. Could help him decide when to advance and when not to.

Shaking his head, he wondered, *Should I narrow it down and see exactly how many words are matched with echoes of the past?* For now, he believed it to be a window of three to eight words.

Nodding, he asserted, *Let's do it.*

So he thought for a while. What would be a good key phrase now that he knew this quirk? *Maybe I should try to jump in the middle of observation record and subjectivity?*

Seemed reasonable enough to get things going. So, he remembered some words from his time reading the actual book but wasn't able to get to them in his prior attempt. *What constitutes objectivity within the context of observation.*

Exactly eight words.

Except it was eight words in Celestine's language. Who knew how many that was in this runic language or the alphabet this echo was originally written in? Surely, it wasn't written in Celestine.

He had a hard time wrapping his head around all the translations that might be happening under the hood. Still, the fact that the echoes showed up as runes could mean two things.

Either the echoes were stored in the weft as translated runes, or the people involved in these conversations actually used these glyphs daily. Vern leaned toward the first option.

If a runic language were so popular, surely common historians and fundamentalists who loved to dig into the past would've found something. From his knowledge, nothing like this had ever been unearthed.

Also, it just made more sense that a grand vision like the Weft of Elyndor had its own internal representation of everyone's messages that wasn't dependent on societal constructs like language, as it would change over time.

The runes that coalesced quickly shook him out of this mental detour, and words formed. *That's a good question, young one. Objectivity? It's akin to using a fishing net to catch the wind. Envision using a quill to sculpt marble. In essence, claiming objectivity in observation is much like trying to read by candlelight during a stormy night; one believes they see the words, but in truth, they're merely guessing the letters.*

Vern's eyes twitched. *That's the worst explanation of objectivity I've read in all my time.*

That wasn't the real problem here though. It looked like it wasn't as straightforward to pinpoint back to that conversation where someone had transcribed the *Observation Record of Subjectivity.*

He rubbed his chin. *Hmm, this word limit actually makes it hard to jump to the middle of conversations.* Because he couldn't add too much context, it was easy to land in other conversations that used the same phrases.

Also, this didn't help me narrow the window of the maximum words in a key phrase at all.

He set his jaw and racked his brain on how to tackle this. In his usual manner, he flipped to a normal page on the pad, made some diagrams and connections, and quickly cobbled together a list of key phrases to test things out.

One set was simply the same sentence shortened by a word each time. Another, he planned to start with one random word and pick the next word from the echo and iterate to see if he could land on the same conversation.

Half an hour later, he sat alone in the hall, his eyes bloodshot and face pale.

Things hadn't gone as anticipated. No matter how much he tried, he couldn't tailor his key phrase to land him on the same conversations, making any direct test that could narrow down this window of maximum words somewhat pointless.

Regardless, after reading fifty or so mundane, out-of-context conversations, he believed it to be somewhere around four or five words. Anything beyond that was ignored.

There were some exceptions though. Every time he wrote *Observation record of Subjectivity*, he managed to reach that exact transcription. The seventh symphony of Visandra was also the same.

He didn't dare to actually read the echo and confirm if it was those whisper-like words. Just the fact that it demanded so much mental focus was a sign that it was the same conversation.

Setting the notepad on the chair's armrest, he massaged his temples and groaned aloud, "Here, I used to think divination was supposed to be simple. King Keras really made it look easy."

Heck, what he was doing was actually one step down the ladder compared to actual divination. After all, they divined the future, whereas he was just trying to stumble his way into the past.

However, there was a common ground between these professions. They both had to understand some bullshit and esoteric laws and find ways to somehow twist them to find out what they needed.

He closed his eyes for a second.

"Damn it, no!" He jolted awake.

He wondered if he'd somehow slept for hours and wasted so much time. He hadn't. The pounding in his head made it clear that he didn't get much sleep. Probably just some quick shut-eye.

Standing, he ran his hand through his hair and jumped for a bit before shouting, "Enough time wasted. Let's get out of here."

Sleep was already trying to claim him. If he didn't do something right now, his odds would only worsen when he started to get hungry too.

"What was I going to do before all this again?"

He smacked his fist on the other palm, "Right. Ask the nexus's spirit."

He opened his notepad and made to write that question once again, but then he suddenly stopped. An introspective gleam appeared in his eyes as he stared at nothing in particular.

Hmm, instead of simply asking the nexus, why not try to apply these echoes of the past to a practical situation like this?

He was a firm believer in balancing theory with practice. He'd spent so much mental energy trying to understand the workings of these echoes that it'd be a wasted opportunity not to put it all into practice for things he might actually want to "divine" through it in the future.

The more he thought about it, the more it made sense. His curiosity was definitely overreaching here, controlling his actions, but the balance had yet to really tip.

Also, I might just get some interesting information out of this topic, he justified.

Alright, let's see. I need to think of a key phrase that's four to five words long, which can give me the information I need.

It was interesting to think about it this way. He had to think about possible conversations his predecessors might have had and find the key phrase that might just land him in the most relevant one.

However, after a while, he stuck to something simple and scribbled, *Nexus of Elyndor.*

An echo surfaced on the paper. *Is where the banquet of gods takes place. You may not know, but I heard the feasts there serve dragon meat as appetizers.*

Vern's nostrils flared in irritation. *Who the hell even gossips about gods? Are you not afraid they'll smite you down for this? And dragons? Really? If such a creature* existed, society before duskfall would've known of it.

But then another idea crossed his mind. What if this conversation wasn't even from this era?

He didn't know. There wasn't enough context.

Not discouraged at all, he tried again. *Nexus of Elyndor representation cost.*

Prior runes dispersed into a harmless explosion, and he waited for them to come back together.

Ten seconds.

Twenty.

They didn't move.

He furrowed his brows. *Did I finally land on a key phrase that had never been used in any conversation before?*

That was unlucky.

Thinking for a while, he scribbled, *Nexus of Elyndor's teleportation.*

An echo came. *Is not what it seems. I have reasons to believe it's more complicated than that. I think it incorporates—*

The runes beyond that became fuzzy, and Vern perked his brows. *Hey, I need more! Don't cut it off like that.*

His eyes landed on a previous key phrase about the seventh symphony of Visandra, and he wondered if his fate would be the same this time, too, if he tried to focus and read what was further ahead in the echo.

He rapped the fingers of his other hand on the armrest and debated what to do. *If only I had some way of divining like Cedric did.* He wouldn't blindly believe the numbers, but it would at least help him make an informed decision.

Made him wonder if he could somehow twist his own viewpoint of balance to help him divine the danger of choices like this.

He sighed. *Well, even if it's possible, it'll have to wait. I can't figure it out right now. Maybe I can ask Cedric for some pointers.*

Not willing to waste any more time, he made up his mind. *I should read this echo. It's different from last time. This responder seems like a logical person rather than some fanatic parroting the words of a god.*

So, essentially, the context—as little he had—wasn't ominous enough to warrant not going through and reading the rest of the echo.

Taking a deep breath, he did it.

His eyes strained further, and runes came together. *Nexus of Elyndor's teleportation is not what it seems. I have reasons to believe it's more complicated than that. I think it incorporates . . . the Institute's ancient research on consciousness vir—*

Vern suddenly sat straighter, squinting harder than ever to try to read what was next. The letters blurred, twisting as if to evade his gaze. Bloodshot veins crept into the whites of his eyes, a stark contrast against the intense focus etched across his face.

His brain throbbed with the effort, the strain pushing him to the brink of endurance. However, despite his best efforts, the final word remained elusive, slipping away into the shadows of his mind, leaving him gasping in frustration and defeat.

Fuck me! Why is the cost of reading this echo so high?

The veins that had just healed themselves a while ago threatened to burst with more blood, and he had no choice but to give up. *Ugh!* He couldn't believe such a sweet secret was almost within his grasp but still just out of reach.

"Fuck," he cursed one final time before letting the pen go. Runes dispersed, and he chewed his cheek in frustration for a while before taking a deep breath and internalizing these revelations.

So . . .

There's a connection between the Institute and nexus? He frowned. He hadn't expected that. Also, the writer alludes to the Institute's research being ancient compared to nexus. Does that mean the Institute is actually older than even the nexus and Elyndor themselves?

That was . . . intriguing. Before he became an observer, his history knowledge only dated back to some nuggets from the last era—one that was supposed to be full of intellectuals who made something like the clock tower of Fulham borough and Elmhurst's bridges without being privy to fundamentals.

This was more surprising than it sounded, given this current era had gone for over seven hundred years—if the historians are to be believed—and still hadn't managed to reach even half the technical heights of the previous era.

At least until fundamentals changed the world a couple of decades ago.

The conversation he just read seemed to hint that the Institute—the founders of axioms—were even older than Nexus of Elyndor—a contraption and a castle that was most likely from a previous era itself.

Just how many eras are there? he wondered with a frown. *How old is humanity?* It was a question that he previously left for historians to waste their time to try to figure out.

Now? These questions seemed indelibly linked to observers and organizations that held terrifying knowledge and the world's secrets in their grasp.

Heck, even Lady Sylphina talked about old paths. Just how many were there? What had they tried? What were their outcomes?

What marked the end of an era?

Terribly curious, he picked up his pen as his mind conjured dozens of key phrases he could try to suss out some information about Prima's past.

Thankfully, his self-restraint stopped it just in time. Feeling the pinch, he sighed. "I first need to go back." Knowing the world's secrets would be useless if they would go with him to his grave in this ancient palace.

I've delayed it long enough.

Let's just ask the spirit first. I can always confirm with the echoes later if the answer I receive is positive. Otherwise, he might have to focus on regenerating his representation and think about how to best explore this palace.

He really was in no position to waste any more time. *I must balance my curiosity with the situation's needs,* he concluded.

So when he finally extricated himself from these runes and looked up, he couldn't believe his eyes.

That half-ring of light on the pillar he'd filled with a big chunk of his own representation was now . . . replaced by three shining rings.

"H-how?"

Chapter 77

RETURN

Vern had spent almost all his representation filling up just one-half of the bottommost ring. To fill the pillar all the way up to the third ring where it was now, he would have had to infuse a similar amount another five times.

That would have taken him more than a day, and that was only if he focused all his mind on just sparking new thoughts and regenerating his representation.

He left the notepad behind and walked to the pillar before kneeling to get a closer look at the thin rings. He furrowed his brows and monitored it closely, wondering, *How did it happen? Does the nexus have some kind of self-regeneration?*

That sounded plausible, except his eyes had drifted to the pillar from time to time during his experimentation, and he hadn't noticed a single change.

He strained and recalled his memories of the past few minutes, and this little introspection gave him a simple answer.

Whatever happened must have taken place in the last couple of minutes. He was so focused on that final echo that he'd forgotten all about his surroundings.

Conjectures ran through his mind, but he soon narrowed his eyes and turned back to the chair where the golden runes floated around his notepad.

Could it be . . . his thought trailed off.

That would make no sense, right? What did his queries and the echoes have anything to do with the representation that nexus just recovered? There was no reason to assume a link between the two except for the weird timing.

He spent a couple minutes brainstorming it and realized the other options were actually less likely than even this. No way that Rupert or any of the visionaries from before suddenly felt generous and sacrificed more representation to keep the nexus running.

Yeah, that is impossible. He bit his lip. *If only I wasn't so engrossed in the runes to miss out on such a change in my surroundings.*

Maybe I could have used my perception to keep an eye on the environment? he thought.

But he soon shook his head. His goal was to conserve his representation so he could funnel it into the nexus later. Using it to survey his surroundings when there were no enemies around would have been a waste.

"Argh, it doesn't matter." He huffed. "It's a good thing there's more energy now."

He briskly walked over to the notepad, stopped dallying, and went right back where he'd stopped. A weird thought surfaced. *I am going to ask the nexus's spirit this question, no matter what. Nothing will stop me.* He'd been interrupted so many times while trying to do this that he almost felt like some higher force was stopping him.

Shaking his head, he imagined Lady Sylphina's trace and wrote, *Is there enough representation in the nexus to send me back?*

He doubted that half a ring that he'd filled would've been enough, but with this unexpected windfall of three rings, it might just do the trick.

Luckily, nothing stopped him from contacting the spirit this time, and his note went through. A few seconds later, a bunch of lists emerged, and he quickly glanced at the proximity list. It was empty. Which made sense but also didn't because then that meant nexus's spirit wasn't located around here.

Regardless, his hand moved on its own, and the response read, *Primary reserves scant of the necessary flux. A minimum of 5 percent is imperative for secure passage.*

However, as these words emerged on the note, his eyes flickered, and he noticed that the almost full third ring suddenly depleted by a small amount.

Ah, hells, he groaned. *Even asking questions costs me representation now? What a scam.*

At least it wasn't too much, or his heart would've bled for having asked the question in the first place. After all, these rings and the "flux" they represented were his ticket out of here.

For some reason, he liked *flux* far more than *representation*.

Dismissing this as collateral damage, he focused on the main point. *So, it needs 5 percent, huh? How much is it at right now?*

Though tempted to query the nexus directly, his innate thrift urged him to figure it out on his own—which he did. Observing the pillar, he estimated it based on the height of each illuminated ring. He deduced that the entire pillar might accommodate a hundred or so similar rings.

Which meant each ring was about one percent of this flux.

Then it's currently at about 3 percent right now?

He paced around the room. According to this logic, his prior infusion amounted to only half a percent. This meant that to reach the required goal of 5 percent, he would have to regenerate his representation—no, flux—about four or five more times and infuse all of it into the nexus.

Fuck. Why is it so expensive?

Thump. He settled on the chair and assessed the new options. He could either spend more of nexus's energy and ask the spirit questions that might help him figure out more about nexus and it's workings.

Or . . . He eyed his notepad.

If his discovery of the echoes of the past related to the nexus or Institute had really somehow recharged these rings, then what if he could do that again? After all, the only cost he had to pay to peruse the echoes was his brain cells.

His own . . . uh, flux was hard to regenerate, and nexus's was even harder. The only thing he could afford to spend freely was his own mental prowess.

Well, maybe not too much, given it's been abused so many times today.

Anyway! This is my best shot for now. He didn't know if it was his curiosity speaking, but if simply finding echoes that had something to do with nexus could regenerate its reserves, then it was a crazy good deal that he'd be stupid to pass up on.

It sated his thirst for the history of observers, all the while helping him get out of here. Where would he get a better deal than that?

Having made up his mind, he cracked his neck and focused on the note once again. *Alright. Give me something about . . .* He wrote, *Elyndor.*

An echo surfaced, and it strained him a bit to read it. *Is at war with Kristswelt. Do you think we can profit off of this? I have some goods that I can't sell in the main continent.*

Interesting. So, Elyndor was like a city or country? Not just an organization of special observers? Also, what's up with the main continent? And at what point in the timeline did this even happen?

Sighing, he gave up on trying to answer these impossible questions and eyed the pillar. There was no change. The first two rings were full, while the third maintained its almost complete state—not increasing or decreasing.

He leaned forward, a thoughtful look on his face. So, just any information about Elyndor didn't trigger the infusion.

In a few seconds, he dismissed the previous echoes and wrote *Elyndor* once again.

Runes came together. *Is erupting with maddening whispers. Do not, and I repeat, do not chart your route through that place. You will lose your mind if you get close. If you really need to go west, go through—*

The words ended there.

Erupting with whispers? What exactly happened there? Also, this note somehow seemed to be from a different time than the previous one.

Regardless, it didn't increase the nexus's flux either. *Am I asking the wrong questions here? Maybe I should stick to the nexus and Institute?* He'd hoped to get to nexus using conversations about Elyndor and work his way up from there. But it looked like the conversations of people from the past didn't work like that.

So he tried something else. *Institute.*

However, the moment the echo formed, he realized how stupid he'd been to use such a common word as a key phrase.

The echo read, *Needs to refund my tuition. It's a scam, I tell you. I learned almost nothing about observation there! It's just some grumpy old monsters who don't even know the first letter about teaching.*

He was speechless.

Yeah, I need to try harder. This isn't the institute I want to know about. This echo obviously didn't do anything to nexus's reserves either. Looked like single-word key phrases weren't getting him anywhere.

That's when he remembered something that Horace—the confluence's initial speaker—had mentioned about the fate of the people from Elyndor.

Vern's hand moved before his heart could match the sudden excitement that coursed through him. This question was bound to be interesting! So, he penned, *Elyndor's assimilation by first observer.*

He waited.

To his utter delight, the runes moved. *Yes!* he cheered. *There's actually something about this in here.*

However, right when the shining symbols were about to merge and form something anew, they halted in their tracks. Almost as if stopped by some magical force, they tried to move closer but failed.

Vern's gaze sharpened. *It's not going to be cheap, huh?*

Well, it just meant the cost of reading this echo was quite high, and even without further thought, he was more than willing to pay it. He was just that curious.

So he strained his eyes, and the runes reluctantly converged.

Elyndor's assimilation by the first observer must be stopped! The cycle mustn't go on! They can't keep—

"Ah! God damn," he cried as a sharp pain rushed up his head. The pen fell sideways, and the runes dispersed without fanfare.

However, before his mind could recover from the shock and register the echo's implications, the room turned a little brighter.

Gripping his head with one hand, his gaze snapped to the base of the glassy pillar. There, the third ring, nearly complete, intensified in brightness before it surged, filling the entire circumference of the pillar.

Immediately after, a fourth ring sparked to life above it. Starting with a faint glimmer, it rapidly spread around the pillar's edge, illuminating fully in a seamless flow.

That did it!? How? Why?

But it wasn't over yet. Soon a fifth ring materialized.

Then a sixth.

And a seventh.

Vern's jaw dropped, his pain momentarily forgotten in the wake of his awe. The successive illumination of the rings filled the room with a dazzling light, each one sparking more intensely than the last. His heart raced as the reality of what was unfolding hit him—this was working, actually working!

The magic electrified his senses, propelling him onto his feet. He watched, wide-eyed and breathless, as the eighth ring blazed alive.

Just what is going on?!

Was the echo that just surfaced really that significant?

Before this attempt, he had remained somewhat skeptical despite evidence suggesting that his inquiry about the nexus and the Institute had boosted nexus's reserves from half a percent to three.

Just how the fuck did his reading old conversations top up nexus's reserves? Energy conservation was the most basic law in mechanical arts, but this chain of events blatantly defied all such principles.

So, the realization that what had happened last time was not merely a fluke but a reproducible phenomenon with some underlying rationale unnerved him deeply.

His gaze oscillated between his notepad and the pillar as the eighth ring mysteriously materialized and filled itself. He even scrutinized it with his own perception to confirm nothing was amiss.

Yet just as he was about to sink deeper into his confusion, the droning from the canopy intensified, followed by a distant, monotonous voice that said, "Flux rekindled. Proceeding with unfinished duties."

"What . . ." he blurted, but suddenly, his arms began glowing blue, and an unnatural tug pulled at his body.

"Wait. No. This . . ." he exclaimed, but the pull was merciless.

Until now, he'd been doing everything to get out of here, but now that things had actually turned out this way, he realized he didn't want to leave just yet. *I still have so much to explore here!*

He wanted to leave here on his own terms.

Panic surged through his body and he envisioned a quick burst of instability in the ground underneath him, hoping to propel himself forward as he made a mad dash toward his notepad.

If I can get my hands on the pad, I should be able to interrupt the process.

Unfortunately, the ground was too sturdy for his vision, and the blue haze dissolved his outstretched arms in an instant, whisking the rest of his body away.

"No. Stop! At least let me grab my notepad!"

What if it wasn't sent back to him because it was not on his person? That would be disastrous. It was his longest surviving notepad.

However, the nexus didn't give a damn. His vision quickly faded to black, and he lost all his faculties.

Fuck! he shouted internally, wanting to break something. That notepad had so many pages of convergence notes too. Yes, he had more of them in the original notepad Esther had gifted him, waiting for him in the hotel, but each and every one of those pages was precious!

He couldn't waste them like this.

Hah . . . Who would've expected nexus's spirit to be so diligent and remember the tasks it had to finish even after losing and getting back its flux?

Not having a body to rage with did wonders in calming him down as he perceived the oversaturated tunnel around him once again. The sight made him forget his woes for a second, and he remembered that one interesting echo.

It had talked about how this whole process wasn't teleportation but something related to consciousness instead.

It almost made him wonder if this was some esoteric vision from an ancient shade sequence. *Maybe even part of Lady Sylphina's weft?*

With a sudden gasp, Vern jolted back to awareness. A warm, comforting sensation enveloped him as the firmness of polished wood pressed reassuringly against his spine. His eyes fluttered open, blinking away the remnants of otherworldly visions.

A sense of serene familiarity settled over him in the dimly lit confines of his chamber. The rich aroma of aged mahogany filled his nostrils, a scent intimately tied to hours spent poring over his myriad studies in this very spot.

He leaned forward slightly, his hands instinctively finding the edges of the sturdy table that occupied the center of the room. Across from him, his notepad sat there—the one he thought might have been left behind.

After all, he had been perusing some notes inside it just before being swept into the confluence.

Now the room was quiet save for the soft ticking of the wall clock, its pendulum swinging with the comforting regularity of a heartbeat.

He sighed, a mix of relief and disbelief coloring his voice. "I'm finally back." And in one piece, no less. His notepad wasn't lost in some ancient meeting place of gods either!

His head still ached, but the quiet moments seemed to dull the pain. Before long, the silence brought back a flood of questions that had been pushed aside, urging him to dig deeper.

Why was everything exactly as he had left it? The unchanged setting almost convinced him that he had never left, that perhaps it was all just a figment of his imagination—a dream.

"That would suck," he murmured. Seeking some reassurance, he flipped through his notepad, the pages rustling softly. One after another, pages filled with bizarre key phrases like *Dear*, *Institute*, and *Elyndor* greeted him, and he chuckled. "Well, if that was a dream, I must still be dreaming."

Shaking his head, he snapped the notepad shut—ignoring the insistent runes— and positioned himself in front of his bed.

Without bothering to extinguish the gas lamp or take off his coat, he collapsed face first onto the bed and rationalized, "I can figure it all out tomorrow."

Sleep enveloped him almost instantly, whisking him away into the realm of genuine dreams.

"Lrd . . . ax . . . lp."

Vern shifted in his bed, his subconscious pushing the pillows against his ears to block out the noise.

"Ar . . . te . . . lnce."

Yet no matter what he did, faint whispers persisted, burrowing into his consciousness.

He couldn't tell the time, but his room shouldn't be this noisy, ever.

"Acc . . . os . . . qa . . . pr."

"Fr . . . gi . . . vo . . . es."

"Zx . . . ph . . . mst . . . w."

"Bv . . . rld . . . qs . . . ny."

Thump. He suddenly bolted upright, cold sweat dampening his forehead.

Frantically looking around, he realized the voices weren't emanating from his surroundings.

Panic surged through his foggy mind, and a singular thought took over.

"Am I losing control?"

The whispers had never been so vivid. So relentless.

Why? What did I do wrong?

"Wq . . . xr . . . lt . . . nz."

No. Stop!

He attempted to steady his breathing, repeating to himself, *Let's not panic. Let's not panic.*

"Gr . . . nk . . . ub . . . lv."

Managing to disregard the voices, he checked his thought space.

It appeared normal, surprisingly more vibrant and cohesive than usual.

He scowled. *Then what is happening?*

Wait!

A realization struck him. *These aren't whispers!*

Rather than trying to shut them out, he decided to concentrate on them—a risky move if they were indeed malevolent.

"Oh, Arbiter of Fate, the Supreme Axiom who reigns above all. I, the seventh son of Ascendant Minthra, humbly seek the honor of your protection and the privilege to serve under your mighty wings. I shall . . ."

As Vern listened to these . . . "whispers," an odd expression spread across his face.

C H A P T E R **78**

DEFAMATION AND FUTURE PLANS

Vern sat on the chair with two notepads in front of him. His eyes switched between them both while his hand moved continuously, copying over text from one onto the other.

Except the new words he wrote came out as symbols and glyphs that should make no sense to most people—including observers. Ever since becoming one himself, being unable to jot down crucial information had been gnawing at his being every step of the way.

So, now that he knew a language that was supposed to be lost to society and couldn't even be cracked without an intuitive understanding of it, the first thing he did was rewrite his notes in this language.

However, he remembered the possibility that this runic language might have been a common language at some point in time, so he went one step beyond to further obfuscate his private notes. He combined it with his former master's cipher.

It used complicated alphabet substitution, shifting, transposition, and a few other tactics.

This is a nightmare, he protested internally. Because of how this language worked, he first had to intuitively write out the whole sentence, then apply the cipher on top of it and rewrite it.

His right hand quickly made drafts, while his left took those papers and destabilized them, their structures crumbling right before his eyes. Because of how thorough instability inducement was, it did a better job destroying the originals than even fire.

Minutes turned into hours, and the sun rose outside as he continued to encrypt all the vital information while adding some things that he otherwise didn't dare to write down.

Given that he still didn't know how safe this was, he didn't go all in and kept many things to himself, but it was less restrictive than his prior setup.

A sudden raving echoed in his head, and he instantly stopped writing, focusing hard on this voice.

He'd realized after interacting with only a couple of "prayers" that they transmitted not just sounds but emotions as well as the sight. Maybe more, but these were the only ones he could process.

Most of the prayers came from random people making unsolicited introductions and one-sided wishes to the new powerful figure in the market that was Axiom.

In his mind's eye, three figures donned in pitch-black robes and hoods knelt in front of an altar with a chaotic mass of something dark, oozing with a putrid liquid sitting atop it.

Suddenly, all three knelt, and the one in the center began, his voice resonating with zeal, "Oh, great one, binder of axioms." He then produced a ceremonial dagger and, with a swift motion, drew it across his palm. Blood trickled down, dripping onto the dark mass, which absorbed it hungrily, emitting an eerie glow.

Vern jolted upright, a dark expression on his face. *What the hell are they doing?* Befuddled, he wondered, *Should I . . . stop them?* He didn't even know if he could. *Would they hear a response if I made one?*

However, his face turned grim the very next instant.

The second figure, a woman, retrieved a glass jar from her robes. She unscrewed the lid to reveal two bloodied eyes, their nerves still attached and twitching slightly. "We offer you these eyes, freshly plucked from the innocent," she said, placing them carefully on the altar. The eyes dissolved into the darkness, adding to its swirling energy.

Vern's hands clenched into fists, nails digging into his palms.

The third follower, a gaunt man with a twisted smile, held up a small, wriggling creature. Its cries were muffled by the cloth wrapped around it. "We sacrifice this newborn bloodling, a gift of pure life to feed your power," he declared, placing the bundle on the altar. The dark mass engulfed the creature—its cries silenced instantly.

Their chant grew louder, filled with fervent hope. "Grant us your strength, Oh Great Axiom, and we shall bring darkness to this world. Empower our hands to wreak havoc in your name. To bring a new balance to the ode of this wretched reality."

This went on for a few more seconds before the sight fizzled away.

A cold mask settled over Vern's features. The table before him trembled, the air around him growing thick and oppressive. The room itself seemed to pulse in rhythm with his mounting tension.

Suddenly, the shaking stopped. Silence enveloped the room, and his eyes snapped open, sharp and clear, cutting through the lingering unease.

"Someone's trying to sully Axiom's name," he concluded coldly. "Someone from the confluence."

There was no other explanation. How would these random people even know about Axiom otherwise? It hadn't even been a dozen hours since he came back from the confluence.

For a while, he sat there in silence, the scene replaying in his mind endlessly. *Blood, newborn of some unknown species, eyes of an innocent.*

His fingers drummed an erratic rhythm on the table, the muscles in his jaw tightening with each passing second. His eyes narrowed, darkening with an intensity that seemed to burn.

Without warning, he slammed his fist down, the force rattling the table. "These motherfuckers!" he snarled through gritted teeth.

He wished he could somehow tear through space and cut them down with Duality right then and there.

Should I reprimand them? It should be possible to respond to the "prayers," right? Given he was the "deity" they were praying to, his rebuke should terrify them.

Clenching and unclenching his fist, he concluded, "It won't do."

Clearly, someone was trying to paint Axiom as some kind of evil god who demanded innocent sacrifices from his worshippers. If Vern responded to these accusations carelessly, what would that do?

These people were clearly the criminal sort—going so far as to kill innocents, sacrificing lives over some vague rumor of an evil new god.

What kind of message would his reprimanding them send to the one orchestrating this?

That the so-called cosmic balancer couldn't even handle such a simple matter? That he was so benevolent he only reprimanded them but didn't stop them with his might?

Yes, maybe that could work with his theme of "balancing" mercy and punishment, but unfortunately, he had no means to punish anyone even if they ignored his warnings and continued their treachery.

Then his failure to punish and "restore the balance" would instead appear as Axiom not having the strength to back up his words or silently approving of such matters. Both of which were terrible outcomes.

What a trap! Gladly, he hadn't been impulsive. *This is fucking crazy! It hasn't even been a day, and someone's trying to shift the perception of the masses against me.* He wondered if there was some kind of backlash for that sort of thing.

What should I do about this?

After getting lost in this thought loop for a while, he let out a deep breath and concluded, *Let's not be hasty. The damage is already done. I need a better solution.*

Him stopping each of these prayers one by one wouldn't even work. The person targeting Axiom's image could just pick a different location and begin anew until this reputation preceded him and his image was tarnished for good.

Repeatedly tapping his pen on the table, he wondered, *Is this Rupert's counterattack?* He couldn't be sure, but the tactic reeked of something that man would do.

"Fuck! I know nothing about how this supernatural mysticism business works."

Whoever used this tactic knew exactly where to hit him. And it hit hard. If left unchecked, it would destabilize the influence this new variable—Axiom—could have on the world.

He tapped the pen one final time on the table and decided, *The confidentiality ritual for the Vigil Irene had talked about should be happening soon. I need to make sure I don't miss it.*

His mission in the Ironhart district gave him enough merit to participate in it, allowing him access to more texts in Vena's archive. *I hope the new array of texts will have comprehensive knowledge regarding this.*

He had to quickly find some ways to restore the balance. One obvious way would be to do good deeds like a benevolent god. Alas, he was a fake one.

"A fake one who's not going to let all his work go to waste just like this." He didn't know exactly how useful his identity as Axiom was going to be. But, he did know that it could very well be the difference between him actually achieving that status one day versus getting lost in the sands of time like most others.

As always, the root cause of all this cajoling and cautious maneuvering was the same. *Weakness.*

He looked out the window with an empty gaze and muttered, "I need to figure out my path forward." He'd delayed thinking about it for long enough.

He tore a piece of paper from his old notepad, planning on disintegrating it once he was done with it, and he wrote, *Lady Sylphina suggested going for one fundamental per shade.*

This meant he needed to shade his perception with a vision that clearly belonged to a different fundamental.

But which one?

Should there be some criteria? Was one choice better than the other? He opened the drawer, and objects within it tumbled forward. Pulling out the insight sphere from the myriad items, which mirrored his thought space, he inspected it.

The eight fundamentals are dissolution, creation, preservation, transformation, cognition, structure, force, and finally relationships.

His root goal was to find a fundamental with which he could shade his perception without risking his sanity.

However, he knew things were far more nuanced than that.

I shouldn't choose something like dissolution for now. As the name suggested, it was a fundamental most heavily tapped by Chaos fundamentalists—the people who reveled in destroying everything. But how would that react to his thought space and current visions?

After some thought, he had an interesting idea. *Hmm, what if I go for dissolution after my perception already has a vision related to creation fundamental? Their opposing nature should balance out each other, right?*

Wait, but then . . .

This led him to a frightening theory. *Is it possible that the combinations of fundamentals, if not handled in the correct order, could cause contradictions inside my thought space?* The simple thought of the whispers that such an arrangement would invite sent shivers down his spine.

That would be . . . terrifying. The whispering repository in the Vigil was a living proof of what happened to people who shaded their perception with visions that didn't mesh well with their perspective.

He took a deep breath and reasoned, *Yeah, something like dissolution would contradict my insights on structure.* After all, structure was all about order, whereas dissolution was literal chaos and destruction.

Without insights on creation to rein in the chaos that would come from the dissolution, structure might crumble before the sheer destructiveness of the potent fundamental.

I need to be careful, he decided with a resolute nod. He hadn't had another serious case of whispers overwhelming him ever since Eleonora's archive, and he wanted to keep things that way.

So, he wrote, *Dissolution is a nonoptimal choice because of lacking prerequisites and incompatibility with existing insights.*

"Then, what about creation?" Vern leaned back in his chair, mulling over the implications of choosing creation as his second shade. It was a tempting option, but he needed to be cautious. Creation, while seemingly powerful, had its own complexities that might not align well with his current position and resources.

As a fundamental, it required a deep understanding of both the intrinsic and extrinsic properties of matter and energy. It demanded not just insight but also resources and conditions conducive to generating something new.

Hmm, the resources at my hand are quite limited, and so is my time.

Creation fundamentalists, which included alchemists, were the secluded kind. Even among their already socially inept brethren, they were the worst offenders. And for good reason. Their discoveries came from thousands of repeated experiments demanding severe time commitment, stable environments, controlled variables, and nigh infinite funding and resources.

Creation is indeed potent, he thought, tapping his finger rhythmically on the edge of the insight sphere. *But it's also resource-intensive.*

He recalled the intricacies of the creation fundamental: it wasn't just about forming new things but also about understanding the essence of existence itself. The process was heavily dependent on an intimate knowledge of various fields—alchemy, mechanics, even esoteric disciplines that Vern had only started to scratch the surface of.

Moreover, he couldn't afford to spend too much time deepening his insights on creation by experimenting in this rapidly changing world. Every day was precious and had to be treated as such.

"Also, there are the resources." He was having trouble sourcing materials to fix his lumenscope, much less the ingredients he would need to delve deep into creation. *And it's not like I will be creating more mechanical constructs after shading my perception with such a thing.*

He would need materials related to mysticism, not cranksteel or the blueprints of some engine. This creation would far surpass anything mechanical and edge into the supernatural. He didn't understand even the basics of it. Forget creating something from scratch.

"Yeah, it would just be a nightmare, given my current channels and resources," he said, shaking his head. The final nail in the coffin was the fact that structure and creation weren't really the most compatible pair.

"Creation might indeed balance out dissolution in theory, but practically," Vern said aloud, "it might instead amplify the complexities I have to deal with."

He jotted down his thoughts. *Creation is not advisable for now due to resource constraints, time limitations, and environmental instability.*

Soon, he had an idea. He held the insight sphere and rotated it freely, murmuring to himself, "Each octant is neighbored by three other octants on its edges, and generally, there's a higher compatibility between the concepts within."

He turned it around to focus on the upper northwestern octant—the one belonging to structure. Its neighbors were the upper northeastern, lower northwestern, and upper southwestern octants.

He added to the paper, *So the neighbors to structure are cognition, preservation, and relationship fundamentals.*

He felt inherently repulsed by preservation because of that bastard who'd kidnapped Ari—Quentin Flowhart. Not only that, but he just didn't think preservation was his best option for the second shade. Stability inducement, to an extent, mirrored what preservation could do.

"Well, maybe not everything." Preservation might be able to stabilize more aspects of reality than just structures, but he wasn't very keen on going too far down the same path and was instead hoping to become a jack of all trades—at least early on.

Anyway, I can look into it again if nothing else works out. For now, he still had four other options to consider, with two in particular being more synergistic with structure.

After spending some time pondering each of them, he didn't find anything too egregious with any. So, he noted, *The priority list for fundamentals I'd like for my second shade: cognition, relationships, force, transformation.*

He would've preferred a vision focused on force due to his prior experience with it, but he didn't want to narrow down his options too much just yet.

Why? Because, until now, he'd ignored the biggest obstacles to shading his perception. He jotted it down too. *The resonance catalyst and the observation record.*

He'd gotten terribly lucky to have the greatest resonance catalyst at hand when he first shaded his perception—the third rune's realm, or the land of dark sun as he casually dubbed it. This was something he'd realized after learning about resonance catalysts.

He recalled the aftermath of his advancement after imprinting stability inducement. It was like he were sitting in the eye of a tornado and everything around him had been ravaged to a terrifying degree.

So much so it had attracted the attention of what very well might have been the Cryptic Constructor. Clearly, that whole space was heavily infused with insights related to structure, courtesy of it belonging to the Cryptic One.

There he'd unintentionally absorbed the surroundings, and they supplemented him with the insights required to consolidate his new vision. By basing his new work on instability inducement—something belonging to the fundamental of structure—he'd created another vision under the same fundamental.

That was to say, had he tried to create a vision of some other fundamental, he might not have succeeded at all.

"Lucky was what that was." And he knew such opportunities couldn't be sought for, only chanced upon.

However, resonance catalyst was only the second requirement. Before that, he had to answer an even more pivotal question: *Which observation record should I follow?*

Should he even follow a record not his own? Or maybe just take inspiration from them? "After all, I know how to create visions from scratch."

But he very quickly gave up on that line of thought. Stability inducement was special. He'd used another vision as the inspiration, had a space where he could test his hypotheses freely without any repercussions, and, to top it all, had a catalyst that couldn't be replicated.

Trying to make a new vision from scratch without all these factors would be nothing short of suicidal. On top of that, he was a firm believer in standing on the shoulders of giants and was against reinventing the wheel.

Hmm, it might be in my best interest to further study existing observation records and work on adapting them to my perspective of balance instead.

After all, these records were legacies of generations, and he would have to be beyond arrogant to think he could conjure better visions for all eight fundamentals than them while not even knowing the limits of what's achievable through observation.

He suddenly slapped the table, his mood turning sour. "If only I could safely return inside the third rune."

That would solve most of his problems. Right now, there was more than a fifty-fifty chance he would be greeted by that gigantic eye the moment he entered the third rune. *And that would be the end.*

No way he could escape that entity's gaze twice.

"Argh!" It felt like sitting on a coal mine in the dead of winter, unable to use the fuel because of the devil lurking inside.

He played with the pen in his hand as he pondered this problem.

"Wait!" A sudden burst of inspiration struck him.

He peered into himself. Beyond his spherical thought space, which used to stand in an empty void, stars now twinkled. These were the nodes representing all the prayers he'd received until now.

He quickly focused on them individually and soon found what he sought—Hensen's prayer.

"I should reach out to him."

CHAPTER 79

IT'S POSSIBLE!

Vern focused on the star that represented Hensen's prayer. It was . . . fading. Not imminently, but he was sure that it was somehow weaker than yesterday.

Filing away this detail for later, he let the star's brilliance wash over him, and a scene played out. Hensen sat there with a top hat on his lap, his eyes closed and hands clasped, murmuring, "Oh, Lord Axiom . . ."

Vern involuntarily glazed over the pretentious preamble, instead fixating on the details of the environment around Hensen. Or lack thereof.

He knew this was a scene from the nexus, but the visuals of the prayer made it impossible to figure that out. Everything other than Hensen and his immediate surroundings was hazy. Another interesting detail which he left for himself to analyze later.

Hensen's seemingly sane voice continued, "Grant me insight to reconquer the third rune . . . For this burden is beyond mine talents and threatens mine very being. Guide me through its tempest . . ."

Before even attempting to try to see if he could respond to this prayer, Vern folded his arms and replayed it again and again, analyzing each and every one of the words carefully.

So, he wants Axiom's help in reconquering the third rune. Not conquering it for the first time? This threw Vern for a loop. Didn't this mean that Hensen had just recently lost control of the rune and had been proficient in its use previously?

"Could it be . . ."

It was a bit presumptuous of him, but he could only think of one event that had the capability to mess with the workings of something in the order of the third rune.

"Duskfall of sorrows . . ."

And what happened beyond time? he added in his mind. *Surely, this has to be a result of him sharing the derivative rune with me.* Then what exactly went wrong with his counterpart?

A sense of unease enveloped Vern as he explored the possibilities and their repercussions. Hensen's warning at Eleonora's archive still rang in his mind to this day. The man had made it more than clear that he would chase Vern to the ends of the world.

And this is the side effect of that?

He even wondered if the Hensen from beyond time wanted things to play out exactly like this. Where only an inconvenience as massive as the current one would force Hensen, who didn't know about Vern's derivative rune, to do everything to chase after this mysterious leech.

Vern couldn't help but shudder at the ruthlessness of the man from that night. This further solidified the seriousness of the death sentence that was waiting for him if Hensen managed to track him down.

Seconds turned into minutes, and he spent all of them analyzing this situation from many angles.

Soon, he concluded, "I shouldn't contact him without a proper plan."

Coming in contact with Hensen was a risky business no matter what. However, not doing so was even worse. Who knew how far Hensen had reached in tracking him down? What if the madman was waiting for Vern to slip up just one more time?

If he wanted to safely use the third rune ever again—and not just as a last resort suicide ground—then he needed to know. Know everything there was about this rune in his head.

It reminded him of the classic saying, which he spoke aloud, "Keep your friends close and your enemies closer."

That's exactly what I need to do. Because Hensen wasn't the only threat. Even if he decided not to touch the third rune and kept Hensen at bay in that fashion, a larger threat loomed like a guillotine over his head.

The Cryptic Constructor.

He remembered Hensen's words: *Every time you make use of this rune, I will sense it . . . and even if you don't use it, once the Cryptic Constructor descends, I will be alerted.*

So not doing anything wasn't an option either. He had no plans of letting the noose tighten around him to the point where Hensen could just waltz into his backyard leisurely and end him on a whim.

I have to sabotage and misdirect Hensen's search, all the while getting more information on how to properly use the rune out of him.

He rubbed his chin and reasoned, *Given that Hensen's the one who reached out first, I already have the upper hand in this interaction. To top that off, Axiom shouldn't have the same concerns as me—a weak first-shade observer.*

If he laid his cards right, Vern could very well control the narrative of how it all played out.

But that's where things got tricky. He couldn't just blindly ask Hensen to reveal everything about his plans and progress in solving the rune's anomalous behavior. He didn't forget. Even though Hensen came off as insane, a sharp and shrewd mind sat behind that facade, calculating everything in terms of personal benefit.

He had no plans of shortchanging him. Not again. Letting down his guard while pretending to be Axiom was the worst mistake he could make on his path as an observer. *Well, except maybe straight up losing control.* He had no plans of letting either of those cases come to pass.

Not just that, there was also a large organization behind Hensen—the Aetheric Collective—something Esther had clued him in on. They surely had vested interest in Hensen's rune, and him being unable to use it meant that everyone in there wanted the culprit of this anomaly—Vern—caught as soon as possible.

"Hmm, this is a great opportunity, as well as a terrible risk."

This reminded him of what Rupert suggested. For Vern—no, Axiom—to act as an information exchange hub for the whole world.

It had been on his mind ever since, and this thought experiment on how to use his position to get what he wanted out of Hensen only made him aware of how stupidly powerful such a position would be.

"If handled right," he murmured.

But how to handle it right? That "right" was doing too much of the heavy lifting here. He had some confidence in keeping up the charade due to his unique knowledge since it could help him pretend to be more insightful than he was, but that would only take him so far.

There were far too many gaps in his understanding of the world and observers, especially about higher shades. He would be beyond doomed if someone asked him things that were otherwise considered common knowledge for that strength.

He probably didn't know many things that even low-shade observers should know, much less insights that eternas and whatnot should have. *I have to be very deliberate in how I shape this persona when interacting with others.*

Ugh, if only I always had a voluntary helper like Keras. The man had done wonders to sell his image to the whole crowd during the confluence.

Even beyond that, he remembered others. There was someone in the fourth row alongside Hensen who had laughed at everyone without fear of any consequences, reducing the pressure he had to face while ascending.

He concluded something from all this experience from the confluence. *The more varied the opinions of the audience, the wilder their conjectures. And the wilder their conjectures, the more bullshit I can get away with.*

He narrowed his eyes and jotted down, *Until Axiom's image is solidified or I have the strength to back it up, I'll need to restrict myself to interactions that involve multiple people with starkly contrasting opinions.*

He nodded. It would be even better if they didn't know each other, as that would force some of their thoughts to be focused on being wary of one another rather than scrutinizing Axiom's responses.

Hmm, what else should happen in an ideal situation? he thought, staring at nothing in particular. Many ideas flashed through his mind. Ideas he could potentially use to further Axiom's image as this mysterious being of immense power.

However, after a bit, he chuckled. "But how?"

As far as he knew, a convergence note couldn't facilitate simultaneous communication between many people. It connected two parties, not ten.

However, it wasn't that big of a bottleneck here. He squinted and remembered the plethora of things he'd read during his studies and quickly realized that this was already a solved problem.

Hmm, I could just receive notes from multiple people and rebroadcast to all involved parties with the senders' names attached.

Steamscript relay stations already did something of the sort to broadcast internal instructions around the empire. They just didn't function in real time and had an overnight waiting period.

However, he was miffed by the very thought of such an arrangement. It felt . . . mundane? Something that didn't suit the majestic image of Axiom.

Surely, many others were already making use of such a tactic to avoid sharing their traces with too many people. Vern even wondered if being such a middleman was a sought-after job.

Yeah, I don't think this is the right setup for my use case. It would make Axiom seem like a second-rate charlatan. He sighed. *I might be better off just interacting with prayers rather than that.*

At least that would lend an air of the divine to everything he said. However, he didn't even know if he could respond to a single prayer, much less bring more than one together.

He made two columns on paper, one for prayers and one for convergence notes, and penned down each of their pros and cons. Both had their advantages and disadvantages.

Unfortunately for him, both missed something crucial he needed to portray Axiom the way he'd envisioned. He needed a better balance.

Annoyed by the awkward limitations of both options, he stood and began pacing. That usually helped untangle his convoluted thought process.

"Wait!" He stopped and shouted, "Of course!" His eyes widened, and a spark of excitement ignited within them. He'd have begun pacing sooner if he knew things would click like that.

He rushed to the table, retrieved the new notepad from the mess, and quickly flipped to a page that had a plethora of golden runes floating around it—buzzing for some reason he was too occupied to consider.

Imagining Lady Sylphina's trace, he wrote, *How can I invite observers to the nexus?*

If the Estefans could do it, surely there had to be a way to make this work, right? And who better to ask than the spirit of nexus itself? It would cost the nexus some flux, but it would be worth it.

With bated breath, he waited for the golden runes to play their part as they channeled themselves into some random list.

In a bit, a shiver coursed through his mind, and he let the sensation guide his hand. The response emerged in elegant, flowing script, completely unlike the one from yesterday. *Ah, kind dreamer. Is that . . . you? Do you . . . wish to summon those from beyond?* Then there was a pause.

Vern looked at the words, befuddled. *Kind dreamer? This . . . isn't like the responses I received from the spirit yesterday. There was a hint of . . . personality behind them. Did something change?*

Yet before he could read more into it, his hand moved again *Mm-hmm, to draw chosen ones from beyond our home and bridge realms, you must pay the price to call forth the grand archivist. Through sacrifice and intention, the archivist will heed your call and discern those worthy from the echoes of existence. However . . .*

The notion made him grip the pen tighter as it wrote, *Beware, what you ask for, kind dreamer. The archivist knows all, but the price . . .*

The sensation ended there.

His brows furrowed as he set aside the unexpected tone behind the words for a moment and considered the answer. It was a little . . . unexpected. *Grand archivist? Sacrifice and intention?*

It almost sounds like this grand archivist determines the trace of people who need to be invited based on the organizer's intention.

Dots began connecting in his head, and he reasoned, *Wait. Is this how the Estefans managed to target every "visionary" who had crossed some threshold in loosening their shackles of subjectivity?*

That sounded plausible. Though he was sure they'd learned the details through a completely different method. Maybe even some kind of vague divination or from some records of the past. After all, he was directly communicating with Lady Sylphina's trace. No one even knew about her existence, much less had a way to contact her.

This made him wonder, *Who is this really on the other end?* It surely wasn't the Sylphina he'd met in the void, right? Her Eminence's mannerisms were far removed from . . . this.

Shaking his head, he refocused. Surely, it all had something to do with his actions yesterday. Regardless, whoever it was, they were far better than a spirit with no intelligence. He might be able to get a real answer to this crucial question.

So he gathered his thoughts and wrote, *Then do I still need to invoke the archivist if I already know the traces of those whom I wish to invite?*

He waited for a while, and his hand moved, *Kind dreamer, you already have their flux's signature? You sure learn . . . fast.*

Then a pause.

Do you . . . wish to summon your guests right now? There's enough flux to invite and attend to . . . two people.

Vern's heart raced as he reread the whole conversation, and the implications settled over him. A grin spread across his face, eyes wide with excitement. Unable to contain his elation, he threw his fist up in the air as his voice echoed in the room, "It's possible!"

This was . . . game-changing!

It altered the very scope of the possibilities! Until now, he'd been thinking of what he could do in terms of basic note exchange or words and the kind of impressions he could give off there to get what he wanted.

But this?

Nexus was like a home ground where he got to set the rules. Its unique restrictions were a godsend to a phony pretender like him. They'd already shown their usefulness during the confluence, where he was up against dozens of naysayers. Now, however, he could even control who was present and who wasn't . . .

He paced around the room, unable to control his excitement. *Fuck fuck fuck. This is too big!*

This actually went beyond just Hensen. It could be a means to something . . . greater. *Yes! I . . . I might even be able to counter the scheme against Axiom's image and be proactive about fixing it!*

His persona as Axiom was like a performer with great potential, but it was limited by his lacking overworld knowledge and meager means. Now, however, he had a stage.

A stage where he could set up the props and the characters, as well as the audience. It was a stage where he could . . .

Suddenly, footsteps closed in on his door and . . . *Knock knock.*

Chapter 80

MAYBE

Someone was at the door. "Ah, crack my cogs," he murmured, eyeing the mess on the table. *I haven't even replied to my correspondent yet.* Given that their responses seemed so . . . human, it'd be rude to leave them hanging.

"A minute, please," he shouted to his visitor through the door and rushed over to the table, penning a quick reply to the last note he'd received. *My apologies for the delay. But no, I don't wish to summon anyone right now. Thanks for your help. I shall get back to you regarding this later.*

He had a lot more thinking to do before committing to anything.

He leaned over and opened the window with one hand, fully extending it and disintegrating the papers that had learned far too much, their white ash scattering in the wind one by one.

Soon, his mind jolted, and the pen moved. *Mm-hmm, I await your instructions. Farewell, kind dreamer.*

Vern was stumped by the opposite party's simple yet . . . kind mannerisms. They felt . . . mechanical? No, maybe that wasn't the right word. He just couldn't put his finger on it.

He didn't have the mind to overthink their words, but they assigned a very specific role to Vern and themselves in this conversation.

Roles that had more depth to them than should have existed, given he was just some random bum who started giving them orders out of the blue yesterday.

Knock knock. "Master Vern, this is Beaumont. I have some important mail for you."

Damn. He'd let himself get lost in the thoughts once again. Shaking his head, he eyed his room one more time, and when he didn't find anything suspicious or culpable, he jogged toward the door and opened it.

Ka-cha.

Beaumont stood in front of him, wearing his perfectly tailored suit. One hand behind his back, he bowed and spoke, "Good morning, Master Vern."

Vern didn't let the butler one-up him in terms of gentlemanly etiquette and bowed back. "Good morning, Beaumont. How can I help you?"

Somewhat of a bitter smile peeked through the butler's otherwise stiff face marred with laugh lines, and he said, "My apologies for disturbing you so early in the morning, but I have some urgent letters for you. A policeman came looking for you a few days ago. Frustrated by your absence, he insisted I deliver this to you at the earliest."

Vern wondered, *Policeman, huh? Is it that guy? The one who gave me the weapon permit?*

Beaumont opened the binder in his other hand and pulled out a few envelopes. Vern received them and quickly checked the names of their senders. There were three.

One was from Oberon Derleth. *Ah, yes. It's him.* It even had the police's seal on it as well as their menacing brown parchment. Second was from . . . Von Industries. *Not Miss Cera, huh?* Then the final letter was from . . . Hotel Inkwell?

Vern isolated the last envelope and looked up at Beaumont, puzzled.

A businesslike expression covered the butler's face as he said, "This is from Lord Kai, the hotel's owner. In my weekly report, when I mentioned that one of our guests—a fundamentalist—had failed to check in for a while, and . . . uh . . ."

Beaumont grew hesitant, and Vern waited patiently for the man to find his words. Soon, he coughed lightly, "Ahem." Then he continued, "I . . . also had to report that you hadn't paid the suite's rent for over a week."

Ah . . . Vern closed his eyes and facepalmed, disappointed in himself.

What if they'd thrown out my luggage? Sold it? If nothing else, just the loss of the original convergence note would have been a disastrous one. All for . . . what? He didn't even have much use for all the money sitting in his wallet. At least not right now.

Before Beaumont could even finish his explanation, Vern shook his head and interjected in an apologetic tone, "That was negligence on my part, Beaumont. Can you tell me how much I owe you?" He returned inside the room and made for his coat, leaving the letters on the display rack.

He pulled out his wallet and asked, "Actually, I'd like to pay in advance for the whole month. How much would the total be?"

However, when he turned back around, Beaumont shook his head with a light smile. "You don't have to pay anything, Master Vern. Lord Kai has agreed to disregard your past dues and is willing to offer you a great discount in the future. Assuming you don't find his proposed arrangement disagreeable."

Vern stopped. "Arrangement?"

Beaumont nodded, gesturing toward the letter.

Vern squinted and grabbed the pocketknife from his desk. Holding the wax-sealed envelope with some noble family's insignia on it, he expertly sliced away the seal and pulled out the contents.

Beaumont stood there patiently, waiting for Vern to finish reading the letter inside.

Vern quickly skimmed through it. It wasn't a fully personalized letter but more of a template commission advertisement with a couple of extra lines tacked onto its end.

It was quite a normal job. The employer, Kai Egrass, wanted someone to help set up . . . mechanical traps and security measures in his basement. Apparently, they were having a hard time finding matter experts.

Vern wasn't one either, but there was no need for him to be because the listed devices were simple to work with. He'd heard about at least a couple of them and knew the rest. Simple trip wires and sirens—nothing too complicated. Which made him lose interest in it all.

He didn't really need money right now. His expenses were next to nothing now that he didn't even pay Ari's tuition.

Ahh. I don't think it's worth my time.

Surely, they can find another person for this job. He eyed Beaumont from his periphery. The man had an expectant look on his face. *Ugh. Did he oversell me in front of his boss or something?*

That would suck.

Vern began to look for good excuses to refuse this proposal while not coming off as ungrateful. After all, the staff had gone above and beyond by not touching his personal property when they had all the right to do so. And he didn't want to repay them by being a sardine about it.

However, that's when he reached the final few lines of the letter written in ink rather than typed like the rest of the commission and noticed something interesting. It read, *I will be happy to disregard all the dues and discount your stay just for that. However, if you have the skills to create a truly door-free sanctuary in my basement, you can ask for anything in the Egrass family's power.*

Vern wondered, *A door-free sanctuary? Why? What's wrong with doors?*

It piqued his curiosity. So he stopped looking for excuses to avoid this job and asked, "Can you tell me more about this arrangement? What is this . . . door-free sanctuary all about?"

Beaumont looked unsure for a second, but then he seemed to come to a conclusion and answered, "Umm, from my understanding of things, Lord Kai has grown a little . . . paranoid. I don't know all the details, but he appears to have a vivid fear of doors. It could be . . . related."

Vern raised his eyebrows. *Could it have something to do with pollution? Or maybe these are the side effects of some vision?*

Did that mean this Kai person was an observer?

Hmm, maybe not. Anyway, it might be worth looking into.

Vern decided to first ask De Flanc or Irene about his schedule before committing to anything else.

Done reading the whole letter, he folded it back and shoved it into the envelope before replying to Beaumont, "I can't guarantee anything, but I shouldn't have much trouble finishing up the first part of the job. For the second part, I'll need to meet the employer and figure out the details. However, I'll need to make some inquiries before I can give you a date."

Beaumont nodded after a bit and bowed. "I shall relay your decision to Lord Kai. If you'd like to know anything else about Master or this job, don't hesitate to ask me."

Vern chuckled. "I'll take you up on that offer, then. Please fill me in when I'm having breakfast."

Beaumont suddenly became alert as if reminded of his duties. He turned around. "Ah, see you later then, Master Vern. I need to check if things are going well down in the kitchen."

Vern smiled and closed the door only immediately to hear another reminder from Beaumont. "Please don't forget about the letter from the policeman. It's . . . hard for us to handle someone of their station."

He sighed. It seemed Beaumont had lost faith in his memory. Shaking his head, he replied, "Will do."

And he indeed did just that. He brought both the unopened envelopes and his new notepad to the bed and fell into the den of pillows before finessing the wax seals on the police letter.

For the one from Von Industries, he tore the envelope from its right edge. Apparently, they were the only ones who knew to use the latest methods of letter-sealing in all of Elmhurst. It was from someone named Alistair.

Not Cera, sadly. He hadn't talked to her in such a long while.

However, at that moment, his perception, which he'd recently begun to passively observe his room with, shifted abruptly.

He became tense, and his head snapped toward the anomaly that . . . flew into his room from the window.

All his senses heightened at that moment, and his eyes each blazed with a white ring as they homed in on the culprit, ready to end this impending conflict before it could begin.

However, when his mind fully registered what had entered the room, he was dumbstruck.

A paper plane, folded with great finesse, glided into the room in a gentle arc and slowly began to crash in circles atop his desk. Vern continued to watch the spectacle with vigilance.

The moment it hit the wooden desk, it unfurled, all its neat folds giving way to remarkable flatness, displaying an array of words.

Vern didn't make a move toward this unexpected delivery and continued to monitor it with his perception for a while.

When nothing happened after a few minutes, he got up, grabbed the vapor blaster from the rack—Duality was farther—and inched closer to his desk.

Gun cocked and aimed at the paper, he slowly reached a point where his eyes could comprehend the words on the unfurled page.

Important information for: Vern.
Today's task: Whispering repository—second shift.
Today's news: There's a sale at Selena's Emporium! Come check out our new armor and weapons!/

Upcoming events: Confidentiality ritual for newcomers.
(Are you short on contribution points to apply for this ritual? Contact us today to purchase exclusive tips and tricks on how to contribute to the Vigil! Fifty percent discount for new customers!)

~Thank you for flying with Selena Aviation Services. Tips appreciated and can be left inside this paper once you're done reading. Make sure to fold it back up and give it a good head start toward the west.

Vern's eyes twitched with every word that he read. Something inside him urged him to aim that gun at his head and pull the trigger.

After a bit, he relaxed his grip on the gun and massaged his forehead. He remembered hearing something about this from Ambrose a while ago. There was someone in Vigil who had a fleet of paper avians, which they used for scouting purposes.

He didn't know they had . . . expanded their business.

Still, what the hell kind of mission briefing was this? The sender barely used five words to provide relevant information, while the rest was just . . . advertisements. They didn't even elaborate on the timing of this "second shift."

Not sure whether to laugh or cry at his own paranoia stemming from this whole ordeal, he decided to take it all in stride and pulled out a crown from his wallet. Placing it in the middle of the paper, he folded it back into a crude plane.

He had no clue how this light paper plane would ensure the bill didn't fly out of it, but that wasn't his concern. *It is surely the aviation agency's fault if they lost the goods in transportation.*

Huffing, he leaned out the window and gave his arm a good swing, and to his surprise, the little plane floated higher and higher instead of falling to its demise as gravity should have forced it to.

The absurdity of this whole charade wasn't lost to him, but he had too much on his mind.

His search for observation records that might suit him.

His image as Axiom and how to best make use of his current advantages and turn them into even bigger ones.

Then there were the echoes of the past, which he'd barely scratched the surface of.

To top it all off, he had three different requests from influential parties that asked him to make use of his fundamentalist skills.

Now he even had to rush to Vigil for this "second shift," which started at lady knows what time.

To his chagrin, a raving voice abruptly echoed in his mind. He grew alert, only to become annoyed in the next instant. It was some fop asking Lord Axiom to bless him to win over his beloved in the battle of the century—whatever that meant.

Is this what gods have to deal with every day? he couldn't help but sigh.

"One step at a time," he reasoned and pumped himself up. "I got this!"

Taking deep breaths, he checked if the bathroom had water—it did. So, he picked out his outfit. It was going to be a long day. He could already feel it.

Hrrrr.

Instantly, his mind buzzed—someone was sending him a note.

"What's wrong with the world today?" he groaned. *That's five different ways that people have tried to communicate with me within a few minutes.*

First Beaumont physically, then three people with letters, then Selena with her "aviation agency," then the fop's prayer, and finally this—a note. Was he always such a busybody? The resolve he'd just made came crumbling down, and he felt like snuggling back into the blanket he'd left too early because of last night's jump scare.

After glaring at everything for a few seconds, he sighed and walked over to his notepad. Without any more drama, he let the notion in his head guide his hand. The words read, *Hello, Vern.*

He squinted. This was a familiar first message. Suspiciously familiar.

She's trying to get back at me, huh? The last time he'd initiated the conversation, he hadn't known to sign off on his first message. Now, she was intentionally skipping it. To mess with him.

Bring it on. He accepted the challenge. Given this is how she started, she was surely in a good mood. To recreate the events from the last time, he decided to ignore her—for now.

He went and took a bath, donned his outfit for the day, actually combed his hair to feel fresher, and filled his pockets with all his gear before finally strapping Duality to his back.

Before he knew it, the clock tower outside chimed eight times. "Great!" he exclaimed. *It's been more than thirty minutes since her first note.*

He took this chance to eye his room one final time. The early morning light filtered through the curtains, casting a warm, golden hue across the room. The familiar scent of his belongings mixed with the fresh, cool air, creating a sense of comfort and nostalgia.

Finding nothing amiss, he grabbed the final item—the notepad.

He opened it in his right palm while the other held the pen. His lips curled into a cheeky grin, and he imagined Esther's trace before his pen flowed and mimicked her response from that day, writing, *Who is it?*

He didn't hold his breath for her reply and locked the door behind him with a chuckle.

Stepping out beneath the vast transparent canopy of the hotel, he couldn't help but look up at the barely visible gash in the sky.

He raised his hand to block out the sun and smiled, thinking, *Maybe, just maybe, I'm not as insignificant as I thought.*

EPILOGUE

Pointing at another misguided and ignorant sheep in the herd that lived in this unnecessarily gaudy hotel, Walter explained, "In her grand design, an individual like him"—then he turned his finger at Elias—"like you"—then finally at himself—"like me, has no significance. Our lives and their trajectories do not matter."

Then in a severe voice that didn't leave room for even a shred of doubt, he guided his beloved project and said, "What matters is the final direction of truth and falseness. Good and evil. Life and death. Virtue and sin. What matters is that her design will bring forth the most positive direction of all."

Letting his words hang in the air for a bit, he patted Elias's shoulder before declaring with a proud smile, "And you, my boy, are the living proof of her justice."

Elias, as tall as Walter and draped in a sleek white shirt and formfitting blue jacket, descended the stairs with a reticence unsuited for a child his age. Seventeen was supposed to be the spring of life, after all.

His chestnut brown hair parted neatly down the middle framed his dark brown almond-shaped eyes, slightly upturned at the corners, giving him a keen, inquisitive look.

The kid listened in with a quiet focus that, at times like this, frustrated Walter. How was he supposed to guide the kid if he gave him no feedback—no reaction? Yes, the boy no longer was a sheep that still needed shepherding, but even the sharpest of knives had to be guided with a steady hand.

He was that hand. He was the hand that created this . . . reaper. The very hand that would wield this reaper's scythe by proxy as his own and bring this city into Seraphine's grand design.

As an observer of shepherd pathway, there was no one better to control this walking god of death. One that was growing stronger by the day.

"Who must I punish today?" asked Elias, his eyes shining with purpose.

Good. Walter nodded to himself. *This is how you should be.* Those eyes told him all he wanted to know. The boy had come a long way in such a short time.

From a failed experiment of Seraphine's angels to forming such a terrifying and disruptive viewpoint. From a boy who shook and trembled for days after punishing a vile criminal to craving the next convict first thing in the morning.

He's come a long way. Walter smirked. Reaching into his breast pocket, he pulled out the photograph of the next target and passed it to Elias.

It depicted a man sitting on a lavish chair with a cane in his hand. The man had soft features that didn't suit his noble station. However, his work was absolutely vile.

The man was a staunch atheist who actively obstructed religious preaching, wishing to enforce fines and jail time as punishment for those who indulged in religion. As a shepherd whose very job and purpose in life was to show people the path to Seraphine's grand design, such a man was Walter's biggest enemy and had to be dealt with swiftly.

After a few seconds, Walter began, "This is Simon Razus, a villain of uncanny proportions. In the mere few weeks after duskfall, he's set up a trafficking racket that is kidnapping young men and women from the outer districts who lost their families to the tragedy, and he has drawn them in with promises of jobs, food, and shelter."

A frown began to surface on Elias's face, but Walter wasn't satisfied with it. *Such a heinous crime, and the kid's only slightly perturbed.*

Narrowing his eyes, he continued the briefing. "Once in his den of sin, he alters them using shapeshifting visions of disgusting observers to meet the demands of his twisted and perverted clients."

Elias showed little to no reaction.

Walter wanted something. So, he let his revulsion emerge on his face as he played one of his hidden cards. "That's not all. He has exceeded the height of depravity. He has created a disturbing . . . product. One where he forcefully enlightens the victims, then makes them lose control."

Elias suddenly stopped in his tracks.

Walter smiled internally but added in a grim voice, "And then he sells these mentally broken individuals to the sick fucks in the inner city."

Well, this one was actually true. When he first learned of it, even his blood had run cold. Except he didn't know who the real perpetrator was.

Well, Mr. Razus will have to take the blame for now.

Walter and Elias stood in silence at the foot of the staircase as the sheep he'd already herded passed all around them, avoiding the pair unintentionally.

This was his doing. This was the reason he'd been speaking about all these events so freely. No one in this hotel really noticed them.

To them, he and Elias didn't even exist. After that first day, where he'd managed to force Elias to pass judgment, he'd realized that they were going to stay at this hotel for a long time.

So he had gone out of his way to mentally erase himself and Elias from every tenant's mind. There were a couple of observers in the mix, but all were first-shade younglings, unable to resist his mental suggestions.

They could have chosen a more . . . isolated place, but the clock tower outside was important for their plans, and so was the touch of society.

Well, the aromatic Southville coffee they served here was one of the reasons too.

On top of that, Elias was a quiet kid. He needed to be around society to keep his moral compass calibrated and not get his insights twisted in the wrong direction. Prolonged isolation would essentially doom his gift into nothingness.

After a bit, Elias turned back toward Walter and replied with a single word, "Evidence."

Walter felt like gnashing his teeth. Just how many times had they had this exact same conversation? Was his word not enough? Why did the kid feel the need to outright distrust him like this? Hadn't he proved himself enough times?

Every waking second since he sneaked Elias out of Citadel had been spent caring for his needs and wants. Then why was there still a need for providing evidence?

Walter sighed. Regardless, he wasn't one to slack. Like all the other times, he'd set up and gathered all the evidence before even bringing up a new case to Elias. This was how he guided the knife for now. Surely, the kid would come around one day or another and stop asking for evidence.

With a flourish of his hands, he pulled out an envelope from his inner pocket and handed the whole thing to Elias. The kid—well, he wasn't really young enough to be a kid, but Walter couldn't not see him as one, given all he'd experienced living with him. So, yes, the kid gripped the envelope tightly, his eyes burning with a silent fury as he walked out of the hotel without even bidding Walter farewell.

He shook his head and murmured to himself, "You'll come to appreciate it one day." Walking toward the bar, he rapped on the counter, his eyes shining a murky green.

The butler cleaning the glasses suddenly became aware of Walter's presence and asked with a confused look, "How can I help you?"

Walter suggested, "Make me a Southville coffee and send breakfast for two to room 319."

The butler hemmed and hawed for a couple of seconds before he got to work without any more questions. Walter had this whole place locked down under his mental suggestions, and no one was any the wiser.

Soon, the butler brought the piping hot coffee in a porcelain cup and a saucer, which Walter took with him back to their room as he sipped and enjoyed the aromatic brew.

Oh, well. One step closer to her grand design, he thought on his way back.

He entered their room, closed the curtains, and placed his cup on the table before opening its drawer and pulling up the false bottom. Inside sat his prized possession—a single page scribbled with tiny words.

Recently, the Marchionists—the biggest underground merchants he knew of— uncovered an ancient artifact that solved a very important problem: the problem of communication.

Convergence notes had existed since forever, but their rarity made them a terrible bargain. However, this artifact changed that. Using its unique methods, they found ways to unlink the pages of a convergence note from one another.

This meant that each page of the note could have its own separate owner and wasn't bound to a single observer. This changed the name of the game completely. One could understand the rarity of these notes by how even he, who was handling such an important matter, wasn't provided with one.

Until recently, that is.

Now that each page could work on its own, suddenly, the impossible had become possible, and he didn't need to travel eight districts to communicate with the angels back in Citadel anymore.

Or, well, their proxies. No one but Seraphine herself knew of her angels' traces.

Shaking his head, he sat down by the table. He sipped his coffee with one hand while the other sent a note to his superior's proxy. After all, he had to report when Elias wasn't here. The kid might be quiet, but he was observant, and it would be a rookie mistake on Walter's end to talk about confidential matters like these in front of him.

He wrote, *Did you know? Gods of life hate apples.*

This was a preestablished passcode between him and the angel's proxy. Hopefully, the poor thing hadn't been sabotaged or disposed of. That would mean he would be without contact with Citadel for at least another week.

Fortunately, nothing of the sort happened, and soon came a reply, which he wrote down in the tiniest of handwriting to save on the space, *Greetings, Shepherd Walter. I am requesting an audience with the dusk angel right now. Please wait a while.*

Walter smiled and took another sip of his coffee. *Everything according to plan.*

Who knew? If he really managed to bring Elmhurst down to its knees, his meteoric ascension to fame in the Citadel was all but guaranteed.

Soon his hands moved once again. *Report, Walter.*

Walter suddenly grew nervous as he set down his coffee cup and sat straighter before writing back in the most formal script, *Greetings, dusk angel. The project is progressing well. Another medium-priority target should be eliminated within a few minutes.*

Passable. How is the child of death faring?

Walter thought, *Always straight to the point.*

He replied, *Under my guidance, he has grown by leaps and bounds. Recently, he managed to instantly end a third-shade necromancer. As things stand, his viewpoint breaks all norms of progression and can bring the observer society down to its knees if handled carefully.*

Walter wrote that from the depths of his heart. Given overwhelmingly incriminating evidence against a target, the kid was one scary bastard. Recently, he'd instantly killed someone two shades above him! There was no struggle. No contest. No back and forth. Just death.

Walter had even gone and collected the perceptual artifact borne out of that necromancer's corpse. Unfortunately, he had to sell it right away, or the kid might have decided to kill him too.

Suddenly, his hand moved. *Don't waste my time with unnecessary embellishments. How long before he ascends to the second shade?*

Walter chewed his words for a second before penning, *I believe that he's all but understood the essence of his current shade. Regardless, the ascension is bound to be a tough one, given how he's walking down a condensed shade sequence. However, worry not, my seraphic lord. I have already arranged for the proper circumstances and resonance catalysts to boost his chances.*

Walter made sure his hands didn't tremble as he wrote these words. This was the biggest roadblock in his plans, and if the angel got wind of how he'd already attempted to push Elias over the edge a couple of times and failed, he might just get replaced.

Under his guidance, the kid had done everything noted in the observation record. In theory, he should be able to ascend any moment, but progress as an observer was a fickle thing, especially for these rare sequences that could only be followed by those with very specific mindsets—like Elias.

For Elias, though, it was even worse. The observation record he followed only had insights from two predecessors, and just because something worked for them didn't mean it would apply to a newcomer like him too. After all, even though Elias imprinted the same visions in his thought space as his predecessors, their constructs of isolation were bound to be vastly dissimilar.

So dissimilar that the record became more of a suggestion rather than a doctrine to be followed.

The kid had even come up with his own tenets to better play as a judge, but it just wasn't working out. With past records, his guidance, valuable catalysts as these, the kid should have long been ready to advance.

Yet, he wasn't.

Unfortunately, Walter was forbidden from peeking into Elias's head, even if for good reasons. Someone who could shade their perception with a condensed sequence had to be dealing with whispers and demons that Walter didn't even dare imagine.

Such was the terror of condensed shade sequences. These paths ended early for a reason. This sequence was gifted directly to the dusk angel by Her Eminence Seraphine, and even then, it ended at the third shade.

Why did it not go any higher? Well, Walter's guess was that even the everflux was scared of such a viewpoint, and the providence of the world itself was against it becoming even more potent.

Given that the requirements were satisfied in the first shade alone, the user could effortlessly annihilate an average third-shade observer. In the second shade, they could bring to heel observers up to the fifth shade. Then, finally, the third was fabled to be able to grant even eternas and angels instant death.

What would a fourth shade of such a sequence entail? Killing gods? *Hah*, Walter chuckled, amused by his own conjectures.

Well, there was actually a more canon reason for the lack of a fourth shade.

It was simple, really. It was the terrifying difficulty of advancing each step in these condensed sequences. Elias was one out of hundreds, no thousands, who managed to actually form a coherent viewpoint for this sequence without losing himself.

Walter liked to believe his guidance was what allowed Elias to pass the hurdles that thousands in the Citadel failed. And even the angels agreed not to mess with Elias's environment and call him back.

It was hard work, really. Walter had almost lost his life to the kid's prowess many times. It had taken them a lot of trial and error to reach the current process where Elias could assassinate the targets without incurring heavy backlashes. And even then, the kid would come back depressed and bloody at times.

Suddenly, Walter's hand moved, and the words read, *Stop with your flowery words.* Walter's expression dropped. *I give you three weeks, Walter. If the ruling class of Elmhurst isn't dead in three weeks, the child of death shall be handed over to a more capable shepherd.*

"No way!" he shouted. He was the one who carved this rough gem into the terrifying onyx he'd become. He was the one who guided him on the path of an observer. How could they hand over his project of blood, sweat, and tears to someone else just like that?

"Argh!" he slammed his fist on the table.

However, he knew he couldn't let his fiery emotions color his words. Not when talking to the angel. It wouldn't end well.

Gritting his teeth, he activated calm mind, and his surging emotions ebbed. With a clearer head, he explained, *I will do my best to fulfill your commands, angel. However, as the seraphic lord may already know, the child of death requires damning evidence against every life he harvests.*

To leave no gaps and avoid future backlash to the child, I have to forge the evidence with the most rigorous standards. I must silence any witnesses who may say otherwise and bury any leads that extend outward from my imitations.

Now, while I revel in doing the lady's bidding, I am but a single man with modest means. My methods of collecting evidence against forth-shade and higher observers are quite limited and can be insufficient. However, if my seraphic lord could lend me the Eye of Seraph . . .

Walter stopped there. He didn't want to overextend himself. He was but an early fourth-shade influencer of the shepherd sequence. He couldn't afford to offend his ruling angel. Yet if he had the Eye of Seraph in his hand, he could surely find ways to help Elias ascend.

And this was all true. He didn't dare lie to the angel. Evidence was how he wielded the knife that was Elias. Perhaps the only way. The kid's morals were absolute, and he wouldn't budge unless it was clear that the target was pure evil.

When there was no response for a while, his heart ramped up, and he sipped the coffee one more time with trembling hands, now finding no comfort in its aroma.

Soon his hand wrote, *Shepherd Leah will handle gathering the evidence and forward it to you. Focus on the child's ascension to the second shade. Don't disappoint me.*

Walter narrowed his eyes. Leah was an orchestrator of the fifth shade. He had to be careful while working with her.

Nonetheless, he replied with deference, *Your will is my command, my seraphic lord.*

Soon came a response, *Shepherd Walter, the dusk angel has dismissed me. Would you like to begin a two-way conversation with Shepherd Leah right now?*

Walter looked at the wall clock. It had only been a few minutes. Elias shouldn't be done by now. The kid always spent a lot of time poring over the evidence.

With a nod, he wrote, *Yes, please.*

Crank.

Elias stepped out of the creaky elevator, greeted by a host of cogs and wheels. Gigantic clock hands and pendulums hummed and clicked in their hypnotic *tick tock* rhythm, not minding his intrusion at all.

Ignoring these contraptions, he made for the door out to the perimeter balcony of the clock tower and opened it a touch.

Cold wind buffeted his face, and his jacket billowed as he took in the sight that still managed to steal his breath. Dozens of disjointed islands connected with each other by nothing but bridges that seemed too frail from up here reflected in his eyes, and he appreciated them in silence.

"A clear day," he murmured. That meant the convict wasn't just evil but unlucky too. After all, the creeping visitor didn't perform as well on a foggy day.

Having checked the weather, he closed the door and walked back in, making his way toward the empty bulletin board tucked in the corner.

With a screech, he pulled it to the center and opened the envelope Walter gave him. Using the plethora of thumbtacks on the board, he hung up each piece of evidence one by one.

Victim's photographs, sigil-bearing letters of communication about the kidnappings, requests of "purchase of broken goods," financial ledgers, personal diary cutouts of victims—everything was here.

In the middle of them all, he nailed the image of the hateful bastard who was the ringleader.

Elias peered over each account and detail multiple times, checking their dates, timings, handwriting, and logical consistency. A narrative formed in his mind in no time.

It detailed the treacherous rise of Simon Razus—an unscrupulous baron who crossed the heights of depravity for greater power and position. Disgust, revulsion, and loathing deepened in his mind as Elias studied the map, which pointed to the man's residence.

After reviewing the evidence again, he uttered, "Filth."

Filth that must be removed.

Duskfall was supposed to be the rebirth of society. What other phenomenon could weed out the deep-seated corruption of the ruling class like an apocalypse that ended a third of the world's population? None.

This was meant to be the change unlike any other that ushered their civilization into a meritocracy. He had noticed a trend where natural selection deleted more of these corrupted nobles rather than the middle class that deserved to rise.

However, things didn't go the way they should have. They never did. Such a massive shake-up of the ruling class instead triggered their defensive instincts, where they ceded control over the outer districts and doubled down on their inner sanctum, slowly reclaiming the lost territories as their internal structure stabilized.

It was a masterful recovery plan that Elias could only praise, if not for its terrible consequences. When the districts were brought back into the fold once again, those filthy rich nobles continued to be the rulers who governed the lives of the masses. Very few positions of power were supplanted by those with merit. The rest were filled by incompetent offspring of those who were the very root of this corruption.

Nonetheless, if things stopped there, Elias might have held out hope for the system and continued his seemingly fruitless endeavor to change it from the inside regardless of what Walter said.

But it didn't.

He stared at all the damning evidence in front of him. It was a horrifying window into the rotten soul of those at the top. How could any city, country, or empire ever really be "good" if it condoned something like this?

He thought that slavery was the worst this city could throw at him.

But this . . . ?

Forcefully creating mentally vegetative observers on the brink of losing control for the sake of fulfilling twisted sexual desires?

His fist crashed into the wall with a resounding *thump* as his blood boiled. With a sharp, deep breath, he eyed the perpetrator, almost doubting that such an innocent-looking man could commit such heinous acts.

But Walter hasn't lied to me. Not even once.

Finding the claims in Walter's evidence preposterous over the past few weeks, he'd gone out of his way to investigate the cases from the ground up on his own, only to arrive at the same conclusion as Walter.

"Filth!" he roared, unable to contain his fury.

Zzzzttt.

The sunlight seeping in from the windows found itself extinguished as a dark haze materialized around Elias. His chestnut hair floated, lifted by an unseen force, and his eyes burned with an intense, otherworldly light. The air around him crackled, heavy with a palpable, dark energy.

Outside the clock tower, beyond his sight, this darkness radiated out in a sphere many meters wide. A crow sitting atop the highest pier of the tower cawed in terror and attempted to fly away but failed. Its body shriveled in the first ten seconds, then decayed, and before the wind could even change directions, it disintegrated into ash and went with the flow.

A deep guttural voice rang out next to Elias. "Heh. Hehe. Hehehaha. Little Elias is playing judge once again?"

Elias didn't respond.

The being behind him floated on dark, tattered wings, its skeletal frame draped in shadowy tendrils with each of its fingers adorned with a shiny ring. Its hollow eyes glowed with a malevolent light, and a twisted grin of schadenfreude spread across its gaunt face. The creature's presence exuded an aura of dread, its long, clawed fingers curling in anticipation.

Seraphs—angels of light—brought life. So, it only made sense for him, a harbinger of death, to bind himself to their counterpart—a shinigami.

Not wasting time on words, Elias stormed out the door to the terrace and strode around to the side that overlooked the Westerleigh borough—the district exclusive to nobles, chock full to the brim with gaudy mansions and unnecessary gardens.

Recalling the location of the bastard's residence, he took a deep breath.

"It's time . . ." he muttered.

Click.

The gigantic minute hand on the clock tower's face settled on thirty, and Elias reached into his jacket.

A low growl echoed out, and his hand trembled as he pulled out a half-shattered mask and stared at it intently for a few seconds before forcing it onto his face.

Like a bony maw constricting its prey, the creeping visitor, a perceptual artifact borne of terror and darkness, gripped at his skull. Its skeletal design covered the upper left side of Elias's face, where the bone-white material clung like the remains of a shattered skull.

The right side was broken, jagged edges framing a single hollow eye socket that emitted a ghastly green glow. Below, a wide, gaping jaw grinned wickedly, teeth sharp and menacing, frozen in a perpetual sneer.

The air around him grew colder than before, carving out a pocket of green haze in the dark sphere visible only to him.

"Feed me," the mask demanded, and Elias did his best not to let the thought overpower his mind. This was the cost of using the creeping visitor. One of the spied beings must die, or there would be untold repercussions. He didn't know exactly what, but Walter's stern face when explaining its usage the first time was more than enough for him not to test his luck.

His vision of the city from his right eye became ghastly and spectral as it suddenly shot toward the skies of Westerleigh borough, closing in like a hawk.

Suddenly, his body shook, and his vision settled on a room. It was as if he were looking into the room through the peephole of its door.

There was no one in the room.

Elias turned his pupil over in a different direction, and his sight jerked to follow it—now displaying another room.

Maids and servants cleaned the lavishly decorated hall, and given that Morwin hadn't interrupted him, these guys were innocent enough not to warrant his wrath.

He shuffled from one door to the next, and then to another, until . . .

"Hehe hehhah haha. Look at the evil oozing from that one . . ." wheezed Morwin.

Elias's sight revealed a gaudy room with its curtains closed, barely lit by purple lamps. A couple slept snugly on a bed fit for kings, but to Elias, it looked like a pile of corpses propped them up.

He clenched his fist, raised it, and . . .

Knock knock.

The couple turned in their sheets.

Knock knock.

The man, Simon, pulled a pillow over his head and frowned, his eyes still closed.

Knock knock.

Simon raised his hand and shouted, "Carlos! What's gotten into you? I told you not to disturb us. We had a late night."

Elias continued without a care, his eyes only growing fiercer. *Knock knock.*

Even the woman stirred. "Honey, could you please go and check? It must be something important."

The man stilled for a couple of seconds before sitting upright and stumbling his way to the door while rubbing his eyes.

"Carlos, is that you? What is it?"

Elias's eyes were glued to Simon's hand, which was about to rotate the knob and open the door. That's all the creeping visitor needed. That's all he needed.

Do it, he dared.

"Carlos . . . ?"

To his disappointment, Simon stopped at the last moment and suddenly became alert, his eyes growing wide. "Carlos? Carlos. Carlos, this isn't funny!"

Elias maintained his pace. *Knock knock.*

Simon turned back toward his wife, blood draining from his face as he exclaimed, "Isa, this . . . this can't be. This can't be!"

Isa sat up in the bed and pulled the sheets up to her mouth. Her body trembled, and she pushed herself back uneasily as she mumbled, "It's . . . it's the grim reaper! It's come for you. For us!"

Simon's knees began shaking, and his balance faltered. He grabbed on to the knob and somehow managed to not fall. Hyperventilating, he rested one hand on his chest and somehow found the courage to look into the peephole.

Elias stared back with the eye of the creeping visitor.

"Agh!" Simon screamed, recoiling from the door, flailing his hands through the air as he pleaded, "I didn't do it! I swear I didn't do it! Please. Please believe me!"

Elias clenched his fist tighter, disgusted by the hypocritical display, and rapped harder.

It was fine even if they didn't open the door right away. It would just become a contest of patience and mental strength. Elias had both in spades.

"Please. Whatever they've told you about me, I didn't do it," Simon begged. Scrambling over to the display table, he snatched the latest newspaper and began rambling, "This . . . this murder. It wasn't me. I . . . I didn't order it."

Knock knock.

"This . . . kidnapping"—he pointed at another headline—"it had nothing to do with me, I swear."

Knock knock.

He repeated this a couple more times before his eyes became bloodshot, the horror of the creeping visitor scrambling his mental defenses.

Simon then turned toward the woman in the room and said, "I . . . I've never even looked at a woman other than my wife. I swear to the lady who gave us knowledge from beyond, whatever crimes you believe I've committed, it wasn't me.

"Please! Give me a chance. I may not have lived a pure life, but I haven't done anything to warrant such a death. Please! Please! I am not like others. I donate a third of my income to charity and set aside another third to help bribe others to pass positive reforms."

"It is my only sin. Please! Please!"

For a second, Elias's wrist hesitated, his eyes wavering.

That's when a macabre face appeared in front of his other eye—the one not seeing through the creeping visitor—and Morwin chuckled. "Our little Elias is having second thoughts again?"

This reminded him of that time when his hesitation had cost an innocent woman her life. Because Elias hadn't been decisive enough, he'd let the convict go, and just a day later, the man decapitated and gouged out the eyes of another tenant, all for some manic ritual.

He was to blame for her death. He had failed his duty as a judge.

To be a judge is to be impartial, to forgo emotions, and to act upon evidence and facts alone. It is to render just punishment regardless of one's station, all the while dissecting all phenomena in the world to better differentiate between good and evil, innocent and guilty. Elias internally recited his shade's core principle, firming his resolve.

The evidence was there. This man who pleaded innocence was nothing but vile filth that fed the cycle of depravity. And he had the gall to pretend to not know anything about it.

Elias's grip became tighter, and he smashed his fist with all his might on the spectral door in front of him.

Knock! Knock!

As if someone had smashed a hammer on his head, Simon suddenly fell on the floor—limp. His wife screamed and rushed to his assistance, but the creeping visitor had gained hold of his faculties.

In a mindless daze, Simon crawled forward. His wife became terrified and attempted to hold him back, but the man's time was over, and his inner self knew it. Death bells tolled in his mind, and he journeyed toward the end himself.

Tap tap.

"Simon, no! Get ahold of yourself! Don't open the door! Don't do it!" she screeched, trying to keep him from moving, but she was too petite to stop him. Elias had nothing against her, so he hadn't pulled her into the effect of the creeping visitor. Also, he could see it. She was just delaying the inevitable.

He continued his rhythmic knocking as if this heart-wrenching scene were nothing but a theater drama in which he was just a mere spectator. It wasn't the time to pass judgment yet.

Knock! Knock!

Tap tap.

Two steps. Three. Six. With the tenth finally bringing him to the door. The woman's choked sobs became hoarser as she tried to call on their butlers, guards, and what not, but creeping visitor blocked it all.

She scratched, punched, and tackled her husband, but nothing stopped him, and he finally reached the door.

Elias's blood grew hotter, and his fury from before came gushing in waves, ready to drown this man in mere moments.

Ka-cha.

The green haze in front of Elias morphed and condensed into a spectral portal the size of a fist—allowing his other naked eye to observe Simon's room.

"Hehheh haha ha. So, little Elias, what's the verdict? Should I harvest his life?" asked Morwin in a low whisper, each word layered with mocking laughter.

Yes, the man may be a charitable person and a loyal lover, but that didn't even come close to overshadowing his crimes. There was nuance in most situations, but Elias—as a judge who wielded only life and death and not the shades in between— didn't have the luxury of being indecisive.

There were only two realities. Good or evil. Only two verdicts.

"And this one"—he pointed his finger at Simon across the space—"is guilty."

"Hehheh haha, don't regret your judgment later, little Elias." Morwin laughed as his wings flapped and he dematerialized from the clock tower before manifesting in Simon's room.

Simon suddenly awoke from the endless nightmare, and only the final words echoed in his head, *This one is guilty.*

"No. No. No. Please, please listen to me! Wait, please! Please!" he shouted with all his strength and backed away from the door at lightning speed.

That's when a . . . ghost. No, a god. No, the god of death appeared at the door—a black angel of decay and rot. With a grin that sent a shiver down his spine, the angel of death slowly flew toward him.

He waved his hands in denial. "No. Please, no! Isa, Isa, help me! Isa, it's here! The reaper. It's . . . it's real! Help me, Isa! It's come to take my life."

He slumped on the floor next to his wife and hugged her with all his being. "Please, please, Isa, I . . . I don't want to go."

Morwin didn't hurry and instead took in the surroundings, going so far as to grab one of the rings from the display rack and put it on one of his fingers—expanding his collection.

Elias clenched his fist. He was not a fan of Morwin's tactics, but he held his tongue for some reason, not feeling like rushing Simon's death.

At that moment, Isa suddenly snapped her head toward the dresser and mumbled something incoherent before forcefully extricating herself from the hug of her treacherous husband.

"Isa . . . Isa . . . I didn't do it. I didn't. I didn't . . ."

Elias didn't understand this turn of events either, but his eyes were beginning to strain, and the sharp whispers had begun to worm their way into his head. The whole combination of visions and artifacts was a big drain on his divine energy.

Ignoring the woman, he narrowed his eyes, crushing any pinch of sympathy for the bastard in his mind. As if aware of his feelings, Morwin suddenly stopped laughing and stopped dawdling.

His stooped, bony spine straightened, and he towered twice as high as Razus and extended his hand. A dark scythe of shadow formed in his hand, and a thread appeared above Simon's head, extending beyond infinity.

Elias closed his eyes for a second and took a deep breath. Morwin matched his pace, and the scythe rose high in the sky, coiling with a strength to snap the very threads of life.

"Your time is up," Elias declared, the finality in his voice echoing like the death knell.

With a swift, merciless swing, the scythe descended, aiming straight for the thread, sealing Simon's fate. It was—

"Please wait!" shouted the woman suddenly, blocking her husband, her arms extended to either side. In truth, her physical form was of no matter for Morwin.

Yet even though her attempt was entirely unable to impede it, for some reason, the shinigami stopped, the smile on its face growing wider.

Elias hadn't asked it to stop.

He was not one to dillydally. He raised his hand high and let it drop back down with a terrifying momentum, and ordered, "End it—"

However, at that moment, he noticed something peculiar in the woman's hand. It was a . . . letter for . . . the Reaper?

"Wait!" he shouted, and Morwin, who hadn't even picked up the scythe, just laughed, his bony body rocking back and forth.

Surprised by her plea actually working, the woman first looked back at her terrified husband, who was clutching on to her tightly, and then extended the letter in her hand toward the empty air in front of her.

She couldn't see the reaper, but she knew it was right there.

Holding back a sob, she pleaded, "Please. Please look at this. Someone gave it to me recently. I . . . I can't remember who, but I just know that you should see it!" Then she added with a mumble, "Oh, gods, why didn't I remember about it until now?!"

Multiple alarms went off in Elias's mind, but Morwin did whatever it wanted. It snatched the paper from her palms with two fingers and strolled back to the door with the paper in hand. It rocked with shallow laughter but still presented the paper in front of the little portal—right in Elias's face.

The unfurled paper had two simple words.

Greetings, Reaper.

Yet the moment Morwin looked at it, a new voice echoed in his mind, *Greetings, Reaper*, and an image followed. At some point as high as his own, a man stood with his back to him, his alabaster locks billowing in the wind. A blindfold covered his eyes, but when he turned back, his eyes hidden behind the veil seemed to peer through Elias's very heart.

Elias's heart grew cold. He was no expert, but even he knew that letting someone else in his mind was a recipe for disaster. With a sharp breath, he decided to cut his losses. "Morwin, get out of there!"

However, in that instant, an eerie reply came from the other side, *Please calm down and listen to me. This is just a pre-recorded illusion. Unfortunately, I can't create illusions that are alive.*

This gave Elias pause, and Morwin just laughed, ignoring his command to retreat, almost as if it knew that there was no risk in letting this man speak. Holding the terrace's railing, Elias steadied himself and watched this illusion with a frown.

Clap clap.

"I must say, it's commendable that you've instilled a primal fear in the nobility of Elmhurst in such a short time."

But then he suddenly stopped. "Yet have you really purged the scum of society like you seem to believe?"

Elias involuntarily stepped back. How did this person know of his convictions? The nobles he'd judged weren't considered scums by the society at all—it's just the deeper evidence that Walter provided that revealed their true colors. Then how did this person know to think it was because of a need for justice?

A soft smile hung on his lips, and the man didn't elaborate. Instead, he said, "What's even more fascinating is that divinations and roundabout visions have little to nothing to say about you." He shook his head. "Let me share some observations I've made regarding this string of murders you've committed."

He waved his hand, and a parchment appeared. "Twenty-seventh of Winterveil, last year, Captain Haytham lost his mind in his own office. Twenty-eighth of Winterveil, Lord Armatage was found lifeless in his estate. Twenty-ninth of Winterveil, Magistrate

Ulric, in his courtroom . . ." Elias listened without a word, reminded of the crimes of each of these criminals he'd judged, only to find his resolve further solidified.

"Seventh of Luminar, Lady Elara in her chambers, and finally the Merchant Guildmaster Roderic on eighth. Each and every death was reminiscent of an observer losing control. Now, I am sure you'll continue to kill on the ninth, tenth, and so on, but hopefully, I will be on your tail before it's too long."

Elias narrowed his eyes. *So this illusion was conjured after the eighth?* He'd already judged multiple convicts since then, after all.

"Anyway, I am sure you already know all of this better than me."

Indeed, he did. What was the point of repeating the names of all these criminals like this?

The blindfolded man waved his hands again, and this time, another parchment appeared in his second hand. "However, did you know that each of these deaths was preceded by multiple deaths of those around your targets?"

Elias frowned.

"Well, I have reasons to believe you don't. So, let me explain. You see, before Lord Armitage died at your hands on the twenty-eighth, his personal butler had asked for a leave the day before, and four days later, his corpse was found washed up down at the docks by a fisherman. For Magistrate Ulric, three of his subordinates went missing around that time and have yet to be found . . ."

Elias furrowed his brows and listened closely, an uneasy feeling growing in his chest. The man listed one cryptic death after another related to the people he'd judged.

"Now, you see, that alone isn't really a proof of anything. So, we had to disturb the dead and scour their memories. Would you believe what we found?"

The man grimaced. "Nothing."

He shook his head. "Fortunately, in our line of work, no evidence is evidence in and of itself.

"There are three known shade sequences that can perform a memory manipulation of this kind. Well, to not give you free knowledge of other sequences, I will jump straight to the conclusion and tell you that when correlated with the positions and tendencies of the murder targets, I believe this is the work of Seraphine's shepherd."

He then slowly paced around the open space. "Now, you see, shepherds are powerful in their own right, but they surely don't have the means to remotely kill such a varied range of individuals, with some even having their personal troops and armies guarding their residences."

He nodded. "You know what that means? Either it was a coincidence that a shepherd just happened to be manipulating records and minds around all your targets. Or . . ."

"There is a connection. One too significant to be ignored."

Elias's breath quickened. *This . . . this couldn't be.* He'd done his own rounds of investigations after Walter and hadn't found a single contradiction.

No. This could just be their way of sowing mistrust between me and Walter. There was a purpose behind this whole illusion, and Elias wasn't about to fall for his enemies.

Why would he believe the words of this man he didn't even know over Walter and his own eyes? Who was to say that the things this guy mentioned really happened?

Wary, he continued to listen with skepticism.

"Hah, since I don't believe in coincidences, I am of the mind to believe that there's not just a link but rather that these shepherds are working for you. Or"—he looked back—"you're working for them?"

"Anyway, we dug deeper, and what would you know, we found all kinds of weird phenomenon going on with people related to these murders . . . even the ones who didn't die. Some had become traitorous overnight and leaked private ledgers, while others forgot the last few days of their lives and were found with the seals of their masters and objects they shouldn't possess. Accounts and financial transactions made no sense, and even worse, letters that senders didn't remember writing were posted."

"You see, to me, that paints a very clear picture. It's the doing of the same shepherds you work for."

Morwin laughed while Elias stared daggers at the blindfolded man.

"But that begs the question. What would a shepherd gain by doing all these silly things? Why manipulate these random records and force servants to perform these illogical tasks?"

Elias's breath hitched in his throat. It was as if someone were tearing down the walls around him one by one. There was a reason they hadn't been caught yet, and that was because of the uniqueness of the creeping visitor and his disruptive shade sequence.

The lack of public information about his sequence was what allowed him to act as freely as he did.

But this . . .

"It is clear now . . . isn't it? They wanted . . ."

"They wanted evidence," he enunciated.

"No. You wanted evidence."

"Hah," the blindfolded man chuckled. "Well, that was the breakthrough I needed, and I have your incompetent shepherds to thank for that.

"It's clear that these shepherds provide you with evidence, which you then somehow use to manifest a reaper that reaps the lives of these targets from afar.

"Now, where this gets interesting is that the evidence needs not be objectively true. It's enough as long as you perceive it to be true."

Elias gripped the railing tighter, his knuckles turning white. It was almost as if this man knew him intimately. He had figured out the intricacies of his shade sequence through the most absurd methodologies.

However, he didn't like the direction of this argument at all. Elias knew Walter was using him to target people who were a nuisance to Seraphine's grand design, but he didn't mind that as long as his and Walter's goals melded. What did it matter if a heinous criminal also belonged to a faction that opposed Seraphine?

What mattered were their crimes and their judgment.

However, this man talked like it was already established that most of the evidence was forged and the targets hadn't really committed the crimes it proved.

What if I'd really judged innocents to be evil? The mere thought sent him into a panic.

"Little Elias," laughed Morwin. "Oh, Little Elias, you already seem more . . . evil."

No! Everything the man said was conjectures and hypotheticals without proof. There was no evidence!

"Stop this!" Elias shouted, glaring at the paper still held in Morwin's hand outside of this illusion. However, all that echoed in his ears was a mirthful laugh.

He closed his eyes, but the illusion remained persistent. *It is Morwin!* he realized. It wasn't going to let Elias go just like that. It didn't really listen to him most of the time.

"Fuck!" he blurted, not sure what to do about this.

The blindfolded man continued his monologue. "Now, you see. I already had enough information to predict the next targets." However, he suddenly let out a defeated sigh. "But you and your shepherds, no matter how sloppy, have some terrifying means at your disposal.

"You managed to kill two more innocents even when they were guarded by a team of experts. Worse, one of my subordinates even had their memories scrambled by your shepherd."

Then he spread his arms and sighed. "And well, that is why we're here. That's why I had to set up all this. That's why I'm talking to you.

"To show you," he began, his voice calm but laced with bitterness. "Tell you that you're not ridding the world of the filth you claim to see. You're slaughtering innocents, whose only crime was being a nuisance to your gods and their twisted plans."

He took a deep breath and continued, his tone cold and precise. "You're nothing but a heartless murderer. A butcher who deserves to rot in the hell you've created for others." He shook his head, a flicker of pain crossing his face. "Do you even realize the depths of your own monstrosity?"

Elias shuddered where he stood as his reflection in Morwin's eyes became redder—oozing with evil.

No. This . . . this just can't be true.

His demeanor as a judge instead helped him block out the guilt that was beginning to surface within his mind. He knew there had to be some truth to these words, but words were meaningless. Evidence was what mattered, and this man had given him none.

However, that's when the blindfolded man looked straight at Elias with disdain and spoke. "Now, I know you're probably trying to justify this to yourself. Justify how there's no evidence to prove my claims, and maybe even succeed in convincing yourself and somehow not lose control.

"No." He shook his head and laughed in a low voice. "I am not going to let you off so easily. Once this illusion is over, the letter will give you a list of methods to publicly verify most of the claims I've just made.

"But I know. I know you won't believe anything I say so easily. After all, it's my word against your Shepherd's.

"That's okay. I will convince you.

"Convince you that you're a monster that needs to be put to rest."

He then pointed back, and the skies in the illusion became transparent, and the sobbing couple entered his sight once again. "You're here to end the life of this criminal, right? I am sure you have damning evidence of how they've committed the most heinous of the crimes, and only you can judge them.

"Wrong!

"Awaken!" he shouted, and to Elias's surprise, the sound reverberated in the room tangibly, and the couple suddenly became dazed. A few seconds later, their grips loosened on each other, and the man asked, "Marie? What . . . what are you doing here?"

"Caleb? I . . ." She suddenly backed out of his embrace and looked around in confusion. "What . . . what is going on?!"

However, before Elias could read more into it, the skies of the illusion recovered, and the blindfolded man scoffed. "You see? The so-called criminal you came to punish today is just a commoner whom we planted with fake memories.

"They have no real connections to nobility, no strings to pull. They aren't even invited to private gatherings and hold no influence. How would they ever commit any crime that warranted a visit from the reaper itself?"

The man slowly turned toward the city and looked up. "Unfortunately, I am neither omniscient nor prescient. So, I don't know which of the fake houses I set up that you've fallen for, but I can still tell you that everything you see there is a sham. There is no noble house. They have no real funds to spend anywhere except where I want them to. And I only spend them in an effort to appeal to your shepherd's ire.

"Heh, but I suppose that might still not be enough for someone who reveres evidence as you do.

"So, let me tell you something even more interesting in the patterns of how your shepherds seeded evidence.

"It was fascinating, really. The evidence of each case was tailored to pin varied types of crimes each time, avoiding repetition. One was painted as a corrupt official who let hundreds die in the cold because he wanted to fill his coffers, while another was framed as a cunning embezzler who siphoned funds from orphanages. A third was depicted as a ruthless gang leader orchestrating violent robberies, and yet another was marked as a serial arsonist burning down historic landmarks and people inside it.

"The list goes on and on, and you can't tell me this is all just a coincidence." He mimed as if he was deep in thought and asked, "But then, what does it all mean?

"Did they just want to throw off the investigation by picking such a varied range of crimes? Well, that would have been plausible if they hadn't already made the link between all these targets so painfully obvious.

"And that's when I realized! That was the point where I managed to rule out all other hypotheses about this reaper being an artifact or some sort of pollution and confirmed that you're indeed just an observer.

"A newly enlightened one at that."

The image of the blindfolded man became taller in his head, and Elias couldn't help but backpedal, only to have the wall stop his retreat dead in his tracks.

"You see, the reason for falsifying evidence for such a varied range of crimes wasn't to scramble connections between murders; it was to give you new experiences. After all, varied insights lead to higher power. Your growth was their goal."

The blindfolded man stopped there and simply looked in his direction in silence for a while before chuckling. "So that finally allowed me to grasp the depth of this so-called reaper. Which meant I finally had everything I needed to triage you.

"So, what did I do?" He chortled. "I invented new crimes. Fake ones, of course. I knew your shepherds couldn't resist presenting fresh evidence of such heinous crimes to broaden your horizons.

"While I'm not sure which one led you here today, I'm certain your evidence includes images of supposed victims." He smiled with a chilling coldness and said, "You see, I spread those for each of these fake crimes myself."

What . . . what does he mean? Elias tried to make sense of these devilish words.

The devil's grin became wider. "Well, surely, if your evidence is solid, the victims mustn't be alive, right? If your shepherd had no intention of faking the evidence, there's no way they managed to link a fake noble to a crime that would need hundreds in manpower, right?"

With a surprising amount of edge to his voice, he repeated, "Right?!"

After a bit, he shook his head a final time. "Before you leave, take a look around this mansion. See if you recognize any faces. Strain your eyes if you must. I'm sure some of them are bound to catch your eyes."

The illusory terrace began to destabilize, and the blindfolded man sighed. "I hope I've dismantled your fake justice and the sham it's built upon. While I wish that this alone would make you lose control and end this misguided justice once and for all, I feel like that's wishful thinking on my part.

"So, go. Take this warning to the heart, and . . . do *not* trust shepherds."

The illusion lost all its energy and exploded into particles of light, which dispersed into nothingness within a few seconds, leaving a final set of words in the air.

I am watching you.

Forgetting to even breathe, the moment the illusion disappeared, Elias hurriedly shifted his pupil, and the creeping visitor jumped over to a different room. To a hall he'd seen earlier.

Maids and servants diligently performed their various duties, and there, his eyes locked on to two faces. He hadn't noticed it the first time around, but now that he was looking for it, he instantly realized.

It's . . . them. They're . . . alive.

The two servants closely resembled pictures of two of the victims he'd seen on the bulletin board inside. Victims who were supposed to have lost control and died after being abused terribly.

"I . . . judged incorrectly. I would have killed an innocent. No, I already did. I already judged many based on false evidence."

He didn't even feel the need to look for evidence any further. If all this didn't make it obvious that Walter had played him like a fiddle, then, he deserved to be used like that.

The ground seemed to slip from under his feet, and the wall behind him felt like a crumbling facade, no longer offering support. His breath hitched, and his hands trembled as he grasped at the air, seeking stability.

"I . . . I was so sure," he whispered, his voice breaking. "So certain I was doing the right thing." His eyes welled with tears, and he clutched at his chest as if to hold himself together. "But I was wrong," he choked out, sinking to his knees. "I've become the very monster I swore to destroy."

Feeling as if the world were closing in, he ripped the mask from his face, and the small portal faltered before snapping shut. Morwin soon manifested above him, standing over him like the death god it was, a scythe in its hands, its eyes reflecting a purely red Elias.

"Hahaha hehahah."

"Oh, little Elias. You were naive. Too naive. Right now, you look like evil incarnate to me. Tell me, should you not be judged in your own court?"

Elias crumbled and hugged his knees, rocking back and forth as the sight of all those nobles' soulless faces after his false judgment flashed in front of his eyes. Their passionate pleas, which he'd heartlessly ignored—all because of evidence that spoke otherwise.

Evidence that was gathered by someone else. Evidence he didn't even fully trust. Evidence whose purpose wasn't even related to justice but rather to some personal agenda of Walter's. Evidence that a part of him always knew could be false.

Yet he had relied on it like it was absolute truth.

Why did I never question it any further? he asked. The blindfolded man's explanation had made it more than clear that any secondary investigations he'd done were nothing but a joke. He arrived at conclusions that Walter wanted him to reach.

Why did I think that was enough?

Was any amount of investigation ever enough to warrant claiming a life? Until a while ago, he would have easily answered with a yes.

Now? He didn't know.

Staring at nothing in particular, he asked, "Morwin, did you . . . know? Know that I was punishing innocents for crimes they hadn't committed?"

It just hovered in silence, a mocking grin on its face.

"Did I punish a real criminal even once? Were they all innocents?"

No answer.

Whenever he asked Walter these questions, the man always assured him that what he did was right. That what he did, while cruel, was necessary to cleanse the world.

Surprisingly . . . Elias still believed that.

Believed that the world was rotten and that he would be a coward not to bear the burden of changing it.

Then where did things go wrong?

"Little Elias, it's time to go."

Elias stood, an introspective look on his face. He leaned over the parapet one more time and took in the sight of this beautiful city. A beauty that was rotten from the inside.

Then he replied, "Indeed. My verdict for myself is that I'm evil." The process mattered, but facts were paramount. He might have stopped a few evil ones, but from the man's words, he'd slaughtered far more innocents.

The evidence was against him, and he had no plans of faking it. Not anymore.

He realized where things had gone wrong.

Responsibility.

It was the fact that he didn't take responsibility of his verdicts as a judge. He allowed Walter to pick the targets and collect evidence for them, all the while staying in his safe bubble where he justified these kills as necessary evils and that Walter knew the best.

"What is a judge who can't even take responsibility for his own verdicts?"

In that moment, Morwin closed his hollowed eyes for a second before snapping them open once again as they shone with an otherworldly light. "Do you feel it, Little Elias?"

He nodded, feeling his insights completely align with that of a judge. The bottleneck that had been plaguing him for a while was gone.

"I need to take responsibility for my actions." That was it. That was the reason his singularity suddenly aligned with his insights and the vision of a judge.

Morwin, who had its scythe resting against Elias's soul thread—ready to end him in a moment—pulled it back with a sharp gleam in its eyes and waited silently.

Elias appreciated the breathtaking scenery without a word as the internal alignment continued at a slow pace, and he realized so many issues with his philosophy.

When he finally felt at peace with . . . himself, with his crimes, he picked up the creeping visitor one more time and forced it onto his face.

With a forlorn look, he turned toward Hotel Inkwell next to the clock tower.

Soon, his vision shifted, and a room appeared in his mind. A familiar room. Walter—the person who had saved him from the hellhole that was the Citadel and its higher angels—sat in a worn armchair, diligently writing.

Wrinkles had begun to etch themselves into Walter's face, a face that had become a source of comfort in a short time. His eyes, once sharp and full of determination, now held a weary kindness, reflecting the toll of their recent battles.

Though their time together had been brief, Walter had been a beacon of hope and guidance, a mentor who had shown him a glimpse of a life beyond the chaos.

"So, little Elias, what's the verdict?" asked Morwin, staring at the seated figure, who was oozing with the crimson of pure evil.

Elias didn't answer. He clenched his fist, raised it, and . . .

Knock knock.

About the Author

FiniteVoid writes computer science concepts disguised as epic progression fantasy. Also, Void is actually just 13m^3. Trust him.

Podium